HILLINGDON HALL

OR, THE COCKNEY SQUIRE

Robert S. Surtees

NONSUCH

TO

THE ROYAL AGRICULTURAL SOCIETY

OF ENGLAND

THIS VOLUME IS INSCRIBED

BY THEIR

OBEDIENT HUMBLE SERVANT

THE AUTHOR

First published 1845
Copyright © in this edition 2006 Nonsuch Publishing Limited

Nonsuch Publishing Limited
The Mill, Brimscombe Port, Stroud, Gloucestershire, GL5 2QG
www.nonsuch-publishing.com

Nonsuch Publishing is an imprint of Tempus Publishing Group

For comments or suggestions, please email the editor of this series at:
classics@tempus-publishing.com

British Library Cataloguing in Publication Data.
A catalogue record for this book is available from the British Library.

ISBN 1-84588-211-3
ISBN-13 (from January 2007) 978-1-84588-211-2

Typesetting and origination by Nonsuch Publishing Limited
Printed in Great Britain by Oaklands Book Services Limited

HILLINGDON HALL

OR, THE COCKNEY SQUIRE

Mr. Jorrock's arrival astonishes the village of Hillingdon

Contents

INTRODUCTION TO THE
MODERN EDITION

ROBERT SMITH SURTEES WAS BORN in 1805, the second son of Anthony Surtees, the squire of Hamsterley Hall in County Durham, where the family had long been established. He was educated at Durham grammar school before becoming a solicitor's articled clerk in 1822. He moved to London and practised law, but his heart was not really in it, country sports, and in particular hunting, being of far more interest to him. He attempted to combine his profession and his love of equestrian activities by publishing a treatise on the law as it related to horses, called *The Horseman's Manual*, in 1831. In the same year he was one of the founders of the *New Sporting Magazine*, which he edited for the next five years. It was in the pages of this publication that he developed his genius for comic writing, creating the character of John Jorrocks, the Cockney grocer.

Jorrocks is the antithesis of a conventional Master of Fox Hounds: a self-made tradesman from the East End of London, he is invited to become master of the Handley Cross pack because of his money and his exploits with 'the Surrey.' However, the refined hunting fraternity of Handley Cross are totally unprepared for the rather blunt, vulgar manners of Jorrocks and his wife and hilarious consequences ensue. He featured in the *New Sporting Magazine* between 1832 and 1834, stories which were collected into book form as *Jorrocks' Jaunts and Jollities* in 1838, with illustrations by Hablot K. Browne ('Phiz,' who drew for *Punch* and illustrated several of Charles Dickens' novels). He reappeared in *Handley Cross* (serialised in the *New Sporting Magazine* 1838–39) and *Hillingdon Hall* (serialised 1843–44); both of these stories were later reprinted in book form, with illustrations by John Leech (who also drew for *Punch*).

When Surtees' elder brother died in 1831, he became the heir of Hamsterley Hall; he finally gave up the law in 1835, resigned as editor of the *New Sporting Magazine* in 1836 and returned to County Durham, where he was able to indulge his love of country pursuits. When his father died in 1838 he succeeded him as squire, and seemed to find fulfilment in the life of a country gentleman. He became heavily involved in local affairs and politics, and kept his own pack of hounds from 1838–40. He stood for Parliament (unsuccessfully), served as a Justice of the Peace for County Durham and as an officer in the Durham Militia and was High Sheriff of the county in 1856. However, he continued to 'scribble,' as he termed it, producing three further (non-Jorrocks) hunting novels, *Hawbuck Grange* (1847), *Mr Sponge's Sporting Tour* (1853) and *Mr Facey Romford's Hounds* (1864), and two 'society' novels (*ie* with slightly less emphasis on hunting, although by no means devoid of it), *"Ask Mamma"* (1857–58) and *"Plain or Ringlets?"* (1859–60); *Young Tom Hall*, sub-titled 'His Heartaches and Horses,' remained unfinished at his death.

In 1841 Surtees married Elizabeth Jane Fenwick, daughter of Addison Fenwick, of Bishopwearmouth; they had a son, Anthony, and two daughters, Elizabeth Anne and Eleanor, the latter of whom married John Prendergast Vereker, later 5th Viscount Gort, in 1885. He died in 1864.

John Jorrocks, having established his credentials as a fox-hunting man in *Jorrocks Jaunts and Jollities* and *Handley Cross*, aspires to the life of a country squire, and so purchases Hillingdon Hall, 'quite a specimen of the old-fashioned manor-house'. Naturally, the *nouveau riche* Jorrocks, the 'Cockney Squire' of the subtitle, does not find himself immediately at home amongst neighbours like the Duke of Donkeyton and the Marquis of Bray, in much the same way as he did not quite fit in amongst the sophisticated inhabitants of Handley Cross. Naturally, much of the story concerns hunting, but it also has an important political aspect: Jorrocks' espousal of modern farming methods and the campaign he fights for election to Parliament as the representative for Sellborough were very topical when it was written.

Surtees intended *Hillingdon Hall* as a satire against the Anti-Corn Law League. The Corn Laws had been intended to protect British agriculture against foreign imports and to encourage exports, but in reality they protected rich landowners from cheaper domestic competition. There was considerable debate within the country as to whether these protectionaist measures should be repealed, which would come to a head at the beginning of the Irish Potato Famine in 1845. Sir Robert Peel, the Tory Prime Minister, suggested that the purchase of cheap American maize could avert the crisis, but he was opposed by most of his own party. The Whigs, who formed the Opposition, supported him. Surtees himself was a major landowner, and was therefore against the repeal of the Corn Laws, on the basis that it would lower the value of his land and so of the rents paid to him by his tenant farrmers. Neither repeal nor the introduction of new ways of farming would bring benefit to him, or to his fellow landowners, and in *Hillingdon Hall* he pokes fun at those who sought to (as he must have seen it) deprive him of his comfortable existence.

Like all of Surtees' stories, *Hillingdon Hall* is filled with a plethora of memorable characters, most of whom sport amusing and apposite names: the Duke of Donkeyton and the Marquis of Bray, Mr Smoothington and Mr Sneakington, Mrs Flather and Mrs Trotter. His descriptions of country life and hunting are detailed and full of enthusiasm, but he does not take matters too seriously, displaying a dry wit and an appreciation of human absurdities. Although in the later twentieth and early twenty-first centuries hunting has become a controversial activity, during the middle of the nineteenth century it was a perfectly natural thing to do in the countryside, and, uncomplicated by animal rights activists and hunt saboteurs, Mr Jorrocks' equestrian escapades still bring joy to modern readers.

PREFACE

THE AUTHOR OF THIS WORK will not trespass on the indulgence of the reader, in the way of preface, further than to say that the agricultural portion of it is not meant to discourage improvement, but to repress the wild schemes of theoretical men, who attend farmers' meetings for the pleasure of hearing themselves talk, and do more harm than good by the promulgation of their visionary views.

HODDESDON, HERTS,
October 1844

I

Oh, knew he but his happiness, of men,
The happiest he who, far from public rage,
Deep in the vale, with a choice few retired,
Drinks the pure pleasure of the rural life.

HILLINGDON HALL WAS ONE OF those nice old-fashioned, patchy, upstairs and downstairs sort of houses, that either return to their primitive smallness, or are swept away for stately mansions with well-arranged suites of company rooms, leaving perhaps the entrance or a room or two to disfigure the rest, and show what the edifice originally was. This at least is the fate of most of them. As soon as the last addition or improvement is completed, down comes the whole; and a plausible architect so confuses the owner with indispensables—things without which "no house can be perfect"—that when at length the masons and joiners and painters and plasterers and plumbers have taken their departure, he finds himself the master of quite a different sort of house to what he wanted, and begins to think the old patched house would have served his purpose very well, and been much more comfortable.

Hillingdon Hall was quite a specimen of the old-fashioned manor-house. Driving through the neat little village, with its pretty white-washed, rose-covered cottages, a simple portico projecting a little into the street, was all that denoted a mansion of pretension; but when the door was opened, and the stranger ushered along a wide but low passage, into a fair-sized hall, with a billiard table in the centre, the numerous carved black oak doors and passages branching off, increased its importance as he proceeded. The old rooms, consisting of a dining and drawing room on either side of the entrance, were of fair dimensions, oak-wainscoted, with deep recesses at either end, closed by sliding shutters, but these had long been converted into a housekeeper's and "master's room," and first one and then another had been added, until a handsome dining, drawing room, and library ranged along the new front. Still there was no attempt at architectural symmetry or display. Each room had been added separately and stuck in, as it were, so as not to interfere with its neighbours, and a verandah accommodating itself to the various angles of the house, and encompassing three sides of it, was the only piece of uniformity about the place; all the lower windows opened into this, and under its fragrant shade a tolerable share of exercise might be obtained on a wet day. The view from it was beautiful.

Beyond an undulating lawn profusely studded with gigantic oaks and ground-sweeping pines, the land stretched away to a high promontory, whose rocky peak was washed by the clear waters of the rapid Dart, which girded the two sides of the angular estate. The fields were large and well divided, and being of that table land frequently found on river margins, showed to the eye as large again as they were. The village with its hail stood about the centre of the angle's base, and diverging from the road, about a mile on the east, there was a sweet saunter along flowery meads up the river's course, until the gradually narrowing hills changed into craggy heights—wild and magnificent grandeur—with drooping, dark green yews, and brighter broom, or gayer gorse, or mountain ash, springing from the interstices of the unscaleable rocks and craggy steeps.

Between these lofty cliffs the rapid river flowed in noisy haste; now foaming and rushing through water-worn chasms in the massive rock, now pouring in regular flood over some breast-high barrier, now dashing and dividing into a hundred channels, against the fragments of a scattered rock, and now gliding noiselessly away into the tranquillity of deeper water.

From the giddy heights of the crag-head, the eye roved over a vast expanse of mountainous wood-clothed country.

Following up the water's course, the rocks and banks again gradually receded; the land drooped towards the river, whose gurgling stream sounded soothingly through the spaces between sweeping spruce, whose lofty and luxuriant forms lined either side of a well-kept grassy ride. Here pheasants fed and loitered in the tameness of tranquil security, squirrels spurted up the trees, wood-pigeons cooed wooingly in the branches, blackbirds and thrushes and nightingales, all the feathered tribe, in short, joined in the minstrelsy of the waters: and as the wanderer pursued his way amid the music of nature and the perfume of wild flowers, a sudden turn brought him again in sight of grass fields beyond the road on the other side of the angle's base from whence he had set out.

This was its out-of-door or walking aspect. From the windows, though the acclivities of the crag were lost, there were two peeps of the silvery water at the extreme sides of the angle where the banks were lowest, and an immense tract of forest scenery, extending from the opposite hill and stretching quite over the mountain brow, broke the sky line with the spiral tops of pines and larches commingled with grey rocks and pointed cliffs, scattered in irregular confusion over the wild surface. No sign of habitation appeared save the clear white curl of smoke from the woodmen's cottages, scattered at wide intervals in the deep bosom of the forest. The animation of village life was all behind the Hall.

This terrestrial paradise had long been the blissful retreat of Mr. Westbury, a man of infinite talent and learning, and about one of the last of the old-fashioned race of country gentlemen who lived all the year round on their estates. The beauty of the spot might indeed plead in excuse for so uncivilised a proceeding, for Mr. Westbury had ample means of partaking of London pleasures in the unostentatious style of personal comfort, which, after all, is the truest way of enjoying them. But year after year rolled on, season succeeded season, without the vacuum occurring that required the filling up of London life.

Happy in the tranquillity of the country, happy in the companionship of a sympathising wife, happy in the society of congenial friends, happy in the seclusion of the woods that his hands had planted, or in wandering over the fields and meadows that his skill had fertilised, age succeeded youth,

> And all his prospects brightening to the last,
> His heaven commenced ere the world was past.

He was the patriarch of the district—the man to whom all disputes were referred, all plans submitted—the man by whom all charities were promoted—the petty king, in fact. The humble inhabitants of the little village looked up to him, the wealthier neighbours were always anxious to consult him; and when death closed the eyes of the amiable owner of Hillingdon Hall, and his comfortable mansion, with its rich and picturesque domain, its woods and waterfalls, varied and romantic scenery, became the subject of newspaper advertisements, people far and wide regretted the loss, and the inhabitants of the pretty little village felt that the sun of Hillingdon's glory had set forever.

Some time elapsed after the sale before it became known who was the purchaser of the Hillingdon estate; some gave it to one person, some to another; the lawyers, as usual, were "mum."

II

… O most delicate fiend!
Who is't can read a woman?

SHAKSPEARE

MRS. FLATHER AND MRS. TROTTER, who had long battled for the honour of being second to the Hall people, and who had only been restrained from downright acts of hostility by the amiable intervention of Mr. and Mrs. Westbury, seemed to have entered into a sort of truce in case the new-comer should require their united opposition.

Mrs. Flather was a simple, apparently open-hearted, but in reality double-dealing, half-cunning sort of woman, extremely candid and straightforward when it suited her convenience, and extremely stupid and dull of comprehension when the reverse was the case. She was the undespairing widow of a clergyman, an old friend of Mr. Westbury's, like him then recently gone to his last home.

Mrs. Flather was a capital figure for a gossip—short and dumpy, with a mild, placid, unmeaning sort of countenance, that banished all fear as to what one might say before her. Moreover, by assuming her late husband's undisguised detestation of gossip and twaddle, she rather inveigled people into communicativeness. "Oh, don't tell me any secrets, pray!" she would exclaim—or, "Don't tell me anything that doesn't concern myself. I never meddle with other people's affairs," and so on; by which means she often got possession of secrets that would otherwise never have been intrusted to her.

Mrs. Trotter was of the masculine order: a great, tall, stout, upstanding, black-eyed, black-haired woman, with a strong, unturnable resolution; and a poor, little, henpecked, Jerry Sneak of a husband, who was of no more account in the house than if no such being existed. He was a kind, mild-dispositioned man, who might have been a useful and amiable member of society, had not his wife's magnificent proportions captivated him at the outset of life, and merged his insignificance in herself. Mrs. Trotter was a busy, bustling woman, with such a strong sense of "duty" as frequently caused her to say and do things that most people would have been glad to leave alone.

If she saw an incipient flirtation, she always thought it her "duty" to caution the parties or their friends; if Mr. Brown called on Mrs. Green oftener than she thought right, she would think it her duty to inform Mrs. Green's husband; if Doctor Bolus hinted that he thought Miss Martin in a delicate way, she would bundle on her bonnet and shawl, and forthwith assure Miss Martin that she thought it her duty to tell her she was going to die, and advise her to prepare accordingly.

It would never answer the purpose of any author to allow two such ladies as these to be without the essential requisites of daughters, and we are happy to say that in this instance there is no need of fiction, for Mrs. Flather had her most interesting, well-blown Emma, coming after a couple of sons—one at sea, the other ashore, whom we only introduce to dismiss as perfectly intractable in our hands; while Mrs. Trotter had her Eliza at the head of a graduating scale of little Trotters, ranging from sixteen years to six. Some links had been broken in the chain, but at the time of which we are writing Mrs. Trotter had her six little followers. As, however, there is no occasion to load the reader's mind with people as an omnibus cad does his vehicle, we may here state that Eliza is the only one of the young ones we mean to deal with.

Emma Flather was of the middle stature, what would be called a good-sized girl, neither too big nor too little, too fat nor too thin, with well-rounded limbs, and altogether a good armfullish sort of figure. She had a fair, clear, alabaster-like complexion, full, oval face, pale and yet not sickly, with light brown hair, well-pencilled eyebrows, darkly-fringed, bluish-greyish eyes, rosy lips, and regular pearly teeth. Perhaps we have hardly done justice to her eyes. In repose they were mild and passionless, lighting up, however, when animated, into a radiance that imparted life and intelligence to a countenance that at other times some perhaps might not have called pretty. Still Emma was never worked into anything like glow or excitement. As some one said of Talleyrand, that you might kick him behind without his countenance betraying a change, so a man might have kissed Emma Flather for half an hour without raising a blush on her cheeks. Indeed, she was a fine piece of animated statuary—and as cold withal. A provoking sort of girl. Not exactly pretty enough to fall in love with for her looks, and yet dangerous with her looks and blandishments combined. She was desperately enthusiastic; could assume raptures at the sight of a daisy, or weep o'er the fate of a fly in a slop-basin. Moreover, she had a smattering of accomplishments, could sing, and play, embroider, work worsteds, murder French and Italian, and had a knack of talking and pretending to a great deal more talent than she possessed. This taste for exaggeration she carried into other matters; she had a fine fertile imagination—frequently fancied herself a great heiress—talked of the beauty of her aunt's place in Dorsetshire—insinuated that she was to inherit it, with a vast number of other little self-enhancements, plainly showing that her *education* had not been neglected.

Emma was a curious mixture of high-mindedness and meanness—of feeling and insensibility. Full of enthusiasm and lofty sentiments— compassionate and tender beyond expression when it suited her purpose—she was, nevertheless, selfish and insensible to the last degree. Cold, calculating, and cunning, she had all the worldly-mindedness of a well-hackneyed woman of fifty—in short, of her mother. As the Frenchman said of his dog, "she was well down to charge," and thoroughly appreciated the difference between an elder son and a younger. She would dismiss the latter at any moment that her mother hinted the probability of anything better. All this told in her favour, she acquired the character of a model of propriety, and Emma Flather was held up as a pattern girl for all young ladies to imitate. Of course, old mother Flather was extremely anxious to get her married, but not having fallen in with anything exactly to her mind, she had just flown her at minor game and checked her off under pretence of not being able to part with the dear girl.

Eliza Trotter was of a different nature. She was warm-hearted, but shy and reserved, and so humble-minded as to be always most anxious to give way to any one that would have the kindness to take it of her. And yet she was a beauty—tall, slight, and graceful, with a clear olive complexion, and the brightest black eyes and hair imaginable. Emma Flather was not to be compared to her in point of looks; and yet, by sheer assumption, she always passed for something infinitely superior. Age, perhaps, might have something to do with this, aided by a certain patronising air that the model of propriety invariably indulged in to those whom she condescended to notice. She set up for something out of the common way, and assumption does a great deal!

We trust the reader comprehends these characters.

III

Ecce iterum Crispinus.
Here's old Jorrocks again, as we live!

Free Translation

THE SUN HAD SUNK BEHIND the distant hills, the whistling ploughman was watering his horses and washing their legs in the pond at the end of the village, and the tired labourers were knocking the clay from their clogs at their rose-entwined porches, preparatory to entering their cottages, when the jingling rattle of a hack-chaise drew all heads to the street. The cobbler dropped his last, the publican his pipe, the basketmaker his willows, and the sempstress her needlework, to look at the destination of so unusual a sound.

Amid the chalky dust raised by a pair of lumbering jaded posters appeared the outline of a yellow po'-chay, so enveloped in packages as to leave little but the side panels visible. A well-matted package of apple trees covered the roof, a desperately-dusted boy in a glazed hat clutched the pot of a huge scarlet geranium in one arm, and with difficulty kept himself on the cross-bar with the other, while the pockets of the carriage were occupied with bundles of carnations, convolvuluses, caper bushes, and cornelian cherry trees, completely screening the passengers from view.

Thus it rolled up the street of Hillingdon, like Birnam Wood on its way to Dunsinane, at the best pace the post-boy could muster to dash up to the Hall door.

"Vell, thank God, ve're 'ere at last!" exclaimed a fat, full-limbed, ruddy-faced man, in a nut-brown wig, bounding out of the chaise as soon as the door was opened, cutting off the heads of a whole bunch of roses that had been riding most uncomfortably in the back pocket of his grey zephyr.

"Oh, Jun, you've done for the roses!" exclaimed a female voice from the depths of the chaise.

"Cuss the roses!" exclaimed Mr. Jorrocks, giving the fallen flowers a kick with his foot. "Votever you do, *come out o' the chay!* for I'm sick o' the werry sight on it. Here, Batsay, come out, and then your missis 'ill get turned round—for vot vith her bastle, and vot vith her flounce, she really is as big as an 'ouse."

Out then came Batsay, stern foremost, exhibiting the dimensions of a well-turned foot and ankle, and altogether a large, stout, well-proportioned figure. Mr. Jorrocks having eased her of her flower-pot on landing, Batsay gave her dusty, bunchy, black ringlets a shake, and then proceeded to help out her mistress.

"Now, Binjimin, vot are you a-sittin' perched up there for, like a squirrel in an acorn tree?" exclaimed Mr. Jorrocks to the hero in the glazed hat with the geranium-pot in his arm, who still kept his place on the cross-bar. "Don't you see ve're at 'ome, man?"

Benjamin would have been very clever if he had, for he had never seen the place before. The boy then descended, and Mrs. Jorrocks, in a stiff, rustling, amber-coloured brocade pelisse, with a crimson velvet bonnet, and black feathers, having been baled out, the old deaf man who had been left in charge of the Hall having fumbled the chain off the door, and got it unlocked, stood, hat in hand, while the party proceeded to unpack the chaise, and carry the luggage into the house.

"Now, gently with them happle trees!" exclaimed Mr. Jorrocks, as the post-boy prepared to roll them off the roof; "and have a care of the lumbagos (plumbagos) and stockleaved 'ound's tongue, for them are exotics, vot don't grow in this country. Paid no end of money for them," added he, in a mutter.

Out then came box, and bundle, and parcel, and bunches of flowers and moss-tied roots without end; and all having been carried into the house, Mr. Jorrocks paid the post-boy, and closed the door upon the curiosity of the inhabitants of the village of Hillingdon.

IV

Oh, what a tangled web we weave
When first we practise to deceive!

"So the new squire's come at last!" exclaimed Mrs. Flather, bursting into the room the next morning, where Emma sat patching and torturing a piece of muslin under the pretence of embroidering a collar. Confound those collars! If women only knew how little men appreciate those flimsy, fluttering, butterfly articles of dress, they would surely betake themselves to some more profitable employment. Embroidering a collar! Spoiling a good piece of muslin, we should say! We never see what is called a "richly worked collar" without thinking how much better it would have been to have got a new one, instead of hiding the blemishes of the old one with wreaths, flowers, spots, dots, caterpillars, and other curiosities.

But to Mrs. Flather and the Squire.

"So the new Squire's come at last," was the exclamation of Mrs. Flather, bursting into the room to her daughter; and as this is to be a regular orderly three-volume work, we may as well describe the locality before we proceed.

Mrs. Flather's husband, as we have said before, had held the living of Hillingdon, the next presentation to which had been purchased for a youth not yet fully japanned, and by a hokus pokus sort of conjuration, it was now held by another; and Mrs. Flather occupied the manse until the new owner, James Blake, was ready to take possession. The manse did not stand in "Neighbour Row," in the village of Hillingdon, but occupied a slightly elevated position about a mile off, giving the occupant a view of the beautifully proportioned church, and spire rising amid the foliage of gigantic trees, without the addition to the prospect of the village. The house itself was of the patchworky order of Hillingdon Hall (of course, on a much smaller scale), for it is observable that the same style of architecture pervades certain districts and the manse was partly stone, partly stucco, partly covered with slate, partly with pantile, though the latter was of the diamond pattern and subdued colour of the new national duck-house in St. James's Park. Still it was very pretty, particularly at the season we are now describing, when gay parti-coloured roses bedecked the lower parts, covering the bare stems and stalks of the more aspiring vines and fragrant honeysuckle, or commingling with the large-leaved ivy or perfumed jessamine, showing every bright variety of hue, and every tint of sober green.

Altogether, it was a pretty, sentimental-looking spot—interesting in itself, but doubly interesting as containing the pattern young lady of the place. It combined all the poetry, without the inconvenience of love in a cottage.

Now, a third time, we will surely get under weigh.

"So the new Squire's come at last!" exclaimed Mrs. Flather to her daughter.

"Indeed!" replied Emma, with equal excitement. "How do you know?" inquired she, laying down her collar, and looking anxiously in her mamma's stupid face.

"I have it from very good authority," said Mrs. Flather, with an important nod of the head, as she advanced into the room. Fools are always mysterious.

"Well, but you surely can tell *me*," observed Emma pettishly.

"Well, I had it from Jane, who's been down for the milk," said Mrs. Flather, after such a pause as she thought would be a sufficient punishment for her daughter's impetuosity.

"And who told her?" asked Emma after a similar pause, during which she resumed her stitching as though she did not care to hear anything about them.

"She saw them," replied Mrs. Flather.

"*Them!*" observed Emma; "I thought you said 'The Squire.' "

"And his wife," added Mrs. Flather.

"Oh, he's married, is he?" observed Emma, with a sneer. "What lies people do tell," added she angrily after a pause. "Every person has been declaring for the last three weeks that he was a smart, handsome young London gentleman, and half the girls in the country are ready to set their caps at him."

"They may save themselves the trouble," observed Mrs. Flather. "He's a regular, steady, *old* gentleman, in Hessian boots and a brown wig."

"*So*," observed Emma, with a look of disappointment: "perhaps he'll have some daughters," added she, thinking to vex her mamma with a little mistimed propriety.

"*Sons* would be more to the purpose, I think," replied Mrs. Flather, eyeing her daughter with a half-angry glance.

Emma worked away without the slightest change coming over her alabaster countenance.

"If there are sons, there'll be no harm in seeing what they are like, you know, Emma, my dear," continued the old lady coaxingly.

"What, and throw James over?" inquired Emma, looking up. James Blake was the third and present rung in Emma's matrimonial ladder.

"Ay, but get well on with the new one *first*, you know; but I'm sure, my dear, you've so much discretion, that there is no need for me to point out what is right and proper on such an occasion."

"Poor James!" observed Emma, looking intently at an ink spot she had just discovered on her white muslin frock. Emma dressed plainly. Her mother prided herself on her daughter having no taste for finery, declaring she never was so happy as when in her little muslin frocks. A very convenient doctrine for mammas, and very taking with the men.

"James will soon get over it," continued the affectionate parent; "but that is very careless of you to ink your frock in that way—clean on to-day, too—got to serve till Saturday; but what I was saying was, that no man ever died of love—at the same time, I don't wish you to do anything hasty or unfeeling— James, you know, can always be had— keep him in reserve—just as you did little Meadows, nothing could be more delicate or lady-like than the way you dropped him. James, no doubt, was a change for the better, just as Meadows was better than Upton. If you can get one with double James's fortune, why drop him, and so on, always changing for the better if you can, and taking care always to have one to fall back upon. Men are easily managed. They believe things said to themselves that they would laugh to scorn in the case of another. None of them ever suppose any girl can prefer another to themselves; and if the point of fortune touches them, ridicule riches, say you would rather live with a man you love upon hundreds, than be the mistress of thousands without the endearments of the heart; in short, my dear, I am sure your fine feelings and sense of duty will prompt you to do what is right."

"Oh, I'm sure they will, my own dear mamma!" exclaimed Emma, rising and throwing her arms round her mother's neck, and kissing her profusely, thinking all the time of half a strawberry tart she had left in the dining-room closet, for, O reader, if the model of propriety had a passion, we blush (which is more than she would do) to say it was—*for eating.*

This scene of domestic life was suddenly interrupted by the creaking of the green gate as it swung back on its hinges, causing an involuntary exclamation from Mrs. Flather of—"Oh dear, here's that horrid Mrs. Trotter! Run, Emma, and put on your canary-bird collar."

"Odious woman, what can she want?" muttered Mrs. Flather to herself, bustling into the drawing-room, and seating herself on the centre of the ottoman, as though she had been using her best room all the morning.

"Mrs. Trotter, *marm,*" announced the man-boy in buttons, and immediately Mrs. Trotter's majestic figure occupied the portal.

"My dear Mrs. Trotter, I am so delighted to see you!" exclaimed Mrs. Flather, jumping up and saluting her with all the *empressement* in her power. "I hope you leave all at home well."

"Quite well, thank you," was Mrs. Trotter's comprehensive reply, as she threw a rich black lace veil over her drawn silk bonnet, and displayed the healthy glow of her fine features, and the lustre of her large black eyes.

"And Emma?" added Mrs. Trotter, looking inquiringly round the room, "how is she?"

"Emma's just stepped into the garden to water her flowers," observed Mrs. Flather, casting an eye towards the garden, as she spoke.

"Dear child," said Mrs. Trotter, "she's so fond of her flowers, it's quite a treat to see her among them," thinking it would be, for she knew Emma cared nothing about them.

After a few commonplaces about the weather, the cleanliness of the roads, and the dirtiness of the lanes, Emma entered, watering-pot in hand as usual, and Mrs. Flather having arranged her collar behind (which the rose-bushes had somewhat deranged), Emma pretending great impatience all the time, she burst into most energetic inquiries after all her sweet young friends at Hillingdon, Eliza in particular. Mrs. Trotter answered in the usual full-measured strain, and then, after a little repetition about the weather and a hit at the rose-bushes, conversation came up short.

"And have you heard of the new-comers at the Hall?" at length interrogated Mrs. Trotter.

"No, indeed!" replied Mrs. Flather; "you know we never hear anything—shut up in this little quiet retreat we feel as if the world was bounded within our gates. Nobody ever tells us anything, and I'm sure I never trouble myself to inquire. It can make little difference to us who comes."

"Nay, then!" exclaimed Mrs. Trotter. "I'm sure, now, I'd have thought you'd have liked to have known. However, never mind—I dare say you're right, only it would have looked neighbourly to have given them an early welcome."

"What, they've come then, have they?" exclaimed Mrs. Flather, with well-feigned surprise.

"*Come*—yes—surely!—bag and baggage—and I've made it my business to ferret out all about them."

"And what have you learned?" inquired Mrs. Flather, merging her indifference in her curiosity.

"Why, I've had a good deal of trouble to make out anything, to tell you the truth, for the post-boy that drove them put me on the wrong scent—at least, so it would seem, from the information our Thomas got of their servant, whom he met at the public-house, though his story doesn't exactly tally with what our Jane got from their lady's-maid—however, I gleaned enough to satisfy myself that their name is Jorrocks, and that they have no family."

"What, just a couple by themselves?" asked Mrs. Flather, with as much indifference as she could muster. "Are they young?"

"No, oldish, I should think—at least their man says his master's been Lord Mayor, and they don't make Lord Mayors of boys. The maid says her mistress is a Lady Patroness of Almack's, and that they've a grand house in the city—Great Lombard Street, I think—and I can tell Miss Emma they are great florists," added Mrs. Trotter, turning to the model of propriety, who sat admiring her fine collar.

"Florists are they!" repeated Emma, looking up. "I am so glad of that. Oh, how I *dote* on flowers!" added she, clasping her hands and turning her fine eyes up to the ceiling.

"Yes, they brought a great cargo of flowers and trees, and the man-servant says his master is enormously rich, and kept a pack of hounds, and altogether I think we may congratulate ourselves upon the acquisition—not that they may perhaps supply the place of poor dear Mr. and Mrs. Westbury—but still we might have done a great deal worse, and altogether I think it is a very nice thing, and I shall consider it my duty to pay my respects to them as soon as ever I hear they are in a situation to receive company, and of course you will do the same."

"Oh, I shall call, of course," replied Mrs. Flather; "but not in such a violent hurry," inwardly resolving to be beforehand with Mrs. Trotter if she could, adding, "in a week or ten days' time, perhaps."

"Well, just as you please about that," replied Mrs. Trotter; "in the meantime, if you have any acquaintance in London, perhaps you may as well write to them, and see if you can get any further information. I consider it the duty of us mothers to be circumspect."

"Not for the world!" exclaimed Mrs. Flather; "I have no curiosity of that sort. It's enough for me to take care of myself and my poor dear child here without troubling myself about other people's affairs."

"Well, just as you think right about that; I like always to know who people are; indeed, I consider it my duty—not that I suppose the Jorrockses are other than highly respectable, but still as a general rule I mean. But I must be off, for I've got to attend a meeting of the Ladies' Anti-Corn-Law Association, and must pop into Mrs. Barber's to give her a hint that her daughter was walking rather late with young Dodd, the blacksmith, last night; and that reminds me that our Book Club meeting is to-morrow evening, and I've to distribute the prizes at the Sunday School after that, and write to the secretary of the Shipwrecked Mariners' Society into the bargain; so now, my dearest Mrs. Flather, good-bye. Emma, my sweetest, good day."

Thereupon the ladies kissed with all the smackiness of affection.

"It wouldn't be a bad plan for you and I to pop down to the Hall while that tiresome woman is on her rambles," observed Mrs. Flather to Emma, as soon as she saw Mrs. Trotter clear of the gate. "You could take your watering-pot in your hand, you know, and say, that hearing they have a taste for flowers, you came to offer them the loan of it till their own arrives, or some thing of that sort."

"Well, mamma, whatever you think right," replied the willing daughter; "only let me finish my tart before I go, for I'm very hungry."

"Certainly, my dear, it's always well to eat before you go out, for young ladies should never be seen to indulge; at least, not to eat as if they were enjoying it. Indeed, that is the only thing I have to find fault with you about; you always eat heartily, as it were, instead of picking and playing with what is set before you. It's all very well at home to stuff and eat, but nothing disgusts men so much as a guzzling girl; so now eat your tart and get a good slice of bread—buttered if you like—and then wash your mouth out and we will set off."

V

Down with the bread tax!

COBDEN'S CRY

But times are altered; trade's unfeeling train
Usurp the land and dispossess the swain.

GOLDSMITH

IT WAS A FORTUNATE DAY which secured to the Anti-Corn-Law League the services of Mr. William Bowker—fortunate to the League, for they gained an able and most unscrupulous coadjutor; and fortunate to Mr. William Bowker, for he had just lost the best part of his income by the demise of his old master, the celebrated Mr. Snarle, the great conveyancer of Lincoln's Inn.

Mr. William Bowker, or Bill, as he was familiarly called, was one of a large class of men about town, who make a very great show upon very slender means. Not that he made any equestrian or vehicular display, but in his person he was a most uncommon swell, gay and gaudy in his colours, glittering in his jewellery (or make believes), faultless in his hat, costly in his linen (or apologies), expensive in his gloves, and shining in his boots. Many a country cousin, and many a one again, has anxiously inquired of his London cicerone "who that smart gentleman was," as Bill has strutted consequentially through the Park on a Sunday, swinging his cane, with the tassels of his Hessian boots tapping the signal of his approach.

Many a time Mr. Jorrocks and him have passed for lords as they rolled arm in arm through the Zoological or Kensington Gardens, *haw, haw, hawing,* at each other's jokes, looking about at the girls and criticising their feet and ankles. This latter, however, was in short-petticoat times.

Mr. Bowker was an extraordinary fellow; over head and ears in debt and difficulties, he was as light and gay as if he hadn't a care in the world. Not a new fashion came out but Bill immediately had it. If a flight of extraordinary neckcloths alighted in the mercers' windows, the next time you met Bill he was sure to have one on. All the rumbustical apologies for greatcoats that have inundated the town of late years had their turns on Bill's back. You seldom saw him twice in the same waistcoat. Variable as D'Orsay, and as gay in his colours. Moreover, there was a certain easy nonchalance about Bill, far different to the anxious eyeings and watchings of the generality of "would-be" swells. He would salute a man immeasurably his superior, with perfect familiarity; offer his richly-ornamented gilt snuff-box, or poke him in the ribs with a smile and a wink, that plainly said, "You and I have a secret between us." His looks were in his favour—rosy and healthy, as though he had never known care or confinement; with wavy yellow locks, slightly streaked with grey, giving him the licence of age over youngsters; while his jolly corpulency and plummy legs, filling his bright Hessian boots, had the appearance of belonging to some swell fox-hunter up at Long's or Limmer's, or some of the tiger traps, for what they call a spree—rouge et noir, feathers, hot port, Clarence Gardens, and the Quadrant.

In the language of the sect, Bill had some breeding in him—by a lord, out of a lady's-maid—and blood will tell in men as well as horses. Hence, whatever his difficulties, or whatever his situation, Bill always retained the easy composure of a well-bred man. His address was good, his manner easy, and his language pure. If fortune had neglected to supply him with the essentials, at all events it had not deprived him of the advantages of birth. He was about the gamest cock with the fewest feathers that ever flew.

Hundreds will exclaim on reading this sketch, "Lord, I know that man as well as can be! Have seen him in the Park a thousand times;" and perhaps no one has caused more "Who's that?" than our friend Mr. Bowker. Indeed, he was a sort of person that you couldn't overlook, any more than you could a peacock in a poultry yard, for there was a strut and a dazzle about him that almost provoked criticism. Of course Bowker was well known to his own set, but what's a man's own set in the great ocean of London society? Moreover, even in his own set he was an object of admiration, for he was friendly and jocose, and we don't believe there was a man among them but would rather have enhanced Bill's consequence than attempted to lower him by proclaiming him the clerk to a conveyancer, and keeper of a miserable tobacco shop in the miserable purlieus of Red Lion Square. Our readers, we dare say, will be anxious to know how Bill managed matters. We will tell them. *He lived by his wits.*

When old Snarle was in full practice, Bill's fees were considerable, and in those days he was nothing but the "thorough varmint and the real swell." As soon as chambers closed, he repaired, full dress, to a theatre, attended a "free and easy" or some convivial society. Here his jolly good humour ensured him a hearty reception, and the landlords of the houses were too happy to hand him anything he called for in return for the amusement he afforded to his customers. He could sing, or he could talk, or he could dance, or he could conjure, lie through thick and thin—in short, do everything that's wanted at this sort of place. He was in with the players too, and had the *entrée* of most of the minor theatres about London. At these he might be seen in the front row of the stage boxes, dressed out in imitation of some of the fat swells in the "omnibus," his elbow resting on a huge bamboo, with a large "Dollond" in his primrose-kidded hand. There he was the critic. Not the noisy, boisterous, self-proclaiming *claquer*, but the gentle, irresistible leader, whose soft plaudits brought forth the thunder of the pit and gallery. He had some taste for acting, and we have read some neatish critiques attributed to him in the *Morning Herald and Advertiser*. This sort of society brought him, of course, a good deal among actresses, and we have heard that several of his "How d'ye do?" great acquaintance arose out of little delicate arrangements that he had the felicity of bringing about. This, however, we don't vouch for; we will therefore thank our readers not to "quote us" on this point.

But to the "baccy" shop.

As fees fell off, Bill set up a snuff and cigar shop, and he who had amused so many, sought for the favours of the fumigating public. But Bill had a great mind. He did not stoop to the humble-mindedness of

appearing as a little tobacconist, but leapt all at once into the station of
a merchant, and advertised his miserable domicile as BOWKER & CO.'S
WHOLESALE SNUFF AND TOBACCO WAREHOUSE—THE TRADE SUPPLIED.
Whether this latter announcement had the effect of keeping off
customers—people perhaps supposing they could not get less than a
waggon-load of baccy at a time—or whether Eagle Street is too little of
a thoroughfare, or not sufficiently inviting in its appearance, or whether
there were too many Bowker & Co.'s in the trade already, we know
not; but certain it is, no wholesale customer ever cast up, and most of
the retail ones were what Bill touted himself or were brought by his
friends. The situation, we take it, must have been the thing; not that
we mean to say anything unhandsome of Eagle Street, but we cannot
account for the bad success of Bowker & Co.'s establishment upon any
other grounds than that the neighbouring shops were not attractive, and
a good deal of a tobacconist's trade consists of what is called "chance
custom." Doors with half a dozen bell-pulls in each post, denoting half
a dozen families in the house, coal and cabbage sheds united, those
mysterious, police-inviting bazaars, denominated "marine stores," with
milk shops, corn chandlers, furniture warehouses, and pawnbrokers
commingled, do not add much to the appearance of any street, and
certainly Eagle Street has nothing to lose in the way of attraction.

Yes, the situation must have been the thing, for if any one will take
the trouble of walking through the thoroughfares, and casting their eyes
into the brilliantly-illumined "divans," they will see men, without a tithe
part of Mr. Bowker's ready wit and humour, handing the cigars over
the counter as fast as they can fumble them, with women immeasurably
Mrs. Bowker's inferior, riveting men with their charms, and sending
them away by the score every night with the full conviction that they
are desperately in love with them all, and only wanting to get rid of
the other chaps to tell them so. *That*, we take it, is the grand secret of
a baccy shop. Keep up the delusion, and you keep up your customers,
but then you must have a bumper at starting. There's the advantage of
a thoroughfare. Fool No. 2 sees Fool 1 smoking and making eyes at a
woman, and in he goes to see what she's like. She's equally affable with
him, and while both are striving to do the agreeable in comes No. 3

on a like errand—4, 5, 6, 7, 8, 9, 10—legion, in fact, quickly follow, and they all go on eyeing and fumigating, as jealous of each other as ever they can be, until the smoke obscures their vision, and they leave, each with the determination of seeing what they can do single-handed next night. The shop is then established.

Mrs. Bowker, when Bill set up, was a fine, big, dashing woman, with as good a foot and ankle as any in London. She was then on the flage at the Coburg, but marrying Bill for the purpose of getting off it, he found to his sorrow that she was likely to be a dead weight, instead of an assistance in housekeeping and theatrical society, which it was then his ambition to enter. Still there were her looks—a clear Italian complexion, large richly-fringed dark eyes, corkscrewy ringlets, swan-like neck and ample bust; and what with gaslight, and the tinsel of a theatrical wardrobe, Bill hoped to turn his better half to some account in the way of decoy duck at a cigar shop. Mrs. Bowker, however, took badly to it. She was above it, in fact, and instead of sitting to display her charms in the gaslight, she was generally sipping brandy and water, and reading greasy novels on a sofa in the back shop. Miss Susan Slummers, her sister, also an actress and a fine handsome girl too, was shortly afterwards added to the family circle; and certainly, if wit and beauty can command success in the baccy line, Mr. Bowker had every reason to expect it. Still, as we said before, we grieve to say it did not come; and debt, and duns, and difficulties soon beset Bill's path of life in most alarming profusion.

Our old friend, Mr. Jorrocks, as kind-hearted and liberal a man as ever stuffed big calves into top-boots, long stood his friend—so long, indeed, that the worthy old gentleman had ceased entering Bill's obligations in his books—and many people trusted Bill on the strength of the intimacy, who would never have let him into their debt upon the faith of any of his own palaverments. Not that he was a bad hand in that line, but they had had too much of it. In short, Bill was better known than trusted.

Thus then matters stood at the time of Bill's enlistment in the League. Old Snarle was dead. The dwindling fees were done. To begin brushing coats and cleaning boots for a new man, in hopes of seeing him rise in

the profession, was out of the question to a man with Bill's ideas, and
at his time of life. The cigar shop did nothing. Mrs. Bowker did a good
deal in the brandy-and-water way. House rent was due—their first-floor
lodger had left them. Gas rent was in arrear—water ditto—and poors'
rate collecting. Income-tax, we needn't say, he was exempt from.

Mr. Jorrocks had retired into the country, and though he had never
turned a deaf ear to any of Bill's representations or petitions, still our
worthy tobacconist could not help feeling that without the aid of the
emollient blarney wherewith to pave the way in jolly half-seas-over
intimacy, the ominous "no effects" might some day be returned to his
epistolatory requisitions, and then what *was* to become of him?

—The law and Mr. Commissioner Fonblanque only knew!

Having now introduced Mr. Bowker, we will let his correspondence
with Mr. Jorrocks speak for his situation and arrangements.

EAGLE STREET, RED LION SQUARE

HONOURED SIR,—You'll be glad to hear that your old
friend Bill has lit on his legs at last. High time he did, for
I really think I was never so nearly stumpt in my life. Old
Snarle, as you'll have heard, has cut his stick. Poor old bitch!
Yet let it not be as our great master says—

——the evil that men do lives after them;
The good is oft buried with their bones.

Snarle had his faults, and so have we all, but for 'parties
in a hurry,' there never was a quicker hand at a settlement.
May his new settlement be to his liking!

T'other night, as I was sitting in my back shop
uncommonly spooney, reflecting on the uncertainty of life,
and the certainty of the tax-gatherer calling in the morning,
a mysterious big black-whiskered, beetle-browed stranger
entered the shop, and asked to have a word with me in
private. As soon as we had coalesced behind the scenes,

'Mr. Bowker,' said he, taking off his broad-brimmed hat and gloves, laying them on the table, and sitting down on the sofa, as if he meant to be comfortable.

'You don't know me?'

'Why, you have the advantage of me,' said I.

'Well,' said he, 'I come to advantage you.'

'Glad of it,' said I, adding aside, 'wonder if it's Joseph Ady?'

'You are to be depended upon?' said he, after a pause.

'Close as wax,' said I.

'Well then,' said he, 'you have heard of the great National Anti-Corn-Law League?'

'I have seen their advertising machine,' said I, 'but I never thought more of it than I should of Toss-pot's crockery cart, or Warren's matchless blacking van.'

'I could let you in for a good thing,' observed the stranger musingly.

'Haste me to know it, that I with wings as swift as meditation or the thoughts of love, may—*jump at it*,' exclaimed I.

'I find thee apt,' rejoined the stranger, rising and extending his right arm, saying—

'And duller should'st thou be than the fat weed
That roots itself in ease on Lethe's wharf,
Would'st thou not stir in this.'

'Oh, my prophetic soul! my uncle!' exclaimed I, interrupting him; 'if it wasn't for that black pow and those d——d heavy brows, I'd swear you were my old friend Jack Rafferty, late of the Adelphi Theatre.'

'You *have me*!' said he, pulling off the wig and appurts with one hand and grasping my hand with the other. Sure enough, there stood old bald-headed Jack, with his little ferrety eyes peering at me with the great black brows still above them. Having taken these off and put them carefully in his pocket-book, he again shook hands, and asking for a squeeze of the old comforter, we stirred the fire, put on the kettle, and prepared for hot stopping.

'Bill,' said he, as soon as he had got the brew to his liking, and one of my best Woodvilles in his mouth, 'one good turn deserves another.'

'Undoubtedly,' said I, 'as the tailor observed when he turned the old trousers a second time.'

'Ah!' said he, 'you're just the same old cove that ever you were. How are you off for blunt?'

'D——d badly,' said I; 'should be glad to join you in raising a mortgage on our joint industry.'

'Well, never mind,' said he, chuckling, 'you did me a good turn when that wicked bailiff, Levy Solomons, came to take me for the butter bill, and I haven't forgotten it. By Jove! I fancy I hear him blobbing into the rain-water tub at this moment. I've seen queer days since then,' added he thoughtfully; 'been all through the Disunited States, Canada, Columbia, and I don't know where, shipwrecked twice, gaoled thrice, tarred and feathered besides. Hard life a player's, forced to appear merry when we're fit to cry; however, that's all done—I've turned over a new leaf—I'm in the respectable line now, and hearing that your occupation in Lincoln's Inn's gone, why I've just stepped in, as Paul Pry would say, to see if I could do anything for you in the respectable line too. You see,' said he, 'the way for talented men like us to prosper is to take the folly of the day and work it. I saw this in the nigger times. Lord, if the compensation money had been taken direct from the pockets of the people, instead of passing through the filtering bag of Parliament, it would have been a good workable subject to this day. John Bull is a great jackass—a thick-headed fool. Unless you empty his breeches pocket before his face, and say, "Now, John, I take this shilling for the window tax, this for the dog tax, this for gig tax, and this for the nigger tax," you can't make the great muddle-headed beast believe he pays anything for the nigger tax, and so by making it a parliamentary grant, opposition was lost, and with it as fine a field for enterprise as ever was seen. However, it's no use crying for spilt milk. Go ahead's my motto, as they say in the Disunited States. But to business.

'The new light is the Corn Laws. There's more sense in this than there was in the nigger question, because if you can persuade a man he'll get a fourpenny loaf for twopence, you show him something to benefit himself, which you couldn't do in the case of the great Bull niggers, that he had never seen or cared to set eyes on. Still John shows his stubbornness, and hangs back as if he thought the Repealers were the only people that would get the fourpenny loaf for twopence. It is to rouse the animal, and convince him that for once there is such a thing as pure disinterestedness in the world, that the League is bestirring itself; and now, my old friend Bill,' continued he, 'for the service you did me, by popping the bailiff over head in the tub, I've come to offer to recommend you, as a man of very great talent, eloquence, experience, and I don't know what; in fact, to supply the vacuum there must necessarily be in the heads of men who are fools enough to subscribe theft money to force a be on people that they don't want.

'The League is about to enlighten the country—north, south, east, and west—from the Orkneys to Portsmouth, from Solway Firth to Flamborough Head—all are to be visited by men of mettle like ourselves, and if we don't astonish the natives, why my name is not Jack Rafferty.'

'Faith,' said I, 'Jack, I'm not nasty particular, and never was about making money, especially at the present time, for to tell you the truth, I'm as near in Short's Gardens as ever I was in all my life; but the devil and all is, I know nothing about either corn or the corn laws, and hardly know wheat when I see it.'

'That's nothing,' said Jack; 'you've a quick apprehension and a ready tongue—lots of jaw—and that's what the League want. You'll have plenty of time to study your part, and rehearsals over and over again. Zounds, man, it's the easiest thing in life! Instead of appearing in one character on Monday, another on Tuesday, a third on Wednesday, a fourth on Friday, and a fifth on Saturday, and having to study and cram and rehearse for them all, here you have nothing to do but repeat the same old story over and over again, which comes as pat off the lips as a child's church catechism. "Infamous aristocracy"—"iniquitous"—"ruinous starvation"—"landlord-supporting tax"—"blasted Quarterly"—and all that sort of thing. Whatever is wrong, lay it to the corn tax. If a man can't pay his Christmas bills, attribute it to the bread tax; say the landlords have grabbed a third of his income. Tell the shipowners theft interest is ruined by the monopolists—nay, you may even try it on with the farmers, and say you verily believe they would be benefited by the abolition of the corn laws; that you really think our climate and system so superior, that they would drive foreign grain out of the market, just as our fat Durhams and Devonshires beat Sir Robert's Tariff fat cattle out of the shambles. In fact, you may say almost anything you like; and should any one oppose you, you will always be ready with a cut and dried answer, which, with an easy delivery, will put your cleverest unprepared arguer quite in the background.'

Just then, in came Mrs. B. 'Cleopatra, my dear, here's our old friend, Rafferty,' said I.

'What, Jack!' exclaimed she, 'that robbed the treasury at the Adelphi?'

'*Hush!*' cried I. 'Jack's respectable. *Encore* the brandy.'

Well, the upshot of it was, that the next day I attended a meeting of the League at the British Hotel, in the best apparel I could muster—light blue, buff vest, drab tights, best Hessians, tartan cravat. Joey Hume was in the chair, and as soon as ever I saw that, I determined to be stiff.

'Who have you there, Mr. St. Julien Sinclair?' (for that is the name Jack goes by)—asked Joe, as we advanced to the table.

'Mr. William Bowker,' replied he.

'The same of whom you spoke at our last meeting?' inquired Joe.

'The same,' answered Mr. St. Julien Sinclair.

Jack had primed me pretty well on the road what I should say, in case they examined me; but I suppose, being well recommended, or knowing it must come to that at last, they thought it better to dispense with all humbug, and having ascertained that I was perfectly disengaged, and ready to embark in the cause, they said that the Council of the League had determined to sectionise the kingdom, to enlighten the lower orders on the monstrous iniquity of the bread tax, and the great advantages of a free trade in corn. That they had been at it for some time without producing much effect, but they had now got a new dodge which they thought would tell. This was, that instead of single-handed lecturers, like Jack Rafferty, going about doing as they liked, and reporting what they pleased, that the leaders of the League should take the thing in hand, distribute themselves over the land along with ladies and lecturers, and make a regular crusade against the monopolists. Lecturers, it seems, they had not had much difficulty in getting, indeed I should wonder if they had, for eight guineas a week and one's travelling expenses are not picked up every day—but the ladies there had been some trouble about. However, as they thought they could not dispense with the influence of the fair sex, they have accommodated matters by hiring a certain number of females who are to take superior characters, just as Jack Rafferty took the part of Mr. St. Julien Sinclair. To each lecturer, therefore, there is to be attached a leader and a lady; and the company are building a lot of Whitechapels, capable of carrying three with their luggage, and we are to be allowed ten shillings a day for a horse to pull them about. There will be suitable devices, with mottoes, such as 'DOWN WITH THE BREAD TAX!'—'FOOD FOR THE MILLION,' &c. &c., along the sides of the vehicles, which are to be painted sky-blue, with red wheels, picked out with green. They will be labelled behind in statutable letters—

'GREAT NATIONAL ANTI-CORN-LAW ENLIGHTENMENT CART'

'FORMS FOR PETITIONS SUPPLIED!'

I think that is all I've got to say, except that I hope your new purchase is to your liking, and that Mrs. Jorrocks approves of the house as much as she did of her mother's at Tooting. Should there be anything I can do for you in town, pray let me know; and after I leave, Cleopatra or Susan will be glad to do their best for either Mrs. Jorrocks or you, to whom we all beg to present our most respectful compliments, and I have the honour to subscribe myself,— Dear sir, your humble and obedient servant,

WM. BOWKER, L.G.A.C.L.L.A.
Lecturer to the Grand Anti-Corn-Law League Association

Mr. Jorrocks, it seems, had commenced a letter to Mr. Bowker, before the receipt of the foregoing. We give it entire, throwing, as it does, some light upon his opinions and movements.

HILLINGDON HALL

DEAR BILL,—We've got here at last, and precious glad I was on it. Tiresome work riding three in a chay—two fat

women and one's fat self. Not that Batsay's werry crummy;
but there's a good lot on her; and we had sich a lot o'
poleyanthus's aboard, that I was forced either to squeeze
her, or squeeze them.

The country is werry different to London! Lord bless ye!
'ow small everything looks. Afore we stopped at the first
station, I felt I was gettin' out o' my element; but afore we
arrived at the end of the rail, I felt quite flummoxed—all
bedevilled. Thinks I to myself, 'Now, John, you old jackass,
what are you agoin' out o' your own line o' life for, into
a land of strangers, with nerve an acquaintance, and all
to begin afresh? Couldn't you have stayed quiet in Great
Coram Street, with the run o' the world before you?'
Then, a little somethin' within whispered, 'But you loved
the country, John. 'Ampstead 'Eath has always had great
attractions for you—you love the hair of Greenwich, and
Shooter's 'Ill is dear to your recollection. 'True,' said I, 'my
frind; and I minds when I started in my prentice prime I
loved figs, but I soon found there was sich a thing as getting
a surfeit on them.' Howsomever, never mind—the country
has its charms—cheapness for one. Fowls, three shillin's a
couple; a goose with his gizzard and all complete, four and
sixpence. But to proceed with our journey.

The further we went, the stupider people got; and when
we were done with the rail and got into a country inn, I
think I never saw such a set of stupexes. Instead of half a
little finger fatching one a coach, it took me ten minutes
to drum into an ostler's 'ead that I wanted a po-chay and
pair. Oh dear, then came sixteen miles of dusty roads, sultry
weather, and fat women. I shall never forget it. Howsomever,
we got here at last; and certainly, though frightfully retired,
the place is pretty. It will take us some time to get all
square, for most of the furniture was sold, and there's
nothin' in two rooms but images—men with beards—
men without beards—some without neckcloths—and two

naked Wenuses. Folks about are monstrous purlite—will lend us anything from a warmin'-pan to a waterin'-pot. We've had some callers—women folk chiefly, who seem to be monstrous taken with us. They are a goodish breed o' women hereabouts—large, well-grown 'uns, and werry agreeable. Altogether things are better than they threatened to be, but there's a deal o' sameness, and the evenin's are long. Howsomever, I s'pose we shall get used to it, and when I get started farmin' I shall have more to do. I means to take a hundred or a hundred and fifty acres in hand, and try all the new experiments on a liberal scale—guano, nitrate o' soder, bone manure, hashes and manure mexed, soot, salt, sand, everything in fact; shall lector on agricultur, and correspond with the Royal Society, and so on—Mr. Jorrocks on buck wheat—Mr. Jorrocks on clover—Mr. Jorrocks on long 'orns—Mr. Jorrocks on short 'orns.

I had written this far when your agreeable favour came to hand, and werry 'appy I am to hear of your luck. If the Leaguers have wot they say (£50,000), you are in for a good thing, but I don't believe it—I think it will prove like a lady's fortin', or the dirty dandy's shirts, who began to count at twelve and went up to fourteen—they may have £5000 or £6000, and an o is soon added. I've lived a long time in the world—a liberal sixty, let us say—and I never found money to be had for axin'—certainly not from *our* party, though I believe the Tory calves bleed sometimes. Howsomever, never mind; £5000 or £6000 will take a deal o' spendin', and if you manage matters well, you'll get them to make another whip when that's gone. The question is better nor the nigger one in some respects, and worser in others. It is better for the subscribers, because they are adwenturin' their money for summut that may profit themselves; but then, on the other hand, it choaks off the whole host of grievance-'unters who are only to be moved by imaginary and inwizible wrongs.

In the language of botoney, to which Mrs. Jorrocks is now dewotin' herself, pure philanthrophy is a bush of curious growth. Its tender leaves expand at the pictor of a great naked nigger claspin' his 'ands with 'Am not I your brodder?' comin' out of a scroll in his mouth, and yet close at the sight of a needy relation comin' to ax for a little golden hointment. Old women, love-sick damsels, and ringey, ringlety, guitar-playin' youths, are the great supporters of 'umbuggeries of all sorts; but then it must be a real useless object to enlist their sympathies—a subscription for a Sunday School on the ivory coast, or a communion service for a chapel among the Copper Indians. Bread is too homely a subject. Wot sentiment is there in a great barley loaf? My maid Batsay would be shamed to be seen givin' a yard o' bread to a beggar if there wasn't a great slice o' beef below. There's where I think the Leaguers will be leaked. They can't show a clear case of sheer uselessness; but, on the contrary, there are some strong symptoms of utilitarian self-interest. Who's to be benefited? The Leaguers themselves. There's the rub! Will you get Mrs. Sympathizer Green or Miss Puritana Brown to come down with the mopusses to benefit Cobden and Co.? I think not. P'raps you'll say the Leaguers don't want their mopusses—only their tears. Who are they to be shed for? The labourin' classes? Not they! The labourin' classes don't want them. Bull, as you say, is a great hobstinate beast, but he has some gumption notwithstandin'. This mornin' I walked up the street of our town, dressin'-gowned and slipper'd à la Margate, just to appetise a bit afore breakfast, and there I fell in with a man called 'Ercules Strong, a-shovlin' on stones with a spade and a barrow. 'Mornin', 'Ercules,' said I. 'Mornin', Squire,' said he. 'Hardish work that,' said I. 'Middlin',' said he, diggin' the pickaxe into the heap. 'Vot do ye get a day?' said I. 'Half-a-crown,' said he. 'That's a good deal,' said I. 'Had three shillin' last year,' said he. 'How came they to reduce

Mr. Jorrocks accosts Hercules Strong

ye?' axed I. 'Things fell in price,' said he, 'and half-a-crown
goes as far this year as three shillin' did last.' 'Then the price
of labour's regulated by the price o' wittles, is it?' axed I.
'Undoubtedly,' said he.

Now, supposin' Cobden (who keeps a print-mill, or
print-works, or somethin' o' that sort) employs two or three
'undred 'Ercules Strongs, it's clearly his interest (on the 'grab-
all-I-can' system) to get the price o' wittles reduced, because
then he can get his 'Ercules Strongs so much cheaper,
and pocket the difference. Time was when the motto of
an English merchant was, 'Live and let live,' but them was
antiquated days. These are the 'get-rich-in-a-hurry' times.

P'raps Cob will say, 'Oh, but then if I get my 'Ercules
Strongs at sixpence a day less, I shall be able to let you have
my devil's dust goods, or *bads*, cheaper.'

I doesn't believe that either. I mind, when the leather tax
was taken off, sayin' to my bootmaker, 'Now, I s'pose I shall
get shod cheaper.'

'Why, sir,' said he, 'the fact is, I was jest a-goin' to raise the
price o' my boots, so this reduction will enable me to keep
them as they were.'

Cob would jest be a-goin' to do the same with his devil's
dust bads, I guess.

I don't think you can bam the lower orders about bread.
The Bull niggers with nothin' but a bishop's apron on,
supplicatin' for mercy with chained and uplifted 'ands,
aided by Mrs. Sympathizer Green and Miss Puritana Brown,
was a fine subject, because there was summut left to the
imagination; and as Tommy Moore or some other popular
and poetical gentleman says:—'Disguise thyself as thou
wilt, still, slavery still thou art a bitter draught; and though
thousands in all ages have been made to drink o' thee, thou
art no less bitter on that account.' But a fourpenny loaf sets
Apollo and the Muses to flight, jest as Binjimin has set a
flock o' crows off my front field.

'Disguise thyself as thou wilt, still, Cobden,' say I, 'still thou art a great 'umbug; and though thousands may roll into your beggin' bag, the poor will never eat cheaper on that account.'

It arn't a bad dodge, but I don't think it'll do. There is no elbow-room for the imagination, and the purpose o' the promoters is too apparent on the face on it. It will require a deal o' sleight o' tongue to make Bully believe you're a-workin' for his good. If I was to adwise the workin' classes, I'd say, 'Don't you sign no petition nor nothin' o' the sort, unless your masters will hire you for sivin years sartin at present wages.' Ay, Cobden, wot say ye to that? In short, this is not a good genuine 'ome-brewed grivance, frothin' up at the bung-'ole of discontent, but a sort of seakaley, hothouse, forced thing; a thing that requires mexin' and stirrin' about with a *spoon* like a seidlitz pooder. No offence to the lectorers in course, who I'm sure are anything but spoons.

But I'm a-deviatin' from my text, which ought to be congratilations to you for bein' taken up by the League, instead of denouncin' the 'umbuggery of its ways. In course *you*, as a traveller o' the concern, will do your best to further its interests—and feather your own nest.

So shall you better yourself, and secure the everlastin' esteem of—Yours to serve,

JOHN JORROCKS

VI

There shall the flocks on thymy pasture stray,
And shepherds dance at summer's op'ning day.
PLEASURES OF HOPE

SMALL AS HILLINGDON APPEARED AFTER London, and insignificant as were the shops, Mr. Jorrocks soon found that he could get most things he wanted. There were two tailors', three shoemakers', a milliner's, a straw-bonnet maker's, two inns or public-houses, where they sold grocery, woollen and linen drapery, hats and hardware, or exchanged them with the farmers for poultry, butter, and eggs; also a beggarly beer-shop, a butcher's, and a bull's-eye or lollypop confectioner's. Besides these, of course there was the doctor's—Dr. Claudius Sacker—with his white house and green rails, and name properly emblazoned on a bright brass plate, with a "night bell" pull in the doorpost. Most of the cottage property belonged to Mr. Jorrocks; indeed, the extreme neatness of the buildings, with their old gables, and rose trees, woodbine, or ivy creeping up the thatches or stone roofs, or apricot or pear trees nailed against the fronts, plainly bespoke which were included in his purchase and which were the property of other individuals. There was an air of substantiality about all the Westbury—now the Jorrocks property.

Of course it was the interest of the new landlord to encourage his own people, and accordingly Mr. Jorrocks set about giving an order to each. His swell London clothes he soon found to be inconvenient and unsuited to the country; and in lieu of his fine blue coat and brass buttons, and buff waistcoat, he devised, in conjunction with Tommy Rumfit, *his* tailor, a new article of dress, which he purposed calling the Jorrockian jacket.

John Brick, one of the mercantile publicans aforesaid, having imported a piece of the queer-figured cotton velvety[1] looking stuff that we see ladies making gowns of, Mr. Jorrocks determined to adopt it as the material for his dress, and accordingly had the requisite quantity, with trimmings, cut off, and sent to old Rumfit's. The colour, we should observe, was brightish brown, with a fine light seaweedy sort of pattern shot through—indeed, we are not sure but it might have been meant to represent wheat-ears—Sir Robert Peel's present—though the word "free" was not apparent in any part of it.

Well, this was cut and contrived into something between a jacket of modern and a jerkin of olden times. The collar was a mere hem, turned up; it did not half cover the nape of his great bull-neck; Mr. J. was terribly thick about the throat—a sad sign of want of breeding. The jacket, or garment, was double-breasted, with slanting pockets on each breast, with very full straight laps meeting, or rather folding over, in front, and reaching about half-way down his thighs. A row of buttons enabled him to fasten them in front. In each lap-front were two tiers of diagonal pockets, the pocket-mouths—for holes would ill describe their proportions—being edged with nut-brown velvet, and the upper-storey ones a size or two smaller than the lower. In these he purposed carrying his hands, halfpence, and trifles of that sort; while the lower ones were for his handkerchief, hand-saw, books, and other bulky articles. The back of the garment presented a most extraordinary aspect. There were no buttons at the waist, nor indeed anything to denote where the small of his back would have been—if *small* he had had any—but just about his girth the garment swelled out as if inflated. Two downward folds, indeed, there were, and a line of buttons up the middle, as if the laps were buttoned together, but this was all deception—or rather attempt at deception—for it was apparent to the commonest observer that the garment was of a piece all round. Such it was, however, and being made entirely out of Mr. Jorrocks's own head, of course let him have the credit of it; and such of our readers as think it becoming, we dare say are at liberty to copy it—as he has not yet gone to the expense of a patent. The waistcoat was of the same material, with large flaps without *any* pockets; and his lower man was clad in drab stockingette tights and Hessian boots. A green neckcloth, a woolly white hat, turned up with green, and a knotty little dog-whip, completed his costume. Rumfit and he thought it extremely fine, and altogether a very good job.

Thus attired, Mr. Jorrocks mounted a most imperturbable old Roman-nosed, dock-tailed black cob that he had picked up cheap in the village, and rode about surveying his estate, looking at pigs and cows and sheep, asking foolish questions, and talking a great deal of nonsense about farming. Thanks, however, to the veneration in which townspeople, above all Londoners, are held in the country, the rustics thought some new lights must be breaking in the husbandry horizon—never imagining for a moment that the owner of so fine an estate, with such a fine open countenance of his own, knew nothing whatever of what he was talking about.

Among the cottagers he did well enough, for he had plenty of small-talk for the old women—how many daughters they had? who they married? how many children each had? how many were bouys, and how many gals ? where they got their cat ? whether she was a good mouser? how the oven baked? if their water-tubs were full, how much they held? what they gave for their pig? how they were off for soap ? and other little family inquiries.

Never was such an estate as Mr. Jorrocks expected he had taken possession of, for, in addition to all the tenants being described as most opulent and respectable, Mark Heavytail, the largest, who farmed what was called the "pet farm," was stated by the rural Robins who "did" the printed particulars, to be a man of such *respectability* and independence of character, as to be above asking or accepting a reduction of rent. Glorious man! There was a tenant! Mark was a fine specimen of an English yeoman, six feet high, large and stout in proportion, with a great, round, nearly bald head, grey eyes, snub nose, and ample chin. His usual costume was a snuff-brown coat—at least when he sported any coat, for it was oftener on a hedge than on his back—a striped toilenette waistcoat, broad patent cords, and grey worsted stockings and thick shoes. The pet farm lying round a hill-side, and the house being on the top of it, Mark had the wind first hand, and, either from that cause or from having a voice a size too large for his body, Mark always roared as if he was holloaing to a man at the mainmast of a man-of-war in a gale of wind. One of Mr. Jorrocks's earliest visits was to the pet farm, and though he might not, like Miss Waithman, [2] expect to find all the shepherds with pipes and crooks, or smartly clad dairymaids with cows and syllabubs under the trees, he certainly expected a different reception to what he met with from Mark. Having kicked his pursy pony up the hill, he sat mopping the perspiration from his brow, and looking down upon the village of Hillingdon, with the silvery Dart winding its tortuous course through a wide expanse of rugged picturesque country, when Mark, who was busy cutting hay in his stackyard, seeing a stranger, who he concluded was the "Squire," put on his coat and proceeded to meet him.

"GOOD MORNIN', SIR," roared Mark, as soon as he got within fifty yards of Mr. Jorrocks. "STOP, LET ME OPEN THE GATE FOR YOU;" and Mr. Jorrocks, thinking Mark was deaf, pitched his voice in the same key. The following dialogue then took place, each bellowing as loud as he possibly could.

"GLAD TO SEE YE AMONG US," roared Mark, taking off his hat as Mr. Jorrocks neared the gate.

"THANK YE, MY GOOD FRIND," replied Mr. Jorrocks; "WERRY 'APPY TO MAKE YOUR PERSONAL ACQUAINTANCE. YOU'VE A WERRY NICE FARM HERE; DOIN' WELL, I 'OPES."

"WANTS A DEAL OF DOIN' TO," replied Mark.

"THEN VY DON'T YOU DO IT?" inquired Mr. Jorrocks.

"BECAUSE IT ARN'T MINE," responded Mark.

"THEN WHO'S TO DO IT?" inquired Mr. Jorrocks.

"YOU, TO BE SURE!" replied Mark, louder than ever.

"ME!" responded Mr. Jorrocks. "MY VIG!—WHY, THEY TOLD ME THE FARM WAS PERFECTION;" adding aloud to himself, "There must be some mistake here; this can't be the 'pet farm.' PRAY, MY GOOD MAN, VERE DOES MR. 'EAVYTAIL LIVE?—MR. JORROCKS'S 'EAVYTAIL, IN FACT?" inquired he, after a moment's reflection.

"HERE," roared Mark; "MY NAME'S HEAVYTAIL."

"Indeed! Vell, I thought so; but some'ow your account don't tally with the auctioneer's description of the pet farm."

"I know nothin' about auctioneers," roared Mark, "But I know our back kitchen 'ill be down this back end if there isn't somethin' done to her; and there's no keepin' the cattle straight for want of a new bier."

"Vell, but I'm a buyer," replied Mr. Jorrocks; "vot is it you've got to sell?"

"Sell! Why, there's no prices to get for nothin'. down corn, down horn! We're all beggar'd; nothin' for us but the onion (union); ye can never keep up your rents."

"My vig!" exclaimed Mr. Jorrocks, adding aloud to himself, "if this is the crack tenant, I vonder wot the rest'll be like."

"The veat's a-lookin' well," observed Mr. Jorrocks, after a pause, anxious to get Mark off the grievances—Mr. J. looking back on a field he had passed in coming up the hill.

"That's barley," roared Mark. "I wishes the wheat was lookin' well. Pray, just ride this way and see it, and then say if it's possible at present prices to keep up present rents."

"Vell, but the clover's a good crop," observed Mr. Jorrocks, not noticing Mark's invitation.

"The old land hasn't a ton an acre on it. The land's all sour—wants draining."

"Faith, I thinks the land's not the only *sour* thing on the premises," observed Mr. Jorrocks aloud to himself.

"Will ye be pleased to step this way and look at our back kitchen?" bellowed Mark, after a pause; "And really i think the dairy'll have to be built new from the ground, for the wet comes tumblin' in by bucketfuls from all quarters."

"So much the better," roared Mr. Jorrocks; "it'll save you the trouble of pampin' into the milk. The Islinton folks always say the *black* cow is the best."

"Ay, that's varry true," rejoined Mark, "Our pump's all gone wrong, too—not been a drop of water come from her this fortnight."

"Oh dear! oh dear!" exclaimed Mr. Jorrocks, "you seem to be all gone wrong together—a bundle o' grievances. If grumblin' makes a good farmer, you certainlie ought to be classed A1. Good mornin', good mornin'," added he, turning his sluggish cob's head downwards as he spoke, and giving it a good double-thonging as he went.

"BUT YE'LL SURELY COME AND SEE THE BACK KITCHEN!" roared Mark. "I DECLARE IT'S NEVER NO USE——"

"IT'S NEVER NO USE BOTHERING ME!" screamed Mr. Jorrocks, kicking the cob and double-thonging the harder to get out of hearing, adding to himself as he went: "I'm dashed if ever I see'd sich a perfect 'urricane of a man. Pet farm, indeed! My vig! reg'lar spoilt child, I declare! Come hup, you hugly beast," to the cob, "come up, and get me out o' hearin'."

And with the word away they went down the hill, a deal faster than they came up, the whip, and the cob's nose being turned towards home, giving an additional impetus to his movements.

1.   "Peel" or Ancoat Vale velvet.
2.   Theodore Hook used to take great liberties with this lady in the "John Bull." Transplanting her into Hertfordshire from the shawl-shop in Fleet Street, he represented her as encountering a shepherd with his crook, and saying in exultation at the realisation of her dreams of rural felicity, "But, shepherd, where's your pipe?"

     "Please, marm, I harn't got no baccy," was the reply.

VII

Neighbour, you are tedious.—SHAKSPEARE

CRUELLY DISTURBED AS MR. JORROCKS had been by his interview with Mark Heavytail, he had scarcely recovered his usual equanimity before he encountered another tenant who again upset his philosophy. This was Johnny Wopstraw, a civil but very concise man; and if there is one more provoking thing than another, it is encountering a slow pragmatical matter-of-fact man when one is in a regular state of combustion. Wopstraw was a big, broad-shouldered, broad-faced, sensible, respectable man, but slow in his judgment, and cautious in his utterance. Moreover, he had a provoking way of lengthening each sentence by the unnecessary introduction of the phrase of "upon the whole," the word whole being pronounced as if there were a couple of "h's" and two or three "o's" in it. He was busy in the field, but seeing the new Squire, he left his work, and introduced himself in the usual way by opening a gate.

"Thank ye, my frind," said Mr. Jorrocks as he approached; adding, as he looked over the hedge into the next field, "You've a fine crop o' barley there."

"That's wheat," replied Wopstraw, taking off his hat; "upon the *who-ole* it's tolerable fair. The low end isn't so good as the high, though."

"Humph," grunted Mr. Jorrocks, "these corn crops rather bother my vig. And vot do you think o' things in general?" asked he.

This was a fine comprehensive question, and just the last one that ought to have been hazarded to Wopstraw, for it was sure to last him till nightfall.

"Why, upon the who-ole," he began, "things are down, and I fear they'll keep so. Upon the who-ole, I think Sir Robert was wrong in meddlin' with us farmers. We were doin' pretty well upon the who-ole—just managin' to scratch on, at least—and then he came and knocked the very wind out of our bodies. Upon the who-ole I—"

"Vell, but 'ave you got ever a bal (bull) to sell?" interrupted Mr. Jorrocks, anxious to turn the conversation, and save himself a political lecture. "I vants a bal, o' the pure Devonshire sort, to give these foreignerin' chaps a quiltin'. It be'oves us to be awake—*wide* awake, I may say, sharp as Durham mustard—and to drain and dust our land with hashes and bone manure, nitrate o' sober, and all that sort o' stuff. The farmers here seem a long way behind the hintelligence o' the day."

"Why, now," replied Wopstraw, scratching his head, and reconsidering all Mr. Jorrocks had said, so as to begin answering at the right end—"Why, now, as to a bull, I doesn't know of one that, upon the who-ole, I can recommend. Dick Grumbleton at Hawkstone has one, but he's of the Herefordshire sort; besides which, upon the who-ole, I don't suppose Dick wants to part with him."

"Vell, never mind, then," said Mr. Jorrocks, anxious to be off.

"As to drainin'," continued Wopstraw, without noticing Mr. Jorrocks's interruption, "upon the who-ole, I should say it's the foundation of all agricultural improvement. It's like the foundation of a house, and unless that's sound it's no use."

"Then you don't know of a *bal* to suit me?" rejoined Mr. Jorrocks, catching impatiently at the cob's head, double-thonging and digging his heel into its side, riding off, and muttering something about "Tiresome chap—slow-coach—bothersome beggar," and other little censurable epithets.

In truth, Mr. Jorrocks found a great difference between London and country people. Bred in City, where his life had been passed, and where "time is money," the contrast between its quickness and the slowness of the country was strikingly visible. No smartness, no quickness, no question answered before asked, everything seemed to lag and drag its weary way on—to-day the same as yesterday, to-morrow as the day before. Evervarying nature supplies the charms of artificial change, but he that cannot read that book had better remain behind the counter. Yet how many are there panting to repeat Mr. Jorrocks's mistake!

> Hackneyed in business, wearied at that oar,
> Which thousands, once fast chained to, quit no more,
> But which, when life at ebb runs weak and low,
> All wish, or seem to wish, they could forego;
> The statesman, lawyer, merchant, man of trade,
> Pants for the refuge of some rural shade.

Mr. Jorrocks soon found he was more at home at the Shades at London Bridge or Leicester Square than in the shades of Hillingdon. It was clear he had a deal to learn. Impressed with the conviction that he was too shrewd to be cheated, and country people too honest to attempt it, he made several very moderate bargains both in the matter of cattle and corn, though the prices were so much lower than in London, that he prided himself upon being very clever, just as Englishmen think they "do" the French when they get five-and-twenty francs some odd sous for a sovereign.

Mr. Jorrocks's jobbing and dealing brought him acquainted with another gentleman whom we will at once introduce to the reader.

Joshua Sneakington was a sort of man to be found in most places—a country mischief-maker, a kind of village lawyer—a better hand at talking than working. Tall in person, with long thinnish grey locks scattered over a finely shaped head, with a marked and expressive countenance, high forehead, grey eyes, Roman nose, slightly compressed mouth, and trimly kept whiskers and chin, there was an air of respectability about Joshua, which, aided by a low-crowned, broad-brimmed hat, a well-brushed coat, and the unusual appendage of a pair of gloves, bespoke him a remove or so from the common herd. Gloves are very unusual wear in the country—the exciseman and Joshua were about the only people that sported them, except on a Sunday; and even on a Sunday they were rare—country people don't feel at home in them. Joshua was precise and methodical in his manner, thoughtful in his looks, puritanical in his conversation, and apparently profound in his calculations. He was a native of Hillingdon, a mason by trade, and his misfortune was having been cast in so contracted a circle, for he had all the ingredients of a great rogue, and only wanted room to exercise his talents. As it was, he had cheated everybody, and set the whole parish by the ears long before he had reached the age of fifty. Joshua was in very bad odour among his own craft, for though a neat workman, and also a good judge of work, he always preferred picking holes in other people's to doing any himself. He was plausible and subtle, and his communications were always so close and confidential that they were of little use to his employers, and only served the purpose of transferring his own delinquencies to the shoulders of other people. All this comes out in time in the country, where a bad name is a serious inconvenience to the bearer.

The appearance of a fresh fly in the spider's web at a time it was almost deserted, was as great a godsend to Joshua as the Anti-Corn-Law League summons was to Mr. William Bowker. Not that we mean to compare Joshua to Bill in point of respectability, for Bill was immeasurably Joshua's superior, inasmuch as he would have been honest if he could, while Joshua's natural inclinations were for roguery and underhandedness. Bill was a fine, bold, daring, dashing sort of fellow, while the other was a mean circumventing animal, that would rather carry his points by stealth and undermining than by honesty and straightforwardness.

Knowing the advantage of early applications, as well for the purpose of securing success, as of warding oft hostile admonition, Joshua very soon contrived to come in contact with Mr. Jorrocks. He knew everything Mr. J. would want, and by anticipating this, pointing out that, and recommending t'other, he soon convinced our worthy friend that he was a "monstrous clever fellow," and might be extremely useful to him. Indeed, an honest man of this description would have been very much so, for Mr. Jorrocks, as we have already said, was superlatively ignorant of country affairs, and landed property is not quite so manageable as money in the funds. But the worst of Joshua was, he persuaded Mr. Jorrocks that all the people about him were rogues. This even he didn't do openly. He looked grave and solemn, and shook his head, when Mr. Jorrocks talked of employing any one he didn't approve of—hinted they were not quite the thing, that he knew some one much better suited, or that they were not first-rate workmen. Among the villagers Joshua announced himself as Mr. Jorrocks's confidential adviser, hinted that Mr. J. would not do anything without his advice, and told them they had better make all their applications through him. Joshua jumped all at once into a great man, and paraded Mr. Jorrocks about the town just as a young lady does a newly caught lover. Then it was, "Sneak" this, and "Sneak" that, and "You must talk to Sneak about it," until Joshua seemed likely to eclipse even the renowned Benjamin Brady himself.

VIII

What! is the jay more precious than the lark,
Because his feathers are more beautiful?
Or is the adder better than the eel,
Because his painted skin contents the eye?

TAMING OF THE SHREW

ODD AS IT MAY SEEM, Mrs. Jorrocks got on better at first in the country than her husband. Whether this was attributable to her earlier rural recreations at her mother's at Tooting—who occupied one of those summaries of London felicity, a paled box containing a pond, a weeping willow, a row of laburnums and lilacs scattered about—or that she found herself of more consequence in the village "Hall" than she did in Great Coram Street, we know not; but certain it is, she took to it much more naturally than our worthy ex-grocer himself, who made a very bungling piece of business of the early days of his squireship.

To be sure, Mrs. Jorrocks jumped all at once into active pursuits, furnishing and arranging her house—the like by the garden and greenhouse. She was at it all day, pulling about carpets, wheeling sofas, doing the becoming by tables and chairs, smelling and tying up geraniums, rowing the gardener, and nailing and training up rose trees, woodbine, and ivy. Weeds too were plentiful, and Emma Flather and she always had their hands full of something. Mrs. Flather, though she could not exactly reconcile the Jorrocks's manners and ideas with those of their predecessors, saw, nevertheless, that they were very moneyed people, and coming from London—the place in her mystified imagination of universal gentility—she was inclined to think the Jorrockses must be the newest fashion, and that the Westburys belonged to a somewhat antiquated day. At all events, she had no doubt the Jorrockses were a desirable acquaintance, and day after day the model of propriety was seen wending her way, watering-pot in hand, to the village Hall.

Mrs. Flather thought it "so nice" that there was no young man in the way, so that their disinterested attentions could not be misconstrued, charging Emma all the time to find out whether there were any nephews, or, who the money was likely to go to. Emma was an apt scholar, and even began clipping the Queen's English and taking liberties with her vowels, either from contagion or for the sake of flattering her new friends.—"Imitation," says Lacon, "is the sincerest flattery."

Joshua Sneakington, too, set up a somewhat similar dialect, and talked to Jorrocks about 'osses, and 'edges, and 'eifers (heifers), and 'ouses, and 'arrowing, and 'oeing, and all sorts of 'usbandry.

Indeed, if it hadn't been that Joshua was *ray*ther too keen, having laid so long out of a victim, he would have been quite an acquisition to Mr. Jorrocks at this period, for he knew all the ins and outs of the country, and where to lay hands on everything Mr. Jorrocks wanted.

The hundred or hundred and fifty acres that Mr. Jorrocks threatened taking in hand, of course, was not yet available, the tedious process of half-yearly noticing and out-going cropping having to be gone through with a greater part of it. This, perhaps, was what made Mr. Jorrocks settle less readily than his amiable and accomplished spouse.

One of the old wainscoted rooms, that we described as the parlour of the original old house, was taken by Mrs. Jorrocks for her *boudoir*. Not that it came up to her idea of what a boudoir ought to be, but it was conveniently situated for the kitchen; added to which, she had an eye to the other for a storeroom. Neither were its fittings-up at all to her taste, but these she thought she could rectify. She had the old richly carved stone mantelpiece painted black and yellow, in imitation of marble. The sun, the moon, and all the stars were made to accommodate themselves in the various compartments of the deeply mullioned, richly corniced ceiling, the ground of which was done cerulean blue; and the gloominess of one side of the oak-wainscoted walls she purposed relieving by all the prints out of "Jun's" Sporting Magazines, while the other was to exhibit a triumph of industry in the shape of a papering of old postage-stamps, done in stripes of twopenny blues and penny reds. This of course was to be a work of time, the completion of which depended a good deal upon the kindness of her friends, to whom she applied most assiduously for contributions. Many of them wondered what she meant by writing to ask them to "save their old heads for her." The Gothic oak door, with its massive wrought-iron bands and knocker, did not please her either. She had the bands and knocker taken off; invisible hinges supplied the place of the former; and a smart brass bell-pull appeared in the door-post instead of the noisy old knocker. The door itself also underwent two or three coats of paint, and shone forth in highly varnished imitation of either mahogany or rosewood: altogether, the old girl made quite a revolution. Out of doors she was equally energetic. The village school, which so long had prospered under the fostering care of the late owners of the Hall, came in for a large share of her attentions. This, however, was not conducted in accordance with her ideas of how things should be; the mop caps and russet brown stuffs of the girls did not meet her approbation, any more than did the corduroys and woollen caps of the boys meet Mr. Jorrocks's. Mr. J. had an idea that the dress had a good deal to do with their learning, and always contended that there were no bouys half so *cute* as those of the red jackets and leather breeches of Islington. It was there, we believe, he got his treasure, the renowned "Binjimin" Brady.

Mrs. Jorrocks's chief objection to the girls' dresses was the dowdyness of them. "No style, no smartness, you see," said she to Mrs. Trimmer, the mistress, after she had got her first visit or two over; "it costs nothin' more havin' them a good colour, and the clothes decently made, than these queer, flat, trollopy-lookin' things," running her parasol down a girl's back as she spoke—"nothin' personal, in course," added she, "to the lady wot does the genteel novels, but a little smartness and fillin' out doesn't do young folks no harm—sky-blue now, I should say, would be werry neat, with plenty of flowers—or sea-green, or laylack, or lavender, or red, anything in fact better than these dismal-lookin' browns. And as to their learnin'—spellin', and cypherin', and sewin' is all werry well; but I'd teach them a little of the genteels—braidin' and ornamental sewin'—satin stitch; worsted work too is werry much in wogue."

Poor Mrs. Trimmer didn't know what to make of it all; but of course she concluded the fine London lady knew what was right.

Mrs. Jorrocks was very much bothered about the girls' dresses, and many were the consultations Emma Flather and she held on the subject. Emma, however, had had no experience in these matters, never having seen any other school of the sort, and her taste for clothes not descending below silks, satins, and muslins. In this emergency, Mrs. Jorrocks bethought of applying to Mr. Bowker's sister-in-law, Susan, whose theatrical knowledge and taste combined had aided her on former emergencies, and she thought would help her to some thing smart. Accordingly she wrote her the following epistle:—

> Mrs. Jorrocks's complaments Miss Slummers, and mam, I'll thank you to see what you can do for me in the way of dressin' my school-girls, as they have at present a very flat, trollopey, dowdey sort of look; Mrs. Jorrocks does not approve of too much finery for girls, thinkin' it likely to lead their minds astray from the cultivation of intelligent vays, particular from their reverence and duty to their superiors in every station of life; but I think, without goin' to any great expense, somethin' smart might be hit upon, that would be neat and not costly or gaudy, and set off their figures a little better to adwantage.
>
> Mrs. Jorrocks will, therefore, thank you to see what you can do for her.
>
> HILLINGDON HALL, HILLINGDON

Susan and Mrs. Bowker had a long consultation on the subject of this letter; both had a taste for finery, but how to apply it to the exigencies of a country school was rather beyond their ingenuity, besides which they knew Mrs. Jorrocks wanted to cut a cheap dash. All the charity schools in London and the environs were examined for ideas, but they were all more in the check, than in the fan, vanity style. Susan's attention was then turned to stage costume; all the characters she had appeared in were canvassed, and at length, all things considered, she determined upon recommending a Swiss costume. Her reasons will be best gathered by a perusal of her letter.

RESPECTED MADAM,—I have the honour to acknowledge the receipt of your letter, and in conjunction with my sister, have given your wants my best consideration. I have inspected the dresses of all, or nearly all the scholastic establishments in London and the neighbour hood, but find they all have a tendency to the disfigurement, rather than a development of the person. The colours vary greatly, and the articles of dress slightly differ, but in no one that I have seen is there the slightest attempt at fashion or elegance. At Kensal Green, they have sky-blue gowns, white caps, capes and sleeves, with yellow stockings; but the girls are one uniform breadth from the shoulders to the heels. At Clapham Rise, they have Lincoln green, with blue stockings; at Peckham, tartans, with tartan stockings; at Balham Hill, scarlet, with green stockings, and yellow worsted shawls; at Pimlico, orange, with orange stockings; at Parson's Green they are red all over; and at Turnham Green, all grey.

The result of my examinations and inquiries has been, that though there is a great deal of strong showy material used for dresses at some of these schools, they all seem to have been chosen with a view to extraordinary and incongruous effect—something to startle and surprise, rather than to please and allure. It may have been the taste of the day in which they were founded, but they have certainly outlived the fashion very considerably. Under these circumstances I turned my attention to other countries, first and foremost among which stand the Swiss for originality and variety of female costume. They are an out-of-door people, and though cleanliness and sewing is very properly inculcated in schools, yet the main object in patronising them being to make a show through streets up to church, I conceived we could not do better than attempt a modification of a becoming Swiss dress. These, as you doubtless know—(having seen many on the stage)—are various, particularly the head-dress. In one Canton (Appenzell) they wear black caps like butterflies' wings stuck on their heads, while the rest of the dress partakes a good deal of that of an English housemaid—short sleeves and long petticoats—bodice lacing in front. The Lucernoise are richer and more foreign—large flat hats, hair in two long plaits down the back, white collars, with large frills, purple dresses, trimmed with orange, with a square of orange and red let in at the back of the waist, white stockings, and an infinity of chains, beads, and crosses, on a richly embroidered waist of purple velvet and black. This, however, I think, would hardly do, save for the monitors or head-girls of the school, besides which it has the fault—which all Swiss dresses have indeed—of extreme flatness and want of *tornure*. I therefore merely describe this dress in case richness and costliness should be what you want. What I would respectfully recommend, would be the costume of the Canton d'Ury. This is a large flat-crowned straw hat, with a wreath of ribbon round the crown, the bonnet placed becomingly on the back of the head. A white sort of bed-gown, well open at the bosom, reaching a little below the waist, with a scarlet petticoat and pink stockings. This, confined at the waist, and well set off with horse-hair petticoats, or even bustles, would have a very stylish, dashing effect, and should you ever think of giving a *fête champêtre*, or any little rural entertainment of that sort, girls dressed in that way might be exceedingly useful and ornamental to the scene. A few lessons in dancing would enable them to go through a figure or two while the servants were laying the table; or if the entertainment wanted varying after dinner, you might have them in to perform. Again, they might be useful in handing about tea or cakes; and altogether the appearance of so many retainers would have the effect of adding consequence to the mansion, and, of course, to the mistress.

Should this suggestion meet your approbation, it will afford me very sincere pleasure to assist in carrying it into effect, and your instructions shall be promptly attended to. My brother and sister unite with me in most respectful compliments to Mr. Jorrocks and your self, and I have the honour to remain, madam, your most obedient and very humble servant,

SUSAN SLUMMERS

EAGLE STREET,
RED LION SQUARE, LONDON

Mrs. Jorrocks was charmed at the idea! She thought it was "the werry cleverest hit that ever was made, combinin' the ornamental with the useful"; and she wrote to Susan Slummers to get her estimates and proposals for furnishing the requisite quantity of stuff and stockings, also for finding and upholding for twelve months a certain number of horsehair bustles. The latter was put in competition through the medium of the advertising columns of the *Times* newspaper in the shape of the following announcement:—

HORSE-HAIR BUSTLES

To be let, the finding, maintaining, and repairing for twelve months certain, five dozen best horse-hair bustles of different sizes, which, with all other particulars, may be had on application to Miss Clarissa Howard, at BOWKER & Co.'s wholesale and retail snuff and tobacco warehouse, Eagle Street, Red Lion Square.

N.B.—Just arrived, a large consignment of real havannahs. Tobacco and fancy snuffs in the greatest variety. The trade supplied.

The schoolhouse underwent an alteration as well as the inmates. This was a modern building of the lattice-window cottage order, entered by a porch, leading into a passage on one side of which was the schoolroom, and on the other the master and mistress's apartment. Its outward appearance bespoke what it was; and as there was no fear of the little girls getting to the wrong house by mistake, the owner had never thought it necessary to put up an inscription either stating that it was a school, or that it was meant to educate so many children, or even that it was built by so and so in such a year. Things were now about to be done as they ought. Under the auspices of Joshua Sneakington, a tablet was prepared for erection over the door, stating that Mrs. Jorrocks was the foundress, &c. &c., and in order that all things might start together it was arranged that the tablet should be put up on the Saturday night preceding the Sunday on which the "merry Swiss girls" were to parade for the first time in long drawn line up to church. Then, as the village bells rang gaily on a balmy summer's morning, Mr. and Mrs. Jorrocks were seen repairing arm in arm "full fig" with Binjimin with his hands full of Prayer Books behind them, to see the grand effect of the new dresses and inscriptions, and walk alongside the children to church; out the children came, hand in hand, the little ones first, with their great umbrella hats and enormous bustles, each couple laughing at those on before, Mrs. Jorrocks admiring the effect of the scarlet and white, and Mr. Jorrocks spelling aloud to himself the over-true inscription Joshua Sneakington's hurry had caused to be stuck over the door.

THIS
SCHOOL WAS FOUNDER'D
BY
JULIA JORROCKS
THE TRULY PIOUS AND BENEVOLENT
LADY
OF THIS MANOR
ANNO DOMINI 184—

IX

Some country girl, scarce to a curt'sey bred,
Would I much rather than Cornelia wed;
If supercilious, haughty, proud, and vain,
She brought her father's triumphs in her train.

OUR HERO'S SHIRE, LIKE MOST counties and shires, was divided into Whig and Tory, whereof the Whigs had rather the advantage, owing, perhaps, to the influence of the Lord-Lieutenant, who favoured the former politics, and had the usual making of great men, in the shape of magistrates, deputy-lieutenants, and, perhaps, excisemen. Still the Tories ran them close, and every vote was of importance. The late Mr. Westbury, like most right-thinking men, was a Whig, and great anxiety was felt in high quarters as to what the politics of his successor might be. The Lord-Lieutenant aforesaid—to wit, the Duke of Donkeyton—was a muddle-headed, garrulous old Whig—liberal, levelling, and mankind-loving out of doors—exclusive, and a bit of a bashaw within. "The greatest good for the greatest number! civil and religious liberty! equality! freedom of the press!" and all that sort of thing sort of man.

The period of which we are now writing was one of great importance to his Grace, inasmuch as the hope of his house—the young Marquis of Bray—had just attained his majority, and Parliament had shown certain unhealthy symptoms, indicating, in the opinion of the physicians (Peel, Goss, and Co.), no distant dissolution. These considerations made the Duke come down a peg or two in his greatness, and mix rather more with the commonalty, not but that he knew of all that was going on in the country, for every great man has his toady—his Joshua Sneakington—to supply him with tittle-tattle and gossip, but the Duke thought it prudent to unbend a little. Accordingly, the Duchess began carding, and the Duke began dining, all the likely birds in the district. Of course the Tory party turned up their noses, wondered "that so-and-so would let themselves be made cats'-paws of"—observing that "it was quite evident what the Duke and Duchess were after"; "*they* wouldn't allow themselves to be made a convenience of," and with such-like declarations, patiently waited to be called upon by the leaders of their own party.

It was with great pleasure the Duke heard that Mr. Jorrocks was a Whig, for what with his farms and what with his shops, he could carry as many as fifteen or sixteen votes to the poll. The consequence was, that not many weeks after Mr. and Mrs. Jorrocks's arrival, a dark claret coach, the wheels picked out in red, with four horses, and postilions in scarlet, and two outriders in dark grey, drew up at the old porch of Hillingdon Hall, much to the astonishment of Binjimin and Batsay, who stood staring at two richly embossed and glazed cards, one bearing the title of "The Duke of Donkeyton, Donkeyton Castle," the other that of "The Duchess of Donkeyton, Donkeyton Castle," until the coroneted coach and its contents had whisked clean out of sight. It so happened that Mr. Jorrocks, on that day, had gone with Joshua Sneakington to look at a "*bal*," about ten miles off; and Mrs. Jorrocks and Emma had been sent for suddenly, to quell an insurrection in the school, arising out of the unpopularity of the new costume. Mrs. Jorrocks was sadly distressed at being out, for in addition to natural curiosity, Mrs. Trotter had the impudence to assert that the coach contained his Grace's gentleman, and her Grace's maid; but Mrs. Trotter having once mistaken these personages for the Duke and Duchess, it was just as likely she might mistake the Duke and Duchess for these personages, especially in a large family coach with the windows up. Be that as it may, however, the coach had been there, as the cards could testify.

Great was Mr. Jorrocks's astonishment when he saw them. "Vell, he thought he never know'd sich a thing in his life—called on by a duke! wonders would never cease." Then he summoned Binjimin to know how it all was. "Vell, Binjimin," said he, jingling a load of keys and halfpence in the upper storey of the Jorrockian jacket, "tell us all about it now—vot did you see?"

The Duke of Donkeyton calls on Mr. Jorrocks

"Vy," said Binjimin, wiping his nose across the back of his hand, "I vas a-scrubbin' and polishin' for 'ard life at your Sunday 'essians, ven all of a sudden there came such a peal at the bell that I thought some waggabone had run away with our new pull; accordin' I throws down the boot, and, seizin' the big vip, ran as 'ard as ever I could, 'oping for to catch them. Vell, I opens the door, and crikey, there stood a man, for all the world like Jack the Giant-killer, dressed in a short coat, leather breeches, and top-boots, with a cockade in his 'at, and a precious long vip in his 'and—just like one of them great, long, lazy, 'ulking London Johnnies, wot we used to see about the warst end, only a *deal* bigger, and a coach with sich a sight of 'osses in it, that I think the leaders' 'eads were at the far end of our town. Just like the Lord Mayor's state boobey hutch, only there wasn't no men in harmour about it, or fools in wigs inside. Vell, I was so flummox'd at comin' out with a vip to sich an assortment, that I dare say the Johnny might have been 'ollerin' to me till now to know if you were at 'ome, if Batsay hadn't come and explained that you were away lookin' arter a bull, but her missus was up at the seminary, and she would run for her; whereupon the great sarcy Johnny, with his upturned nose, jest shoved the two cards into her 'and, and the coach and all the party were off and bowlin' away out of sight afore one could say—Jack Robinson."

"My vig!" exclaimed Mr. Jorrocks in astonishment at the honour.

The first blow was speedily followed up by another.

Ere the Jorrockses had fully digested the compliment, and settled the order of march for returning the visit, an enormous card—larger than one of these pages—arrived, done up in a richly gilt and figured cover, sealed with a prodigious seal containing the coronet, crests, arms, and supporters of the Donkeyton family.

The card was not less gorgeous. Under a canopy formed by a ducal coronet, surrounded by a glittering halo, a richly coloured royal party sat at a sumptuously spread table; stars and feathers and orders abounding, while the word "BANQUET," in gilt letters below, denoted the nature of the entertainment, and prepared the receiver for the invitation which followed. Thus it ran, or rather thus it was filled up, the names of the inviters and words of course being printed in gilt letters:—

> The Duke and Duchess of Donkeyton request the honour of *Mr. and Mrs. Jorrocks's* company to dine *and stay all night on Tuesday* the *21st of July*.
>
> R.S.V.P.
>
> DONKEYTON CASTLE

There was a go!

Mr. Jorrocks was staggered, and Mrs. Jorrocks dumb-founded. They thought it must be a hoax. The idea of them, whose most aristocratic acquaintance was old Lady Jingle, at Margate, jumping all at once over the heads of baronets, baron lords (as the late lamented Sam Spring used to call them), earls, and marquises, and arriving by one flying leap at a dukedom, was altogether incredible. Couldn't be the case. Must be some mistake. Perhaps a trick of the boys at Dr. Rodwell's academy, who had always been a nuisance to the neighbourhood, as Joshua Sneakington avowed. But then the coach and horses and cards; there was no hoax in them, for both

Batsay and Binjimin saw them, as well as every man, woman, and child in the village. No, it must be right. The Duke was a farmer, and had heard of Mr. Jorrocks's fame; the Duchess was a florist, and had heard of Mrs. J.'s garden. Thus each settled the matter to their own satisfaction.

"*Honour* too!" observed Mrs. Jorrocks, looking again at the card, "calling it an *honour*—the Duke and Duchess of Donkeyton requesting the honour of Mr. and Mrs. Jorrocks's company."

"R. S. We. P., too," observed Mr. Jorrocks, taking the glittering pasteboard out of the mistress's hand. "Wot can that mean, I wonder? R. S. We. P.—I have it! Remember six werry punctual. So ye vill! Six o'clock and no waitin'—I hates waitin' for my dinner."

Mr. Jorrocks, being the penman of the house, having deliberately unlocked his great brass-bound mahogany writing-desk, and drawn forth a sheet of the best super fine double-wove satin post, thus proceeded to answer the invitation in a good round old-fashioned hand.

"Mr. and Mrs. Jorrocks have the honour of accepting the Duke and Duchess of Donkeyton's inwitation to dinner at six o'clock on Tu——"

"Ah, but Jun," said Mrs. J., when he had got thus far, "are you sure you're right about the hour?"

"No doubt!" grunted Mr. Jorrocks; "vot else can it mean?"

"Vy, S. may stand for seven," replied Mrs. Jorrocks, "as well as six. Remember seven werry punctual."

"So it may!" exclaimed Mr. J., throwing down his pen, and sticking out his legs like a man regularly floored. "Confound these hieroglyphicks. Shall be makin' a hass of myself. Jest like my friend Christopher's clerk, who, when the chap left his P. P. C. card for his master, would have it was a horder for wine, and forthwith dispatched a cart with a pipe o' port and claret. Vell, it's one thing to be *green*, and another to show it," so saying Mr. Jorrocks tore up the note and wrote another, saying "Mr. and Mrs. Jorrocks would do themselves the honour of dining and staying all night at Donkeyton Castle," and let the R.S.V.P. part alone.

News of this sort doesn't keep. In less than an hour after receipt of the card, Mrs. Jorrocks was seen turning out of the Hall in her Sunday hat and shawl, and wending her way "up street," taking the chance of who she might fall in with. As luck would have it, Mrs. Trotter was coming "down," and they met opposite the pond.

"Ow dey do's?" "Charmin' weather, &c.," being exchanged, and Mrs. J. having no place in particular to go to, joined Mrs. Trotter, who was on her way to a district meeting of the Samaritan Society, just for the pleasure of a little of her company that fine day. Mrs. J. very soon broached the subject of the invitation. "Could Mrs. Trotter tell her 'ow far it was to Donkeyton Castle?"

"That she could, for she had been there once, and hoped never to be again: it was just fourteen miles."

Mrs. Jorrocks was rather dumbfounded, for she had never met anyone high enough up the ladder to be able to sneer at a lord, let alone a duke.

Mrs. Trotter, seeing Mrs. Jorrocks's embarrassment, kindly undertook to raise her that she might have the pleasure of knocking her down again.

"And so they were going to Donkeyton Castle, were they? She had heard the Duke's break had been in the town a few days back."

"It was the Duke's coach and six," observed Mrs. Jorrocks—"the Duke and Duchess were callin' on Mr. Jorrocks and me; and now they've sent to ax us to stay."

"Sooner you than me," observed Mrs. Trotter. "I always pity anybody I hear going there—but, however, don't let me prejudice you against it"—so saying, having reached the door of the meeting-house, Mrs. Trotter bid Mrs. J. a good morning, and turned in.

"Jealous, I guess!" muttered Mrs. J. to herself—"howsomever, she'll not put me out o' conceit on't—sour grapes, I guess, as Jun would say."

Nothing daunted by Mrs. Trotter's snarlishness, Mrs Jorrocks wended her way to the Manse, where she found the model of propriety and her mamma in full conclave on the very subject that caused them the honour of her visit. On the parlour table lay a duplicate "banquet card"; and Miss Emma and her mamma were in full discussion as "to what it meant," not that they were puzzled about the R.S.V.P. or anything of that sort, but in the enlarged womanish sense of the term, they wanted to know what it "*meant*." And here we may observe that we believe it to be a well-established fact that every young lady, and many young ladies' mammas, consider at the outset of life that they are destined for duchesses. The model of propriety and the model's mamma were discussing the meaning of the card at the moment. Their argument was this—The Duke of Donkeyton and Mr. Flather were intimate because Mr. Flather was a Whig, and Whig parsons are scarce. Moreover, a parson, Whig or Tory, is a sort of a necessary appendage at a great man's table. Then, in addition, Mr. Flather was a man whose judgment was looked up to, and even dukes are sometimes better for a little guidance. Mrs. Flather therefore satisfactorily settled why Mr. Flather and she had been guests at Donkeyton Castle, but then came the question why her daughter and she should be invited now that there were neither politics nor guidance to get in the way of return. The thought seemed to strike them simultaneously. "My *dear, dear* child!" exclaimed Mrs. Flather, kissing her daughter profusely. "Oh! mamma, if I *should*!" exclaimed Emma, as a slight tinge of pink passed across her alabaster countenance, like a fleeting cloud before the moon.

Just then in came Mrs. Jorrocks.

It were needless following these old girls through their open congratulations and hidden disappointments at finding each other invited, for, of course, each expected to have the "crow": suffice it to say, they thought it prudent to coalesce, and see what could be done in the way of mutual accommodation.

As to rivalry, Mrs. Flather had nothing to fear from the Jorrockses being invited—indeed, she told Emma, all things considered, she didn't know but it was better that they should, for it looked less marked and particular than asking them alone; and if the Marquis's attentions were not palatable to her, it would prevent his feelings being hurt by its bruiting abroad; an overture of that sort being a thing no woman ever *thinks* of mentioning.

Fully impressed with the conviction that the Duke and Duchess of Donkeyton had determined on perpetuating their line through the medium of some artless, guileless, unsophisticated country nymph—

such a one as described in our motto—after the manner of divers well-authenticated greasy novel couples, Mrs. Flather (who was obliging enough to believe us ladies and gentlemen who lie upon paper—called authors) most magnanimously ordered her daughter such a rig-out as she thought becoming for the next taker of the title. Not that she went to Vouillon and Lawrie, or any of the accredited dispensers of fashionable feathers and furbelows, but she expended some pounds in the purchase of a piece of uncommonly good blue silk for a morning dress; which with the aid of Mrs. Smith, the village sempstress, was made to display the fine swelling figure of the new marchioness to great advantage. Nay, more, it imparted a shade of colouring to her eyes, and made them quite blue. A Leghorn bonnet, lined with blue crape, and a white feather tipped with the same colour, did the business, and made the model perfectly killing. Give Emma her due, she was a fine girl—straight as a milkmaid, fine drooping shoulders (which she exposed so much when dressed as to make bystanders fear she might be enacting Mrs. Eve), splendid bust, tolerably small waist, and good feet and ankles.

Before starting with Emma Flather on her new matrimonial speculation, it may be well "to advertise the reader," as the old writers used to say, as to her past and present position. We have already intimated that she was then in the third step of her matrimonial ladder, in the person of James Blake. The previous ones it is immaterial to mention, further than to say, that Mrs. Flather had made each believe her daughter was desperately smitten with them both, but that a sudden reaction had taken place on finding that neither had anything to live upon. It is wonderful how many people achieve the feat of living upon nothing. James Blake was differently situated, for Mrs. Flather had the advantage of knowing the exact minimum at all events of his fortune. He had been in the dangerous position of a pupil to Mr. Flather, who had been in the habit of putting the finishing touch to young gentlemen before going to College, and Emma and James had been sort of schoolfellow playfellows—dangerous situation for a young man, especially an orphan as he was. Well, on Mr. Westbury's death, as we said before, the next presentation of the living had been purchased for James;

and the period of his taking possession drawing nigh, and nothing better having presented itself, Mrs. Flather had fully settled in her own mind that it would be much better both for him and her daughter to marry, and then they could all live together, and she could keep things in order, and save them and herself a world of trouble.

In this arrangement Mrs. Flather did not contemplate any difficulty, for James had lived with them long enough for her to know that he was easily led, especially by such a charming conductress as her daughter. Indeed, wiser men than he might have willingly surrendered themselves to such prepossessing guidance. James was not very bright, however, partaking rather of the nature of what is called *soft*. Just the sort of youth for Mrs. Flather to have to deal with, she being what the Yorkshire people call both *soft* and *hard*. Few are so stupid as not to know their own interest. To look at James, though, you would have thought he was wise—he was a good-looking young man—tallish, with a lofty forehead, bright brown eyes, Roman nose, and altogether with what ought to have been an expressive sort of countenance—only it had no exact expression. Still he was what would be called a gentlemanly-looking young fellow; particularly in the country, where the half-buck, half-hawbuck order preponderate.

Our readers perhaps will say, "Why, you make both James and Emma rather of the negative order." Perhaps we do—however, we can't help it, so there's an end of the chapter.

X

Thou know'st how guileless first I met thy flame,
When Love approached me under Friendship's name;
My fancy formed thee of angelic kind,
Some emanation of the 'All-beauteous Mind,'
Those smiling eyes, attempering every ray,
Shone sweetly lambent with celestial day.
Guiltless I gazed; Heaven listen'd while you sung;
And truths divine came mended from that tongue.
From lips like those what precept fail'd to move?
Too soon they taught me 'twas no sin to love:
Back through the paths of pleasing sense I ran,
Nor wish'd an angel whom I lov'd a man.

THE PREPARATIONS FOR THE VISIT to Donkeyton Castle occupied the attention of Mrs. Jorrocks and Mrs. Flather most uninterruptedly. The rose bushes and flowers were left to train and look after themselves and the household department received little attention. Silks, satins, and sarcenets usurped the place of card-tables, carpets, and counterpanes. Mrs. Jorrocks had a new dress made for the occasion—an amber-coloured brocade, with large bunches of scarlet geraniums scattered about, and flounces three-quarters of the way up her middle. Her bonnet was white chip, with an amber-coloured feather tipped with scarlet, above a Madonna-shaped front, plastered down each side of her forehead—"Mutton, dressed lamb fashion," as Mr. Jorrocks observed.

Mrs. Flather was equally assiduous—more so if possible—having higher and more important objects in view. Many were the tryings on, and alterings of, Emma's dress—a little fulness here, a little tightness there, a little pinching in the arm, and a little puffing elsewhere. She was regularly fitted out for conquest. Many were the confidential dialogues held between mother and daughter, as to Emma's proceedings, after she had captured the coronet. How she should ride in a coach and six, how she should call on Mrs. Trotter, how she should appear at Court, and how condescending she should be. Poor James Blake was shelved, or seldom mentioned, save as a *dernier ressort*.

Emma's appetite was the only thing Mrs. Flather feared. Men she knew—marquises she imagined in particular—disliked guzzling girls; and she was most anxious that Emma should appear a pure ethereal being—a sort of compound of love, sentiment, and omelette *soufflée*.

"I think, my dear, it will be well to take a little bit of something to eat with you," observed Mrs. Flather to the model of propriety as they sat in solemn conclave on the oft-discussed and all-important visit, "and then you can trifle and play with your dinner, and be able to give your undivided attention to—whoever happens to sit next you. A great deal may be done at a dinner-table, especially when people are hungry. Suppose we tell Jane to bake you a few buns, and then you can eat some before breakfast as well?"

"Oh yes, mamma, and let her put some currants in them," replied the embryo Marchioness.

"Pshaw, you and your currants," observed Mrs. Flather snappishly, "I wish for once you'd give up thinking of eating, and turn your attention to something else—consider what a prospect you have before you": with which admonition Mrs. Flather left the room to look after buns and other matters.

The getting to Donkeyton was the next consideration. Mr. Jorrocks swore no power on *airth* should induce him to ride three in a po-chay again; and having imported his valuable old rattle-trap fire-engine vehicle, he settled in his own mind that the old Roman-nosed cob should go in it, and convey Mrs. Jorrocks and himself in front, with Binjimin and Batsay stuck up behind. The weather was fine; the roads were good; the cob was strong, and what was to hinder them? Mrs. Jorrocks, however, was the one to hinder them. "She'd jest as soon think o' flyin' as goin' to Donkeyton Castle in a hamber-coloured dress in a one-'oss chay. Wot! when the Duke and Duchess had come in a chaise and six! She'd rather not go at all, than not go as she ought." Mr. J. was quite willing to let her stay at home. However, there were two to one against Mr. J. there; three indeed, Mrs. J., Mrs. Flather, and Emma. These cases generally end in a compromise, and so did this.

Mrs. Jorrocks of course wanted to get herself there in good order—without the derangement to dress and complexion consequent upon sultry weather and dusty roads. Mrs. Flather wanted to get Emma there in like manner, and, moreover, would rather ride with Mr. Jorrocks than his wife, so they arranged to hire one of those forlorn attempts at gentility—a coachmaker's job carriage—with a "neat and careful driver," from the neighbouring town of Sellborough, to which we shall by and by have the pleasure of introducing our readers. Between this and the old fire-engine the following distribution of parties was made:—Mrs. Jorrocks and Emma inside, with Batsay and Mrs. Flather's boy in buttons on the box, and Mr. Jorrocks, Mrs. Flather, and Binjimin in Mr. Jorrocks's old rattle-trap. Mr. J. wanted to argue that there would be too many for the cob, and thought it would look better for Batsay to go inside, and Binjimin and the boy in buttons to occupy the box of the job-chaise; but Mrs. Jorrocks indignantly spurned the idea, and stopped the argument by asking how he could have the imperence to say *that*, when he had proposed taking her, Batsay, Binjimin and all. Poor Mr. J. was posed.

The important morn dawned a lovely summer's day. The sun rose clear and bright. The sky was of azure blue, scarce a cloud obscured the heavens, nor did a breath of wind disturb the leaves. But for the bustle of packing and arranging, with the fear of forgetting, it would have been a day of enjoyment. Mrs. Jorrocks's knuckles got sadly reddened before she had done.

Mr. Jorrocks took it "werry easy." The Jorrockian jacket being still in high favour, of course he sported that with drab tights, and Hessian boots. His shave had been accomplished with extra care, and a neat sea-green cravat supported his jolly chin. He got a little help from Binjimin that morning, and the old cob would have gone without his corn but for the timely services of Mr. J. Tiresome work these sort of "jaunts." What with preparing, lounging about waiting for the right time, so as to nick the proper hour for arriving, and, above all, getting a lot of women with their goods under weigh—there is no doing anything; and unless a man has a letter back, or something in his pocket whereon to vent his mind in the shape of an article for a paper or magazine, he's sure to blow up his wife, or the maid. "Now, *are* you ready? *Con*found it, you're *always* late! Didn't I tell you so? Lauk, what a woman you are! Now, where's your bag? D—n the bags! *Do* come away. We shall never get there. Wish I'd refused the invitation. Never go again, however."

The job-chaise—a terribly dirty, drab-lined old green, with greasy red leather cushions and back—was dispatched to the Manse to import Emma and her mamma, and after keeping Mr. Jorrocks dancing about at the door with the white reins of the old cob in his hand a good half-hour, it at last hove in sight buns and all, and Mr. Jorrocks having moved the fire-engine on a pace or two, it presently drew up at the door. The model of propriety really looked beautiful. It's wonderful what miracles dress accomplishes. We have seen girls who were really quite plain, expand into beauties under the hands of a good milliner. "*Expand*" we may well say, for they generally make them look about half as big again as they are. Emma, as the reader may remember, did not want any filling up—fining down would have been more to the purpose with her. However, that is matter of taste, there being, fortunately, admirers of women in all shapes. Indeed, if it would not shock the delicacy of our male readers, we might mention that Emma had had an extra tug at her stays, and reduced her waist by an inch and a half or so. Emma had a good foot and ankle, pulled her stockings well up, and didn't mind showing her legs a little. Indeed, pulling up their stockings is a great thing with girls. The finest satin dress that ever was worn, will not compensate for untidy ankles. It is not the value of the article, but the fit and style of the thing that does a man's business. A cotton gown has proved many a man's "fix," as the Americans say. Still, when one's been used to a girl in cotton, the emergence into the radiance of silks has frequently a very favourable effect. So it was with Emma. Mr. Jorrocks—a great admirer of beauty, and an excellent judge of the points of a woman—albeit he hadn't shown any great taste in his selection of Mrs. J.,—was struck "all of a heap," as the saying is, with the elegance of Emma's appearance, and could he have been sure that Mrs. J. would have let Emma sit in the middle he wouldn't have minded riding "three in a chay" again. Nothing would satisfy the old cock but Emma should get out and show herself, an invitation she readily complied with, and having praised the tightness of the sleeve, the breadth of the flounces, and the curl of the feather, Mr Jorrocks handed her back again, and shoved Mrs. Jorrocks in after.

Mrs. Flather and he then mounted the front seat of the fire-engine, Benjamin left the old cob's stupid head to jump in behind, and yielding the *pas* to the chaise, they fell in behind just at a sufficient distance to avoid the dust. At the first turn of the road they met Mrs. Trotter; glorious encounter. Mrs. Jorrocks kissed her hand at her, as if she would never see her more. Mr. Jorrocks pulled up for the double purpose of a little chat, and of letting the chaise get out of sight, for he had a wholesome dread of those little nasty back windows, that coachmakers will stick in behind.

"Vell, Mrs. Trotter," said he, after mutual salutations were over, "this *is* summut like summer—the real unadulterated article, I guess—and where are you atravellin' to?"

Mrs. Trotter was bustling about trying for subscriptions for the "Shipwrecked Fishermen and Mariners' Benevolent Society; annual subscription, two and sixpence—donations *ad libitum*"; and liking Mrs. Flather as little as Mrs. Flather liked her, and, moreover, objecting to let her "Donkeyton Castle" her, she hurried away, vowing she hadn't a minute to spare, commenting in her own mind on the abandonment of Mrs. Flather in riding about publicly with another woman's husband.

Mr. Jorrocks, who always did everything like a workman—or at least what he thought like one—having folded a natty new zephyr across his thighs, so as to leave the upper part of his well-filled drab stockingette pantaloons visible between the laps of the Jorrockian jacket, turned a little to his left, and commenced a voluble battery—not to say love-making—with his fair friend. Our young readers, we dare say, will turn up their noses at this, just as the boarding-school miss did, when she begged her mamma not to marry her to an old man of thirty; but as we get older we get wonderfully lenient in the matter of age, and see no reason why two old fools should not amuse themselves as well as two young ones. Besides, if our accommodating friends will refer to the first portion of this tale, or whatever they please to call it, they will find that we expressly stated, that Mrs. Flather was an undespairing widow—as indeed all widows are, that have anything—so there is nothing improbable, though it may be a little improper, in a steady old gentleman, like Mr. J., doing as we have described. Well, right or wrong, J. did it, and but for the encumbrance of Benjamin, we fear he would have been far worse. First he flopped the nag—"There was a goer, neat, clean, straightforward, dartin' action, none o' your lumberin', rollin', dishin' beggars, wot go like crabs, all vays at once, and none in particklar. Took to his collar like a tramp (trump), didn't run arter it all day, never tryin' for to ketch it." Then he gave old Roman-nose another flop—"Nice nag! all over right, he did believe. He called him Dickey Cobden, not out o' compliment to him o' the League but simply because he was wot is called a cob 'oss—a useful, underbred nag. If he'd been a dun 'un now, he'd ha' called him Tom Duncombe, but he should have had a trifle more breedin'. Finsbury's pride was werry well bred. Howsomever, all things considered, Dickey did werry well. Some might think him a trifle too old; but he thought nothin' o' that, age was nothin' either in 'osses or women. Fat, fair, and forty, was his motto. Binjimin!" exclaimed he, turning short round as he heard the boy snicker at hearing this oft-repeated assertion, "take the drivin'-seat out from an under me, and make me a comfey place for my back. I'm far too 'igh; nothin' to rest agin,—there, take cushion and all out, and I shall get a nice nest."

This arrangement had the desired effect. It brought Mr. Jorrocks a few inches below the level of Mrs. Flather, and enabled his lower notes to ascend to her bonnet without travelling over the back to Benjamin. At least so Mr. J. thought. He then began afresh—"Nice day for a drive?" observed he aloud, flourishing his whip over his head like a French postilion; adding, in an undertone, "and rare weather for billin' and cooin'. I'm dashed if a day o' this sort don't rejuvenate one—knocks full five-and-twenty per cent off one's age. I feels like a four-year-old. Binjimin!" exclaimed he, "jamp out and see if Dickey hasn't picked up a stone."

On Mr. J. drove, keeping the boy running after the carriage, vociferating that Dickey "hadn't done nothin' o' the sort." Mr. J. availing himself of the opportunity to sweetheart Mrs. Flather. "Stones," said he casually, as if he really thought the cob had taken up one, "are bad for the feet—and talkin' o' feet," continued he, "wot beautiful feet and ankles your daughter 'as. Now, if I was a young 'un—that's to say, a little younger than I am——"

"*There ain't no stone in his foot!*" roared Benjamin.

"Five-and-thirty or so," continued Mr. Jorrocks, without noticing the interruption, "I'd have a shy at her. She's jest the sort o' figure I fancy—clean, full limb'd, up-standin' sort o' gal; with as fine a figur-'ead as ever I——"

"*I tells you there ain't no stone in his foot!*" screamed Benjamin, toiling after the dust-raising vehicle, Mr. Jorrocks jerking the old cob's mouth to keep him going, and prevent Benjamin overtaking them.

"Your boy's left behind," observed Mrs. Flather, not exactly comprehending Mr. Jorrocks's manoeuvre.

"Oh! never mind the bouy," replied Mr. J., "he finds his own shoes."

"It's the '*ind* foot, Binjimin, I think, the stone's in," holloaed Mr. Jorrocks over his left shoulder; adding to Mrs. Flather with a wink, a nod, and an emphasis, "Emma's her mother's own child, I calculate— like as two peas."

"*I tells you there ain't no stone in his foot!*" screamed Benjamin again, relaxing from his run into a walk; and Mr. Jorrocks, guessing he had had about enough, pulled under the shade of a roadside tree to wait his coming. Meanwhile he busied himself tucking Mrs. Flather into her cloak, and arranging the rug for her feet.

"Dear me!" said he, lifting her gown a little, "them's Emma's feet all over. Werry rum," continued he, half to himself, and half to the tree, "but 'oss maxims often 'old good with women too. No feet no 'oss, no fut no ankle. Never troubles to look at a woman's face if she's clumsy and beefey about the pins. *Con*found them long pettikits! There's never no sayin' wot's an under them. I wonders G——y B——y, or some o' them '*emollit mores*' ladylike legislators, don't bring in a bill to make draggle-tails felony. I declares they drives me perfectly mad. Unless a man spends 'alf his time at 'Owell & James's, or Swan & Hedgar's, or some o' them man-milliner sort o' shop doors, waitin' for to see the gals get into their chays, he has no possible chance o' knowin' wot sort o' understandin's they have."

"Come up, Dickey!" said he to the cob, as Benjamin soused himself sulkily into his seat, and leaned forward to hear what was going forward.

On they went.

Women in general have no idea about roads, or distances, or places, and will travel the same way over and over again, without making an observation or a landmark of any description on the line. Indeed, some men—fox-hunters too—are not much better; and will ride over a country season after season, without getting a bit better acquainted with it. No wonder Mrs. Flather was not of much assistance in directing the route or timing the journey, when the natural indifference of the sex on these matters, and the exciting nature of her companion's conversation, are taken into consideration. The day was fine and pleasant, and the road picturesque. Not that the latter was any great recommendation, for Mrs. Flather was own cousin to the ladies Lord Byron met sleeping in the char-à-banc between Porte St. Martin and Chillon, while Mr. Jorrocks's eye for a country was chiefly directed to the nature of the soil, the quality of the crops, and the advantages it exhibited, either in an agricultural or fox-hunting point of view. "That's nice turnip land!" he would exclaim in a loud voice for Benjamin to hear, pointing to a field on the right, after indulging in a long murmur of amatory sentiments; or observing, on looking at another, that he'd "be bund with a good dustin' o' nitrate o' sober to make it grow ten quarters a hacre. There's a Balfinch!" he would say, pointing to a high quickset fence next the road. "Stop Hashton Smith and Craven Smith, and all the Smiths wotever were foal'd. Lord! 'ow I used to show them the way with the immortal old Surrey. Would lip anything a'most—anything that my 'oss could lay his nose on." Then in an undertone he would indulge in a strong panegyric on fox-'unters, ascribing to them every desirable matrimonial quality under the sun, which, by a dexterous adaptation of his subject, he contrived to bend into an exemplification of himself—Mr. J. was tolerably vain. "There's lazy farmin'!" then he would exclaim—"see 'ow the beggar's shirked the fences, as if he thought they'd set fire to the plough. Be bund I'd grow as much grain on the land he's wasted, as would pay a quarter the rint o' the farm. My vig, but that chap wants a lector on agricultur."

"That's Donkeyton Castle!" at length exclaimed Mr. Jorrocks, breaking off in a long tirade about ladies' legs and the advantages of lime as a manure.

"Good," we fancy we hear some cavilling critic, who has dogged us thus far on our path, exclaim, "Mr. Jorrocks, who has never seen Donkeyton Castle, pointing it out to Mrs. Flather who has."

It *was* so nevertheless, for no sooner did his eye catch the flag floating on the keep, rising above the octagonal towers among the trees in the distance, as a sudden Derbyshire or Dorsetshire twist of the road brought them full on the valley of Borrowdale, with the broad Dart swelling in the middle, than he immediately pointed with his whip, and exclaimed, "That's Donkeyton Castle!" as aforesaid. Mrs. Flather thought it was too, and, looking at her watch, expressed her surprise at the hour—and astonishment, mingled with something like regret, at the apparent shortness of the distance.

Mr. Jorrocks, ever "wide awake," gave her a gentle nudge with his elbow, and pretending to arrange the apron strap on the splashboard, whispered, *sotto voce*,
"*You and I'll ride 'ome together.*"

A change now came over the spirit of their dream.

Their minds became occupied with anticipations about their visit, the ceremony of presentation, and the necessary palaverment. The vision of the ducal coronet gracing Emma's brow again returned in full force, as Mrs. Flather looked with an eye of ownership on the proud scarlet flag floating lazily on the evening's breeze. It was a lovely scene. The road wound gently round the lofty river banks, fringed with stately trees in all the luxuriance of full summer foliage, reflecting their gigantic shapes in the crystal-like clearness of the water; while Donkeyton Castle rose tower above tower in the distance, in all the massive grandeur of feudal pomp and unconquerable strength.

The road now bent into the valley, and it required all Mr. Jorrocks's coachmanship to prevent the fire-engine running the old cob off his legs, which began to fail just at the time the hill was steepest. At length they accomplished the descent, and a short piece of level road brought them to the massive, deeply-ribbed, many-arched bridge across the smoothly gliding Dart; and a few paces farther on, and they were at the castellated gates, forming a triumphal arch into Donkeyton Castle Park. The great black-nailed oak doors were closed, and the rattle and jingle of the fire-engine died out on the pavement, without procuring the attendance of any one.

"*Now then!*" cried Mr. Jorrocks, in the orthodox London twang, putting his whip in the case, preparatory to making his final arrangements.

"*Come, Mr. Slowman!*" squeaked Benjamin, as he stood up behind with all the importance of a grenadier; "*look alive!*" added he, without moving his station.

"Jest get out, Binjimin," said Mr. Jorrocks quietly, "and give a leetle '*tinctum nabulum sonat*' to that 'ere bell I sees perched i' the corner."

Out Benjamin got, and seizing the chain, rung a peal that made the old entrance echo, and scared the owls out of the ivied battlements.

"*What's happen'd now?*" inquired a big-bellied, brandy-nosed porter, bustling out of a side-door, dressed in green plush, with a yellow waistcoat, and lace-bedaubed hat; "no one's allowed to pass through our park."

"Pass through our park!" repeated Mr. Jorrocks, "vy, I'm a-goin' to dine with the Duke—I'm Mr. Jorrocks the grocer—Mr. Jorrocks of Hillingdon 'All, that's to say——"

"Beg pardon, sir," replied the porter, all humility, taking off his laced hat and throwing back the massive doors with an ease non-comportant with their heavy appearance.

Mr. Jorrocks then passed on a few paces, and drew up under the arch.

"Fatch me a lookin'-glass," said he, pulling off his gloves, and putting them into his hat, at the same time diving into one of the lower Jorrockian jacket pockets, and pulling out a hairbrush and comb.

Mr. Jorrocks then made a formal arrangement of his wig and whiskers; and having, by the aid of the glass, wiped the dust from his face and green tie; he handed it to Mrs. Flather, who made a hasty review of her features, while Mr. J. flopped the dust off his Hessians with his handkerchief.

"There, old bouy," said Mr. Jorrocks, handing back the looking-glass to the owner, "there's your mirror, and see you learn to know a genl'man agin I come this way again;" so saying, he put Dickey Cobden in motion, and commenced the ascent to the castle.

It was a noble place. On a lofty hill in the centre of a large, well-stocked deer park, exhibiting almost every variety of grass on its undulating surface, and profusely dotted with gigantic trees, stood the moss-grey towers and terraces of the ancient castle, forming a feature in the country for many miles around. The clustering trees around its base seemed unable to cope with the towering altitude of the castle. Centuries upon centuries had rolled on since the first part of it was built, but succeeding additions had adhered to the Gothic architecture of the original.

"I *do believe* Dickey Cobden's agoin' to knock up," observed Mr. Jorrocks, with a shake of the head, as the old nag relaxed into a walk on feeling the collar against the now approaching hill. "Binjimin, jemp out and ease the beggar a bit, or we shall be planted, and then there'll be a pretty kettle o' fish."

"That's the worst o' these underbred beggars," observed Mr. Jorrocks confidentially to Mrs. Flather, "they're all werry well so long as the road's 'ard and smooth, but, *con*found them, as soon as ever they get into a difficulty, or the collar begins to pinch, they shut up. Come, Dickey, old bouy," continued Mr. Jorrocks, rubbing the colt's back with the crop of the whip, "be o' good cheer, and sink the old Sussex ploughman for once."

Dickey stood still.

"Nay, then!" exclaimed Mr. Jorrocks, "it's all U P with us. Ease his bearin' rein, Binjimin—ease his bearin' rein, or loose it altogether, and turn his 'ead to the hair—block the wheel, or he'll run back with us, and we'll lose wot he's done."

"Come, old bouy," resumed Mr. Jorrocks, after a few seconds' pause, during which he sat eyeing the old nag intently, "I vouldn't expose myself afore all these deer, and other signs o' genteelety"; Mr. J. looking at a herd of deer watching them from a neighbouring clump of trees on a gently swelling hill on the right; "rouse the spirit o' the cobs, and at it like a man."

Dickey shook his head.

"Vell, it arn't no use argufyin' with such a muff," observed Mr. Jorrocks, throwing the reins to Benjamin, and sticking the whip in the case; "he's jest von o' your—if he *vill*, he *vill*, and if he *von't*, he *von't*—sort o' beggars, and he played me jest the same trick agoin' up the 'ill to Mr. 'Eavytail's pet farm t'other day, and neither coaxin' nor quiltin' had the slightest effect upon him—so vot do you say, my dear Mrs. Flather; s'pose you and I get out and valk, and leave Binjimin to follow ven he gets his quadruped out o' the sulks?"

Mrs. Flather readily assented, and divesting themselves of cloaks, shawls, and outer habiliments, Mr. J. handed her out of the fire-engine, and off they set arm in arm for the castle.

"It's a deal plisanter walkin' nor ridin'," observed Mr. Jorrocks, kicking his legs out before him on the grass—"at least plisanter nor ridin' curled up like a cod-fish as I was. Not but the hutch is a good 'un, comfey hutch I may say, but it don't do, when a lady and gen'lman want to be a *leetle* confidential, to have a servant stuck in behind, listenin' to all what they say. Lord, I should like nothin' better than to be cast on a barren land, a sort o' Heel-pie island on a large scale, with an agreeable companion—*female* one, in course," added Mr. Jorrocks in an undertone, squeezing Mrs. Flather's arm, "with no bother o' servants, or nothin' o' that sort. Jest a maid to milk the cows, and another to make the beds and lay the cloth, with a silvery sailin' boat, with a blue streamer at its mast'ead, to come every Saturday night, with poultry, and pastry, and preserved fruit, and bottled stout, hoysters, marmeylad, eggs, and wermacelli, and may be a few yards o' bombazeen: not that dress would be any object, for beauty, says I, when unadorned's adorn'd the most," Mr. J. giving Mrs. Flather's arm another hearty squeeze; "but I'm sick o' the hartificial state

o' society—the cards, and the compliments, the *so* glads, and *so* sorrys, the
grinnin', and the gammon and spinnage o' the thing, and my wiggorous
'eart yearns for natur' unalloy'd, and the habolition o' bustles and 'oss-'air
pettikits. Cuss me if here arn't Dickey Cobden a-comin' again!"

Sure enough there was Dickey—Dickey in a canter too, for Benjamin,
by the aid of what the old "stage coachmen" called a "short tommy,"[1]
had succeeded in getting Dickey into motion, who, with the now much
lightened vehicle, came jingling along at a sort of donkey's canter, with
Benjamin grinning in the driving-seat.

"*Cut along, Binjimin! cut along!*" exclaimed Mr. Jorrocks, waving his
arm onwards towards the castle; but Dickey was one of your regular
marplots, and came to a standstill immediately opposite his master and
fair friend.

"Oh, but you're a beast!" grinned Mr. Jorrocks with vexation, "*do* get
him out o' the way, Binjimin, for the dust he raises is quite obfuscatin',
and Mrs. Flather here's got her Sunday gown on, and not never no
cloak, nor nothin' to protect it."

Benjamin didn't like showing the short tommy to his master, so
he hit on another expedient for making Dickey go. Leaning over the
splashboard, he took off his hat, and rattling his hand in it, produced a
noise like distant thunder at Dickey's tail, who, cocking his ears, set off
at a canter which very soon bore him out of sight.

"Cute bouy that Binjimin," said Mr. Jorrocks, eyeing the receding
vehicle with delight, "he's up to sn*aff*. Nice wehicle, too," continued
he, following it with his eye. "Had it a long time—done me a deal o'
work. Charley Stubbs, wot married my niece Belinda—as neat a little
trout as ever you set eyes on—christen'd it the fire-engine; or, rayther,
one of them sarcy toll-takers on Vaterloo Bridge christen'd it so; but,
howsomever, they never could put me out o' conceit on it, and there it
is, and there it isn't," concluded he, as it passed out of sight, where the
road wound round a clump of trees.

"I reckons the coachmaker's trade's a particklar good 'un," observed
Mr. Jorrocks thoughtfully; "almost equal to the possession o' the

philosopher's stone, for they certain*lie* do conwert wood and iron
into gold in a most *mir*akilous manner. Nothin' under a hundred and
thirty-eight guineas for elliptics, and a hundred and eighty-five for C
springs; and yet if you takes them a boobey hutch back, they'll hardly
give you thirteen for it: offer you ten, p'raps. I gave eight for that; you
couldn't have a nicer one for sweet'eartin' in, or no manner o' purpose,
though it has neither ornamented lamps, nor a double-compass'd
dashin' iron. Crikey, vot a shop!" exclaimed Mr. Jorrocks, breaking off
in his discourse, as the whole castle front, with its terraces and towers,
stood full before them. "Vot *can* a man do with so much 'ouse room
as all that: I wonder now if he pays winder tax on all them funny little
pigeon 'oles, and crosses, and things wot are stuck all about the towers.
I reckon the Lumber Troop, or even the City Light 'Oss, would look
uncommon blue if they'd been order'd to 'take' that castle! Fancy a
panful o' 'ot lead comin' down on one's cocoa-nut from one of them
'igh places, such as one reads of in Clarendon's 'istory of the Rebellion,
or Marryat's Jacob Faithful, I doesn't mind whether." Mr. Jorrocks stood
staring.

"Oh! but the hart o' love's far afore the hart o' war, isn't it, my little
d*a*ck?" continued he, moving on again, with a squeeze of the arm of
Mrs. Flather.

"Them 'ill be the gardens to the left, where I sees all the glass a-
glitterin' through the trees," observed Mr. Jorrocks, pointing them out
to his fair friend. "It don't seem much out of our way now to take them
as we go to the castle, and if there's a short cut, I'll be bound to say I
find it. Let's see 'ow the enemy goes."

Having pulled out his great ticker and forgot to look at it, he felt
a sudden conviction that a few *gus*berries before dinner would do
them both an infinite deal of good, especially himself, having, as he
said, a slight tendency to headache, from having incautiously taken a
thimbleful of indifferent brandy the previous evening; that's to say, from
having had a glass too much.

His company was so agreeable that Mrs. Flather could not refuse, so
leaving the carriage-road, they struck up a path across the park to the
left, leading apparently in the direction of the garden.

"Nothin' like fox-'unting," observed Mr. Jorrocks, "for makin' chaps cunnin' about country. Now your reg'lar Cockney chaps never think there's a shorter way than by the road, and go trudgin' jest the same way as they go on 'oss-back. James Green, now, for instance, though he saw the glass a-glitterin', would have gone to the castle, knocked at the door, and axed which was the way to the garden, instead of settin' off on a woyage of discovery like you and I are a-doin'. To be sure an agreeable companion makes any place plisant, and I never thinks of poor Hadam alone in his beautiful garden and plisure grounds, without feelin' a sort o' compassion for him. To be sure he lived in good times, no income-tax—no 'oss-'air pettikits; but then, on the other 'and, he had no 'unting. When you marry again, Mrs. Flather, marry a fox-'unter," said he.

"Oh, my dear Mr. Jorrocks, I've given up all idea of anything of that sort," replied Mrs. Flather, who at length got a word in sideways, "my poor dear children occupy my only thoughts in this world."

"*Fiddle-de-dee!*" replied Mr. Jorrocks, squeezing her arm more violently than before—"never say *that*—a nice comely little woman like you—*for shame* of yourself—you're any man's money—any man's, at least, wot knows the good pints of a woman."

"Oh, Mr. Jorrocks, you flatter!"

"Never such a thing! never such a thing!" retorted our gallant Squire, waxing warm, "I *wow——*"

"*There ain't no road this way, my old covey*," roared a green-and-yellow watcher (who, unseen to our friends, had dodged them for some time), right into Mr. Jorrocks's ear.

"B— your imperence!" screamed Mr. Jorrocks, doubling his fists, and putting himself into an attitude of defence before his trembling friend. "B— your imperence, I say! you confounded rebellious-looking ruffian, I'll knock you neck and croup into the middle o' the week after next, and spit you like a sparrow afore the fire. Vot do you take me for?"

"Take you for!" repeated the man, "why, a trespasser, to be sure—maybe a poacher, looking after *our* leverets. A regular snaring-looking chap," continued the man, eyeing the Jorrockian jacket-pockets.

"I'll snarin'-lookin' chap you," roared Mr. Jorrocks; "stop till I gets to the Castle, and I'll let you see who you've been insultin' of——"

The man looked foolish, and thinking he might have made a mistake, pretended to be taken by the sight of some one else in the distance, and hurried away, with a view of watching theft manoeuvres again. Mr. Jorrocks's equanimity was soon restored, and before the keeper was out of sight, his feathers were down, and he was arm-in-arming it with Mrs. Flather over the green sward as before.

The sombre tint of a massive yew-tree-lined walk led the eye onwards to the garden, which they entered by a triumphal arch through the gardener's house. The garden was an immense place, five or six acres at least within the walls, with forcing and succession houses of every sort and kind. Vineries, pineries, peach houses, melon frames, and cucumber beds, without end. A dozen gardeners were lounging about, some with watering-pots, some with spades, some with fruit, some with vegetables, some with their hands in their pockets.

"They must be werry fond o' fruit," observed Mr. Jorrocks, as, Mrs. Flather on arm, he stood eyeing the premises and retinue. "Wegetable diet altogether, one would think, judging by the quantity they grow. S'pose we have a bunch o' grapes," added he, advancing towards a glass-house. "Oh! I declare it's a pinery! real pines a-growin' quite nattural, instead of perched on plates, as one sees them in Common Garden, or Bond Street. Sarcy meat there, I guess—a guinea at least—howsomever, we'll have our rewenge here, and get one for nothin'." Thereupon our worthy friend opened the door, and having selected an exceedingly fine pine, rejoined Mrs. Flather, who waited his return outside. "Where there's ceremony, there's no friendship, I always says," observed he, diving into the lower pocket of the Jorrockian jacket, and producing a large pruning-knife, wherewith he cut off the bottom of the pine as he held it by the top in the other hand. "There now," said he, paring and presenting Mrs. Flather with a most liberal slice, "eat that, and then we'll take a turn at the gusberries."

Mr. Jorrocks then cut and commenced eating a similar slice himself.

"Werry good," said he, munching and eating away. "Werry good indeed—fine-flavoured—ripe—juicy—declare the juice's a-runnin' down my chin."

A very important-looking personage, who, but for the attendance of a couple of followers with flower sticks and bass matting, Mr. Jorrocks might have taken for the Duke of Donkeyton himself, now bore upon them right up the centre of the walk. "This is Mr. Tuliptree, the head gardener," whispered Mrs. Flather, seeing her companion was rather puzzled.

"Indeed!" exclaimed Mr. Jorrocks, resuming his wonted gaiety, and staring most unceremoniously—a feat that Mr. Tuliptree was perfectly equal to; for, making a dead halt before them, he stood making an apparent mental calculation whether the rum-looking figures he saw could possibly be Castle company or not.

"Vell, old Cabbage-stalk!" exclaimed Mr. Jorrocks as they met, " 'ow are you, this fine weather?—'ow's Mrs. Stalk, and all the little Sprouts?"

Mr. Tuliptree stared.

"You grow grand pines," continued he, holding the half-finished one up to Mr. Tuliptree's nose. "Excellent, I may say; but there's an old sayin', and it's a werry true un, too much puddin' 'ill choke a dog, and too much pine 'ill do the same by a gen'lman, so now show us the way to your best gusberry bushes—not your great overgrown prize sorts, all skin and seeds, what have no more flavour nor a turnip, but some o' the nice little prickly old-fashioned sort, scarlet or green—you know wot I mean, old buoy."

"Pray, sir, may I ask if you're staying at the Castle?" inquired Mr. Tuliptree.

"*Goin'* to," replied Mr. Jorrocks, taking another cut at the pine; "but first," said he, "give me a bit o' that bass mattin', and get me a cabbage leaf, for I really think I shall be makin' myself sick with this pine, and that would have a werry nasty appearance, you know, old Cabbage-stalk, not to say ungenteel; there now," said he, when he had got what he wanted, "we'll tie it up, and so keep it fresh, and maybe i' the mornin' I may like to take another cut at it;" so saying, Mr. Jorrocks popped the remainder of the pine into the lower Jorrockian jacket-pocket, leaving the top of it sticking above the diagonal pocket hole.

Mr. Tuliptree was posed; but having seen some queer looking customers at the Castle, who afterwards turned out to be lords, he thought he had best put on his servitude manners, which he immediately did, and most obsequiously led the way to the gooseberry bushes.

Mr. Jorrocks then fell to.

"Our old gal 'ill be a-wonderin' wot's got me," observed Mr. Jorrocks at length, gathering a parting handful of gooseberries, and thinking what a wigging he was running the risk of. " 'Ark! there's the clock— one—two—three—four—five—six—*six* as I live—my vig—there's a go—they'll be a-sittin' down to dinner without us—tempus fuggit, money flies certainly."

"Oh, they don't dine till seven," observed Mrs. Flather, "and I think the Castle's not far off—there used to be a bridge somewhere about here, between it and the garden, I think, over a brook, if I recollect right."

"Ah, yon 'ill be it!" replied Mr. Jorrocks, pointing to a bridge a little way off, nearly obscured by foliage—"the Castle can't be werry far off, or that clock must be own brother to the one at Saint Paul's. Well, I'd a deal rayther walk in these nice shady humbrageous walks with sich a sweet hen-angel as you, nor go and stuff wenison and fizzy with my Lord Dukeship up there—deary me now, it's been jest these sort o' summer, sunshiny valks that Dean Swift meant when he talked 'bout the greenest spot on memory's waste. Ah! it must be a plisant waste wot's a-covered with sich spots. There's a deal o' plisant sentiment I always thinks in them nice lines o' Peter Pindar's:

> And say, without our 'opes, without our fears,
> Without the joy wot plighted love endears,
> Without the smile from partial beauty won,
> O vot were man? a vorld without a sun!

"Ain't there, my darlin'?" asked Mr. Jorrocks, looking under Mrs. Flather's bonnet, and squeezing her hand as it rested on his arm, a pressure, we are shocked to say, Mrs. Flather slightly returned.

Mr. J. then kissed her.

"*You and I'll ride 'ome together*," said the steady old gentleman, beginning to puff as the ascent of the hill announced their approach to the Castle. Presently they were on the terrace.

Those who have stood on the ramparts of the city of Berne—the Aar at their feet—and the setting sun shedding a roseate hue over the snow-clad encircling Alps, can form an idea of the splendour of the scene from the terrace of Donkeyton Castle, inferior of course in magnificence, but wonderful when found in our not over-picturesque country of England. Mr. Jorrocks, however, was not much of a man for scenery, and Mrs. Flather was too busy thinking of her reception from the Duchess and other things, to give it a thought, so they turned to the massive, richly-carved portico of the Castle to await the answer to the summons of the bell.

"The chap must have had a wast o' grandfathers, as D——è R——e would say," observed Mr. Jorrocks, eyeing the many time-worn shields studding the walls of the centre tower, the arms on some of which were mouldering into decay.

"I'd take them old things down if I was the Duke, and put up some pretty images—shepherds and shepherdesses, Wenuses, or Diannas, or things o' that sort, summut more in the taste of the times—might have them in wood or Mulgrave cement, if he didn't like to go to the expense o' carvin' in marble or stone."

A fat porter in state livery—his pea-green coat and yellow waistcoat almost concealed with gold lace, and a court bag to his collar, opened the massive door to admit our guests into the hail. Here they were met by two gigantic footmen similarly attired, and the groom of the chamber in full dress.

"You cut it fat here, old bouy," observed Mr. Jorrocks, handing his hat to the porter and a glove to each foot man, " 'ope you don't injure yourselves with work. These chaps," observed Mr. Jorrocks to Mrs. Flather, "are jest like wot the Lord Mayor and Sheriffs o' London 'ave."

"What name shall I say, sir?" asked the groom of the chamber in the politest manner possible, motioning them across the lofty baronial hail, the stained glass of the deeply mullioned windows casting a variety of shades over the armour, and banner-displaying rafters of the oak ceiling and walls.

"Mr. Jorrocks, to be sure," exclaimed our hero, "who else should it be? Mr. Jorrocks and Mrs. Flather, in fact."

Passing onwards into what would be a large room for a house, though a small one for a castle, the groom of the chamber opened a lofty door on the right, and ushered them into a sixty by thirty feet library, fitted up in the extreme of Gothic style; old oak chairs, old oak tables, old oak sofas, old oak screens, old oak wainscoting half up the walls—at least half up those that were not covered with old oak bookcases.

"Mr. and Mrs. Jorrocks, your Grace," whispered the well-trained menial in the low funereal sort of voice that distinguishes the servants of the nobility from the name-mangling brawlers of High Life Below Stairs, as his Grace reclined in a luxuriously-cushioned, richly-carved black oak chair, taking a skim of the *Morning Chronicle*.

Down went the paper, and up got his Grace. He was a fine, tall, noble-looking man, quite bald, with a little snow-white hair behind, and full whiskers and beard under his chin. Indeed, he looked as though the hair had been scraped off his head and made into a fringe for his face. There was a glow of health upon his countenance, and a straightness in his gait that took considerably from his age, which (on the wrong side of sixty) might, with the aid of Persian dye to his "snow wreaths," have passed for five and forty or fifty. He was dressed in a black frock-coat and waistcoat, with drab trousers and wore eyeglasses affixed to a massive gold chain across his waistcoat.

"How do you do, Mr. Jorrocks? I'm very happy to see you," said his Grace, offering his hand, and bowing very low.

"How do you do, Mrs. Jorrocks? I'm monstrous happy to make your acquaintance," continued his Grace, extending a hand of fellowship to her, his naturally misty memory making him forget that he had greeted Mrs. Jorrocks not very long before, who was since gone with the Duchess to her bedroom.

"This is *Mrs. Flather*, your Grace," observed Mr. Jorrocks, after their hands were released, "she's comed with me"—adding, with a sly look and shake of his head, "nothin' *wrong* though, I assure you."

"Ah, true!" exclaimed his Grace, pretending the evening shades had dimmed his vision, and seizing Mrs. Flather again by the hand, "My old friend, Mrs. Flather, to be sure, I'm very glad indeed to see you;" adding, "and where's my old friend, your husband; he's coming, I hope?"

"*I rayther think not*," replied Mr. Jorrocks, with a grin and a wink, pointing downwards with his forefinger.

"Ah, *true!*" replied his Grace, with a shrug and solemn look—"I remember now he died of the————"

Just then the Duchess, who had piloted Mrs. Jorrocks and Emma to their rooms, returned to see if any more of their dear friends had arrived, and relieved the trio from their embarrassment.

"Susan, my dear, here are our good friends, the Jorrockses," exclaimed the Duke, seeing the Duchess making her way up behind them.

"Mr. Jorrocks and *Mrs. Flather*," observed Mr. Jorrocks with an emphasis, turning short round and making a very low bow—"nothin' *wrong*, my lady, I assure you, only Mrs. Flather likes an open chay, and Mrs. J. don't—a little *stommach*, you understand," added Mr. Jorrocks, tapping his own with his forefinger.

Her Grace was delighted to see them of course, and, after a few commonplaces, proposed showing Mrs. Flather her room. The Duke volunteered the same office by Mr. Jorrocks, notwithstanding his assertion that if Mrs. Jorrocks "wasn't long gone he be bund to say he'd run her to ground by her scent, she musked herself so uncommon 'igh when she went to fine places."

---

1.   A short, heavy, knotty whip.

X

I'll make my heaven in a lady's lap,
And deck my body in gay ornaments,
And witch sweet ladies with my words and looks.

BATSAY, BINJIMIN, AND MRS. FLATHER'S boy in buttons, not being much used to company-making, thought the visit to Donkeyton was quite as much for their amusement as for that of their master and mistresses; accordingly, instead of unpacking and laying out the things for the latters' dressing, they contented themselves with carrying the boxes upstairs, and leaving the parties who were to wear the clothes to unpack and sort them out at their leisure, while they, trustworthy individuals, underwent the ceremony of introduction and acquaintance-making among the servants of the Castle. The consequence was, that what with the time consumed in pulling at bells—the confusion attendant upon the influx of a houseful of strangers, and the difficulty of appropriating each peal to the proper servant, our fair friends were hard run in the matter of dressing. Mrs. Flather was in a desperate state of excitement, for, independently of only having Batsay's services at second-hand, that rascal Binjimin had smelt the buns and carried them away bodily; and the model of propriety, whose naturally good appetite was greatly heightened by the ride, was really ravenous for want of food. Like many home-made arm-chair projects, the possibility of accomplishing the coronet seemed suddenly to dissolve as they came within sight of it. Still, like a man with a middling race-horse, Mrs Flather determined to run, and take the chances of luck in the tussle; she had paid her stakes, in fact, in the shape of dresses. The buns, however, were a desperate blow, and the worst of it was, Mrs. Flather durst not ask point-blank

about them for fear of exciting Mrs. Jorrocks's curiosity, and much time
was consumed in Batsay's running between Mrs. Jorrocks's room and
Mrs. Flather's, inquiring for a "brown paper parcel tied up with blue
ribbon."

"No, there was nothing of the sort."

"Then, perhaps, the blue ribbon had slipped off, and it would just be
a brown paper parcel."

"No, there was no such thing."

Binjimin had taken better care of them than that. The buns were
under the cushion of the carriage, and bag in the harness-room fire.

The Duke and Duchess of Donkeyton had had weary work all the
morning of this important day marshalling the order of their guests
according to their ideas of each visitor's importance, and the service
they could be of in the event of a contested election. As usual on such
occasions, their Graces' ideas, and the ideas of the parties themselves,
were greatly at variance; and the more trouble they gave themselves to
please everybody, the further they were from attaining their object. Each
guest had an accurate idea of his own consequence, but unfortunately
no two tables of ideas tallied.

The ingredients of an electioneering Whig party of this description
are rather curious. The "don" Whigs, of course, are not asked; or, at all
events, only those who from similar necessities are able to tolerate the
nuisance of such gatherings. The guests are generally the exception
to the general order of guests. The politics of middle life are chiefly
personal. The first great man that is civil to a person generally gets his
interest, and Whig or Tory is just a toss up which comes first. We admit,
however, there has been a change within these twenty years—we might
almost say within the last dozen—since the passing of "the Bill," in fact.
Men that never thought of anything but their shops, now talk of their
politics just as their fathers used to talk of their wives, their horses, or their
watches. Times are changed indeed. Whether for the better is another
matter not important to this dinner. We leave it to Young England.

The guests mustered strong. Their Graces had taken a pair of
compasses and drawn a circle of seven miles round the Castle, within
which radius the parties were only asked to dine, while those beyond

were accommodated with beds. The consequence was, that great
anxiety had prevailed relative to the accuracy of the different village
clocks and hall timepieces, so as to nick the *juste milieu* of time, each
visitor being duly impressed with the conviction that the eyes of that
inquisitive and observant gentleman, "all England," were turned upon
him; and that upon his individual accuracy depended the success or
failure of this great party. Indeed, though there was scarcely an appetite
amongst them, and though they were all most horribly frightened, there
wasn't one who would not have taken it seriously amiss if he or she had
been omitted. It is wonderful what pain people will undergo for pride
or (what ought to be) pleasure. A tight boot is nothing to it. There was
a great stir of one-horse chaises within the seven miles' circle towards
the hour of six.

Of course the host and hostess were anxious to show every honour
to their guests—make *real* company of them, in short; and the best of
everything was put in requisition—state liveries, first-class china and
plate in profusion; the whole brilliantly illumined with wax and oil.
His Grace didn't use gas—the only piece of sense he was known to be
guilty of.

A little before seven the Duke and Duchess of Donkeyton had planted
themselves on a sumptuous rug, before a brightly-burning wood fire,
in a glittering, profusely-mirrored drawing-room, fitted up with fawn-
coloured satin, with gold coronets worked on the chairs, sofa-cushions,
ottomans, screens, and so on. His Grace was in full dress. His star
glittered on a richly-buttoned blue coat with velvet collar; waistcoat
and cravat vying with the whiteness of his hair and whiskers; the broad
blue ribbon of his "order" crossing gracefully over his chest; the garter
relieving the monotony of his breeches and black silk stockings.

The visitors then began to arrive. Those who were all-nighting in
the Castle, walked into the drawing-room with an "at-home" sort of
air; while the dinner guests passed into the presence with an anxious,
hurried, sidelong-glance sort of walk, that looked very like wishing
themselves back again. Each looked as if he were playing a part. The
Duke—who was a very loquacious old gentleman, though terribly
given to making mistakes—received his guests with the easy dignity of

high life, and asked each a question or two that he thought would show a familiarity with the parties, and an interest in their concerns;—just as he asked Mrs. Flather after his "good friend, Flather," who had been dead some years. For instance, Mr. Tugwell and the Rev. Mr. Webb having come together, and his Grace recollecting that one was a great farmer, shook hands with Mr. Tugwell, observing it was delightful weather; and hurriedly turning to the parson said, "Well, Webb, how are you? How's your bull?"

"Please, your Grace, the bull belongs to——"

"Ah! *dead*, I suppose," replied his Grace, shaking his head with a look of concern—"sorry for it, indeed; very sorry—excellent man."

"By the way, how's your daughter, Mr. Tonikins?" he asked another, almost in the same breath.

Mr. Tomkins stared.

"Dangerous attack, I heard?" observed the Duke, shaking his head.

"Beg pardon, your Greece; it was the other Mr. Tomkins's daughter"— at length replied Mr. Tomkins—Mr. Tommy Tomkins's."

"Ah, true! you are Mr. Jeems Tomkins—glad to hear she's better— fine girl!—*monstrous* fine girl!" and so he turned away to say something civil to some one else.

Our Hillingdon friends having been nearly the last in arriving at the Castle, and having had the difficulties we mentioned to contend with, were the latest of the late, and the Duke had twice taken his repeater out of his waistcoat pocket to compare it with the French clock on the mantelpiece, when Mr. and Mrs. Jorrocks made their appearance. Mrs. Jorrocks was magnificent. On her head she wore a yellow-and-gold turban, with a full plume of black ostrich feathers, such as one sees on a mute's head before a great funeral, while long full ringlets (false, of course) streamed down the sides of her fat red cheeks, and rested on her shoulders. Her gown was crimson brocade, stiff and rustling, with many flounces of black lace; and her arms and neck were decorated with a profusion of mosaic jewellery in the shape of bracelets, armlets, chains, brooches, and lockets.

Our "Cockney Squire" was in the full-dress uniform of the Handley Cross Hunt—sky-blue coat, lined with pink silk; canary-coloured shorts, and white silk stockings. A good large frill protruded through the stand-up collar of a white waistcoat, and a roll puddingy white neckcloth replaced the sea-green silk one of the morning. Altogether they were a most striking couple. Mr. Jorrocks's big-calved, well-shaped legs—the feet encased in large gold-buckled, patent leather pumps—and the general brightness of his colours, rendered him quite the object of attraction in the room, and threw the "star and garter" of the Duke rather into the shade—more over, most of the guests had seen the "star and garter" before, but they had only heard of Mr. and Mrs. Jorrocks, the new opulent owners of Hillingdon Hall. Accordingly, there was a grand stare and nudging as they made their way up the spacious drawing-room, Mr. Jorrocks strutting with his usual bantam-cock air, as much as to say, "There's a pair o' legs for you—find fault with them if you can."

"Well, Mr. Jorrocks," said his Grace, not exactly knowing what question to hazard to him, "I hope you feel hungry after your ride?"

"Tol-lol—thank ye, your Greece," replied Mr. Jorrocks, squaring himself before the fire, taking a coat lap over each arm, and turning full upon the company—"feedin' time's near at 'and, I s'pose—wot o'clock may it be by your Greece's gold watch?" continued he, eyeing the awestruck company around—"you're uncommon well lodged here," continued Mr. Jorrocks, staring about without waiting for an answer—"excellently, I may say—dare say this room is fefty feet if it's a hinch—doors o' 'hoggany too," added he, looking at them. "Put up afore Bob Peel's new Tariff came in, I guess. Gilt cornices I superb mirrors! and satin damask, I s'pose," added Mr. J., stooping down and nipping one of the sofa cushions. "I likes this room a deal better nor the first one I was in—more glitter, more sparkle about it. If I was you now, I'd furnish t'other same way—that's to say if you have the tin—but don't go tick whatever you do; things cost jest double when you buy on credit. Tick's the werry divil certainlie," continued Mr. Jorrocks, turning his eyes up to the splendid cut-glass chandelier sparkling from the centre of the ceiling, and jingling a handful of half-crowns in his breeches pocket. "I minds, my Lord Duke, when I was in the tea-trade—indeed I'm in it still, only I doesn't attend the shop—when your swell 'ouse-stewards or powder-monkey Peters used to come axing the price o' tea, pekoe, hyson-skin, twankay, gunpooder, and so on; I always used to ax whether they were purchasers or buyers. *Purchasers*, you see, my Lord Dukeship, are chalkers up; *buyers* are money *down* and discount coves. Well, if they were purchasers I jest doubled the price—to cover long credit and the risk o' not gettin' the money at all; besides which, these confounded fine gen'lemen always expect a compliment for the horder, and a compliment when they pay the tin, that's to say, if the 'appy day occurs in their reign, for great folks in general don't keep their flunkies long; but, howsomever, never mind," added Mr. Jorrocks, eyeing the opening door at the end of the room.

Mrs. Flather and Emma then entered; Emma in a well-fitting, pale pink satin, made *drapée* at the breast. She was a decidedly fine-looking girl, held herself up, and walked with an air. The composition of the party was in her favour, there being nothing but country dowdies; no London-milliner-turned-out lady to eclipse her, as we have seen too many country belles eclipsed in London. Lord, what a place London is! How it takes the shine out of the country conceit—girls, horses, equipages, *men*, and all. We met a friend t'other day at a country fair, who didn't seem much in his element; accordingly, we asked him what brought him there. "I've got a pony to sell," said he—"and by the way," now added he, "as you understand these sort of things, I should like you to see it, for it is, *without exception*, the neatest and most perfect animal I ever set eyes on—*a perfect model*. If you had it in London now, and rode it up and down the park, every dealer in the town would be after it. There it comes!" cried he, pointing to a shuffling, ginger-coloured chestnut (of all colours the most detestable) looking thing, with a full tail and a hog mane, and a great white ratch down its face,—a sort of animal that none but Van Butchel, Claudius Hunter, or some such appearance-defying genius, would be guilty of riding. So it is with girls. If a girl has a tolerable figure, and a face not amiss, they immediately set her down for London—for the Duke of Devonshire, in fact. "Indeed, Mister Brown," says his amiable spouse, "I don't consider we should be doing Jemima justice if we didn't give her a season in London."

"Nonsense, my dear, you know I can't afford it—can hardly pay my way as it is."

"Then you must just give up your hunters, *Mister* Brown."

"*I'll be d——d if I do, though!*" says *Mister* Brown.

But suppose Mister Brown is of the "genus Jerry," as Linnaeus would say, and gives in (poor Brown), what does he see when he gets to London? Why, that every other girl he meets with is quite as good, and many a deuced deal better-looking than Jemima.

Take an author's advice, Brown, and stay at home.

But let us on to the Duke of Donkeyton's dinner.

"Now, Bray, don't you make yourself such a swell," said young Lord Aubrey, entering the Marquis's room, who, with the aid of his valet, was settling himself into one of Jackson's particulars, blue coat, velvet collar and cuffs, silk facings and linings, with Windsor buttons. Nature meant the Marquis for a girl, and a very pretty one he would have made. He had a beautiful pink and white complexion, hair parted down the middle of his head, and falling in ringlets about his ears, blue eyes, Grecian nose, simpering mouth, with a dimple on each side, very regular pearly teeth, and incipient moustache on his upper lip, and a very incipient imperial on a very pretty unshaved chin. In stature he was about the middle height, five feet ten or so, thin, with a deal of action in his legs and backbone; indeed, he had a considerable cross of the dancing-master in him, and was considered one of the best "goers" at Almack's or the Palace. In short, he was a pretty Jemmy Jessamy sort of fellow.

Now, this sort of man is generally desperately disliked by their own sex, particularly by the hirsute, rasping, bullfinching breed of fox-hunters; and just in proportion as men are abused by each other, they are petted and praised by the women—particularly if they are marquises, and *in the market*.

Accordingly, our hero stood as an "A1" lady-killer in London; and that being the case, our readers may imagine what a desperate man he would be in the country. Indeed, these sort of fellows ought not to be allowed to go about unmuzzled (that is to say, without a wife), for country girls are monstrous inflammatory, and having little choice beyond the curate and the apothecary's apprentice, are ready to worry anything in the shape of a man—to say nothing of a lord—a hand some Marquis beyond all conception. Then the greasy novels put such notions into their heads. We really believe they think the great people go into the country for wives, just as the Cockneys go to Kensington for strawberries and cabbages; and that there is nothing of the sort to be had in London. Unfortunately for rural belles, London beaux look upon them in quite a different light. They consider them a sort of strop to keep the razor of their palaverment fresh against the return of another London season, and think they may go any length short of absolutely offering; and that the girls wash the slates of their memories just as they wash their own on passing Hyde Park, down Portland Place, or by the Elephant and Castle, on their way back to town. The Marquis of Bray was just one of this sort. He knew perfectly well the Duke would no more think of letting him marry anything below a Duke's daughter, than he would think of sending him off for a trip in one of Mr. Henson's air carriages; and being well assured of that fact, he thought the girls must know it also, and would just take his small talk for what it was meant. Moreover, the Marquis having had the unspeakable misfortune of being brought up at home, had conceived the not at all unnatural idea that the world was chiefly made for him, and that he might do whatever he liked with impunity. No greater misfortune surely can befall a young man than such an education; and lucky it is that so few of them get it. Eton knocks and Eton kicks save many a "terrible high-bred" lad (as the Epsom race-list sellers describe the horses) from ruin.

But we must get the Marquis downstairs. Behold him, then, in his blue coat aforesaid, with a delicate bouquet in the button-hole—a most elaborately-tied white cravat, the folds of the tie nestling among six small point-lace frills of an exquisitely embroidered lawn shirt front over a pink silk under-waistcoat, and diamond studs of immense value, chained with Lilliputian chains—his waistcoat of cerulean blue satin, worked with heart's-ease, buttoned with buttons of enormous bloodstones, the surface of the waistcoat traversed with Venetian chains and diminutive seals—pink silk stockings, and pumps—gliding into the drawing-room, with an airy noiseless tread, and a highly scented, much-embroidered, lace-trimmed handkerchief in his hand. How he bowed! how he smiled! how he showed his teeth! He was so d—d polite, you'd have thought he'd got among a party of emperors, instead of among all the John Browns of the neighbourhood. Then the old Duke, like all blunder-headed men, being monstrously afraid lest his son should make mistakes, must needs take him in hand, and introduce him to those he didn't know. "Jeems, my dear!" cried he, as the elastic back began to slacken in its salaams round the awestricken circle, "come here, and let me introduce you to our excellent friend, Mr. Jorrocks, who's been kind enough to come all the way from—from—from—to dine with us."

"To dine and *stay all night*, your Greece," observed Mr. Jorrocks to the Duke, letting fall his coat laps, preparatory to offering his hand to the Marquis.

The Marquis bowed and grinned, and laid his hand upon his heart, as if perfectly overcome by the honour—proudest moment of his life!

"Where I dine I sleep, and where I sleep I breakfast, your Greece," observed Mr. Jorrocks, resuming his position, finding it impossible to compete with the Marquis in bows.

"Let me introduce you to Mrs. Jorrocks," said the Duke, taking his son by the arm, and leading him up to the plume, the bearer of which rose and bobbed and curtsied till the Duke and Marquis passed on to Emma, whom the Duke introduced as Miss Jorrocks; and the Marquis, thinking she seemed more like the thing than anyone else in the room, continued to bow and simper and shuffle before her, leaving the Duke to finish the circuit alone, and bear up before the now triumphant and all-gratified Mrs. Flather—who was listening to the painful recital of how Mrs. Smith's little girl had got two double teeth, and how her brother George had gone through the whole of—

> Whene'er I take my walks abroad,
> How many poor I see!

without a single mistake or wrong pronunciation.

The author of "Cecil," we think, says there is nothing so difficult of settlement (except a pipe of port), as a peer's eldest son; and some other conjurer says, it is less difficult to arrange a party of duchesses than a string of justices' wives. On this occasion it certainly was so. Notwithstanding the Duchess had done all she could to drum into the Duke's dull head how they were to go, his natural obtuseness and self-sufficiency made him confound them all together; and at the moment that the folding-doors were thrown open, and dinner announced, he knew no more than the man in the moon whether Mrs. Hamilton Dobbin's husband, or Mrs. Grumbleton's, were first on the commission, or whether Jorrocks or Jenkins had most votes at command. Indeed, he forgot which was Mrs. Jorrocks; at all events, he went bolt up to Mrs. Flather, who could by no possibility do them any good; and the Marquis having reconnoitred the room, and satisfied himself that Miss Hamilton Dobbin and all the Miss Smiths were infinitely inferior to the model of propriety, offered her his arm in the most supplicating manner, and tripped through the now greatly agitated group with an air as though he were leading her out to a dance instead of a dinner.

Mr. Jorrocks, thinking there seemed likely to be a good deal of bother in the arrangement of couples, very considerately tendered his arm to the Duchess, to the exclusion of Lord Aubrey, and a couple of Honourables; and the two having got in the rear of the flock, drove them "pell-mell" before them, some with their neighbours' wives, some with their own, some without any body's wives at all.

The Marquis being much out of practice, was glad of an opportunity of rubbing up his small talk, especially with a girl who did not look sheepish, and be-lord and be-lordship him as country dowdies are in the habit of doing. Indeed, before he had got through his soup, he found that Emma was quite a "half-way meet" sort of girl; and looking upon everything below a nobleman's daughter as fair game, he began to make play very strong.

Of course the conversation began about flowers. Flowers in the country, fancy-balls in London. Fancy-balls are safe specs: they are within the reach of every one.

"Was she fond of a garden?" Oh, Emma doted upon a garden! Nothing she liked so much as running about with her watering-pot, picking up daisies, pulling up weeds, tying up roses. "Was the Marquis fond of flowers?"

"He adored them!" at the same time diving his nose into his bouquet.

Emma admired them.

"Would she allow him to present her with one?"

Emma pressed it to her lips, and put it into her bosom. We forgot to say that the pink satin was made with a peak.

Then they talked about horses. Was Emma fond of riding? Oh, nothing she liked so much! just riding about the country alone, wherever fancy led her.

"*Alone!*" rejoined the Marquis; "you should always have a gentleman with you." He liked sauntering along a green lane, with a pretty girl in a nice tight-fitting habit, and a well-set-on hat—not those confounded butter-and-eggs-poke sort of bonnets country misses rode the family horse about in. Then he asked Emma to take wine, and gave her a look as he bowed, that as much as said, "You are the girl for me."

Meanwhile the Duke, having exhausted his small talk with Mrs. Flather, and made as many blunders as he could during the time they had been together, began to look up the table to see whom he should inflict his politeness upon. Mr. Jorrocks's sky-blue coat and rubicund visage forming an attractive feature at the top of the table, procured the honour of a holloa from the Duke's voice, who had good lungs, and made free use of them.

"Pray, Mr. Jorrocks," roared he, "how old are you?"

"Please, your Greece, I'm fefty-five," replied Mr. Jorrocks, knocking half a dozen years off at a blow.

"Indeed!" exclaimed the Duke, "quite a young man! may live these twenty years yet!"

"I intend so, your Greece!" replied Mr. Jorrocks.

"Take a glass of wine, Mr. Jorrocks!"

"With all my 'eart, your Greece—champagne, if you please."

"Pray, Mr. Jorrocks, who was your mother?" inquired his Grace, after he had bowed and drank off his wine.

"Please, your Greece, my mother was a washerwoman."

"*A washerwoman, indeed!*" exclaimed his Grace—"that's very odd—I like washerwomen—nice, clean, wholesome people—I wish my mother had been a washerwoman."

"I vish mine had been a duchess," replied Mr. Jorrocks.

Mrs. Flather, who sat on the Duke's right, on the opposite side of the table to that at which Emma and the Marquis were planted, was in ecstasies at the apparent prosperity of the scheme. Scheme indeed, she thought, it could hardly be called, seeing it was a mutual arrangement—the Duke taking her, the Marquis taking Emma, and so on. The consequence was, Mrs. Flather felt far more at ease, and underwent far less trepidation than her opposite neighbour, Mrs. Thomas Chambers, who would have given anything to have been restoring her old spangled turban to the band-box, for another twelvemonth's slumber. A country turban lasts for ever. Meanwhile the Duke chattered, and talked, and ate, and drank, and called people by their wrong names; and as the wine began to operate, confidence began to creep in, and before the sweets commenced their circuits, neighbours began plucking up courage sufficient to ask each other to wine; and the popping of champagne corks formed a pleasing variety to the chatter and clatter of the table.

So the dinner progressed.

The Marquis's left-hand neighbour, Mrs. Tomkins, having at length found her tongue, and got into the midst of a most interesting, oft-repeated ramble, about a ragged-coated man, who had knocked at their door, and asked for some cold chicken and punch, the Marquis and Emma went at it harder than ever, a listener always acting as a clog on the free vent of conversation, as Mr. Jorrocks and Mrs. Flather had found in the morning.

"Have you much gaiety in your part of the world?" asked the Marquis; "many balls, many parties?"

"Oh dear no," replied Emma, "we are shockingly dull."

"Short of beaux, perhaps?" observed the Marquis.

"Indeed, we haven't such a thing in our part of the country: there are only five young men at Sellborough, and four of them are engaged."

"And you have bespoken the fifth, I suppose."

"*Not I, indeed,*" replied Emma, with a toss of the head.

"But are there no officers? Surely it's a garrison town."

"It's a new regiment," observed Emma; "besides, you know, we are a good way from the town. We never see such a thing as a redcoat in our little village, except perhaps a stray fox-hunter, now and then asking his way. Do you hunt?"

"*God forbid!*" replied the Marquis, with a shake of his head and shrug of his shoulders, for he had gone out once, and soon found himself in a wet ditch, with his horse on the top of him.

"I hate fox-hunters," observed Emma, half to herself and half to the Marquis.

"Horrid fellows!" ejaculated the dandy. "It seems a sort of uncivilised process, fit only for heavy dragoons, and flying artillery men. By the way, though, your pa is a fox-hunter, is not he?" continued the Marquis, looking significantly at Mr. Jorrocks.

"He's not my pa," observed Emma, somewhat disconcerted, more at the unfavourable aspect it threw on affairs than any shock the insinuation occasioned her feelings.

"But didn't my pa introduce you as Miss Jorrocks?" inquired the Marquis.

"It's not the case for all that," observed Emma tartly. "My name is Flather; that is my mamma sitting beside the Duke."

"True!" observed the Marquis, "how stoopid I am. Lor', I know your ma as well as I know myself. Your pa, too, I knew, poor man. Well, but tell me now about the old boy in the sky-blue and yellow shorts—the fireman's or Thames waterman's uniform, in fact. Isn't he some relation? Your uncle, or something?"

"Mr. Jorrocks, allow me the honour of taking wine with you," continued he, seeing his eyeing had attracted our hero's attention.

"Champagne, if you please!" replied Mr. Jorrocks.

"No, he's no relation whatever," replied Emma "only a neighbour."

"He seems a desperate old quiz," observed the Marquis, putting down his glass, after touching his lips with it. "I wonder what he'd take for his wig."

"Vulgar old man," said Emma, "but country life makes us acquainted with strange companions."

"You are a great fox-hunter, I understand, Mr. Jorrocks," screamed his Grace, down the table. "Have you killed many foxes this summer?"

"No, your Greece, we don't 'unt in the summer," replied Mr. Jorrocks, with a slight curl of his upper lip—"*farm* i' the summer, fox i' the winter, that's the ticket."

"True!" rejoined his Grace. "I'm glad you're a farmer—am a great one myself—prize bull, prize pig, prize ram, prize turnip, prize spade—should like to talk to you about farming."

"Nitrate o' sober! guano! sub-soilin'! Smith o' Deanston! top dressin' wi' soot, and all that sort o' thing!" added Mr. Jorrocks. "Shall be 'appy to take wine with your Greece."

"With all my heart," replied the Duke. "What shall we have?"

"Champagne, if you please," said Mr. Jorrocks; adding, in an audible whisper to himself, "can get sherry at 'ome."

"The Duke don't 'unt, I think," observed Mr. Jorrocks to the Duchess, setting down his glass with a thump that almost broke the slender stalk. "Wish he'd got some 'ounds; winter'll be dull without them—knows a man with five-and-twenty couple to dispose on—fifteen couple o' dogs, and ten couple o' betches—no offence, my lady," added he, with a bow and shake of the head, "*betch* is female dog."

The sweets were now in full swing. Mrs. Flather sat on thorns as the dishes were taken to Emma; and she helped herself in succession to pastry, jellies, creams, tipsey cakes, and all sorts of trash.

Oh, how she grieved for the loss of the buns, and dreaded the effect on the complexion in the morning! In vain she tried to catch the model's eye—she either would not see her, or was too absorbed with the sweets on her plate, or the sweet things the Marquis was saying to her, and ate and crammed away in a most determined way. Fortunately, the Marquis was a spoon-food man, and having been laying back for the sweets, was too busy "dieting" himself, as the Poor-Law people call it, to pay much attention to his neighbour. At length both Emma and the Marquis got surfeited, and the latter having let off the old piece of sentiment "about sweets to the sweet" as Emma magnanimously declined a third offer of Maraingues, again took wine with her; and laying his napkin across his legs, turned slightly in his chair, and began whispering soft nothings in her ear—

"Was she fond of dancing?"

"Oh! she delighted in dancing!"

"Would she be in London next spring?"

Emma feared not—oh! she should like it so much—but she had nobody to take her.

She should get her ma; everybody should go to London in the spring, Paris in the autumn, Italy in the winter. Almack's was not what it was, still the rooms were good, and the floor excellent. The little anteroom was so nice for platonics—his ma was a patroness. Did she know the Princess of Quackenbruck?

(How could the poor girl? But these London chaps always fancy that everybody knows whom they do.) Well, the Princess Orel Quackenbruck was going to be married to Lord Plantagenet Hay, the Duke of Drossington's son. Did she know Taget Hay?

(How the devil should she?)

Well, he understood it was all settled. Indeed, he *knew* it was; for he had it from Storr & Mortimer, who had been sending him down some pattern wristband studs that morning, and the diamonds were ordered there—fifteen thousand pounds' worth—no great quantity, to be sure, but then she would come in for the family ones at last. His ma's diamonds were worth forty thousand.

Emma wondered when they would be hers.

"Matrimony seems all the rage just now," observed the Marquis, breaking off in the middle of his strawberry ice. "Lord George Noodleton wants to marry Miss Dumps, the banker's daughter, but his pa won't hear of it unless old Dumps will come down with a hundred thousand pounds."

"Mercenary creature!" exclaimed Emma, stuffing her mouth as full as ever it would hold.

The Marquis then rehearsed several weddings that had taken place among his friends during the previous year, to all of which Emma listened with the greatest interest; for though she had never heard the names before, still there is a something about weddings, high or low, that all women like to listen to, and the Marquis having about exhausted his stock of matrimonial reminiscences, observed casually, as he drank off his glass of sherry, that all the world seemed marrying mad, and he supposed it would be "their turn next."

Just then the Duchess gave the signal, and Emma rose, with a maiden blush upon her maiden cheeks, having, as she considered, *all but* captured the coronet.

XII

Look on this picture and on that.

A RATHER DIFFICULT PASSAGE IN OUR history now draws near—namely, what the ladies did when they got back to the drawing-room at Donkeyton Castle. In these points authors disclose their sex. A lady would be *great* here, whereas we of the breeches, at least *legitimately* of the breeches, are "quite out." In this dilemma we inquired of a female friend, who happened to be teaing with our grandmamma (a most remarkable old lady of eighty-three, who reads without specs), what ladies did when they retired from the dining- room. "Oh," said she, "they generally go to the fire, dawdle and stand about a little, and then sit down and talk scandal."

We will then, gentle reader, with your permission, suppose the fire, and standing about part done, and that the ladies are pairing off, or grouping for the scandal stakes. Emma, who could hardly contain herself, and had given sundry nods, and made several significant grimaces at her mamma, all indicative of "*I've done it*," now got to her, and giving her a most loving squeeze of the elbow, whispered in her ear, "*All right.*"

"*All right, my dear*! what d'you mean?" inquired Mrs. Flather.

"*All right*," repeated Emma, with a most triumphant smile.

"*You don't say so!*" exclaimed Mrs. Flather, in a somewhat louder tone. "Has he offered?"

"Have you seen these beautiful views of Copley Fielding's?" inquired the Duchess, with one of those bugbears of company a portfolio of drawings. What iniquitous work that is. The Duchess had set three groups to their books, just as a jailer would set his prisoners to their task work. Indeed, we think the prisoners have the best of it, for they see what they have to do; while, in a case of this sort, you must reckon on having to run the gauntlet of all the portfolios in circulation, without knowing how many more there may be in reserve.

Oh, Emma was *"so obliged"*—"there was nothing she liked so much as drawings—scenery of all things." So the Duchess, having pushed her into a chair, and placed her mother beside her, went and got Mrs. Hamilton Dobbin to join the party to make up the trio, and left them to the enjoyment of their intellectual treat. How Mrs. Flather wished Mrs. Hamilton Dobbin at home. Here let us leave them for a time.

The ladies being comfortably swept out, and the champagne having supplied a certain degree of animation and confidence, the gentlemen drew towards the Duke with less apparent embarrassment than had marked their approaches during the earlier part of the evening. Mr. Jorrocks, whose maxim of "Perfect ease being perfect gentility" never allowed him to feel out of his element, having got rid of the Duchess, took his napkin and large wine-glass (very large it was too), and strutting to the other end of the room, planted himself most consequentially on the right of the Duke, to the great relief of Mr. Thomas Chambers, who, but for him, would have been driven into that dangerous position on the retirement of Mrs. Flather.

"Vell, your Greece, and 'ow d'ye feel arter your feed?" inquired Mr. Jorrocks, sousing himself into one of the soft capacious arm-chairs with which the table was encircled. "I reckon I've had an unkimmon good tuck-out."

"Ah! I'm glad to hear you say so, Mr.—Mr.—Mr.—Jorrocks; very glad to hear you say so," replied the Duke. "Nice dinner—good dinner—very good dinner—*monstrous* good dinner, indeed."

"And good eatin' requires good drinkin', I always says, your Greece," observed Mr. Jorrocks, jingling his wineglass against his buttons.

"Ah, true!" exclaimed his Grace, laughing at the hint, and throwing back his white head. "Good eating does require good drinking,"—so saying, he helped himself to a bumper of claret, and passed the bottles. "Here's your good health, Mr. Jorrocks. I'm very happy to see you— *monstrous* happy to see you. And so you are a great fox-hunter? Glad of that—fine amusement fox-hunting—monstrous fine amusement.

I remember Burke saying he would willingly bring in a bill to make poaching felony, another to encourage the breed of foxes—that he would make, in short, any sacrifice to the humour and prejudices of the country gentle men in their most extraordinary form, provided he could only prevail upon them to live at home. Fine speech of Burke's; monstrous fine speech."

"He was 'ung for all that," observed Mr. Jorrocks to himself, with a knowing shake of the head, as he availed himself of the opportunity of the bottles coming round again to take a "back-hand" at the port.

His Grace then had a word or two with Mr. Tugwell and afterwards with Mr. Grumbleton, but being unable to get more than "Yes, my Lord Duke," and "No, my Lord Duke," out of either of them, he soon returned to his voluble neighbour, Mr. Jorrocks.

"You're a great farmer, aren't you, Mr. Jorrocks?" asked the Duke—"tell me now, have you an Agricultural Association at your place? Prize for the best bull, best cow, best ram, best two-year-old tup?"

"Vy, no, I doesn't think we 'ave, your Greece," replied Mr. Jorrocks, "and I think if we had, they'd a been *at* me for a subscription—town and country's werry much alike in that respect—never lose nothin' for want of axin'—I minds—"

"Well, but you should get up an Agricultural Association," interrupted the Duke. "Independently of the good it does in promoting neat and scientific farming, it's a good thing for getting acquainted with the farmers—keeping your interest together—*you understand*. Good thing, indeed—capital good thing—*monstrous* good thing," added the Duke, rubbing his hands, and laughing at his own cunning.

"I twig!" replied Mr. Jorrocks, with a wink. "*True blue!* Please yourselves, genl'men, but if you don't please me, I'll *make* you—haw, haw, haw. Rum world this we live in, your Greece—werry rum world, indeed. I'll have a Hagricultural 'Sociation though. President, Mr. Jorrocks—or say, President, Duke o' Donkeyton. Wice-President, Mr. Jorrocks."

"Very proud of the honour, I'm sure," replied the Duke, bowing very low, and shaking his head over his plate as though he were quite overcome—"*monstrous* proud indeed. But I'm getting old, Mr. Jorrocks, I'm getting old—suppose you take Jeems—it's more in his way."

"With all my 'eart," replied Mr. Jorrocks; he don't look much like a farmer, though. President, the Markiss o' Bray—Wice-President, Mr. Jorrocks—that'll sound well, and look well in the papers too; call it the 'Illingdon 'Sociation, and have it at our place—dine in a tent—dance in a barn—band in open hair—school-gals to skip. Or sheep-shearin' i' the mornin', tea i' the evenin'—ball for the ladies—'ands across and back again, down the middle and hup again." Mr. Jorrocks suiting the action to the word, bumping about on his chair and crossing his arms as if he were at work.

"Very good!" exclaimed the Duke; "extremely good! *monstrous* good, indeed—but you must instruct as well as amuse—encourage science, experiments, chemistry; teach them the virtue and use of manures."

"Guano! nitrate o' sober! soot! and all that sort o' thing," interrupted Mr. Jorrocks.

"Farmers are a long way behind the intelligence of the day; a *monstrous* long way," continued the Duke, "too much of 'what my father did, I'll do' style about them. They want brushing up. You take yours in hand, Mr. Jorrocks—make them drain."

"Smith o' Deanston! Tweeddale tile! furrow drainin'!" exclaimed Mr. Jorrocks.

"Apply their land to proper purposes," continued his Grace, "don't force it to grow crops that it has no taste for—much may be done in the way of judicious management. For instance, where land won't grow corn, try trees—much of the land in this county is too poor for agricultural purposes—would grow wood well. All the pine tribe flourish in this country and pay well for planting; very well indeed; monstrous well."

"Grand things they are too!" observed Mr. Jorrocks aloud to himself, thinking of the pine-apple he'd had before dinner; "I'll teach them a trick or two," added he, "pine dodge in particklar—address them— 'Frinds and fellow-countrymen!' " throwing out his arm and hitting Mr. Thomas Chambers a crack in the eye, and so closing the conversation for the moment.

The Marquis of Bray, not being a great man for his liquor, took advantage of the commotion to throw up his napkin and steal out of the room to the ladies. These he found in full employment: three groups of three, looking at pictures; the Duchess knitting a purse and superintending the portfolios, occasionally addressing a word to her toady, or "companion," as the poor devils are called, in derision one would think, for they are generally less thought of than the lap-dog; while Mrs. Smith inflicted a recital of how her little boy had gone through

> Whene'er I take my walks abroad,
> How many poor I see!

without a single error or wrong pronunciation, upon Mrs. Somebody whom she had inveigled into a corner for the purpose.

The butterfly Marquis having saluted the Duchess with a kiss, fluttered away to chatter to the ladies; who all thought it "so nice" of him coming in so soon. The first group was a turbaned one, busy with Colonel Batty's Swiss Views. The Marquis didn't stay long with it, but glided into the middle of the room where Emma sat between her mamma and Mrs. Hamilton Dobbin, turning over a portfolio of water-colour sketches, mother and daughter most heartily wishing Mrs Hamilton Dobbin further. Nor did the Marquis's approach at all disconcert Mrs. Dobbin, for she had known him from a boy, and perhaps had not established to her own satisfaction that he was anything else yet. Living near the Castle, and knowing the awe in which the neighbourhood held the family, the idea of such a thing as the Marquis marrying a girl like Emma Flather never entered her head, or, indeed, the idea of any girl being foolish enough to think of such a thing; consequently, instead of drawing out her chair to let him into the centre, she merely moved a little nearer Emma, and kept the Marquis outside. Mrs. Flather immediately counteracted the movement by rising and joining another group, and the Marquis presently sidled into her seat. The imperturbable Mrs. Hamilton Dobbin remained rooted to her chair. The Marquis then began chattering, and turning over the drawings. "Was Emma a painter?"

"Only a *very middling* one—she doted on pictures though."

The Marquis dared say she was a very good one.

"Oh no, she wasn't! Nobody about them cared for drawing but her."

"Oh, that was a pity," replied the Marquis. His pa and his ma were both great artists. "My *pa* did *that*," continued he, holding up a picture.

"Oh! how beautiful!" exclaimed Emma.

"My *ma* did *that*," added he, producing another.

"Oh! how beautiful!" repeated Emma.

"My *pa* and *ma* did that between them," continued he, producing a third.

"Oh! how beautiful!" reiterated Emma. Meanwhile the guests came dropping in from the dining-room, each with considerably more confidence than he felt on arriving, and Mr. Jorrocks and the Duke at length were the only two that remained—still they talked about farming, until a stranger would have thought they were the only two people that knew anything about the matter, instead of one being a mere theorist and the other a mere fool—we beg pardon—we mean *in farming*. Indeed, the Duke of Donkeyton might be called more than a theorist, for he had some most extraordinary notions about farming and the management of property—a system so peculiar that it generally ended in beggaring the tenants and impoverishing his estates. Still he chattered and talked so glibly, that poor Mr. Jorrocks was thoroughly convinced he was a most "wide-awake" farmer; and what with the wine and what with the twaddle, he got a brainful of most confused ideas. The dominant idea, however, was that farmers were all asleep, and scientific farming was the only thing to make money of.

"Allow me to give you a toast, your Greece?" inquired Mr. Jorrocks every time the decanters came to a stand, and his Grace dabbled in his finger glass, or applied the napkin to his lips, symptomatic of going.

"With all my heart, Mr. Jorrocks."

"I'll give The 'Illingdon 'Sociation and the 'ealth o' the Markiss o' Bray, again!" exclaimed Mr. Jorrocks. (This was the third time he had given it.)

"Thank ye, Mr. Jorrocks, most kindly—Jeems I'm sure will be most flattered when I tell him of this repeated mark of your attachment."

"Not at all," replied Mr. Jorrocks, "not at all—werry fine young man—werry fine young man indeed—werry like my frind, James Green, of Tooley Street. Perhaps your Greece doesn't know Green o' Tooley Street."

His Grace did not.

"Allow me to give your Greece another toast?"

"With great pleasure, Mr. Jorrocks."

"It must be a bamper," observed Mr. Jorrocks, drinking off his heel-taps, and filling his goblet as full as it would hold.

His Grace did the like.

"I'll give you the 'ealth o' the Duchess o' Donkeyton," observed Mr. Jorrocks. "Her Greece has given us a most capital dinner, and your Greece has given us a most excellent drink:" so saying, Mr. Jorrocks quaffed off his tumbler.

"Thank ye (hiccup), Mr. Jorrocks," replied his Grace. "The (hiccup) Duchess, I am sure, will be (hiccup) most proud of the (hiccup) honour, which I'll tell her (hiccup) directly when——"

"But drink off your lush," observed Mr. Jorrocks, seeing his Grace sat with the bumper before him—"wine first—speech arterwards"—added he, as if in explanation.

"True!" observed his Grace, laughing—"thank ye, Mr. (hiccup) Jorrocks, for the hint—capital (hiccup) hint — monstrous (hiccup) good (hiccup) hint." So saying, his Grace drained off the glass, and set it down with the face of a man who has taken a black draught.

"Now, if your (hiccup) Greece has anything to (hiccup) say, we shall be 'appy to 'ear it (hiccup)," observed Mr. Jorrocks.

"Thank you, Mr. (hiccup) Jorrocks," replied his Grace. "I can't (hiccup) express the (hiccup) obligation I'm (hiccup) under to you (hiccup). Shall we (hiccup) have a little (hiccup) coffee?"

"Jest (hiccup) bazz the bottle (hiccup)!" exclaimed Mr. Jorrocks, holding it up to the light, "there's (hiccup) only jest a glass apiece (hiccup)!" So saying, Mr. Jorrocks helped himself and then the Duke, measuring the quantity out most equitably. "There's (hiccup) honesty!" hiccuped Mr. Jorrocks, banging the decanter down in the stand. "No (hiccup) drucken man (hiccup) could do that (hiccup), I guess."

The Duke looked at his glass as if it contained poison, and turned very green.

Mr. Jorrocks having drunk his wine off, washed his mouth out, and ran the pocket comb through his whiskers, set off for the drawing-room, leaving the Duke, as he said, to "put the bottle ends away if he liked."

"*Holloa* (hiccup), *Mister Jorrocks!*" hiccuped our hero, finding his legs didn't carry him as straight as they ought, and he bumped with his shoulder against the door-post. "*Holloa there!*" Mr. Jorrocks then got his land legs and proceeded.

Towards ten o'clock the groom of the chamber whispered a reprieve in the ears of divers of the male guests, who were all suddenly seized with a desire of looking at their watches, and wondering what sort of a night it was. This is a question that great people do not understand, thinking (like the little Princess who wondered that people should starve when there were such nice buns to be had for a penny) that every one keeps a close carriage.

If the Duke had gone to the door, he would have seen a curious mêlée of half-drunken, three-quarters drunken, whole drunken servants and post-boys, exchanging compliments and civilities with his accomplished domestics. Great men's great men, butlers, and so on, being equal to the conveyance of any given quantity of liquor, measure the capacities of their rural brethren by their own, and without intending to make them drunk—or even *perhaps thinking* of doing so, generally give them what makes them very nearly so. This is a serious inconvenience to those outside the ring— or who do not, like Mr. Jorrocks, sleep where they dine, and breakfast where they sleep.

There were such cuttings in and jostlings out, such threats of running the shafts into each other's "chays," and such exchange of country jokes among country Johns. Of all abominations, save us from the impertinence of servants! the *open* impertinence at least, for few are totally free from it, and talk of their masters and mistresses as though

The guests depart from Donkeyton castle

they were something inferior to themselves. The drink frequently brings it out. At Donkeyton Castle there was a grand display. If a master had availed himself of the sombre castle shadow reflected in the moonlight for diving into the carriage ring, he might have heard his own character, and perhaps that of his wife, sketched with all the fidelity of a daguerreotype portrait.

Then, when the Jehus got their masters and mistresses cooped into their melon frames and leathern inconveniences, they began putting their boastings of the merits of their respective steeds to the test, by setting off at a pace down hill that perfectly terrified the inmates, and drove all the observations they had made as to how things were done at the Castle, clean out of their heads. Mr. Tugwell had been charged by Mrs. Tugwell (who had got the influenza, and could not come) to mind and see whether the butler handed the wine about with a napkin or not; Mr. Webb had been especially ordered to see whether the footmen took off the bread with a fork or a spoon, also how they got rid of the crumbs; and divers others had made knots in their minds to pay particular attention to certain points, all of which vanished as the jingling of the rattle-traps, and the darting disappearance of roadside objects, convinced them they were getting run away with; and the horrors of drowning, and quarry tumbling, and dashing to pieces, with sundry acts of omission and commission, darted across their minds, with a velocity equalled only by their movements. Horrible work getting run away with! There is something humiliating in the idea of getting into a one-horse booby hutch (booby hutches they are well called, for a man does feel like a fool riding in one), and committing oneself, and three per cent. Consols, to the rash indiscretion of a half-fledged three-quarters-drunken yokel, in black velveteens and baggy Berlins. Talk of the jurisdiction of magistrates over husbandry servants! What is the jurisdiction of magistrates over husbandry servants, compared to what it would be if they had it over their own? Every large house would have a treadmill, and the parson, the lawyer, and the apothecary, would club for one among them. On this night it would have been in requisition, for Mr. Tugwell's boy, having set down Mr. Webb, very coolly deposited his sleeping master in the coach house, where he remained till the morning.

There had been fine doings in the servants' hall and housekeeper's room at Donkeyton Castle. Betsey, whose propriety—at least sobriety—of conduct had never before been impeached, evinced the hospitality of the establishment, by a very confused statement of what a delightful evening she had spent, and how the Markiss's gentleman had shown her great attention, and asked her to wine twice during the supper; and how the servants—*upper* servants at least—had wine twice a day, and how Benjamin had insisted upon being among the upper servants—swearing he was a "walet at 'ome"; and how he had rooked them of their money at cards, and won two pounds nine and sixpence. Indeed, the wine being in, and the wit being out, Benjamin, contrary to his usual custom, could not contain himself for his exploits, and let out all to his master, he (Benjamin) having, in order to sustain his character of valet, gone up to Mr. Jorrocks's dressing-room at the time the other valets went to their masters', under pretence of helping Mr. Jorrocks out of his clothes. Lucky it was that he did so, for Mr. Jorrocks, having soused himself on to a sumptuous sofa, had fallen fast asleep when his trustworthy domestic entered and discovered him.

"Vell (hiccup), Binjimin," said Mr. Jorrocks, opening one eye and cocking up a leg, "vot are you arter now? (hiccup). Marmeylad, I dare say."

"Please, sir, did you ring?" inquired Benjamin.

"Vy, no (hiccup), Binjimin—I didn't—(hiccup) ring—at least not that I minds (hiccup)—but here, turn (hiccup) about, and let's have my (hiccup) tops off; for this 'ere one's a-pinchin' o' my (hiccup) corn;"— Mr. Jorrocks raising a leg for a lever, and lifting the other to put between Benjamin's legs, to make what sportsmen call a new-fashioned boot-jack of the boy.

"Pleaz, sur, you harn't got your tops on," replied Benjamin, knowing it was only a hunting day practice.

"Ah (hiccup), vell, never mind (hiccup)," replied Mr. Jorrocks, starting up, thinking he was falling from the sofa. "They're my pamps, are they? I thought I'd been out an 'unting. Vell, left me up, I s'pose (hiccup) it's about (hiccup) bed-time (hiccup)."

"Nigh *von!*" replied Benjamin.

"Nigh von?" hiccuped Mr. Jorrocks; "impossible (hiccup), Binjimin! I've only jest (hiccup) come upstairs (hiccup)."

"Nigh *von* for all that," replied Benjamin. "They keep rum hours at these great shops. Never goes to bed afore midnight."

"Queer coves," hiccuped Mr. Jorrocks, sitting up on the sofa.

"Deed are they!" replied Benjamin, "but I've put the leak into some o' them great long lazy London Johnnies. Won a 'atful o' money of them!"

" 'Atful o' money 'ave you (hiccup), Binjimin?" hiccuped Mr. Jorrocks, "that was (hiccup) werry clever (hiccup) o' you—you'll be a (hiccup) great man, Binjimin (hiccup)."

"Yes, sir," said Benjamin.

"A *werry* (hiccup) great man," hiccuped Mr. Jorrocks; "(hiccup) sobriety and (hiccup) cleanliness are (hiccup) great things in the world. Never (hiccup) degrade yourself, Binjimin, to the (hiccup) level of a (hiccup) beast by intemperance (hiccup). Drunkenness is a shockin' (hiccup) sin. Drink (hiccup) will do nothin' (hiccup) for no man."

"Yes, sir," replied Benjamin, looking at his master. "Where (hiccup) moderation dwells (hiccup), the mind (hiccup) expands with mutual (hiccup) ardour (hiccup), and all that sort o' thing (hiccup)!"

"Yes, sir," said Benjamin.

"Then (hiccup), Binjimin, 'elp me out o' my (hiccup) coat," rejoined Mr. Jorrocks, rising and extending an arm to the boy.

Benjamin took hold of the sleeve, and in the jerk to disengage himself of the garment, Mr. Jorrocks lost his balance, and fell souse on the floor with Benjamin atop of him.

XIII

O that men should put an enemy into their mouths
To steal away their brains!—SHAKSPEARE

THE DUKE OF DONKEYTON HAD a very bad headache the next day, and could not come down to breakfast.

Mrs. Flather was sorely disappointed at this, for she got down early in hopes of a kiss from his Grace, by way of sealing the bargain. This, we believe, is the usual form in such matters. The young people kiss as a matter of course, and the old ones do ditto, at least when both parties are pleased with the match—a thing of such unusual occurrence, as not to have happened in our recollection. Emma had detailed to her mamma, with such few additions as her fertile imagination supplied, all that had passed between the Marquis and herself, particularly the tone and manner in which he made the observation or declaration, and, above all, the exact degree of warmth with which he squeezed her hand at bed-time. Young ladies, and young gentlemen too, should be cautious in these matters—young gentlemen not to give utterance to ambiguous expressions—young ladies not to put interpretations upon words they are not meant to convey. Had it not been that Emma, and Emma's "ma," to whom Emma attributed superior sagacity when it suited her convenience, had gone to Donkeyton Castle, with the full conviction that the Duke and Duchess wanted Emma for the Marquis, there would have been something ridiculous in their taking hold of such a commonplace observation as "it will be our turn next," and construing it into an offer of marriage; but when that impression, together with the rusticity, and the "greasy novelling" of the parties, is taken into consideration, we think our indulgent readers will acquit us of taxing their credulity beyond the stretch of literary latitudinarianship in stating such to have been the case.

Moreover, there is another observation we wish to make on the subject. Young ladies and mammas who have only been accustomed to the jog-trot day-book and ledger courtship of common life, cannot imagine that all the *empressements* and soft nothings of high life are in fact "*nothings*," but are apt to take them as the pure current coin of courtship, and contrasting the earnestness of the one with the snoring sleepy-headedness of the other, fall into a very excusable error in supposing a great deal more meant than is really intended.

Fair ladies; beware of the small talk of young gentlemen in cerulean blue satin waistcoats worked with heart's-ease, and pink pantaloons.

Mrs. Flather and Emma had little sleep that night. Everything was talked over three or four times, and the darting rays of the morning's sun found them talking still. Mrs. Flather rose, and drawing the costly curtains, looked out on the lovely landscape, wood and water, hill and dale, with an eye of ownership. What a conquest! Mrs. Trotter would die of envy. Then Emma talked of the diamonds. Told how the Marquis had said they cost fifty thousand pounds. Then Mrs. Flather wondered how old the Duchess was. If she could get into the library before breakfast she would have a look in the "Peerage." Already the Duke and Duchess began to be looked upon in the light of encumbrances.

Mr. Jorrocks, who had one of those remarkable heads that take very little harm from drink, came strutting into the breakfast-room with his hands in the upper tier of the diagonal Jorrockian jacket pockets, and the massive silk tassels of his Hessian boots tapping against the leather as he went, and found Mrs. Flather, bag in hand, pacing up and down pretending to look at the pictures, but in reality waiting for the arrival of the Duke. Mr. J. "was so glad to see her! Now that was werry kind of her," and thereupon he gave her such a smack, as caused the footman, who was coming in with the urn, to start and snicker outright. Mrs. Flather looked very black, inwardly resolving to put the steady old gentleman to rights as soon as ever she became a Marchioness's mother.

The guests then came dropping in, and presently the Duchess and Jeems arrived, when salutations became general, together with inquiries after the health of his Greece—how each had slept, and unanimous approval of the appearance of the day—"splendid weather!"

The guests again ranged themselves to the now much shortened table, each with a new neighbour, like the survivors of a regiment after a battle, and tea and toast, coffee and eggs, became the order of the day.

As the breakfast party were in full cry, the Duke of Donkeyton made his appearance, looking very seedy, and having made his circuit of politeness, drew up beside Mr. Jorrocks, who was sitting next the Duchess, giving her a lecture on the varieties of tea and the usual modes of adulterating them, much to Mrs. Jorrocks's annoyance, who sat looking as if she would eat him.

"Ah, Mr. Jorrocks, and how do you do?" inquired his Grace, stopping short at his over-night friend, who had a plateful of cold meat, with a circle of muffin plates, toast racks, sweet cakes, and egg-shells before him.

"Tol-lol, thank your Greece; 'ow are you off for 'ealth?" replied Mr. Jorrocks, adding, "That *last* glass was *ray*ther too much for me; howsomever, never mind—I carried it upstairs—had a Seidlitz pooder this mornin', and am all right again now. 'Ow's your Greece, I says?"

"Thenk'ee, Mr. Jorrocks, thenk'ee; I'm middling—pretty well, I thenk you—I was imprudent enough to eat a little lobster *paté*, which I think has rather disagreed with me."

"That's a bad job, your Greece," observed Mr. Jorrocks, diving his fork into three or four slices of cold ham, as the footman brought the plate past him. "That's a werry bad job," added he—"I s'pose it's a complaint peculiar to 'igh life though, for I see Cockle has almost every great name in the kingdom down as patrons of his antibilious pills—I doesn't place much faith i' pills and physic. My frind, Roger Swizzle, says, eatin' does far more 'arm nor drinkin'! Roger tries the drink at 'igh pressure too—howsomever you'll be better when you mend, as the nusses say to the children. Here's a werry fine mornin', your Greece—one ought to have been among the dandylions, these two hours—us farmers should be early."

"Ah! by the way, you're a great farmer," observed his Grace, pricking his ears—"delightful occupation, farming—monstrous nice occupation—wish I'd been born a farmer."

"Wish I'd been born a duke," grunted Mr. Jorrocks, as he stuffed a large piece of tongue into his mouth.

"Tell me now," continued his Grace, without noticing Mr. Jorrocks's observation, "have you an Agricultural Society about you? Society for promoting science, agricultural chemistry, improved farming? Best cow, best bull, best two-year-old horse?"

"No, but I intend *to*, your Greece," replied Mr. Jorrocks, "shall teach them a thing or two—farmers are a long way behind the intelligence o' the age, your Greece."

"That's just what *I* say, Mr. Jorrocks!" replied his Grace; "that's just what *I* say!" repeated he. "Too much of 'what my father did I do' style about them—want brushing up: you take yours in hand, Mr. Jorrocks—make them drain."

"Drainin's a grand diskivery, your Greece. It's the foundation of all agricultural improvement." (Mr. J. borrowed that idea from Johnny Wopstraw.)

"That's what *I* say, Mr. Jorrocks," replied his Grace.

"Vell, and I say it *too*," rejoined Mr. Jorrocks, with a jerk of his head, as much as to say he would not be done out of his idea. He then began his third egg.

"Smith o' Deanston should be knighted," observed Mr. Jorrocks, as he put in the salt.

"A *baronetcy* wouldn't be too much," replied his Grace; "greatest benefactor the world ever saw—makes two blades grow where one grew before—*monstrous* benefactor."

"Guano! nitrate o' sober! gipsey¹ manure!" continued Mr. Jorrocks.

"I see you understand it all!" observed his Grace.

"Trust me for that," replied Mr. Jorrocks, diving deep into the egg.

"We'll have sich a Hagricultural 'Sociation. President, John Jorrocks, Esq. Dine in a tent—dance in a barn—cuss it, there goes the hegg all over my chin. But stop," added Mr. Jorrocks, wiping it off—"Didn't we say—'President, the Markiss o' Bray? Wice-President, Mr. J.?' I think that was the way."

"Jeems I am sure will be *most happy*," replied his Grace, who now began to recollect something of the overnight conversation. "Jeems, my dear!" exclaimed he to young hopeful, who was just cutting Emma a fourth slice of white bread, to the indescribable horror of Mrs. Flather. "Jeems, my dear! Mr. Jorrocks does you the honour of proposing you for President of his Agricultural Association."

"Mr. Jorrocks does me great honour I'm sure," replied Jeems, almost bowing his face into his plate; adding to Emma, "What a curious old man he is!"

"He'll be rather young in the business, you know, Mr. Jorrocks," observed his Grace *sotto voce*.

"Oh, I'll put him up to it all!" rejoined Mr. Jorrocks with a knowing wink, and a dig of his elbow into the Duke's ribs; "give him a lector aforehand—South Downs—'Erefords—Durhams—subsoil plough—liquid manure—Deanstonizing, and all that sort o' thing. We'll inwent a manure together. The Donkeyton dung—or maybe a drainin' tile—Mr. Jorrocks's tile. We'll be werry famous. Write in Stephens's Book o' the Farm. Mr. Jorrocks on balls. The Markiss on milch cows. We'll make the grass grow, the grass grow, the grass grow, as my 'untsman James Pigg used to sing about his coal barge."

If ever there was a man Mrs. Flather more heartily wished *further* (as people delicately say, when they consign another to the devil), it surely was this loquacious old man, Mr. Jorrocks. Fancy the stupid old fellow intruding in the morning at a time he was never wanted, and then monopolizing the Duke and Duchess in this scandalous manner! This most delicate and important transaction kept open by the ill-placed garrulity of the old grocer. Never was anything so provoking. Never was a woman so thwarted as Mrs. Flather was—*did it on purpose too*. We certainly must admit it was very trying; but these sort of interruptions frequently occur just at the critical moment, either of an offer or a declaration. The footman with the coal-scuttle, or a carriage-full of company, grinning and kissing their hands through the window with delight at finding you at home, and the anticipations of spending a long day. From all "long-day spenders, good Lord deliver us!"

At length Mr. Jorrocks's appetite was appeased, and pulling out his watch, he discovered that it wanted but ten minutes to eleven. "Tempus fuggit," said he, putting it up to his ear to ascertain that it had not stopped at that hour overnight. "We must be mizzlin'. Don't do for us farmers to be away too much. Old saying, when the cat's away, the mice will play. Dare say your Greece finds it true."

"Well, but there's no great hurry, my good friend," observed his Grace—"sorry you're obleged to go. Should like to show you my farm—the Duchess's dairy—my bull—Jeems's rabbits."

"Oh, vy you know I'm not *forced* to go; only I harn't brought another shirt—clean shirt, clean shave, and a guinea in one's pocket, is wot constitutes a gen'leman in my mind. Howsomever, I'll ride over again some day, jest in a friendly pot-luck sort o' way; meanwhile," added he in a low tone in his Grace's ear, "Mrs. Flather and I are engaged to ride 'ome together, and ven a lady's in the case, your Greece *knows the rest.*"

"Well then, Mrs. Flather, you and I ride 'ome to gether," observed Mr. Jorrocks, strutting down the table to where Mrs. Flather sat in agony, twisting the cord of her bag into a thousand different forms under cover of the table.

Mrs. Flather looked very black.

"S'pose we order the hutch round in ten minutes, or a quarter of an hour. It von't take you long to put on your bonnet, and," added he, in an undertone, "if we start afore the chay, we shall 'scape all the dust. *You twig?*" added he, with a wink.

"*Say half an hour,*" whispered Mrs. Flather, in agony.

"Sorry you're obleged to go, Mrs. Flather," observed the Duke, rising and passing down the table to where Mrs. Flather sat. An example immediately followed by the company, who were now all on their legs together.

"I'm sure we are extremely obliged to your Grace——"

"Not at all," interrupted his Grace, "not at all; nothing can give us greater pleasure than——"

"Your Grace's partiality—*preference*," faltered Mrs. Flather—"for my daughter is most flattering, and——"

"Not at all, Mrs. Flather—not at all; she's an extremely fine girl—very fine girl indeed—*monstrous* fine girl! Your husband and I are very old friends, Mrs. Flather—most gratifying to the Duchess and myself to renew our intimacy in such a satisfactory way."

"I'm sure you do us infinite honour. It is what I never could have expected. I trust my poor child will show herself worthy of the high honour."

"No fear of that, Mrs. Flather—none whatever. The Duchess likes her amazingly—*monstrous* fond of her," saying which the Duke shuffled on to Mr. and Mrs. Hamilton Dobbin, to express his regret that they too were obleged to go.

"Now then!" said Mr. Jorrocks, touching Mrs. Flather's elbow, "let's be startin', they're all a-goin', and we shall get into the ruck if we don't mind, and ketch all the dust."

"Don't be in such a hurry, *pray*," said Mrs. Flather peevishly.

"My vig!" said Mr. Jorrocks, aloud to himself, drawing back, "shows a little wice I think."

"Your carriage is at the door, sir," and "Please to order my carriage round," now became general, and the headachy Duke and complacent Duchess began hugging their departing friends, most heartily glad to get rid of them.

"The Markiss and I must have a talk about this 'Sociation some day," observed Mr. Jorrocks to the Duke.

"True!" exclaimed his Grace, who had gumption enough to keep the main chance in view. "Jeems!" holloaed he to young hopeful, who was pinning a bouquet into Emma's breast, "come here, my dear! Mr. Jorrocks wants to speak to you."

"You and I must have a talk together about this 'ere 'Sociation," observed Mr. Jorrocks, eyeing the butterfly figure before him. Pink-striped shirt, tied with a blue ribbon for a neckcloth, pea-green duck-hunter, pitch-plaister-coloured waistcoat, white jean trousers, pink-striped silk stockings, pumps and buckles.

"Ah! the farming thing!" replied the Marquis, "true, I suppose we must say something to the people."

"You had better drive over to Mr. Jorrocks's, Jeems, and talk it all over," observed the Duke.

"Do," replied Mr. Jorrocks; "and bring your nightcap with you—you mustn't come in the coach-and-six though, for I can't put up sich a sight of 'osses."

"Whereabouts do you live?" inquired the Marquis, who had as much idea about the country as a cow.

"Oh, twelve or fourteen miles from here," observed Mr. Jorrocks, "nothin' of a ride."

"This hot weather though, it would, I think," replied the Marquis, with a shake of the head—"however, I should like to pay you a visit" (the Marquis meant Emma), "and I dare say my ma will lend me her brougham; however, I'll write you word, Mr. Jorrocks:" so saying, he whisked away to jabber and prattle with the ladies.

Mrs. Jorrocks having got herself into her bonnet and shawl, the Duke offered his arm to conduct her to her carriage, while the Marquis followed with Emma, telling her how soon he would be over to see her, and kissing her fair hand as she ascended the steps of the carriage, with all the devotion of a lover, sent her away as happy as a duchess.

Mr. Jorrocks stuck so close to Mrs. Flather that she could not get a word in sideways, either with the Duke or Duchess—at length she yielded to the teasing importunities of the tiresome old man, and resumed her yesterday's place in the fire-engine, without the anticipated salute from the Duke, and greatly incensed at Mr. Jorrocks for his untimely persecution.

How they "rode 'ome together" the reader can guess, nor will it be supposed that Binjimin had any trouble in looking for stones in Dickey Cobden's feet.

1.   Query Gypsum.

XIV

Abused by some most villainous knave!
Some base notorious knave, some scurvy fellow!—
O heaven, that such companions thou'dst unfold;
And put in every honest hand a whip
To lash the rascal naked through the world!

SHAKSPEARE

THE FIRST PERSON MR. JORROCKS met on his return to Hillingdon Hall was Joshua Sneakington. Joshua was prowling about on his travels, backbiting and making mischief, and occasionally displaying his newly-acquired importance by bullying some unfortunate cottage tenant. Mr. Jorrocks was full of the farming project, and Joshua was just the man he wanted to see.

"Yell, Sneak," said Mr. Jorrocks, in his usual free-and-easy style, when Joshua's broad-brimmed hat regained his finely-shaped head after the salute it gave the Squire; "vell, Sneak, 'ow are you gettin' on here?"

"Why, middling, I think, Mr. Jorrocks—can't expect perfection all at once—but I strive all I can to keep things right and comfortable. It's really an un pleasant office looking after a great estate like this, one gets a deal of ill-will—many mischievous ill-disposed people about."

"I thought all the ill-disposed people had been in London," observed Mr. Jorrocks.

"Oh no, sir," replied Sneakington, with a shake of the head, "town and country's pretty much alike for that, I dare say."

"The farmers are a long way behind the intelligence o' the day," observed Mr. Jorrocks, after a pause.

"Oh, a long way," replied Mr. Sneakington.

" 'What my father did I'll do' style about them," said Mr. Jorrocks.

"Just so," rejoined Joshua. "They have no life about them—no energy."

"No taste for nitrate o' sober, subsoil, Smith o' Deanston—Smith's the greatest benefactor the world ever saw."

"Indeed!" replied Joshua Sneakington, an answer that may mean anything.

"I a-thinkin'," said Mr. Jorrocks after a pause, during which he kept digging a Suffolk weed-spud into the ground in a fanciful sort of way, "it would be a good thing to get up a Hagricultural 'Sociation here—*monstrous* good thing, I think."

"No doubt," replied Joshua.

"Put a little life into the farmers," said Mr. Jorrocks. "Teach 'em the use o' manures—book-keepin' by double entry—rural economy—meadow fox-tail grass. Fine thing fox-tail grass—'unters should be fed on it."

"Indeed!" replied Joshua.

"You are an intelligent man, Sneak, and enjoy the confidence of the country in a remarkable degree. I wish you would take the thing in hand, and talk to some o' the farmers, and let us get the thing started."

"Why, sir, I shall be very happy to do anything to serve you," replied Mr. Sneakington, "and agriculture is a thing I have given my mind to very particularly; but the world's ill-natured, Mr. Jorrocks, and perhaps some of the people might think I was taking too much upon me."

"Never sich a thing! never sich a thing!" replied Mr. Jorrocks; "you are jest the man—Hillingdon 'Sociation—President, the Markiss o' Bray; Wice President, Mr. Jorrocks; Secretary, Mr. Sneakington—I tells you, you *shall*."

"Well, sir, what you please," replied Joshua; "only my time is precious just now, for I have an application from a gentleman in North Wales to build him a castle, and in course, if I take the secretaryship, I can't build the castle."

"Never mind the castle," replied Mr. Jorrocks, "never mind the castle—dare say he never meant to pay you for it—castle-builders seldom do; you stir your stumps, and go among the farmers—tell them they are all benighted—that we want to enlighten them; give them premiums—gold medals!—silver medals— lectors!—frinds and fellow-countrymen! walk in procession! band o' music! flags flyin'! dine in a tent, dance in a barn, tickets for tea, all that sort o' thing, in fact."

"Well, sir, what you please, sir," replied Mr. Sneakington, who was now about to undertake the character of agriculturist at short notice. "What you please, sir. There is no doubt such a society would be a great benefit—encourage activity—early rising. Your tenants, Mr. Jorrocks, though I shouldn't like it to go further, are a very indolent set of men. Mr. Westbury let them their farms too easy, dare say they would stand raising ten or fifteen per cent some of them. But then you know it's not my business to interfere, and I shouldn't like to make mischief; but you may rely upon it, your estate should produce a deal more than it does."

"Vy," said Mr. Jorrocks, "that's all werry well, I'm glad to hear it. Ven we've stuck the new lights into their candlesticks, may be it'll produce twice as much, and then we may get a leetle more tin. Smith o' Deanston should be knighted—baronet'd indeed! greatest benefactor the world ever saw; makes four blades grow where one grew before. You go, brush up my tenants, tell them to drain, subsoil, guano, nitrate o' sober, and gipsey manure."

"If I had a horse," observed Mr. Sneakington, "I should be able to make a survey of each farm, so as to judge of its capabilities, and talk to the tenant at the same time. It doesn't look well to see the agent of a great man going about on foot," added he, seeing Mr. Jorrocks did not exactly relish the proposal.

"Vy, as to an 'oss, you know, Sneak, it would only be a bother to you; for instance, if you came to a field with a large stone wall, and never a way out, you wouldn't know what to do with the nag while you was over a-lookin' at the crop; and as to leapin'! vy, you *know* you'd tumble off!"

"Oh, but the tenant would be there to hold the horse you know. There's work enough, I assure you, for a horse to look after all your concerns, and keep things square; farmers want a deal of looking after. It would be a saving in the end."

"Vy, time's tin in the City, certainly," replied Mr. Jorrocks, tinkling his silver in his breeches pocket; "it's all 'ow d'ye do? and oft again—state your case and away you go; but some'ow the day seems a many 'ours longer i' the country. No one's ever in a hurry here. Howsomever, I've no objection to lend you Dickey Cobden now and then; only you must mind and not overmark him, for he's only one o' the buttery sort—werry soft—can stand a deal o' rest—you twig."

"Thank you, sir," replied Sneakington, who thought riding the Squire's cob would have a grand effect—"then if I go to your stable, perhaps you'll tell Mr.Benjamin to let me have it to-morrow.Your rent-day's coming on, and I should like to go my rounds before, so as to make a proper report of the state in which everything is at present."

"Jest so," replied Mr. Jorrocks, "and then we shall see what improvement is made. Farmers should keep journals, write down everything they see and do, make obserwations on the weather, and so on—signs o' the sky; be philosophers as well as farmers in fact."

The next morning Joshua was seen riding Dickey Cobden slowly up the village of Hillingdon, with an armful of plans and a green gingham umbrella for a whip. His low-crowned broad-brimmed Sunday hat was well brushed, he had a clean white neckcloth, and his second-best black coat and waistcoat, and every-day trousers and gaiters on; also a pair of gloves, an appendage denoting that the wearer is going "from home." The cottagers eyed Joshua with suspicion and astonishment, and Beckey Brown ran into Polly Jones's to ask where Jos could be going to; while sundry of the "betterly people" who kept servants were sorely annoyed at the grievous length of time they stayed at the "well"—a sort of rural parliament, where James and Marys talk over their masters and mistresses, and tell all the secrets of the house. A little thing makes a great talk in the country.

Never did a Lord Mayor ride through Cheapside in his gingerbread coach and six, on his way (like his web-footed brethren the geese) to "take water" to be sworn in at our Lady the Queen's Exchequer, with a more inflated mind than Joshua Sneakington possessed as he rode through the village of Hillingdon on that important morning. Twice he was for turning back under pretence of having forgotten something, but

Dickey Cobden had a will of his own, and feeling Joshua had a loose seat, he gave certain indications of dissent that caused Joshua to alter his resolutions, and proceed on his journey rejoicing.

It was a fine day, clear and sunshiny, and Joshua's mind partook of the apparent happiness of nature.

Firfield—Johnny Wopstraw's farm—was the first in Joshua Sneakington's circuit, and he timed his visit so as to arrive as Johnny was sitting down to his twelve o'clock dinner, with his wife, children, and servants. Potatoes and bacon, and gooseberry dumplings. Jos, like most lazy dogs, was a good eater, and didn't require a second invitation to induce him to sit down and partake of the frugal meal.

After it was over, and the party were dispersing to their respective occupations, Joshua began broaching the subject of his mission.

"Well, and how are you getting on in the farming way?" inquired he.

"Oh, why, upon the whoole, middling well; times are bad, but the land's pretty good, and the situation not amiss, and I hope the Squire will not be over hard with us."

"The Squire's a-thinking," observed Joshua, with a hem and a stroke of his puritanical chin, "of having a fresh survey made of his estate, and letting the farms according to the times."

"*So-o-o*," replied Wopstraw, wondering how that would cut.

"The farmers in this country, he thinks, are a long way behind the intelligence of the day—too much of what-my-father-did-I-do style about them."

"Just so," observed Johnny Wopstraw.

"The Squire you see's a very clever man—and has been used to first-rate farming—patent ploughs—gipsey manure—fox-tail grass—and he wants to encourage activity and emulation among his tenants. There's a grand discovery just made, for making eight blades grow where one grew before."

"*So-o-o-o!*" ejaculated Johnny Wopstraw.

"And the Squire thinks if he can get the farmers to adopt it there will be like twopence gained to them and a penny to him."

"Just so," observed Johnny Wopstraw; "upon the whoole, I should think it must be a grand discovery."

"The man should be made a lord," replied Joshua, rubbing his chin and looking very sagacious—as much as to say that he had had a hand in the pie.

"Upon the whoole, I think he should," replied Wopstraw.

"If you'll bring me out my horse I'll just ride over your farm, now that I have got the plan in my pocket, and then we'll be better able to talk the matter over at our rent day," observed Joshua, drawing on his gloves most consequentially.

Wopstraw, somewhat astonished at the sudden elevation of the scamp, though not at all surprised at his airs, brought out the nag, and Joshua mounting, desired Wopstraw to take him such a circuit as would lead him on to the next tenant's farm, so that he might not lose time by going over the same ground twice. Off then they set, Joshua on Dickey Cobden, and Wopstraw walking alongside, opening gates, handing up specimens of soil, and replying to Joshua's interrogatories.

"Give me a piece of that!" Joshua would exclaim on entering a allow; then he would break the clod, and eye it, just as Master Homer eyed his Christmas pie, to see how much fruit there was in it. "Ah, I see," Joshua would observe thoughtfully, as if to himself, but in reality to Wopstraw—"Silicious sand—clay—calcareous sand—carbonite of lime—humus"—and thereupon he would make a memorandum, as if he was entering the quality in his book.

Having played at this game over a few fields, and glanced at the crops generally, during which operation he imparted no small degree of astonishment to Johnny Wopstraw's sin mind, he at length observed he had no doubt the farm was capable of very great improvement, particularly if this new system of making ten blades grow here only one grew at present was introduced; and that he thought it would be well for Mr. Wopstraw to secure a lease, intimating at the same time that the usual custom in farming was to make the steward a present in proportion to the rent and length of the term.

A word here to landowners.

It has long been remarked that whatever becomes of the owner of an estate, the steward invariably thrives, and we have often heard wonder

The surprise

expressed how this happens. Having made what to us was a discovery, the other day, on this head, we will here impart it to you in case you may be ignorant of it also.

We were fishing in the neighbourhood of a water corn-mill, and the trout not being inclined to be taken, we were about shutting up shop, with some half-dozen in our creel, when we encountered an old farmer riding on his cart for a sack of flour. The usual country courtesies, "What sport have you had?" and "How are you getting on?" having been exchanged, a conversation sprang up about the farmer's landlord (who was an absentee) and his agent, Mr. Jeremiah Jumps. Jumps was a new broom, and, of course, sweeping clean—we don't mean to say he was racking the land, but he was displaying a little unusual activity on behalf of an absentee landlord—well, the present Jumps brought up the previous Jumps, or whatever his name was, and the present Jumps' activity was contrasted with the indolence of the former, and then the former Jumps' riches came to be talked of.

"Ah, he had a grand time of it," said the farmer; "no trouble—no one to check him—just did what he liked—granted leases to whom he pleased, and every tenant down with his five or ten pounds on each letting, as regular as could be."

"The agent got *that*, then, did he?" asked we.

"Oh, to be sure—that's the *custom*, you know—always make the steward a compliment on taking."

"Indeed," said we, "that's a wrinkle we weren't up to—do us the pleasure to accept these trout—two and two's four—five and one's six—there you are—and good morning to you—good morning— knowledge should not be had for nothing."

Reader! take care your "Jumps" isn't playing you that trick.

Willey Goodheart was the next tenant in Joshua's route. Willey was one of the very old-fashioned, tarry-at-home school of farmers—neat, careful, prudent, honest, and cheerful. He had been on the estate "man and boy," as the saying is, for sixty years, and his little farm was a perfect model of neatness and productiveness. Age had now bowed a once upright manly form, and time had strongly marked the handsome features of his face; but there was a mild, gentlemanly, patriarchal air about old Willey, corresponding with his manners; and his venerable grey hair fell in curly locks on the upright collar of his straight-cut, single-breasted, large-buttoned blue coat. On Sundays, his costume partook still more of the character of bygone days, by the addition of a pair of nearly sky-blue worsted stockings, and square-toed shoes, with large silver buckles—shoes that must either have been much better than they make them at the present day, or been devoted exclusively to Sunday wear, for they had seen "square toes" in and out three times since they were bought. Willey seldom went from home except to church. Markets even he did not trouble. His corn was sold to a neighbouring miller; his daughter carried his butter and eggs to the truck shop at Hillingdon, from whence his few wants were also supplied. He was one of the draining, manuring, land-working breed of farmers—always some little improvement in hand or in view—some hedge to run straight—some land to lay better away—some slack to fill up—or some gate to remove to a more convenient position; but he knew nothing of "guano, nitrate o' sober, or gipsey manure," as Mr. Jorrocks would say. Having in early life been in a gentleman's service at Grampound (Cornwall), an intimacy he had then contracted with a fellow-servant had continued, and showed itself by his sending Willey the county papers; but the friend most likely being one of Willey's breed, instead of availing himself of Her Majesty's post for the conveyance of each paper, hoarded them up till he got a year or two's papers in hand, when he transmitted them to Willey per waggon. The consequence was, that Willey read the papers like history, and was generally a year or two behind-hand—sometimes more, in the harvest-time. Farmers and fox-hunters are not great readers in a general way.

We knew a fox-hunter, who borrowed the first volume of one of Scott's novels, and, having kept it a long time, his friend asked him if he would not like to have another.

"Oh no, thank you," said he, "that does very well. By the time I get to the end, I've forgot the beginning, so I just begin over again, and it serves my purpose quite as well as a new one."

Willey was rather better than this, for he studied the *Grampound Gun* and *Tregony Times*, as the paper was called, with a patient and persevering assiduity, beginning with the title, and ending with the printer's name of each number, and remembered what he had read, for he could refer to the file of his authority with great accuracy whenever a difficulty arose in his mind. Indeed, his Bible and the *Grampound Gun* were the only two works that Willey considered worth having; and, in his younger days, when he mixed more among the farmers, he had acquired the *sobriquet* of the *"Grampound Gun,"* from generally prefacing his stories or observations with—"I see by the *Grampound Gun and Tregony Times* that" so and so has taken place.

Well, on this particular day Willey had been taking a suck at his old friend after his frugal dinner, and the last bundle of *Guns* was on the table before him, a Joshua's dry cough and the tread of Dickey Cobden's feet arrested Willey's attention. Taking off his tortoiseshell-rimmed spectacles, he hurried to the woodbined porch of his door to greet the visitor.

There sat Joshua, looking as consequential as could be, with a supercilious smile on his hypocritical countenance, that as much as said, "I'll astonish the old man."

"Well, Mr. Goodheart," said he, how do *you* do to-day?"

"Why, middling, thank ye, Mr. Sneakington," replied Willey, for he didn't like Joshua a bit—"middling, thank you—mustn't complain—cannot work as I used though—and I'm nabbut seventy-two. A-dear—but this is a bad job in Lunnun, Mr. Sneakington—shocking bad job. Do you think he'll be hung?" inquired Willey, with anxiety depicted on his fine expressive face.

"What's the matter now?" inquired Joshua, who felt himself in a manner connected with London, from his master having come from there.

"A-dear, haven't you heard," replied Willey, "of this tarrible rascal shooting at the Queen? A-dear, Lunnun must be a tarrible place—lucky our Squire's got away from it, I'm sure."

"Well, but who's been shooting at the Queen now?" inquired Sneakington.

"A villain called Oxford! 'ord rot him; but if I had him I'd strangle him—I'd knock the very soul out of him, spiflicate him," replied Willey, his still bright eyes sparkling as he spoke. "The idea of shooting at a beautiful young lady like that—a queen too! But won't you alight and come in, Mr. Sneakington, and I'll show you all about it?"

"*Stuff and nonsense!*" exclaimed Joshua Sneakington, with a sneer and an indignant curl of the lip—"that's as old as the hills—you're always finding a mare's nest. Good day, old boy! good day!" adding to himself as he kicked Dickey Cobden along, "no use bothering with such an old fool as that. He's too far behind the intelligence of the day for me. Leave him for the Squire."

Willey then, somewhat shocked at Joshua's want of loyalty, re-entered his house, and resuming the tortoise shell-rimmed spectacles, returned to his reading of Oxford's attempt on the life of the Queen.

Before Joshua Sneakington had accomplished the hill leading up to Mr. Mark Heavytail's farm, Mark having returned from his dinner, had stripped off his coat, and was working away in the fields. Josh owed Heavytail a grudge, and he was a great man for paying his debts—debts of honour at least. He had done some very indifferent mason's work for Mark, and had charged about double what he ought, which of course made him owe Heavytail a *good* turn—as people say when they mean the contrary—for resisting the imposition.

Seeing a horse and a low-crowned hat on the sky line of the hill, Mark hurried from his work to greet the Squire as he thought. When he got within hail, and saw it was Josh, he was for turning back.

"HOLLOA THERE!" exclaimed Joshua, waving his arm for Heavytail to come to him.

"WHAT DO YOU WANT?" roared Heavytail at the extremity of his voice.

"Come and open this gate!" cried he; "I want to speak to you."

"OPEN IT YOURSELF! YOU CANNOT HAVE A BETTER SARVANT," roared Heavytail.

"CONFOUND YOUR IMPITTANCE!" bellowed Josh, "I've come with a messuage from the Squire."

"WELL, AND WHAT DOES THE SQUIRE WANT, THAT HE'S SENT AN 'ARD BRICKLAYER LIKE YE TO TELL?"

"You had better sink all *that*," replied Josh, with an emphasis and look of authority. "The Squire wishes me to look over his estate preparatory to his rent day, to see that the rotation of crops is properly kept, and give him a report as to——"

"Ye!" roared Heavytail, pointing at Josh, and then holding his sides as though he would split with laughter—"Ye!" repeated he, "an 'ard bricklayer like ye! I'd as soon think of setting my 'ard sow to survey an estate—haw! haw! haw!—he! he! he!—haw! haw! haw!"

Heavytail's unwonted mirth roused the ire of his dog, who, not exactly understanding matters, but seeing his master was not pleased, at this juncture jumped over the wall with his bristles up, when Dickey Cobden shied off at an angle, and, finding his head loose, set off down hill as hard as ever he could lay legs to the ground, with the colley dog at his heels.

Josh lost his umbrella, and scattered his plans as he went, and the impetus gained sent Dickey and his rider clean through the gate at the bottom of the hill with a most terrible crash of the timber.

XV

We think our fathers fools, so wise we grow;
Our wiser sons, no doubt, will think us so.

GREAT ANXIETY PREVAILED AMONG THE farmers to hear the grand discovery the "greatest benefactor the world ever saw" had made for making "two blades grow where one grew before"; a number that increased in the telling till they got it up as high as sixteen—sixteen blades, where only one grew before. As Mr. Jorrocks's rent-day approached, anxiety became quickened, and Joshua Sneakington's importance increased, by the mysterious gravity he observed in his rounds among the farmers, and the obscure hints he dropped, that he was at the bottom of the secret.

Meanwhile Mr. Jorrocks busied himself reading up anything he could lay hold of upon farming, for the purpose of making them a grand oration on the importance of establishing an Agricultural Association, and of the virtue of scientific farming in general. And here let us observe, that many people talk as if they imagined theoretical—that is to say, book farming—is a thing of modern introduction—that our fathers had no "Books of the Farm," no "Quarterly Journals," or other experimental trying works in their times. It is quite a mistake—our forefathers were quite as well off as ourselves in that respect. We have whole bookshelves loaded with farming lore of former times, the property of our grandfather, the husband of the old lady we mentioned before, who, at the age of eighty-three, reads without specs. Indeed, we may add, that the old lady herself thinks very lightly of the virtues of what is called scientific farming.

"Such farming, indeed!" she exclaims, whenever we pump her on the past; "why, a hind nowadays is as good as a farmer used to be in your poor grandfather's time—driving about in their gigs, with their names painted up behind; and writing nonsense to the papers instead of ploughing their land." But the wives are what anger her most. "Silks, ay, and *satins*, and sofas every day; and pianneys skelping at night. Lauk! we never heard of such things as pianneys in my time!" she says. "The churn was the farmer's daughter's instrument, and a precious sight better wives they made, than the fine gadabout be-feathered breed we see nowadays." So much for our granny. But, as we said before, we have yards upon yards of books on every possible subject relating to land, leaving after-comers the chance of starting anything new apparently out of the question. One consolation, however, is, that there are always new farmers coming on—to whom the old theories are new—as our friend B—— says, when we tax him with riding the same joke rather often.

We have just run our eye along our bookcase, and see what a haul we have made in the way of farming literature. Alongside some twenty vols. of the Farmer's Magazine, we have Mills's Husbandry (1762).—Du Hamel's ditto.—Hunter's Georgical Essays, in numberless volumes.—Pott's Farmer's Cyclopaedia, or Agricultural Dictionary of improved Modern Husbandry, in one large quarto.—Anderson's Essays.—Farmer's Letters to the People of England, containing the sentiments of a Practical Husbandman, on various subjects of great importance (1768).—Farmer's Guide in Hiring and Stocking Farms (1770).—The Farmer's Instructor, or the Husbandman and Gardener's useful and necessary Companion, being a new treatise of Husbandry, Gardening, and other Matters relating to Country Affairs, by Samuel Trowell, Gentleman (1747).—A Philosophical Account of the Works of Nature, printed for J. Hodges, at the Looking-glass, over against Magnus Church, on London Bridge.—The New Farmer's Calendar, or Monthly Remembrancer of all kinds of Country Business, in the New Husbandry, with the Management of Live Stock, inscribed to the Farmers of Great Britain, by a Farmer and Breeder (1802).—Marshall's Agriculture of the Southern Counties, with a Sketch of the Vale of London (1799).—Curwen on Feeding Stock.—Cully on Live Stock.— Davis on Land Surveying.—Bailey's Agricultural Survey.—Rennie's Essays on Peat Moss.—Practical Husbandry, or the Art of Farming with a certainty of Gain, by Dr. John Trusler, of Cobham, Surrey; together with Directions for Measuring Timber (1780),—and no end of pamphlets and letters, and "observations on similar subjects."

Let us not, however, be supposed to decry agricultural improvement. Far from it. We are quite sensible of the many defects in our present system, which we believe chiefly arise from the want of capital, energy, and observation; but we wish to counteract the evil people in high stations frequently do by talking wildly at agricultural meetings, for the mere purpose of astonishing the farmers, without really knowing or caring any thing about what they say. They do far more harm than good, for farmers get confused; and, frightened at their own ignorance, despair of coming up to the mark, and so remain as they were; or else attempt fanciful experiments, which, after endless expense, they find unsuited to their climate or soil, or unproductive of the anticipated ends. The great difficulty under which farming labours, however, is want of capital; and so long as people look upon it as an exception to all other trades, and requiring no capital to set up with, so long we fear will be the want of energy and taste for improvement. But to our tale. Mr. Jorrocks having determined that his "let off" should be one of great magnitude, resolved upon inviting the principal neighbours to dinner, and winding up the evening with a ball to their wives and daughters. Accordingly, Mr. Jorrocks and Joshua Sneakington went about beating up for recruits, and, as usual on such occasions, were very successful. Indeed, one of the grand differences between town and country is this—that invitations cannot be refused without offence. By town and country, of course we mean any place out of London for the latter. Now, in London, Mr. and Mrs. Brown request the honour of Mr. and Mrs. Green's company to dinner, on Tuesday the 26th of June, at half-past six; and if Mr. and Mrs. Green either don't like Mr. and Mrs. Brown, or have reason to think that they may get a pleasanter invitation elsewhere, Mr. and Mrs. Green make no bones whatever of saying they are sorry that a prior engagement prevents them the honour of accepting Mr. and Mrs. Brown's kind invitation for Tuesday, June the 26th; and Mr. and Mrs. Brown never trouble their heads to inquire whether there was any truth in the story or not; but in the country it is quite another thing.

Take a small town for instance. Every small town has a "professed cook,"
a sort of brandy-bibbing body, who can cook a little when she's sober,
but who has not what servants call conduct enough to keep in place,
consequently she confines herself to making "blows out" for the party
givers, among whom a few days' work will furnish several days' drink,
and victuals too, if she is skilful, which most of them are, in carrying
away. Well, these sort of people know every movement and every party
in the town—know exactly beforehand who will be at each feed;
and if Mr. and Mrs. So-and-so are not there, they immediately set to
work to ferret out what's happened that Mr. and Mrs. So-and-so are
not asked—that they never cooked a dinner there before without Mr.
and Mrs. So-and-so being there—wonder what can have happened
that Mr. and Mrs. So-and-so are not there—think Mr. and Mrs. So-
and-so must have fallen out; for when people of this sort get a thing
on their tongues, there is no end to the repetitions they indulge in. If
the servants can't solve the mystery among them, cookey most likely
performs the same office of blow-out maker for Mr. and Mrs. So-and-
so that she is performing for the present party givers, consequently she
can drop in the next day (if she's sober enough to walk) and inquire
of their everyday cook, if they had had anybody dining the day before,
or if their "people" dined out, and so the story gets afloat, and truth is
drawn out of the well.

However, this is a capital world for lending or giving things away in,
and people need not be much put to, who only want to give others a
treat. Mrs. Flather and Emma were the only persons who refused Mr.
and Mrs. Jorrocks's invitation. They were sorry that they had a previous
engagement. Our readers will perhaps remember that Mrs. Flather had
been sadly disconcerted by Mr. Jorrocks's attentions at Donkeyton Castle,
when she wanted to bring the Marquis "to book," and her anger had not
yet subsided. She determined to snub him. Well, as luck would have it, just
as her boy in buttons delivered her answer at Hillingdon Hall, a messenger
arrived from Donkeyton Castle with a note from the Marquis.

Jeems had taken it into his head that he would like to see Emma, and
under, pretence of paying Mr. Jorrocks a farming-electioneering visit,
he thought to accomplish that object, and either by accident or design

had pitched upon the very day our Cockney Squire had fixed for his party.

This was the letter:—

DONKEYTON CASTLE

DEAR MR. JORROCKS,—My papa and you had some conversation about a farming thing that you thought would further our interest in your neighbourhood, and my mamma thinks I had better go over to Hillingdon Park and see you about it. If it will be convenient to Mrs. Jorrocks and you to receive me, I shall be very happy to dine and stay all night with you on Thursday next. Pray write me an answer by the bearer, and with compliments to Mrs. Jorrocks, believe me to remain, dear Mr. Jorrocks, yours very truly,

BRAY

To JAMES JORROCKS, ESQ.,
Hillingdon Park

Of course Mr. Jorrocks was too happy to see the Marquis, and he wrote him to that effect, adding that he had better come early, in order that they might talk matters over, as he would have some friends to meet him, and they kept early hours in the country. There was also this postscript. "*P.S.*—My name's JOHN, not James. My place is a Hall, not a Park. If you want wenison, you'd better bring it with you."

Mrs. Flather's boy in buttons having gone into the kitchen to have a game of cribbage with Binjimin, made himself sufficiently acquainted with the "ins and outs" to be able to tell their cook that Jorrocks was either going to Donkeyton Castle again, or that Donkeyton Castle was coming to Jorrocks. This news soon found its way into the parlour, and mother and daughter were uncommonly struck and hurt at the intelligence. Mrs. Flather was sure it would be that the Marquis was coming to the Hall, for she had overheard some of the conversation between the Duke and Mr. Jorrocks at Donkeyton, and she thought she never could sufficiently censure herself for refusing the invitation.

How to repair the error was now the consideration. Emma should step down with a bouquet, and see if she could not put matters right. Accordingly, having selected a smart one, she set out on her errand. Mrs. Jorrocks was delighted to see her, and was werry sorry she was not to have that pleasure on Thursday. Emma was very much obliged for their kindness in asking them, so was mamma—the latter rather expected an old friend of dear papa's calling that day, and if he did call he might stay dinner; but—

Oh, Mrs. Jorrocks "wouldn't wish to interfere in such a case—of course, an old friend o' the family must take precedence of them."

"If, however, their friend did not come," resumed Emma.

"Oh, think no more about it," interrupted Mrs. Jorrocks; "any other time would be equally agreeable to Mr. Jorrocks and her; indeed, here was Mr. Jorrocks himself," added she, as our hero emerged from a laurelled walk, and came suddenly upon them.

Mr. Jorrocks would fain have forgiven the poor girl, but Mrs. J. stood up stoutly, and gave Mr. J. a look that plainly told him he had better be quiet; so as our farmer friend did not care much about the matter, he left them, and went away to stare at some sheep.

We will not trouble our readers with a recital of the preparations, the borrowing, and joining, and contriving, and managing, nor will we give a programme of the entertainment, but let the thing speak for itself.

The great, the important day at length arrived—clear, bright, sunshiny, and cloudless—a real summer's day—one that English people appreciate most thoroughly from the circumstance of their coming so seldom. Mr. Jorrocks bustled about, in a terrible stew, reciting his speech, and bothering and running against every body.

Towards two o'clock, a claret-coloured brougham, with red picked wheels, and a ducal coronet on the panel, drove down the village of Hillingdon, to the astonishment of the natives, who had never seen anything of the sort before. The noble, lofty-actioned iron grey stepped and carried himself with becoming dignity, champing the richly chased bit, and throwing his head about as though he had a bowing acquaintance with all the people in the street. In fact, he went just as he may be seen any day of the season going up and down St. James's

Street. Horses, unlike dandies, have only one action. Beside the driver, for, we believe, "one-'oss guiders" are not admitted among the fraternity of coachmen, sat the Marquis's French valet—a profusely-whiskered much-bejewelled individual; and an imperial, containing his lordship's clothes, covered the roof of the carriage.

Mr. Jorrocks, who had begun to wax uneasy, and had stopped the recital of his speech for some time, listening for the noise of approaching wheels, no sooner heard the sound drum-like roll of the well-built London carriage, than he shoved his notes into his pocket, and ran to the entrance to greet his guest. The Marquis alighted just as Mr. Jorrocks got to the door. He was dressed in the extreme of, the London fashion. A gold-laced, gold tasselled, blue foraging cap sat jauntily on his well-waxed light brown ringlets; the ample tie of his rich blue and gold satin cravat, secured with enormous pearl pins, covered the wide opening made by a very broad, roll-collared white waistcoat, loose down to the two bottom buttons, while the narrow hem of a collar to his blue coat barely came up to the nape of his neck, and the nippy waist began considerably higher up than nature had put his own. His trousers of lavender-coloured merino were shaped over the instep, and buttoned under a pair of laced lavender-coloured boots, which would have been stockings but for a morsel of patent leather over the toe and round the soles. He carried a gold-headed cane and a richly embroidered lace-fringed handkerchief in his hand.

"I'm werry 'appy to see you," exclaimed Mr. Jorrocks, greeting his unagricultural-looking guest; "werry 'appy indeed—thought you weren't comin'—howsomever you're in plenty of time—only I wanted to have a little talk with you afore'and you know—as to what you shall say to the chaps. We must be werry knowin'—scientific in fact."

"True," replied the Marquis, "I've got off part of an agricultural article in the Encyclopaedia by heart, and—"

"Ah, but they want facts," replied Mr. Jorrocks, "*drainin'*, science, and steam's the ticket—howsomever, come into my sanctum, and I'll talk it all over with you."

"Couldn't we walk, and call on Mrs. Flather, and talk it over as we go?" inquired the Marquis.

"No, no," replied Mr. Jorrocks, "no time to look arter the pettikits. Let's to business—this way—mind the step—now take a chair, sit down, and I'll tell you all about it."

The Marquis having complied with Mr. Jorrocks's request, our friend soused himself into his red-morocco hunting-chair, and folding one leg over the other, turned to the Marquis, and began talking with his fingers and tongue. "You see," said he, pressing his forefingers together, "we're come to enlighten these muffs, and a pretty benighted, bewildered, bedevilled lot they are; and the first thing is to conwince them they are all wrong, and the next to instruct them wot is right. Farmin' in fact's in a benighted sort o' state, and we must break the shell o' their ignorance, and set the boobies at liberty. Now I've got a werry fine composition in my 'ead, if I can only draw it out when the time comes—for that's the deuce and all in oratory—one's so werry apt to lose the thread, and get carried right up among the clouds, just like a chap on a wet mornin' on the top of Mount Riega; howsomever, I expect I've got it pretty pat, and, with the aid of cheers, and referrin' to my notes, I dare say I shall get through with it; and in course, arter I've lathered and soaped the chaps well, I shall want some one to shave them, and there's when I want you to come in. I shall start by 'busin' of them, then do a little instructin', and finally finish by flatterin' of them, and proposin' a 'Sociation for the encouragement of everything relatin' to farmin'—with you for the President, and all that sort o' thing—with your health—three times three—one cheer more, and all that sort o' thing. Then in course you'll get up and make them a werry hoiley oration, say whatever you think will be most palatable, pay them all sorts of compliments, and all that sort o' thing." Mr. Jorrocks finished this long sentence by releasing his hands and flourishing the right one about in the air.

"But that won't suit the speech I've got by heart, Mr. Jorrocks," replied the Marquis, in a state of perturbation at his friend supposing he could take a part at short notice.

"Vell, but vot's your speech about?" inquired Mr. Jorrocks; "it'll surely be about farmin'."

"Oh yes, I begin with the antiquity of the thing, showing that the greatest poets and generals and states men of all countries and times have encouraged agriculture."

"Werry good," said Mr. Jorrocks.

"Then I take a look at the beautiful harmless simplicity of life it engenders, contrast the robust farmer with the pallid artisan, and their beautiful and rosy offspring with the children of town-bred parents; talk of the importance of a 'bold peasantry' to a country's welfare, and finish with the advantages of improving the farmers' condition by putting them in possession of the newest fashions, or whatever you call the things in farming, and express the great interest I take in this district, and the pleasure I experience in becoming the President of a Society of such praiseworthy people, or something of that sort," concluded the Marquis.

"Werry good," said Mr. Jorrocks, "werry good in deed—capital I may say; nothin' can be better. Folks have a wonderful likin' for what they don't understand, and if you finish by a little that they do understand, they'll take all the rest for granted, and say you are a *tre-men-dous* clever feller! I'm agoin' to do a bit of antiquity myself—cribbed of course, but that's nothin'. But *con*found it, I'm forgetting the werry pint wot I wanted to talk to you about. Drainin's the ticket, as I told you before. Stick *that* into them. Let drainin' be the great gun of your discourse. Nothing like drainin'; say it's the grandest diskivery wotever was made—that the inwentor, Smith o' Deanston, 's the greatest benefactor the world ever saw; and finish off by tellin' them 'ow you've turned your attention very extensively to the subject, as applied to this part of the country, and with the aid of a certain degree of geological knowledge, you have inwented a tile that you have no manner of doubt——"

"But I've done nothin' of the sort I" exclaimed the Marquis, throwing up his hands in alarm, his ma having taught him never to tell fibs.

"Never mind that," replied Mr. Jorrocks, "never mind that; I've done it for you—I've done it for you—and it's as old as the 'ills, that wot you do by another, you do by yourself. Here, see," said he, pulling an old letter back out of his pocket, "here are the component parts of the tile; and whether they adopt it or not, it will show your great interest in agricultural concerns, and make you poppilar with the farmers; but

I think comin' from you they *will* adopt it, for it's extonishin' how even the commonest people are led away by great people and great names. Well, howsomever, never mind, this is it (reading). Take of stiff, strong clay two stun (stone) four punds, add to this two stun of fine river or sea gravel, and one stun three punds of finely sifted lime, mex them well together, by stirrin' for a couple hours, and when of a proper consistency add one stun of coarse brown or Muscovado sugar, sluice the whole with 'ot water, and then pour it into the tile shapes, and you will have for, for, for—you may say—werry little tin, one 'undred werry good tiles. In course," added Mr. Jorrocks, "this calkilation is not quite perfect; indeed I've not had time to work the thing out properly, but you can give it as a werry promisin' experiment, and one that will amply repay further inwestigation."

"But I'm afraid I don't sufficiently understand the thing myself, Mr.—Mr.—Mr. Jorrocks, to be able to explain it to the farmers."

"Oh, never mind that," replied our worthy friend, "never mind that. No questions axed on these occasions: state broadly and confidently, and unless they've tried the experiment themselves they can't contradict you. In this case I'm sure they haven't tried it."

"But the sugar rather puzzles me," observed the Marquis.

"Not at all," replied Mr. Jorrocks, "not at all; at all ewents it only shows you don't rightly understand the natur' o' sugar—nothin' so glutinacious as sugar—sugar is of four kinds, brown or Muscovado, refined or loaf, sugar-candy, and clayed sugar; clayed sugar of itself would bespeak a connection with drainin' tiles. The old ancients used to think it was a gum collected from the canes, strong as glue."

"But why not use the *clayed* sugar, instead of the Muscovado?" inquired the Marquis.

"Jest as you please," replied Mr. Jorrocks, "jest as you please;" adding aloud to himself—"only there must *be* sugar in the concern, or it won't suit my book botherin' my 'ead about it."

"Vell then, now you understand," resumed our grocer-farmer Squire; "you can let off wot you like at startin'—talk about Julius Caesar, Romeo Coates, or any of them old codgers, but you must lower your steam down to ordinary levels; and when you talk about the newest fashions in farmin', you can introduce that tile as one of the newest fashions you have heard of, if you don't like to say it's your own. When you've done that, you can finish with my werry good 'ealth, and refer with satisfaction to the adwantage of your appearin' before a body o' farmers under the auspices of a gen'lman so distinguished in the annals o' agricultur' as myself—you twig? *Sugar* again, in fact!"

Just as our farmer friends had got thus far in their arrangements, the "clatter *versus* patter" of Batsay's tongue and dishes in the kitchen, together with certain savoury smells, caught Mr. Jorrocks's nose and ear and raising his hand as if in the act of tallyhoing a fox, he exclaimed, "'Ark! there's the joyful sound—feedin' time's at 'and."

"What time is your breakfast?" inquired the Marquis.

"*Breakfast! it's dinner!*" replied Mr. Jorrocks.

"What! dinner at *three*?" rejoined the Marquis, taking the most diminutive Geneva watch out of his waistcoat pocket.

"You surely wouldn't *breakfast* at three!" observed Mr. Jorrocks.

"Why, no; but I thought it was what London people call a breakfast— soups, poultry, venison, pastry, everything except fish—something between three and seven you know."

"Call it vot you like," said Mr. Jorrocks, "I means to make it *my* dinner—and precious 'ungry I am too; been up since six—'mong the dandylions—only had four heggs, two chops, and a kidney: don't do for us farmers to lie long in bed."

"I had better be dressing then," said the Marquis.

"Dressin'! Vy, you're smart enough, I'm sure."

"Oh, but I can't appear in public in these travelling things; must be got up properly—dress you know is half the battle in speaking. My governess used to tell me that if Tully himself had pronounced one of his orations with a blanket about his shoulders, more people would have laughed at his dress than admired his eloquence."

" 'Ang Tully," replied Mr. Jorrocks, in a fidget lest the Marquis should keep his entertainment waiting; "you can jest wesh your 'ands, and put your fine clothes on arterwards; I'll bring you a basin and *towl* in here, and save you the trouble of goin' upstairs."

"Oh, but I want Adolphe!"

"Adolphe! Who the devil's Adolphe?"

"My valet."

"Your walet! Surely your walet don't wash you, does he?"

"No, but he arranges my hair—it's all out of curl—helps me on with my clothes, and saves me a world of trouble; I'll ring for him, if you please." So saying, the Marquis gave the bell a pull; and Mr. Jorrocks, seeing there was no alternative, conducted him up to his room, charging him over and over again not to be above five minutes at most.

XVI

When we have stuff'd
These pipes and these conveyances of our blood
With wine and feeding, we have suppler souls
Than in our priest-like fasts.—SHAKSPEARE

JOSHUA SNEAKINGTON HAVING PERSUADED MR. Jorrocks that he had better
leave the receipt of rents and putting off requests and complaints to
him, had taken his seat in great form in Mrs. Jorrocks's postage-stamped
boudoir, with a portfolio, inkstand, cash-box, and other paraphernalia
of money-taking before him. He had each tenant ushered in separately,
and was uncommonly pompous and precise with them all. Joshua, like
most country people, had just a sufficient knowledge of farming to
be able to put proper questions, and of course he was at home when
discussing the state of farmhouses and buildings; moreover, there was
a certain solemn thoughtful manner about Joshua that looked like
wisdom and calculation. He would place his elbows on the table, and
rest his chin upon his hand, and draw a loquacious tenant on by means
of little coughs and monosyllabic responses until he had got everything
out of him. His main object was to sift whether they were desirous
of leases—on the usual terms, of course—a handsome douceur to the
steward. Joshua having at length dismissed the last tenant, old Willey
Goodheart, and replied to a strong expression of fear he had charged
his mind with from the *Grampound Gun and Tregony Times*, relative to
the injury the importation of foreign cattle was likely to do farmers,
by assuring Willey that his fears were past date, for the cattle had come
in and injured none but the importers, and the teeth of those who
had tried them; and having counted the money and found it all right
and put everything away in a style becoming a scientific stone-mason,

went to join Mr. Jorrocks, who was now receiving his farmer friends, who were fast assembling with enormous appetites. Mr. Jorrocks was coming the agriculturist in costume—the Jorrockian jacket, with a wheat ear and two or three heads of oats in his button-hole, a bright buff waistcoat and gilt buttons, patent cord shorts and rather baggy drab gaiters, showing the whiteness of his stockings and the jolly rotundity of his calves. He received his friends in his usual "hale fellow well met" style, asked after the farmers' wives and daughters, talked of turnips, aftermaths, and potato prospects, wishing all the time the Marquis would come down. At length he appeared; not with a coronet on his head, as some of them expected to see him, but clad in the height of ballroom fashion, affording a striking contrast to the rural attire of the company around.

Dinner, as the country servants say, was then "sarved." It was in the usual style of Jorrockian liberality—rounds of beef and saddles of mutton, fillets of veal and sucking-pigs, with puddings, pies, custards, jellies, tarts, all crammed on together. There was a novelty in the centre of the table, in the shape of a new horse-pail for an epergne. This was intended to serve a double purpose, an epergne at dinner and a punch-bowl after. It was painted white within and pea-green without, with a plough on each side, and the mottoes, "Speed the plough" and "Live and let live," above and below, while tasteful garlands of real flowers encircled the parts where the hoops came round. Altogether it was a splendid affair and quite novel—Mr. Jorrocks is a great man for novelty. The Marquis, of course, was on the host's right, Mr. Trotter was on his left, and down the long table were ranged tenants and neighbours—higgledy-piggledy, just as they came. The Marquis, who had been the object of attention, was now deserted for the substantial viands heaped before them. At them each man went, with a vigour known only to rural appetites whetted by a long fast. Jorrocks commenced by helping the Marquis to a piece of beef that perfectly astounded him. Then there was such ladling in with knives, such calling for ale, such smacking of lips, such runs upon favourite dishes, until at length the human voice divine, rising above the clatter of knives and plates, announced that nature was knocking under, and in due time the decks began to be cleared. The horse-pail, with a soup ladle for a spoon, having resumed its position in the middle of the table all smoking and reeking with rum punch, and such of the company as were too genteel to drink "grog" being supplied with wine, Mr. Jorrocks ran through the usual loyal and patriotic toasts, as the newspapers phrase them, at a brisk pace, in his usual felicitous manner, and then gathered himself together for his great let off of the day. Having called upon Joshua Sneakington, the vice, and Mr. Heavytail, who sat in charge of the horse-pail, to see that their neighbours charged their glasses, he gave a substantial *hem* and thus began:—

"Frinds and fellow-farmers! lend me your ears! that's to say, listen to wot I've got to say to ye. Omy beloved 'earers, I've come to teach you a thing or two—a thing or two wot'll make men instead o' mice on ye if you will but follow my adwice (applause). Believe me, I'm so chock-full o' knowledge that I can hardly get it out o' the bung'ole o' my 'ead—knowledge o' the purest kind, cull'd in the fairest fields o' farmin' science (applause). Ah my beloved 'earers, that's to the pint, and your intelligent minds cap forrard to the find. The first step towards knowledge is to be satisfied of your ignorance!—there then you must all join!—write your selves down jackasses, and John Jorrocks will put you on your legs again. Lord, wot a set o' benighted-lookin' cocks you all are," added Mr. Jorrocks, casting his eye up and down the lines of bald heads all turned towards him. "I dare say there isn't a man among ye wot ever heard o' Columella, or o' Cato, or o' Mr. Warro (Varro), three o' the greatest farmers whatever were foal'd Wirgil, too, I dare say you are ignorant on, and Smith o' Deanston, the greatest benefactor the world ever saw—monstrous benefactor!"

Here Mr. Jorrocks swigged off his punch, and from a bundle of papers before him having selected one, he resumed.

"Having," said he, "introduced you to Columella, who I take it was a sort o' Roman Smith o' Deanston, I will read you wot he said about this all-important subject.

"'Many people imagine,' says Columella, 'that the sterility of our lands, which are much less fertile than in times past, proceeds from the intemperance o' the hair, the inclemency o' the seasons, or the alteration o' the lands themselves, that weakened and exhausted by long and continual labour, they are at length incapable of producing their fruits with the same wigour, and in the same abundance as they were wont to do afore. But this is all an error.'[1]

"There, frinds and fellow-farmers," said Mr. Jorrocks, "is the selfsame story that we have nowadays. The seasons are changed!' says each lazy 'ound, throwin' himself on his bed, or bustin' into tears in a fit o' despair. 'The intemperance o' the hair destroys all one's efforts,' says another, as he sneaks off to the public-'ouse. 'The land's worked out!' says another, slopin' off[2] in the night without payin' his rent.

"That's all my eye!" exclaimed Mr. Jorrocks. "I minds the fable o' the dyin' man and his sons, who he summoned about him. 'My sons,' said he, 'I'm a-goin' to cut my stick, wot I leaves behind you'll find buried a foot and a 'all under ground.' Well, the old gen'lman was as good as his word, and went; and after they'd got his remainders interred, they set about lookin' for the silver, each with a spade, a-diggin' for 'ard life a foot and an 'aif under ground. Howsomever, nothin' wotever turned up, and in all 'umane probability the old gen'lman was jest a 'oaxing on 'em to make 'em work the land well, for the consequence of all this diggin' was that they got sich amazin' crops as proved a treasure of themselves. That was werry well done," observed Mr. Jorrocks, handing his glass up for some more punch. "Believe me, beloved frinds and fellow-countrymen, the intemperance o' man has much more to do with the misfortins o' the land, than the intemperance o' the hair. The intemperance o' the hair is a mere matter o' inexpensive moisture, but the intemperance o' man is a double drain, a drain on his self and a drain on the soil. Not that J. J. would deny a farmer a cheerful glass, or conwert a

Bold peasantry, a country's pride,

into a lot o' cantin', lily-livered, water-drinkin' 'umbugs; but drunkenness and farmin' cannot thrive together, and the sooner a man wot opens a reglar account with the lush crib shuts up shop, the better.

"Then as to the land bein' weaken'd and exhausted by continual labour, that too is all my eye. If men, from want o' farmin' knowledge, will force crops upon the soil wot it has no taste for, no doubt you may make the land sick, jest as you might make yourselves so by eatin' figs if you don't like them, or have served an apprenticeship to a grocer. It's jest the same thing. A grocer surfeits his 'prentices with figs at startin', and the youth never wants none after: so if you surfeit your land with wot we Frenchmen call '*toujours perdrix*,' goose every day, you can't be surprised if it at length refuse to grow whoats.

"Farmers are a long way behind the intelligence o' the day—a monstrous long way. They seem to me to travel by the 'eavy Falmouth, instead o' the dartin' rally. By and by, when Mr. 'Enson accomplishes flyin', p'raps they'll take to steam. You all go too much in the old track; wot your fathers did, you do; confound your stupidity. I want to put some new sky lights into your 'eads. There was a great man, his name was Bacon—he wore a conical pointed hat, with a frill round his neck, and wrote a book which they call Bacon's Essays, and among other sensible things he put in it was one about peoplin' a country; says he, 'In a new country, first look about what kind o' wittle the country yields of itself to 'and, as chestnuts, walnuts, pine-apples, and make use on 'em. That, gen'lmen, is wot I adwises you to do. If your land won't grow barley, try summut else, pine-apples[3] for instance. Nothin' pays better nor pine-apples, nor can anything be finer eatin'. Byron, I think, said that 'critics *alone* are ready made'; but there he was wrong, for farmers are also 'eaven-born, thick 'ead and thick shoes seems all that is wanted to make one. There was a gen'lman called Smith, in all 'umane probability he was the father of that now werry numerous family, for his Christian name was Hadam. Hadam Smith, I say, wrote a book, and among other intelligent things he put in it was the following, which I cut out for the purpose of stickin' into my speech.

"'No 'prenticeship has ever been thought necessary to qualify for 'usbandry, *the great trade o' the country*; but after what are called the fine arts, and the liberal professions, there is no trade which requires so great a wariety of knowledge and experience.'

"Werry true," observed Mr. Jorrocks, swigging off his punch. "Farmin my frinds, is in its infancy, nay, hardly that. You've all seen a butterfly afore it is hatch'd, when in its chrysillis state, dead and inanimate. You are jest like them, and I'm a-goin' to break the shell o' your ignorance, and start you into life! set you on your legs! make men instead o' mice o' you! so give me some more panch.

"No one knows what human skill may accomplish," continued he, as soon as his glass was returned. "I've lived a liberal allowance: not that I'm old, far from it; but I've seen summut o' life, and not gone through the world with my eyes shut; indeed a man can't travel that way in the City, and I minds the time when steam and gas were thought all my eye and Miss Elizabeth Martin, and coachin' was looked upon as the perfection o' travellin'. A hunt in Surrey was all a Cockney could aspire; now Mr. Lockhart, that great man wot does the Quarterly Review, says that they can take the cream o' Leicestershire for their day. 'Stonishin' work! But that's beside the question; another pair o' shoes, as we say in France. Farmin' is the subject o' this discourse. There's no sayin' what skilful farmin' may do—science, machinery, and the use o' manures. Folks talk o' Peel, but I thinks nothin' o' Peel; Graham neither. Smith o' Deanston's the man! the greatest benefactor the world ever saw—*monstrous* benefactor! Who ever 'eard o' drainin' afore Smith o' Deanston inwented it?" Something like murmurs of dissent follow this inquiry.

"It is a mistake to suppose that any fool will make a farmer. A farmer should be a philosopher, an astrologer, a chemist, an engineer, a harchitect, a doctor, I don't know what else.

"This werry mornin' I made a remark that may be the foundation of a most important diskivery. As I was a-shavin', I looked out o' the window, and there I saw Mrs. J.'s 'ens a-scratchin' and scatterin' the new-mown grass with all the regularity of 'ay-makers. Who knows but by the application of—of—of—application of somethin', those useful birds may be made still more serviceable by conwertin' them into 'ay-makers. Turnin' a whole drove into a field, and making them do on a great scale wot I saw them this morning doin' on a small one. Why shouldn't the cold-water cure be successful in stables, and the homoeopath be tried among cows?

"But them are twopenny affairs compared with the great golden sovereign pound-cake of steam and engineerin' skill. I've got an inwention in my 'ead—in course I tells you this in *strict* confidence, lest some unprincipled waggabone should filch me of it. But I've got an inwention in my 'ead—at all ewents, the notion of an inwention, that I wentures to say will work wonders in the terrestrial globe— flabbergaster the world! It's a steam happaratus or hengine that will do at one 'go' wot now takes I doesn't know how many 'ands, and how many 'osses, or how many hours to accomplish. It is, I say, an inwention so complicated in its detail, and yet so simple in its performance, that unless I am half asleep on my pillow o' repose, I am sometimes bother'd myself to compass its extraordinary capabilities.

"Then as I lay all at ease, 'alf sleepin', or 'alf seas over, I sees its every part working away with all the ease imaginable, jest like a thing I've been used to all my life.

"O Mrs. Ceres and Mr. Morpheus," continued Mr, Jorrocks, casting his eyes with supplicating air up at the ceiling, "look benignantly down and grant your worshipful admirer power to describe to these enduring boobies all wot I have seen in balmy somnifulo, somnifulorum. And you, Mr. Bacchus, or, at all ewents, Mr. Brandy and Waterus, give us a left in this most *mo-men-tous* crisis, to explain this most laudable but werry complicated affair! I've caught the idea," continued Mr. Jorrocks, "and thinks I can go oh. In my mind's eye, I see a ten-hacre wheat-field, yellow as gold, and level as a die, and my monster reaper a-snortin' at the gate. The gate hopens, the steam's hup, and in he comes. Forrod he moves straight up the rig, and, as he goes, the yellow grain is cut by the ground—not a hinch o' stubble left—and falls upon plates like the receiving plates of a paper mill—then it turns suddenly round and ascends the second floor, where the heat o' the biler seasons the grain, and a wop of a flail sends it bang out of the hear. Again, it takes another turn, and behold it's landed on the third floor, all dry and mellow for Teddy the grinder—round go the stones, crush goes the grain, and in the twinklin' of an eye, the waving wheat is turned into flour, jest as one sees an old coat in a paper mill go in at one end and come out a sheet o' paper at t'other. Wondrous miracle! but still more wondrous yet is Mr. Jorrocks's miracle, for the same monster engine wot does all this upstairs, ploughs the land by machinery down in the area, so that reapin' and sowin' go 'and in 'and; like the Siamese twins, or a lady and gen'lman advancin' in a quadrille, or the poker[4].

"Oh, but science is the ticket; neat genuine unadulterated science. Everything now should be done by science. The world's on the wing, and why shouldn't farmers take flight? Look at Mr. 'Enson! There's a man o' pith for you. If I had 'ounds, I'd take a great hair ship, and fly to 'Merica, to Jones of Faire Knowe, and give him a good quiltin' for his imperance to me in Jonathan's Magazine; then I'd 'unt the 'red and grey,' and fly back to my farm surrounded with brushes, all in three days—'three glorious days,' as Monsieur Frog-eater Frenchman would say. Flyin' and farmin' may seem ill assorted, and certainlie you don't look like likely birds; but there's a deal in 'Enson that may be useful to agriculture. Had he got his machine under way, we should have heard nothin' o' Rebecca and her darters, for farmers would have put their corn, and their pigs, and their poultry, and their charmin' wives and accomplished darters into their flyin' machines, and bilked all the pikes in the land (loud cheers). Ah, my frinds and fellow-farmers, I see you're awakin' from your long trance of indolence to the day-dawn of intellect and sunshiny times. Look again, I say, at science and Mr. 'Enson! Suppose you alighted at your accustom'd country town, and found the market glutted, and prices fallin', wot would you have to do, but bundle up your traps, take wing again, and cut to other places? (Renewed cheers.)

"No pikes, no tickets, no tolls, no market dues, no mayors, no corporations, no inns, no ostlers no 'orrid exactions.

> Corn, by the hair, at sight o' 'uman ties
> Cuts its light stick, and in Mr. 'Enson flies.

(Repeated cheers.)

"There, gen'lmen—frinds and fellow-farmers, I should say," continued Mr. Jorrocks, as the applause subsided, "I've got your steam up, by the hargumentum ad pocketum. Let us now take a good swig o' punch."

The punch having been liberally dealt out, and the bottles having made their movements, our worthy Squire resumed his legs, and again

proceeded to address the company. "Having now, my beloved 'earers,"
said he, "given you an insight into the deplorable state of puppy-like
blindness in which you've been livin', I now come to the means of
improvin' the light wot has bust upon you, and overtakin' science afore
it runs clean, away from farmin' altogether. You have all doubtless heard
of Agricultural 'Sociations, and 'Sociations for the encouragement of
Long 'Orns and Short 'Orns, and all that sort o' thing; and though it
would ill become us to follow in the beaten track of seven pund for
the best tup, three pund for the biggest pig, or five pund for the man
wot has the biggest family of little 'uns; still we may learn something
from the 'sociations in existence, and take their plans for our outline.
Poor example, as we say in France, I would elect a President, a Wice-
President, a Sec, and a Committee of white wands; and I would also
have shows, and give premiums for best balls, best boars, best black-
faced gimmers, with in course dinners for gen'lmen to butter each
other at; but I'd extend the scheme, and have punishments as well as
prizes.

"I knows in these 'umanity, ante-'angin' times, punishment is quite
out o' fashion, and everything must be done by the noble spirit o'
emulation, jest as if you could make a string o' donkeys race like
Newmarket 'osses. I heard tell of one o' them peripetetic 'umbugs, wot
all administrations pawn on the public, called a commissioner, or Paul
Pryer, who was a-goin' about, inquirin' into the management of those
modern palaces called gaols, and he stopped at ours to pour his quart of
ignorance on the gaoler; well, he went his rounds—into this cell, out o'
that cell, up to this apartment, down to that apartment, and wonderful
to relate, he hadn't a hole to pick. 'Werry well manish'd,' said he, takin'
a consequential pinch o' snuff, 'werry well manish'd indeed—does
your beaks great credit—werry quiet—werry orderly—the ladies
and gen'lmen whom you 'ave in charge seem werry 'ealthy—werry
'appy— werry comfey—pray wot's your system?' 'Oh, the system's
simple enough,' replied the gaoler, 'when they don't be'ave we trounce
'em well.' 'All wrong!' exclaimed the commissioner, throwin' up his
hands in 'orror, '*all wrong together!* reward should be the incentive o'
wirtue, and not the fear of punishment.'

"'That may do werry well in ladies' seminaries,' replied the gaoler, 'but it von't act here.'

"So much for 'umanity and 'umbug. I really believes much o' this nonsense has been engender'd by the poppilar melody,

> If I had a donkey vot vouldn't go,
> Do you think I'd wollop him? oh, no, no!

and the hauthor has much to answer for.

"It's all my eye applyin' the same rule to everything—some may be led, but others must be driven. My frind Willey Goodheart, there, for instance, wants no tellin', he sees all wot's wanted, and does it of himself; but old Tommy Sloggers waits and waits to see if the thing won't do itself, and at length, findin' it doesn't, he either leaves it alone altogether, or does it at the wrong time. Wotever may be the season, whatever crops may fail, Tommy Sloggers is sure of one thing, a good crop o' weeds. I found a thistle at his back door t'other day, carryin' its wood from the ground like a hoak, and branchin' out like the genealogical tree of a ducal family. It was a superb specimen o' the genus— it must have grown and flourished for weeks; for it had flowers, and it had seeds, and as many 'eads as a hydra—it was well calculated to stock ten hacres o' land, and yet Tommy Sloggers had passed that werry thistle mornin', noon, and night, and had never taken the trouble to give it a back 'ander with his stick. Few men, perhaps, have magnanimity enough to knock thistles off their neighbour's 'edges, but surely one would think they would do so off their own. Not so my frind Sloggers; he would see them spring, and flower, and seed, and droop, afore he'd be at the trouble of raisin' his 'and. Wot can one do with sich slugs? Will the brightest medal o' the purest gold, with the most flowering superscription wotever was wrote, put life and activity into sich lubbers? Assuredly not. Then, I say, let us try wot the rewerse will do. Let us add to our premiums and prizes a distinguishin' emblem for the greatest lout in the country. In addition to five or ten sovs. for the best-managed farm, let us give somethin' to the worst. Let us strike a medal with the evil gen'lman on one side, and a big thistle on t'other, to be worn round the neck of the fortinate obtainer for one whole year, so that, wherever he goes, to church, or to market, or to the public, where he is most likely to be found, people may pint and say, 'There goes the most slovenly farmer in the county'; and let us show to England—to Europe—show to Europe, Hasia, Hafrica, and 'Merica, that while we foster talent, encourage hemulation and industry, we put our big toe of detestation and obbrobrium on slovenliness, hignorance, and sloth."

Mr. Jorrocks sat down amidst loud and long-continued cheering.

When the applause had subsided, and our friend had quaffed off a large glass of punch that had been cooling before him, he again rose and said—"Gen'lmen, I sat down because I wished to finish my speech with a splash, and hear what quantity of applause my eloquence would obtain. I have now ascertained that; and I'm bund to say, you have done the genteel by me. I am quite content; and I now come to wot I should have finished the speech with if I hadn't been desirous of keepin' the two accounts separate. We are honoured this day, as you doubtless all know, with the presence of the distinguished scion of the most noble 'ouse in this county—a nobleman young in 'ears, but old in 'usbandry—one who, while cultivatin' the classics, has also had an eye to the clay—one who looks proudly forward to protectin' your interests in that august assembly called the 'Ouse o' Commons (cheers)—one who, moreover, takes sich delight and interest in our doin's as to have signified his intention of becomin' the President of our 'Sociation (loud cheers). Need I after sich an announcement entertain a doubt as to its success? Oh, surely not! The sun of science has bust upon us from the portals of Donkeyton Castle, and though no President likes to hear another more loudly cheered than himself, I do assure you from the bottom of my breeches pocket, that I shall not take it the least amiss if you wisit the name o' the Markis o' Bray with the heaviest round o' Kentish fire wotever was issued. Gen'lmen, I beg to propose, with all imaginable 'onours, the health o' the Marquis o' Bray, the noble President of our 'Sociation."

The toast was drunk with tremendous applause, Mr. Jorrocks acting as fugleman—"but as we mustn't over-egg the pudding," as the Yorkshire

farmers say, we will reserve the other proceedings of the evening for
another chapter.

1. This is part of Mr. Jorrocks's prigging. It will be found nearly word for word
    in one of Nimrod's agricultural articles, in the New S Magazine.
2. "Sloping off" was a new term to us for the old trick of boltiixg without
    paying the rent, and perhaps it maybe so to the reader.
3. The Duke of Donkeyton, if our readers remember, observed to Mr. Jorrocks,
    that farmers tried crops that the soil had no taste for; adding, "that corn did
    not grow well in their country but wood throve, the pine tribe in particular."
    Our worthy friend seems to have mistaken pine for pine-*apples*.
4. "La Polka," we presume.—Printer's Gentleman.

XVII

We see no difficulty in organizing a College of Agriculture and we can suggest a few of the probable professorships. Of course there will be a chair of new-laid eggs, which the professor of poultry would be well qualified to occupy. Degrees will be conferred in guano; and a series of lectures on the philosophy of making hay when the sun shines would, no doubt, be exceedingly popular. We should propose that, previous to matriculation, every student should be required to undergo an examination on moral philosophy in connection with chaff, and the efficacy of thrashing by hand when the ears are unusually lengthy. Corresponding with the university Masters of Arts, there could be Bachelors of Barley; and the undergraduates might be brought direct to the Agricultural College from plough, as they are now brought to the universities immediately from Harrow.—*Punch*

THE LAST CHAPTER LEFT MR. Jorrocks and friends at the critical point of drinking and applauding the Marquis's health. When the cheering had subsided, our butterfly friend rose, and with one hand resting on the table, and the other stuck in his side, thus proceeded to address the meeting:—

"Mr. Jorrocks and Gentlemen,—I do not know that I can adequately express the very great pleasure and satisfaction I experience at the flattering manner in which my health has been proposed by my valuable friend," turning to Mr. Jorrocks with, "if he will allow me to call him so."

"*Certainly*," replied our worthy host, "certainly," adding aloud to himself, "wonders who wouldn't."

"And," continued the Marquis, "received by this great and enlightened assembly (loud cheers)—an assembly composed of a class of men second to none in loyalty, attachment to the constitution and the crown, and renowned for their intelligence, independence, and spirit."

Renewed cheers, increased perhaps from the sentence being so unlike the style in which Mr. Jorrocks had addressed them, and the description he had given of them.

"Gentlemen, in all times, in all ages, the science of agriculture has been fostered and encouraged by the greatest of men—by all whom the page of history records as famous in the annals of countries (cheers). The greatest statesmen—the greatest scholars—the greatest generals—have each found, in turning from their schemes of government, their studies or the toils of warfare, solace and enjoyment in the harmless simplicity and the interesting relaxation it affords. Every man whose opinion is valuable—every man whose breast glows with a genuine feeling of patriotism—joins in testifying the importance of agriculture. Columella, the author so happily referred to by our classical and distinguished host, wrote ably and ardently on this interesting point. He insisted on the importance of agricultural training and scientific improvement. 'I see at Rome,' says he, 'schools of philosophy, rhetoric, geometry, music, and, what is more astonishing, of people not solely employed in the arts of luxury—some in preparing dishes, intended to sharpen the appetite and excite gluttony, and others in making artificial curls for adorning the head; *but not one for agriculture.* The rest,' he adds, 'might well be spared; and the republic have flourished long without any of these frivolous arts; but it is impossible to dispense with that of husbandry, because upon that life itself depends (applause). Besides,' asks this enlightened man, 'is there a more honest or legal method of increasing a patrimony than by good cultivation of it? Is the profession of arms of this kind? Is the acquisition of spoils, dyed with human blood, and amassed by the ruin of our fellow-creatures? Or can commerce be compared with it, which, tearing citizens from their native country, exposes them to the fury of the winds and seas, dragging them into unknown worlds in pursuit of wealth? Is the trade of *usury* more laudable—odious and fatal as it is, even to those whom it seems to relieve? Are any of these occupations to be compared with wise and innocent agriculture, which the depravity of our notions alone can render contemptible, and, consequently, unprofitable and useless?' We read," continued his lordship, "that Numa Pompilius, one of the wisest of kings, divided the whole Roman territory into cantons, and had an exact return made of the manner in which each department was cultivated, and the names of the most scientific farmers of that day. Ancus Martius, the fourth king of the Romans, trod in the steps of Numa; and Hiero the Second wrote a work on agriculture, as did Attilus, king of Pergamus; whilst Mago, the Carthaginian general, wrote no less than twenty-eight volumes upon farming, which were preserved by Scipio at the taking of Carthage, and presented as a treasure to the Roman Senate. Attilus was found sowing corn when ambassadors from Rome came to invite him to the consulship; and the story of Cincinnatus being taken from the plough to the dictatorship is doubtless familiar to you all." —Cheers followed this piece of confidence in their knowledge.

Mr. Jorrocks hemmed and stroked his chin.

"If we look at home, who can for a moment doubt the advantages the virtuous simplicity of a country life possesses over the confinement of cities? Look at the robust offspring of country parents, and compare them with the squalid objects in town streets. Who would barter the wild freedom of rural life for the impure and pent-up atmosphere of the crowded city?"

"It's not so *bad*, nouther," remarked Mr. Jorrocks aloud, with a shake of his head, thinking of the salubrity of St. Botolph's Lane, where the greater part of his days had been passed.

"Gentlemen," continued the Marquis, "can I, with all the bright examples of antiquity before me—with all the noble emulation of modern times around me—can I remain insensible to the paramount importance of agricultural energy and improvement? Can I see the tenfold return of other parts, and not wish to witness the same efforts and the same success at home?"

"Mind the *shug*," whispered Mr. Jorrocks, in one of his audible whispers.

"And, gentlemen, how is it that so desirable a consummation is to be obtained? By the co-operation of parties and the communication of ideas! By Agricultural Associations in fact!" (Cheers.)

"*Shug*," repeated Mr. Jorrocks.

"My noble friend—that is to say, my excellent friend on my left—with his all-powerful and comprehensive mind, has imparted a discovery to this meeting of which I really am at a loss to say whether the originality of the conception or the boldness of the execution is the most astonishing. My noble friend—that is to say, my learned friend—that is to say, my excellent friend, is indeed a man to whom a country—nay, an universe—may well look up with the all-inspiring confidence of perfect security. I know no man so qualified to lead the sons of darkness into the lights of science as our excellent and most distinguished host." (Loud applause.)

"Werry good," said Mr. Jorrocks; "werry good—mind the *shug*——"

"His monster reaper will make the name of Jorrocks famous wherever farming science spreads, and English honesty is respected. It is by the interchange of ideas such as these that science is promoted, and farming flourishes. Instead of keeping the noble invention to himself and astonishing the country with its performances on his own property—instead of amassing wealth—as wealth most assuredly must be amassed by such an admirable contrivance—my noble friend—that is to say, my agricultural friend, with all the generous openness of confiding liberality, assembles his friends and fellow-farmers here this evening, in all the bounty of old English hospitality, and frankly tells them the discovery he has made. And in what a fine vein of poetic spirit did he make the announcement! Instead of saying, 'I've got a machine that will cut your corn and grind it at the same time——' "

"*And plough the land!*" roared Mr. Jorrocks.

"Instead, I say, gentlemen, of saying, 'I've got a machine that will cut your corn and plough your land at the same time——' "

"*And grind your corn!*" screamed Mr. Jorrocks.

"Instead, I say, my lords, of saying, 'I've got a machine that will cut and grind your corn and plough the land at the same time'—he invokes the aid of the heathen mythology to describe its performances.

And here it is where all after speakers must feel the feebleness of their own resources (applause and cries of "No, no") at all events, other discoveries or other communications must sink into insignificance by the side of our excellent host's. His monster reaper swallows all up! Yet, my lords and gentlemen, there are matters connected with farming, though apparently trifling compared with the topics on which our noble—that is to say, our scientific host, has touched with such a master hand, that nevertheless may not be wholly beneath your consideration and attention. Our noble host—that is to say, our hospitable host, has glanced with prophetic spirit at the flights by air and steam farming may yet undergo. But leaving those lofty altitudes, so well befitting the soaring genius of his capacious mind, I will venture to request your attention for a few moments while we look at the humbler preparations for calling that noble and comprehensive engine into play, or freighting the car of the aerial ship. It is too trite a truism perhaps to observe, that without proper preparation of the ground, monster engines will have little to reap; and there is one subject connected with the preparation of the ground for productive sowing that at the present day occupies no small portion of public attention—I allude of course to the grand discovery of draining. Draining, gentlemen, I believe, may be looked upon as one of the greatest discoveries of modern times. More over, it is not included in the comprehensive performances of our host's monster reaper. Had our forefathers been acquainted with the merits of draining, I think I may venture to say, the land would have been doubly productive at the present day. That operation may be carried on in a variety of ways; but as there are constantly improvements turning up in this very important branch of domestic industry, if I may so call it, I think it is very important that farmers should be in possession of the latest and most improved invention, because the saying is as old as the hills, that whatever is worth doing at all is worth doing well; and it would be very provoking to find, after you had gone to a certain degree of trouble and expense about a thing, that if you had made inquiry you would have found there was a process both cheaper and better. The invention, gentlemen, to which I allude, I understand is allowed to supersede all others, by reason of an extraordinary ingredient that would never enter the head of any but a most scientific and practical chemist to add—namely, the glutinacious, saccharine matter, called clayed sugar."

"Werry good," observed Mr. Jorrocks, tapping his fork against the table to raise applause and suppress a slight disposition to titter; "*werry good*, I say!"

"The recipe, with that exception, gentlemen, is very simple, the ingredients being generally come-at-able—clay, river-sand, and gravel, lime, well mixed and stirred up together, and then poured into the shapes, when, for a very trifling expense, you have some very capital tiles."

"*Werry durable*," whispered Mr. Jorrocks.

"And very durable also," continued the Marquis; "no small recommendation, I imagine, to any invention."

"Werry good," observed Mr. Jorrocks, adding aloud to himself, with a jerk of the head, "the chap has summut in him."

"Having now, my lords and gentlemen," continued the Marquis, "trespassed, I fear, already too lengthily on your valuable time, in glancing at the importance of agricultural science, little remains for me to say but to repeat to you my most cordial and heartfelt thanks for the kind and enthusiastic manner in which the toast of my health has been proposed and received; and allow me to assure the meeting that the cause of agriculture and the farming interest is deeply engraved on my heart's core; and in whatever situation of life I may be placed, the honour you have conferred upon me, in electing me President of your Agricultural Association, will ever remain the proudest—the most gratifying recollection of my existence, and the farmer's interest and my own will henceforth remain irretrievably interwoven together."

His lordship resumed his seat amidst loud and long-continued applause.

The punch and bottles again began to circulate, and the usual criticism of Mr. Jorrocks's speech, that had been averted by the immediate rising of the Marquis, now began to flow, each man turning to his neighbour, or groups of three or four laying their heads together, and discussing what they had heard.

"Ah, but he has a grand tongue!" exclaimed old Willey Goodheart, as he ceased rapping the table with his fork, in mute astonishment. "Ah, but he *has* a grand tongue!" repeated he to his neighbour, Johnny Wopstraw.

"Why, now, upon the *who-o-ole*, I should say our Squire's full as fine a talker as him," replied Wopstraw.

"Ah, the Squire's a grand tongue, too," exclaimed Willey; "I'll lay he'd make a grand speech about anything."

"What sort o' things are these pine-apples our Squire talked about?" asked another of his neighbour. "I never see them mentioned in the papers."

"He's all wrong about draining," whispered another to his neighbour; "it's nothing new—my grandfather drained—I'd have had all the wet off my farm before now if I had had the money."

"I wish these gen'lmen mayn't be o'er-wise for the country," observed Mr. Heavytail, in his usual loud and audible voice, to his opposite neighbour, as he ladled him a bumper of punch; "I've been a farmer, man and boy, these fifty years, and heard a vast of fine speeches, but I never heard nothing to ekle this about the air carriages. What will my old girl say when I bid her spread her wings and fly to market instead of riding old Dobbin or Smiler?"

"Ah, but the engine's the thing!" interposed another; "there'll be no use for horses at all, if we're to plough by steam, and fly to market. I wish I was well shot o' mine, for when this gets wind, nobody will take a horse in a gift."

"Dear, what would old Squire Westbury say, if he could rise from his grave, and see all this, poor man?" observed another. "I'm sure when they got the railway made, I thought that was a wonder that never could be beat; but now down comes a new Squire with new wonders that quite beat the old wonders out of sight."

"These Lunnuners are terrible wise people. I sure I don't know how I shall carry all home what they've said," observed another, turning a tumbler of punch down his throat, as if to keep the knowledge safe.

A loud knocking at the top of the table arrested the noise and conversation; and Mr. Jorrocks having obtained silence for his noble guest, the latter again rose and addressed the company.

"Mr. Vice-Chairman and Gentlemen," said he, "with the permission of the chair, I rise to propose a toast that I feel well assured will meet the enthusiastic approbation of this meeting—a meeting composed of friends and neighbours, who must as thoroughly appreciate the amiable, hospitable, and truly patriotic character of which it is the subject—a character, permit me to observe, gentlemen, known only in this highly-favoured kingdom, and one which, when it shines forth in its brightest, purest light, as in the present instance, needs fear no comparison with coroneted, or even with crowned, heads—the character of an English gentleman." (Loud cheers.)

"Quite true," observed Mr. Jorrocks aloud to himself; "*quite true*," repeated he, with an emphasis.

"I know no more delightful sight," continued the Marquis, "than to see an English gentleman surrounded by his friends and tenantry—dispensing with liberal hand that generous hospitality of which we have all partaken so largely this day, and radiating the minds of all with the lights and erudition that his well-applied means, leisure, and genius enable him to glean and cull in every field of science and information (loud cheers). No one, I feel assured, could have listened to the eloquent language of my noble friend, that is to say, of my honourable friend, without being struck with the perfect mastery he exhibited of his subject—a mastery acquired by clear-headed judgment and observation, combined with long experience and practical husbandry. I cannot sufficiently felicitate this country on the acquisition of so truly valuable an ornament (cheers). I feel that under his fostering care, prosperity, bright un equalled prosperity, will reign triumphant throughout this vale, and that all eyes will be turned to a man who promises such miracles to farmers. Without trespassing further on your attention, I beg to propose, with all the honours, the health of our excellent host, Mr. Jorrocks."

The toast being received with most uproarious applause, amid the bountiful replenishment of the horse-pail, considerable time elapsed ere silence was sufficiently restored to enable our worthy Squire to make his acknowledgments. At length he began.

"My Lord Markis and gen'lmen," said he, sticking a hand into each breeches pocket, "you have certain*lie* served me out a considerable deal o' butter and applause, which I feels considerably your debtors for. My Lord Markis has one adwantage over me in the way of talk; he has his jawin' tackle much handier nor I have, for though I can make you a werry hoiley, beautiful oration when I've time to consider my subject, I'm not quite so good a 'and at reply; runnin' heel as it were, and observin' on another gen'lman's discourse—at least, not unless he's told me afore'and wot he's a-goin' to say, which is not the case on the present occasion. Howsomever, it's a deal plisanter to be praised nor abused, and I'm sure I may say I'm always ready for praise, because I thinks I deserves it; I feels extremely grateful for all the fine things the Markis has said on me. I'm sure he thinks what he says. There's no manner of doubt at all whatsomever, that between us we shall make farmin' a werry different thing to what it has been. The diskivery my noble frind has communicated respecting the drainin' tiles is worthy the serious consideration and trial of every man. Bein' particular well acquainted with the wirtues o' sugar, I can take upon me to say that it is wonderful well calkilated to accomplish what my noble frind has suggested. It sticks things together uncommon. Howsomever, upon that pint perhaps my Lord Markis and I have said enough. The proof o' the puddin' is in the eatin'; and talkin' of eatin' reminds me o' drinkin'. We're a-goin' to have a little ballet dance this evening—'ands across and back again, down the middle and hup again; and I think we cannot do better than propose the 'ealth of the ladies (applause); there'll be sich a bevy o' beauties—Mrs. J. in her best bib and tucker, surrounded by her schoolgirls in their bran new bustles, and I doesn't know what else besides; so without further palaver, let us drink their good 'ealths, and when you've all had as much lush as you can carry, we'll adjourn the meeting and go and help them to foot it."

"Will Miss Flather be here?" whispered the Marquis in Mr. Jorrocks's ear, as the latter sat down after his speech.

"Miss Flather—Emma! let us see—yes—no—no, she won't; got a toothache or summut o' that sort; werry sorry previous engagement—red nose p'raps, or summut o' that sort."

"O dear, I'm sorry for that" whispered the Marquis. "Fine gal, Emma," observed Mr. Jorrocks confidentially, "werry fine gal—good figure—good figure'ead too, as the sailors say—but there'll be quite as diver a one as her here to-night, darter o' this rum lookin' little fish on my right," whispered he; "how somever, she hasn't taken arter her dad, but arter her dam, who's a real strappin' huzzey—great hupstanclin', black-'air'd, black-eyed, clean-limb'd wench, *nous werrons*, as we say in France; meanwhile I must be giving them another toast." Mr. Jorrocks then proposed "Honest men and bonny lasses," then "Live and let live," "Speed the plough"; after that, "Guano," "Nitrate o' sober," "Smith o' Deanston," "Soot," and a variety of local and agricultural toasts.

"How far does Miss Flather live from here?" inquired the Marquis of his host, as soon as he could get a word in sideways.

"Oh, close at 'and," replied Mr. Jorrocks, "mile—'aif a mile p'raps; wot are you a-wantin' with her?"

This question was rather a poser, and the Marquis's countenance showed it.

"Nothin' wrong in course," continued our friend, "only you know she ha'nt got no dad, and it's my duty as Lord o' the Manor to see that all's on the square—*you twig*. If you wants to marry her, in course that's another thing."

The Marquis thought he had better not.

The parting rays of the setting sun now shot into the room, imparting an additional glow to the heated faces of the punch-drinkers, while the bright red sky tinged the landscape with its hue, chiding, as it were, the sitters for their depravity. Added to this, the sound of music was borne ever and anon on the gentle evening breeze, and sundry smart bodices had been seen flitting past the windows, diving among the shrubberies and gay flower-beds, betokening the mustering of the dancers. The heat of the room, the smell of the punch, and the feeling of repletion, made even the most inveterate toper wish for fresh air. At length the host rose, and the folding windows opening from the ground being thrown open, the party streamed out on to the close-shaven lawn, and inhaled the fresh air in deep-drawn, hearty gulps. How different from the tainted atmosphere they had just been breathing!

XVIII

You, who the sweets of rural life have known,
Despise the ungrateful luxury of the town.

UNDER A SPACIOUS HAY-RICK, PITCHED beneath what had been
a couple of ground-feathering spruce of gigantic size, now
trimmed half-way up to admit the awning, sat Mrs. Jorrocks in stately
pride, decked out like a tragedy queen, surrounded by her schoolgirls
in their Swiss costumes—white bedgowns, with scarlet petticoats, set
off with large horse-hair bustles, pink stockings, and large flat-crowned
straw hats, looking as unlike nature as anything could do. Mrs. Jorrocks
wore a splendid red and white turban, entwined with enormous bands
of sham pearls, and a bird-of-paradise feather reclining gracefully over
the left ear, and sundry mosaic chains, necklaces, bracelets, and lockets
about her shoulders and arms. Her dress was of many-coloured muslin,
done in tiers like house-slating; next her dumpy waist came a pea-green
tier, immediately below it a bright yellow, followed by red, then a sky
blue, and a white, fringed with broad black lace at the bottom. Each tier
was understood to be a separate affair, though, as we did not dissect her,
of course we cannot speak confidently on that point. The presumption,
however, is that it was so, for she "stood out," looking like a rainbow
dumpling.

Tea had been liberally supplied to the ladies at their pleasure, some of
whom loitered in the tent with Mrs. Jorrocks, instead of taking advantage
of the balmy fragrance of the summer's evening, and wandering about in
the sweet air, loaded with the perfume of jessamine, roses, and the lime-
tree flowers. The little folk, too, had been entertained with amusements
becoming their juvenile years, and several bluff little urchins wandered
about the shrubberies with stained faces and clothes, got by blobbing

in a treacle barrel for half-pence; while shouts of laughter rent the air from the far side of the enclosure, as boy after boy came sliding down a greasy pole, at the top of which was stuck an inviting leg of mutton, or a soapy-tailed pig eluded the grasp of a clown, and upset a fair lady or two as, grunting, it dived among the crowd.

The appearance of the dinner party added fresh impetus to the scene, and a course being formed down a smooth green alley, several of the village nymphs contended in a race for a petticoat, after which Mr. Jorrocks and a select party of friends, being blindfolded, tried their hands at a wheelbarrow race, and either from the novelty of the situation, or the confusion consequent on the drink they had taken, they severally landed at very different places to what they intended. Others then tried their hands with like success, and Joshua Sneakington being inveigled into an attempt, was deluded by the false cries of the boys in a wrong direction, and before he knew where he was, was soused over head in the pond. Out he came like a drowned rat, blowing and spluttering, with a green sort of net all over his person, formed by the slime and the weeds of the surface. Great was the joy at the sight, for Joshua was thoroughly detested. Even Mr. Jorrocks joined in the mirth his appearance created.

Twilight now drew on, and the sultry heat of the day was succeeded by a cool refreshing dew. The dining-room having been cleared of its tables and furniture, showed lights in various directions, enticing the company back to the house. The Marquis, who had been in waiting on Mrs. Jorrocks since his appearance in the garden, was now seen wending his way along with her on his arm. The fiddlers were scraping their catgut on the spot where the sideboard recently stood, and the flute-player was sucking and licking the joints of his flute, as if he was extremely fond of it. The appearance of the hostess, followed as she was by a train of her big-bustled girls, was the signal for the musicians to begin, and accordingly they struck up the usual "See the conquering hero comes," though who was the hero, or whom he had been conquering, seemed somewhat problematical.

"We are to have a dance, are we?" said the Marquis, as they approached the window; "I'm glad of that. I wish Miss Flather had been here."

"Miss Flather's engaged at 'ome," observed Mrs. Jorrocks, rejoicing that she had *done* her. "Who would you like to dance with?" added she, sidling through the sash.

"Won't you allow me the honour of opening the ball with you?" asked the Marquis.

"Thank you, my lordship, I'm only a werry poor dancer; howsornever I'll try my 'and; only it's werry 'ot work. Jun," said she, going up to her spouse and giving him a shake of the shoulder, "get your partner, and let's set to. Who are you a goin' to dance with?"

Mr. Jorrocks had booked Mrs. Trotter, who, decked in a rich green and yellow Ancoat Vale velvet, made extremely tight, and short at the shoulder, and peaked at the waist with a cord and large tassels, as if to tie her up with, now responded to his summons, and stationed herself next Mrs. Jorrocks.

"She's a grand 'un, isn't she?" asked Mr. Jorrocks in a subdued tone—at least a subdued tone for him, with a nudge of the elbow in his lordship's ribs, and a nod of his head forwards. "Clean made, hupright, cleveraction'd thing; what a harm she's got! *you see her step.*"

A long line of dancers had now fallen in, and the Marquis began to be puzzled what to do. Twice the leash of musicians ran over the "White Cockade" with out their getting away; at length Mr. Jorrocks, anxious to foot it, said, "I think you'd better start next time."

"I don't know what it is!" exclaimed the Marquis in alarm.

"Vy, a country dance to be sure," said Mr. Jorrocks, " 'ands across and back again, down the middle and hup again; simple as can be, nothin' simpler, there, see, our ould gal 'ill put you in the way of it; off you go!" said Mr. Jorrocks, stamping with his foot and clapping his hands Mrs. Jorrocks seizing the Marquis by the hand, and the three setting him a going, just as willing coach horses start a restive comrade, pulling him along in fact.

The figure was soon learnt, and the Marquis and Mrs. Jorrocks bumped and danced most vigorously up and down, turning every couple till they got through the last juvenile pair at the end, and our now profusely-perspiring hostess leant against the wall and mopped herself. Presently her place was wanted by another couple, and gradually, by dint of turning and elbowing, they again accomplished the top of the dance.

The Marquis, whose eyes had been attracted in going down by a graceful sylph-like figure, about the middle of the dance, now availed himself of the opportunity of inquiring who the beautiful dark-eyed girl, in white muslin with a broad blue sash, was.

"A tallish gal do you mean," inquired Mrs. Jorrocks, "with werry black eyes?"

"This one," said the Marquis, "with the swan-like head and neck; just dancing towards us," pointing to a couple approaching from the bottom of the dance.

"Oh, that's Eliza," said Mrs. Jorrocks; werry pretty gal she is too, good gal too, nice modest gal, beautiful figure, all nattural. P'raps you'd like to dance with her."

"Yes, I should very much," replied the Marquis, who now stood admiring her richly-fringed, downcast eyes, and clear Italian complexion. "She certainly is an uncommon pretty girl," observed his lordship confidentially to Mrs. Jorrocks.

"And as good as she's pretty," observed our hostess, who, without any particular partiality for the Trotters, was willing to use Eliza for the purpose of extinguishing Emma.

We will not make Eliza so unwomanly as to prefer Jack Smith of the Hill Farm, whom she was then dancing with, to his lordship; but the unexpected demand, and novelty of her situation, drew such a mantling blush over her beautiful features when the Marquis was presented to her as further ingratiated her in his favour. Finding he was nothing very awful, she gradually recovered courage, and turning her large lustrous languishing eyes upon him, she whispered forth such sweet silvery notes as perfectly enchanted him. We will not say how often they danced together.

Capricious youth! Morning's dawn found the finely rounded figure, greyish blue eyes, and alabaster-like complexion of Emma Flather banished from the Marquis's recollection—at all events, completely eclipsed by the graceful form and Italian skin of the beautiful dark-eyed Eliza. That is the worst of these young men; they are so very fickle, you never know where you have them. Mammas have terrible times with them, for they are scarcely to be trusted out of sight, and the only way of securing them is by tying them up tight (matrimonially of course) as quick as ever they can. They are easily caught, but as easily lost.

The Marquis was desperately smitten. This he candidly admitted to himself, and there is no mistake when a man does that. He tossed and tumbled about in bed, bemoaning the inequality that prevented his thinking of her. That was a step beyond what he had got with Emma, his ideas respecting her never having got further than the degree of simple flirtation—flirtation that he might be carrying on with half a dozen girls in different parts of the country at the same time.

The result of the Marquis's musings was that though he knew that it was very naughty and very dangerous too, he would spend that day with Mr. Jorrocks. Accordingly, when Adolphe made his appearance in his bedroom, he inquired about the state of his wardrobe, and finding that he had about as many clothes as would serve a moderate man a week, he resolved on sounding his farmer friend whether it would be convenient to keep him.

Of course it was, and Mrs. Jorrocks, like all women, being uncommonly quick at smelling a rat, as soon as ever she got her tea-caddy locked after breakfast, and the dinner ordered, put on her bonnet and shawl, and went to the Trotters to bid them spend the day and dine at the Hall. Need we say that she went a little further, and dropped in at the Manse? Assuredly not, for the triumph would not have been complete without. With what eagerness she watched the countenance of mother and daughter as with becoming circumlocution and embellishment she detailed the doings of the previous evening—how delightful the Markis had been—how genteel he was—and her decided conviction that he was *desperately* smitten with Eliza. Neither could she resist the additional mortification of adding, that she expected her to spend the day to meet the Marquis, which must be an apology for her hurried visit.

Poor Mrs. Flather! Never were such unwelcome tidings conveyed with such apparent indifference; and it was only a pretty intimate knowledge of the sex that made Mrs. Flather sensible of the cutting cruelty of Mrs. Jorrocks's conduct. A man would have thought it odd, a "curious coincidence," telling a mother whose daughter had had designs on a man; but ladies know each other better.

Cobbett, who understood the sex well, was fully conscious of their discrimination. "Women," he said, "are much quicker-sighted than men; they are more suspicious as to motives, and less liable to be deceived by professions and protestations; they watch words with a more scrutinising ear, and looks with a keener eye; and making due allowance for their prejudices, their opinions ought not to be set at naught without great deliberation." Still, though all women know this perfectly well, they can't help *playing* at deceiving each other.

Mrs. Flather knew what Mrs. Jorrocks came about just as well as Mrs. Jorrocks knew herself; and Mrs. Jorrocks knew that Mrs. Flather knew that she did, just as well as if she had told her. However, *vive la* humbug!

Now, Mr. Jorrocks was not at all quick at smelling a rat—at least not unless the rat was after some of his bacon; and moreover, being tolerably conceited, he concluded the Marquis had prolonged his visit from sheer enamourment of himself, and cut out quite a different day's work to that of his missis, and quite contrary to what would have suited his lordship. Having got the breakfast disposed of, and the usual stare out of window and lounge about the door that follows that repast in the country, Mr. Jorrocks looked at the Marquis's paper boots, and proposed investing him in a pair of his thick shoes for what he called a "stretch" across country seven or eight miles, to see "a fine ball"—a bull being the object of Mr. Jorrocks's ambition at that time. The Marquis was horrified—such a walk would be the death of him— such a sultry day too. Besides, he knew nothing about bulls, and had talked farming nonsense enough over night to serve him some time—better keep himself cool—take a stroll about the grounds—see the garden, and admire the beauties of the place.

Mr. Jorrocks started off alone.

Towards the afternoon Mrs. Jorrocks and Mrs. Trotter were seen wending their way up the village of Hillingdon at that usual flirtation-encouraging distance which all mammas know so well how to measure, followed, of course, by Eliza and the Marquis at a proper elbow-touching, side-bumping sort of space. Mind, not arm in arm. What the old women talked about is immaterial—perhaps they didn't talk at all, but kept their ears cocked back to try what they could catch from the conversation of the juvenile pair in the rear.

It would puzzle a shorthand writer to make sentences of what the Marquis and Eliza said; it was so mixed, so general, and so broken by such pleasing interruptions from the stares of the villagers and the dazzling novelty of her situation as her luminous dark eyes met the Marquis's flashing blue ones. Suffice it to say, they were both very happy, and their conversation, if not very enlightening, was very agreeable to each other. But let us take a glance at the Manse.

Mrs. Flather could have eaten Mrs. Jorrocks—whether she could have digested her or not is another thing, for she declared she *always* thought her a disagreeable-looking woman, and now "perfectly disgusting." The conduct of parties has a great deal to do with their looks. If they are *for* us, let them be ever so ugly, there is always a certain something in their favour; whereas, if they are *against* us, the best-looking are little better than monsters in our eyes. Mrs. Flather, as we said before, could have eaten Mrs. Jorrocks.

Emma was desperately hurt too; for though cold blooded, calculating, and passionless, and willing to jump from one suitor to another, as she would from one dress to another, just as the "turn of the market," as Mr. Jorrocks would say, seemed in his favour, still she could not be insensible of the value of attentions from a man like the Marquis, even though they went no further than "attentions"; but, in her case, she thought she had fair legitimate claims, if not a downright hold upon him. Indeed, the line of policy to be pursued in consequence of what had passed at Donkeyton Castle had occupied mother and daughter many anxious hours both by day and by night, and nothing but the natural pride and delicacy of their sex, of which they both had a large stock in theory, prevented their making a crusade against the Castle. It would have been a grand sight to see the old Duke blundering to a conception of what they were after, and bowing them out with all the dignity of offended pride. "*A duchess* forsooth!" he would say, as he saw them bundling away in their rattle-trap.

The question now was, whether to go boldly down and demand the Marquis, or try what a little circumventing would do. Had the engagement been satisfactorily ratified by the Duke and Duchess, Mrs. Flather would have had no hesitation in demanding the Marquis, or, at all events, in writing to his "ma," to bid her come and look after her boy; but that confounded old marplot, Mr. Jorrocks, if our readers remember, interposed his troublesome old person at the critical moment that Mrs. Flather was bringing the Duke to book. The Flathers clearly saw the mistake in their policy had been snubbing the Jorrockses, by which they had not only set the Jorrockses against them, but had played them into the hands of the Trotters. They censured themselves, but protested nobody could foresee the turn the agricultural concern had taken. They should have nailed the Marquis at the moment, and never given him a chance of getting into the hands of the Trotters; had a regular understanding with the Duke—pocketed their delicacy, in fact. Mr. Jorrocks, Mrs. Flather thought, would befriend her; but time pressed, and perhaps she could not lay hold of him; and then the affair was more in the ladies' department, and there was little to hope from Mrs. Jorrocks, who had stolen the Marquis from them. The thing was how to get him back; a man's never fairly lost till he's churched. The only plan was to pique him—play some one off against him. In these emergencies, very forlorn hopes are sometimes resorted to—in short, anything in the shape of a man. Mrs. Flather and Emma were too good generals to be left totally destitute, and James Blake, whom we have already slightly introduced to our readers, was raked up for the enviable appointment of cat's-paw. James was one of those desperately over-righteous, cushion-thumping, jump-Jim-crow breed of parsons, so sanctified that he could hardly suffer the light of heaven to shine upon him, and he ate cold roast potatoes to save his servant the sin of cooking on the Sunday.

Well, James Blake, like many weak young men, was desperately violent. He had preached two sermons that had enraptured all the servant-maids, and astonished the quiet-going people. As the chemist said, "they were full of sulphur." Common people like to be d——d in heaps.

James was fished up to rescue the Marquis from the clutches of the designing Mrs. Trotter—not by the persuasive eloquence of his tongue, or the admonitions of a Christian minister, but simply by being "played off" against his lordship. It may seem an odd game to men, but it is a very popular one among women.

Since the visit to Donkeyton, James had been nearly discarded, at least they had commenced the operation of "letting him down gently"; now, however, they had to draw him up again at short notice, and we hope our fair readers will not close the volume in disgust when we say how they set about it. We know they will say it was very wrong—shockingly indelicate—improbable! perhaps impossible!—and we fully agree with them—only mind, fair ladies, that you don't do it yourselves some time.

Emma dressed herself in what she thought her most bewitching attire—white chip bonnet with a bunch of blue flowers inside, and the new blue silk dress she had got for her visit to Donkeyton Castle, with clean white kid gloves, and uncommonly well put on patent leather shoes, and open cotton stockings—so smart, indeed, that she a good deal over-did it for the country. Thus attired, with a blue and white Chinese-shaped parasol over her head, mamma and she repaired to James's lodgings, to invite him to take tea with them that evening; and if they happened to find him at home, they—or rather Mrs. Flather, for they had a great deal of propriety between them—would ask him to come out and take a walk.

Emma's dress was not exactly the thing, perhaps, to angle for a tight-laced, sanctified parson in, but then she had higher game in view; and even as it was, we question whether James, with all his sanctity, would not rather give her absolution for looking so bewitching to *him*, than have had her come down in a little puritanical print, with a Dunstable straw on her head; stiff-backed parsons are but flesh and blood, notwithstanding all their thunder, sulphur, and pretension. It so happened that James was mixing his sulphur for Sunday, and was sitting, as many parsons do, in his back-room, *sans* neckcloth, in his dressing-gown and slippers; and the stiff tapper of the door not making a greater noise than a crockery vendor or other itinerant merchant might aspire to, he unceremoniously opened it himself, and stood before the beauty and her mamma in all the homeliness of that comfortable costume.

The parson blushed to find himself in such a situation, but the offer of Emma's soft ungloved hand, and the bewitching beauty of her smile, put all straight, and drove her right back in his affections. He very soon had on a stiff white starcher, his best black coat and waistcoat, Wellington boots, Sunday hat, and—we blush to add—a pair of lavender-coloured kid gloves. Altogether he was a very passable swell.

Mother and daughter then joined arms, and the mid day sun being obscured by a passing cloud, Emma put down her parasol, and turned the whole battery of her attractions upon the young parson—now trotting by her side. Her eyes glistened, her alabaster complexion assumed a slight roseate hue, her pearly teeth shone resplendent between her cherry lips; and she really looked remarkably handsome and kissable. The poor parson was vanquished—he forgot all her transgressions; all her cold looks, all her stiff bows, all her iniquitous piano-playing, all her still more flagrant dereliction in dancing. We really believe he could not have refused to dine with them off hot meat the next Sunday. All-powerful womankind!

Thus they proceeded towards the village of Hillingdon, and as they turned down the street, and Emma's vivacity was at its height, and her countenance more than usually brilliant—for hers was a beauty that required lighting up—who should they meet but the "Hall" party progress-upwards, as already described. Nothing could be better.

They met with all the extra ardour of people cordially detesting each other. Mrs. Jorrocks was so *werry* sorry Mrs. Flather couldn't come (never having asked her) and Mrs. Flather was as *much* obliged to Mrs. Jorrocks for her kindness in thinking of her; and Mrs. Trotter smiled as she looked at the Marquis and her daughter; and Emma clung to the parson, as she greeted his lordship with the freedom of an old friend. Altogether it was a most charming business-like meeting; and if each had not the satisfaction of thinking they had "done" the other, at all events they had the gratification of feeling they had done their best to attempt it.

The sequel is soon told. The next day the Marquis's brougham was seen standing at Mrs. Flather's door, and no sooner was it gone than

Mrs. Flather went down the "town" to tell Mrs. Trotter and Mrs. Jorrocks in "confidence, to go no further of course, for Emma wouldn't like to have it mentioned,"—that she had reason to think the Marquis was about to become her son-in-law; while Mrs. Trotter was busy paying a similar visit to the Manse, "urged by a strong sense of what was due between friends," to make Mrs. Flather acquainted with a similar conviction on her part.

The post-mistress observed that the Hillingdon letter-bag was fuller than usual that evening.

XIX

He's a justice of peace in his country, simple though I stand
here.—SHAKSPEARE

The remainder of the crown was settled on the heirs of the
Princess Sophia, the Electress of Hanover; but what this
remainder was, when some one else had got it all, we leave
our arithmetically disposed readers to calculate.—*Punch's
Comic Blackstone*

O N THE MARQUIS'S ARRIVAL AT home, he reported so favourably of
the Jorrockses and the pleasure he had derived from his visit to
Hillingdon Hall, that the Duke and Duchess of Donkeyton were quite
taken with their conduct. They made no doubt they were most worthy,
respectable people, with considerable influence. A few days afterwards
Mr. Jorrocks received the following note from his Grace:—

DEAR SIR,—I beg to return Mrs. Jorrocks and your self the
Duchess of Donkeyton's and my thanks for your attention
to the Marquis of Bray, who I assure you feels extremely
gratified by his visit to Hillingdon Park.

In looking at the arrangements of the county, I see there
is no magistrate in your immediate neighbourhood since
the lamented death of Mr. Westbury; and it occurred to me
that it might perhaps be agreeable to you, and beneficial to
the public service, if you were placed in the Commission of
the Peace. Should it be so, and you will have the kindness
to notify such your desire to me, I beg to say I shall have
great pleasure in submitting your name for the approval of

the Lord Chancellor. With the repeated expression of our thanks, and with the Duchess's and my compliments to Mrs. Jorrocks, I remain, dear sir, yours very obediently,

DONKEYTON

Donkeyton Castle

G. JORROCKS, ESQ.
Hillingdon Park

Joy shows itself in various ways. Some people run and kiss their wives, some shout, some sing, some dance, some cry, some kick their hat-crowns out, some get blazing drunk, some throw money about, while a few fall on their knees and return thanks.

Mr. Jorrocks's joy generally went off in a few clumsy pirouettes on alternate legs, and then a sudden subsidence into contemplative reflection in his great arm-chair. Our friend having indulged in a few of his usual antics, sunk, letter in hand, into its roomy recesses, and gave his memory a refresher through the bygone days of life.

He then rang the bell for Benjamin.

"Binjimin," said he, as soon as the latter appeared, with his usual hang-gallows countenance, for he had just been robbing the larder; "Binjimin," repeated Mr. Jorrocks, not knowing exactly how to begin, "Binjimin," said he, for the third time, "greatness has come down upon me this mornin' in a shower—a regular clothes-basketful of honour."

"Yes, sir," said Benjamin.

"That great man, the Duke o' Donkeyton, has appointed me one of Her Majesty's jestices o' the peace."

"Yes, sir," said Benjamin.

"And, Binjimin, you have always been an honest, sober, meritorious, and industrious servant, and wirtue shall not be its own reward in your case—I'll make you my clerk."

"Crikey O!" exclaimed Benjamin, clapping his dirty hands.

"But," said Mr. Jorrocks, eyeing his dirty paws, "now that you will 'ave to do with pen and ink and wite paper, you must contrive to keep your hands clean."

"Yes, sir," said Benjamin.

"Also your mug," observed Mr. Jorrocks.

"Yes, sir," said Benjamin.

"And talking of mugs," continued Mr. Jorrocks, "now that we are worshipful, it becomes us to be grave and respectable-lookin'. You are goin' to be adwanced to a post of honour and distinction above your years, therefore it will be necessary to endeavour to make your years come up to the post, as the post will not come down to your years. I shall therefore get you a Welsh wig, and a pair of green specs, also an usher's gown, so that when you sit below me in the justice-room, you may have an imposin' and wenerable appearance, and may awe the waggabones by your looks."

"I think a big vip would be better," observed Benjamin, not relishing being made a guy of.

"A big vip's a good thing in its way, Binjimin," replied Mr. Jorrocks, "but a wig's the thing for strikin' awe into the be'older. It's an old sayin', that there were ten men 'ung for every inch they curtailed in the judges' wigs. Howsomever, you must wear one," observed Mr. Jorrocks determinedly, and Benjamin, knowing it was no use resisting, quietly withdrew, to communicate his elevation to Betsey, leaving his master ruminating in his arm-chair.

Joshua Sneakington was next sent for, and after somewhat of a similar prologue, was invested with the order of constable—an order exceedingly to his mind, as it gave him legal authority to bully the township.

Our old friend, Bill Bowker, was next written to, with similar information, and a request that he would rummage the book-stalls for a second-hand copy of Burn, Mr Jorrocks being determined to do justice in the old-fashioned way—substantial justice—every man his own clerk. Bill was still touring for the "League," on a "diminishing-influence salary." But we have forgotten to give Mr. Jorrocks's reply to the Duke. It was as follows:—

My Lord Duke,—I have the honour to acknowledge the receipt of your agreeable letter, and note the contents. I

will not, my Lord Duke, indulge in the episcopal language
of mock 'umility, and say, 'nob beakopari,' but I will use the
language of J. J., and say, I shall be werry much obleged to
your Lordship to make me a beak. I looks upon a beak as
the greatest of men! He says to number a hundred and one,
'You go and catch me a waggabone,' and forthwith he grabs
a man called John Brown. 'Now, John,' says his worship,
'you're an interminable rogue, you've been arter my fizzants
and my 'ares, and I'll transport you to all eternity.' Then he
axes him what he has got for to say; and John tells his story,
and his worship orders him off to the 'ulks. But I need
not inform your Grace of all the greatness that belongs to
the grand order of beak; how they sit with their hats on,
how they order people out o' court, and how they return
thanks for their healths at farmers' dinners, and ex pound
the grand duties and dignities of beaks. All this I shall be
most happy to do, and, therefore, not to trouble your Grace
unnecessarily on the subject, I shall only add, that the
sooner you makes me a beak, the sooner I shall begin to
'execute jestice and maintain truth.' Not that I thinks the
truth will be werry easily maintained, for, betwixt you and I
and the wall, people lie uncommon 'ard when they can get
anything by it. Howsomever, never mind that: and so with
the respectful compliments of Mrs. Jorrocks and myself to
her Grace and the Marquis, I have the honour to subscribe
myself, my Lord Duke, yours to serve,

JOHN JORROCKS, not G. JORROCKS

Hillingdon Hall, <i>not</i> PARK

The Duke was rather shocked when he got this epistle, for though
he knew Mr. Jorrocks was not very refined, still he did not expect
finding him making such a "hash" of himself upon paper. However, the
mischief was done; he had offered to make him a magistrate, and could
not now back out without giving offence. Moreover, Mr. Jorrocks was a
Whig.

In due time an intimation arrived from the Clerk of the Peace
that Her Majesty had been pleased to approve of the insertion of Mr.
Jorrocks's name in the Commission of the Peace, and that he could
take the oaths at any adjourned session, if he would give the Clerk a
week's notice. Accordingly, our hero returned answer that he was ready
to take the oaths immediately, and would attend at the next sessions for
the purpose.

Mr. Jorrocks, many years before, ere fame had marked him for her
own, had been "hauled up," as the saying is, for a little poaching trespass,
and had imbibed his first impression of a county justice from the
one before whom he was taken, or rather before whom the case was
ultimately tried at the Croydon Sessions, for our hero appealed against
the original conviction. From this suburban beak—Mr. Tomkins of
Tomkins, near Croydon—Mr. Jorrocks drew his first impression what
a solemn magistrate should be like, and, overhauling his wardrobe, our
worthy friend converted himself as near as he could into the prototype
of his great original. First, he floured his wig—powder he would not
use, because he had no notion of being taxed for his consequence;
and he gave his blue coat collar a dash behind, as though it had been
done by the rolling of a pig-tail. His blue coat and buff waistcoat
were both his best, and a pair of antediluvian leather breeches, much
cut and slashed about the waist and knees, met a pair of exceedingly
scratched mahogany tops, adorned with a pair of heavy lacklustre spurs.
Thus attired, with Benjamin in a suit of plain clothes, converted out of
some of his master's cast-offs, beside him, and Joshua Sneakington, in
his Sunday apparel, in the seat behind, magistrate, clerk, and constable
set off for the ancient town of Sellborough, in the old rattle-trap fire-
engine-looking carriage, drawn by Mr. Jorrocks's horse, the renowned
Dickey Cobden.

Sellborough, as its name would imply, was formerly a parliamentary
borough; but having had the misfortune of being Schedule A'd, it had lost
a considerable part of its commerce and consequence. It was a drowsy-
looking place—a wide, scrambling sort of town, forming something like
a square, with little off-shoot streets, starting off in all directions. There
were two churches and two parsonage-houses, enclosed with high walls,

among trees, and the usual sort of store-shops—grocers selling ribbons and British wines, booksellers dealing in candles and confectionery, and milliners in soap and crockery-ware. Trade there was none, save on a market day, and that was purely agricultural produce, varied, perhaps, by an itinerant hawker and pedlar pitching his cart and selling his edgeless knives and pointless needles—pointless as his jokes—by auction. It had also its two inns—Whig and Tory—which was about the only vestige of the "good old times" that remained. The "Duke's Head," of course, was the Whig house—the "Crown and Sceptre" the Tory. We need hardly say the "Duke's Head" was the Duke of Donkeyton's, for as in London there is but "one Duke," so in the country the "Duke's Head" always denotes the caput of the great man of the district. The "Duke's Head" was then in the ascendant, as appeared by the newly-painted green window-shutters and a booted postboy lounging about the door in conversation with a crooked-legged ostler. It is very odd how many hangers-on there are about inns with a leg on a curve. Mr. Jorrocks's rattle-trap, bumping and jingling over the grass-grown cobble-stone pavement, drew countless ringlets to the windows, a noise of any sort being a real godsend to the young ladies of Sellborough, who were terribly moped. A race and a new-year's-eve ball were all the gaiety they could raise in the year, and men were lamentably scarce. This is generally the case in towns without trade; the young men leave them as soon as they are fledged in search of more bustling places, from whence they are seldom suffered to return—*single*.

The Court-House was in the centre of the town, raised on stone pillars above the old shambles of the market place—a place containing, perhaps, a dozen stalls; and hither our hero repaired, after he had seen Dickey Cobden put up, attended by his suite.

The Court was in full flower when Mr. Jorrocks entered. The Chairman, a red-hot Tory, sat with his hat on, with three brother Tories on his right, and a solitary Whig on his left. This was Captain Bluster, a most unpalatable magistrate, who had thrown the Tory bench into convulsions when he appeared, about a year before, to take the oaths. There is nothing so sensitive as a bench of magistrates. With the exception of those who take their seats as a matter of course, and who elevate the office, rather than the office elevating them, the envy, jealousy, and detraction that take place on the appearance of a newcomer is truly ridiculous. Each questionable occupant man feels himself personally injured—*lowered*. Gentlemen who were scouted when they came, now scout with double vigour in return.

Captain Bluster was a fine instance of the scouting principle. All eyes were turned up with horror when he came. It was a downright insult to the bench. The Lord-Lieutenant must wish to drive all gentlemen from it. Captain Bluster!—late master of a trader—now dealer in "pigs, treacle, and all other game," as the song says, to be forced upon them—it was not to be borne. *They would all resign.*

We wonder how many benches have threatened to do the same?

However, Captain Bluster was not to be put down. Indeed, he was one of those coarse-minded, hard-bitten, vulgar beggars, that cannot understand any coolness short of a kick, and had horrified the Sellborough bench so by his forward impudence, that several had left it altogether, and the Captain seemed likely to have it all to himself, when the Lord-Lieutenant intimated that he should be obliged to make some more magistrates if they did not pull better together. This had the desired effect, and the Tory tide was on the return, when Mr. Jorrocks again raised the storm.

If a man goes into Guildhall—at a session, for instance—he cannot help being struck with the resemblance there is among the loose purple-robed, white-faced, flabby, live turtle looking things ranged on each side of the chair, called Aldermen or Common Councilmen, that all look as if they were made in the same mould; and a similar resemblance runs through mankind generally, breaking them into classes. There was a strong sort of likeness between Mr. Jorrocks and Captain Bluster—so strong, that any one at a glance would say, "Those men are of the same breed." Not that they were like when you came to compare their faces, but the style and general appearance were the same; the same bull heads, the same big broad backs, the same great clumsy limbs, the same manner, or want of manner. In point of looks, Mr. Jorrocks had the advantage, the twinkle of his cheerful eye and humorous expression of his countenance giving an air of good nature to his face; while Captain

Bluster's coarse bristly-red hair, stiff scrubbing brush-looking whiskers under his chin, freckled face, ferrety eyes, broad, flat-ended, snub nose, and thick-lipped mouth, gave him a very bull-dog sort of air. The general harshness of his appearance was heightened by a blue coat and metal buttons, ugly spotted waistcoat on a buff ground, blue trousers, and "high-lows."

An evident shudder ran along the Tory end of the bench as Mr. Jorrocks entered at the other, and all eyes were turned upon the new Justice. The Chairman, who was just disposing of a case, made Mr. Jorrocks a very low bow; and the Clerk having produced a great skin of parchment, and informed their worships that there was a gentleman going to take the oaths—forth with turned to Mr. Jorrocks for the purpose of administering them, amid half-suppressed expressions of disgust from the bench. "Downright insult!—Resign tonight!—Political purpose!—Disgrace to the country!—Greasy old chandler!—The Duke must be mad."

Mr. Jorrocks, having taken the book in his right hand, proceeded to repeat, after the Clerk, the following oath:—

"I, John Jorrocks, do sincerely promise and swear that I will be faithful and bear true allegiance to Her Majesty Queen Wictoria: so help me God." And thereupon he gave the Testament a hearty smack.

"Please to repeat after me again," said the Clerk—

"I, John Jorrocks, do swear that I do from my 'eart obor, detest, and abjure, as impious and heretical, that damnable doctrine and position that Princes excommunicated or deprived by the Pope or any authority of the See of Rome, may be deposed or murthered by their subjects, or any other whatsoever. And I do declare that no foreign prince, person, prelate, state, or potentate, hath, or ought to have, any jurisdiction, power, superiority, pre-eminence, or authority, ecclesiastical or spiritual, within this realm: so help me God."

"No more they ought," observed Mr. Jorrocks, kissing the book.

"Now, again," said the Clerk, commencing with a third oath—

"I, John Jorrocks, do truly and sincerely acknowledge, profess, testify, and declare, in my conscience, before God and the world, that our Sovereign Lady Queen Wictoria——"

"Not Wictoria, but *Victoria*," observed the Clerk.

"Victoria," repeated Mr. Jorrocks, "that our Sovereign Lady Queen Wictoria is lawful and rightful Queen of this realm, and all other Her Majesty's dominions and countries thereunto belonging: and I do solemnly and sincerely declare that I do believe, in my conscience, that not any of the descendants of the person who pretended to be Prince of Whales——"

"Not W*hales*, but Wales," observed the Clerk.

"I said Whales," observed Mr. Jorrocks, adding, "but I don't know who you're a talkin' about. The Prince o' Whales can't 'ave no heirs, he's only a babby."

"Never mind that," replied the Clerk, "you follow me, if you please, sir."—"And I do solemnly and sincerely declare, that I do believe, in my conscience, that not any of the descendants of the person who pretended to be Prince of Whales, during the life of the late King James the Second——"

"I doesn't know nothin' about King James the Second," observed Mr. Jorrocks, breaking off again, with a shake of the head, amid the hearty laughter of the bench.

"That's nothing, sir," observed the Clerk; "it's a mere matter of form."

"Well, but why should I swear agin a gen'lman that I knows nothin' whatever of, and wot has never done me no 'arm?"

"Oh, sir, it's a mere matter of form," repeated the Clerk.

"So chaps always say when they come to get one to accept a bill for them," observed Mr. Jorrocks; "*mere matter o' form—I doesn't like* these mere matters o' form."

"Well, but all these gentlemen on the bench have sworn the same thing. Indeed, you can't be a magistrate unless you do. Pray let us go on, for you are not half done yet, and it only wants a quarter to twelve."

"And I do solemnly and sincerely declare that I do believe in my conscience, that not any of the descendants of the person who pretended to be Prince of Whales during the life of the late King James the Second, and, since his decease, pretended to be and took upon himself the style and title of King of England——"

"Never heard of the gen'lman," observed Mr. Jorrocks. "By the name of James the Third, or of Scotland by the name of James the Eighth, or the style and title of King of Great Britain, hath any right or title whatsoever to the crown of this realm——"

"Certainly not," said Mr. Jorrocks, "it's *our* Queen's, and I'll stand up for her!"

"Or any other the dominions thereunto belonging," read the Clerk, followed by Mr. Jorrocks, "and I do renounce, refuse, and abjure any allegiance or obedience to any on 'em."

"So I do," said Mr. Jorrocks, giving the book another hearty smack.

"But that's not all," said the Clerk; "you must swear a little more yet. Please repeat after me again—"

"And I do swear that I will bear faith and true allegiance to Her Majesty Queen Wictoria, and her will defend to the utmost of my power against all traitorous conspiracies and attempts whatsoever, which shall be made against her person, crown, and dignity."

"So I vill," observed Mr. Jorrocks, panting for breath. "And I will do my utmost endeavour to disclose and make known to Her Majesty and her successors all treasons and traitorous conspiracies which I shall know to be again' her or any on 'em."

"And 'ow am I to do that?" inquired Mr. Jorrocks; "write to her, or how?"

"Oh, just let the Clerk of the Peace know—Her Majesty won't trouble you to write to her yourself."

"No trouble—*rayther* a pleasure," observed Mr Jorrocks.

"And I do faithfully promise to the utmost of my power to support, maintain, and defend the succession of the crown against the descendants of the said James."

"I dare say none o' them will trouble it," observed Mr. Jorrocks.

"Very likely not," replied the Clerk, adding, "please to repeat after me— "And against all other persons whatever," read on the Clerk, "which succession, by an Act intituled 'An Act for the further limitation of the crown, and better securing the rights and liberties of the subject,' is, and stands limited to the Princess Sophia, electress and Duchess-Dowager of Hanover, and the heirs of her body, being Protestants.

And all these things I do plainly and sincerely acknowledge and swear, according to these express words by me spoken, and according to the plain and common-sense understanding of the same words, without any equivocation, mental evasion, or secret reservation whatsoever."

"Wait a minute till I get wind," begged Mr. Jorrocks; "you really run me off my legs, you go so fast."

"And I make this recognition, acknowledgment, abjuration, renunciation, and promise, heartily, willingly, and truly, upon the faith of a true Christian."

" '*Deed do I not*," observed Mr. Jorrocks aloud to himself.

"So help me God. Kiss the book."

Thereupon Mr. Jorrocks kissed it again.

Having gulped these, and one or two other similar and equally sensible oaths, our excellent friend sank exhausted on the bench—a full-blown beak.

Captain Bluster, who had been waiting the completion of the ceremony, now seized him by the hand, and congratulated Mr. Jorrocks on "becoming one of them."

"Thank'ee," puffed Mr. Jorrocks; "thank'ee," repeated he, adding, as he looked at the Captain, "you have the adwantage o' me."

"My name's Bluster," observed the Captain, "Captain Bluster; I've heard of *you*—glad to see you on the bench—very proper appointment;" adding confidentially, in a whisper in Mr. Jorrocks's ear, "these Tory beggars want looking after; we'll keep them in order."

"You're one o' the *right* sort, I s'pose," observed Mr. Jorrocks.

"*True blue*," observed Captain Bluster, with a wink; "*down with the bishops!*"

"Civil and religious liberty, the greatest good for the greatest number—gover'ment without patronage, as it was in *our* day," observed Mr. Jorrocks.

"You had better put on your hat," observed Captain Bluster; "there's no doing justice with your hat off."

"No more there is!" replied Mr. Jorrocks, sticking it a-top of his wig, and giving it a thump on the crown that sounded through the Court, and sent a shower of flour over his own face.

The Clerk having pocketed Mr. Jorrocks's ten pounds for all the oaths he had made him swallow, now called on the next case—"Mortimer Green against John Tugwell."

The parties being ranged at the bar, the Clerk, taking up the information, addressed himself to the defendant, saying—

"This is an information charging you with having, on Friday night last, put your ass into a field of oats belonging to the complainant, Mortimer Green. You will hear the evidence against you."

Mrs. Mortimer Green was then sworn "to speak the truth, the whole truth, and nothing but the truth."

This being Mrs. Green's first appearance before that august tribunal, a bench of magistrates, she was rather nervous; and Captain Bluster, thinking to show off before Mr. Jorrocks, addressed her fiercely with—

"Now, ma'am! why don't you speak?"

"Please, gentlemen, I was going to say——"

"*Going!* Why didn't you say it?"

Mrs. Green stared.

"Now, what are you gaping at? why don't you speak? who are you? where do you come from? what's your name? what's brought you here? Tell us all about it!"

"Please, gentlemen," recommenced Mrs. Green, "last Friday—no, last Thursday as is gone a fortnight——"

"Now, whether do you mean Thursday or Friday?" roared Captain Bluster; "remember you're on your oath."

"Please, gentlemen, last Thursday as is gone a fortnight, my husband took badly in his stomach——"

"Good God! what has your husband's stomach to do with the case? Why don't you tell us about the ass?"

"I was going to, sir, when you interrupted me," observed Mrs. Green, addressing Captain Bluster.

"*Me* interrupted you! I never interrupted you! Why don't you tell us about the ass?"

"Perhaps we had better let her tell the story in her own way," observed the Chairman; "it will, perhaps, save time in the end. Now, my good woman," continued he, addressing the witness encouragingly, "tell us as shortly as you can what you have to say about this man and his ass."

"Please, gentlemen," observed Mrs. Green, gathering herself together for a third effort, "last Thursday as is gone a fortnight, my husband took bad in his stomach, and I went down to Doctor Bolus's to get a penn'orth of peppermint water—peppermint water, you see, gentlemen, is recommended in these cases——"

"Hang your peppermint water," growled Captain Bluster; "I'll be bound to say you're a regular old thief."

"And as the doctor wasn't in when I got there," continued the witness, "I sat down in the back kitchen to smoke my pipe and wait till he came."

"Nasty stinkin' old beast," grunted Mr. Jorrocks, who hated tobacco.

"It so happened, you see, gentlemen, that the doctor's people had been washing that day, and all the wet clothes were in the front kitchen, or I should have gone in there."

"Well, never mind that," observed the Chairman; "tell us now what happened to you as you sat in the back kitchen?"

"Well, and I hadn't sat there very long, not more than a quarter of an hour at farthest, when just as the young lady of the house—that's the third little girl like—came in with her kitten, and she asked Susan, that's the cook, for a saucerful of skim milk for it, and——"

"Oh dear me, can't you tell us about the ass?" roared Captain Bluster again, regardless of the Chairman's recommendation.

"I was going to, sir, when you interrupted me," again observed Mrs. Green.

"*Me* interrupt you! I didn't interrupt you—I *never* interrupt anybody—I *can't* interrupt anybody."

"Well, now, what happened," continued the Chairman, anxious to help the complainant on; "did the girl go for the milk?"

"That was just what I was going to tell you, gentlemen," observed the imperturbable witness. "Said she, that's Susan—said she, that's the third saucerful of skim milk you've asked me for to-day, Miss Elizabeth; and really if you stuff your cat so full, it'll catch no mice; however, the

young lady was so pressing, that Susan at last consented, and getting
the key of the dairy off the kitchen range, just from behind a plate
like," continued the witness, running her hand along the rail at the bar,
as if in the act of feeling for a key, "she took the empty saucer off the
floor, and went away to get it. Well, she hadn't been gone I dare say the
length of a minute, when I heard a knock at the door—one knock, like
that," giving the bar a rap with her knuckles, "and thinking it might be
somebody wanting the doctor, I laid down my pipe and went to open
it. Well, you see, there was a small chain on the door, which I didn't see
at first, and so before I got it open there was another knock. 'Who's
there?' said I. 'Open the door,' said some one, 'and see;' and according*lie*
I did, and there stood this man, with an arm full of brooms, and an ass
laden with more at his side."

"Well now," interrupted the Chairman, we don't want to hear about
any bargaining that took place or anything that passed about the
brooms, but tell us as shortly as you can when you saw the ass again."

"Yes, gentlemen," replied the old lady, evidently disconcerted, and
giving her nose a wipe with a folded-up red handkerchief. "Well then,
but I should tell you that by this time Susan, that is the cook, had got
back with the milk—the skim milk, and——"

"D—n the milk!" roared Captain Bluster, "didn't you hear the
Chairman tell you to stick to the ass? Do you think we've got nothing
to do but sit here and listen to your rambling stories?"

"Well, then, sir, I'm sure you're very welcome to go," replied the old
lady with great *naïveté*, producing a burst of laughter from the bench
and bystanders.

"Can't you tell us about finding the ass in the corn without going
into other particulars?" asked the Chairman.

"Well, sir, your worship, what you please."

"Nay, it's what *you* please, only we should like you to get on with
your story."

"Well then, gentlemen, on Thursday night, or early on Friday
morning, my husband took badly in his stomach again, and after trying
if the pains wouldn't go off with warm flannels and ginger, he asked me
to put on my clothes and go to Doctor Bolus's for another penn'orth of

peppermint water. This was just about daybreak; but there was a heavy mist that morning, and it might be rather later than we thought, for our clock had run down, and as we were going to have her cleaned, my husband thought it wasn't worth having her wound up until that was done. Well, as I went down the lane, I saw a pair of long ears bobbing up and down in our corn, and being struck with astonishment, I stood debating whether to go back to my husband or to see to it myself; but thinking of the badliness of his stomach, and the dampness of the morning, I considered I had better face it myself; and so, on I went, and just as I got to the gate at the turn of the road, I saw this villain coming over the hedge, pulling his ass after him through the hedge."

"Very good," said the Chairman, glad to get to the end of the story. "You swear that you saw a man bringing his ass out of your field, and that this is the man?"

"Oh, I swear that's the man, for I went up to him, and abused him right well."

"We don't doubt that," observed Captain Bluster.

"Now, Tugwell," said the Chairman, addressing the defendant, "you hear what that witness says. Do you wish to ask her any questions?"

"Undoubtedly I do, your worship," replied the man—a swarthy, herculean-looking fellow, with corkscrew ringlets, open neck, green plush waistcoat with yellow sprigs, and a double row of blue-bead buttons, cord breeches, dirty white stockings, and heavy laced ankle-boots. "Didn't I forewarn you," with great gravity asked he, "when I saw you at Doctor Bolus's, to make up your gap, otherwise my ass would be getting into your field?"

"Never such a thing!" screamed the old lady, "never such a thing! We talked about nothing but the price of the brooms: you said you could sell cheaper than anybody else, for though they all stole their stuff, you stole yours ready made."

"That's all gammon! I'd scorn the action!" replied the defendant, with an indignant curl of the lip. "I'm *noted* as the honestest besom-maker on our circuit. Your worships, my character stands too high to be damaged by such an old devil as this."

"We can't allow such language here," observed Captain Bluster sharply.

"Your defence is, I suppose," said the Chairman, "that the field was not properly fenced, and so your ass got in."

"Precisely so, your worship," replied the man, adopting the idea, or rather assenting to it, for it is the usual defence of the brotherhood.

"Pray, then, may I ask where you keep your ass?" inquired the Chairman.

"Sometimes in one place, sometimes in another, your worship. Mercantile men like us, your worship, are generally on the move, and we are obliged to put up with such quarters as we can get."

"Ay, but had you, on the night on which your ass is charged with being in Green's corn-field, any place to put him?"

"Why, not exactly, your worships. I was intending to be on the move by daylight, and I just turned the poor beast into the lane, and this stupid old woman persisting in not making up her gap, why, I'm ashamed to say he so far forgot himself as to go in. It's the first time, your worships, I assure you, such a thing ever happened, and it will be the last, for, without any disrespect to your worships, I feel this is not a place for a respectable man to be in."

The Clerk, on referring to his books, contradicted Tugwell's assertion, by observing that he had been convicted of a similar offence in a clover-field about a twelvemonth before.

The Chairman observed that depasturing an animal on a highway was an offence punishable by fine. The justices then considered their sentence. Mr. Brown had no doubt Tugwell was an old offender. Mr. Green would have been better pleased if he had been caught going into the field instead of coming out. The Chairman inquired what state the fence was in, and found it was very good. Captain Bluster thought, if he broke the fence, he might be caught under the Wilful Damage Act.

"What does Mr. Johnson think?" inquired the Chairman, addressing Mr. Jorrocks.

"*Jorrocks* is his name," observed Captain Bluster, with a growl.

"I beg his pardon," said the Chairman, with a low bow. "Pray, what does Mr. Jorrocks think?"

Mr. Jorrocks then, with great gravity, delivered himself of the following opinion:—

"Every man wot keeps a jackass is a waggabone," said he very slowly. "Every man wot keeps a jackass keeps a pair of big panniers also, and there's no sayin' wot on airth goes into them."

Mr. Jorrocks paused.

"Then what do you think should be done to him?" asked the Chairman. "What punishment shall we inflict upon him?"

"*Skin him alive!*" exclaimed Mr. Jorrocks, looking as if he would eat the defendant.

"I'm afraid that's hardly 'law,' " observed the Clerk, looking respectfully up at his ten-pound friend.

"If it's not law, it's what law ought to be," observed Mr. Jorrocks, with great gravity.

"A very good observation! very capital observation!" observed Captain Bluster, as soon as Mr. Jorrocks had done; "you'll make an *excellent* magistrate."

"I think I shall," said Mr. Jorrocks, "I think I shall, as soon as I get up a little law at least."

Captain Bluster: "Oh, hang the law! The less law one has in a justice-room the better. Get Stone's 'Justice's Pocket Manual,' it'll keep you all right as to form; and if you read 'Sam Slick,' it will do you more good than all the rubbishing stuff the lawyers write put together. Stone for the law—Slick for the sense."

"Stone for the law and Slick for the sense," repeated Mr. Jorrocks.

"Yes; and the first time you're in London go to the Judge and Jury Court at the 'Garrick's Head' in Bow Street, and learn some Latin sentences from Chief Baron Richards—Latin tells well from the bench."

The Chairman then informed the prisoner that he was convicted, and had to pay to Her Majesty the Queen the sum of one pound over and above the costs of the prosecution and the amount of the damage done by the donkey.

The defendant pleaded hard in mitigation.

"No," said the Chairman; "we have dealt very leniently with you."

"You are liable to a month's imprisonment, with hard labour, in the House of Correction," observed another.

"*One* month! *six* months!" rejoined a third; "this is a second offence."

"Whipping also!" exclaimed a fourth, "this conviction being before a bench of magistrates."

The mercantile man then begged for time, his trade being seriously depressed.

"By the police protecting the woods, I suppose," observed the Chairman.

"You must pay the money down," grunted Captain Bluster, "*nullum tempus occurrit Regi.* The Queen stands no nonsense."

Mr. Jorrocks, on leaving the Court, which he did after hearing a few more cases similar to the foregoing, strutted very consequentially down the middle of the street, making the quiet monotony of the place more apparent by the noisy clamour of his boots. He felt like a very great man.

He ran his mind through the backward course of life—thought of the time when he swept out his master's shop for his meat—then when he got a trifle for wages—next how he was advanced to a clerkship—how he bought his first pair of top-boots—how he stamped out two pair before he got a horse; his horses then came in chronological order, like kings and queens in a Memoria Technicha. His first, a white one, that tumbled neck and croup with him down Snow Hill, and broke both its own knees and his nose; his second, a brown, that always tried to kick him over his head when he mounted; and so he went on through a long list, the recollection of each bringing with it many other interesting associations.

Then he thought of the day when he was elected a member of the Surrey Hunt, and of the glories and honours he had reaped in that sporting country. Then of his advancement to the mastership of the Handley Cross Foxhounds, his short though brilliant reign at the Spa, and now how a whole wheelbarrowful of greatness had been heaped upon him in the shape of a J.P.-ship.

"Vell," said he, feeling his chin with one hand, and sliding a whole handful of half-crown pieces down the smooth inside leather of his breeches pocket with the other; "vell," said he, "for all this I am but mortal man."

Just as our friend had indulged in this humble-minded observation, he crossed the street at an angle to get back to the "Duke's Head," and the mail-gig hurrying up at the time, rather drove him from his point, and caused him to land opposite Mr. Pippin, the fruiterer's.

Mr. Pippin was a game-seller as well as a fruiterer, and the 12th of August drawing nigh, he had stuck a newly gilt and lettered sign to that effect over his door:—

"Pippin, Fruiterer, and Licensed Dealer in Game," read Mr. Jorrocks, in that vacant sort of way that people read anything that comes in their way.

"Pippin, Fruiterer and Game-seller," said he to himself, shortening the sign. "Wonders if he's got any cranberries." Mr. J. was very fond of cranberries.

"Have you got any cranberries?" asked he of Pippin, who, on the look-out for "squalls," now rushed to the door.

"Not any cranberries, sir; particular nice gooseberries, strawberries, cauliflowers, radishes, fish sauces of all kinds, sir; cucumbers, cigars, pickles—expect some peas in to-night, sir—step in, sir; step in."

Mr. Jorrocks complied, but oh! what a sight greeted him on the opposite wall—"three brace of grouse hanging by the neck!" Mr. Jorrocks stood transfixed.

"*How now?*" exclaimed he, as speech returned, and with staring eye-balls he turned to the shopkeeper.

"*How now?*" repeated he, pointing to the birds, "grouse for sale before the 12th of August."

"Five shiflings a brace," replied Mr. Pippin, quite unconcerned; "we generally charge six, but the season's coming on, and we shall soon get plenty more."

"Plenty more," roared Mr. Jorrocks; "aren't you 'shamed of yourself?"

"Oh dear no, sir, not at all; take the whole for fourteen shillings."

"*I'll fourteen you!*" repeated Mr. Jorrocks, stamping with rage, "I'll fourteen you, you waggabone. I'm one of Her Majesty's jestices o' the peace—'*nullum tempus occurrit*' somethin'—the Queen stands no nonsense—I'll fine you!"

"What for, sir?" inquired Mr. Pippin.

"For havin' game afore the twelfth—I'll summons you directly," added Mr. Jorrocks, hurrying out of the shop.

"Please say *they're stuffed*!" roared Mr. Pippin after him.

XX

This done, he took the dame about the neck,
And kissed her lips with such a clamorous smack,
That at the parting all the room did echo.

CRANIOLOGY.—A science that virtually professes to discover
how the interior of a house is furnished, from a mere
examination of the inequalities upon the roof of it.

WE HAVE NOT SEEN ANYTHING of our friends the Flathers since
the Marquis's brougham drove away from their door, and they
contributed their quota (as it is supposed) to the heaviness of the
Hillingdon letter-bag.

What passed on the occasion of the Marquis's visit we are not at
liberty to mention. Indeed we don't know— most probably Mrs. Flather
would have him a little to herself at first, during which she would hint
at her great esteem for him—but her duty to guard her daughter
from the risk of forming hopeless attachments; and then at the proper
period Emma would appear suffused in tears, and Mrs. Flather would
possibly leave them to themselves a little. All this, however, is chiefly
conjecture—or at best mere servants' gossip, formed from an outline of
what Mrs. Flather's boy in buttons communicated to Benjamin, who
detailed it to Betsey for the information of Mrs. Jorrocks. Our readers
must therefore just give such credence to the story as they consider it
worth. It will be remembered that each party claimed the victory, and
each indulged in the usual "crow."

The story was—for we may as well tell it out now that we have
begun—that the boy in buttons having taken it into his head to water
the myrtle below the window, saw the Marquis with Emma's head

on his shoulder, administering consolation to her eyes with his blue bandana. As a justice would say—that may, or may not be—it may be true, or it may be a lie—it may be Betsey's lie—it may be Benjamin's lie—or it may be the boy in buttons' lie—it may be true and yet have nothing in it. The Marquis might merely be doing what any man in such a situation would do, trying to soothe the poor girl. Had she been on his knee, we think the case would have been different. The presumption then would have been that he had got her there—at least we hope so. As it was, there was very little but supposition in the case. Our own opinion, however, is that there was something in it, though whether intentional on the part of the Marquis, or merely one of those involuntary, inadvertent, consolatory acts a man sometimes commits when suddenly beset by a pretty girl in tears, is another question. We dare say the Marquis would be very tender—very soft, and very likely say many things he never intended. A pretty girl in tears is a very dangerous thing, more especially when the tears are caused, or supposed to be caused, by one's self. We fear the Marquis said more than was prudent. Very possibly he thought no more of it after he had bowled away in his brougham; but Mrs. Flather's more than insinuation to Mrs. Jorrocks that her daughter and the Marquis were engaged, with the profusion of letters that showered into the Hillingdon letter-box, were presumptive evidence that the words had made some impression on her daughter.

A country post-office is a queer place. The postmistress—for they are generally kept by ladies—has a sort of intuitive acquaintance with every letter that comes or goes, knows who they are from, and can guess pretty nearly what they are about. There is none of that tranquil, easy security one feels, or rather used to feel, when dropping a letter into the well-accustomed depths of a large town post-office, where the variety of writings, the number of letters, the hurry of sorting, put all idea of curiosity out of the question. The country post-office generally consists of a black pane, with a slit in the middle of it, put into the parlour window with the words "Post-Office," done in white letters, above or below; and the letter, instead of passing, as the sender perhaps supposes, from all observation until it greets the eyes of the expectant receiver, drops through the hole into a plate or a table in the parlour, or perhaps in the bar of a public-house, where the landlady or her daughters are sewing, or drawing drops of comfort for the customers in the kitchen. Down it glides, and is immediately whipped up; and if the hand-writing is unknown, and the seal uninforming, the post-mistress has nothing to do but open the sash and look up and down street to see who was the party putting it in. Townspeople wouldn't believe the curiosity there is in the country.

But to return to Emma Flather and the Marquis of Bray.

The usual answers of congratulation, with the usual amount of sincerity—some with good-natured, ill-suppressed wishes that the news might not be too good to be true, or hopes that such an alteration might not injure the head of either party—having been received, each party rested on their oars in expectation of a "move" from the Castle. The "cock-a-hoop ness" of both mammas was considerably lessened on finding that each had similar expectations, and a thought occasionally glanced across their minds that it might have been better had they waited till they were a little more certain ere they announced the thing. One Marquis for two ladies would do nothing, still we dare say our readers will agree with us that it would not have been natural not to have announced it immediately. Indeed, the Marquis's manner was so truly love-making, that the villagers all set it down as a fixed thing; and even Johnny Wopstraw, who happened to be passing along on the top of his wain, observed to his wife when he got home that he thought "upon the who-o-ole there was a young gentleman making love to Miss Eliza." The change in the Marquis's costume, and the height from which Johnny overlooked down, prevented him recognising his over-night orator and draining-tile maker.

Thus things stood for at least a fortnight, each day adding additional uneasiness to the ladies. Every post delivery was anxiously looked for; every large seal that passed in review as Mrs. Medler sorted the letters was conjured into the impress of a ducal coronet, or a marquis's at least, with the reverse side directed to Mrs. Flather or Mrs. Trotter. Still it came not, neither was there anything heard of the Marquis, except that he had got a bad cold. This, however, was some consolation, enabling them to account in some measure for his silence. As a set-off against this, however, they had to take into account the Duke's letter to Mr. Jorrocks offering him a J.P.-ship, in which nothing was said of the marriage, or even hinted at. All this was very perplexing.

Mr. Jorrocks had now got himself into all his honours. Mr. Bowker had furnished him with a fine old edition of Burn's Justice; and Mr. Jones, the bookseller at Sellborough, had supplied him with a copy of Stone's "Pocket Manual" and "Sam Slick," according to Captain Bluster's recommendation; while Benjamin had been rigged out in a Welsh wig, and a pair of green spectacles with tortoise-shell rims, and a sort of beadle's dress, formed out of Mrs. Jorrocks's old bombazine gowns. Moreover, Mr. Jorrocks being a great believer in phrenology, or bampology, as he called it, had furnished himself with a copy of Combe's " Outlines," as also with a plaster of Paris head and phrenological chart, for the purpose of examining such culprits as might be brought before him, and ascertaining their bumps. His sanctum was now converted into a justice-room. In the centre, behind a high desk, stood an important old carved black oak arm-chair, on a raised stand: while below the desk were stools and a table, for Benjamin and Joshua Sneakington to sit and cry silence and take the depositions upon.

In other respects the sanctum underwent little change; the old red morocco hunting-chair occupying one side of the fireplace, a sporting picture screen and a coal scuttle the other.

Here, as his worship sat in the hunting-chair, thinking first of one thing, then of another—when his apples would be ripe, whether he should buy Brown's bull, whether Thompson's wouldn't be better—one loud knock at the door informed him that Benjamin was there, and before our friend had let his leg down that he had been nursing, in came the boy and stood before him.

"Please, sir, you're wanted, sir," said Benjamin.

"Vanted, Binjimin," repeated Mr. Jorrocks, pulling his wig straight; "who vants me now, I wonder—jestice or gentlefolk?" Mr. J. had now two sorts of visitors.

"Gentlefolk, I thinks," said Benjamin; "at least, she wants you alone. It's a 'ooman—old mother Flather."

"*Mrs. Flather*, you should say, Binjimin; there are no old women in this world. I'll see her in a minute," added he, running to a small mirror, and adjusting his neckcloth and frill.

"My dear Mrs. Flather, I'm werry 'appy to see you," exclaimed Mr. Jorrocks, as Mrs. Flather came sidling in past Benjamin, who stood with the door in his hand, arranging the latch so as to see through the key-hole. "Take a chair; pray take a chair," added he, passing her on to the one he had just vacated, and motioning Benjamin to leave the room.

"Here's a werry fine day," observed he, pressing her shoulder to get her to sit down in the hunting-chair, at the same time drawing a smaller one close to it. "How's Emma?" said he.

"Pretty well, I thank you," replied Mrs. Flather, throwing up her veil, and setting herself forward, as if for business.

"Fine gal, Emma," said Mr. Jorrocks, "fine gal! I always says though," added he, *sotto voce*, squeezing Mrs. Flather's arm, "that the gals of the present day ar'nt to be compared to their mothers."

Mrs. Flather smiled.

"*It's a fact*," observed Mr. Jorrocks, smacking his lips as he looked at her. "And 'ow's she getting on with the Markis? I hear there are two on 'em arter him."

"That's just what I've come to talk to you about," observed Mrs. Flather in a low tone, laying her hand confidentially on Mr. Jorrocks's wrist, as his arm rested on the elbow of her chair. "I want a little of your advice."

"Always 'appy to adwise the ladies," observed Mr. Jorrocks, "particklar 'appy. We'll jest bolt the door," added he, bundling up and making for it, "and then we shan't be interrupted. You knows wot Byron said about interruptions," observed he, as he bustled towards it.

Having locked it and bolted it too, he resumed his place by the side of Mrs. Flather.

"It's a very delicate situation we are in with regard to that young man," observed Mrs. Flather, after a pause; "he's engaged my daughter's affections, and I really fear he's only making a fool of her."

"Werry naughty o' him," observed Mr. Jorrocks, "werry naughty o' him"—muttering over the word "affection, affection," wondering if it was in Stone—(Mr. Jorrocks did everything judicially now). "Vot's he done? Kissed her, I s'pose," added he; "kissed her, kissed her; no sich title as that; come under the 'ead of assault, though. Kissin' ar'nt altogether right," added he to Mrs. Flather, "unless, indeed, she Consented, and then it is wot us jestices call justifiable kississide."

Mr. Jorrocks turned to Mrs. Flather, for the purpose of demonstrating the law, when one of Benjamin's loud knocks at the door, and attempt to open it, arrested his movement.

"Vot's 'appen'd now, Binjimin?" exclaimed Mr. Jorrocks, starting back; " vot's 'appen'd now?"

"A waggabone!" squeaked Benjamin through the door.

"Confound them waggabones," muttered Mr. Jorrocks, thinking how to get rid of the charge without bothering himself.

"Wot'un a nob 'as he, Binjimin?" inquired Mr. Jorrocks; "wot'un a nob 'as he?

"I harn't examined his nob," replied Benjamin; "Jos has only just cotch'd him, Jos has only just cotch'd him!" repeated he.

"Oh! *con*found it, Binjimin, 'ow can you trouble me in this ere way. Here am I inwestigatin' a *desp'rate* bugglary, nd you comes interruptin' of me, without havin' taken the dimensions of his coacoa-nut I tells you, never bring a waggabone forrard until you've examined his perrycranium"

"Yes, sir," said Benjamin.

"Then go and do it."

"Yes, sir," said Benjamin, muttering as he went, with a shake of the head, "desperate bugglary, indeed! I knows better nor that."

"Capital thing, that *crazeyology*," observed Mr. Jorrocks to Mrs. Flather, as he heard Benjamin's foot steps dying away in the passage; "gives one a capital idea of a waggabone's character; or any one's indeed," added Mr. Jorrocks, looking smilingly at Mrs. Flather, after the frown Benjamin's ill-timed interruption had brought over his good-natured countenance had passed away. "I should say, now," added he, "that your 'ead would pay a bampologist well for examinin'."

"Oh, you flatter, Mr. Jorrocks," said Mrs. Flather.

" 'Deed I doesn't, though," replied Mr. Jorrocks, " 'deed I doesn't, though," repeated he; "I always says you're the neatest little 'ooman I knows; neat, *pretty* little 'ooman."

"Oh, fie! Mr. Jorrocks," said Mrs. Flather diving into her bag, and producing her best pocket-handkerchief.

"Fiddle, O fie!" replied Mr. Jorrocks, "it's the truth, and that's all how and about it. I always says you're the neatest little 'ooman I know. I likes a little 'ooman."

"I thought you'd like big ones," observed Mrs. Flather, looking archly at our friend.

"Never such a thing!" exclaimed Mr. Jorrocks, "never such a thing! Little 'uns for my money."

"Well, I'm sure I always thought you admired big women," observed Mrs. Flather.

"Quite a mistake," replied Mr. Jorrocks, "quite a mistake; I says big 'uns are only fit for grenadiers."

"Well, that's my opinion," rejoined Mrs. Flather; "especially when they've moustarche," added she, with as sagacious a smile as her unmeaning face could muster. (Mrs. Trotter had a slight pencilling that way.)

"Just so," said Mr. Jorrocks, giving her a poke and a wink.

"Let's have your nob examined," said he, wishing to turn the conversation before Mrs. Flather made him commit himself further against Mrs. Trotter, a thing our friend had no intention of doing. "I should think," continued he, "you'll have some remarkable fine bamps—observin' faculties, knowin' faculties, reflactive faculties—all sorts o' faculties, in fact."

"Oh dear no! no such thing!" exclaimed Mrs. Flather, resisting Mr. Jorrocks's untying of her bonnet-string.

"*Jest me*," said Mr. Jorrocks, as if he was nobody. Our friend then divested Mrs. Flather of her bonnet.

"We'll begin with number one," said he, getting his outlines, and feeling Mrs. Flather behind the ear.

"Bamp of amitiveness," said he, looking at his paper with a great black head at the top, marked into divisions corresponding with a classification below. "Bamp of amitiveness, werry large—marriage, love. 'A man shall leave his father and mother, and cleave to his wife;' and I s'pose, by the same rule, a 'ooman shall leave her father and mother and cleave to her 'usband. Ad 'esiveness," continued he, feeling a little forward, "that means attachment —friendship, and social sympathy, such as exists between you and I," said Mr. Jorrocks, giving Mrs. Flather a kiss.

"*Oh, Mr. Jorrocks!*" exclaimed Mrs. Flather.

"Nobody will hear," said our worthy friend, giving her another.

"Well, but now, let's talk about the Marquis," said she, pushing him aside, as he prepared for another salute.

"Vell," said he, "let's talk about the Markis; wot's the specific charge again' him?"

"Why, I can't say that I have any regular charge to make against him," replied Mrs. Flather, putting on her bonnet; "indeed, I believe if he was left to himself, he would do what is right and proper; but that odious—you know who I mean—is doing all she can to get him away from us, for her own gawky copper-coloured daughter."

"Vell, but that would be 'larceny,' I should think," observed Mr. Jorrocks with a sagacious shake of the head; "that would be larceny, I think—stealin' a sweetheart;" at the same time diving into his pocket to consult his friend "Stone."

"Larceny has been defined to be," read he, the wrongful takin' and carryin' away of the personal goods of any one from his possession, with a felonious intent to conwert them to the use of the 'fender, without the consent of the owner."

"That seems werry like the thing," observed Mr. Jorrocks, looking full at Mrs. Flather; "she wants to conwert the Markis to her own use—at least to the use of her darter—*sed quoere*, as us lawyers say, is the absolute possession of the Markis in your darter?"

"But I don't want the law of him," observed Mrs. Flather; "indeed, I come to ask your advice more as a friend than as a magistrate."

"Always 'appy to see you in any capacity, my leetle duck observed Mr. Jorrocks, giving her another kiss that sounded right through the room.

"Bump of acquisitjven werry big!" holloa'd Benjamin through the door; and "bump o' philopro—somethin' werry small!"

"*Con*found the bouy!" growled Mr. Jorrocks, wondering if he had heard the Sound; "confounded young rascal—does it on purpose I do believe."

"Bamp of acquisitiven Binjimin!" replied Mr Jorrocks, collecting his faculties; "bamp of acquisitjveness, did you say? that's the priggin' bamp; wot's the rascal been a stealin'?"

"Gooseberries!" replied Benjamin.

"Gooseberries!" repeated Mr. Jorrocks; "wot's the punishment?"

"Don't know!" replied Benjamin through the door.

"*Don't hnow, bouy!* Vy didn't you look it out in the book afore ever you came botherin' 'ere? Look out gooseberry, I say, or I'll pull your gown over your 'ead, and send you to the treadmill yourself. These bouys are the devil's own," muttered Mr. Jorrocks, half to himself and half to Mrs. Flather. "I *really* sometimes think that bouy takes a pleasure in interruptin' o' me when I'm particklarly engaged—at least *plisantly* engaged," added he, giving Mrs. Flather's arm a squeeze.

"There ar'nt gooseberry in the book," holloa'd Benjamin through the door, after a long pause, during which he had been listening.

"Ar'nt gooseberry in the book!" repeated Mr. Jorrocks; "impossible, Binjimin!"

"There ar'nt, howsomever."

"Look out goose then!" replied Mr. Jorrocks, adding to himself, "wot's sauce for the goose is sauce for the gander; and wot's law for goose will most likely be law for gooseberry."

"There ar'nt goose neither!" replied Benjamin—gold plate—good be'aviour—"

"Ay, good be'aviour, indeed," grunted Mr. Jorrocks, "that's a thing you knows precious little about."

"Goods forfeited—grand jurymen—grey'ound—grouse—guide-post—guest—gunpowder—gipsies," continued Benjamin, reading on while his master was muttering.

"Ord rot it, 'old your noise, Binjimin!" roared Mr. Jorrocks, "you are long past goose. Let me look," said he, getting up and making for the door.

"Let me look," said he, after he had got it fumbled open, taking Burn's Justice from the boy, who stood with the fifth volume open at the index. Mr. Jorrocks began with the G's at "game," and went regularly through them: "Gaols—garments—general—gentlemen—gins—glass—gleaning—gloves—to gold plate," where Benjamin had begun, but there was nothing about "gooseberry." "Let me look in my 'Stone,' " added he, pulling out his pocket manual again. Dare say it will be under the 'ead of gardens."

"Here it is, 94—Stealin', &c., wegitable productions in gardens."

Mr. Jorrocks then turned to page 94, and read as follows:—

"Wegitable productions growin' in gardens—stealing' or destroyin', or damagin' with intent to steal any plant, root, fruit, or wegitable production growin' in any garden, orchard, nursery ground, 'ot-'ouse, green-'ous or conservatory. Punishment on conwiction afore one jestice for first offence, imprisonment with or without 'ard labour in gaol or 'ouse of Correction for not exceedin' six calendar months, or penalty above the walue not exceedin' twenty pounds."

"My vig!" added he, "but that's tight work. Makes gooseberry stealing werry expensive."

" 'Ow old's the waggabone, Binjimin?"

"May be a dozen," replied Benjamin.

"A dozen—twe that's to say," repeated Mr. Jorrocks; "six months at twelve years old—sharp work. Twenty punds—deal o' cash."

"You're sure he stole them, Binjjmin?"

"Jos caught him in the garden; he had both pockets chock-full, and a cabbage in his 'at."

"Cabbage in his 'at," observed Mr. Jorrocks; "wegitable production, that's to say. Well, Binjimin, I think he's too young to send to quod; I'll deal sammarily with the case. Take him to Batsay with my compliments, and say I'll thank her to take him into the laundry and give him a good basternaderin'—good strappin', that's to say."

"Yes, sir," said Benjamin.

"A dozen or so," observed Mr. Jorrocks.

"Yes, sir," said Benjamin.

"And bid her put a pair o' stockins in his mouth, so that we mayn't be troubled with his noise."

"Yes, sir," said Benjamin.

"Dirty 'uns!" added Mr. Jorrocks, as Benjamin went away.

"And now, my little darlin'," said he, patting Mrs. Flather on the back as he shut the door, and returned the pocket manual to the Jorrockian jacket pocket, and resumed his seat, "let us 'ear all about this naughty bouy and your pretty darter, and let's see if we can deal sammarily with him too; bad bouy, I fear! bad bouy: always pullin' the gals about."

"Well, you see, Mr. Jorrocks, as I said before, it's not the Marquis I blame so much as those who entice him away. I'm quite sure he's very much attached to Emma, and would do what is right if other people would let him."

"Jest so," said Mr. Jorrocks.

"There's something now going on that we can't at all fathom. Nothing could be kinder or more lover-like than he was the morning he called at our house, and yet from that day to this we've heard nothing from him."

"Fallen in with summut he likes better p'raps," observed Mr. Jorrocks.

"But that is very wrong, you know, Mr. Jorrocks," observed Mrs. Flather.

"No doubt," said Mr. Jorrocks, with a shake of his head, "no doubt—but it's wot Sam Slick calls 'uman natur'."

"Well, then, you see, Mr. Jorrocks, I want to ask your advice what is best to be done."

"Best to be done," repeated Mr. Jorrocks, "best to be done? Dash my vig if I *know*. Do you think you could make out a case if I was to summons him?"

"Oh! I shouldn't like to take any step of that sort— it's not as a justice, but as a gentleman that I come to consult you—*friend*, rather, let me say," giving the steady old gentleman a sweet smile.

"Jest so," said Mr. Jorrocks, giving her a hearty kiss in return. "Let us see now," added he, preparing to look at the case in another light. "Has he written her any sweet letters?"

"Why, no; he's not," replied Mrs. Flather, sorry to have to admit the fact. "His attentions have been all verbal and personal."

"Jest kissin' and squeezin'," observed Mr. Jorrocks. "You've nothin' to show, then?" inquired he.

"Nothing," replied Mrs. Flather, with a sigh. "No little lockets or bracelets, or poetry pieces— nothin' o' that sort?"

"No," responded Mrs. Flather.

"*Humph!*" grunted Mr. Jorrocks, not knowing what to do.

"Please, sir, will you have the mutton boiled or roasted?" inquired Betsey, who, having noiselessly opened the door, now stood with it in her hand, as the saying is.

"*D—n the mutton!*" screamed Mr. Jorrocks, starting up in a perfect fury. "That's jest the way! if ever I'm particklar busy—either beakin', or odein', or anything, I'm sure to be interrupted by some cussed inquiry about the wittles."

"And a pretty row you'd make if they warn't to your liking, you nasty ugly old crockadile," replied Betsey, with upturned nose and most indignant look at Mrs. Flather. "But I see how it is," added she, throwing her apron up to her face and bursting into tears, "I see how it is!" repeated she, banging the door to, and hurrying away.

"That 'ooman's mad—full o' beans," observed Mr. Jorrocks with a shake of the head, as Betsey's step died away. "Well flow, my leetle darlin', let's resume about your darter, and see what we can do in the matter," said he to Mrs. Flather, anxious to return to the subject. "I'm afeard he's not put his foot quite far enough in it yet."

"Not gone far enough, you think?" asked Mrs. Flather.

"I think not," replied Mr. Jorrocks. "I'd allow him a leetle more line."

"But he offered to her almost the first day; it was love at first sight."

"Then you should have book'd him," observed Mr. Jorrocks. "There's nothin' like takin' these young chaps when they're in the 'umour—'safe bind safe find's' a beautiful axiom of sweet'eartin' law."

"How do you think we had better do?" asked Mrs. Flather, recollecting who it was that prevented her booking the Marquis at Donkeyton Castle.

"Do, now?" repeated Mr. Jorrocks; "do, now?—faith, that's a difficult question to answer. She's a nice gal's Emma, and a neat gal is Emma—puts her clothes on well—tidy about the pins too; but Lor' bless you! she ar'nt to be compared to her mother."

"Oh, Mr. Jorrocks you flatter."

"*Not a bit*," replied Mr. Jorrocks; "*not a bit*. I've always said, and I still maintains, that the gals of the present day are miles behind their mothers."

"You are so complimentary always, Mr. Jorrocks."

"They may be as fine, you know," continued Mr. Jorrocks, without noticing the observation "when they get to their hage—that in course I can't say—but at present, I'm quite decided in that opinion; gals are nice, pretty, dollish-lookin' things, but I says a 'ooman isn't a 'ooman till she's forty—fat, fair, and forty! *that's* the ticket—that's my motto."

"Well, but about the Marquis," resumed Mrs. Flather, anxious to keep the volatile Justice to the point. "What do you think we had best do?"

"*Best* do?" repeated Mr. Jorrocks; "best do? Vy, I'd try fair means fair, and then—and then—and then——"

"*What?*" ejaculated Mrs. Flather.

"I'm cussed if I know," replied Mr. Jorrocks. "It's hardly, as I said before, exactly within the jurisdiction of a J.P. No doubt our commission is werry extensive—keep the peace—chastise and punish all wot offend again' the laws and ordinances—inquire the truth upon the oath of good and lawful men of the county of all manner of felonies, puzzonin's, inchantments, sorceries, arts majig, trespasses, forestallin's, regratin's, ingrossin's, and extortions whatsomever; and also of all those who in the counties aforesaid in companies against our peace, in disturbance of our people with armed force have gone or rode or hereafter shall presume to go or ride, and also of all those who have lain in wait, or hereafter shall presume to lie in wait, to maim or cut or quilt or kill our people; and also of all wittlers, and all and singulars other persons who in the 'buse of weights or measures or in sellin' wittles——"

"Oh, none of those would apply to the Marquis," interrupted Mrs. Flather, fearful Mr. Jorrocks would recite the whole commission to her.

"I thinks not either," replied Mr. Jorrocks. "We might catch Emma p'raps as an '*enchantress*,' " observed the gallant old Justice, "but, as you say, the person you want to catch is the Markis."

"Just so," replied Mrs. Flather.

"Well, then, it's a ticklish thing," observed Mr. Jorrocks; "werry like fly-fishin'—if you strike too soon, you may lose him altogether. Let him play with the 'ook a little longer."

"But then he doesn't come to play with it, you see," observed Mrs. Flather; "*that's* the difficulty."

"I *twig*," winked Mr. Jorrocks. "S'pose you take the 'ook to him."

"But we have no excuse for going; besides, nobody ever goes to the Castle without an invitation. Couldn't you get the Marquis over again?" at last asked Mrs. Flather.

"Vy, I don't know," replied Mr. Jorrocks, considering how the thing would cut. "I doesn't know, I'm sure. There's a many rings in the ladder atwixt a young Markis and a middle-aged grocer—J.P.; at all events, I should be a'most afraid of offendin'."

"Oh, I don't think you need be under any alarm about that," replied Mrs. Flather; "the Duke seemed to like you amazingly, and the Marquis invited himself before."

"That's jest why I think I'd best let him inwite him self again," replied Mr. Jorrocks.

"You'd oblige me very much if you would," observed Mrs. Flather, looking at him most lovingly.

"It's bad to resist such a hen hangel as you," said Mr. Jorrocks, getting up and bolting the door; but as we dare say our readers have had enough of this dialogue, we will not accompany the parties any further.

XXI

State your case.

SCARCE WAS MRS. FLATHER GONE, and ere Mr. Jorrocks had arranged a composing speech in his mind for Betsey, Benjamin made his appearance to announce the arrival of another "customer."

"Another customer, Binjimin!" exclaimed Mr. Jorrocks, starting up, "not another waggabone, I 'opes?"

"The same as the last," replied Benjamin, with a grin; "Mother Trotter this time."

"*Missis* Trotter, you should say, Binjimin," observed Mr. Jorrocks; "I shall be 'appy to see her."

"Don't doubt you, old boy," said Benjamin to himself, as he went away to bring her.

"Good mornin', Mrs. Trotter!" exclaimed Mr. Jorrocks, as the majestic lady sailed into the room in all the rustle of petticoats and stiff ringlets. "Werry 'appy to see you; pray take a chair—this 'ere harm one, if you please," drawing the recently occupied red morocco hunting-chair towards her. "You needn't mind waitin', Binjimin," said he to the boy, who kept fussing about the desk, as if he was going to act clerk. Benjamin reluctantly retired, carrying with him his wig and gown and spectacles.

"Vell, my beauty," said Mr. Jorrocks to Mrs. Trotter, as the door closed, "Vell, my beauty," said he, his countenance assuming quite a different appearance "and 'ow are you to-day? Needn't ax that, though," said he, squeezing her elbow, "that fine, clear complexion, bright eye, and these full cherry lips, answer that; he's an 'appy man wot has the kissin' on them, I guess!"

"Oh, Mr. Jorrocks you shocking man I what would Mrs. Jorrocks say?"

"Oh, never fear Mrs. Jorrocks," replied our hero; "she's away at her school or some of her wagaries."

"But if I was to tell her, *you'd* mind," observed Mrs. Trotter, with an emphasis; "and I really don't think I'm doing my duty in not."

"Trust *you* for that," said the old Cockney Squire, with a wink—

> Wot passes *inter nos*,
> Mustn't be proclaim'd at Chain' Cross,

you knows," added he. "Come, set down, I say, and tell us all about it," continued he, pushing her into the large chair.

"Well, now, I've come," observed Mrs. Trotter, after a pause, during which she equalised the strings of her reticle; "I've come to ask your advice in a little delicate matter connected with my daughter."

"I twig," said Mr. Jorrocks, with a wink.

And I'm sure that in confiding to you I may rest satisfied it will go no further."

"Certainly not," said Mr. Jorrocks; "close as wax."

"You see," continued Mrs. Trotter, in an undertone, "that the Marquis, we think, took a violent fancy to Eliza, and, I make no doubt, would have offered to her, only she was so shy that she didn't encourage him enough."

"Jest so," replied Mr. Jorrocks; "wants a little practice, p'raps."

"Why, she's very young, you see," said Mrs. Trotter.

"Her mother wouldn't 'ave been so green, I guess," observed Mr. Jorrocks, giving Mrs. Trotter's arm a squeeze. "I always says," continued he, "that the gals of the present day are not to be compared to their mothers."

Mrs. Trotter smiled.

" '*Deed I do*," said Mr. Jorrocks, smacking his lips; the gals may be nice and slim, and slight and pretty, but they've none o' that fine hupstandin', commandin', majestic, knock-me-down, squash-me-flat hair of the women of the present day. I'll pund it, you'd have brought the Markis to book in a minute. If there was a prize for fine women you'd get it."

"Oh, Mr. Jorrocks, how you *do* talk! It's lucky Mrs. Jorrocks isn't here."

"P'raps it is," said Mr. Jorrocks, in an undertone; "you know it wouldn't do for everybody to hear all wot passes 'twixt his worship and those wot come to consult him."

"Certainly not," said Mrs. Trotter, hoping her mission would be kept snug. "Well, then, you see, Mr. Jorrocks," continued she, "as I was saying, I make no doubt the Marquis took a violent fancy to Eliza; and if she had known how to play her cards, she might have nailed him at the time; but, as ill luck would have it, he went away without exactly offering, and I fear that sneaking, nasty woman on the hill got him to have an interview with her mealy-faced daughter, and rather put him off Eliza."

"Humph!" grunted Mr. Jorrocks, not exactly seeing his way between the rival claimants.

"Well, then, you see," continued Mrs. Trotter, "what's passed since, we have no means of knowing. One would naturally have expected that a young man so desperately smitten would have taken an early opportunity of returning to see the young lady."

"Certainly," said Mr. Jorrocks, with a sagacious nod of the head; "I would, I knows."

"But no! from that day to this," continued Mrs. Trotter, "we've heard nothing of him; and I really now am so puzzled what to do, that I've come to you in confidence, as an old friend, and one that, I'm sure, would be glad to do me a good turn."

"*No doubt on it*," said Mr. Jorrocks, patting her plump back, "no doubt on it."

"You're very good, I'm sure," resumed Mrs. Trotter, with a smile that displayed her beautiful pearly teeth; "I've just come to ask, in fact, what you think we had best do under the circumstances."

"Do under the circumstances?" repeated Mr. Jorrocks, regularly posed—"do under the circumstances?" repeated he, casting his eyes up to the ceiling. "Vy," said he, looking especial grave, "if you axes me as a jestice o' the peace, I should tell you that the law on this point is werry doubtful—indeed, I may almost say, werry dubersome; there certain*lie* are cases in the books—Barnewall and Halderson, and six Wesey Junior——"

"Oh, but it's not the law of the point—it's the prudence of the point I want," interrupted Mrs. Trotter.

"The prudence o' the point," said Mr. Jorrocks, "is another view o' the matter. In these cases, I always think it well to be prudent—'Si sit prudentia,' as the poet has it. Eliza's a werry nice gal—werry pretty gal, and it would be a grand thing to see her a Duchess."

"Wouldn't it!" exclaimed Mrs. Trotter, clasping her hands.

"But I'm rayther inclined to think," continued Mr. Jorrocks, "that the Markis will be difficult to catch."

"Why so?" exclaimed Mrs. Trotter.

"Vy, in the first place, you see, there's a great demand for Markisses in London; and wot sells readily there, are seldom disposed of in the country."

"But one's heard of such cases, you know, Mr. Jorrocks."

"Vy, one has certainly," replied our friend, with a sagacious elevation of his brows, "read on them, at all ewents."

"Well, but, however, it's on the cards," observed Mrs. Trotter, "and trying costs nothing."

"Tryin' costs nothin', as you say," observed Mr. Jorrocks; "not like a jestice's petty session—information—summons—conwiction, and all that sort of thing."

"Well, but you'll do what you can to assist Eliza and me, won't you, Mr. Jorrocks?"

"*Certainly*," replied our Squire—"always ready to serve the ladies; you must give Eliza a lesson or two in love-makin' though," observed Mr. Jorrocks; "she don't take arter her mother in that respect, I guess," added he.

"How do you know?" inquired Mrs. Trotter.

"Those sparklin' black eyes tell a different tale," replied Mr. Jorrocks. "I never see'd sich a pair o' pierces afore—no wonder little T. knocked under at once. Vell, I don't know," added he thoughtfully, "but somehow or other I doesn't think the gals of the present day are to be compared to their mothers. They're nice and pretty, and hulegant, and so on, but they haven't the gumption o' women—a 'ooman isn't a 'ooman, I say, till she's forty—tall, dark, and forty's my motto," added he, giving Mrs. Trotter a touch under the chin.

Mrs. Trotter laughed.

"You've a beautiful 'ead for bampology," observed Mr. Jorrocks, looking under her bonnet. "Twenty's werry prominent; that's the bamp o' wit—have it myself—quick perception o' the meanin' of others; presence of mind, readiness to perceive the incongruous and ridicklous. Bamp of amitiveness too—behind the ear" (feeling her there). "No. 1, marriage, love, and all that sort o' thing; werry fine 'ead indeed—am a great bampology man—wonders wot'un bamps the Markis has; should say he has the bamp of amitiveness—most young chaps have indeed."

"Some old ones too, I think," observed Mrs. Trotter, with a laugh.

"Doesn't know nothin' about old 'uns," replied Mr. Jorrocks. "Never mean to be old—stick where I am—jest the right age—wiggour blended with discretion."

While all this was going on, Joshua, who had been uncommonly active that day, arrived with a half drunken, roystering, tramping mechanic, who had been ordered out of the public-house for creating a disturbance by wanting to fight.

Benjamin saw them coming, and sent B to desire Joshua to shove his prisoner into the wash-house, and let them have a word together.

Accordingly Joshua did so.

"The old 'un's werry busy to-day," observed Benjamin, "and werry grumpey, too; I dar'nt go in to him again—should 'ave the boot-jack at my 'ead, p'raps."

"What's happen'd?" inquired Joshua.

"The old game," replied Benjamin, "the old game—a woman, a woman."

"The old fellow!" exclaimed Joshua. "Well, then, we must just keep the chap till he's more at leisure," added he.

"What's he been a doin' of?" inquired Benjamin.

"Getting drunk, and threatening to fight," replied Joshua.

"Getting drunk, and threatenin' to fight," repeated Benjamin, "the warmint! wot'un a chap is he? Does he belong here?"

"No, he's a stranger—a Londoner I should say, by his tongue."

"The Lunnuners are queer chaps," observed Benjamin; "I lived there myself. Howsomever, drunkenness ar'nt no great wice in the eyes of the old 'un; indeed, in the eyes of a vast of the beaks. It's just one of those pints that is either right or wrong, as occasion suits. If a chap commits a gross assault and pleads drunkenness, they immediately flare up with, 'Drunkenness is no excuse! rather an aggrawation.' Then, if he pleads sobriety, they tell him 'he'd better 'old his tongue, for drunkenness would be the only excuse he could make for his conduct.'"

"Just so," observed Joshua, digesting the law as Benjamin proceeded.

"I knows nicely wot the old 'un would give him," continued Benjamin; "he'd storm, and threaten, and bully, as if he were a goin' to transport him for life, then talk about the disgraceful, degradin', disgustin' situation of a drunken man, finish by finin' of him a shillin' or 'alf-a-crown, and werry likely throwin' it at his 'ead as he went away, sayin', 'Take your tin and be off with you! It's a poor 'eart wot never rejoices!'"

"Indeed!" observed Joshua; "why, we could do better than that ourselves!"

"No doubt we could," replied Benjamin; "no doubt we could—save the old boy all the trouble too. If you'll fetch the waggabone forrad, I'll sarve him out 'andsomely, and we can divide the fine for our trouble."

"Well, I've no objection," replied Joshua.

"Fetch him forrad quickly, then," observed Benjamin, "and let us get the case heard—we'll not trouble none of his bamps," added he, imitating his master.

"Not we!" said Joshua, closing the door, as he went in quest of his friend.

Benjamin then proceeded to array himself in his judicial habiliments— Welsh wig, with broad-rimmed green spectacles and black gown. His own mother wouldn't have known him. Having taken an arm-chair at the end of the kitchen table, and ranged a few old books before him, Joshua made his appearance with the prisoner—a strapping young joiner in his working trousers and Sunday coat and waistcoat—a sort of half dress. He was handcuffed.

"Who have you got there?" growled Benjamin, as they made their appearance.

"A prisoner, please your worship," replied Joshua, with a low bow.

"Fatch him forrad, fatch him forrad," rejoined Benjamin, imitating his master's voice and dialect.

"Who prefars the charge?" inquired Benjamin, as they reached the end of the table; "who prefars the charge?" repeated he.

"Me, please your worship," replied Joshua.

"Then take this 'ere book in your right 'and," said Benjamin, handing Joshua Mrs. Glass's Cookery Book; take off your glove, and I'll swear you."

Joshua did as desired.

"Now listen to me," continued Benjamin. "The evidence wot you shall give before this grand court shall be the truth, the 'ole truth, and nothin' but the truth. Kiss the book."

Joshua kissed it.

"Now then," continued Benjamin, receiving back the book, and taking up an old goose-quill, "you are on your oath; now state your case as shortly as you can: tell me all about it, in fact."

Joshua having cleared his voice with a preparatory hem, thus commenced.

"Please your worship," said he, "as I was going my rounds this morning, I was called into the public-house, the sign of the 'Man loaded with Mischief,' to quell a disturbance created by this hero, who had challenged all the company round to fight——"

"*That's a lie!*" observed the man.

"You scoundrel! how dare you speak in such a way before his worship—a justice of the peace of our Sovereign Lady the Queen?" inquired Joshua.

"And one of the jorum," observed Benjamin.

"And one of the quorum," remarked Joshua.

"I'll skin you alive," added Benjamin, with a shake of the head. "Well, come, get on with your story," said he to Joshua.

"Then, please your worship, when I went into the 'Man loaded with Mischief,' I found this fellow standing with his hat cocked on one side before the kitchen fire, bragging any of the company out to fight."

"*That's a lie!*" interrupted the man.

"*Silence, you waggabone!*" screamed Benjamin, "or I'll make mince-meat on ye—chop you into sarsingers! Go on with your story," added he to Joshua.

"Then, please your worship, I ordered him to sit down and behave himself like a gentleman, if he was one; and thereupon he used most abusive language to me, too shocking for me to repeat."

"*Dreadful!*" observed Benjamin, with another shake of the head. "Wot 'ave you got to say for yourself?" asked his worship of the man.

"I mean to say," replied the prisoner, with a lurch, "that all that (hiccup) blackguard has been saying's a (hiccup) lie."

"That won't do," replied Benjamin; the gen'lman's on his oath—couldn't tell a lie if he would. I makes no doubt you're a great waggabone, werry great waggabone. Every man," added he very sententiously, "wot cocks his 'at on one side is a waggabone. Every man wot cocks his 'at on one side would cock his gun at a fizzant or an 'are if they were to come in his way. That's the law o' the case. I conwicts you in the penalty of five shillings for being drunk; and for God's sake," added he in an undertone to Joshua, "get the tin and shove him out of sight as quick as ever you can, for I hear the old 'un a letting his woman out, and there's no saying but he may be poking in here after Batsay."

XXII

Now I state in the presence of many of my tenants, that I am willing to do everything in my power for the improvement of stock. If a committee selected from among themselves will first go into Birmingham, the great metropolis of this part of the country, and ascertain there what description of stock is in the greatest demand, which fattens best, or yields the greatest produce of milk, or is best adapted for the food and pasture of this district, I will, regardless of price, introduce the best bull I can find of such species, and my tenants and their cows shall have free access to the animal (loud laughter).—*Sir Robert Peel's Agricultural Speech at Tamworth*

L ET US PAY A VISIT to Donkeyton Castle.

The Duke of Donkeyton sat in state in the midst of his spacious library, fitted up in rich Gothic style, with every appliance of modern luxury. Noble bookcases, glittering with well-bound, rarely touched books, rose from the softly carpeted floor towards the deeply mullioned ceiling, between the top of the bookcase and which were ranged, in close-drawn line, exquisite marble busts of poets, of statesmen, of orators, of heroes, of great men of ancient and modern times, of every clime and country—the wisdom of the world looking down on the folly of the day. Antique and easy chairs of every shape and make were scattered about among Gothic tables, portfolio stands, busts, banner screens, and globes. A clear-ticking, curiously wrought, and beautifully inlaid timepiece on the elaborately ornamented stone mantelpiece alone disturbed the solemn repose of the large, light-subdued apartment.

His Grace sat in an easy chair, at a small black oak table, with gold mother-of-pearl-cased eye-glasses in hand, surveying the county map, particularly the part about Donkeyton Castle. The inner and outer circles were clearly defined, like the errand circles of a London club, and his Grace was bewildering himself in the attempt to draw a sleeping and non-sleeping party from among the omitted, prevented, and excused of the last gathering. Three attempts had he made, and thrice had he failed, owing to the usual confusion of his mind, and the impossibility of remembering whether it was Mr. Tom Brown of the Hill, or Mr. John Brown of the Vale, who had honoured him on a former occasion; or whether it was Mr. T. Smith or Mr. G. Smith who was on their side in politics.

Just as his Grace began his fourth list, the Marquis entered the library. "Ah, Jeems!" exclaimed his Grace, looking up, "come here, my dear; I am so monstrously puzzled, I hardly know what to do. Three lists have I drawn up of people to be invited, and three times have I destroyed them, owing to mistakes of some sort or other. Just come now and tell me, have the Tompkinses of Lintley been here this summer, or not; or have they been invited, or how?"

"The Tompkinses?" repeated the Marquis.

"You know there are *two* Tompkinses," observed his Grace: "Tompkins of Lintley, and Tompkins of Whitley, and between the two I'm always making some confusion. One is in the outer circle, the other in the inner circle, and it is the outer circle Tompkins I am puzzled about—I have some idea that he dined here, and his wife had a headache, and stayed at home."

"Oh yes, I remember now," replied the Marquis. "He is a little round squat man, with a very red face. He dined here, and went home after. His wife was disappointed of her dress, and could not come in consequence."

"Oh, that was the way, was it," observed the Duke.

"Yes; so their servant told ma's French maid."

"Very good," rejoined his Grace; "then he'd been dined, and there's no occasion to have him again. Now about Heslop of Bustan. Has Heslop been here this year?"

"No, I think not," replied the Marquis. "He was asked, but excused himself on the ground that his Sister-in-law was ill."

"Then I think he had better be asked now. I understand he was a Tory, indeed most of his relations are, so he should be looked after—a doubtful man should always be watched. Now do you know anything about Crossman of Chiswick?" inquired the Duke, writing Heslop's name down.

"Crossman is dead," replied the Marquis.

"*Dead*, is he?" exclaimed the Duke. "Poor fellow—sorry for it, good man. Then he's out of the question."

"Brown Jones, then—do you recollect when Brown Jones was last here?"

"Brown Jones," replied the Marquis, laughing; "that's not his name."

"Oh yes, it is, I have him in my list—own handwriting too," showing it to the Marquis.

"I know all that," rejoined the Marquis, laughing, without looking at the proffered paper. "His nick name is Brown Jones, because he is so very dark, and to distinguish him from another, who is very white; but his real name is John."

"*John* Jones! are you *sure* of that?" exclaimed the Duke.

"*Quite certain!* I remember your setting the table in a roar of laughter by calling out, 'Mr. Brown Jones, may I have the pleasure of taking wine with you?'"

"Well, I do recollect something about that," observed the Duke, laying down his pen and looking especial wise. "I do recollect something about that. Binks whispered in my ear as he helped me to wine—'Mr. *John* Jones is ready to take wine with your Grace'— awkward mistake— *monstrous* awkward mistake; people should never use nicknames—how was I to know his name was John? who knows but I've offended the man, and he's turned Tory? sad mistake, monstrous sad mistake—never heard him called anything but Brown Jones in my life—could have *sworn* his name was Brown Jones—must be asked, however—make it up—shall take your mamma to dinner—mind that, Jeems, and *you* be very civil to him, *monstrous* civil."

Thereupon his Grace added John Jones's name to the list.

"He shall have a bed too," added his Grace, putting a cross to Jones's name, "though he lives in the inner circle."

"Have you got Mr. Jorrocks's name down?" inquired the Marquis, after a pause.

"Mr. Jorrocks! Mr. Jorrocks!" repeated his Grace. "Mr. Jorrocks, of Hillingdon Hall, you know—the old gentleman I stayed with," explained the Marquis.

"Ah, true!" observed his Grace; "I know who you mean—the old gentleman who came here, and sat drink—drink—drinking such an unreasonable time. No, *I've not got him*," said his Grace, with a shake of his bald, white-whiskered head.

"You had better, I think," observed the Marquis.

"Can't stand him! can't stand him!" exclaimed the Duke, shaking his head again; "far too hospitable for me, far too hospitable for me—no getting him away from the table—no getting him away from the table."

"Oh, but you might get some one to drink with him. Old Hobanob, of the Raw, for instance, is fond of his wine, or Mr. Lushman, or Captain Fairdrinker."

"Ah, true; but Mr. Jorrocks is a *desperate* sitter," observed his Grace. "Then he *will* give toasts; I assure you I have hardly got over the headache he gave me when he was here before—desperate sitter! desperate sitter indeed!"

"He's a good old fellow, too," rejoined the Marquis. "Oh, I dare say he's all that—good man—monstrous good man; but he's a hard drinker—monstrous hard drinker—headache-giving old man."

"You have made him a magistrate, too; I think you should have him if it is only for the sake of appearances."

"Ah, that's another misfortune!" exclaimed his Grace, "that's another misfortune. I have got the whole commission up in arms again; all swear they'll resign. Bag full of letters—disagreeable—monstrous disagreeable."

"He's just as good as half of *them*, I dare say," replied the Marquis, determined to stick up for his friend.

"Very true—very true, my dear!" observed the Duke, throwing his white-bearded head up in the air. "Still they do make a great outcry;

they say he can neither speak English nor write it. Certainly his letter to me wasn't first-rate. However, that's done, and we must just make the best of it."

"Then I would have him to dine, if it was only to show you are not ashamed of him," observed the Marquis. "Besides, it is our turn to ask him, you know."

"True, my dear—true; you should keep up your interest, and not lay yourself under obligations: but I think we may do it without sacrificing ourselves too much. That headache I *never shall forget*," added his Grace, with a shudder. "Does he drink much at home?" inquired he.

"Oh no," replied the Marquis, "not to any excess. The first day, you know, we had a public dinner, and there was more speaking than drinking; then, the second, he had a few neighbours—ladies chiefly—and we had music and singing, and so on."

"His daughter's a fine girl," observed the Duke; "monstrous fine girl—ladylike girl."

"He has no daughter," replied the Marquis.

"Oh yes, he has—oh yes, he has," rejoined the Duke; "she dined here—she dined here. Don't you remember her?—blue satin gown on, feather in her head."

"That was not his daughter—that was Mrs. Flather's daughter," said the Marquis, colouring slightly, for he hadn't given over blushing.

"I am sure they called her Miss Jorrocks."

"*You* did, I know," observed the Marquis. "The fact was, she came with Mrs. Jorrocks, and you supposed of course she was Miss Jorrocks."

"Ah, that was the way, was it?" observed the Duke—"that was the way, was it? Very likely—very likely; the servant made the mistake in announcing them, and I adopted it, I dare say. Then he has no children?"

"No," replied the Marquis.

"What does he do when he's at home?" asked the Duke.

"Oh, he's a great farmer," replied the Marquis; "most scientific farmer."

"Is he indeed!" exclaimed his Grace. "Is he indeed," repeated he; "well, now, I should have guessed as much: fine farmer—*monstrous* fine farmer, I dare say."

"Invents all sorts of ingenious things, draining tiles, thrashing machines, and I don't know what else."

"Clever man, I dare say," rejoined his Grace; "monstrous clever man."

"Oh, very clever man," replied the Marquis. "He has a most elaborate piece of machinery in hand now, that is to do I don't know how many things at once."

"Indeed," replied his Grace; "monstrous clever thing, I dare say."

"You had better ask him to dine, and he will tell you all about it," added the Marquis, returning to the old point.

"Ah, that's another question," added the Duke—that's another question—should be very glad to see him to dine—monstrous glad to see him to dine—only he is such a man for his bottle—such a man for toasts—such a man for speeches—such a man for drinking things three times over—gives me a headache to think of it," added his Grace, pressing his hand on his forehead.

"But I dare say we could manage him somehow," observed the Marquis; "get Mr. Slushbucket to meet him—he is a regular two-bottle man."

"Ah, but then Mr. Jorrocks wouldn't be content with him—wouldn't be content with him—besides, Slushbucket would go—Slushbucket has some tact—knows when to go—Jorrocks has none—Jorrocks has none—would victimise me again, to a certainty—couldn't help myself, you know, and then I should have a headache for a week—fortnight perhaps—drinking's a thing quite exploded."

"Except among farmers," observed the Marquis, anxious to shelter his friend.

"Ah, true," replied his Grace; "they take a great deal of exercise—monstrous deal of exercise. Mr. Jorrocks is out all day, I dare say—ploughing, or sowing, or harrowing, or something. No," added his Grace thoughtfully, "I really *cannot* sacrifice myself again so soon to the old gentleman. If I thought Mr. Slushbucket and he would do the business together, I'd have no objection to find wine—none at all—like it rather—for Mr. Jorrocks is a very conversable man—agreeable man—monstrous agreeable man; but then I know exactly how it

would be—Slushbucket would go, and then it would be, 'If your Grace
will allow me, I'll propose the health of the Duchess of Donkeyton,'
whenever Mr. Jorrocks saw me make a move to leave the table—or,
'With your Grace's permission, we'll drink the Marquis of Bray's good
health again;' and so he would go on till midnight. No, we had better
give him something—make him a present—haunch of venison—saddle
of southdown—sucking pig—something of that sort."

"Oh, I dare say he has mutton enough of his own," observed the
Marquis.

"Ah, true," exclaimed his Grace, with an assenting chuck of the
head—"true, true. Well, something else—something farming. Dare
say Jobson could spare us something that might be useful to him—
Dorsetshire ewes—lamb at Christmas—Hampshire hog, or there's that
young bull he talked of taking to the fair—give him that—handsome
present—monstrous handsome present."

"I dare say that would please him," observed the Marquis, who
had heard of Mr. Jorrocks's peregrinations and cogitations about a
bull. Moreover, the Marquis saw the Duke was not to be talked into
having Mr. Jorrocks again, and thinking the present of the bull would
furnish excuse for another visit or two to Hillingdon Hall, he was
content to accept his father's offer. The fact was, the Marquis wanted a
little change—a little excitement. The seclusion of Donkeyton Castle,
though well suited to his Grace's maturer years, was ill adapted to
the warm temperament of the Marquis's juvenile blood. A homebred
youth, reared at his mother's apron strings, he had none of the suitable-
aged companions a public school and college enable a youth to select;
and now, as he advanced to manhood, he felt that yearning after
something—that desire to be doing, incident to youth—and upon the
right direction of which depends so much the happiness of life. The
Duke of Donkeyton was a thick-headed, self-sufficient old man—one
who thought that everybody must like what he liked—and who
could not make allowances for the different tastes difference of age
produces. More over, he wrapped himself in the mantle of his order,
and procured as much ignorance of the world by exclusiveness as his
son possessed from inexperience. Now and then his Grace unbent,

and did a little popularity, as we have seen him on the occasion of
Mr. Jorrocks's visit, and as he now threatened to do by others; but
he soon relapsed into his former stateliness, after having offended as
many by his blunders and want of tact as he pleased by his laboured
condescension. Notwithstanding all this, however, his Grace believed
himself extremely popular, and a perfect pattern of what an English
nobleman ought to be. The Duchess was an amiable woman, but her
sphere of action was naturally contracted, nor is her character important
to our story, further than as her amiable qualities were inherited by the
Marquis.

But to the bull.

His Grace having determined to compliment Mr. Jorrocks with a
bull, in preference to undergoing his agreeable company at dinner, a
messenger was despatched to the farm, to counter-order the animal's
march for the fair, while the Marquis indited the following letter to his
friend, begging to offer him for Mr. Jorrocks's acceptance.

DONKEYTON CASTLE

DEAR MR. JORROCKS,—When I was with you the other day,
you were anxious to procure a fine bull, and as my papa
has a particularly good breed, he has kindly allowed me
to select one for your acceptance, which I have very great
pleasure in offering to you. Our steward tells me he is of
the pure Durham breed, descended from Mr. Collings's
Bolinbroke; his mamma, or whatever you farmers call the
old cow, a descendant of the Godolphin Arabian cow, if I
recollect right—but you shall have his pedigree regularly
drawn up, if you think him worth your acceptance. His
colour is milk white, and he is very tame. I hope Mrs.
Jorrocks is quite well, and that you are getting on with your
thrashing machine. I should like to drive over and see how
you advance. Perhaps you would have the kindness to say
if you are at home, and whether it will be convenient to
you to receive me. My papa and mamma unite with me in

best compliments to Mrs. Jorrocks, and I remain, dear Mr.
Jorrocks, very truly yours,

BRAY

P.S.—I am not quite sure that I am right about the pedigree
of the bull. The steward showed me a young horse at the
same time that was going to the fair, and perhaps I may have
confounded the two; but he will put it all right for you, I
make no doubt.

Mr. Jorrocks was overjoyed at the receipt of the foregoing. A bull was
all he wanted to complete the measure of his happiness. A bull that
would go about the country, and sweep away the prizes, and cause
his master's name to be hailed in booth and tent with plaudits and
acclamation. Now he had got one—*given* too. The following is a copy
of his answer:—

HILLINGDON HALL}
TO WIT}

DEAR MARQUIS OF BRAY,—Yours is received, and note the
contents.

You have conferred an honour on John Jorrocks that
he can never repay—your noble father did me proud by
makin' of me a beak, but your noble self has done me far
prouder by givin' of me a bull. The possession of a bull is
the tip-top rail in the ladder of my hambition. Allow me to
call him the Marquis of Bray; I feels assured he will never
disgrace it—nay, that he will add fresh laurels to those
you have gained. Never mind his pedigree—if he's a good
handler, and straight in the back, I'll make him one from
the Herd Book that can't be surpassed. Collins is a name
jestly dear to us farmers—*dear*, long afore Collins's axles
were inwented. Bolinbroke was indeed a grand bull. His
grandson was the sire of the cow 'Lady,' who at fourteen

was sold for two hundred and sixty guineas. Countess, her daughter, fatched four hundred guineas at nine years old—Major and George, two of her sons, the former three years old, the latter a calf, fatched one two hundred guineas, t'other a hundred and thirty; and, indeed, 'Lady's' progeny are famous throughout the universe. Who knows but your lordship, in givin' of me this bull, has laid the foundation of fame for the name of John Jorrocks, equal to that of the Collins, the Masons, and the Coates' of Scotland? With your permission, I'll go over to Donkeyton on Thursday, to accompany the noble and valuable quadruped 'ome, and the sooner after that your lordship comes to drink his 'ealth at my 'ouse, the better Mrs. Jorrocks and I will be pleased. Dinner at five, and no waitin'; so no more at present from, my dear Lord Marquis, yours to serve,

JOHN JORROCKS, J.P.

P.S.—The Godolphin was an 'oss—not a short'orn— possibly you've mexed the pedigrees, but no matter. Wot you calls my threshin' machine is I s'pose my grand reaper, plougher, sower, thresher, grinder, &c.—'Jorrocks's Generaliser,' or 'man of all work,' as I calls it. I haven't had time to get it stuck together yet; indeed, I'm a thinkin' whether it wouldn't be possible to add a baker's shop and oven; but when you comes over I'll have the joiner at work, and we'll see what we can do. It'll be a grand concern; but at present the bull's the ticket.

On the appointed day Mr. Jorrocks and Benjamin set off in the old rattle-trap to bring the bull from Donkeyton Castle to Hillingdon Hall. Mr. Jorrocks had provided a suitable domicile for him near the house, and laid in a most liberal allowance of straw, cut clover, and every luxury a bull could require. The news of the Marquis's letter was known both at the Manse and Mrs. Trotter's ere our worthy friend had mastered its contents, and both ladies dropped in casually at the Hall to try if they could learn anything about it. Unfortunately Mr. Jorrocks had not returned from his usual stare about the country; and though Mrs. Jorrocks kept turning the letter about on its corners, letting them see who it was from, she did not muster courage to open it. Mr. J. had her in better order.

The Duke of Donkeyton being afraid to encounter Mr. Jorrocks at luncheon even, deputed the Marquis to do the honours of the house to the distinguished visitor; but Mr. Jorrocks having a great contempt for luncheon at all times, and a violent desire to see his bull at the present one, could hardly find time to exchange common civilities with his noble host, who met him as he drove up to the door.

"And how is Mrs. Jorrocks?" asked the Marquis, after he had shaken hands with our worthy friend on alighting from his antediluvian vehicle.

"Quite well. 'Ow's my ball?" inquired he.

"I thought you'd have driven Mrs. Jorrocks or some of the ladies over with you this fine day," observed the Marquis.

"Mrs. J. couldn't have driven the ball 'ome, you know," replied Mr. Jorrocks.

"No; no more can your boy, for that matter, I should think," observed the Marquis, looking at Benjamin's insignificant figure.

"Doesn't know that," replied Mr. Jorrocks, adding, "wot the big 'uns does by strength, the little 'uns does by hartifice."

"Well, but you'll walk in and take a little jelly, chicken broth, or something, after your long drive," said the Marquis.

"I think not, thank you," replied Mr. Jorrocks—"never takes the bloom off my appetite by luncheon—s'pose we walk and see the ball, while Binjimin gets Dickey Cobden a feed o' corn."

"With all my heart," replied the Marquis only it's a long way from here."

"Three or four miles, perhaps," observed Mr. Jorrocks, looking at the soles of his Hessians, and wondering whether Dickey Cobden could draw them there.

"Oh no, only outside the wall—a mile or so."

"A mile's nothin'," observed Mr. Jorrocks with a smile, giving the reins to Benjamin.

The two then set off on foot.

"It is a charming day," observed the Marquis, throwing back his pea-green cashmere coat, lined with silk, and displaying his embroidered braces, pink rowing-shirt, and amber-coloured waistcoat adorned with many chains. "Pray, how are all the ladies?"

"All werry well," replied Mr. Jorrocks; "take care they don't make you the rewerse," added he, with a knowing leer.

"What for?" inquired the Marquis.

"*You* knows wot for," replied Mr. Jorrocks, with a jerk of the head. "Mrs. Trotter'll stand no nonsense," added he; "she's a real knock-me-down man o' business."

"But I've had nothing to do with Mrs. Trotter," replied the Marquis, colouring brightly.

"No; but you've been havin' to do with her darter, she says, and she won't stand no nonsense."

"Oh, the silly woman!" exclaimed the Marquis; "it was Emma Flather I was flirting with."

"Ay, Emma *too*," said Mr. Jorrocks. "Her mother wants to take you through 'ands. Howsomever, never mind. Don't you go too far, or they'll be bringin' of you afore my worship—haw, haw, haw."

"Well, but what do they say?" inquired the Marquis, anxious to know how the land lay.

"Vy, jest *that*," replied Mr. Jorrocks, "that you're a courtin' on 'em both—and the mothers are wise enough to know they can't both get you."

"That's awkward," observed the Marquis aloud, thinking he might flirt with half-a-dozen in London without the others being much the wiser.

"Mrs. Trotter's a fine woman, but I shouldn't like to be basted by her," observed Mr. Jorrocks, shrugging up his shoulders—"she's a divil of a harm."

The Marquis shuddered. "You are joking, Mr. Jorrocks," at length said he.

"Deuce a bit! deuce a bit! they've been at me, both on 'em— layin' informations—layin' informations—trespass on the feelin's—trespass on the feelin's—how somever, as I said before, *don't go too far*."

"*Far!*" exclaimed the Marquis; "why, I've really said nothing!"

"Then you've been a squeezin' their 'ands, or lookin' sweet at them, or somethin', for both the mothers are hup in harms, and when an old 'ooman takes a thing in her, the deuce and all won't drive it out again."

The long silence that ensued brought our friends to the encircling wall, and the Marquis, applying a key to a small green door, let them out on the vulgar world beyond.

They were flow upon the Duke's farm. Lucky it *was* a Duke's farm, for it would have ruined any other man. The spacious house was of the Elizabethan order, guarded by a haw-haw and a shrubbery in front, which rose into forest trees towards the sides, shutting out the huge range of farm buildings behind. The house seemed to possess every requisite for a "genteel family," as the auctioneers advertise. Mrs. Jobson was basking in an arbour on the west side, in an elegant morning dishabille—white muslin, with lavendercoloured ribbons—reading a pocket edition of "Don Juan," when the well-known clap of the door, as the Marquis closed the Park one after him, sent her hurry skurry into the house, to arrange a more attractive attire, beginning, of course with that all-important article in female eyes, an elaborately worked collar. Mr. Jobson was loitering about in a brown sporting buttoned cut-away, duck trousers, and Wellington boots, giving orders to sundry clowns in clogs, who looked far too white and puffy to work. Seeing the Marquis, he came deferentially forward, and, hat in hand, stood to receive his commands His lordship proposed showing Mr. Jorrocks round the establishment, and accordingly a bell was rung at the back of the house, which served as a dinner bell for Jobson, and a summoning bell for the servants. The drones were suddenly called into activity. John Tolpiddle, the Dorsetshire dairyman, came forward in a brown holland blouse, and a short whip in his hand, to show the Cows, some five-and of which stood *dos-à-dos* in a sky-lit byre, littered like Newmarket racers, with a tramway down the centre, for the double purpose of carrying down forage and carrying up litter. The cows were beautifully clean, and the byre as sweet as a drawing-room. The loss upon this branch of the establishment was something under two hundred a year, including

Mr. and Mrs. Tolpiddle's wages, and that was considered very low. It had been as high as four hundred a year, but that was in consequence of his Grace having insisted upon making Cheshire cheese, which the poverty of the pasture had not allowed them to accomplish. The Tolpiddles however, made very good white cheese; and Mr. Jobson with a consideration that did him the highest credit, sooner than his noble master should be disappointed in his prophecy, that ere long they would make as good cheese at Donkeyton as they did in Cheshire, had arranged with another nobleman's Jobson in that county to exchange a certain quantity of cheese annually, and his Grace now ate Cheshire cheese with a hearty gusto, and a firm conviction that it was of his own making. "Let me send you a little Donkeyton Cheshire," he would exclaim, down the table; "excellent cheese—*monstrous* good cheese indeed! Shows what science and perseverance can accomplish. This cheese was made on my own farm, at Strawberry Hill; everybody said it was impossible. I said there was no such thing as an impossibility, and by persevering I've accomplished it. Let me send *you* a piece—just to taste." And so his Grace praised and distributed his cheese round the table, which of course his guests praised also. "Excellent! nothing could be better! better than Cheshire!" "Well, I think so too," his Grace would exclaim. "Binks! the burgundy."

The pigs were next inspected. John Jolter, late of Martyrs Worthy, in Hampshire, had been lured from his native hogs to superintend his Grace's piggery at Donkeyton, and with Mrs. Jolter, and a numerous family of little Jolters, occupied a sentimental-looking cottage in one corner of the spacious square forming the farmyard.

Mrs. Smith, late of Leatherhead, superintended the Dorking fowls; while Mrs. Tubs, late of Pakenham, in Norfolk, had the charge of the turkeys; for each of which a beautifully clean, well-lighted, flued and stoved apartment was kept, above which were pigeon-houses, under the direction of Mr. Kite, the Islington bird-fancier. There were two shepherds, one from Cheviot, the other from Old Shoreham, in Sussex; also goose-driver, from Spalding, in Lincolnshire; and a horse-breaker, from Malton, in Yorkshire. The confusion of tongues, and the confusion of animals, was great.

Mr. Jorrocks went the rounds, as we have seen many a man go the rounds of a house, with ill-assumed interest. All he wanted to see was his ball. At length they arrived at the bull department. These were under the charge of a Durham man, John Topham, late of Middleton St. George. He first brought out one bull, then another, until at length he produced Mr. Jorrocks's "Young Goliah," as he was called. He was a noble animal, milk-white and silky coated, with a curly pow, and a deep dewlap reaching to his knees. He roared and bellowed and pawed the ground, and lashed his tail, as though all the world were his, and the bystanders mere intruders.

"He's an uncommon fine 'un!" exclaimed Mr. Jorrocks, advancing towards him, a liberty the bull resented by rushing headlong at our Squire, and landing him on the top of the midden.

"Take care, my lord! take care, my lord! For God's sake, take care, my lord!" exclaimed half-a-dozen hangers-on, rushing to his assistance, and raising Mr. Jorrocks from his soft, though impure position. "He's not to be trusted with strangers, my lord," added Mr. Jobson, lording our Squire like the rest, for noblemen's servants always fancy noblemen's visitors must be noblemen.

"I fears Binjimin won't be able to take him 'ome," observed Mr. Jorrocks, adjusting his wig, and cleaning himself of the straw.

"Oh, we'll send him for you," observed the Marquis, still laughing at the upset.

"Ah, but I should like to take him 'ome with me," replied Mr. Jorrocks; "there's to be a little festival in our willage in honour of his arrival, and you see we can't rejoice without he's there. He must be introduced as a b*a*ll of his great consequence ought to be—a b*a*ll of consideration, in fact. I fears he will be rayther too many for my bouy Binjimin, though," observed Mr. Jorrocks, eyeing the bull's enormous proportions.

"Oh, a boy would have no chance with him," observed the keeper; "he'd knock a whole troop of them over with his tail. *So*, my man, *so*," added the keeper coaxingly, to the bull, rubbing his hand into his curly pow.

" 'Owever shall I get him 'ome?" inquired Mr. Jorrocks aloud to himself, as the bull began bellowing and roaring and lurching to and fro.

"He's a hawkward customer, I'm a-thinkin', with them polished 'orns of his. He may be a *short* 'orn, but I shouldn't like to have one o' them in my bread-basket, 'owever short."

"Oh, we will send him for you to-morrow," said the Marquis, "in the van; we keep a carriage for the quadrupeds on this farm."

"That's cuttin' it fat," observed Mr. Jorrocks—"'opes he won't expect to have a chay kept with me; but howsomever, you see, I must have him 'ome to-night by 'ook or by crook, or the willagers'll be disappointed of their rejoicin'—bells to ring—children to dance—chaws to shout—self to make a speech, and all that sort of thing. Are there no posters to get in this country? Wouldn't mind standin' eighteenpence a mile for sich an unkimmon fine quadruped. The finest b*a*ll wotever was seen!—b*a*ll of all b*a*lls!"

"Oh, we can manage all that for you," observed the Marquis, who had only to give the order to be obeyed. "Tell them," said he to Jobson, "to put horses to the caravan, and take Mr. Jorrocks's bull home."

"Yes, my lord," replied Mr. Jobson, bowing respectfully.

The cart-horses, however, were all down at the Flemish farm, as a certain portion of Strawberry Hill was called, preparing a piece of ground for another triumph over nature, that of planting potatoes in autumn; and when Mr. Jorrocks and the Marquis returned from paying their respects to Mrs. Jobson, who had got herself and some seed-cake elegantly arranged in the lavender-coloured, silk-furnished drawing-room, notwithstanding the time Mr. Jorrocks had consumed in prefacing the healths of the lady, and of Jobson, and of the Duke of Donkeyton, and of the Duchess of Donkeyton, and of the Marquis of Bray, and of the "Marquis secundus," as he called him, that was to say his b*a*ll, to each of which he drank a bumper of sherry, still, on his return, no horses had arrived. Jobson and Jorrocks then went to seek them; and the Marquis, fearful of walking himself into a fever, took leave of his respected friend, first intimating that he should soon pay him a visit at Hillingdon Hall, and after spending half an hour with his *premier amour*, Mrs. Jobson, he returned alone to the Castle.

Things then relapsed into a very lethargic mood, and the day was far spent before Mr. Jorrocks got his bull into the caravan. Having seen it in and off, he returned to Donkeyton Castle, to get Benjamin and the carriage to follow; but we are ashamed to say, the servants had taken their revenge of Benjamin for winning so much money of them when he was there before, and not bringing any to play with them again, and had made him so drunk that he could not stand. Shocked at the boy's depravity, Mr. Jorrocks curled him up like a codfish, and stuffing him in behind the carriage, drove away as hard as ever Dickey Cobden could lay legs to the ground, to overtake the caravan with the bull. This he was not long in doing, for the driver had pulled up at the first public, and was regaling himself with a pot and a pipe. The consequence of all this was, that the villagers were disappointed of their festival. In vain the big-bustled girls strained their eyes along the turnpike. In vain the chaws climbed on the gates. In vain Joshua Sneakington walked on as far as Old Moor Hill. No symptoms of Mr. Jorrocks or his bull appeared. At length the shades of summer night drew on; the beetles blundered in the waiters' faces, the bats hovered round and round, and the bark of the shepherd's dog was heard more plainly in the evening still. At length Mrs. Jorrocks and her girls beat a retreat. The chaws gradually cleared off, some with their sweethearts, some in couples, some by themselves, and when Mr. Jorrocks arrived a couple of hours after, the road was as clear as if it had never known bustle. The only symptoms of the movement that remained on his arrival was a letter from James Blake, upbraiding him severely for having written to ask to have the bells rung in honour of his bull.

XXIII

And if the night
Have gathered aught of evil, or concealed,
Disperse it, as now light dispels the dark.

EARLY RISERS SEE STRANGE SIGHTS. Mr. Jorrocks's bull kept him in
a state of excitement the whole night. He dreamt all sorts of
horrible dreams. First that the bull-house was on fire, and the bull
wouldn't come out. No, not all the bran mashes and chopped turnips
in the world would induce "the Marquis" to come out. Then with
a last desperate effort, just as he thought he saw the flames catching
the straw behind the bull's tail, he succeeded in landing Mrs. J. with a
terrible flam on the floor; next after he had got Mrs. Jorrocks appeased,
and himself composed to sleep again, he dreamt he saw some idle
boys pull the animal's tail off, and some idle girls join it and another
bull's tail together, and make a skipping rope of them. Then he dreamt
he saw a blue-aproned butcher, with a knife in his hand, and a steel
at his side, arrive for the purpose of slaughtering "the Marquis," and
the effort he made in roaring out *That ar'nt him!* again awoke him.
No sooner was he composed to sleep after this, than he dreamt he
had the bull at the Smithfield Cattle Show, and the judges wouldn't
look at him—next that they gave him the premium, and Sir R. Peel
snatched it from him as he carried it out of the bazaar. Then that Lord
Spencer inveigled him to Althorp, and kept him on oil-cake till he
declared himself an anti-corn-law repealer. That when he was released,
he had grown so fat he couldn't get out of the door. Then that his
lordship put him and his Durham ox, and Prince Albert's Suffolk and
Bedfordshire pig into a caravan, and sent them round the country
as a show—a penny apiece, or twopence for the three. That he (Mr.

Jorrocks) was continually getting stirred up with the long pole to show himself.

At length, feeling the impossibility of procuring anything like comfortable repose, our worthy Cockney Squire determined to vacate his couch altogether, and rose just as a lovely summer sun beamed its first rays upon the beautiful landscape, gilding wood and water, hill and dale, with the luxuriance of its effulgence. Autumn was coming on. The reapers had been busy in many parts, and the golden corn stood in sheaf and stook in all the early places. Mr. Jorrocks surveyed the all-beauteous landscape from his room, and dressing himself in thick shoes, drab shags and gaiters, instead of the blue stockingettes and Hessians of the previous day, determined upon taking a ramble about the country, ere the harvesting population were abroad. Having first visited his bull, and found none of the direful calamities he had dreamt had befallen him, and having foddered him, and littered out his stall, and admired his just proportions, now seen to greater advantage without the competitors of Mr. Jobson's establishment, Mr. Jorrocks set out on his rambles. First he looked at Tompkins's sheep winding round the side of Holford Hill, then he stared Johnny Wopstraw's cows out of countenance—wondered how much milk each gave—whether the milk made good cream—and how much cheese the dairy produced. Then he sauntered on, and admired Willey Goodheart's cart-horses enjoying their rest, during the progress of the harvest—calculated how much each could draw—priced them separately—thought how much each would sell for at Tatt's; then lumped them all together and struck an average. Then he hung over a gate opening into Tommy Sloggers' fallow—counted the thistles till he couldn't count them for thickness—calculated their probable produce next year—admired the brackens, and wondered whether the fallow was meant for a wheat or a bracken crop. Thought nothing could beat Sloggers for dirt—was sure he would get the prize for slovenliness. Had a good mind to walk on and knock at his door and tell him so. Thought perhaps he'd better not. Didn't like to be bit. Thought how often he had been bit in horse-dealing. Run his hunters through his mind, and thought he might write a paper, headed, "My 'Osses, by Jorrocks." Stared at Smith's stack, wondered how many tons of hay it held. How long his bull would be in eating it. Thus our farmer friend sauntered over hill and over dale, now standing with his mouth open inhaling the fresh morning air, admiring the prospect, or wondering whether it would be a good harvest—whether the yield would be deficient—whether the straw would be short or not—and considering whether money in the funds or money in a farm was the safest spec; thought it very odd that while all the farmers swore everything was ruinously cheap, yet if he happened to want anything, that article was invariably dear. Tried to make out how it was that lime was only a manure when given by the landlord, and possessed no "wirtues" when the tenant had to buy it. The more Mr. Jorrocks thought, the more he was puzzled about farming.

He had now got upon Mr. Heavytail's, or the "pet farm." Here he saw people astir on the side of the hill, and looking at his watch, and finding it yet wanted twenty minutes to five, he gave Mr. Heavytail or his people credit for great industry. They were in a corn-field setting up the sheaves that no doubt had toppled over. No, they were on the part where the corn had been led. What could they be after? They crawled about as if they were after no good, now down the hedge side, now across the field corner, now flat on their bellies. They must be waggabones. He would go and see.

Accordingly our friend crept stealthily round the hill, keeping under the walls and the hedges, taking an occasional peep to see that he was going in the line of the objects he had seen. At length he reached the adjoining field. He buttoned his coat, drew his breath, and availing himself of a deep ditch on his side, passed quickly along.

"Crikey, but here's a plummy one!" from a shrill voice, told him that he was close upon the delinquents, and starting up by the side of a big tree, Mr. Jorrocks came upon Benjamin just as he was wringing the neck of a partridge that Joshua Sneakington had handed him from the net.

Benjamin stared like one possessed, for the fumes of the Donkeyton Castle drink were still upon him, and he gave a half-frightened idiotic sort of laugh, as though he didn't know whether to cry or be pleased.

Joshua Sneakington turned deadly pale, his compressed lip quivered, and his hand shook so that the unslaughtered partridges availed themselves of the commotion, and slipt out of the net.

"YOU INFERNAL WILLAINS!" roared Mr. Jorrocks with doubled fists from the top of the hedge, "I'LL TRANSPORT YOU ALL AND 'ANG THE REST," a declaration that had the effect of sobering Benjamin, who dropped on his knees, and with clasped hands began clamouring for mercy—"*Mercy! Mercy! Mercy!*" exclaimed he "it was all this infernal willain wot forced me to it— there weren't a better-disposed bye in all the world afore I got acquainted with this great hugly thief," casting an indignant glance at the still trembling Joshua.

"You warmint," grinned Mr. Jorrocks, still standing with clenched fists, gasping for rage, and meditating whether to jump atop of Benjamin or not.

"Indeed I'm innocent, sir," continued Benjamin, looking imploringly at his master. "There weren't a more wirtuous amiable bye than I was af ore I got corrupted by that amazin' great willain. He's enough to ruin a county."

Joshua now began to recover his senses, and looking beseechingly up at the still bristling, eye-glistening Squire, was beginning, "Oh, your worship!"

"Don't vorship me!" roared Mr. Jorrocks, "you unmitigated scamp. No wonder my partridges are few, and the fizzants don't crow as they used. Get out o' my sight, you double-distilled essence of roguery, or assuredly I'll murther you; I'll ram your 'at down your puritanical throat, and stuff a stockin' arter it."

Joshua took the hint and strode quickly away, cursing his unlucky stars for having embarked in such a speculation, and wondering what would come of it all.

Benjamin, like a licked cur, then came to "heel," and followed Mr. Jorrocks, exonerating himself and inculpating Joshua as he went. Benjamin had had enough of Joshua, and wasn't sorry to get rid of him. First he told all about the netting, and how Joshua had a pheasant call that would draw all the pheasants out of the covers, and how he had been making pies of the young ones already. He also showed Mr.

Jorrocks where he had fed the partridges, and the sticks and furze bushes he had used to prepare them for the mysteries of the net, and how Joshua took them, and all how and about it in fact.

Mr. Jorrocks having learnt all he could, put Dickey Cobden to his carriage immediately after breakfast, and drove himself and Benjamin over to his friend Captain Bluster's, where, after a full disclosure by Benjamin of all, and perhaps a little more than he knew, they concocted a three months' committal for Joshua, which our friend thought it better to put up with than risk a severer sentence at sessions. So great was his popularity, that half the village of Hillingdon visited the prison during the time he was there, for the pleasure of seeing Joshua in gaol.

XXIV

Soon as the morning trembles o'er the sky,
And unperceived, unfolds the spreading day,
Before the ripened field the reapers stand,
In fair array, each by the lass he loves,
To bear the rougher part, and mitigate
By nameless gentle offices her toil.

THOMSON'S SEASONS

JOSHUA SNEAKINGTON BEING COMFORTABLY PROVIDED for in gaol, Mr. Jorrocks had an inward inquiry as to how it was that he, a sharp London merchant, had been done by such a country lout as Joshua—Jorrocks, who had once got to the windward of Rothschild in a deal, and who was reckoned the second-best judge of treacle in the trade. To carry the inquiry out, our friend called in the assistance of his neighbours, who, as usual, "knew it all before." "Oh, they knew all about it! Didn't *he* know? Well, now, that was odd! If they'd only thought *that*, they'd have told him directly. Joshua was the greatest rogue in the country; Joshua had cheated everybody—had cheated them, had cheated Brown, had cheated Green, had cheated Brown Jones, had cheated White Jones—would rob a church—should have been transported long since;" in short, gave Mr. Jorrocks such information as caused him to doubt whether all the knavery was really settled in London, and all the honesty in the country.

An Uxbridge, a Watford, or a Twyford waggoner, in his gosling-green embroidered breasted frock, round-crowned ticketed hat, clumsy packthread-pointed whip, and enormous hob-nailed highlows, wending his way along Holborn or Oxford Street, with his rough-coated, mud-stained team, and a rickety wain, had always appeared to Mr. Jorrocks the impersonification of simplicity and rural honesty. If he had wanted his washing sent into the country, or a goose brought from it, he felt as if he could have trusted one of these simple-looking chawbacons, without "noting" the contents of the bundle, or limiting him as to price for the goose. Far otherwise did he feel with regard to any of Meux's, or Barclay and Perkins's "hey the whays!" with their red nightcaps, plush breeches, dirty cotton stockings, and bluchers. They, he felt certain, would put the bundle "up the spout," or make purl or "half-and-half" of the goose money.

Such were the ideas with which Mr. Jorrocks had emigrated into the country—ideas not uncommon, we believe, among those whose lives, like his, have been spent in the great city of London; and now, at his age, to awake to the unpleasant conviction that there were as big thieves in the country as in London, was rather startling and unpleasant; worse still to think that he had been victimised by one of the fraternity. Joshua had had a fine time of it. His respectable appearance, his plausible tongue, his subtle management, aided by Mr. Jorrocks's unsuspecting confidence and self-sufficiency, had afforded him opportunities that his able mind knew well how to make the most of. *He had bit him.*

Joshua had certainly been of use to Mr. Jorrocks—but for him, our worthy friend would have paid about double for everything that he bought, and been desperately cheated in bulls, and all farming transactions; and now that Joshua was on the "mill," Mr. Jorrocks began to feel the loss of his managing mind. Benjamin was of no use whatever out of doors; indeed he candidly told his master one day, when he wanted him to lead ashes out with Dickey Cobden, that "he didn't profess to be a farmer."

Plenty of people offered for the vacant situation, but Mr. Jorrocks was afraid and durst not venture. His time and thoughts were divided between his bull, and the question who should be Joshua's successor. The bull was very expensive. Before Mr. Jorrocks had had him a week, he had been the means of consuming half a dozen of sherry and a suitable quantity of seed-cake, everybody that called being supposed to have come to see the quadruped. Indeed, he was the cause of a sore disappointment to Mrs. Flather. "You must come and see the Markis," said Mr. Jorrocks in an offhand sort of way to her, coming out of church on the Sunday after the bull's arrival; and, accordingly, Emma and she arrived, tricked out in their very best, and found that the "Markis" he meant was the bull.

The factotum question was very perplexing. Mr. Jorrocks thought over everybody, from Bill Bowker downwards, and could not hit upon any one qualified for the post. The farmer's instructor was floored. In truth, it was rather a difficult office to undertake, having to lead the blind leader of the blind. Mr. Jorrocks began to suspect that he was not quite so wise as he thought. That, however, he kept to himself.

It was on a bright summer afternoon, when the harvest was at its height, and joyful cheers rang ever and anon on the surrounding landscape, denoting that now another and another farmer's fears were over, by the last of his corn getting cut, that Mr. Jorrocks, still meditating and uncertain, sauntered from his house by the more unfrequented paths, and sought the sweet communion of nature, without the interruption of mankind. The country was in full beauty. The green grass shot forth vigorously, obliterating the scythe marks of the mower; the clover presented a fragrant second crop; turnip fields were unfolding their leafy honours; and all these, commingled with the waving corn, or dotting stooks of golden grain with the purple heather of the higher lands, or sky-line breaking larch or pine of the hill tops, presented a rich mixture of primeval nature and agricultural improvement. The trees were still in full leaf, and though autumn's later tints were wanting, still there was a goodly mixture of foliage, by the dotting of the gay larch, or sombre spruce, or darker pine, among the masses of oak wood, while the white birch stood outside in gay relief against the rest. The loaded corn-fields scattered here and there among the woods diversified the landscape, and presented a rich picture of bounteous plenty.

Mr. Jorrocks sauntered on, now across the green sward, now hip-high in waving corn through the field path, now forcing a way through the rank grass and concealing brambles of the wood track, and now roaming again upon the wilder turf, sprinkled with heather and field flowers. At length he got into one of those now rarely met with passages, a green

lane. It was a real green lane. Scarce a cart-rut broke its even surface, and
its verdure was kept so close nipped by cattle, that the traveller had not
sufficient temptation to keep in any track, so as to form one decided
foot-way. It was one of those continuous lines of by-roads frequented
chiefly by cattle-drovers. The woodbine-entwined and rose-bending
bushes of the high hedges in the narrow parts formed a cool shade,
while broader places, widening into patches of common towards the
hill-tops (over which these roads always pass), furnished cheap pasture
for the loitering cattle.

As luck would have it, just as our Squire got to the narrowest path of
this green lane, and within a hundred yards of where he meant to turn
off, to make a circuit back to Hillingdon Hall, he encountered a large
drove of Scotch kyloes, picking their way as they went. There might
be fifty or sixty of them, duns, browns, mottles, reds, and blacks, with
wildness depicted in the prominent eyes of their broad faces.

"*Hup! How! How!*" cried our Squire, throwing up his arms to get
them to clear a passage for him, a movement that only threw confusion
into the herd, and caused them to butt and run foul of each other. They
didn't seem to care twopence for the Justice.

"Had bye, ar say, there!" holloaed a voice from behind, accompanying
the demand with a crack of his stick on the quarter of the hindmost
kyloe.

"*You* get out o' the vay, I say!" roared Mr. Jorrocks, indignant at being
spoken to in such a manner.

"God smash! how can ar get out o' the way?" replied the same voice,
again visiting the hindmost kyloe with a crack. "De ye think a kyley's
like a huss, that yean (one) can pull about by the gob?"

Mr. Jorrocks again raised his arms, and by dint of *shew! shew! shewing!*
and keeping close to the hedge, succeeded in forcing his way through
the herd.

He now got a sight of the drover, as the latter rose a short hill that had
kept him below the level of the cattle. He was a tall ungainly-looking
man, in a Scotch cap, with the lower part of his face muffled up in a
plaid, which, spreading in ample fold across his chest, was confined
by the fringed end under the right arm. A rudely-cast brass shamrock

and thistle decorated the red and grey border of the woollen cap, in which was stuck a splendid eagle's feather, that stood boldly above the crown. Long, straggling, iron-grey locks escaped from below the cap's close-fitting sides, making the aquiline nose and bright hazel eyes of the wearer more conspicuous.

The upraised arms, now employed in frightening, now in beating the cattle, displayed the dark green tartan, of which the wearer's little butler's-pantry sort of jacket was made; while a very short, much-stained, red waistcoat kept at a very respectful distance from a pair of very baggy, drab, shag breeches, confined at the knees with buttons of various colours and patterns. First, on the right leg came a large white one, with a fox, and an L below it; then a black horn one; then a large yellow one with a fox and an N; then a button with a coronet and a bunch of hieroglyphics; followed on by a white button with a fox's mask. On the left leg the row began again with a large button of the fox and L pattern, followed on by a black horn one, then a gilt one, with a ducal coronet and a B below; then came another yellow one, with another bunch of hieroglyphics; and the bottom one was a gilt one, with a fox's mask, and three letters.

The jean gaiters, which were uncommonly tight, as if to show the spindleness of the wearer's shanks and the profuseness of his breeches, were decorated, if possible, with a greater variety of buttons, there being, in addition to the yellow and white ones, some of a mixed species, and some few non-sporting ones, of coloured glass.

"Vy don't you get out o' the way with your nasty lousy Scotch cattle?" exclaimed Mr. Jorrocks, as he neared the uncouth figure.

The eagle-plumed hero stood transfixed.

"Don't you hear vot I said, man?" inquired Mr. Jorrocks, speaking louder, and standing on a green hillock, as if to increase his importance by height.

"God smash, if it ar'nt the ard Squire!" exclaimed the figure "why, dinnut ye ken yean?" added he, taking off his Scotch bonnet, and lowering the plaid from before a very tobacco-stained mouth.

"Vy, *it's James Pigg!*" exclaimed Mr. Jorrocks, jumping down and running towards him. "James, my good frind, 'ow d'ye do?"

"Nicely, thank ye; how's theesel?" replied James, pulling off a greasy old glove, and offering his hand, saying, "Give us a wag o' thy neif."

Mr. Jorrocks and he then shook hands.

"D—n, but ar's glad to see thee," said James, as soon as their hands were released. "Ah, God, what a belly thou's getten," added he, eyeing his late master's corporation.

"And vot are you arter now, James?" inquired Mr. Jorrocks, without noticing the observation.

"Ah, ar's getten a livin' just how ar can—whiles yean thing, whiles another. Ar's travellin' beast enow. Ye dinna want ne beast ar's warn'd, de ye?" added he, pointing to the drove.

"Vy, no, I thinks not, James," replied Mr. Jorrocks; "but vere do you come from now—vere are you livin', in fact?"

"Ah, ar's livin' aside canny Newcassel. You ken canny Newcassel, where the coals come frae?"

"Ah, the Vallsenders," replied Mr. Jorrocks; "then you've left your uncle, Deavilboger, 'ave you?" added he, remembering his late huntsman's former locality.

"Why, no, ar's not; ar's drivin' for the ard Deavil enow. He's mar coosin, not my uncle."

"Vell, but tell us all about it. Here, set down on this bank," continued Mr. Jorrocks, pointing to a hillock under the high hedge near where they stood. "Take off that rambustical thing," added he, touching Pigg's plaid, "and let's sit on it."

"Ay, to be sure," said Pigg, unfolding it from his chest. "It's mar *plaide*: ar's getten mar frilled sark, everyday breeks, and Sunday shun (shoes) in it," pointing to a bump at the sewn-up end of the plaid, which he placed for himself to sit down by.

"Vell, now," said Mr. Jorrocks, adjusting himself comfortably, "tell us all how and about it—the cattle'll pick quietly along the green lane, and a rest'll do you no 'arm this 'ot day. Tell us now, vot 'ave you been a doin' since we parted?—'ow does the world use you? Wot's there a goin' on in Scotland? How's Deavilboger? 'Ave you got a wife yet? 'Ow are the markets with you?"

"Ay, the Deavil's gay and well," interrupted Pigg, knowing his late master's propensity for stringing on questions; "how's theesel? ye did not chew neane, ar's warn'd," added he, producing a japanned tobacco-box, and offering Mr. Jorrocks a quid.

Mr. Jorrocks declined.

Having replenished his own mouth, James clasped his hands upon his rugged oak staff, and sticking out his legs, leant forward upon it.

"Vot a lot o' rum *battons* you've got on your breeches and gaiters," observed Mr. Jorrocks, looking at Pigg's legs.

"Ay," replied Pigg, cocking up one of his spindle shanks, "the breeks is a pair o' yeer ard 'uns; they're what ye had on the day t' ard huss coup'd ye into the bog."

"I minds it, James Pigg!" exclaimed Mr. Jorrocks, brightening up at the recollection. "I minds it," repeated he, taking hold of the old shags—"many a good run I've seen in them breeches, many a one again in Surrey and elsewhere—dear old things," continued Mr. Jorrocks, rubbing his hand down them as he would down a horse. "You've done them justice in the batton line, I'm glad to see," observed he. "Lots o' foxes! lots o' fine things! Coronets, and I don't know wot!"

"Ay, *lots*," replied Pigg, with an emphasis. "Sink it, ar's glad ar put them on to-day. They're mar lucky breeks. Ah, they're a grand sight o' buttons! Ah, they're worth a vast o' money! Ah, they're good for sore eyes! That yean," putting his thumb on the white button, and polishing it up a little, "was Squire Lambton's. Ah, a grand man! Sic a man for the hoont. Ah, as canny Codlin used to say, ye may get prime beef, and prime mutton, and prime ministers, but ye'll niver get sic a prime sportsman as Ralph Lambton again. Ah, he was a grand 'un," added Pigg, polishing it again. "The next yean's Sir Matthew's, a fox and a B for Blagdon," continued Pigg, putting his thumb on the yellow button; "grand man, Sir Matthew, grand kennel, grand stable."

"That's an N, James," observed Mr. Jorrocks, looking attentively at the button.

"No, it's a B," replied Pigg, "at least it should be a B; or else' it's an R for Ridley."

"This is Elcho's," continued he, proceeding with the exhibition—"a lord's hat, with a lot o' sarpents below."

"Them's letters," observed Mr. Jorrocks, trying to decipher them.

"Elcho's a grand man," observed Pigg, without noticing his late master's observation; "ar's thinkin' of shiftin' him to t'other leg," turning the left one partially round, "and then ard Squire Lambton and he may glower at each other. Take these black 'uns off," said Pigg, "and put an Elcho on each side, perhaps. Ah, he's a grand man, Elcho! Ah, how he can ride! Ah, how he can go! Ah, what a pack o' hunds he has! Ah, how he does dust the foxes! Ye should see his ard dog Contest. Faith he's gotten wor ard huss, Arterxerxes."

"Arterxerzes! you don' say so, James," exclaimed Mr. Jorrocks.

"Ay, has he," replied Pigg, turning the quid in his mouth; "grand huss he is too—not the best Elcho has though, by mony."

"Vell, I'm glad to hear the old 'oss is in good 'ands," observed Mr. Jorrocks cheerfully; "he carried me well sometimes."

"He was ower mony for *thou*," observed Pigg. "He was aye tumblin' of ye down. Do you mind when we had to saw ye out o' the thorn hedge?"

" 'Deed do I!" exclaimed Mr. Jorrocks, in ecstasies; "wot a run that was! saw them pin the warmint in the corner of the stubble-field by the stacks, as I was stuck up aloft in the thorn. Those were fine times, James! those were fine times!"

"*Ay were they!*" replied Pigg, wiping his tobacco-stained mouth across the back of his hand. "Sink it, what brandy we used to drink! Have never had a real good drench since, but yance at Squire Russell's. Sink," added he, giving his knee-cap a haarty slap, "if the butler didn't give me as much brandy as ever I could haud (hold). Grand man, Squire Russell! That's his button," added Pigg, pointing to a gilt one, with twisted letters. "Ar'll have him put higher up when ar shifts Elcho," added Pigg, eyeing its present position. "Thir, on the gaiters, are most deadly 'uns," observed Pigg, glancing down his legs. The twe top 'uns are Handley Cross, wor ard buttons. This yean, with the raised sarpents," taking hold of a yellow button with raised letters at the top of the right leg, "was Lord London darry's. He got the Sedgefield country when Squire Lambton gave it up. Ard Price gave me the button. That plain yean was Squire Williamson's. Ah, he was a grand man for the hoont. The next was the ard Duke o' Cleveland's. Got a duke's hat, you see," added he, turning the button for Mr. Jorrocks's inspection. "Raby hoont, as it was called," added Pigg, letting it go again. "Ar's getten another duke's button some where," continued the showman, looking at his legs. "Buccleuch's; ay, here it's," said he, "among the whick 'uns," pointing to one at his breeches knees. "Duke's hat, you see," said he, "and B, for Buccleuch—grand man, Buccleuch; Mr. Williamson, the hunts-man, gav me the button—grand man, Mr. Williamson!"

"Ay, ay, you're all grand men you Scotchmen, accordin' to your own accounts," interrupted Mr. Jorrocks; "it's the old story of 'claw me, and I'll claw ye.'"

"Sink, ar's ne Scotchman," replied Pigg, indignant at the observation. "It's all gospel what I've telled ye."

"Vy, if you're not a Scot, you're next door to one," observed Mr. Jorrocks; "jest as much a Scot as a Borough man's a Londoner."

"Why, ye ard gouk," exclaimed Pigg, "doesn't ar tell ye ar lives aside canny Newcastle; how the deavil then can ar be a Scot?"

"Vy, I don't know," replied Mr. Jorrocks soothingly, "you certainly speak rayther Scotchy."

"Hoot, that's all fancy," replied Pigg; "it's just because ar's getten a *plaide*," added he, taking hold of the thing on which they were sitting.

"Vell," observed Mr. Jorrocks smilingly, "it may be—it may be, my good frind—let us talk about Deavilboger and his farm."

"Sink the farm!" exclaimed Pigg, "ar niver talks about farmin' when ar can talk about huntin'—yean wad ha thought now you'd have liked to have heard tell all about mar grand buttons," said Pigg, looking lovingly down his legs.

"*Dash your buttons*," grunted Mr. Jorrocks aloud; "tell me what do you do when you're not cattle-drivin'?"

"Why, I works for mar cousin, Deavilboger," growled Pigg; "ploughs, dikes, sows, reaps—aught in fact."

"Tell me, now," asked Mr. Jorrocks, has Deavilboger a ball?"

"Bull! Ay!" exclaimed Pigg, "grand bull, best i' the country, took two prizes—gold shoe-horn—silver wine-funnel."

"And you're not reg'larly hired to Deavilboger, I s'pose?" inquired Mr. Jorrocks.

"Not by the year," replied Pigg; "I warks piece wark."

"Vot's that?" inquired Mr. Jorrocks.

"Why, se much for dein' se much—ten shillin's for turnin' a midden— five shillin's for cleanin' a fard and se on."

"Humph," grunted Mr. Jorrocks, not catching all the last sentence. "I s'pose," observed he, "that reg'lar wages are better than piece-work."

"Ne doot," replied Pigg, "ne doot; but yean cannot always get them, ye ken."

"Humph," grunted Mr. Jorrocks, considering how he should sound him. "I s'pose you'd like to get a good place?"

"Ne doot," replied Pigg, "ne doot, where there are some hunds."

"You wouldn't like a farm-servant's place, I s'pose?" observed Mr. Jorrocks.

"A faith, ar's not sarcy! ar'd turn my hand to aught."

"Or go anywhere?" asked Mr. Jorrocks.

"Ah, arll places is alike to me," replied Pigg. "Ar's getten a bit shop enow that mar missus keeps, but ar could soon shut that up."

"Vot, you've got a missus, 'ave you?" observed Mr. Jorrocks.

"Housekeeper, that's to say," replied Pigg, "housekeeper—*ar niver marries them*," added he, with a shake of the head.

"And vot do you sell?" inquired Mr. Jorrocks.

"Why, tape, pins, thread, buttons, galluses, ony thing—ye didna want ne galluses, ar's warn'd, de ye?"

"No vot?" inquired Mr. Jorrocks.

"*Galluses*," repeated Pigg—"things to had your breeks up by," explained he.

"No, but I thinks *you* do," replied Mr. Jorrocks, looking at the great interregnum between Pigg's red waistcoat and shags.

"Ah, sink, ar never wears neane," replied Pigg, turning his quid; "but I mun be gannin," added he, with a start, it's foour o'clock, I see!"

"How do you see that?" asked Mr. Jorrocks.

"By the shearers yonder," replied Pigg, his keen eye glancing to a distant hill where the workpeople had just left off. "Well, ar's main glad to see thou," said he, rising himself from the bank with his staff—"*deed is ar*," continued he, standing and looking at his late master, adding—"ye dinna drink ne brandy now, ar's warn'd."

"I'll give *you* summut to get a glass with," observed Mr. Jorrocks, with a smile, diving his hand into his breeches pocket, and producing a great five-shilling piece. "There," said he, "there's a dollar for you, and when you've delivered your cattle, if you come back this way I'll give you another, and meanwhile I'll try to get you a place."

"Ah, you're a grand man," replied Pigg, taking the five-shilling piece, with a duck of the head. "Ah, you *are* a grand man," repeated he, as he eyed it. "Ye dinna want ne sarvant yoursel, ar's warn'd?"

"I lives about a mile and an 'alf from here," observed Mr. Jorrocks, pointing in the direction of the village of Hillngdon. "You ask for Squire Jorrocks; anybody can tell ye where I lives."

"Ne doot," replied Pigg, "ne doot; ar' warned ye, ar'll find ye out," added he, hitching up his breeches, and adjusting the plaid as it was when we found him. Having taken leave of his former master, he then proceeded, *hup howing*, on his way.

"Rum betch, that fellow!" said Mr. Jorrocks aloud to himself, as Pigg left him; "shouldn't wonder if he might suit me."

XXV

That well-known name awakens all my woes.

ANOTHER LETTER WITH THE MARQUIS'S coronet again threw the village of Hillingdon into commotion. His lordship wanted another turn with his agricultural friend, or rather a little flirtation under pretence of a visit to him. Thus he wrote:—

DONKEYTON CASTLE

DEAR MR. JORROCKS,—I was glad to hear your bull arrived safe, and sorry to hear that your coachman was taken ill at our house the other day—I hope, however, he is better, and that there is nothing to prevent your receiving me at Hillingdon Hall on Thursday next, when I purpose driving over, and staying all night. Pray write me a line, saying if it will be convenient, and with best regards to the ladies, believe me, dear Mr. Jorrocks, yours very truly,

BRAY

The following is Mr. Jorrocks's answer:—

HILLINGDON HALL}
TO WIT}

MY DEAR LORD MARQUIS,—Yours, of no date, is received, and note the contents. We shall be most proud to receive you on Thursday—dinner at five, and no waitin'. My bull arrived safe; thanks to your lordship for lending of me your wan. It would have taken *his* lordship a precious long time to waddle here. I don't think he can go much above a mile

an hour. But he's a noble quadruped! Uncommon! The admiration of
the country. All the ladies come to look at him. Dare say he's cost me
a dozen of wine already—sponge biscuits in proportion. Wot you calls
my 'coachman,' is my bouy Binjimin, I s'pose; some o' your long, lazy
Johnnies made him drunk. Scandalous work! Howsomever, I licked him
uncommon; and if your chaps had their licks too, it wouldn't do them
no harm. Intoxication is a beastly wice. Bad in a man, but shockin' in a
bouy. I wonders you great men don't keep a private treadmill for your
Johnnies. Howsomever that's enough! so 'oping to see you, I remain,
my dear Lord, yours to serve,

John Jorrocks, J.P.

August 29th, 184—.

To the most noble the Marquis of Bray

Mr. and Mrs. Jorrocks had a most solemn argument as to who they
should have to meet the Marquis. Mr. Jorrocks rather inclined to Mrs.
Flather, while Mrs. Jorrocks insisted upon inviting Mr. and Mrs. Trotter
and Eliza. In fact, she had done it before she argued the point; and
finding that to be the case, Mr. Jorrocks invited the Flathers also, so
that between them they made what Mr. Jorrocks called "a pretty kettle
of fish."

The day but one before that fixed for the Marquis's visit, Mr.
Jorrocks, while taking his daily stroll, ascended the hill leading up to
Mr. Heavytail's pet farm. Mr. Heavytail was exceedingly busy, preparing
for his harvest home. The shearers were at work on the north side of
the hill, and the golden grain stood in well-filled stooks in most of
the fields around. It had been a capital harvest. The weather had been
all that could be wished, and Mr. Heavytail was going to evince his
gratitude by giving his servants and labourers a plentiful repast at the
close. The large barn was swept out, rustic chandeliers hung from the
rafters, and block-tin candle-holders were stuck promiscuously into the
walls. Mrs. Heavytail was equally busy. She was making mountainous
plum-puddings, and skewering corresponding rounds of beef—cheese,
too, appeared likely to be abundant.

"Vell, Mr. 'Eavytail," said Mr. Jorrocks, poking his way into the barn, with his hands behind his back, in his usual vacant sort of way, "vot are you arter now? goin' to give a lector, are you?" added he, looking at the illuminatory preparations.

"GOOD MORNIN', SIR," roared Mark, as if Jorrocks was half a mile off; "GETTING READY FOR OUR HARVEST HOME, YOU SEE," continued he, pointing to the candles and some old banners, with the usual agricultural mottoes, "Live, and let live," "Speed the plough," and so on, upon them.

"So," said Mr. Jorrocks, eyeing the proceedings, "goin' to 'ave a little procession, are ye? speech—frinds and fellow-farmers!" continued he, extending his right arm.

"IT'S FOR OUR SUPPER NIGHT, SIR," roared Heavytail—"FINISH OUR HARVEST ON THURSDAY—GIVE THE MEN A SUPPER, WIVES A TEA, THEN COME IN HERE AND DANCE—ALL DRESSED UP, MEN AS WOMEN, WOMEN AS MEN, AND SO ON."

"Vot fun!" exclaimed Mr. Jorrocks, shuffling with his feet, as if he would set to.

"FIDDLERS TO PLAY!" continued Mark, pointing to a chair, "STRONG ALE FOR THE MEN, TEA FOR THE LADIES AGAIN."

"Tea for the ladies again!" observed Mr. Jorrocks; "I'd give them a little strong ale too I thinks! And is this annual?" asked Mr. Jorrocks, "once a year, in fact?" seeing Mark didn't take the first question.

"OH YES," replied Mark, "EVERY YEAR—GRAND FUN."

"So I should think," observed Mr. Jorrocks aloud to himself; "vish I was a *real* farmer," added he, "instead of one of these harm-chair 'umbugs—*phee*losiphers what they call."

But to return to the ladies.

When Mrs. Flather and Mrs. Trotter found they were both invited (which they speedily learned from the servants, from that rural parliament, "the well"), each made up her mind not to go, and nothing but the dread of the other stealing a march prevented theft sending excuses. It was quite clear how it was—Mr. Jorrocks wanted to keep in with both; at all events he wouldn't give either of them a lift. The result was, that each mother strove her utmost to set her daughter off to advantage. Mrs. Flather adhered to the blue silk that did so much execution at Donkeyton Castle, while Mrs. Trotter arrayed the beautiful brunette in a new pale pink silk, with an old rich point-lace berthe, that varying fashion had twice seen in favour. She had also got her a new bustle of very liberal dimensions.

The Marquis arrived in his brougham, as before, in ample time to allow his French valet to make an uncommon swell of him. His fair hair hung over his ears in longer ringlets than usual, and his shirt frill and front were perfect curiosities in the way of lace and needlework. A very stiif starcher rose above the low velvet Collar of his light blue coat, the neckcloth matching in whiteness the purity of his waistcoat, while his nankeen trousers were slightly shaped over the instep, to display the exquisite texture of his stockings, and his small buckles and French-polished pumps. Rings, brooches, buttons, chains, &c., were in their usual profusion.

Scarcely had the Marquis flourished round the drawing-room, and lisped out the usual nothings about the company, worsted work, the view, and the weather, ere Benjamin announced Mrs. and Miss Flather, who greeted the visitor in a motherly and half-bashful lover-like sort of way. Before he had got in full swing with the fair Emma, the door opened again, and lo! the goodly proportions of Mrs. Trotter filled the portal, followed by her diminutive husband and her eye-dazzling daughter.

The Marquis was thunderstruck. He never thought his agricultural friend would be such a fool as invite them together, especially after the hint Mr. Jorrocks had volunteered on his way to Mr. Jobson's. The consequence was the Marquis was tongue-tied, and instead of indulging in all manner of high-flown sentiment in a lover-like undertone, he was obliged to speak up, while the mothers sat watching each move like the lookers-on at a chess table.

A most tedious dinner was the result. Nor did the Marquis's misery end with the retirement of the ladies, for little Trotter stayed, and the conversation turned upon turnips. At length the trio returned to the drawing-room, and after a yawning, uneasy hour, Mrs. Flather said something about avoiding the evening dew, and having forced Mrs.

Trotter into an assent, cloaks, shawls, and bonnets were sought out, and the meeting dispersed.

"It's a werry fine evenin'," observed Mr. Jorrocks to the Marquis, as he returned from setting them to the door—"werry fine evenin' indeed," added he, looking at his great noisy watch, and finding that it still wanted a quarter to nine. "Wot shall we do with ourselves?"

"We might have set the ladies home if we'd thought of it," observed the Marquis, who had thought of it very intently, but did not know how to manage it.

"We might so," replied Mr. Jorrocks, with a vacant yawn.

"I've 'alf a mind," said he, after a pause, "to stroll up to Mr. 'Eavytail's pet farm, and see what they're a-doin' in the dancin' line. It's only right for us jestices to patronise the amusements of the lower horders," continued he, anxious for an excuse to do what he wanted.

"Oh, is it his harvest home?" asked the Marquis.

"Yes," replied Mr. Jorrocks, "it's a sort of a masquerade thing, as I understands it. Dress up, King o' Bohemia—Timour the Tartar—William the Conqueror—Doctor Pangloss—then 'ands across and back again, down the middle and hup again." Mr. Jorrocks suiting the action to the word, and throwing himself about in attitudes.

"We might have some fun, I think," observed the Marquis, anxious for anything rather than bed; "only it wouldn't do to go as we are."

"Oh no," replied Mr Jorrocks—"dress up certainly. I've got a werry fine Scotch dress—kilts, filly-bag (philibeg), and all, wot I used to cut about in London in, that I could sport, only I don't know wot to put you in. My tops would be too big for you," added he, glancing at his own legs and at the Marquis's, "or I could rig you out as an 'untsman."

"Oh, both my legs would go into one of your boots," observed the Marquis: "besides, I should be lost in the coat."

"It would be rayther like a dressin'-gown, p'raps," replied Mr. Jorrocks; "it's roomy for me even," added he, feeling his great fat sides.

"I'll tell you wot we could do, though," exclaimed he, after a few minutes' consideration. "We might dress you hup as a gal, and deuce a soul will ever know you. We've got some o' my niece Belinda's things, wot she left when she got married, that'll jest about fit you," continued Mr. Jorrocks, eyeing the Marquis's dimensions. "Werry pretty gal you'll make, too," added the Cockney Squire.

The Marquis rather hesitated. He would have preferred being a hussar, or a light dragoon, or something in the military line; but fancy dresses not being procurable at a moment's notice in the country, he at length consented, and with the aid of Mrs. Jorrocks, accomplished a very becoming attire. White silk bonnet with a blue feather, blue and white striped dress, with his own Wellington boots.

Mr. Jorrocks was rotundity itself. The thick, well-puckered plaid stood from his plump person, while his corpulent calves loomed magnificent above his striped hose.

"There's an 'Ighlander for you!" exclaimed he, bounding into the apartment where Mrs. Jorrocks was dressing the Marquis, balancing himself on one leg like an opera-dancer, extending his arms with a lighted candle in the right hand.

> Ighlands gay, foots away,
> Appy on the weddin' day,

continued he, whizzing himself round, teetotum-like, which had the effect of inflating his kilts and blowing out his candle.

"I wonders now," continued he, "if there really are people wot dress in this style," looking at his bare legs, "or if it's jest one o' Walter Scott's wagaries. My vig, but you makes an uncommon pretty gal," added he, getting in front of the Marquis, and eyeing his bright ringlets and fair complexion, "werry pretty gal indeed. Mr. 'Eavytail 'ill wonder who the deuce it is—real lady!—swan's-down muff and tippet, and a feather in her 'at, I do declare," continued he, eyeing the whole attire.

"Well, now," continued he, adjusting his peacock-feathered cap before the mirror, "we'll jest steal quietly out at the back door, and you, Mrs. J., must see that it's left open when Batsay goes to bed, and I'll jest put the spirit-stand key in my filly-bag, and you must put glasses and vater in the closet for us again' we come 'ome, for we shall most likely be drinkey for dry; so now let's mizzle, or we shall be losin' 'alf the fun."

Our friends then set off. The night air had assumed an autumnal coolness, and our Cockney Highlander felt the want of his stockings before he had got across the second field, on his way by the back of the village. The young moon shone brightly in the sky, occasionally obscured by a passing cloud. Mr. Jorrocks strode hastily on, followed by the Marquis, laughing ever and anon at the grotesque shadow his fat friend cast on the fields.

Thus they proceeded for a mile or so, the Marquis still keeping in the rear.

Presently lights appeared on the hill-top, and the sound of revelry fell on the country round.

"That's the place," observed Mr. Jorrocks to his friend, as they halted at a stone stile and looked towards the lights. "You're not tired, are you?"

"Oh no," replied the Marquis. "My petticoats are rather inconvenient, and catch the briars as I pass along, otherwise I could manage well enough."

" 'Old them up," replied Mr. Jorrocks. "My kilts are werry cool, I know, and expose my legs desperate to the gnats."

Presently the lights became more apparent, and seemed to move about in greater numbers; and as they reached the foot of the hill, music and the clattering of the dancers sounded more distinctly.

"The game's begun," observed Mr. Jorrocks, pretending to listen, but in reality drawing breath before commencing the steep ascent.

"We'll soon be there now," continued he, making a fresh start.

They then commenced the climb.

As they neared the summit of the hill, the noise of voices, the clapping of hands, the stamping of heels, the twang of the music, with here and there a rustic couple loitering about making love, announced a numerous gathering.

"There's a precious sight o' company," observed Mr. Jorrocks, turning round to the Marquis, when a man with his face blacked, and a pair of horns on his head, trod on Mr. Jorrocks's foot.

"Oh, you great clown!" roared Mr. Jorrocks; "you've trod on my toe—my corney toe!" added he, catching his foot up in his hand.

"Why don't you look where you're going, you great woolpack?" replied the man, pushing past.

"*Voolpack!*" grunted Mr. Jorrocks, letting down his leg, adding, in a lower tone—"I'll lick you within a barleycorn o' your life. Stop a bit 'ere," said he to the Marquis, "till I gets my mask on, or they'll be twiggin' on me."

Having got this adjusted, the Cockney Sawney took the arm of his fair friend, and, drawing a faded green-baize curtain aside, they passed at once from the open air into the barn ball-room.

The game was in full play. Amid clouds of smoke the dim, tallow candles shed an indistinct light upon a most miscellaneous collection of maskers and mummers. Here might be seen a man with an ass's head, coquetting with the tapster for another jug of barleycorn there a sailor footing it with a ram, or a haymaker with a billy-goat, many of the characters being from animal and agricultural life.

Our friends were some time after entering before they could discriminate objects.

Not so with those already in, for the appearance of our Squire and his fair friend caused an instantaneous outburst of exclamations, some not very complimentary to Mr. Jorrocks's proportions and his country, others in approbation of the fair companion of his travels. "Here's a Scot!" exclaimed one, pushing Mr. Jorrocks forward to show himself. "A real fat 'un," added a butcher, poking him in the ribs. "A bare-legged 'un, too!" exclaimed a horse-jobber, feeling Mr. Jorrocks down like a purchaser. "Take care, he'll maybe give you the itch!" observed a fourth, dressed as a sailor. "I once got it from a chap at Arbroath very like him." "Hang him, he's no Scot!" observed another, dressed as a woman; "are you, old joggle-belly?" continued he, giving Mr. Jorrocks a crack across the stomach. "Is he your dad, my bonny lass?" asked another half-drunken clown, taking a pipe from his mouth, and giving the Marquis a chuck under the chin, and a face full of smoke at the same time.

Mr. Jorrocks was rather abashed by their rudeness at first, but having often taken his own part among the frolicsome maskers in the days of the immortal Charley Wright, of gooseberry champagne celebrity, and in later times at the "Crown and Anchor," and Lowther Rooms, he soon began to peck up and move freely about the barn. Not so the Marquis, who was sadly disconcerted at the rude liberties of the clowns, who pinched him and pulled him about, and made all sorts of observations upon his figure and appearance. At last, having got separated from his bulky protector, he could no longer put up with the tender advances of a liquorish young husbandman, who, with his arm round his waist, insisted upon kissing him, so getting to the door, he made his escape, and ran away as hard as ever his petticoats would let him lay legs to the ground. Meanwhile our gay-hearted Squire rolled joyfully about, thrusting his uncouth mask under the bonnet of every pretty girl, and replying in most Cockneyfied Scotch to the numerous inquiries that were hazarded as to his country and kindred—"Oh, he was from Inverness! Would they gan to Inverness? &c. He could eat nothin' but oatmeal! he could drink nothin' but whisky! He was all for the mountain hair!" The fiddlers, as if in compliment to his country, presently struck up a reel, but Mr. Jorrocks did not regard the invitation, until a very gaunt-looking figure, in a very old white mask, with large red spots on the cheek-bones, dressed in a soldier's coat, with nankeen shorts and gaiters, and a regular bulge of shirt round his waist, appeared with a buxom wench on the floor, and with a youth dressed as a barn-door cock, commenced a three reel. The woman was masked, but her figure was tall and plump, and finely formed. She tripped lightly through the figure, and set to the soldier, whose toe and heel work and lanky lugubrious appearance contrasted with the nimble jollity of his partner. Still the soldier seemed to have some notion of the dance, for he snapped his fingers and stamped with his heel, and screamed *eu heu!* at every period for changing the figure. Chanticleer, however, made very poor work of it, and seeing the Scotchman standing by, he said, "Here, *you* dance it," and giving Mr. Jorrocks a shove forward, left him to fill up his place in the reel.

Our lumpy Squire then commenced frolicking with a very clumsy cow-like sort of action, imitating, however, to the best of his ability, the stamps and yells of the soldier. The fair masker seemed to prefer the fat Scotchman, and turned and set to him much oftener and with more

The harvest home ball

grace than the equity of the dance required. In vain the soldier cut and shuffled, and snapped his fingers, and cried *eu heu!*—Mr. Jorrocks bumped and jumped, and cried *eu heu!* also.

At last the soldier began to get angry. "D—n it," said he, "if that great muckle Scotch thief isn't a takin' mar pairtner from me. Sink him, ar'll fell him," continued he, cutting and shuffling, in hopes that he might reclaim her by superior activity.

Still she set to the Scotchman.

"Ye stand up here," said he to a youth dressed as a duck, "and tak mar place whilst ar gan and get a neif full o' nettles for yon lubber. Sink, *ar'll gar him loup!*" added he, eyeing one of Mr. Jorrocks's awkward bounds.

The dance gained converts, and ere the soldier returned several more reels were formed. Still the Highlander frolicked with the fine-figured masker, and the admiring crowd pressed round to look at them. The duck, too, danced much better than the cock. The soldier having provided himself with a handful of nettles, took a position behind

Willey Goodheart and a group of unmasked countrymen, and, as Mr. Jorrocks came rolling round, he very quietly drew the nettles across the inside of his knees.

Mr. Jorrocks bounded across the floor.

The soldier then changed his position, and wiped him across the front of his legs; but an extra bound was all the acknowledgment Mr. Jorrocks made.

"Sink, arll stuff them up bodily," observed the soldier, shortening the stalk of the nettles, and changing his position again.

Presently Mr. Jorrocks was frolicking before him, and up went the nettles.

"Be'ave!" roared Mr. Jorrocks, with a tremendous bound; an exclamation that caused the soldier to start, and the fair masker to fly.

XXVI

O may the silver lamp from heaven's high bower
Direct my footsteps in the midnight hour!—GAY

THE MARQUIS OF BRAY WENT like a lamplighter down the pet farm hill, after escaping from Mr. Heavytail's harvest home ball, inwardly resolving never to assume female attire, or expose himself to such undignified rudeness again. It was his first appearance in any other character than that of a lord, and as he went he thought there was none so convenient. The night had changed for the worse, and the flitting clouds that had occasionally obscured the young moon's brightness had become heavy rolling masses. On the Marquis went, stumbling, tripping, and tearing his petticoats, following the first path he struck into, without considering whether it was the one he came by or not.

At length a narrow plank of a foot-bridge across a rushing rivulet startled him into the conviction that he was not returning by the way he came. When a man once loses himself, no matter how well he knows the country, it is wonderful how soon he gets confused. Everything looks different. The Marquis was bewildered. He had lost all idea where he was, if indeed he ever had any, for not being used to take lines of his own, he had most likely relied on Mr. Jorrocks bringing him safe home again. Still over the plank, and on he went, in the delusive hope of being right, until a dark wood stood full before him. The moon at that moment gleamed bright upon it, and a driving gust whistled through the leaves. The wood was a poser. The Marquis was sure he was wrong. The awkwardness of his situation now flashed upon him. Dressed as a girl, and lost in a strange country. The night was getting darker—the wind whisked his petticoats about, and the scared screech-owl fluttered about, hooping clear shrill full hoops upon the surrounding country.

The weak bat,
With short shrill shrieks, flitted on leathern wing.

"I must try to find my way back," observed the Marquis to himself,
"or I shall be getting benighted;" adding, as he turned and tripped over
a boundary stone, "confounded mess this is, to be sure; I wish I hadn't
been so foolish as to accompany Mr. Jorrocks. Oh dear! I do believe
there's a toad!" added he, jumping off the foot-path, as a sudden gleam of
moonshine flashed upon a slimy-looking gentleman, jumping leisurely
before him. "*Two! three! four!*" added he, as they successively hopped in
view. "Oh dear, the place is alive with them—*horrible* beasts!"

The foot-way now became more indistinct, and on arriving at the
next field, from which the corn had been led, the Marquis stood
doubting whether to take the track to the right or to the left. Which he
had come by he had no idea, nor was that material, as he did not wish
to get back to Mr. Heavytail's, if he could find his way to Hillingdon
without. At length he took the track to the left. He had not proceeded
many paces before, with a sniff, grunt, and snort, up jumped a sow with
a litter of pigs, giving him such a start as to drive the idea of following
the path out of his mind. On he went, lost in meditation and fear,
walking, as it were, involuntarily, for he could not but feel that he was
just as likely to be going wrong as right, while the fear of meeting any
one in his present disguise almost overcame the desire to do so, for the
purpose of getting put right.

Another loud sniff, grunt, and snort again disturbed his reflections,
causing him to start and think there must be a sow with a litter of pigs
at each corner of the field, until, getting to the stile by which he had
entered, he found he had made a circuit of the enclosure. That was a
clencher, and stuffing his hands into his muff, he leant against the rough
railing next the stile, in a state of despondency. He had never known
difficulty before. His had been a bed of roses, instead of which he seemed
in a fair way of getting into one of nettles. The night was bitter cold—
the wind howled, and a drizzling rain began to threaten saturation to his
flimsy garments. "Well, it's no use stopping here," said he to himself, as

he eyed the fleeting clouds driving before the dull moon; "I must walk, if it's only to keep myself warm." So saying, muff in hand, he proceeded at a half-walk, half-run, along the path he had before rejected.

"I've a great mind to holla," said he to himself, stopping and resting against a stile, after crossing three or four more fields, at the same time undoing the belt of his gown to get at his diminutive gold watch, which he long held up, in hopes of a moon's ray enabling him to see what o'clock it was. He could make nothing of it. A gold face was all that was visible; the tiny ticking all he could hear. "Oh dear, Mr. Jorrocks is a stupid old man," said he, returning it to his waistcoat pocket; "I really think my pa was right about his being a vulgar old fellow. Who but a clown could find pleasure in such revelry as that? Well, I wish I was home again—I wouldn't be caught at another, I know." So saying, the Marquis again set off at a sort of amble, brushing his silk gown against the protruding thorn-hedge as he went.

A hare's meanders are not more curious than the Marquis's wanderings on this unlucky night. The ground he covered and the little progress he made were truly ridiculous. At the end of two hours he was not more than two miles from where he started, though he was fully of opinion that he had walked ten. The time, too, seemed equally long, and by eleven o'clock he began to expect daybreak. Though not boisterous, the wind was noisy, and blowing the contrary way to the pet farm; no sounds of mirth or music reached the low country about which the Marquis wandered; while the festivities, being confined to the back of the house, and the window shutters being closed in front, no indications appeared from that side. Cold and fatigue had so tamed his lordship that he would have made for them if there had, even at the risk of a second hugging from the clown.

If the Marquis lived to a thousand years, he would never forget the horrors of that night. It would have been bad enough to have been lost in his own clothes; but to be lost without daring to holla, because he was dressed as a woman, was something vexatiously ludicrous. What would his ma say, if she could see him? O Jorrocks! Jorrocks! you had a deal to answer for, old cock.

Still the Marquis moved about till cold and fatigue almost overcame him. The heir of Donkeyton Castle would have been thankful for the shelter of the meanest cottage on the estate. At last, when almost sinking under his difficulties, a sudden gleam of moonshine disclosed a stack of chimneys, between clumps of tall trees. The Marquis darted towards them. Another gleam showed some common railing round the trees, and just at the same moment a melancholy-looking candle flickered past a lattice window high in the roof. A few seconds, and he was over the rails.

"Holloa!" exclaimed he, as loud as he could shout, immediately below where he saw the light, when out rushed a dog with such force as to throw himself over with the check of his chain, as he darted to within a few feet of where the Marquis stood.

"Get away, *you beast!*" exclaimed he, bounding away with such a spring as made him assume a similar position on the ground.

The rattle of the chain grating at full tension against the wooden dog-box sounded like music to the Marquis, as he gathered himself up from his dirty fall, and prepared for a fresh attempt below the window.

"*Holloa!*" repeated he, amid the whistling of the wind, the *bow-wow-wow-wowing* of the dog, and the rattling of the chain.

"Who's there?" at length exclaimed a voice from below a white cotton nightcap, out of the little window.

"Me! me!" exclaimed the Marquis, delighted at the sound.

"*Me, me,*" mimicked the voice; "who's me, I wonder?"

A fitful gleam passed over where the Marquis stood, displaying his dress, and the draggled state of his clothes.

"Stand back!" holloaed the voice from above, "or I'll shoot you."

"For God's sake don't!" exclaimed the Marquis, holding up his muff like a shield, amid the increased baying of the dog.

"Then make yourself scarce, and don't be after disturbing a respectable family at this time of night."

"Don't be silly!" exclaimed the Marquis, "I don't want to hurt anybody; I want shelter," added he, advancing a few paces.

"*Stand back!*" repeated the voice, "or I'll shoot!" the speaker at the same time popping a mop-handle out of the window.

"*Hold!*" screamed the Marquis, couching to avoid the discharge, " I'm not a robber."

"I know what you are well enough," replied he of the cotton nightcap, "but we don't want such cattle as you here."

"What's the matter? Who's there? Thieves! murder! fire help!" exclaimed a voice from below a frilled night-cap, out of a larger window a little lower down.

"It's nobody that will hurt you," exclaimed the Marquis, waving his muff in a supplicating way towards the house. "*Only hear me!*"

"But who are you?" inquired the frilled night-capped voice. "What do you mean by disturbing the house at this time of night?"

"I've lost my way," exclaimed the Marquis, "and am perishing with cold. Do let me in, and I'll tell you all about it," added he, pulling up his wet petticoats.

"*I dare say!*" replied voice number two. "We don't harbour such people as you here, this is not a lodging-house. If you don't go quietly away I'll rouse the house; call the coachman, butler, groom, and all the footmen; have you taken up, taken before a magistrate."

"Pray don't!" exclaimed the Marquis, "pray don't; I really won't hurt anybody; just let me sit by the kitchen fire till morning; I assure you I'll go quietly away, and be most thankful."

"Who *can* it be?" inquired another female voice, now joining the first one. "She doesn't speak like a common person, somehow. How many are there of you?" asked she, now looking out of the window.

"Only myself!" exclaimed the Marquis, "only myself!" repeated he, with upraised muff.

"She's got an ermine muff and tippet, I see," said the second female voice, drawing back, "and appears well dressed. We can hardly let her stand shivering there."

"If I was sure there was no one else, I'd let her in, but it may be a plan to rob and murder us," observed the other; "we can't be too careful."

"Oh dear!" exclaimed the Marquis, "don't keep me shivering here; I shall get my death of cold," added he, his teeth chattering as he spoke.

A long consultation ensued in the lower room, to which the cotton cap of the upper one was summoned. At length slipshod footsteps were heard descending an uncarpeted staircase, and presently the rattling of bolts and loosening of chains denoted the withdrawal of the barricade.

"There's none but herself," exclaimed the cotton-capped hero, after an inspection from the upper window, whereupon the key turned in the lock, and the last bolt flew back. The door then partially opened.

"Come in, young woman!" exclaimed a female voice through the aperture, through which no sooner had the Marquis squeezed, than clap the door went to again, and the lock was quickly turned. A dim swealing candle, in a block-tin candlestick, in the hand of a figure a little further in the passage, threw an indistinct light along it, enabling the Marquis to see two frilled nightcapped figures, muffled up in white flannel dressing-gowns, with thick red worsted shawls about their shoulders; and a short figure in dark trousers, with a white cotton night-cap sticking off his head, like a cardinal's hat. They were evidently the people he had held communion sweet with outside. The walls of the cold flagged passage showed symptoms of decay in the plastering; and the unpainted rails of the staircase at the end had the appearance of belonging either to the front of a very bad house, or the back of a very middling one.

"Come this way," said the figure who had let him in, retreating till she got the candle from the one near the staircase, which she flourished up and down, so as to throw as much light as possible on our friend.

He certainly was a most forlorn figure. The smart blue and white feather that Mr. Jorrocks had admired, now drooped like a wet cock's tail over his ear, his hair hung in wet, dishevelled ringlets about his face, and his blue and white dress was torn and covered with mud stains.

"You're a pretty creature," said the figure with the candle, retreating and beckoning the Marquis to follow her into the kitchen.

A poke of the fire threw additional light on the subject—a light that removed all doubt as to what the wearer was.

"And pray, young woman," said she, with upturned nose, and most contemptuous sneer, "and pray, young woman, what do you mean by disturbing respectable people at this time of night?"

"Oh, I assure you I'm not to blame," exclaimed the Marquis. "It's not from choice I'm this way!" said he, looking at his dress.

"*I dare say,*" sneered the figure with the candle, "*I dare say,*" repeated she. "The old story, I suppose. But *I'll* put you to rights in the morning."

"Hear me!" exclaimed the Marquis.

"I won't hear a word you've got to say," interrupted the figure, starting and stamping with her foot. "*I'll* have you taken before a magistrate! I'll have you taken before Mr. Jorrocks!"

"Oh, Mr. Jorrocks is a friend of mine," exclaimed the Marquis, delighted to hear a name he recognised.

" *The more shame for you!*" screamed the threatener. "*The more shame for you*, you bold—*impudent* hussy. I'll tell Mrs. Jorrocks of you!"

"Nonsense!" exclaimed the Marquis, "nonsense!—I'm not a woman—I'm a man—Lord Bray, in fact."

Scream! screech! scream! went both the dressing-gowned figures, followed by a hurried exclamation—"*Run, Emma, and change your cap!*"

XXVII

Sweet Auburn! loveliest village of the plain,
Where health and plenty cheered the lab'ring swain:
Where smiling spring its earliest visit paid,
And parting summer's ling'ring blooms delayed.

"THERE'S GANNIN TO BE A grand beast show hereabouts,"
observed Pigg to his master (for the sagacious reader will have
conjectured from Mr. Jorrocks's parting observation, as Pigg left him
with the cattle, that the relationship of master and servant was likely
to be re between them); "there's gannin to be a grand beast show
hereabouts," observed Pigg, entering his master's sanctum, with one
of the usual autumnal-issuing handbills, offering such a premium for
the best bull, such a premium for the second best—such a premium
for the biggest boar, and such another for the best pig; with the usual
intimation at the bottom, that dinner would be on the table at two
o'clock precisely, with a band in attendance.

"Is there?" observed Mr. Jorrocks, taking the proffered bill, headed
in great letters:—

ST. BOSWELL
AGRICULTURAL SOCIETY.
GRAND CATTLE SHOW
ON THE FAIR DAY.

"Humph!" grunted Mr. Jorrocks, "I s'pose we must be after sendin'
the Marquis. Wot do they give for the best ball?" added he, glancing at
the prizes. "Here it is. 'For the best ball of any age, ten punds; for the
second best, five punds; for the best yearling ball, six punds.' I thinks

we'll send the Marquis. 'Ow far is it from here do you suppose?" for Mr. Jorrocks had not learnt the country as yet.

"Why, they say it's a gay step frae here," replied Pigg, "maybe fourteen or fifteen mile; yean should set off the day af ore, se as to travel the maist o' the distance, and get the boole there in good order."

"Jest so," observed Mr. Jorrocks, "jest so; but that'll ran up expense. If I shouldn't get a prize, I should be out o' pocket."

"Ne doot," replied Pigg, "ne doot; but he'd stite stay at heam as gan in i' bad order. Lose his *caracter*, ye ken."

"Vell," said Mr. Jorrocks, "there's summut in that, to be sure; nothin' wentur, nothin' gain." Thereupon our friend jingled his money in his pocket as if he was counting the premium.

St. Boswell, though little more than a village, was a place of some note, from its cattle shows and fairs. To this it was indebted for its locality, being midway between several larger places, to which it acted as a centre of attraction. Moreover, it was a place of surpassing beauty; not that we mean to insinuate that its beauty would be any attraction to a cattle-drover, it being merely mentioned here as a lure to the reader to go on. Situate deep in a narrow valley in a wild moorland region, sheltered with lofty hills, whose grey rock-studded summits were barely sprinkled with the hardy larch or stunted fir, growing ranker and stronger down below until they mingled with beech, oak, elm, and other forest trees in the bottom, St. Boswell was placed in the prettiest part of the narrowing valley, where the mountain's base was swept by a clear, sparkling stream, hardly to be called a river in summer, but when swelled with the mountain torrents of the thunderstorm or wintry falls, it rushed and foamed in terrible and almost irresistible velocity; each mountain chasm showed its tributary streamlet, now rippling noiselessly down, or gliding over the well-worn rock, from whence in winter it flowed a noisy brawling cataract.

Everything about St. Boswell was sunshiny and pretty. The little fields on either side of the river looked fresher and greener than anywhere else. The hedgerow and other trees looked larger, healthier, and fuller of foliage, while the pine tribe clustered on the mountain side with an air of naturalisation. Many of the larches were of great size; some full of cones, and covered with the grey moss of age, while here and there a broken top or shattered branch showed the effects of resistance to the hurricane. The river, too, bore marks of wildness and devastation. The wide bed was scattered with enormous fragments of rock, breaking the stream into minor channels, while wearing jetties on either side showed the efforts of the landowners to keep the torrent in its course.

Over this river was a sloping bridge of many arches, down which the unsuspecting traveller shot, losing half the beauties of the place. From the high end of the bridge a complete view of the little square forming the town might be obtained. The old grey-roofed houses were irregularly built; but the battlemented edifice, under whose Gothic arch the road passed to the north, gave the place the appearance of some little fortified Swiss capital. On the right of the square was a large inn, with a tinge of Gothic architecture in its doorway and mullioned windows; while here and there similar windows might be seen scattered about the square, some brightening with smart shawls, or parti-coloured ribbons, others exhibiting the more humble stores of flour or groceries. The church was a large square-towered, stone-roofed building, standing aloof from the square, and forming a beautiful feature as the traveller progressed up the valley; while a neat-looking little parsonage-house was stuck into the hillside, overlooking the place from its shelving, garden-laid-out terraces. Luxuriant evergreens were trained against its white walls, while a world of forest trees clustered round, sheltering it alike from summer's heats and winter's storms.

The fair was the great event of the year, and the visitor on that day saw the village attired in its best—the capital of moorland life. At other times it presented a pleasant picture of quietude and primitive simplicity.

James Pigg having thoroughly identified himself with his master's interest, did all he could to set the Marquis off to advantage. He cleaned him, and rubbed him, and fed him with oil-cake, and made his coat shine like a horse's. James soon persuaded himself that he was the finest *boole* that ever was seen, and took it as a personal insult when any one attempted to disparage him. Mr. Jorrocks encountered Pigg early in the morning on the day previous to the show, in marching order, just as we found him in the lane with the cattle. The eagle feather stood from his

Highland bonnet, and the *plaide*, divested of its wardrobe, was thrown over his chest, with the fringed end across his back. He had given the sporting buttons an extra polish, and had made the alterations he spoke of between the knees and the gaiters. Altogether he was uncommon smart.

"Vell, James, then you're off," said Mr. Jorrocks, as he met him in the passage.

"Ay, ar's gannin," replied Pigg, taking his oak staff down from the rafters of the kitchen ceiling. "A *boole* taks a vast o' travellin'—ye'll be comin' yourself ar's warn'd!"

"Not till to-morrow, James," replied Mr. Jorrocks, "not till to-morrow—but howsomever you see and get *me* the prize—and don't *you* get *drunk*."

"*Ar niver gets drunk!*" replied Pigg, with a growl, bundling past his master.

Off then James set; and Mr. Jorrocks having seen him and the bull away, returned to his study, where he had a very important scheme in hand—the establishment of a periodical to combine the features of the *Justice of the Peace, The Farmer's Magazine, The Sporting Magazine*, and the *Quarterly Review*, to be called *Jorrocks's Journal of General Genius*, with which he purposed knocking all those periodicals out of the water.

For the present, however, we must request our readers will accompany Pigg.

James did wise in starting early, for an extremely powerful sun dissipated the coolness of the autumnal air; and long before noon it was excessively hot. The flies too teased the Marquis, and rendered him very fractious: indeed, none but an experienced drover, like Pigg, could have got him along. Sometimes his lordship would stand stock-still, and bellow till he made the surrounding country echo. At other times, when he came within sight of a stream or river, he would rush at it as hard as ever he could go, pulling Pigg along like a straw; then again he would charge a stiff bullfinch into a field when he saw a cow, riddling Pigg's face, and nearly scratching his eyes out, as, grinning like grim death, he held on by the chain. At length, towards evening, Pigg had accomplished his journey, and had the satisfaction of housing the Marquis in good order, whatever he might be himself. This was at a small village a few miles off St. Boswell, a distance that left him little to do next day.

A country fair being a great event in rural regions, the little place was astir at an early hour in the morning. The servant lads and lasses had their work to do, or arrangements to make for taking each other's places, and the varied countenances plainly showed who were for the fair and who were not. A crowd collected to see Pigg start. "What a fine bull!" exclaimed one. "What a beauty!" exclaimed another. "He'll come from Scotland," observed a third, eyeing Pigg's habiliments. The urchins gave three cheers as he passed before them.

A turnpike gate stood across the road, about half-a-mile from the village, and presented the unusual sight of a country toilkeeper ready for his money—not that they are averse to taking it, but they are never on the lookout for it. Perhaps this one's activity was caused by its being the fair day. At all events, it is an unusual sight, as unusual as a country servant being ready with his money when he gets to one. There, however, stood Tommy Sacker, with his friend Jacky Green, and as Pigg and the bull approached Tommy seemed more intent on the animal than the toll.

"Here's a fine day," observed Pigg, as he approached the gate.

"Deed is it, master," replied Tommy, "and you've got a fine bull with you."

"Grand boole," said Pigg, rubbing the animal's curly pow, "grand boole—get the prize this yean ar guess."

"Whose is he?" asked the gatekeeper.

"Dinnut ye ken him?" asked Pigg, thinking how he could "do" him.

"No, I don't," replied Tommy, examining the bull attentively all round.

"Ah, come, ye de?" replied Pigg inquiringly.

"*No*," replied the man decidedly, with a shake of the head.

"Why, it's Sir Robert Peel's grand boole," observed Pigg.

"Sir Robert Peel's grand bull!" exclaimed the man. "Bless us, you don't say so! Come here, Mary," cried he to his wife, "come here, woman, and see Sir Robert Peel's grand bull."

"Ye dinnut tak pay frae Sir Robert, ar's warn'd," observed Pigg, driving the Marquis through the gate.

Scarcely had the turn of the road, as it wound round the heathery mountain-side, screened Pigg from sight, than up came Goliah, the crack bull of the country a great red and white animal, that moved like an elephant. He was towed along as usual by the nose by a countryman, while his master, Farmer Cheesecake, followed on his grey pony behind, giving the bull a crack on the hind-quarters every now and then with his stick to keep him going.

A country turnpike-gate being as unlike a London one as possible, Farmer Cheesecake pulled up to have a little talk with Tommy Sacker, as he paid him the toll.

"Well, Tommy," said he, "here's a fine mornin' for the fair."

"Fine mornin', sir," said Tommy, "fine mornin'."

"Many cattle gone through?" asked Cheesecake.

"Only one bull, as yet," replied Tommy, "but he's a fine 'un: I doubt Goliah won't gain the prize to-day."

"I don't know *that*," replied Cheesecake, with a smile, as much as to say, "what do you know about bulls?"

"Well, but you may depend on't he'll be an awkward customer," replied Tommy Sacker.

"Why, it will be Harry Tugwell's bull—a strawberry roan," observed Cheesecake.

"No, it's not," said the gatekeeper. "So you're wrong for once."

"It's Mr. Chub's, then."

"No, nor Mr. Chub's."

"Whose is it, then?" demanded Cheesecake, at the same time tendering his toll.

"Why, what do you think of Sir Robert Peel's grand bull?" inquired Tommy, with an air of exultation.

"*Sir Robert Peel's grand bull!*" exclaimed Cheesecake at the top of his voice, in horrified amazement. "*Sir Robert Peel's grand bull!* What the deuce business has Sir Robert Peel to send his d——d bulls here? We want none of Sir Robert Peel's bulls. No, nor none of Sir Robert himself," growled he. "Had enough both of him and his bulls, and his tariffs too—ruined the country—done it on purpose that he might come and sweep up what's left. D——n him! *I'll Sir Robert him!*" added

"It's Sir Robert Peel's grand boole"

Cheesecake, clutching his stick and laying it into his pony, as if he saw Sir Robert in the distance, and was going to ride at him.

Cheesecake was sore perplexed; Goliah had gained three prizes in his own part of the country, and it had been a matter of argument with his owner whether he should send him to St. Boswell or to a more distant show to take place a few days after. Cheesecake's evil genius had induced him to decide on St. Boswell, and now he found the Queen's Prime Minister's bull was to be there to compete with him. "It was a monstrous shame," he said, as he kicked and jagged his pony along to overtake the bull. "It wasn't fair. No bull could stand against a Prime Minister's bull. The judges would be sure to give the prize to him. It was no use wasting money by going. Only be laughed at. Would go home and try his luck at Moorsley instead." So saying, he overtook the ponderous quadruped and, much to the astonishment of its leader, directed him to take a cross-country road home.

XXVIII

He rides a race.
'Tis for a thousand pounds.

JUST AS MR. JORROCKS WAS getting on to Dickey Cobden to follow his bull to St. Boswell, he espied Hercules Strong lugging a couple of urchins along in a way that plainly said there was work for the justice. His worship was sore perplexed, for as it was he was half an hour behind time, having split his stockingette pantaloons in the rear in drawing on his Hessian boots, and when he had got them replaced by another pair, one of the Hessians flew at the instep, and one of his shirt wrist-buttons came off, which he was obliged to get Batsay to replace before he was what he called "comfey rumph." The arrival of the "waggabones" was a pleasure he could have dispensed with. However, there they were, and his worship felt bound to hear the case.

The youths had been stealing peas, and Hercules Strong had caught them in the act. They had their pockets full. The case was quite clear, and Benjamin, with more than his usual dexterity, having fished out the law in the Justice's Pocket Manual, Mr. Jorrocks proceeded to read aloud, "Stealin', or destroyin', or damagin' with intent to steal, any plant, root, fruit, or wegitable production"—"such as peas," observed Mr. Jorrocks, looking off the book at the malefactors, "growin' in any garden, orchard, nursery ground, 'ot'ouse, green-'ouse, or consarvatory—Pun.: on conwiction afore one Justice, for first offence, imprisonment with or without 'ard labour in gaol or 'ouse of C."—"which means Correction," observed Mr. Torrocks, again looking off the book at the urchins, "for not exceedin' six calendar months," read he, "or penalty above the walue not exceedin' twenty pund."

"Now, vot 'ave you young warmints got to say," asked he, "why I shouldn't send you each to the 'ouse of C. for six calendar months apiece; to be fed on worms and potato parins'—and whipped with stingin'-nettles?" added he, thinking of his own experience that way.

"Pray don't!"exclaimed both the lads.

"Please, sir," observed Hercules Strong, in a whisper, "the peas were growing in a field."

"'Ord rot it, vy didn't you tell me that?" exclaimed Mr. Jorrocks, starting round in a rage. "Here have I been a-treatin' the case as one of a garden, and jest as I'm a-goin' to pass sentence on the malefactors, you tell me they were growin' in a field! Who the deuce can do jestice for you? All the labour to go over again, without knowin' where to look for the law! I'll not bother my 'ead," added he, throwing the book over the back of the judicial chair, "I'll not bother my 'ead with a case so ambiguously mysterious. I'll deal sammarily with it. Take that bigger bouy to Batsay," said he to Benjamin, "and make my compliments to her, and say I'll thank her to flog him well. And 'ark ye, young 'un," added he, with a shake of the head at the other, "if you are caught at this 'ere game again, I'll 'ave you flogged too! *desperate!*" concluded he, with a shake of the head, as he rose from his throne.

At length our worthy friend got started, and worked Dickey Cobden along so vigorously, that he nearly pumped the wind out of him before he got five miles. The day too was hot, and both Mr. Jorrocks and the nag were in a running-down perspiration at the end of that distance.

"Dash those waggabones," said Mr. Jorrocks to himself as he pulled up into a walk, and began mopping his head with a great blue and white bandanna. "Didn't give them '*alf* enough," said he, thinking he should have flogged them both for detaining him so long.

"Come hup!" exclaimed he, jerking the cob's mouth, and kicking its lathered sides. "Will take all the shine off my 'essians, I do believe," added he, looking inwards at his legs.

On they jogged again, though only in a slovenly way, Dickey raising the dust, and playing the castanets with his feet as he went. "Confounded noisy beast," said Mr. Jorrocks, trying to get him to alter his pace, so as to avoid the noise; "lumberin'-actioned beggar—goes like a crab—all vays at once and none in particklar."

On they went, Dickey going very near the ground, and knocking the loose stones about as if he were playing at marbles.

"Do believe the beast will tumble with me," observed Mr. Jorrocks, tightening his hold of his head. "Oh, but you are a *brute!*" added he, grinning with rage and vexation.

"Confound it, I must be near there now," at length exclaimed he, pulling up into a walk, fairly exhausted with working the nag— throwing the reins on his neck, and fumbling out his great watch. "I'm dashed if it ar'nt near twelve," added he, eyeing the chronometer. "Show to commence at eleven. Shall be a day after the fair. Come hup, you hugly beast," added he, again seizing the reins in a bunch and cracking Dickey Cobden across the shoulders with the ends, a compliment that he merely acknowledged by boring and shaking his head.

"'Ord rot you, but I'll get a stick to you," said Mr. Jorrocks, running Dickey alongside a hazel bush in the hedge, from which Mr. Jorrocks helped himself to a stout stick.

"Now, my man," said he, as he broke the twigs off, "we'll see who's to be master—you or I;" saying which, Mr. Jorrocks turned sideways in his saddle, and gave Dickey a good lamming in the ribs.

Away they went in a canter.

"Ah, I thought as much!" exclaimed Mr. Jorrocks, as he felt Dickey easing himself down into a trot again at the end of a hundred yards or so. "I thought as much," repeated he, "short and sweet, like a donkey's canter;" adding, "if I rides a donkey, I rides a donkey; but if I rides an 'oss, I rides an 'oss," whereupon our friend turned sideways again, and proceeded to lam the other side of Dickey's carcass.

Away he went again—left foot leading.

This canter, however, did not last much longer than the first. Dickey kept bobbing up and down, it is true, but the pace was no better than a trot—hardly so good. He construed the first touch of the bridle into an intimation to stop, and obeyed on the instant.

"*Ah, you slug!*" groaned Mr. Jorrocks in disgust, "vouldn't give tappence a dozen for such brutes as you;" thereupon our friend pocketed his wig, and proceeded to mop himself again after his unwonted exertion.

"Must be near there now, surely," exclaimed he, looking again at his watch, after progressing a mile or two. "It's a weary long way to be sure—wouldn't have gone if I'd thought it had been so far—at all ewents not on 'ossback—the exertion of quiltin' and workin' this stinkin', curly-coated beggar is too much this 'ot weather."

Our friend now came within sight of the gate—the turnpike gate through which Pigg had passed in the morning.

" 'Ow far is this to St. Boswell?" inquired he of Tommy Sacker, riding up to the gate, money in hand.

"How far is it to St. Boswell?" repeated Tommy Sacker very slowly.

"Yes, St. Boswell!" exclaimed Mr. Jorrocks "come, quick, man, *you're* not fit to keep a pike."

"Why, it's four miles and better," drawled the man.

"Four miles and better!" exclaimed Mr. Jorrocks, looking angrily around at him—"four miles and *wuss*, I should say. *Impossible! Can't be!* you know nothin' about it."

"It's the case, I assure you," drawled Sacker, astonished at our friend's impetuosity.

"Dash my vig, I shall never get there!" exclaimed Mr. Jorrocks, preparing his stick to give Dickey Cobden another quilting.

"Has my ball gone through!" roared he, looking back at the gatekeeper.

"Oh, I axes your pardon, sir—Sir Robert," replied Mr. Sacker, taking off his hat, and advancing respectfully towards Mr. Jorrocks; "that's to say—I really didn't know you, sir—yes, Sir Robert, sir, your bull's gone through. sir."

"Sir Robert! I'm not Sir Robert!" growled Mr. Jorrocks "who d'ye take me for?"

"Why, Sir Robert Peel," replied the man; "Sir Robert Peel's bull's gone through."

"Sir Robert Peel's ball," roared Mr. Jorrocks; "wot on airth business has Sir Robert Peel to send his beastly ball down here? *I'll Sir Robert Peel him*," added he, grinning with rage, as he whacked Dickey Cobden's quarters with his stick.

"*Con*-found it, what a shame that is now!" muttered Mr. Jorrocks aloud to himself; "there's Peel, with his I don't know 'ow many thousands a year for doin' *nothin'*, and yet he must come and rob us poor farmers of our prizes. It ar'nt right—*I'm shot if it is*." So saying, he shortened his reins, and laid the stick smartly into Dickey Cobden's withers.

Dickey shook his head, and poked it down, and winced as if he would kick; but before he had summoned resolution to do so, Mr. Jorrocks brought him such a crack across the hind-quarters as set him off in a canter.

Up and down, up and down, up and down, he went tit-tupping along, with great labour and little progress.

"Vish I may find a fool at the fair to stick you into," observed Mr. Jorrocks, eyeing Dickey's bobbing ears with disgust—adding, "you certain*lie* are the most worthless beast that ever was lapped in leather. 'Oss, by Jove! I've seen a cow wot would go quicker."

Thus he went working along.

" 'Ow far will this be to St. Boswell?" asked our perspiring friend, as he overtook a drab-coated farmer in similar coloured overalls, riding a mealy-legged, mealy-muzzled, lumbering bay cart-horse, with a brass-cantrelled, brass-pommelled saddle. " 'Ow far will this be to St. Boswell?" continued he, repeating the question that he had hazarded at the traveller's back.

"Why, upon the *wh-o-o-le*"—commenced the drab-coat, without looking round.

"Oh, it's you. Mr. Vopstraw?" exclaimed Mr. Jorrocks.

"Your servant, sir I your servant, sir!" replied Wopstraw, raising his hat respectfully to the Squire.

"I didn't know you," said Mr. Jorrocks, pulling up alongside of him— "I didn't know you—vot 'ave you got your great hupper binjimin on for?" asked Mr. Jorrocks, lifting one of the enormous laps with his stick.

"To keep the heat out, sir—to keep the heat out," replied Mr. Wopstraw; "upon the *wh-o-o-le* it's very warm to-day."

"*Werry*," said Mr. Jorrocks, with an emphasis.

"And 'ow far is it to St. Boswell?" again inquired Mr. Jorrocks, after they had looked each other over.

Wopstraw still kept staring.

" 'Ow far will this be to St. Boswell?" asked Mr. Jorrocks in a sharper key.

"Upon the *wh-o-o-le*," said Johnny Wopstraw, transferring his eyes from Dickey Cobden to the rider, "I think your nag must be better than he looks, Mr Jorrocks."

"He can't look wuss nor he is," grunted our friend; "howsomever that's not the question—wants to know 'ow far it is to St. Boswell?"

"St. Boswell?" repeated Wopstraw, very deliberately, "upon the *wh-o-o-le* I should say it's five miles."

"*Five miles!*" screamed Mr. Jorrocks. "Impossible! the pike-man told me it was only four."

"Well, I don't know," replied Mr. Wopstraw, apparently conning the thing over in his mind, "I don't know, but upon the *wh-o-o-le* I should say it was *full* that."

"'Ord rot it, 'ow can that be?" exclaimed Mr. Jorrocks "if it was four miles from the gate, and we're a mile from it, 'ow can it possibly be five?"

"Why, upon the *wh-o-o-le*, I never was there before," replied Wopstraw "my brother's always gone, and I've met him and the sheep about half-a-mile from this, just at yon plantation end you see."

"Oh, then, upon the whole, good day!" exclaimed Mr. Jorrocks, seizing Dickey by the head and working him up again into a canter, muttering execrations as he went, upon cross roads, country stupidity, and want of milestones. On they went for half-a-mile or more, when the sight of white petticoats and smart shawls lining the road as it wound round the hillsides greeted his eyes. All the country round was pouring in, and every little mountain track was contributing its quota of healthy, blooming lasses, escorted by sunburnt, stalwart sweethearts. St. Boswell Fair was the great event of their year: a series of them furnished the epochs of their lives.

"And 'ow far will this be to St. Boswell, my pretty gal?" asked Mr. Jorrocks of the first group he overtook, consisting of three couple, all in their Sunday best; the girls in light gowns, with artificial flowers in their caps, and many ribbons on their bonnets, all laughing and talking of their anticipated enjoyment.

"Four miles, sir!" cried a couple of the ladies; "rather more than four," replied the third.

"Nay, not so far!" exclaimed Mr. Jorrocks; "it *can't* be so far," repeated he softly.

"You'd say it was, though, if you'd to walk it," observed the first, with a smile on her pretty dimpled cheeks.

"Not if I vas to valk with you," replied our gallant Squire; "your laughin' blue eyes would shorten the distance."

A loud guffaw followed this gallant sally. "Will you give us our fairings?" asked Blue-eyes.

"If you'll give me a kiss," rejoined our Squire.

"No," replied she, looking at her sweetheart, who didn't seem to relish the proposal.

"Then I'll give it you without," said our liberal friend, fumbling in his pantaloon pockets for some money. Presently he made a great haul—silver, copper, keys, rings, knife, pencil-case, all in a handful. "See," said he, picking a couple of sixpences and a five-shilling piece out of the mélange—"see, there's a shillin' apiece for you," giving it all to Blue-eyes to divide.

"Thank you, sir!" exclaimed she, with a curtsey; "thank you, sir!" exclaimed the others. "Good luck to you," exclaimed the youths, and amid the hearty good wishes of the party, Mr. Jorrocks again set Dickey Cobden a-going. Shorter and shorter still grew Dickey's canters. He seemed to have taken it into his head that his master wanted to speak to everybody they overtook, and dropped short at each group he came up to.

"Oh, you're an 'umbug!" exclaimed Mr. Jorrocks, jerking the curb sharply in his mouth.

Presently they overtook an equestrian—a stiff little man on a very slight bay pony. He had on a very low, dish-crowned hat, with a broadish brim, and a couple of fly-hooks and a twist of line round the band, a red cotton neckcloth, with an old dirty Witney blanket greatcoat cut down into a frock, with enormous mother-of-pearl buttons, and a very long dirty Meg-Merrilies tartan waistcoat. His breeches were of broad patent cord; and leggings of a similar material, though of a smaller pattern, met a pair of very stout ankle boots. He had a fair, but desperately freckled face, with curly yellow locks, and a pair of little, roving, ferrety, grey eyes that took everything in at a glance. His pony, as we said before, was small and slight, high in bone and low in flesh, while the indented mark above the eye gave evidence of age.

"'Ow far will this be to St. Boswell?" exclaimed Mr. Jorrocks, as he tit-tupped up within a few yards of the man.

"To St. Boswell?" repeated he of the hat, pulling his left hand out of the Witney coat pocket; "three miles or so."

"Humph!" grunted Mr. Jorrocks, pulling up along side of him to indulge in a little talk with a man who seemed to have some London quickness about him.

Mr. Jorrocks scanned him attentively, and his eye caught the hooks. "Fisherman," grunted he to himself.

"You've a niceish nag there," observed the stranger, breaking the silence.

"Yes, he is a *werry* nice nag," replied Mr. Jorrocks, patting Dickey's neck. "Rather 'ot jest now," added he; "come a long way—werry quick too."

"You'll not be for selling him perhaps," observed the man, after they had ambled on a few paces in silence.

"Vy, I'm not particklar about sellin' of him," replied Mr. Jorrocks; "that's to say, I'm not anxious. In course," added he casually, "if I could get my price, I *might* part with him."

"And what are you asking for him?" inquired the man, after a good survey.

"I'll tell you in a word," replied Mr. Jorrocks brusquely—"twenty guineas! Not a fardin' less, so it's no use offerin' of it; wouldn't take punds even."

"What age is he?" asked the man.

"He's eight," replied Mr. Jorrocks, with the greatest effrontery.

"He's long in the tooth," observed the man, looking into Dickey's mouth, as he yawned and bored at the bridle.

"You must have length somewhere," replied Mr. Jorrocks, "and I'm blow'd he ain't got it nowhere else."

"Will you let me lay my leg over him?" at length asked the man.

"Certainly," replied Mr. Jorrocks, "certainly," stopping and preparing to dismount. "You must mind he's come twenty miles though," observed he, dropping himself quietly on to the ground, "and ar'nt fit to show. We can ride on together, you know," added he.

The man leapt off his pony, and turning it round for Mr. Jorrocks to mount on the right side, prepared to get upon Dickey.

"You've a fine roomy saddle," observed the stranger, laying hold of the pommel of one of "Wilkinson and Kidd's" biggest.

"You can't put a round of beef on a plate," replied Mr. Jorrocks, adding, "vish I could say as much for yours, my frind," as he eyed the little old flat-flapped jockey-looking thing he had got in exchange, and began to fumble at the stirrups. Ere he got them adjusted, the man had stuck his little sharp-rowelled wiry-looking spurs into Dickey Cobden's sides, and got him away in a canter.

"Vot a rambustical apology for a saddle," grunted Mr. Jorrocks, hoisting himself on to the little pony, with a swag that nearly sent it over. 'Vish I mayn't lame myself trying to ride in it."

With this prudent reflection, our friend thrust his feet into the rusty old stirrups, and turned the pony round by the thick weather-bleached reins, just in time to see Dickey Cobden's stumpy tail disappear at a bend in the road a long way further on. A high wall hid all from view, except the dish-crowned hat of the rider, which kept bobbing up and down in a way that satisfied Mr. Jorrocks Dickey Cobden was cantering.

"I vish that chap mayn't be priggin' the agitator," observed he, eyeing the hat.

Another moment, and he had his heels in his new mount's sides, and was whacking him along with his hazel.

Away he went, as hard as ever he could lay legs to the ground.

Whether the man had overrated Dickey Cobden, or underrated his own nag, or may be underrated Mr. Jorrocks's equestrian powers, we know not; but, certainly, a looker-on would have thought the stranger had the worst of the game. Mr. Jorrocks sat like a jockey, and hustled the shambling little beggar of a pony along in a way that perfectly astonished him. The dust rose, and the loose stones flew, and the dogs barked, and the country lads and lasses jumped aside, as our eager-eyed friend pressed onward in the chase.

"It's a race! it's a race!" exclaimed some. "Bay for a shilling!" "Black for a guinea!" "Go along, guts!" "Lawk, what a man for a jockey!"

Whack, whack, whack, Mr. Jorrocks's stick went into the pony, then elbows and legs went working away and the unbuttoned Jorrockian jacket-flaps flew about, exposing a figure that fully justified the last ejaculation. "Cuss me if I'll be done by a fisherman," said he to himself, hustling along *à la* Chifney.

The road was undulating—not exactly hilly, but up and down, up and down for the first half-mile or so, and there was little diminution in the space between the parties at the end of that distance; but after that it became more level, and also took a straight line up the valley, instead of winding round the hill-sides.

On making the last turn, Mr. Jorrocks espied Dickey in the distance, lobbing along amidst a terrible dust, and the view lent impetus to his energies. He put on all the steam he could raise, declaring as he went that "it must be a werry bad nag wot couldn't beat Dickey Cobden."

Droves of cattle and flocks of sheep, coming from the fair, now occasionally intercepted the view; but every time our worthy friend got a fresh glimpse, he thought he saw Dickey's "galloping-dreary-done" sort of action more and more distinctly.

The white tents, with their many-coloured flags floating in the sunshine on a flat by the moor edge in the distance, roused the last spark of latent fire, and caused him to press forward ere the crowd of the fair baffled the pursuit.

The fugitive saw how things stood, and made play too. With steady legs he kept his spur-rowels digging into Dickey's sides, and urged him by every appliance of the bit, and every noise he could make with his mouth, to the utmost. Thus they clattered along, the thief riding in a most comfortable home seat in Mr. Jorrocks's capacious saddle, while our worthy friend was constrained to stand up in his stirrups, every now and then, to ease himself in his little apology for one.

What vows of revenge Mr. Jorrocks made as he went! He'd skin him alive! he'd transport him! he'd sus per col.; tuck him up short! He'd grind his bones to make him bread.

The foot people mistook his energy for zeal, and shouted and applauded "fatty" as he went. They now understood why the man on the black rode so hard; it was a race, though why he should get the start they could not conjecture; all the way behind people were running and straining their eyes to try and see the result of the race. Betting at this time two to one on the black. Some few backed "fatty" for his pluck, but these bets were chiefly in kisses with their sweet hearts, and would not have been quoted in the regular odds at the "corner."

"Whack, whack, whack," went Mr. Jorrocks, his eagerness increasing as he drew sufficiently near to descry the fugitive looking over his shoulder to see where he was.

"S-t-o-r-p t-h-i-e-f!" gasped Mr. Jorrocks, grinning and hustling along as he found he was drawing upon the runaway: "s-t-o-r-p t-h-i-e-f," repeated he, hitting and holding for hard life.

Another glance and the thief saw the game was up.

Dropping his hands and his heels at the same time, he coolly settled into a walk, while he listened for Mr. Jorrocks coming up. Presently he heard the clatter of his pony, and Mr. Jorrocks gasping and ejaculating, "You villain! you waggabone! you unmitigated thief!"

The pony stopped short so suddenly on overtaking Dickey Cobden as to start Mr. Jorrocks on to its neck; betting, three and four to one that our friend came off.

"He's off! no, he's on! he holds by the mane!"

"Take care, sir! take care, sir!" exclaimed the man with the greatest effrontery; "you'll be hurting yourself!"

" 'Urtin' myself!" roared Mr. Jorrocks, hugging at the neck; "take care

I doesn't 'urt you," added he, balancing himself on the withers. He then got back into the saddle.

"He's a niceish cob this of yours," observed the man very coolly; "but hastn't quite pace enough for me."

"I thinks not!" screamed Mr. Jorrocks, "I thinks not!" repeated he, dismounting and seizing the man by the collar.

"A fight! a fight!" exclaimed the astonished fair goers, stopping short.

"A thief! a thief!" exclaimed Mr. Jorrocks, pulling him off Dickey Cobden.

"Lawk, it's Tom the Tinker!" shouted one—"he that stole my brother's mare."

"So it is," roared another; "I didn't know him in that hat."

"Duck him," cried several, pointing to a pea-green soup-looking pond.

"*Have at him!*" screeched Mr. Jorrocks, as if he was worrying a fox.

Up they took the little vagabond, and, throwing him high in the air, down he splashed over head into the stagnant filth.

"*Now again!*" cried another, seizing him as he crawled out.

"There's nothin' like sammary conwiction," observed Mr. Jorrocks, as he disappeared a third time, adding, "*who the deuce would be done by a fisherman!*"

XXIX

These tidings nip me; and I hang the head
As flowers with frost, or grass beat down with storms.

SHAKSPEARE

WE LEFT OUR RESPECTED FRIEND just as he had overtaken the horse-stealer, and was witnessing his submersion in the horse-pond. Having mopped and cooled himself after his unwonted exertion, Mr. Jorrocks readjusted his wig, and proceeded to recover Dickey Cobden, who was now grazing quietly by the roadside, having had quite enough galloping.

"Confound him," observed Mr. Jorrocks aloud to himself, eyeing first his own quadruped and then the other; "if it hadn't been for the saddle, I really believes the bay's the best of the two." So saying, he hoisted himself on to Dickey Cobden, and plumped down in the capacious saddle.

He then "moved on," as the old watchmen used to say.

The crowd of foot people going, and cattle coming from the fair, would have prevented any great activity in the way of pace, even had our friend been desirous of using it; but having ridden such an uncommon race, on such a tremendously sultry day, made Mr. Jorrocks well inclined to take the thing quietly at the end; accordingly he let Dickey Cobden poke along at his own pace, while his master kept peeping under the girls' bonnets.

Mr. Jorrocks was a long way behind time for the show. The foot people were all for the dance and the gingerbread stalls, having enough of cattle and sheep at home; but Mr. Jorrocks seeing they were in no hurry, thought there was no occasion for him to be in any either. Dilatoriness is very catching. If you see a man in scarlet going quietly, you are very apt to go quietly too; whereas, if you see one blazing along as hard as ever he can clatter, you are very apt to clap on too, and perhaps find the wearer is going to breakfast with a friend on his way. The same with a railway, a coach, or anything tied to time.

"Vich vay's the cattle show?" inquired Mr. Jorrocks of the first countryman he could get to look at him, at the junction of the roads between the village and tent-covered plain.

"Up there," replied the man, pointing towards the southern hills, "but the show's over."

"Humph," grunted Mr. Jorrocks, stopping his cob against the stream of population, thinking what he should do. Presently the boom of a drum and the twang of a trumpet fell upon his ear; and sundry blue and white flags emerged in sun-bright splendour from among the tents. A large double-poled flag, borne by two men, with an inscription in gilt letters on a white ground, came first; followed by the band, consisting of some half-dozen performers; and then divers trades' banners, mingled with an old Union Jack, and sundry smaller insignia, preceded a long-drawn line of pedestrians walking two and two; most of them with very blotched and pimply noses, and white cheeks.

"Vot's all this about? Vot's all this about?" inquired Mr. Jorrocks, keeping Dickey Cobden's head up towards the music, in spite of all his efforts to turn tail.

"You're just in time, sir, you are just in time!" cried a man in advance, who acted as a sort of drum major, having a broad blue rat band over his shoulder, and a constable's staff in his hand. "We're just going to sit down," added he, waving his hand for Mr. Jorrocks to turn and head the procession.

Accordingly our worthy friend did, riding in front, the band playing, "See the conquering hero comes!"

Thus they proceeded from the moor edge towards the little town, the rush of spectators increasing as they neared the bridge. The procession made the angle of descent, and the music sounded among the crowds who surrounded the shows and stalls of the itinerant dealers. The hardware auctioneer stopped his eloquence, the teachers of the noble art of self-defence stood in their gloves, the wonderful conjuror ceased his exhortations to the gaping clowns to enter his magnificent pavilion, and the musicians belonging to the respective establishments of the five-legged horse, the fat boy, the learned pig, the white-haired lady, the American savages, &c., ceased their clamour to witness the grand procession of the day.

"*A God's wuns!* what's happened now?" exclaimed a voice, rushing out of a stable, as Mr. Jorrocks rode most consequentially past the bridge end, prior to entering the town.

"A dear! a dear!" exclaimed Pigg, wringing his hands in despair. Wot's happened now? here's wor ard ancient gouk gean and joined the Tea-to-tallers! Why, ye ard fondey!" exclaimed Pigg, forcing his way, bare-armed, bare-headed, and coatless, through the crowd, "what's come o'er ye now? Sink, if ar wasn't afear'd of boggin mar neif, ar'd give ye seck a crack in the guts," added he, seizing Dickey Cobden by the head to arrest his master's further progress.

"Vot's 'appened now, James Pigg? vot's 'appened now?" exclaimed Mr. Jorrocks, astonished at his bull-keeper's impetuosity.

"MATTER!" roared Pigg, "why, what are ye disgracin' yoursel' for? *Ye* join the Tea-to-tallers! Sink, but ar'd niver ha' hired mysel' if ar'd ha' *thout* sich a thing!"

"*Tea-to-tallers!*" screamed Mr. Jorrocks, in horrified amazement, looking back at the flag with "ST. BOSWELL TEMPERANCE SOCIETY" glittering across the street.

"Ay, *tea-to-tallers!*" repeated Pigg, pulling Dickey Cobden across the road by the head, so as to let the now impeded procession get on, adding, as he led his rescued master along—"Sink, if thou's fit to be trusted frae heam by thysel'!"

"God sink, but thou's parfectly disgracin' thysel'," observed Pigg, as he got his master off the cob and hustled him into the stable alongside the bull. "Get in there and hide thysel'," added he, pushing his master into the next stall.

"Vy, James, they told me it was the dinner band, or I never would have thought of joinin' them," replied Mr. Jorrocks, anxious to explain.

"Dinner band!" exclaimed Pigg; "couldn't thou read 'TEMPERANCE' on the colours? What's the use of all thy grand larnin', ar wonder?"

"Vell, never mind; they haven't cotched me, at all events," replied Mr. Jorrocks. "Tell me, now, all how and about it; wot do they say about my ball; am I to have the prize?"

"Thou get thysel' dusted over," replied Pigg, giving Mr. Jorrocks's back a crack that sent a volley of dust out of it, "and gan to the dinner, and they'll tell ye all about it; it's ne use axin' me, ar's not the judge."

No sooner had the band—Which was "open to all and influenced by none"—deposited the teetotaller in their Temperance Hall, than off they set again to the moor, to escort the diners to the tent. The same sort of processions with a change of flags, marked the progress of the farmers: "Speed the Plough" usurped the place of the great Temperance banner; while "Live and let live," and similar mottoes, floated on smaller flags. Perched on the hillside, by a belt of wood, and commanding an uninterrupted view over the village below, was a spacious tent, whose patched and tattered canvas bespoke it better adapted for a sultry sun-bright day, like the present, than an exposure to those ruder elements with which the place was frequently visited. The interior was in keeping with the canvas: rude benches formed of planks nailed upon posts driven into the ground, ranged by the side of long, uneven deal tables, covered with snow-white linen. The cross-table at the head of the tent was a good deal elevated; and a venerable, carved, black oak chair stood in the centre, ensconced amid a profusion of dahlias, sunflowers, evergreens, and heather, giving the chairman's seat somewhat the appearance of the tenements that in former days used to be occupied by Jack-in-the-green. The seats on the right and the left were reserved for the big and such like. The tables were also decorated with bouquets, and wreaths and crowns of flowers dangled from the roof. There had been great anxiety all the morning for the arrival of our worthy friend. His acquaintance were desirous of his company, while those who had not seen him were anxious to have a sight of him. His bull, too, had created no small sensation, and it was strongly suspected by those who had watched the countenances and manoeuvres of the judges, as they moved, mysteriously and solemnly, from animal to animal, that Jorrocks's bull stood a very good chance of a prize. The bull-show had been rather deficient, and Jorrocks's, though not a first-rate animal—or most likely the Duke of Donkeyton would not have given him it—cut a very good figure among the inferior animals by which it was surrounded. Whether the deficiency in the bull department had been caused by Mr. Pigg's repeated assertion that his was Sir Robert Peel's bull (as in the case of Mr. Cheesecake), is not material to inquire—the fact is as we state it.

Pigg having rubbed his master over, and Mr. Jorrocks having righted his wig, combed his whiskers, and flopped his Hessian boots over with his handkerchief, reached the tent just as the band and its followers, headed by Captain Bluster, rounded the turn of the road above, and Mr. Fortescue, the intended chairman of the day, dismounted from his horse, and gave him to his groom. At the same moment a rush of blooming damsels came scuttling up from the town, bearing smoking dishes on their heads or in their hands, with which they hurried into the tent, where they were judiciously interspersed by the landlord of the inn among the cold joints, salads, and sweets, that had for some time been attracting the attention of the flies on the flower-decked tables.

The chairman, a neighbouring squire of large estate, combined the polished manners of the modern school with the sterling characteristics of the old-fashioned English gentleman. He was at home everywhere, from the palace of the sovereign to the cottage of the labourer. Liberal, high-minded, and gentlemanly, he was looked up to and respected by all. The fair and cattle show of St. Boswell mainly owed its existence to him; and being held in the autumn, when London no longer possesses attractions, he seldom missed the opportunity of meeting his friends and neighbours by presiding.

Having passed up the tent to his seat, the places on his right and left at the cross-table were immediately filled by the foremost of the procession, and the last comers crowded the tent up to the very entrance. The band having deposited the party, then sheered off, to divide themselves into parties, to open the dances at the various public-houses.

It being an hour or two after most of the farmers' usual dinner-time, and their appetites being whetted by the fine mountain air they had been inhaling as they wandered about among the cattle show, or stood making their bargains, there was little mercy shown the viands when they once sat down; and grace had hardly escaped the clergyman's lips ere the clatter of knives and forks commenced. It was a half-crown ordinary, and each person called for and drank what he liked. Londoners who order dinner at two guineas a head for half-fledged appetites, would wonder how such ravenous maws could be appeased on the best roast and boiled at half-a-crown a head. There were capons, and ducks, and hams, and tongues, and boiled legs of mutton, and roast legs of mutton, and boiled beef, and roast beef, and trembling jellies, and decorated tarts, with the finest vegetables that had been exhibited for prizes at the flower and vegetable show of the morning. Talk of the cheapness and plenty of a French ordinary! it's not to be compared to that of an English one—a good English farmer's ordinary.

It used to be an old school recommendation, to "let one's meat stop one's mouth"; and most assiduously the farmers acted up to the injunction. After they once set to, there was little heard but clatter, clatter, clatter; varied by an occasional request for another slice of beef or ham, or another piece of bread. Then the fluids began to be called for; wine was only seen at the cross-table, and a very short way down the centre one; most of them indulged in ale or bottled porter. At length the most ravenous appetites were appeased, and eyes gradually began to wander from the plates to the surrounding faces. Friendly nods of recognition took place. "How is't, Jack?" "How is't, Tom?" "Good day, Mr. Brown." "Hope you're well, Mr. Green." "How's the missis?" Then the cross-table was scrutinised. "There's Mr. Lumpington," said one. "Who's that next Mr. Patterson?" inquired another. "Oh, that is Mr. Smith of Grittleton," replied a third. "No, not him; the gentleman on the other side, with the figured-velvet coat on." "Oh! I don't know him; he's a stranger." "Mr. Wopstraw," continued the last spokesman, stretching back towards the next table, "can you tell us who that is on Mr. Grittleton's left?"

"On Mr. Grittleton's left?" repeated Mr. Wopstraw, very deliberately, his eye turning slowly towards the cross-table; "upon the *who-o-ole* I should say it was Mr. Jorrocks."

"Oh, that's Mr. Jorrocks, is it?" exclaimed the inquirer, recovering his equilibrium to communicate the intelligence at his own table; "it's Mr. Jorrocks," observed he, "the owner of the White Bull."

"Is that him?" exclaimed half-a-dozen voices; and in a very short time Mr. Jorrocks had the eyes of the majority of the meeting upon him.

From this he was relieved by grace, followed by the Chairman rising to propose the health of the Queen.

"Gentlemen," said he, "I rise to propose to you the health of our gracious Queen (cheers); I am satisfied that in this company your loyalty will induce you to drink the toast with every honour (loud cheers). But, in addition to your loyalty, you cannot forget that in drinking the health of your Sovereign, you are drinking the health of a youthful Queen, who, as a wife and a mother, has in the highest station set the brightest example of domestic virtue. Gentlemen, I give you the Queen, upstanding, and three times three." The toast was received with the loudest cheering.

"The next toast on my list," said he, "is the health of His Royal Highness Prince Albert. In addition to the high station he holds as consort to the Queen, and the popularity he has gained since his arrival in this country, he has a claim on our affections as the ardent promoter of agriculture." (Cheers.)

The Chairman then gave the toast, which was drunk with three times three.

The third toast was, "The health of the Prince of Wales," whose high breeding, the Chairman thought, would be allowed by agriculturists to give fair promise of future renown.

"Queen Adelaide, and the rest of the royal family," then, with similar honours. Then came "The Army and Navy," and "The Bishop and Clergy of the Diocese," for which latter toast the Rector of St. Boswell returned thanks.

The Chairman then rose to propose "Success to the St. Boswell Agricultural Association." After congratulating the company on the excellence of the cattle show, the number of competitors for premiums, and the large attendance of yeomanry and farmers, he observed that in days like the present, when they had foreigners to compete with,

British farmers must depend chiefly upon the excellence of their breed of cattle, and every exertion ought to be made to produce the greatest possible quantity of consumable food from the land; but when he saw the great improvements which had been effected and were in progress, he felt they might exclaim in the words of a homely saying—"Who's afraid?" (Cheers.) He trusted the St. Boswell Agricultural Association would long flourish and prosper, because he was convinced an increase of agricultural skill and industry was of vital consequence to the country, and identified with the maintenance of its independence and happiness. Meetings like the present, where a number of persons whose interests were identical, were assembled in social intercourse—the enterprising farmer and the honest, industrious labourer—must produce good results (loud cheers). He heartily wished well to agriculture; it was an art in which he took great pleasure—a pursuit dignified in every age by being practised or encouraged by men in the highest rank and of the highest talent. He concluded by giving "Prosperity to the St. Boswell Agricultural Association," and sat down amidst loud cheering.

The Chairman then announced that he should call upon the Secretary to read the report of the committee on the transactions of the past year, and then the awards of the judges for the present one.

On hearing this, Mr. Jorrocks immediately found himself on a seat of thorns, on which the worthy gentleman continued to recline during the infliction of a somewhat lengthy document. It glanced at all the transactions of the year—ploughing, hedging, reaping, cattle-show, sheep-show, horse-show, pig-show—and how the Society, though flourishing, would be better for a little more money; all of which was listened to with that impatient inattention that usually characterises meetings anxious to get to the point.

At length the Secretary concluded, and after wetting his whistle with a mouthful of hot port, he drew a document from his pocket, and announced that he would now proceed to read the awards of the judges of the present show.

Mr. Jorrocks bit his lips, and squeezed his hands till he sent all the blood to his fingers' ends.

The Secretary, however, with painful prolixity, took another sip of "black strap," and gave two or three hems that did not seem to satisfy him, for he took out a great blue-silk pocket-handkerchief, and having unfolded it very deliberately, and ascertained the exact centre, blew his nose with a long and melodious blow.

He then began reading. "The following are the awards of the judges," said he, unfolding a long slip of manuscript. "For the best bull of any age, above two years, five entries, Mr. Johnson, ten sovereigns."

Mr. Jorrocks's countenance fell five-and-twenty per cent. "He may have got the second, however," grunted he.

The Secretary again read—"For the best bull under two years of age, seven entered, five sovereigns, Mr. Grumbleton." (Applause followed this announcement.)

Mr. Jorrocks tried to look unconcerned, and, in doing so, knocked a glass of port into his lap.

The Secretary then proceeded with his light reading, showering sovereigns upon the owners of cows, and heifers, and calves, and tups, and lambs, and ewes, boars, sows, and cottagers' pigs, each announcement being followed by more or less applause. At length he got through his list.

The Chairman then rose to perform what he said was to him one of the most gratifying tasks of the day— namely, proposing the healths of "The Successful Candidates." He had attended many meetings in St. Boswell—almost every meeting that had taken place—and he could safely say that each succeeding one outstripped its predecessor in the number and value of the stock, and he felt confident they would go on improving until their shows would be second to none in the kingdom. He concluded by proposing the healths of "The Successful Candidates."

After a long pause, caused by the successful candidates waiting for the head prize-man, Mr. Johnson, to return thanks for the body, Mr. Grumbleton at length rose, and was followed by the representatives of cows, tups, heifers, calves, lambs, ewes, &c., all standing and looking as solemn as judges. Thank God! farmers are no orators. They are almost the only class exempt from the curse of eloquence. They say what they've got to say, and are done with it, instead of yammering and "honourable friend-ing," "honourable gentlemaning," and moving, seconding, amending, using all the jargon of Parliament, in fact. Mr. Grumbleton dribbled out what he had to say, and all the horned and other cattle were speedily in their seats again.

The Chairman having filled a bumper, held it up before him, and called upon the company to imitate his example. Those who drank wine having complied with his request, and those who drank spirit having replenished their glasses, the Chairman again rose to address them. "I call," he said, "for a bumper, for two reasons: first, because the toast I am about to propose is one where a little consolation and encouragement is required; and, secondly, because in that toast is included a gentleman whose name is famous throughout the universe"— ["That's me," observed Mr. Jorrocks aloud to himself]—"and who has honoured us with his presences for the first time, this day."—["I said so," said Mr. Jorrocks, jingling his money in his breeches-pocket. All eyes sought out the great unknown.]—"Gentlemen," continued the Chairman, "the toast I have to propose to your notice is that of 'The Unsuccessful Candidates' (applause). I could wish that at the first appearance among us of a gentleman so distinguished in many enterprising undertakings, we could have had the satisfaction of drinking the health of Mr. Jorrocks as a successful candidate"—["Indeed, so do I," observed our friend aloud to himself, with a deep sigh and a shake of the head—an observation that elicited a laugh from those who heard it]—"but," continued the Chairman, it is not for mortal to command success, though I am sure all of you who witnessed the noble animals our distinguished guest exhibited this day—["I'd only one," grunted Mr. Jorrocks, adding, "and that was one too many"]—"I should say, gentlemen, those of you who saw the noble animals our distinguished guest and the rest of the unsuccessful competitors exhibited here this day, will readily admit that they deserved success"—["The judges were all wrong," grunted Mr. Jorrocks aloud to himself; "wouldn't give tuppence a dozen for such fellows"]—and in drinking their healths I am sure you will cordially join me in wishing one and all 'better luck next time.'"

The toast was drunk amidst great applause, Mr. Jorrocks sticking his legs out before him, and looking very like having taken the rest.[1]

A considerable pause ensued, all eyes being anxiously turned on the "lion of the day." Mr. Jorrocks, however, didn't seem at all inclined to acknowledge the compliment, and crossed one leg over the other, as much as to say—"Some one else may return thanks." How long this humour might have prevailed is uncertain, had not a familiar voice, exclaiming, "*Now then, ard man!*" in a cheering tone, risen above the knockings of knives and forks and the clatter of glasses and spoons.

"That's James Pigg!" observed Mr. Jorrocks aloud to himself, with a start that brought him on to his legs to see where his misleader was. "Rot him," added he, "it was him wot did all the mischief." Loud cheering followed this movement, which Mr. Jorrocks acknowledged with his usual affability. Better humour returned with the restoration of silence.

"Mr. Chairman and gentlemen," at length said he, looking uncommonly wise, and dancing his glass about among the biscuit crumbs before him—"Mr. Chairman and gentlemen," repeated he, "if I was to say that I am gratified at the result of this day's exhibition, I should be tellin' you an uncommon crammer—I shall not do no such thing—I'm not the man to thank you for nothin' (laughter and applause). On the contrary, I'll candidly confess, that I'm quite down in the mouth at the result of this day's show—I'm mortified to think that my quadruped—my noble quadruped—my beloved quadruped—should not appear in your eyes wot he does in mine."—["Weall done, ould 'un!" exclaimed James Pigg, tapping his oaken staff against the table, adding, with a shake of the head, "Sink him, he can jaw a bit."]—"It would, indeed, have been a proud feather in my cap," continued Mr. Jorrocks, "if I had carried the prize back to my shop, and been hailed as the wictor at this great gatherin' (applause). Not as I cares for the money—oh no! it's the honour I look to."—["Sink the honour!" exclaimed Pigg, "the *brass* is the thing!"]—"It's the unsullied reputation of that spotless b*a*ll—that milk-white beautiful critter"—(Here Mr. Jorrocks's voice faltered, and he was apparently overcome by his feelings.)

"Haud up, ard 'un! haud up!" exclaimed Pigg cheeringly, amid the applause and shouts of the company.

"'*Old your noise!*" replied Mr. Jorrocks, with a shake of the head, looking very indignantly towards the spot from whence the voice proceeded; for the dense volleys of smoke that now filled the tent, and a large pot of flowers and evergreens behind which Pigg ducked, screened him from his master's view. Mr. Jorrocks was quite put out.

"Well," said he, after the applause that was raised to give him time to collect himself had subsided—"well," said he, "it's no use botherin' about the matter. I've not gained the prize, and the loss is yours as well as mine. I had as fine, hoiley an oration as ever was uttered, all ready to let off in case I had won; but I'll candidly tell you, losin' was not taken into my kalkilation: if it had, I would not have come here (laughter and applause). You may laugh," observed Mr. Jorrocks, "and I makes no doubt them as laughs *have* won; but I can tell you it's no jokin' matter, comin' swelterin' 'ere as I've done this 'ot day. But, if there's any of you gen'lmen," looking at the unsuccessful upstandets "wot would like to disembogue anything, I'll not stand atwixt you and the chair." So saying, our friend soused himself into his seat again.

Mr. Jorrocks having delivered himself of his speech, the curiosity of the meeting seemed a good deal subsided, and the landlord of the inn who supplied the entertainment having made his appearance for orders, there was a considerable tendency exhibited for ardent spirits, and ruin, and brandy, and gin, and Hollands were loudly called for from all quarters, the demand being occasionally accompanied by an order for a pipe. Great good-fellowship appeared to prevails especially at the lower end of the tent, where Pigg's voice was frequently loudly conspicuous. James was entertaining his auditors with wonderful accounts of farming in the north, and particularly the farming of his cousin Deavilboger's land, which, from his account, was a perfect model farm. His auditors entertained him with spirit in return, and as each glass went down, James's voice became louder. The Chairman having run through the usual routine of toasts, rested a little on his oars, and all tongues were gradually let loose into one general cry. Wheat, and beans, and ruin, and cattle, and whisky, and baccy, and barley, and pigs, and sheep, and turnips, and tares, and long horns, and short horns, and protection societies, and corn-law leagues: all sorts of farming and agricultural concerns were severally discussed.

Even those fertile subjects seemed to fail at last, and the noise slackened till it gradually died down, and Pigg's and half-a-dozen other voices were the only ones that kept going. Mr. Jorrocks sat comforting himself with a bottle of uncommon strong port, fresh from the wood. At length the Chairman rose to announce that the Rev. Mr. Prosey Slooman would favour the company with the result of his experiments with guano upon turnips.

"*Sink your guarno! Muck's your man!*" exclaimed Pigg, at the top of his voice—an assertion that caused a roar of laughter throughout the meeting, and somewhat disconcerted Mr. Prosey Slooman, who kept fumbling about in his pockets for his spectacles while he had them on his nose all the time. At length he ascertained where they were, and having lowered them, he proceeded to unfold a very bulky bale of manuscript, that caused an involuntary shudder among those who were acquainted with his tedious prolixity. Slooman being on the best of terms with himself, coughed and hemmed and stroked his chin, and looked complacently around, as much as to say, "I am Sir Oracle, and when I ope my lips let no dog bark." He was a little, bristly-headed, badger-pyed, pedantic, radical schoolmaster, who farmed his own glebe, and managed matters somewhat in the style of the celebrated Wackford Squeers, frequently recreating the boys with a little work on the farm. He was a great turnip and root grower, which the ill-natured world said were largely consumed in the house, as well as in the foldyard. Mr. Prosey Slooman had given the boys a whole holiday's work on the farm that day, in order that he might inflict his tediousness on the assembled farmers at St. Boswell. Having somewhat recovered from the unwonted interruption occasioned by Pigg's exclamation, he gradually screwed his coarse features into a self-complacent smile, and proceeded to address the meeting.

"Gentlemen," said he, "after the very flattering appeal that has been made to me by our distinguished Chairman—a gentleman not less remarkable for his urbanity than for his scientific acquirements—I cannot hesitate for one moment in complying with his request, backed, as it appears to be, by the unanimous wish of this enlightened assembly. I cannot, I say, hesitate in laying before you, as shortly and succinctly as the extensiveness of the subject, and the humble talents with which nature has endowed me, will allow, the very important—I might almost say, nationally interesting—experiments I have made upon the valuable, and, to farmers, never-to-be-sufficiently-appreciated agricultural production called turnips, with various kinds of manures and compositions—particularly guano—upon different soils."

Mr. Slooman paused, in expectation of applause; but a dead silence prevailed, save a slight noise at the low end of the tent, caused by Pigg's drinking off his neighbour's brandy—as he said, in mistake for his own—an awkward mistake, as his glass happened to be empty.

"Gentlemen," continued Mr. Slooman, taking off the top layer of the ponderous pile of papers, and pompously unfolding it, "my first experiment was with an acre of globe-turnips with one hundred pounds of guano."

"*Sink your guarno! Muck's your man!*" again roared Pigg, to the convulsion of the company.

"*Silence!*" exclaimed Slooman, with flashing eyeballs, or "*I'll*——"

He would have said "flog you," but returning presence of mind saved him.

"*Order! order!* pray keep order, gentlemen!" interposed the Chairman.

"It's that beggar Pigg," grunted Mr. Jorrocks, helping himself to a bumper of port; "doesn't seem to care a copper for the misery he's brought upon me."

"I am obliged to the chair for interposing so promptly on my behalf," observed Mr. Slooman, bowing very obsequiously; "interruptions so coarse, so unmanly, so unseemly, only recoil upon the brainless head that makes them."

"*Ay, ay!*" grunted Pigg; "ar'll sarve ye out e-now!" clutching his oaken staff as he spoke.

"Mr. Chairman and gentlemen," resumed Mr. Slooman, returning again to his paper, "I was saying, when that stupid blockhead interrupted me, that my first experiment was with an acre of globe-turnips, with one hundred pounds of guano, upon ten single-horse cart-loads of farmyard manure, which produced twenty-two tons of turnips when weighed in December; while upon a second acre of the same land, with twenty single-horse cart-loads of the same farmyard manure, without guano, I only got fourteen tons."

"*Muck's your man!* for all that," exclaimed Pigg.

"There again!" started Mr. Slooman, laying down his paper and throwing out both hands, "am I, Mr. Chairman," continued he, addressing the President, "am I to be protected in the gratuitous performance of a public duty, or am I——"

"Who is it makes that noise?" asked the Chairman, for he could not see for the smoke.

"Gan on, ard 'un! gan on!" exclaimed Pigg; "there's nebody fashin' ye!"

"That Pigg's drunk," observed Mr. Jorrocks aloud to himself, as he *at* the port again.

Mr. Slooman again essayed to proceed.

"A third acre of Swedish turnips, gentlemen," continued he, "with two hundred pounds of guano, mixed with four bushels of sifted house-ashes, produced fourteen tons; while an acre adjoining the above, with twenty-five single-horse cart-loads of the farmyard manure, produced only ten tons sixteen hundred weight."

"*That's a lee!*" roared Pigg. "MUCK'S YOUR MAN!" repeated he, louder than ever.

Mr. Slooman dropped his hands, and stood transfixed. Laughter, groans, hisses, and all sorts of discordant noises prevailed, mingled with the Chairman's cries of "*Order!* order!" and a few exclamations of "Turn him out, turn him out!"

"Ay, torn him out!" roared Pigg. "Torn him out!" repeated he, thinking they meant the Chairman; "and ar'll come and sit up there, and sing ye a sang," added he.

"Really, gentlemen, this noise and interruption is very indecorous," observed the Chairman, rising as soon as the uproar began to subside.

"If it is not the pleasure of the meeting to hear the reverend gentleman, I am——"

"*Raverend!*" roared Pigg. "Ar'll give ye a raverend toast: ar'll give ye, 'Mair pigs and fewer parsons!' " (Roars of laughter.)

"Who is it that makes that disturbance?" again demanded the Chairman.

"'OLD YOUR NOISE, JAMES PIGG!" exclaimed Mr. Jorrocks, rising, and speaking as loud as he could; an order that had the effect of restoring silence on the instant. James couched behind the flower-stand.

Mr. Slooman stood in expectation of some reprimand from the Chairman on the offender; but the former seemed satisfied with the restoration of silence, and Mr. Slooman again proceeded, and exhausted half-an-hour in a disquisition on the miraculous qualities of guano, which, in his opinion, beat everything else out of the field.

Pigg kept up a sort of running commentary on Mr. Slooman's observations, sufficiently low, however, not to reach his master's ears.

The next incident of the evening was the appearance of Mr. Wopstraw, who, at the earnest request of many admiring friends in his neighbourhood, rose to acquaint the company with the result of his experience in the article of guano. Mr. Wopstraw was still attired in the costume of the morning, drab greatcoat and drab overalls then worn, as he said, to keep the heat out, and now retained perhaps to keep the smoke out. Under them appeared a respectable black coat and waistcoat, with drab breeches; and he had a snuff-coloured bandanna round his neck. Mr. Wopstraw was considered a very safe man—one that never did anything without due consideration, and who weighed the *pros* and *cons* of everything in his mind. His rising caused an outburst of applause.

"Mr. Chairman and gentlemen," said he, plastering his straggling hair flat over his head with his hand—"Mr. Chairman and gentlemen," repeated he, "I have heard what the Reverend Mr. Slooman has told about the guano, but as I've used some myself, upon the *wh-o-o-le* I think I may say he's not altogether right. He thinks little of foldyard manure compared to it; but, upon the *wh-o-o-le*, I think guano and foldyard mixed is the thing."

"Ay, ay," said Pigg, "that's mair like the ticket."

"I had some turnips," continued Wopstraw, "sown with guano alone, and some with foldyard manure, and, upon the *wh-o-o-le*, I should say the guano took the lead at starting, and kept it well to September, when the foldyard began to tell, and came on when the flush of t'other was over."

"*Muck's your man!*" again roared Pigg.

"Therefore, upon the *wh-o-o-le*," concluded Wopstraw, "I should say guano was a good thing for setting turnips a-going; but you should have muck, as that gentleman calls it, to come up when the effect of t'other is over." Mr. Wopstraw resumed his seat amid considerable applause.

Mr. Smith now rose to perform a duty in giving a toast that ought to have been given at an earlier period of the evening, namely, that of the health of their worthy Chairman, to whom they and the country in general were under so many obligations, not only for the honour he invariably did them of presiding at their annual meetings, but for the very exemplary manner in which he discharged every duty of a country gentleman. (Drunk with three times three, and one cheer more.)

The Chairman returned thanks with his usual felicity. He then called upon Mr. Hogger to detail the result of his experiments with nitrate of soda as a manure, which that gentleman did with great perspicuity on various crops—oats grass, barley, wheat, &c.

Shortly after he sat down, and some of the company were beginning to look at their watches to see how much longer they might sit, when the Secretary was observed to proceed, with an air of importance and mystery, to the Chairman, with a paper in his hand, on which they held a conference for some seconds. The Chairman rose to address the meeting.

"Gentlemen," said he, "at an earlier period of the day I had the honour of proposing two toasts for your acceptance—one, 'The health of the Successful Candidates,' the other, 'The health of the Unsuccessful Candidates on the present occasion.' Since then our able Secretary has discovered that we have placed a distinguished stranger in a false position—a position that it affords me, as I feel certain it will you, the liveliest satisfaction to rectify."

"Vot's all that about?" said Mr Jorrocks, pricking his ears.

"You will perhaps remember, gentlemen," continued the Chairman, "that the premium for the best bull was said to be awarded to Mr. Johnson; and perhaps it may have struck you, as it certainly did me, as rather singular that the taker of the first prize, neither in person nor by proxy, returned thanks for the compliment."

"Werry true," observed Mr. Jorrocks, who had observed nothing of the sort.

"That circumstance is now explained by the recent discovery," continued the Chairman. "The bull, it appears, was known to the judges as Mr. Jobson's bull."

"*Mine*, for a guinea!" exclaimed Mr. Jorrocks.

"The prize was unanimously awarded to him," continued the Chairman.

"Hurrah!" exclaimed Mr. Jorrocks; "hurrah!"

"What's thou hurrain' for?" roared Pigg. "Thy name's not Jobson."

"But the Secretary in writing the name down, amid the hurry and pressure of the crowd, it seems, wrote it *Johnson* instead of Jobson. Now, Mr. Jobson, as many of the present meeting are aware, is the farm-steward of his Grace the Duke of Donkeyton—the intimateally of my honourable friend, if he will allow me so to call him, on my left," observed the Chairman, turning to Mr. Jorrocks.

"Certainly!" replied Mr. Jorrocks. "Certainly!" repeated he.

"Among other flattering, honourable, and I am sure I may add well-deserved, marks of distinction conferred by his Grace on my honourable friend, was that of making him a present of this bull."

"Quiet true," observed Mr. Jorrocks, "quite true. The Duke gave me its 'ighest compliment he could pay me."

"And therefore, gentlemen," continued the Chairman, "not to trouble you with the particulars of a story whose conclusion you have doubtless anticipated. I have to beg that you will join me in rectifying the unintentional error of our Secretary, by receiving the name of Mr. Jorrocks as a successful competitor on this occasion, with such bumpers and such acclamations as will testify our sincere delight at his well-merited success, and will soothe, at the same time, the feelings of mortification he must have suffered at the late erroneous announcement." The Chairman concluded by drinking Mr. Jorrocks's health in a bumper, with three times three, amidst great applause.

"Your good health, Mr. Jorrocks!" "Your good health, Mr. Jorrocks!" "Your good health, Mr. Jorrocks!" then flew at our worthy friend, like arrows at a target, from all parts of the tent; and the Chairman having drained off his glass, stood forward to mark the time. Three times three and one hearty cheer more were thundered forth with tremendous effect. Mr. Jorrocks sat nursing a leg, and bowing his head like a Chinese monster on a chimney-piece.

"Now for an *o-ra-tion!*" exclaimed Pigg, as silence gradually prevailed, and our friend let down the leg preparatory to rising.

"Mr. Chairman and gentlemen," exclaimed Mr. Jorrocks, rising, and waving his hand for silence, "I should, indeed, be unworthy the name of a true-born Briton if I didn't confess that this unexpected honour has completely unmanned me (applause). Gentlemen, I haven't the wanity to suppose that the enthusiastic reception you have given the name of John Jorrocks is attributable to any 'umble merits of mine, but simply paid me as the owner of that able and distinguished ball, the Markis o' Bray (applause). In the name of that able, that amiable, that magnificent quadruped. I return you the most 'artfelt thanks (loud applause) would that he could speak and do it himself! But believe me, gentlemen, the Markis's master's 'art is a bustin' with gratitude for the kindness you have shown the Markis. You have conferred on him the 'ighest honour a 'igh-bred ball can attain—awarded him the first prize. Oh! but it was a noble act, and nobly has that ball desered it! Gentlemen, excuse my saying' more, my feelin's overpower me. As my friend, Tarquinius Brown, of Friday Street, sublimely sings—

> If ever fondest prayer for other's weal awailed on 'igh,
> Mine shall not all be lost in hair, but waft thy name above
> the sky.

So shall my best wishes, and the best wishes of my ball, waft your names into the attics o' the hupper regions o' the sky" (great applause). Mr. Jorrocks resumed his seat, apparently overcome by his feelings, amidst loud cheers. Presently he arose, and spoke as follows:—"Mr. Chairman, with your permission I'll give a toast—a toast that will find its way 'ome to the 'arts of you all, without any soft sawder from me. It is the 'ealth of one most jestly dear to me—dear in every pint of view, but bound in stronger union by the result of this day's show. Oh! it's a proud thing to carry off the prize in the manner my ball has done, beatin' every ball in the country, from the Prime Minister's down'ards."

"Ay, ay," grunted Pigg, adding to himself, "thou'd best say nowt about *that*."

"But oh! gentlemen! gentlemen! you've got no liquor!" continued Mr. Jorrocks, looking about him and holding up his own empty bottle. "Here, waiter!" roared he; "you man in the shirt-sleeves!" added he, hollaing to the landlord, who, coatless, had come in with a basket to gather the empty bottles; "fatch in a dozen of your strongest military port, and let me have the 'ealth of my ball drank as it ought to be."

"Ay!" roared Pigg; "and fetch me a bottle o' *roum!*" adding, "wine's o'er strang for mar stommack."

"Yes, sir," exclaimed the landlord, hurrying off to execute the order, or as much of it as the state of his cellar would allow.

Presently the drawing of corks was heard, and the bottles began to be scattered down the table; Pigg's rum, too, made its appearance; and master and man seeing to the charging of their friends, the bull's health was drunk amidst tremendous applause.

Mr. Jorrocks then tried to let off the speech he spoke of as having prepared, but the day was too far gone, and it hung fire; so after a few unsuccessful efforts, he resumed his seat amidst loud cheers. The Chairman having proposed "The health of the gentlemen who had so ably performed the difficult and delkate duty of awarding the premiums," as also "The health of the Secretary and Committee of Management," shortly after withdrew; and, on the motion of Mr. Nobody, Mr. Jorrocks took the chair—Pigg placing himself as vice.

"The health of the bull" was then drunk again, Mr. Jorrocks ordering the necessary supplies, and returning thanks as before. Many other toasts followed.

Captain Bluster at last rose to propose Mr. Jorrocks's health in another capacity, namely, that of a magistrate. The Captain's articulation was now rather thick, and he spoke as if his tongue were a size too large for his mouth; his eyes, too, looked glassy and queer.

Mr. Jorrocks again rose to return thanks, labouring as he was under the influence of his old friend the hiccup.

"Captain (hiccup) Bluster, and (hiccup) gen'lmen," said he, rising, and lurching considerably as he attempted to take hold of his glass, "this is the proudest (hiccup) moment of my (hiccup) life. (Cheers.) I feel considerably obligated to my friend the (hiccup) Captain for the considerable (hiccup) compliments he has (hiccup) paid me as a beak. I believe I may say that there is not a more (hiccup) independent one on the (hiccup) bench. Some, p'raps, may know a little more (hiccup) law, more (hiccup) Coke upon (hiccup) Littleton (hiccup), pig upon (hiccup) bacon, or whatever you call the (hiccup) thing; but for real substantial (hiccup) jastice such as our (hiccup) forefathers used to (hiccup) out, there is none like John (hiccup) Jorrocks. Before I (hiccup) down," continued he, looking very wise, "let me propose a (hiccup) toast, the health of a (hiccup) gen'lman second only to (hiccup) Wellington in arms, and (hiccup) Lyndhurst in law—my (hiccup) friend Captain (hiccup) Bluster; I dare say (hiccup) Waterloo was as much gained by him (hiccup) as by any (hiccup) else. 'Captain Bluster's good (hiccup) health,'" concluded Mr. Jorrocks, draining his glass preparatory to resuming what he thought was his seat, but in reality a vacuum, which had the effect of sending him neck and croup through the back of the tent, just as a clown disappears in a pantomime.

"*God sink!* t'ard man'll be lamin' hissel!" exclaimed Pigg, jumping up as he saw his master's heels disappear above the level of the table.

---

1. Turned sulky.

XXX

Oh, cruel was the justice that took my love from me.

WE HAVE TO APOLOGISE TO our, or Mr. Jorrocks's noble friend, the Marquis of Bray, for the very unceremonious way we have left him during the last three chapters, dripping in his woman's attire over Mrs. Flather's fire, after the fair Emma disappeared on the announcement of who he was. It is difficult, in novel-writing, to drive the two parts of the story (into which all orthodox three-volume ones should be divided) like phaeton horses, and prevent one part outstepping the other, and at this point our farmer friend has shot considerably ahead of the ladies. We have got them no further than where the Marquis of Bray becomes the unconscious guest of the equally unconscious Mrs. Flather, after his midnight ramble on escaping from Mr. Heavytail's harvest-home ball, whither he had been seduced by the Cockney Highlander, Mr. Jorrocks.

Before Mrs. Flather and the Marquis had got the matter explained, and his lordship removed from the kitchen into the parlour, and the fire resuscitated, the fair Emma returned, very unlike the Emma that had run away. In lieu of the common drawn and frilled nightcap she had on when she left, she appeared in a fine embroidered muslin one, trimmed with Valenciennes lace, and tied with a blue ribbon; while her swelling bust and rounded figure were well set off by a blue and white foulard wrapping gown, trimmed and tied down the front with blue ribbons, and a cape trimmed with plaiting of the same coloured ribbon, open cotton stockings, and blue velvet slippers, trimmed with swan's down.

The Marquis was then invested in the flannel dressing-gown Emma had discarded, in lieu of his drenched and tattered silk, as also a pair of Emma's white worsted stockings, and her second-best slippers;

and having got himself tolerably comfortable, Emma and he seated themselves before the now brightly burning fire, while Mrs. Flather fussed for the keys of the cellaret, and drew on a pair of stockings and other little articles of female attire, now rendered more necessary in consequence of the midnight visitor having changed her sex. The fire burnt cheerfully, the room was warm and comfortable, and as the Marquis rolled about in his easy chair by the side of the smiling, pretty Emma, he forgot all the troubles he had passed—all the toads, all the sows, all the clowns, all the dogs, all the guns. Emma and he laughed, and smiled, and looked sweet at each other, until Mrs. Flather's propriety could no longer delay appearing with the sherry and water, but she soon took her departure for the purpose of seeing about the Marquis's bed. Emma did her best; she had tact of a certain order, which, if it did not amount to cleverness, was quite enough for an occasion like the present. There is no time, perhaps, when the soft blandishments of the fair sex are more telling than after an exposure to the rude elements out of doors. Cold and passionless as Emma was, she had the art of pleasing, and the animation the incident inspired threw a natural air into her generally studied conduct; indeed, here there was no occasion for study or calculation. The question was not like one between James Blake and any other of her humbler suitors, where the present state and prospects of each required mature deliberation—there was no need of weighing or considering; the point was to secure the Marquis, and that too as quickly as possible. She did her utmost; whatever subject he touched upon she declared her devoted attachment to; music, painting, poetry, scenery, dancing, all were enthusiastically expatiated upon by her as he severally led them on the *tapis*, with occasionally little sly exclamations at the extraordinary similarity of their ideas. Mrs. Flather, too, was struck at the coincidence; and declared, with more zeal than prudence that they "really appeared to be made for each other." The Marquis, however, was not one either to take fright or a hint, and they would have had to press him much closer before he would have understood them, at least in the light they intended. Thus they chatted on; the Marquis sipping hot sherry and water, inwardly wishing Mrs. Flather anywhere but where she was; Emma, too, would gladly have dispensed with her common-minded mamma, but, like all half-witted people, Mrs. Flather thought there was no management or ingenuity equal to her own.

At length, the relentless clock struck one, and Mrs. Flather insisted upon the reluctant Emma going to bed, whither she retired with sad misgivings as to what might be the result of her indiscreet parent's *tête-à-tête* with the Marquis, which certain significant looks too plainly intimated she meant to have. Mrs. Flather was far too eager, plain-spoken, and matter-of-fact, for her delicate daughter's refinement, though their objects were always the same, viz., to get a good match if they could.

"Well," observed Mrs. Flather, with one of her half-cunning simpers, when she heard Emma's slowly retiring footsteps die out on the landing, after receiving a parting squeeze of the hand from the Marquis as he bid her good-night—"well, Emma and you seem to get on uncommonly well to-night," said she.

"Very well," replied the Marquis, running his fingers through his dishevelled curls—"she's a very fine girl."

"She *will* be," observed Mrs. Flather—"wants taking out a little; she's very shy."

The Marquis thought "middling," but that he kept to himself.

"To be sure she seems less shy with you," simpered Mrs. Flather; "indeed, I never saw any young man she seemed more—more—more at home with than she does with you."

Mrs. Flather rather bungled that sentence; she forgot she was not talking to one of Emma's common place sweethearts, and she felt the words "young man" were not exactly those she ought to have made use of.

The Marquis smiled and bowed—a very convenient course when people don't know exactly what to say.

"She's very amiable," observed Mrs. Flather, rather posed for want of an answer to the last observation.

"I'm sure she is," replied the Marquis. "She looks it all."

"She'll be a great loss to me," sighed Mrs. Flather, anxious to sustain the loss.

The Marquis hemmed assent.

"However, I must put up with it as best I can," added she, still simpering and driving to her point.

"You could not expect to keep so pretty a girl long," replied the Marquis with a yawn, for he had had about enough of the old girl, and wanted to be off to bed.

"Oh, your lordship flatters," simpered Mrs. Flather. "However, I must only think of her happiness. Of that I am sure there can be no doubt," added she, casting a most motherly eye on the Marquis.

"I hope not, I'm sure," said he, finishing his sherry and water, and looking at his diminutive watch. "Bless me I but I'm keeping you up a most unconscionable time," exclaimed he, as he saw it was a quarter past one; adding, "I had no idea it was so late."

Mrs. Flather in vain pressed the sherry and water upon him, in hopes of getting him to the point in the course of another glass; but the Marquis was on his legs and resolute, and she at length most reluctantly rang for candles, and showed him to his room.

She then repaired to Emma, who was sitting in an agony of suspense, figuring to herself all sorts of *gaucheries* being committed by her zealous but indiscreet parent.

Meanwhile the Marquis curled himself up in his bed, congratulating himself that he had not had to pass the night under a hedge.

Mother and daughter then talked the matter anxiously over, each being most desirous of taking the management alone; Emma thinking she could do much better than Mrs. Flather, who insisted that no person could manage these matters so well as herself.

The result of these deliberations will presently appear.

A nice neat breakfast welcomed the Marquis in the morning, to which he sat down with the increased comfort of being in his own clothes. His valet had been sent for from Mr. Jorrocks's, and arrived with the magnificent dressing-case, and all the paraphernalia of dandyism— brushes by the dozen, combs by the score, powders, perfumes, washes, oils, essences, and extracts; while the staple of his costume—coats, waistcoats, trousers, &c.—were supplied in equal profusion.

He came down uncommonly smart; his well-waxed ringlets dangled over each ear from the division of his hair up the centre of his head; an immense pearl pin fastened the folding ends of a lilac satin scarf with white flowers, filling the full rolling collar of his waistcoat, and almost concealing the elaborate workmanship of his shirt front; he wore a bright mulberry-coloured frock-coat, with almost white kerseymere trousers, and very thin patent leather boots.

Emma's toilet was of the happiest order—neat, simple, and well put on. Her glossy hair, worn in the Madonna style, was confined by a sweet little cap—scarcely coming over the parting place of the hair—and ornamented with sprigs of forget-me-not, imparting a little of their blueness to the paler colour of her eyes; while her alabaster complexion gained a slight tinge from the pink ribbons with which the cap was made up. Her healthy cherry lips and pearly teeth accorded with the general freshness of her morning air. Late hours had made no inroads on Emma; on the contrary, there was the full glow of country health without its coarseness. But we have forgot the lady's dress. It was a checked white muslin, well washed, well starched, and well set out, fastened down the front with pink ribbons. Her petticoats were of a rational length, instead of trailing an inch or two on the ground, and showed the symmetry of her well-turned feet and ankles.

Mrs. Flather was too good a manager to lose the advantage of a *tête-à-tête* between Emma and the Marquis; indeed, the whole arrangement had been made during the night. Accordingly, when Mrs. Flather heard his bedroom door close as he vacated his dormitory, she quietly slipped out of the parlour, and went to superintend the toasting and buttering in the kitchen. The Marquis, like all youths of his age, was delighted at finding the fair Emma alone, looking so fresh and blooming, exhibiting such a contrast to the pale and haggard features of a hackneyed London belle at breakfast time. Moreover, the absence of competition and rivalry was greatly in Emma's favour, hiding or softening any little coarseness of figure, and bringing the more captivating points prominently forward. She was a fine-looking girl at all times, but only a beauty when alone. One often sees these sort of girls in the country; girls that rustics rave about, and whom some practised eyes really think something of, but who sink into utter and irretrievable insignificance the moment they enter the competition of a London room.

"Good morning, my dear Miss Flather," said the Marquis, advancing gaily towards Emma, who had just begun fussing among her myrtles and geraniums before the window, in order to be found busy among her flowers as the Marquis entered. "Good morning," repeated he, extending his hand, and squeezing Emma's with a considerable degree of *empressement*. Emma smiled bewitchingly, as she accepted the proffered hand, displaying her beautiful pearly teeth, and establishing a couple of little dimples on her cheeks.

"And how do you find yourself this morning after your night's adventures?" inquired Emma, throwing all the enthusiasm she could muster into her eyes.

"Oh dear!" exclaimed the Marquis, shuddering, "don't mention it; I wouldn't have last night's performance repeated for the world. Fancy wandering about the country all night, getting shot at for a robber, or worried by sheep-dogs. I *do* wonder what pleasure that extraordinary old man sees in these sort of *deliveries*."

"He is a curiosity," laughed Emma, anxious to have a cut at old Jorrocks, but afraid to lead the charge.

"He's a good old fellow, too," rejoined the Marquis, "but really, to see a man at his time of life playing such pranks is rather extraordinary. However, he will not get *me* to accompany him again."

"I should think not," observed Emma, smiling sweetly.

"And yet," continued the Marquis, "I ought not to find fault with the old fool, since it procures me the pleasure of your society."

"Oh!" replied Emma, "that is a pleasure, perhaps, you would as soon have dispensed with."

"Indeed, no!" exclaimed the Marquis, seizing her receding hand. "I assure you the charm of this interview outweighs all the over-night *désagremens*."

"You flatter me," faltered Emma, with a sigh.

"*Don't say that*," rejoined the Marquis, still keeping and pressing the slightly withdrawing hand.

His lordship then kissed it, and Emma flattered herself she was a marchioness.

"You must cause sad devastation among the country swells in these parts," observed the Marquis, eyeing Emma's fair alabaster complexion, now tinged with the slightest possible pink.

"Me!" exclaimed Emma. "Oh no. Indeed, I know nothing of anybody about here."

"You know the Jorrockses, at all events," observed the Marquis.

"Oh, I thought you meant *young* men," replied Emma. "Of course I know the Jorrockses," added she.

"You don't mean to say you've no admirers?" observed the Marquis, eyeing Emma with an air of incredulity.

"Why, as to admirers," replied Emma, with a toss of her head, "I don't mean to say that there are not those who are kind enough to think flatteringly of me; but I'm quite sure all the admiration is on their side."

"But all young ladies should have a lover or two," observed the Marquis.

"I'm afraid my ideas differ from your lordship's there," said Emma, slightly bridling up; "I look upon matrimony as anything but a jesting matter."

"True," replied the Marquis—"true; but matrimony and a little simple flirtation, you know, are different things."

"I don't approve of flirting," replied Emma, looking grave.

"But you don't object to admiration?" rejoined the Marquis, eyeing her now slightly animated eyes.

"If it's accompanied with respect," observed the fair Emma.

"Well, but admiration always precedes love; and you have no objection to the latter, I suppose?"

"If the admiration was *mutual*," replied Emma, casting one of her sweetest looks upon the Marquis; "but, for my own part, I don't profess to be able to fall in love with anybody."

"I should think not," said the Marquis, feeling the compliment.

"My idea is that a person is never *really* in love but once," observed Emma; "and so they should be very careful not to misplace their affections,"—a favourite assertion with ladies angling for offers.

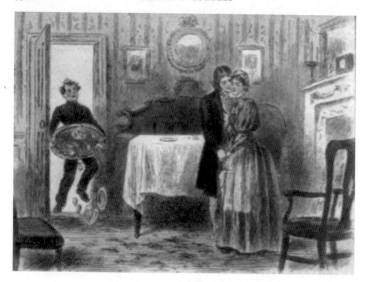

The Marquis of Bray kisses Emma

"And has your *once* not come yet?" asked the Marquis.

Emma blushed slightly, and hung her head—whether conscience-stricken, or in hopes, we cannot say.

"He'll be a happy man who gains that victory," said the Marquis, taking her hand and squeezing it as before—a proceeding that, we are shocked to say, Emma slightly returned.

The Marquis then put his arm round her waist, and gave her a kiss—such a kiss as sounded along the passage, and startled the boy in buttons, who was coming along with the breakfast-tray.

"There'll be white ribbons for me," said he to himself, tripping against the low step leading into the room, and landing head-foremost among the contents of the tray, with his cheek in a preserve-plate. Great was the crash!

It brought Mrs. Flather in an instant from her neighbouring ambush, where she had been forming all sorts of anticipations as to what might be going on in the parlour. The downfall of the best crockery, however, is more than female nerves can withstand, and she was on the spot almost before the boy had gathered himself up. Lucky for him that the Marquis was there, otherwise she would have visited the unpreserved side of his face with a hearty slap. As it was, she said, with an ominous shake of her head, "You *stoo*pid boy!"—and then proceeded to greet her intended son-in-law with as little unconcern as she could muster under the circumstances. Fortunately for all parties there was not much damage done. Two swans had been ejected from the butter-boat without injury to the vessel itself, the cream ewer had been upset over a currant-cake, while some bread and butter had coalesced with a saucer of marmalade. The eggs and dry toast had escaped.

The mischief was soon repaired, and mother, daughter, and Marquis were presently at their morning meal. Tea and coffee, butter and eggs, then occupied their attention for some time. During the repast, however, Emma managed to convey, by signs, to her mother that the Marquis had still not come to book; and, by previous arrangement, Emma retired a little while after breakfast, leaving his lordship in the skilful hands of her mother. The old lady presently began screwing herself up for action; and again commenced with the old question—How he got on with Emma?

"Oh, very well," replied the Marquis. "She's a very fine girl," added he.

"She'll improve," again observed Mrs. Flather. "She wants taking out a little—lost here—no suitable companions for her."

"A London milliner would brush her up," rejoined the Marquis.

"Oh dear, yes," replied Mrs. Flather; "make her quite a different person."

"No doubt," said the Marquis.

"And what does the Duke think of her?" asked Mrs. Flather, after a pause, during which she determined to go to her point.

"Oh, my pa thinks very highly of her, I assure you," replied the Marquis.

"And the Duchess—what does she say?"

"Oh, my ma likes her too, uncommonly. It was only the other day she was talking about asking you both to come and stay with us."

"How very kind!" exclaimed Mrs. Flather, in ecstasies.

"You'll come, I hope," observed the Marquis.

"Indeed, we shall be too happy," replied Mrs. Flather, scarcely able to contain herself.

"You have not *spoken* to Emma yet, I suppose," observed Mrs. Flather, very significantly.

"Not yet," replied the Marquis; "I thought I'd better hear what you had to say first."

"Oh, I'm sure you need anticipate no objection on my part; on the contrary, every—— *Oh dear!* here's that horrid old man!" exclaimed Mrs. Flather, breaking off as she heard a carriage-wheel grinding up to the door, and saw Dickey Cobden's nose poking past the window. What an interruption!

It was too late to say "Not at home;" indeed, Mrs. Flather did not know how the Marquis might like to have his old friend denied. She was, therefore, again doomed to sit on thorns, while the following dialogue sounded through the thin partition wall of the passage into the room; the Marquis sitting listening and laughing as it proceeded.

"Now, young man," said Mr. Jorrocks to the boy in buttons, as the latter replied to the lusty pull our Squire gave the bell. "Now, young man," repeated he, "take off your glove and take this 'ere book in your right 'and."

"The glove is off," replied the boy sulkily.

"Then you've got a werry dirty paw," observed Mr. Jorrocks. "Howsomever, take this 'ere book in it, and listen to what I've got to say to you."

"Yes, sir," grunted the boy.

"You swear that you will true answer make to all sich questions as I shall ax on you: you shall speak the truth, the 'ole truth, and nothin' but the truth, so 'elp you God! Kiss the book."

The boy kissed it.

"Now, young man," continued he, taking back the book, "you're on your oath, and mind you speak the truth, otherwise I'll—I'll—make a present on you to General Tom Thumb: is your missis at 'ome?"

"Yes, sir," replied the boy.

"And is the Markis 'ere?"

"Yes, sir," replied the boy.

"Then you go in and say Mr. Jorrocks is 'ere—Mr. Jastice Jorrocks, in fact—and then you come back and 'old my quadruped."

Presently the boy returned with Mrs. Flather's compliments, and she begged Mr. Jorrocks would walk in; whereupon our friend alighted from his fire-engine, and left it in charge of the boy. Mr. Jorrocks then rolled in, in his usual free-and-easy way, upsetting all Mrs. Flather's and Emma's arrangements, and finally carried off the Marquis before their eyes.

XXXI

Old age laments his vigour spent.—SOMERVILLE

"YE DINNA WANT NE HUNDS, ar's warned?" said Pigg, popping his head into his master's sanctum, where the worthy Justice was busy hammering away at his Journal of General Genius.

"No vot, James?" asked Mr. Jorrocks, scarcely looking up.

"Ye dinna want ne hunds, ar's warned?" repeated Pigg; "harriers, that's te say?"

" 'Arriers! not I," replied Mr. Jorrocks. "Vy do you ax?"

"Why, here's a man o' mar acquentance has getten five couple of uncommon nice 'uns at the door—beagles, that's to say, and he nabbut wants five pund for them."

"Humph!" grunted Mr. Jorrocks; "vot should I want with beagles?"

"Ah! hunt hares with them, to be sure—grand divarsion; ye like hare-soup, ar's warned."

"Vy, 'are-soup's werry pleasant," replied Mr. Jorrocks. "But I can buy an 'are for half-a-crown, what will make as much soup as will serve me and Mrs. J. five days."

"Ay, but ye dinna get the exercise, the divarsion, ye ken. Sink, ye'll be gettin' o'er fat."

" 'Ang the exercise; I'm an exercisin' of my intellect—my mental faculties," replied Mr. Jorrocks. "See," said he, holding up a pile of manuscript; "see wot a heap o' matter I've got for my Journal o' General Genius."

"Hoot ye, and yer larnin'!" exclaimed Pigg; "ye'll never de ne good that way, it's nabbut wastin' paper."

"*Is it though?*" replied Mr. Jorrocks, with a look as much as to say, "you know nothing about it." "This is to teach farmers 'ow to farm,

beaks 'ow to do jastice, fox-'unters 'ow to feed and ride their 'osses—
'old the mirror up to natur, as it were, show virtue its own featurs, wice
its own form, and—ll that sort o' thing," concluded our worthy friend,
not being able to finish the quotation.

"Why, why," said Pigg impatiently, "ar'll tell mar frind he needn't stop
wi' his dogs. Ar see thou'll just stuff and eat and write on till thou dees
of apperplexy."

"I hopes not," replied Mr. Jorrocks starting up in alarm.

"But thou will," replied Pigg, "if thou doesn't take mair exercise."

"Exercise!" exclaimed Mr. Jorrocks "arn't I always on the move, either
ridin' Dickey Cobden, or drivin' him, or quiltin' him, of which he takes
an uncommon quantity?"

"Ay, but that's ne exercise for a man that eats and drinks as ye de
barn collops and eggs for breakfast, roast beef and plum for dinner,
with a quart of wine after it, and a hot supper again at bed-time. Sink,
ye should shake yourself up with a bout; thou'll dee to a certainty if
thou doesn't."

"Don't talk that way, James Pigg; don't talk that way," interrupted Mr.
Jorrocks looking down at his plummy legs, the calves of which appeared
rather too large for his Hessian boots. "I'm no fatter nor I was," added
he, nipping his waist with both hands.

"Deed but thou is; thou'll be seventeen stone, if thou's a pund."

"Nonsense, Pigg, nonsense!" replied Mr. Jorrocks snappishly. "Well,
tell your friend I'm busy just now, and take him into the kitchen, and
give him a run at the wittles to eat and drink, you know; and by the
time he's done, I'll have got through my papers, and shall be able to
speak to him," continued our friend, turning his papers, so as to give
Pigg a hint to retire.

"Cuss that Pigg's imperence," observed Mr. Jorrocks to himself, rising
and stalking up and down the little room a few times. "Fat indeed!"
continued he; "apoplexy, indeed! likes that." Saying which, our
friend brought-up before the little looking-glass against the wall, and
proceeded to examine his features. "Nonsense!" exclaimed he, after a
short survey; "doesn't look a bit older nor I did twenty years ago, may

be a leetle stouter," added he, tapping his stomach, "but, as to seventeen stone, that's quite out o' the question."

Pigg, however, had frightened Mr. Jorrocks. Our fat friend had felt himself not quite the man he was, and he feared, from Pigg's telling him of it, it must be more apparent than he imagined. Mr. Jorrocks was still rather conceited about his looks. Our friend threw himself into his arm-chair, and thought the matter over.

"Strong exercise is a great promoter o' health," observed he to himself at length, rising and ringing the bell. "Somehow, I felt a deal better after the race with the 'oss-stealer—at least, I should if it hadn't been the wrench I got in my back from the un'andsome trick they played me in pullin' of my seat out from an under me. Tell Pigg I want him," said he to Benjamin, who now answered the summons.

"I think you said somethin' about there bein' a man here with some 'ounds," observed Mr. Jorrocks, as Pigg made his appearance.

"*Think!*" exclaimed Pigg; "why, didn't ar tell ye as plain as ar could speak that there was an acquentance o' mine here with some?"

"Possibly you might," replied Mr. Jorrocks; "possibly you might. I was werry busy at the time, arrangin' the Journal o' General Genius. Are they fox'ounds?" inquired he.

"Foxhounds! No; harriers—beagles, that's to say."

"Beagles!" repeated Mr. Jorrocks; "quite little things in fact. I doesn't know wot to say about beagles. Be rayther *infra dig.,* wouldn't it?" asked he, eyeing his factotum.

"*Infra what?*" exclaimed Pigg.

"*Infra dignitate,*" stammered out Mr. Jorrocks.

"Why, ivery man to his pretension," replied Pigg; "but, for mar pairt, ar should say hontin' was far finer fun nor diggin' taties."

"Ah, you misunderstand me, I see," observed Mr. Jorrocks; "I mean to say that it will hardly do for an ex-'M.F.H.' to keep 'arriers."

"Hoots, ye and your X. 'M.F.H.'s'! A hont's a hont. Call them *mine*, if you like. Sink, ar wonder what mar cousin Deavilboger wad say, to hear tell ar'd set up a pack o' hunds! See Mr. Pigg's hunds in the papers!"

"That would be a go!" replied Mr. Jorrocks.

"Yer tied to have a pack," observed Pigg, interrupting a reverie into which his master had fallen. "What the devil are ye to de with yoursel' all the winter? Ye canna gan glowering about the country with your bull, makin' fond speeches at fairs, and ye say the birds winna wait for you to shut them—ye' get as fat as a bullock!"

"Let's see the 'ounds," observed Mr. Jorrocks, getting his hat, desirous of putting an end to so uncomplimentary a conversation.

"Come this way," replied Pigg, leading the way, "ar's getten them in the stable."

"Here, Jovey," excaimed Pigg to his acquaintance, who was taking his ease in the kitchen. "T'ard Squire wants to see hunds."

Forth sallied a very dog-stealer-looking fellow, clad in a very greasy cut-away brown coat with fancy buttons, tartan waistcoat, drab breeches, and square-toed leggings buttoning over the knee-cap, and thick shoes.

"Your servant, sir," said he, ducking a thick, black, curly head, surmounting a copper face, to Mr. Jorrocks.

The hounds were a most primitive lot. A couple of blue mottled beagles, a couple and a half of black-and-tan harriers, a couple of large, yellow, twenty-inch, Cumberland drag-hounds with docked sterns, and a couple and a half of long-backed long-eared dew-lapped, crooked-legged southern hounds, that could run under the bellies of the drag-hounds.

"My vig!" exclaimed Mr. Jorrocks, as they poured out of the stable, and the southern hounds set up a howl that seemed well calculated to last for ever. The harriers frisked about, and one of the drag-hounds dashed at a turkey and very nearly got him down.

"*Steady* there!" cried Jovey, running to the rescue, and giving Bouncer a tremendous crack with the couples. "Ay, but ye should see them hont!" cried he to Pigg, anxious for the credit of the establishment.

"Five pounds!" exclaimed Mr. Jorrocks; "vy, they're only fit to put under a pear-tree."

Mr. Jorrocks stars the hare

"Ar'll put saddle on t'ard nag," said Pigg, without noticing his master's observation, "and ye can ride up t'fell, and see sport like; ar kens where there's a hare sittin'."

"Vell," said Mr. Jorrocks aloud to himself, "I can go and see the fun at all events; looking costs nothin'; but I shouldn't like the editor o' *Bell's Life* or none o' the sportin' perihodicals to see me." So saying, our friend was quickly on Dickey Cobden, and set off by the road for the high ground, while Pigg and his "acquentance," with the motley pack at their heels, took the short cut through the fields.

It was a fine autumnal day, moist, without much sunshine. The cobwebs hung upon the bushes, and the heavy night dew remained in full force where the sun had not touched.

"Shouldn't wonder if there's a scent," observed Mr. Jorrocks, looking at the dew under the wall.

On our friend rode, gradually rising the high hill on the south side of the valley, above the village of Hillingdon, the enclosures getting larger and larger, as he approached the table-land of the summit, which had lately been heathery common, and was divided into those great fields that generally denote recent enclosure. Mr. Jorrocks stopped to puff as he gained the summit of the hill, under the usual "corpulent gentleman's" excuse of admiring the landscape. It was a fine prospect too. The silvery thread of the sparkling river wound among well-wooded banks, whose trees were now diversified with all the rich autumnal tints. The river separated fertile pastures of alluvial soil, mingled with the bright-coloured stubble and rich green turnip fields. The country was thrown into sudden undulating hills, displaying the rude grey stone rocks on the summits of those that were not capped with plantations or forest trees.

"Now," said Pigg, coming up with Jovey and the motley pack, "here's a grand country for a hont. Sink, ar believe we may trail up tiv her," added he, dashing the dew from the heath with his foot. "Which is your finder now?" asked he of his friend.

"This yean," replied Jovey, pointing to a little fat blue-mottled bitch, with very bright prominent gazelle sort of eyes, looking more like a dowager's lap-dog than a hound.

"What de ye call her?" asked Pigg.

"Trusty," replied his friend; adding, "*yooi* Trusty, good bitch."

Trusty acknowledged the compliment by wagging her fat stern.

"Then let's uncouple her," said Pigg, "and see if she can make aught of the trail: ar kens where she'll be sitting, but we may as well see if the hunds can tell us."

Accordingly, the plethoric Trusty was released from one of the dock-tailed drag-hounds, called Tapster, which Jovey kept in the couple by his side. Trusty then began her inquiries. First, she dashed a little semicircle in advance, sniffing and smelling with curious nose at every bit of heather or tufty grass against which the game might have brushed; Pigg looking on with critical eye, calculating when she was likely to hit it off. Presently Trusty began to feather, but spoke not.

"Sink, she's been there!" exclaimed Pigg, eyeing the bitch, and getting forward himself to see if he could prick puss upon a sandy piece of ground formed by the rain washing over a cart track.

"Ay, has she," added he, stooping and pricking her.

Trusty now gave a flourish and a whimper, and then struck forward with a scent and full note.

"Keep them i' the couples, Jovey," exclaimed Pigg, as Trusty's note drew a deep lengthened howl from the southern hounds, and the dragmen and harriers dashed to get to her. "Sink, ar say, get a haud on 'em!" added he, as a couple of the southern hounds caught the fat little bitch in the rear, and sent her sprawling neck and croup a few yards in advance. "Sink, ar say, get a haud on 'em!" added he, "or they'll play the varra deuce with t'ard bitch."

Pigg ran to Trusty's rescue, who, sadly disconcerted at this uncourteous treatment, lay yelping and sprawling on her back. "Poor thing!" said Pigg, taking her up in his arms and patting her pretty sleek sides, "did they upset thee?" asked he, putting her face towards his: "they shanna come nigh thee again though," added he, coaxing her, as he set her down on her legs, saying, as he patted her, "now, canny bitch, try for her again."

Trusty, however, was sadly disconcerted, and some minutes elapsed before she had sufficiently recovered her composure to proceed with the unravelment of the Gordian knot of puss's rambles. At last she touched a scent, and, forgetting her grievance, set too again as briskly as ever. Mr. Jorrocks sat on Dickey Cobden, eyeing her critical examinations and bustling movements.

"Ah, she's a grand bitch!" exclaimed Pigg; "she's worth five punds hersel," added he, pointing her to his master.

"Humph!" grunted Mr. Jorrocks, thinking he'd never give it.

She now made a wider flourish forward; and again a whimper, followed by a full note, proclaimed her on the line of the morning scent.

"She'll be i' yon whin," observed Pigg, in a whisper, to his master, pointing to a patch of gorse on a hillside at a little distance. " Ye keep them great beggars quiet," added he, turning to Jovey, who was well-nigh pulled away by the united exertions of the nine hounds, all striving to get "to cry."

On Trusty went, now bustling and flourishing, now stopping and turning to pick puss's trail step by step; now twisting and bending as she had done whenever a green blade had tempted her out of her way.

Pigg was right as to puss's line. Trusty's tender nose led her towards the gorse patch, and Jovey, by Pigg's request, having given the noisy hounds a crack on the head apiece, to keep them quiet, stood while the bitch worked the trail towards it.

Now she got among the green prickly furze, and sniffed this way and that among the straggling bushes, while Pigg peered in to see if he could detect puss sitting. Now he took his stick and gently divided the bushes, lifting up those that laid low, and poking the grassy tufts in the neighbourhood. No puss.

"Sink, she's gean on," said he, filling his mouth with tobacco, and eyeing the bitch flourishing outside. "Ar ken where she is, thoogh," continued he, eyeing some brown rushes higher up. "How way! canny man, how way!" cried he to his master, waving his arm onwards, "she's oop hill!"

"*Sink, ar sees her!*" at length cried he, catching the little bitch up in his arms as she was rolling more noisily and energetically upwards.

"Vere, James? Vere?" exclaimed Mr. Jorrocks.

"Haud thee gob," said he, "haud thee gob," repeated he, putting his finger to his nose; "ye tak t'ard bitch down to Jovey, and then ye come back and we'll put her away quietly, and lay hunds on after she gets fairly started." So saying, Pigg put Trusty on to Mr. Jorrocks's saddle-pommel, and our worthy Squire trotted down hill with her to Jovey.

Our friend was quickly back, all anxious for the start.

"Vere is she now, James?" exclaimed he, as with staring eyeballs he jerked and jagged Dickey Cobden up the hill. "*Vere is she, I say?*" repeated he, looking all ways but the right.

"*Why, here!*" said Pigg; "God sink, ye're lookin' half-a-mile off!"

"*Vere?*" again exclaimed Mr. Jorrocks, as wise as before.

"*God bliss mar soule!* t'ard man must be blind," said Pigg; "why, here she's, just aside ye, not two yards frae your huss's foot."

"Get off t'ard nag," said Pigg, seeing his master could not catch the place, "and ar'll show ye her," added he, laying hold of Dickey Cobden's bridle. "Now thou sees yon bit rough grass," said Pigg, pointing to a tuft two or three yards in advance.

"Yes," said Mr. Jorrocks.

"Why, then, doesn't thou see her great muckle eyes starin' at ye?" asked Pigg.

"No," replied Mr. Jorrocks.

"No!" exclaimed Pigg; "why, thou *must* be blind. Here, tak mar stick," said he, "and give her a poke," handing Mr. Jorrocks his oaken staff.

Our friend then went as directed.

"Touch her *ahint*," said Pigg, motioning his master which way to use the stick.

Mr. Jorrocks did so, and out puss started.

"*My vig! there she goes!*" exclaimed Mr. Jorrocks, as a great banging hare bounced out before him; "who'd have thought there was anything but a tuft of grass?" added he, climbing on to Dickey Cobden to be ready for a start.

Pigg shaded the sun from his eyes with his hand, while he ran up the hill and watched puss's course.

"Vy don't you lay on the 'ounds?" exclaimed Mr. Jorrocks, astonished at Pigg's slowness.

"Let her get cannily away first," said Pigg, running on to the brow of the hill to watch her course. Presently he returned. "Now then, sit quietly there," said he to his master, "while Jovey uncouples the hunds, and we'll just let them take up the scent by theirsels."

Pigg then went to Jovey, and the motley lot were soon uncoupled, frisking, howling, and towling, according to their respective makes.

"Gan quietly up hill," said Pigg, "she's away o'er back on it, just past low end of quarry like."

The drag-hounds dashed forward expecting to be laid on the line; while the southern hounds, Jingler, Jumper, and Towler, having struck a trail scent, sat on their haunches, proclaiming, with upturned heads to heaven, the grand intelligence, bringing the beagles and harriers to them to confirm their story and partake of the scent. On they went, slow and sure; now a blue mottle, now a southern; now a southern, now a blue mottle; proclaiming, and the rest certifying, the truth of

the statements. Presently they worked up to puss's form; and then there
was such a rush at it, as if they would eat the very grass of which it was
composed.

"Get them forrard, Jovey," said Pigg, "or, sink them, they'll sing there
all day; and let's put the couples on to them greet yellow hunds, or
they'll kill her at view," added he, coaxing one of the dock-tail drag-
hounds towards him.

The pack was now reduced to four couple, of which the black-and-
tan harriers seemed inclined to take the lead. They all clustered on the
scent, and each hound having satisfied himself that there was no mistake,
they dropped their sterns and began to run.

"Now, they'll gan!" exclaimed Jovey, eyeing them; adding, "*ah they're
a grand lot!*"

Forward they went, all in a cluster, much music and little progress;
and just as they swung a cast to assure themselves that puss had passed a
gate, the great drag-hounds broke away from Jovey, and served the pack
the same trick with the couples that they had practised upon Trusty.

"Sink them brutes!" exclaimed Pigg; "ar've a good mind to fell them,"
added he, eyeing the pack scattered and sprawling in all directions.

"Stop till t'others get o'er the wall," replied Jovey; we'll be shot on
'em then."

Jovey was a true prophet. The hare, after passing the quarry, had
struck through a meuse in the wall a little lower down, through which
the big hounds could not pass; and Pigg having fastened the gate as
soon as his master got into the field, the great dock-tailed drag-hounds
were left yammering, yelping, and jumping, each pulling the other back
as he attempted the wall. Puss had taken along the inside of the wall,
and the scent being good, the pack lengthened out like a telescope, and
away they went at a famous pace, Pigg and Jovey running their best,
and Mr. Jorrocks rising in his stirrups, and holding Dickey Cobden hard
by the head.

"Beautiful country!" exclaimed our friend, casting his eye over the
vast enclosures, some fifty, others near a hundred acres; "I'd no idea
there was sich a country about 'ome," added he. "Hooi, you, sir!"
exclaimed he to a man at plough in the adjoining enclosure; "run and

open me that 'ere gate!" pointing towards one to which they were fast approaching.

The man obeyed orders, and Mr. Jorrocks trotted through. The hounds now turned a little to the left, but Mr. Jorrocks seeing a cart track, and knowing that it would lead to a gate or place of exit, preferred keeping his own line to running the risk of being pounded. The next fence was a young quickset one, protected by a rail, over which the hounds quickly scrambled, and then, having passed through a small turnip field near a shepherd's hut, they came to a very high boundary-wall that seemed to present an insuperable barrier to further progress. Mr. Jorrocks ran his eyes up and down the wall, but could see nothing like a gate. It was a long, straight, formal, newly-built thing, with the coping-stone dashed with lime. The hounds could no more get over it than could our friend, and with loud clamour they all threw up.

"'*Olloo!* you chap with the red tie!" cried our now puffing friend to a shepherd who had just appeared outside in his cabin; "vy don't ye come and 'elp these ere 'ounds over the wall, and *me* over the wall?" adding to himself, "or I'll summons you for an assault."

The man came, and pulling up a flag from before a square aperture in the wall, the hounds got through, and casting themselves on the far side, quickly took up the scent again.

"Vell, but 'ow am I to get over?" inquired Mr. Jorrocks, staring at the man; adding, "you don't s'pose I can squeeze through there?"

"There's no way for you but round by Tommy Miller's," replied the man.

"'Ow far's that?" asked Mr. Jorrocks.

"Three-quarters of a mile and better; just to the right by yonder cottage, see," pointing to a dwelling on the outline of the hill, up to which the wall ran.

"Confound it, that's not the way the 'ounds are goin'!" exclaimed Mr. Jorrocks, as he stood erect in his stirrups, and saw them bending to the left, with Pigg and Jovey running inside them.

"Well, then, there's no way in," replied the man, "till you come to Mr. Coxon's boundary-wall, and the gate's kept locked."

"'Ord rot the beggar!" exclaimed Mr. Jorrocks, "I wish he had the padlock on his nose; was ever sich an uncivilised wall as this seen? D'ye think I could squeeze through there?" inquired he, pointing to the place through which the hounds had passed.

"No doubt," replied the man, "no doubt; but what will you do with your nag?"

"Vy, I must leave him with you," replied Mr. Jorrocks, clambering down. "It's only an 'are 'unt, and we'll soon be done; valk him about quietly till I return, and I'll give you a shullin'," added he.

So saying, our bulky friend laid flat on the ground, and, heels first, backed and squeezed through the hole in the wall. Up he scrambled, and seeing the hounds rather tying on the scent, and Pigg and Jovey on a neighbouring eminence, Mr. Jorrocks rolled away quite fresh, the tassels of his Hessian boots clattering against his legs as he went.

"*Forrard away!*" cried he, as the hounds settled again to the scent, with all his old hunting energy, and away they all went full cry.

The enclosure was a large one, but being in grass, and the ground sound, our fat friend made a good fight across it. He was rather blown, however, when he came to the stone wall at the far side; and after he had lifted Trusty and Towler, who were in a somewhat similar predicament, over, he found he would be better of a little assistance himself. Twice his toes slipped out of the places he attempted to get them in, but a third effort succeeded in landing him on the top, where he sat for a minute eyeing the

Strange confusion in the vale below,

and taking breath.

The hare had run into a brushwood-covered bank, forming one side of a small dell, through which ran a purling brook, and the southern hounds could not satisfy themselves that she had gone on. They made several advances towards the front, where old fat Trusty bustled with the scent, and as often returned to where they had last felt it themselves, as much as to say they did not believe her.

"Cuss your unbelievin' souls," muttered Mr. Jorrocks to himself, as he sat eyeing their proceedings; "those psalm-singin' beggars require every step to be sworn to," added he.

At last one of the black-and-tan harriers carried the scent out on to the fallow across the brook, and putting his head straight down the furrow, went away at a rattling pace across a very rough fallow.

"By jingo! they're away again!" exclaimed Mr. Jorrocks, who had not half recovered his wind.

He slid himself down the side of the wall, to the great damage of the Jorrockian jacket-buttons, and prepared to follow notwithstanding. Patter, patter, patter, went the Hessian boot-tassels—blunder, blunder, blunder, went Mr. Jorrocks among the hard clods. Now up, now down; now along the furrow, now across the ridge.

"Oh dear; it's 'ard work!" said he to himself, before he had got half across the field, and he saw the hounds were running away from him. "Oh dear! vot a pain I've got in my side!" added he, stopping, and clapping his hand to his side.

On again he went, still tripping and stumbling across the fallow, with "bellows to mend" becoming more apparent at every step.

"'Ord rot it, but I can't run as I used," added he, stopping and clapping his hand to his forehead.

On again he went, unwilling to give in. A little strip of grass by the wall now rather favoured him, and as he jogged up it he heard the hounds more distinctly, though he had no time for looking.

"'Ard work 'unting on foot," gasped he, as he approached the cross wall. A projecting stone favoured his footing, and he mounted pretty briskly, just in time to see the hounds bend inward to the left.

"Thank God, they're a turnin'!" said he, as he pulled out a great blue-and-white-spotted bandanna and began mopping his head.

"How way, canny man! how way!" holloaed Pigg, waving his hat in the distance for his master to come on.

"Werry good howwayin'," grunted Mr. Jorrocks; "but we're not all sich 'erring-gutted beggars as you, wot can run all day." However, our friend complied with the request by dropping down the wall, and again started away in a trot.

It was a very poor one, a mere make-believe, and he would have got on quite as quick in a walk. Patter, patter, patter, still he went, puffing and wheezing, puffing and wheezing.

A projecting root at last caught his toe, and sent him rolling heavily over on the headland.

"There's a go!" said he, turning over, and seeing he had split his drab stockingette tights at the knees, and crushed his low-crowned hat in. "Vell, can't be 'elped," said he, scrambling up, and adjusting the hat as he went.

Our friend, however, was beat, and before he got half over the next field he acknowledged it. "Well, it's no use!" exclaimed he, dropping down into a walk, as he eyed the hounds growing.

Small by degrees, and beautifully less,

as they followed each other in long-drawn frie up the rising ground in the distance. "*It's no use,*" repeated he, with a melancholy shake of the head. "It's all U.P. with J. J. Ah!" continued he, "*age will tell! I never thought to come to this*," added he, with a deep sigh. "I'm gettin' an old man," said he, in a low tone, as he laid his hand on the wall to hoist himself up.

"Vell, I've had a fine time on it," added he, seating himself astride it, for a view; "werry fine time on it. Deal o' shug I deal o' barley-shug! deal o' sugar-candy too! but my day's gone by. I feels I'm one o' the 'as beens. Melancholy thought!" ejaculated he; "who'd have thought it twenty years ago, or ten—ay, or even five, or yet one? Howsomever, never mind; care killed the cat! Dash my vig, I do believe 'ere comes the 'are!"

Sure enough it was puss coming lobbing along, inside the wall that joined the one across which our worthy friend was seated. She was coming at an easy listening sort of pace, with her trumpet ears pricked to catch the sound of her pursuers.

They were a long way behind, and puss knew it.

"Dash my vig, but she's a fine 'un!" observed Mr. Jorrocks, eyeing her white legs, clean fur, and vigorous canter. "Will take the shine out o' Trusty and Co. before she's done, I guess. It can't be the 'unted 'are," continued he, eyeing her fresh appearance, as she sat listening and looking at our fat friend seated astride the wall. Having satisfied her curiosity, puss gave a tremendous jump backwards, and running her foil a short distance, quietly disappeared through a hedge, a little above where it joined the wall.

"It is her though; and yonder come Jovey and Pigg," added Mr. Jorrocks, looking at the two toiling in the distance, with the hounds towling along a little on the left. " 'Ope they've got their nightcaps with them," observed Mr. Jorrocks, eyeing their pace.

"*Which way? which way?*" cried Pigg, as soon as he got within hearing.

"To the left," cried Mr. Jorrocks, waving his hat; adding, "*she's dead beat!*"

"Glad on't, for wor hunds are maist beat tee. And Trusty's run hersel into fits, and Boisterous and Thunderer are baith done," replied Pigg.

The pack being thus reduced, Pigg and Jovey had to do the work of hounds as well as huntsmen; keeping a look-out for puss, and pricking her where they could. They had now to run with the hounds, instead of keeping inside them on the high ground. This, however, did not require any great exertion, for the hounds had long settled down into what hackney-coachmen call Parliament pace—six miles an hour.

"They von't ketch her," grunted Mr. Jorrocks to himself, lowering himself down the wall, thinking he might chance to see the finish with so reduced and dribbling a pack. As if to thwart our friend, the hounds took to running as soon as he got established on his legs and had started into an involuntary trot. It was, however, a very short one. The stitch in his side soon returned, and in less than two minutes our old friend was *hors de combat*.

"There's an end of *my* 'unting," said he, dropping on to a large stone and bursting into tears.

XXXII

Ye generous Britons, venerate the plough.—THOMSON

"AR WISH T'ARD MAN MAYN'T ha' lost hissel," said Pigg to Jovey, as, after a long-continued effort with the remaining couple of hounds, they at last gave up the chase of poor puss, and commenced gathering the scattered pack, preparatory to returning home. "Hast seen owt on him?" continued Pigg, casting his eye over the surrounding country.

"He was sittin' astride a stone wall the last time I see'd him," replied Jovey.

"Ay, but he came away after that," replied Pigg; "ar see'd him blunderin' o'er the fallow below, makin' after the hunds as it were. Ah dear! ar wish he mayn't ha' lamed hissel, or happen'd a misfortin," observed Pigg anxiously; adding, "sink, he's 'ardly fit to be trusted frae heam by hissel."

"Is he a very old gentleman?" asked Jovey.

"Why, no, he's not se ard," replied Pigg, "but he's se daft—he's lived i' great towns all his life, and he thinks to see gas-lights and poliss stuck all about the country. Let's call hunds together, and, maybe, while we're callin' them he may cast up;" so saying, Jovey and Pigg got on to an eminence and began halloaing—"Cop, come away! cop, come away! cop, hunds, cop! Here Trusty, here Jumper! cop Jumper! cop Jingler! *evooy, evooy*, hunds, *evooy!*" being a corruption of the words "here away, away hounds, away."

The hounds came slowly crawling to halloo, from different parts; and, after half-an-hour spent in this way, our sportsmen had scraped three couple and a half together, and, no more appearing likely to cast up, Pigg proposed that Jovey should take one route, and he another, and try to recover Mr. Jorrocks and the rest. "Ye tak dogs wi' ye," said Pigg, "and gan round yon way," waving his arm to the left, "and keep halloain' as ye gan, and see," added he, "and keep an eye on the grund, and try to prick t'ard Squire by the heels; he's getten a pair o' Jemnly London bouts on, wi' small taper heels, that gan a lang way into the grund, and, if ye keep a sharp look-out, ye may chance to come upon him by the track;" so saying, Pigg gave such of the hounds as seemed inclined to follow him a kick, and Jovey, by dint of coaxing, got them away after him.

"Ar wonder what's getten t'ard man," said Pigg to himself, striding along, looking in all directions, and taking an occasional peep at the ground to see if he could prick Mr. Jorrocks by the heels. "He'd flyer gan heam," said he to himself, "as long as hunds could run, surely, and yet there's nout to see on him. Ar'll dim this hill, for ar really think he mun ha' happen'd a misfortin;" so saying, Pigg legged it up the hill as though be were just turning out fresh for the day.

"Yonder's t'ard nag," said he, as be reached the top and saw Dickey Cobden in the distance, pacing slowly up and down, in charge of the shepherd. "Where *can* t'ard Squire ha' getten? Sink, he *mun* ha' happen'd a misfortin!" added he, as broken legs and collar-bones flashed across his mind. "He's safe enough afoot, though," continued Pigg, recollecting himself; "he may ha' brust hissel or died of apperplexy though," added he, as the prophecy of the morning returned to his recollection.

Pigg was in a great stew—he ran here and there, stood on walls, and climbed every eminence that commanded the surrounding country, and, like most people in a pucker, cast far away, and never thought of looking near home. The consequence was that Mr. Jorrocks who had ensconced himself amid a group of projecting rocks, at the top of a narrow deli, with which the country abounded, was wholly overlooked by James Pigg.

"Sink, is yon a corby?" said Pigg to himself, as Mr. Jorrocks's hat moved above the top of the stones.

"*Hup, hawway! hup! hup!*" shouted Pigg, knocking his stick against a stone to try and frighten the bird. Mr. Jorrocks then popped his great red face over the rocks, to the great joy and astonishment of his man.

"God sink, if there bain't his ard mug poppin' over the stean!" exclaimed Pigg, starting off at full speed down bill to the place.

" Why, canny man," said he, rushing breathless to the spot, "we'd ha' thought that was ye? Sink, ar've been lookin' for ye all o'er, and took thy hat for a corby! Gin ar'd had mar gon, there's ne sayin' but ar'd a shot thee. But what's happened?" continued he; "thou's not lamed thysel, hast thou?" continued Pigg, eyeing his master's melancholy countenance.

"Vy, no," replied Mr. Jorrocks, "not exactly, at least; I've had a bad fall, though," added he, pointing to his breeches' knees.

" 'Deed, has thou?" said Pigg, eyeing Mr. Jorrocks's legs; "broken thy knees, I declare. 'Why, that *is* a bad job; however, they'll mend; but, ah dear, thou's het!" added Pigg; "thy face looks just as though it had been blow'd red hot in a furnace. Ar's warn'd thou's tired," added he, "thou's not made for runnin'; bide where thou is, and ar'll fetch t'ard nag to carry ye home."

"Oh, I can valk to the nag well enough," replied Mr. Jorrocks, starting up, unwilling that Pigg should know the extent of his failure.

"Why! why!" said Pigg, "walk if ye like; but ar kens where t'ard nag is, and ar could seun get him for thee. Ah, but we've had a grand hont!" added he, wiping the tobacco streams from his mouth with his sleeve.

" 'Ave you killed her?" asked Mr. Jorrocks, with a spice of his old ardour.

"Why, *noo,*" drawled Pigg, "we didn't kill her, somehow; but that's all the better, ye ken—she'll mak a grand hont another day."

"Another day, indeed!" replied Mr. Jorrocks, "I should think *one* was enough."

"Ay, but thou mun hont, if it's nabbut te keep thysel out o' mischief," replied Pigg; "grand exercise—de ye far mair good nor farmin'."

"But it von't be so profitable," observed Mr. Jorrocks, with a shake of his head, as he trailed slowly along by the side of his man, with his hands behind his back.

"Ar doesn't ken that," said Pigg, with a shrug of the shoulders; "should say it wad de ye mair good nor farmin' *as ye farm.*"

"That's all you knows about the matter," grunted Mr. Jorrocks. "The new lights o' husbandry haven't broke in upon your wooden 'ead yet."

"Ar wish they mayn't *brik* ye," replied Pigg; "ar think thou's gannin' a fair way for the dogs."

"I see you're one of the old-fashioned, stubborn, stupid sort o' sinners," grunted Mr. Jorrocks. "Jest blunder on in your old ways, without either talent to strike out a new inwention, or spirit enough to follow up what others diskiver—Want enlightenment *desp'rate*."

"They'll lighten ye af ore they're done with ye, I'll be bund," replied Pigg, with a sniff of his nose across his hand.

"I thought you chaps had been clever in the north," observed Mr. Jorrocks, after they had trudged on some time in silence.

"Cliver? ay," said Pigg, "o'er diver to make sic asses o' ourselves as they de hereabouts."

"*Humph!*" grunted Mr. Jorrocks, not relishing the reception of his overture at reconciliation, "and vot'n hasses *de* ye see 'ere, pray?"

"Ah, asses!" exclaimed Pigg, at the top of his voice, "ar niver see'*d* sic wark! folks all gean clean mad together, ar think!"

"*Humph!*" grunted Mr. Jorrocks again, wondering what Pigg had seen to astonish him.

"It was nabbut yesterdays" continued Pigg, "that ar called on Mr. Heavytail, and instead of findin' him in his fields, sink if he wasn't rollin' a hogshead o' sugar into the barn. 'How now, Mr. Tail? ' says ar to him, says ar, 'are ye gannin' te torn grosser?' 'Why, no,' says he to me, says he, 'Mr. Pigg,' says he, quite pertly, ar's not gannin' to tarn grosser.' Then says ar to him, says ar, 'What the deavil ar ye gannin' to do wi' all the sugar?'—for ar see'd twe mair casks a standin' where he was rowlin' this yean te."

"Indeed!" exclaimed Mr. Jorrocks, perking up, "wonders if they came from our place; was there a great J. & Co. at the end, done in black paint with red dots?"

"Can't say, ar's sure," replied Pigg; "but, howsomever, there was Mr. Tail a rowlin' this yean in, and varra heavy it was, and varra hot it made Mr. Tail, se I took and gay it a shove along wi' him; and when we'd getten it placed to his likin', at seed a vast o' sand, and gravel, and rubbish, lyin' about o' barn floor like, se ar axed him what it was all for——"

"And what did he say?" eagerly inquired Mr. Jorrocks, darting to a conclusion.

"Why," said Pigg, turning the quid in his mouth, "he brak out just as ye de—talked about new leets [lights], old-fashioned farmin', and march o' somethin'. Then he pointed at the sugar, and says he to me, says he, 'Ar'll be bound to say, Mr. Pigg,' says he, 'with all your north country knowledge, you can't tell me what that's for.' So, says ar to him, says ar, Ye have the advantage of me, Mr. Tail——' "

"Just so," observed Mr. Jorrocks; adding, "well, go on."

"Why, then," said Pigg, "he tell'd me he'd been to a lector on farmin' some chap ganning about the country, talkin' nonsense, had given, who'd tell'd him of a grand imposition for——"

"*Com*position!" observed Mr. Jorrocks, with an emphasis.

"Ay, grand composition," continued Pigg, "for makin' tiles—drainin' tiles. Ar doesn't ken how many things had to be put into it, but there was *chark*, and sand, and gravel, and I doesn't ken what else, and the whole had to be mexed and stirred up wi' brown sugar."

"Vot a jackass the chap must be!" grunted Mr. Jorrocks, wondering how Mr. Heavytail ever could be so foolish as to adopt the idea.

"Why, that's just what ar said," observed Pigg. "Says ar to Mr. Tail, says ar, 'Ye surely mun be gannin' clean daft, Mr. Tail, to think o' wastin' the sugar in this way. Hey ye ne quarry, nor ne gravel bed, nor ne place nigh at hand, where ye can get steans, instead of makin' sich a mess as this?' But I might as well ha' saved my breath, for arli ar gat was sarce and bad words."

"Oh dear! Mr. 'Eavytail must be a werry stupid man," observed Mr. Jorrocks, wondering how a tenant of his could have fallen into a trap he had only set for other people.

"Why, that's what ar telled him," said Pigg; "says ar te him, says ar, 'Thou may fancy thysel a wise man, and may be ye may fancy the chap that tell'd ye all this a wise man; but for mar pairt, ar should say, it wad be hard to say whether on ye's the bigger feul.' "

"*Did you, indeed?*" exclaimed Mr. Jorrocks, wondering if Mr. Heavytail floored him.

"Faith did ar," said Pigg, striking his staff against the ground—"them was just the varra words ar used—hard to say whether on ye's the bigger feul."

"And vot did he say?" asked Mr. Jorrocks.

"Why, he just glowered and garped, and grinned, and talked about the new leets in husbandry, and said, ar was a lang way ahint the information of the day—that this was the newest London invention, and that the newest things always cam frae there, and that Lunnuners knew mair than all other folks put together."

"Vell, and what did you say?" continued Mr. Jorrocks, still anxious to hear all about it.

"Why, ar said, ar thought nou't o' Lunnuners—that they might de varry well for makin' women's bonnets, and sich like; but as for makin' drainin' tiles, or kennin' ou't about farmin', ar wadn't give a button-top for all their heads put tegither."

"Humph!" grunted Mr. Jorrocks; adding, "well, Mr. 'Eavytail certain*lie* is a bigger fool nor I took him for. Three 'ogs'eads o' sugar, and, very likely, not got at our place either! The man'll be ruined!"

"Ye'll be lossin' your rent," observed Pigg; adding, "it ar'nt possible for a man te farm i' that way and pay rent tee."

"I 'opes I shalln't lose the rent," observed Mr. Jorrocks—"can't afford to do that, howsomever precious little one gets as it is—land-ownin's a *werry* poor trade."

"It *mun* be poor the way yeer folks gan on," rejoined Pigg. "Sink, thou's not much better nor Heavytail thysel. It's nabbut t'other day like, I came upon old Tommy Sloggers, hangin' his great beastly brandy-bibbin' neb over the yeat, gannin' into his faller, his coat all stains, his breeches loose at the knees, his stockins hangin' down, and the land as chock full o' weeds and dirt as ever it could haud. 'Well, Mr. Sloggers,' said ar, '*ad*mirin' yeer weeds! *ad*mirin' yeer weeds! ye'll have a grand crop, ar expect—you've much to be prud on—ye'll not be disappointed in nettles, whatever ye are i' the wheat.' 'Hoot, ye fond boddy,' said he, quite sarcy like, 'what do *ye* knaw about farmin'? Ye're nou't but a boole leader!' 'Why, why,' said I, 'ar can tell a dirty faller from a clean 'un, however; and, of all dirty fallers that iver ar set eyes on, yeers is the dirtiest.' 'Ay, but stop till wor Squire's new invention comes on it,' said he, with a wink of his blear eye, 'and ye'll see how clean it'll be.' 'What invention?' said I. 'Ah, what a man thou is to talk o' farmin'!' said he; 'hasn't thou heard tell of our landlord's grand machine for doin' all farmin'-work at once—ploughin', cleanin', sowin', harrowin', reapin'! Hoot, get away wi' ye!' said he; 'get yeer boole out; ye're mair at heam wi' him nor ou't else.' "

"Ay," said Mr. Jorrocks, "but I didn't say nothin' about weedin'; besides, it was a mere speckilation altogether, and I never said nothin' about when the machine would be ready, or who I would lend it to, or nothin'."

"But then, ye see, the warst o' ye grand folks talkin' is that chaps like Sloggers just tak haud of as much o' yeer jaw as sarves their torn, and then, if things dinna gan right, they say it's yeer fault that ye telled them, and that they mun have a reduction o' rent. Now, Sloggers won't clean his land; and he'll say, thou tell'd him not, and that he kept it to try thy engine on."

"I'll Sloggers him, if he does," observed Mr. Jorrocks, with a shake of the head—"besides," added he, "I'm sure I never said nothin' about the machine cleanin' land—didn't know land required cleanin', indeed," added he, aloud to himself.

"But ye may depend, Sloggers 'ill look to ye for satisfaction," rejoined Pigg.

"Humph!" grunted Mr. Jorrocks, thinking he wouldn't get it.

Master and man trudged on some time in silence, each occupied with his respective thoughts, Mr. Jorrocks considering whether, as "scientific farming" seemed likely to be expensive, he had better employ Pigg to undeceive the people, and Pigg muttering anathemas and strange oaths against dung-doctors, man-doctors, horse-doctors, cow-doctors, and all sorts of doctors. At length they came to the boundary wall through which, our readers will remember, Mr. Jorrocks had squeezed, leaving his cob on the far side.

"We mun be o'er here," said Pigg, striding up to the wall, and laying a hand on the top.

"That's easier said nor done," replied Mr. Jorrocks, eyeing its great height. "Better return the way I came, I thinks," added he, looking about for a place.

"Ah, ye'll seun get o'er!" replied Pigg; "it's nou't of a wall."

"Isn't it?" replied Mr. Jorrocks, as much as to say, *it is to me*."

"Stick yeer toe in it like a man!" rejoined Pigg, placing his own on a projecting stone, to show his master the way.

Mr. Jorrocks tried, but down it slipped again. It wouldn't do.

"God sink, t'ard man's gettin' numb!" growled Pigg, as, lowering himself, he came to his master's assistance. "Here, now," continued he, "put thy foot in there," said he, showing his master the place, "and then give thysel a good hoist, and thou'll soon be atop."

Mr Jorrocks did as desired; but the hoist was a very ineffectual one. He did not even get his hat-crown level with the top of the wall.

"*Try again!*" exclaimed Pigg; adding, "give a good loup."

"Ah, 'non sum qualis *eram!*' " said Mr. Jorrocks, with a strong accent on the "ram"—as he made a still more ineffectual effort than the first.

"Hoot, a ram wad think nou't of such a wall!" muttered Pigg; adding, "come now, put thy toe in again, and ar'll give ye a shove up ahint."

Mr. Jorrocks obeyed the order, and, with the aid of a strong hoist from Pigg's shoulder, succeeded in landing on the top. Pigg was quickly beside him, and master and man dropped down into the enclosure, where the shepherd was still pacing leisurely about with Dickey Cobden.

"Fatch him this way!" roared Mr. Jorrocks, waving his hat to the man; adding, "it's as cheap ridin' as walkin'."

> When I'm rich, I rides in chaises;
> When I'm poor, I walks like blazes."

"You've had a long wait," observed our friend, hoisting himself on, and giving the man a shilling for his trouble.

Mr. Jorrocks then set off homewards.

"Vell, Pigg," observed Mr. Jorrocks, overtaking his man, who had gone striding on before, as he saw his master preparing to mount— "vell, Pigg," repeated he, "I can't get the idea of that unmitigated stoopid old 'Eavytail and his sugar-casks out of my 'ead. The man must be werry soft to swallow all he's told—Lord! if they had him in London, 'ow they would rook him."

"Ar's warn'd ye," said Pigg—"they're gay and sharp there;" adding, "but there are as big feuls as Heavytail hereabouts."

"Possibly," replied Mr. Jorrocks—"possibly; but that's not the question."

"Ar see'd a man t'other mornin'," continued Pigg, without noticing his master's observation, "pepperin' the land just as ye'd pepper a plate o' cabbish. 'God sink,' said ar, 'what's thou about?' 'Giarnoin,' said he. "Giarnion!' said ar, 'what good can that de the land?— gan and get a few cart-loads o' muck, and keep the giarno for thy puddin'—*Muck's your man!*' say I," exclaimed Pigg at the top of his voice.

"Well, but one must do summut i' this world to make oneself known," observed Mr. Jorrocks, still anxious to put matters right and propitiate his man in order to get Pigg to help him.

"Varry true," said Pigg; "varry true," repeated he, filling his mouth with tobacco, and wiping the brown streams from his mouth with his sleeve; adding, "mun de summut to mak worsels conspikious—cannot all grow whiskers under our chins like Captain Bluster."

"Well, but farmin's quite the go, you see, jest now," observed Mr. Jorrocks, "and it don't do for us landlords to appear behind the tenants in information. If it wasn't for the promotion o' science I'm sure land-owning would never pay. Talk o' money i' the funds!" added he, "money i' the funds may pay small interest; but blow me tight, funds pay punctual, and the gates never want repairin'."

"Ar doesn't knaw much about the funds," replied Pigg, "but thou'll find the yeats a small matter i' thy repair—mar cousin Deavilboger always said that ne man is fit to be called a farmer what isn't a good grumbler."

"Faith, then, I've some uncommon good 'uns," replied Mr. Jorrocks, "for I never goes to inquire after the 'ealth of the farmers' wives, or the state o' their 'ouses, but I gets sich a torrent of complaints that I thinks that my 'ouses must be all a tumblin' down together. One's roof rains in—another's barn beams are rotten—a third's 'edges are all dead—a fourth's pump's gone wrong; and so they go on."

"Ay, now, that's jest the way ye cul chaps de," replied Pigg; "ye seek for complaints. Instead o' ridin' into a man's fard, and axin' if his barn's wattertight and his missis i' the family way, ye should gan in ramin' and swearin' and blawin' everybody up that comes in your way, and the man will be o'er glad to slip out the front way, and niver say nothin' about repairs."

"Ah, but the wives are far wuss nor the men!" exclaimed Mr. Jorrocks.

"Ay, that's because you're o'er kind wi' them," replied Pigg.

"Humph!" grunted Mr. Jorrocks, not relishing the answer. "Some of the men are so whimsical," observed Mr. Jorrocks, thinking he might as well turn the conversation, "one sometimes wants exactly the reverse of another."

"Ar's warn'd ye," said Pigg, "ar's warn'd ye; some'll want parlours made into kitchens, and other some, kitchens made into parlours. A parlour, i' mar mind, is varra little use to a farmer. They aye shut them up and sit i' their kitchens, or want a sort o' second parlour to save the best; just like mar coosin Deavilboger. He grumbled and fund fault wi' his 'om'stead till the Squire rebuilt the whole on the largest and most improved plan—cost a sight o' money; and when it was finished the Deavil shut up twe-thirds on it, say-in' it was far o'er big for the farm."

"That's the way they go on," said Mr. Jorrocks, digging his heel into Dickey Cobden.

"There was Harry Grumble of Clottergate," said Pigg, "wadn't take his farm till the landlord would build him a porch to his front door, because he said he'd always been used to a porch, and he liked to see his missis sittin' knittin' in it when he came home half drunk frae the market; and se, what with his wishes and what with his wants, the landlord at last built one—cost the matter, ar dare say, of ten pounds. Well, Harry was so varra punctual i' the drinkin' way that he forgot to provide his rent, and the consequence was, he was soon bundled out again, and the farm was to let. John Brick was the man to take it; but nothin' would sarve Brick but the porch should come down. He'd never been used to a porch, and didn't like the look of a porch, so down cam porch again."

"The beggar," grunted Mr. Jorrocks.

"Jonas Hen's pigs were aye on Mr; Blatherington's coach-road," continued Pigg, "and he swore till he was maist black i' the face about it; but Hen persisted that the pigs must have room to wander about, for if they were kept cooped up i' the sty, their legs wad get crook'd, and they'd want far mair meat, and so on. At last yean night the Squire was comin' home either varra drunk or it was varra dark, for he tumbled over t'ard sow as she lay across road like. 'Sink it,' said he i' the mornin', 'I'll build this ard beggar a new range of sties, with airin' yards in front, for ar can't stand splittin' my kerseymeres i' this way'—just as you've done," observed Pigg, looking at Mr. Jorrocks's knees; "se at it he went—built an uncommon fine range of sties, with ar's warn'd ye a quarter of a yacre of ground walled in; and when it was done, Squire Blatherington said to Hen, 'Now, Mr. Hen, ar hopes yeer pigs will have the kindness to keep off mar coach-road, for ar can't stand them, and they've plenty of elbow-room and everything pigs should have in this spacious yard.' 'Ay, ay, sir,' said Hen; 'but for mar pairt ar always think they're just as well i' the sty altogether.' Queer devils, farmers," added Pigg, replenishing his mouth with tobacco.

"They are that," assented Mr. Jorrocks.

"The best way of stoppin' their gabs," said Pigg, "is gannin' about the country with a great armful o' plans; and as soon as ever a man begins with his wants, unroll the plan, and say you propose buildin' his premises afresh and want to talk to him about the leadin'."

"That's a good idea," said Mr. Jorrocks, with a nod—"a werry good idea."

"Or if they talk about yeats [gates] say there's yeat wood provided, and they've nothin' to do but employ a joiner to work it up. They'll make the ard 'uns last a long while when they've to pay for makin' the new 'uns, and t'ard housin' 'ill stand tee if they've te lead to the new 'un."

"Ar wad say now," observed Pigg, after a long pause, during which he trudged on beside his master, "instead o' talkin' nonsense to the farmers, and gettin' them to try fond expariments, it wad be far better, if ye mun make yoursel conspikious, to train a few lads on, as they de i' wor country, and gar them pay for yeer knowledge."

" 'Ow's that?" inquired Mr. Jorrocks, thinking it sounded like money.

"Have what they call mud-students," replied Pigg; "some of the great farmers i' the north have them, and they pay well whether they lam ou't or not."

"Vot! a sort of an agricultural college, is it?" asked Mr. Jorrocks.

"No! college; no," replied Pigg, "jest a youth or two i' the 'ouse, that you may give lectors to if you like."

"Keep in the 'ouse?" observed Mr. Jorrocks; "shouldn't like that—be pulling the gals about, p'raps."

"Ah, sink ye can de that yersel," muttered Pigg. "If ye dinna like them i' the house," observed he, raising his voice, "ye can lodge them wi' some o' the tenants, and jest have them in when ye want to extonish them with your larnin'."

"That's more like the ticket," thought Mr. Jorrocks aloud to himself; adding, "but wot am I to do with them on intermediate days, when I'm not a lectorin', in fact?"

"Why, thou mun send them out into the fields to kick the clods about, and ax fond questions."

"But they must 'ave somebody to go with them, to answer them, and tell them wot's wot."

"Let them find out theirsels, they'll like it far better if they de," replied Pigg.

"That would hardly be fair, though; if one under takes to instruct them, one ought to be as good as one's word," observed Mr. Jorrocks. "We shouldn't 'ave them in any numbers, though," observed Mr. Jorrocks, "a lecturin' to empty benches is werry poor sport."

"Ay, but ye can get in the ard wives and bairns, anybody but the farmers," replied Pigg; "there's ne fear of misleadin' t'ard women."

"No, that won't do," observed Mr. Jorrocks, half to Pigg, half to himself. "If they'd have the agricultural college they talk of in the *Mark Lane Express* here, and make me principal, *that* would be summut like; but to tutorise a few bouys would never suit J. J."

"Ay, but ye may teach them to hont as well as farm," observed Pigg. "Sink, you've nou't to de but get a beuik and read a lesson aforehand yersel; talk of strang lands, and light lands, and marle, and the rotation of crops; tell them if wheat is full of poppies it's a sign o' poor land, and if full o' thristles, it's a sign o' good strang land, and se on."

"Vell, that seems all werry sensible," observed Mr. Jorrocks, "and wot they ought to know."

"Then ye can tell them the cause why gentlemen farmers never make money is that they all overdo the thing. If ye wish to profit by farmin', ye mun content yersel with tolerably clean fields and good savin' crops; but if ye stoody to ornament your farm wi' fine clipped hollin hedges, representin' booles, and horses, and sows, as ye de, or dinna clean your land till ye get a machine that will plough it and all, like Sloggers, or put sugar into drainin' tiles, like Tail, why, ye cannot but lose. Land needs a sartain quantity of ploughins and harrow-ins, and a sartain quantity of muck, and will pay for all that; but if ye over-egg the puddin' the money's wasted, for the land may yield as good crops wi' five or six ploughins as wi' ten; and ye may have ower strang crops, that the first wind or rain will lodge and lose ye the whole."

"*Humph!*" grunted Mr. Jorrocks; adding, "I think they must make you professor of agricultur' in the new college."

"Then, after you've talked all sich matters as these over, ye may say, 'Now, gentlemen, there's James Pigg i' the yard wi' the hunds, and he'll show ye how to find a hare setten, and how to hunt her when she is fund.'"

"Ay, ay, I thought that would be the upshot of it all," observed Mr. Jorrocks with a smile; "they'll be 'unting students—not mud-students—if you have anything to do with them."

"And a varra good way to teach them farmin' tee," said Pigg.

Mr. Jorrocks re-entered Hillingdon Hall a sadder man than he set out. He found age creeping upon him, and that he was unfit for the life his earlier aspirations had sighed for; farming, which he thought was a sure fortune, seemed attended with no end of trouble; and he now felt that country life owed half its charms to frequent contrast with the crowded, heated, busy, bustling city.

"I'll shut up shop!" exclaimed he, throwing himself into the judicial chair, "and return to Surrey and Great Coram Street. Winter's a coming on, and I'm a gettin' into the sere and yellow leaf. These farmin' fools

will never do for a man of intellect like me. Confound them! they
are a century and a half be'ind the Lunnuners: old Wopstraw, with his
drawlin' 'upon the *who-o-ole*'—Willey Goodheart, with his year's arrears
of news—and Mr. 'Eavytail, with his sugar-casks, and a woice enough
to split a barn-door—*I'm tired on 'em all!*"

So saying, our worthy friend stuck out his legs, and throwing himself
back in his chair, dozed for some time in silence. At length he got up
and rang the bell.

"Send James Pigg here, Benjamin," said he, as soon as the boy came
sneaking into the room, thinking Mr. J. had seen him stealing plums,
and meant to convict him summarily, and inflict substantial justice upon
him. Presently James made his appearance. He had been cleaning the
bull's stall out, and showing him to some ladies.

"Vell, James," said Mr. Jorrocks, eyeing his tobacco-streaming mouth;
"I've been a thinkin' this here farmin' don't exactly suit with me; not
quite the ticket, in fact."

"*So*," said James, thinking he had soon tired.

"And I've been a thinkin'," continued Mr. Jorrocks, "as you seem
full o' knowledge and science, of puttin' you in to manage and keep
matters right, and then you can take mud-students, and teach them the
difference atwixt a stick and a stone."

"*So*," said Pigg; adding, with a sniff of his nose across his hand, "to be
hind, that's to say."

"No, you mustn't be be'ind," replied Mr. Jorrocks, with a shake of the
head; "I must have so much rent accounted for every half year."

"Ne doot," said Pigg, "ne doot. But ar's to be manisher like; that's to
say *hind*."

"Ah, *'ind!* I twig," replied Mr. Jorrocks. "Bailiff, what we call."

"Why," said Pigg, "ar can do all that; but we munnut have ne sugar
i' the drainin' tiles."

"Humph!" grunted Mr. Jorrocks, not relishing the observation, and
considering how he should put the next point. "Vell, then, you see,"
continued he after a pause, "as Mrs. J. and myself will only be here
now and then, jest by way of a leetle recreation, instead of buryin'
ourselves alive altogether, so you'll have a deal to attend to out o'

doors, and p'raps it will be well to get somebody to assist you in the 'ouse."

"Ar's warn'd ye," said Pigg; "ar's warn'd ye, 'specially if ar's to have the mud-students."

"Then I was a thinkin'," observed Mr. Jorrocks, rubbing his chin and casting his eyes up to the mullioned ceiling of the room; "I was a thinkin' that Batsay, p'raps, might be useful to you."

"*So*," said Pigg.

"She's a fine woman," observed Mr. Jorrocks, "and I should like to place her in good hands."

"Ne doot," replied Pigg, "ne doot;" adding, "why, ar dare say ar could inanish her too."

"There'll be a *leetle* incambrance," observed Mr. Jorrocks, in an undertone.

"Why, why," replied Pigg, with a jerk of the head, "why, why;" adding, "ar expects it's mar *owne*."

"*Vot, another!*" exclaimed Mr. Jorrocks. "Who'd ha' thought it?"

XXXIII

To be, or not to be: that is the question.

IF EVER MAN GOT WELL "blessed" by woman, it was our fat friend, Mr. Jorrocks, for carrying away the Marquis of Bray—carrying him away just as Mrs. Flather was bringing him "to book." Two minutes more, and she would have run into her game. As it was, she had nothing to do but con over what had passed, recalling the Marquis's every word and look as he underwent the interesting scrutiny—how he said he got on very well with Emma—that the Duke thought very highly of her, and the Duchess liked her uncommonly.

Then she recalled her inquiry as to whether the Marquis had *spoken* to Emma yet, and half upbraided herself for not going a step further and saying, "about their intended marriage." Still she consoled herself that her unmeaning look was so significant, and the Marquis's answer, "that he had not spoken to Emma, because he thought he had better hear what Mrs. Flather had to say first," so conclusive as almost to render greater explicitness superfluous.

Like many over-anxious people, she banished such parts of the conversation from her mind as did not suit her purpose. She forgot that they had been talking about the proposed visit to Donkeyton, and that the subsequent conversation might in the Marquis's mind have had reference to that. This she either could not or did not choose to remember, because the short pause that followed, during which she was working herself up for the grand effort, seeming to her like an hour, she was pleased to consider it as such, and so to separate the parts of the conversation.

Emma also encouraged her in her self-deception; she had no doubt that the Marquis meant to offer—what else could he mean? Still the awkward fact presented itself, that he did not return to conclude the ceremony. A whole day passed over, and no tidings of his lordship; another succeeded—then a third—Mrs. Flather could contain herself no longer—she resolved to be doing, but somehow did not know what to do—whether to write to the Marquis, or the Duke, or the Duchess, or go to Donkeyton Castle and take the bull fairly by the horns.

The latter was a bold step. No one ever went to Donkeyton without an invitation, or some very cogent reason. This latter Mrs. Flather certainly had, but whether it was the prudent course she could not decide. Mother and daughter had slight misgivings of each other's judgment, and each doubted the policy of the other. Emma thought she could have managed the Marquis better by herself; while her mother thought Emma wanted all the assistance she could give her.

No doubt Emma was right—she had all her mother's cunning, with double her tact, and would have worked the Marquis up to the point if she had only been allowed line and time. Mrs. Flather, like many old women, was in too great a hurry. Moreover, each had a slight misgiving, which neither cared to communicate to the other, that there might be some slight misconception or misunderstanding in the matter. Had either been acting separately, she would perhaps have given the weak parts more weight. It is extraordinary how a little assistance makes us believe anything we wish.

Mrs. Flather argued that the Marquis had gone as far as he ought without a specific declaration; and that he would have made one, but for the untimely intrusion of old Jorrocks. If, however, by any possibility, it could happen that such was not his intention, and he was only trifling with Emma's feelings, it was her undoubted duty to stop the thing immediately. If, again, as most probably was the case, the Marquis was anxious to make a declaration, the sooner the opportunity was afforded the better, and then the thing might be announced, and their friends could not feel hurt at one being made acquainted with it sooner than another. Ladies are very considerate in these matters.

"Upon the who-o-ole," as Johnny Wopstraw would say, Mrs. Flather determined to go to the Castle. If she went, and things did not look promising, she could beat a retreat, under pretence of having gone on other business— writership in India, or promotion for Edward.

The resolution being taken, the next thing was how to put it in execution. Whether to take Emma, or go alone, and how to get there. Emma's appearance might have a beneficial effect, particularly if they could be sure of meeting with the Marquis; but then, on the other hand, Emma would very likely insist upon having her own way, and Mrs. Flather wanted to have hers. Perhaps the best plan was not to broach the subject of Emma's going at all—take it for granted she could not.

"How to get there" then came on. "Neat carriages by the day, month, or year" are unknown in the country, and post-chaises are fast disappearing. Omnibuses are all the go. An omnibus for a picnic is all very well, but for a morning visit rather incongruous. Besides, they don't leave a certain line of road; all drawing towards the railway stations, as true as the needle to the pole.

Donkeyton Castle was clear of railways. You could not hear the sound of a whistle on the calmest day, or with the most favourable wind. The Duke had a great dislike to them—*monstrous* dislike. Would have thought the constitution destroyed if one had come near him—not his own constitution, but the constitution of the country. But to the tale. Question proposed—How to go?

Mr. Jorrocks's rattle-trap would have been the most convenient, that is to say, the cheapest conveyance, but then she was afraid if she applied for it, the Squire would insist upon driving it himself, and very likely mar the object of her journey. Farm inspecting gives a man unlimited range over a country. The Sellborough glass chaise was the *dernier ressort*; but then, how was she to get it? The post was gone, and she knew if she sent the boy in buttons on foot, he would never get back. She might beg the loan of Mr. Jorrocks's horse, and send him over on it. Accordingly she wrote the following note:—

> Dear Mr. Jorrocks,—Could you kindly accommodate me with the loan of your horse, for my servant to go to Sellborough, to get a prescription made up? He is a very careful rider, and will take great care of it.

Hoping dear Mrs. Jorrocks is well, I remain, with our
united best regards, dear Mr. Jorrocks, yours most sincerely,

E. FLATHER

"Humph!" grunted Mr. Jorrocks, as the above was handed to him
in his bull-house, where he was busy with Pigg washing the Marquis.
"*Humph!*" grunted he again, "rayther cool of her this. Batsay tells me,
Mrs. F's Susan told her, she heard her missis call me a wulgar old beast;
and now she wants to borrow Dickey Cobden," added Mr. Jorrocks, in
a tone that reached Pigg's ear as he turned the contents of the bucket
into the manger.

"Ar wadn't be a woman's huss at nou't," observed Pigg, knocking the
pail against the side to clean out the bottom.

"Nor I nouther," replied Mr. Jorrocks, turning sharp round, and
making for the house to write an epistle while he was yet warm.

Having unlocked the great brass-bound mahogany desk, with "John
Jorrocks" on the lid, he took a sheet of paper, and in a good round hand
wrote the following answer:—

HILLINGDON HALL}
TO WIT}

DEAR MRS. F.,—Three things I never lends—my 'oss, my
wife, and my name. Howsomever, to-morrow being our
beak-day, when us Jestices of our Sovereign Lady the Queen
assemble to hear all ma of treasons, sorceries, burnins,
witchcrafts, felonies, puzzonins, trespasses, and naughty
be'aviour generally, if you'll send me the prescription, I'll be
'appy to bring the physic 'ome in my pocket. Meanwhile
I sends you a couple of Seidletz, and if you want anythings
else, Mrs. J. will be 'appy to lend you a few 'Cockle's
Antibilious'— werry extensively patronised. A leash o'
Dukes, five brace o' Markisses, sixteen Earls, one-and-
twenty Wiscounts, Barons, Lords, Bishops, and Baronets
without end.—Yours to serve,

JOHN JORROCKS,
J.P., and one of the quorum

P.S.—Dissolve the powder in the blue paper first, then add
the white—stir 'em up, and drink while fizzin'.

Nothing daunted, though sore annoyed, Mrs. Flather then sent off
the boy in buttons on foot with a note to the innkeeper, charging him
to send the job-carriage, in the charge of a neat and steady driver, over
with the bearer in the morning.

Accordingly, about nine o'clock, a wretched copy of a wretched
original, a London glass coach, was seen crawling along, drawn by a
pair of antediluvian-looking horses, a grey turned white, and a rat-tailed
roan, driven by a postboy transmogrified into a coachman—at least, as
far as a napless hat, greasy-collared olive frock-coat, short buff waistcoat,
ornamented with rows of blue glass buttons, could counteract the effect
of a pair of most palpable postboy's legs encased in the usual very long
breeches and very short boots.

The carriage itself was a lofty old landaulet, built towards the close of
the last century, and now containing little of the original material, save
the roundabout tub-shaped body. The leather top was hard, lustreless, and
weather-bleached, with large hollows formed between the ribbing of the
roof, showing the high-water mark of the last shower in the dust. All the
plating had vanished from the side-joints, and huge creases established
themselves at the folds. Half the crests were knocked off the sides.

The body, as was said before, was of the washing-tub order, better
adapted for concealing the inmates than for surveying the country. The
windows were like pigeon-holes, and the seat being low, a short person
would just see the bobbing of the postboy's hat as he "rode and drove."
On the present occasion he drove, being seated on a lofty perch rising
above the level of the roof.

Such was the vehicle that arrived at the Manse to convey Mrs.
Flather to Donkeyton Castle.

A postboy's care of his horses being always considerable when there is
anything to be got in the kitchen, our hero quickly unharnessed his, and

had them in an out house, enjoying a pail of pump water between them, while he hobbled into the house in quest of cold meat and orders.

Mrs. Flather was in marching order, all but putting her bonnet on, and had been hard at work all the morning, undergoing a rigid examination from Emma as to what she would do and what she would say, the inquiry being adapted to every variety of circumstance that could be contemplated—just like one of Madame de Genlis' conversations in the immaculate "Manuel du Voyageurs."

"Well, but if the Duchess is not at home, what will you do?"

"Oh, if she's not at home, and not likely to return soon, I suppose I must just come away," replied mamma.

"You wouldn't think of speaking to the Duke, I suppose," observed Emma suggestingly.

"I don't know," replied Mrs. Flather, thinking the scheme not altogether unfeasible.

"But the Duke would most likely be away too," said Emma.

"They are not likely to go far though, I think," rejoined mamma; "at least not more than a morning drive, for they never visit anybody further than calling, and then they only leave cards."

"They have begun to go in now," observed Emma. "How do you know?" inquired Mrs. Flather. "James told me so," replied Emma, affecting the familiar.

"They want to make themselves popular, I suppose," observed Mrs. Flather.

"Well, but if they are out," continued Emma, resuming the question, "will you wait till they return?"

"I suppose I must," replied Mrs. Flather, after a pause.

"I think I would," said Emma musingly.

"Very well, my dear," assented Mrs. Flather, knowing that by going alone she could do as she pleased when she got there.

"*How awful!*" exclaimed Emma, clasping her hands, and turning her pretty eyes up to the ceiling, as she thought of her mamma sitting waiting the return of the Duchess.

"*It must be done,*" said Mrs. Flather, compressing her lips, and looking as solemn as her vacant countenance would permit. "You're *sure* he kissed you, now?" added she, glancing anxiously at the model of propriety.

"Oh, certain of that, and squeezed my hand too," replied Emma, which she seemed to think about as material as the kiss. Kissing and squeezing are thought more of in the country than they are in London.

"I dare say it will be all right," said Mrs. Flather encouragingly. "He's a young man, but his principles, I hope, are good; indeed, if I thought otherwise, I wouldn't let you marry him if he was an emperor."

"I dare say not," observed Emma pettishly, thinking her mother might as well keep her rodomontade for Donkeyton Castle, her parent's maxim always having been "to get wealth and station, becomingly, if she could, but anyhow to get wealth and station;" a fine doctrine, and frequently acted upon.

"Supposing there's anybody with the Duchess when you go," continued Emma, after a pause, during which she recovered her equanimity, "what will you do?"

"That's not likely, I think," replied Mrs. Flather; "nobody ever goes there, you know, without an invitation."

"But there *may*," continued Emma, "for all that. You don't know what invitations she may have sent out; or, now that they are beginning to entertain, who may take upon themselves to call."

"There's nothing so bad as great people making themselves too common," observed Mrs. Flather; a sentiment of very frequent use in the country, meaning that great people should just patronise ourselves and no one else.

"Nothing," observed Emma. "I'm sure the Duke must feel he's lost caste since he took up with that horrid old idiot down at the Hall."

"Don't *mention* him," rejoined Mrs. Flather; "*abominable old man!* and by the way, that reminds me, I wish you would walk down there this afternoon, and borrow their mouse-trap, for ours is all gone wrong, and the place is literally overrun with mice."

"Now, tell me, how will you broach the subject?" inquired Emma, again returning to her speculations. "Will you go at it at once, or nibble and beat about the bush a little?"

"Upon my word I really think I'd better go at once to the point," replied Mrs. Flather, after a pause.

"But I wouldn't go open-mouthed, as if you were bursting with anxiety," observed Emma.

"Oh, certainly not," replied Mrs. Flather, with a bend and toss of her head, as much as to say, "I know what I am about."

"Will you say that you have come to talk to them about settlements, as if the thing was all fixed; or that you've come to talk about the—the—the—niceness of it, or something of that sort?" asked Emma.

"I don't know, I'm sure, my dear," considered Mrs. Flather; "much will depend upon how they receive me; if they are very affectionate, and so on, we may go to the point at once, but not, I think, about settlements."

"That would look mercenary, perhaps," observed Emma; "still I *should* like to have some diamonds."

"There's no doubt you'll have everything of that sort," rejoined Mrs. Flather.

"Necklace, and earrings, and a tiara. I should so like to go to the New Year's Eve ball in diamonds—splendid diamonds! Jeems told me mamma's cost seventy thousand," observed Emma.

"That's a great deal of money," observed Mrs. Flather.

"I wonder if Mrs. Trotter would go to the winter ball if she knew I was to be there?" inquired Emma. "How delightful it would be if she was."

Just then the old rattle-trap hove in sight, and the debate was forthwith adjourned for the more important business of "getting ready."

XXXIV

Not yet on summer's death, nor on the birth
Of trembling winter.

AFTER THREE "PUT BACKS," FIRST to get her keys, which she had left on the drawers; secondly, to tell Maria to roast the mutton instead of boiling it; and thirdly, to charge Emma not to make herself sick at luncheon, and not to forget the mouse-trap, Mrs. Flather at length got under way.

The bright sun had warmed the air of the autumnal day, and the country round was in the rich luxuriance of declining beauty. The corn-fields were clear, the leaves were changing colour, and an occasional gunshot echoed upon the clear transparent atmosphere. Mrs. Flather, having had the landaulet head put back, settled herself in the middle of the chaise, and hoisting her green parasol, prepared to gather her faculties for the approaching conflict.

On they jingled, but just as a white three-armed guide-post denoted the divergence of the road to three different points, a loud "*Hooi! stop!*" (from behind) caused the driver to pull his horses up with such a jerk as sent Mrs. Flather forward against the front—she nearly broke her nose!

Another second, and her old tormentor, Mr. Jorrocks had his old rattle-trap alongside the carriage, and was putting his whip into the case preparatory to having a confab.

"Vell, Mrs. Flather," said he, with one of his knowing grins, "and vot are *you* arter with your pair 'oss chay? Takin' your medicine in a vehicle, as the doctors write on their labels, eh?" added he, with a leer.

"Oh, Mr. Jorrocks, how do you do?" exclaimed Mrs. Flather, shuffling herself back into her seat, and interposing her parasol between herself and the Squire.

"Vell, and wot's 'appen'd now?" asked Mr. Jorrocks, reaching over and lifting it up, so as to get a view of her face. "Where are you a goin' to? Sellborough, I dare say," added he, without waiting for an answer. "Am a goin' there myself—better come in here with me. Binjimin shall get in there," continued he, unhooking the apron of the fire-engine for the purpose of letting Mrs. Flather in.

"Oh, thank you, Mr. Jorrocks, thank you!" exclaimed she, "but I'm not going to Sellborough; I'm much obliged to—up this other road—here to the right—to the left I mean, thank you; or I should have been most happy."

"And *that's* the Sellborough road," replied our friend. "I knew you was a goin' there. Come, get in—get in! It's no use you and I 'umbuggin' each other."

"I meant the other road! I meant the other road!" exclaimed Mrs. Flather. "The road to the far left," continued she, extending her arm in that direction.

"She's a goin' to Donkeyton Castle," whispered Benjamin from the back seat into his master's ear.

"Donkeyton Castle!" exclaimed Mr. Jorrocks aloud. "Vot, you are a goin' to Donkeyton Castle, are you?" asked Mr. Jorrocks. "Vot's a takin' you there?—thought you'd been a goin' to the chemist's. Has the Duke a blow out? Has the Duke a blow out?"

"I'm going *towards* Donkeyton; I'm going *towards* Donkeyton," replied Mrs. Flather, anxious to get away from her tormentor.

"*Towards* Donkeyton," grunted Mr. Jorrocks; "towards Donkeyton," repeated he, adding aloud to himself, "who *can* she be goin' to see there?"

"Well, good morning, Mr. Jorrocks, good morning," repeated Mrs. Flather; adding, as she desired the coachman to go on, "I'm only wasting your valuable time."

" 'Ang the time," at length observed Mr. Jorrocks, taking the whip out of the case and gathering the reins together, preparatory to setting Dickey Cobden agoing again. "Where *can* the 'ooman be goin' to?" mused he, his eye following the receding chaise.

"She's a goin' to Donkeyton Castle, I *tells* you again," said Benjamin from the back of the chaise.

"Impossible, Binjimin!" exclaimed Mr. Jorrocks.

"But she is, *though*," replied Benjamin, in a confident tone.

"And 'ow do you know that, Binjimin?" asked Mr. Jorrocks, jerking and flopping Dickey Cobden into motion.

"Cause I was hup at their 'ouse when their young man came back with the chay, and he'd peep'd into the iwte and seen the horder," replied Benjamin.

"*So-o-o!*" ejaculated Mr. Jorrocks, "there must be somethin' goin' on—some leetle mystery, I guess;" and musing and wondering what it could be, Mr. Jorrocks proceeded on his way to Sellborough.

There had been a great dinner at Donkeyton Castle the day before, and some of the outer ring visitors having accepted the Duke's invitation to visit his example farm, the last rattle-traps had hardly jingled under the Gothic arch of the battleinented gateway, when Mrs. Flather appeared at the opposite side for admittance. The porter stared as he threw back the old nail-studded oak doors, and his wife observed with a significant smile that "she wished the lady mightn't be a day after the fair."

On Mrs. Flather crawled, at that weary, dilapidated pace that ill-fed, hard-worked horses exhibit—walking, if it were not for the appearance of trotting—along the winding drive through the undulating and picturesque scenery of the richly wooded, water-glittering park.

It was a lovely place. Hundreds of deer herded on its hills, or followed in lengthy files along its ravines; while water-fowl of every description splashed or sported on the extensive lakes, where snow-white swans were gliding majestically about, or noble herons rising slowly and noiselessly to heaven.

The now browning fern and faded heath waved and drooped on the wilder ground, affording shelter to the game and adding wildness to the scene.

It is odd how few visitors at great houses see the beauties of the places. In going they are generally in too great a fright; the ladies pulling on their clean gloves—the gentlemen adjusting their whiskers or neck-cloths. In returning, they are apt to get clear of the premises ere they have done congratulating themselves and each other on their escape;

applauding their courage and sagacity in going, and commenting on their great patron's marked attention to themselves. Some people really seem as if they expected to be "catermauchously chawn up" by great people, as the Americans say.

Mrs. Flather saw nothing. As the rattling of the carriage on the pavement under the arch announced her arrival at the awe-striking castle gates, she gathered herself into a state of desperate compression, and sat eyeing the front joints of the old landaulet, now folded before her, with all the energy of a person enjoying a dentist's arm-chair.

Grind, creak, grind, creak, went the old vehicle over the Kensington gravelled carriage road. *Jip!* crack, flop, went the persuasive Jehu to the pottering screws; coachey looking more lively as the emblazoned banner on the castle glittered in the sun, and bespoke good cheer within.

At length the carriage sounded on the moss-grown walls of the stately castle, as it drove past the open cloisters at the side.

The driver, having deliberately thrown his reins upon the horses' backs (as if in the fullest confidence that they would not run away), descended, whip in hand, from his perch, and applied his hand with the greatest *nonchalance* to the bronze bell-handle in the richly carved doorway, with far different feelings to those which now agitated the bosom of his fair passenger.

"Please, marm, who shall I ax for?" inquired he, limping back to the carriage, with a grin at the peal that answered his pull.

Ere Mrs. Flather had time to reply to the inquiry, the lace-bedizened porter loomed large in the doorway. He was the *beau ideal* of a porter— a great, big, broad, stout, overfed-looking fellow, with well-powdered bald head, pimply nose, and swelling ankles—a spoiled figure footman! Having eyed the wretched vehicle and the humble charioteer, whose old olive-coloured coat assumed a still dingier hue by the bright pea-green ducal livery, the porter, standing in the first position in the exact centre of the top doorstep, with upthrown head, indicated that he was ready to answer questions.

"Is your missis at home?" asked the driver, without waiting for Mrs. Flather's instructions.

"Is the *Duchess* of Donkeyton at home?" inquired Mrs. Flather.

"*Who is it?*" asked the porter of the coachman.

"Mrs. Flather," replied he.

"Not *at home*," rejoined the porter, with a slight inclination towards a bow.

"I have particular business with the Duchess of Donkeyton," exclaimed Mrs. Flather, in a state of desperation.

"Perhaps you'd have the kindness to send in your name," observed the porter, advancing a couple of steps, so as to be able to announce into the carriage, without unnecessarily exerting himself, "that her Grace was rather indisposed, but perhaps she would be able to see her."

Mrs. Flather having dived into her bag, and fished up a carved ivory case, produced a card, with which the porter presented a footman to hand to the groom of the chamber to carry to the Duchess.

Who shall describe her feelings as she waited his return?

Her Grace was in the drawing-room, superintending the arrangement of her portfolios, after the overhauling of the previous evening's party. Castles were joining cascades, and sea-views coalescing with sunsets. Her first impression on seeing the card was, that Mrs. Flather had made a mistake, and come the day after she was invited. This idea, however, was quickly set at rest by inspecting the lists of invited, accepted, and refused, which ended in the Duchess desiring the servant to show Mrs. Flather in. The unfortunate performer of her toils, yclept companion, made her exit through an invisible door in the richly gilt walls as Mrs. Flather sidled through the half-opened folding ones at the far end.

Her Grace of course was charmed to see her, and restored confidence to her now palpitating heart, by that easy affability and kindness of manner almost invariably the attribute of the high-born. Nay, more, it cheered Mrs. Flather onward in her course; and before the Duchess had run over the commonplaces relative to the weather, the roads, and the distance, the parching dryness that almost prevented utterance as Mrs. Flather entered gradually dissolved, and she sat by the side of the awe-inspiring Duchess far more at her ease than she would have been in conclave with Mrs. Trotter.

Conversation with people one really has nothing to say to soon comes short up, and the Duchess presently looked at Mrs. Flather, in hopes that she would "lead the gallop," as they say at Newmarket. Twice Mrs. Flather faltered. "Your Grace," was all she uttered before the tongue-tying dryness again assailed her; and the Duchess at last tried to turn her to her old friend the portfolio, in hopes of engaging her till luncheon was announced.

"Your Grace," again attempted Mrs. Flather, with the desperate energy of a person bent on a subject, "I am sure you, as a mother, will excuse the——"

Her Grace was surprised at Mrs. Flather's vehemence. She was too high-bred a woman to be put out of her way, and had, besides, a certain constitutional inclination for taking things easy. Mrs. Flather, being wound up, proceeded.

"I am sure I need not say," continued she, "how deeply I appreciate the honour conferred on my poor girl."

Her Grace smiled and bowed courteously, thinking it merely had reference to the party she had had them to, and said, "Pray don't mention it."

This rather put Mrs. Flather out, and her Grace was just going to draw her attention to the flower-stand beaming radiant before the window—another safety valve for country stupidity—when Mrs. Flather again went on. "It is certainly a most unexpected—a most unlooked-for honour," said she, drawing her best cambric handkerchief out of her bag; "but I trust Emma will so conduct herself as to prove she is not unworthy of the high confidence your Grace and the Duke have reposed in her."

The Duchess was "quite sure she would; indeed they both thought most highly of her. She was a remarkably fine girl. Wish Mrs. Flather had brought her with her."

This was great encouragement to Mrs. Flather. She proceeded to explain that it was merely a point of delicacy that had prevented her doing so, but that after the kind assurance her Grace had given, of course there could be no difficulty about it, and she would take a very early opportunity of doing so.

"Her Grace hoped she would—would always be most happy to see them," making a knot in her mind at the same time to tell the servants to deny them.

Luncheon was then announced.

"Your Grace, perhaps, wouldn't like it to take place very soon?" said Mrs. Flather, still sticking to her seat.

"Oh, any time," said her Grace, motioning her to obey the summons. "Wouldn't she take a little luncheon?"

Mrs. Flather, however, having heard that "any time was no time," thought she might as well get that point settled.

"It will require a good deal of preparation," observed she, rising and standing by her chair with her right hand resting on the back.

The Duchess stared, wondering if Mrs. Flather thought she was invited to stay.

"I mean that the settlements, and such-like, will take some time doing."

"*Settlements!*" exclaimed the Duchess, staring with astonishment.

"Oh, just as your Grace pleases," replied Mrs. Flather most submissively; "of course we don't insist upon anything of the sort."

"I fear we misunderstand each other," said the Duchess, reconsidering all that had passed. "It surely isn't Jeems you're thinking about? *It can't* be Jeems!" added she, as the ancestry of twenty generations flashed upon her mind. Mrs. Flather felt as if she would drop through the floor before the Duchess's withering glance.

"My dear Mrs. Flather," said she, in a low tone, pressing her on the arm to get her to resume her seat; "my dear Mrs. Flather, I fear there is some misunderstanding between the Marquis of Bray and yourself. Of course I don't know what has passed between you, or what reasons he may have given your daughter to think he is attached to her, but I must tell you, as a friend"—and the Duchess said it in the kindest manner possible—"I must tell you as a friend, that it would be the death of the Duke to mention such a thing to him."

"But his Grace encouraged it!" exclaimed Mrs. Flather, in the greatest agitation.

"*Impossible*, my dear Mrs. Flather!" replied the Duchess, calmly but firmly. "Impossible, I assure you; you must be under a mistake. The Duke is too proud; has too great regard for his station to think of such a thing; far too much regard!"

"Nay, then——" said Mrs. Flather despondingly.

"Here *is* the Duke," observed the Duchess, as his Grace popped his snow-wreathed head into the door, to see what kept the Duchess away from her luncheon.

"Here's Mrs. Flather, my dear!" exclaimed the Duchess, as he was jerking back, in hopes he had not been observed.

"Ah, Mrs. Flather!" exclaimed he, with the gaiety of sham delight, as he thought of the hot chicken he had left and "My dear Mrs. Flather," repeated he, advancing up the spacious room with extended hands, to give her a hearty welcome—"how do you do?" said he, seizing her by both—"glad to see you, *monstrous* glad to see you; come and have a little luncheon; on the table quite ready." So saying, his Grace bowed, and waved, and drove her along into the privacy of viands and powdered menials.

The Duchess followed.

"And how are you all at home?" asked the Duke, as he helped Mrs. Flather to a wing and a piece of the breast of one of his own high-fed Dorkings. "Fine fowl that; monstrous fine fowl," said he; "reared at my own farm, great farmer, monstrous great farmer. Potatoes of my own growing too," said he, as a footman handed a dish of fine white mealy ones to the appetiteless Mrs. Flather. "And how is Mr. Jorrocks? neighbour of yours, isn't he? good neighbour, monstrous good neighbour, I should think."

"*Very* good neighbour *indeed*, your Grace," replied Mrs. Flather, with an emphasis, seeing which way the wind blew.

"Clever man," said his Grace, putting the first mouthful of the delicate white meat, with the nicely browned outside, into his mouth. "Monstrous clever man," continued he, chewing away. "And how's his bull?"

"Quite well, I believe, your Grace," replied Mrs. Flather.

"Fine bull," said his Grace; "monstrous fine bull—got premium I saw in the papers."

"Take a glass of sherry with me—there's Madeira if you prefer it," said his Grace, seeing Mrs. Flather played with her luncheon. "Your good health," said his Grace, bowing, and drinking off his wine at two gulps.

"And how's your daughter?" asked his Grace, after a pause, as he worked away at the chicken, and considered whether the daughter belonged to Mrs. Flather or to Mr. Jorrocks. His Grace knew there was a daughter between them, but he had never been able to get the confusion of the chaise arrangement set right in his head.

"Quite well, I'm much obliged to your Grace," replied Mrs. Flather, with fervour.

"Fine girl," said his Grace; "monstrous fine girl," added he, cutting again at the chicken.

That observation determined Mrs. Flather to make one effort with the Duke ere she gave up all hopes. Accordingly she recollected all her scattered energies, and prepared for the first opening she saw after they left the luncheon room. It was some time before the Duke gave her a chance. He jabbered and talked so fast about flowers, fruits, pheasants, footstools, farming, that she could hardly get a word in sideways. At last he got back to Jorrocks and Hillingdon.

"And how does Mr. Jorrocks acquit himself on the bench?" asked the Duke. "Good magistrate, monstrous good magistrate, I should think." added he, answering himself—"keeps the country quiet, I dare say; peaceable, respectable; good thing to have an active magistrate in your neighbourhood, monstrous good thing."

"Oh, Mr. Jorrocks is an excellent magistrate!" exclaimed Mrs. Flather, as soon as she allowed an opportunity.

"And a good neighbour, I make no doubt," added the Duke; "sociable, agreeable, sensible," thinking Mr. Jorrocks would be like himself.

"Most agreeable man!" exclaimed Mrs. Flather.

"Great farmer, I suppose?" observed the Duke; "talented farmer, monstrous talented farmer; disciple of Smith of Deanston's? Smith is the greatest benefactor the world ever saw; monstrous benefactor!"

"The Marquis of Bray is a great farmer, isn't he?" asked Mrs. Flather, seizing the opportunity.

"Oh, Jeems is a great farmer—monstrous great farmer," replied his Grace, with a series of nods of the head—"fond of guinea-pigs—monstrous fond of guinea-pigs—has a whole drove up at Mrs. Jobson's."

"His lordship was kind enough to express his partiality for my daughter," observed Mrs. Flather, with desperate resolution.

"Did he indeed," exclaimed his Grace, not exactly catching the sentence Mrs. Flather's hurried articulation rendered doubtful. "Good judge—monstrous good judge," added the Duke, thinking he would beat a retreat to his country paper, *The Dozey Independent*, which was published that day.

"I am glad it meets your Grace's approbation," observed the emboldened Mrs. Flather.

"*Quite*, I assure you," said his Grace—"good thing—monstrous good thing indeed."

"Well, I think there is nothing like young people settling early in life," rejoined Mrs. Flather.

"*Nothing* like it!" said his Grace; "nothing like it," repeated he, looking at his watch. "However, I am sorry I must bid you good morning," added he, with a feigned start, as if he had discovered he was behind time. "I hve a despatch from the Home Office: the Duchess will be glad to take a walk with you—show you the aviary—the *goold* fish—Jeems's rabbits—her Italian greyhounds." So saying, with a wave of the hand towards where the now horrified Duchess stood, his Grace sidled and backed out of the drawing-room.

Mrs. Flather was not a great hand at reading physiognomies, or she would have seen astonishment and indignation mantling on the Duchess's brow. As it was, she thought she had rather got a "crow" over her—the Duke having so eagerly ratified what her Grace had so lately derided.

"The Duke, you see, is quite in favour of the match," observed she, advancing towards the Duchess, with a smile on her vacant countenance.

Her Grace deigned no reply.

"I'm sure," continued she, rather taken aback by the Duchess's manner, "it will be our study to please and make ourselves agreeable—and—your Grace—"

The Duchess bowed slightly.

"It is an honour we had no right perhaps to aspire to," simpered Mrs. Flather; "but I hope we shall conduct ourselves becomingly. I'm sure," added she, "I hope it may be many years before my daughter occupies your Grace's place." The Duchess bridled up, but still held her peace. "The Duke too, I'm sure I hope he may live a long time," simpered Mrs. Flather; "no two people, I can assure you, your Grace, can be less desirous of an early change than my daughter and myself." The same provoking silence greeted this handsome announcement.

"Titles are nothing compared to happiness," simpered Mrs. Flather; "I wouldn't my daughter should marry a prince if he were not a man of good principles."

"Really, Mrs. Flather," said her Grace, unable any longer to contain herself, "you must allow me to tell you that you are labouring under a strong delusion."

"How so, your Grace?" and Mrs. Flather stared.

"In the first place, in supposing that our son would ever think of marrying your daughter; and in the second place, in supposing that the Duke and myself would ever sanction such a thing."

"But he stated his positive delight at the prospect of it not two minutes ago," exclaimed Mrs. Flather, with the most determined confidence.

"You quite misunderstood him," said the Duchess; "you quite misunderstood him," repeated she; "the Duke is the last man in the world to approve—nay, *hear* of an unequal match. What!" exclaimed the Duchess, her eyes flashing as she spoke, "the representative of twenty generations throwing himself away in such a manner!"

Mrs. Flather was dumfoundered.

"No, my dear Mrs. Flather," continued her Grace, her features softening as she proceeded, "let me advise you to get rid of the idea— dismiss it from your mind—it can only make your daughter and every one concerned ridiculous."

"I couldn't use the Duke so badly, so ungratefully," replied Mrs. Flather, now fully impressed with the idea that the Duchess was deceiving her.

"I *again assure you*, you misunderstood the Duke," observed her Grace, "or the Duke misunderstood *you*. He is rather deaf, and perhaps did not hear what you said."

Mrs. Flather looked incredulous.

"I assure you it is the case."

Mrs. Flather was silent. She still doubted. The Duchess, she thought, must be deceiving her. The Duke seemed to expect the observation, and to jump at it. His manner, too, was most impressive when she arrived—most affectionate. The Duchess saw the turn things were taking in Mrs. Flather's mind, and gave her time to think them over.

"Would you like to see the Duke again?" at length said she, "and ask him the question yourself?"

Mrs. Flather muttered something about "Mistake somewhere. The Duchess might be mistaken, perhaps."

"But is it likely," inquired her Grace, "that on a subject so deeply affecting the interests—nay, the happiness—of our son, that there should be any mystery or misconception between the Duke and myself?"

Mrs. Flather was silent; she thought it more evident that the Duchess wanted to get rid of her and try and dissuade the Duke from it.

"Nay, you are a mother yourself," observed the Duchess; "would you, if your husband was alive, have any concealments from him on such a subject?"

"Certainly not," said Mrs. Flather, who had always prided herself upon being a pattern wife. "But your Grace and the Duke may differ on the point," boldly observed the aspiring mother.

"Nothing of the sort, I assure you," rejoined the Duchess most emphatically; "nothing of the sort, I assure you. The Duke and I have no secrets, no disagreements on any subject."

Mrs. Flather didn't know what to say.

"Let us take a turn on the terrace," at length said the Duchess, really feeling for Mrs. Flather's situation. "Forget what has passed," said she, rising, "and it shall never be mentioned or referred to by me."

"Well," said Mrs. Flather, in a tone of despair, still thinking it was a *ruse* of the Duchess's to get her away.

"But don't let me take you if you would like to see the Duke again on the subject," observed her Grace, reading reluctance in Mrs. Flather's countenance.

"Well," said she, after a pause, during which she thought of the enormous stake she was playing for—a coronet and coach and six—the distinction of strawberry leaves not being much understood, a coronet being a coronet in the country; when she thought, we say, of the stake she was playing for, she resolved not to lose a chance. "Well," said she, "in so important and delicate an affair, an affair involving the happiness of my daughter, perhaps her life—for I will not deny that her affections are deeply engaged—I really think I should not be acting right were I not to avail myself of your Grace's proposition; not that I in the slightest degree doubt the—the—the accuracy of your Grace's assertion—at least not the—the—the accuracy of your Grace's belief that the Duke is—is—is—I dare say your Grace knows what I mean; but still, in so delicate a matter, I'm sure you'll forgive the feelings of a mother and—" here she applied her cambric to her eyes.

The Duchess assured her she could make every allowance for her. If seeing the Duke again would satisfy her, she would advise her by all means to do so. She would find him in the library, and she would either accompany her or not as she liked; meanwhile Mrs. Flather had better compose herself, and thereupon the Duchess urged her to sit down, knowing, as she well did, that the Duke abominated a scene. Perhaps the Duchess thought that a little reflection might make Mrs. Flather think better of it, but there she was mistaken, an old woman being as bad to turn as a sheep.

Mrs. Flather sat counting the silk fringe on her shawl, giving herself a certain length, and settling that if the bunches came even it should be a sign of luck; and if odd, the reverse. She had got through her task, and declared for even, when the radiance the circumstance threw into her countenance made the Duchess think she was ready for something, and accordingly she addressed her by inquiring what she would like to do.

"Oh, to see the Duke, by all means," observed Mrs. Flather, now more than ever convinced that the Duchess was deceiving her.

"He is in the library," observed her Grace; "would you like me to go in and tell him what you want to speak to him about, or shall I accompany you, and leave you to broach the subject yourself?"

Mrs. Flather would rather have gone by herself, but she had no notion of letting the Duchess have the first word, very likely prejudicing, or maybe intimidating, the Duke. However, as she could not well tell her Grace she would rather have nothing to do with her, she very politely begged she would not give herself the trouble of going; if she would just show her where his Grace was, she would not trouble her Grace any further.

The Duchess assented, and led the way to the library.

XXXV

Sleeping within mine orchard,
My custom always in the afternoon,
Upon my secure hour Mrs. Flather stole.

THE DUKE OF DONKEYTON, ON retiring to the library after the exertions of the luncheon table, *Dozey Independent* in hand, had thrown himself into the deep recesses of the easiest of the many easy chairs with which the apartment was supplied. In truth, it was a noble chair—a chair well becoming a Duke. The curiously carved, black oak frame-work glided on the highest finished castors; while the back, sides, and arms were stuffed with puffy, rich-cut velvet cushions, with invisible springs. Though copied from the antique, it had none of the inconvenient height or inverse propensities of the original. On the contrary, the Duke's head just rubbed above the back cushion, as in the abandon of his easy hour he stuck his legs out before him, straight as a deal-board, or a lay figure in a studio.

Here, in one of the deep recesses formed by the windows in the massive walls, the Duke was in the habit of wheeling himself, just sufficiently far to enable him to enjoy the perfume of the flowers wafting from the terrace, and the scenery of the distant hills, without being visible to those below.

A little more luncheon than he usually ate, with a little more talk than he usually indulged in, together with the extreme heat of the day, aided perhaps by the autumnal dulness of his newspaper and the seductive qualities of the easy-chair, had sent his Grace off in a nap sooner than usual; and when the Duchess and Mrs. Flather entered the room, his shining bald head appeared above the crimson, bullion-fringed cushion in such a position as, without the deep snore he every now and then emitted, clearly proclaimed that his Grace slept.

He was quite comfortable. His mouth was wide open, his legs were stretched out before him, his eye-glasses hung on his unbuttoned buff-waistcoat as they had fallen from his nose, and the well-ironed *Dozey Independent* stood from the carpet just touching his right hand, as it hung negligently over the chair side. A large "blue-bottle" fly buzzed and bumped and noised about the room, now exploring the Duke's bald head, now settling on his nose, now apparently determining to enter his noble mouth. The impudence of a blue-bottle passes all comprehension.

"Perhaps we had better not disturb his Grace," observed Mrs. Flather, in a whisper.

Mr. Flather used not to like being disturbed when making his sermons, and Mrs. Flather recollected this.

"Oh, he'll not mind," replied the Duchess, in her usual tone, thinking to awake him by the noise.

A loud snore.

The blue-bottle buzzed away, making a small circuit in the air—scared perhaps by the intruders. They proceeded slowly and noiselessly over the soft Turkey carpet, Mrs. Flather half inclined to stop the Duchess, lest awaking the Duke should have a prejudicial effect. Before she could make up her mind to do so, however, the Duchess had reached the occupant of the easy-chair, and placing her hand on his shoulder, gave him a half sort of shake, with—"Jeems, my dear, here is Mrs. Flather wishes to speak to you." Just then the blue bottle, after buzzing round about the Duke's nose, had paid a visit to his nostril, and his Grace started in his chair with a perfect cannon of a sneeze.

"*Ah-whitz!*" sneezed the Duke again, as if he would blow himself to pieces. "*Ah-whitz!*" repeated he, getting up and diving into his pocket for his handkerchief. "*Ah-whitz!*" he went again, with the water streaming from his eyes.

Mrs. Flather trembled for her mission.

"*Ah-whitz! ah-whitz! ah-whitz!*" sneezed the Duke in succession. "Cold—monstrous bad cold," said he, mopping his eyes.

"Mrs. Flather wishes to see you, my dear," observed the Duchess, amidst a tremendous "*ah-whitz*," from his Grace.

"*Me!*" exclaimed the Duke, in astonishment, "*ah-whitz!* What can she want with me? *ah-whitz*," said he, smothering his face in his handkerchief.

The Duchess, fearing his Grace might say something he ought not, here drew Mrs. Flather forward, and when the Duke took his face out of its bandanna bed, his would-be relative was full before him.

"Ah, my dear Mrs. Flather, how do you do?" asked his Grace, offering one hand, while he mopped his face with the other; "*glad to see you— very glad to see you.*" His Grace could not say "monstrous," for where is the man who likes to be interrupted in a sneeze? "Hope you are all well at home?" asked his Grace, running on in the usual form.

"Quite well, I'm much obliged to your Grace," replied Mrs. Flather, nothing disconcerted at his apparent forgetfulness of her. "I wish to speak a few words to your Grace respecting my daughter," faltered Mrs. Flather, amid a long protracted *ah-whitz* from his Grace.

"She's quite well, I hope?" observed his Grace. "*Ah-whitz*—oh, I beg your pardon—*ah-whitz*—I saw you before," he added, giving his nose a final blow, and returning his handkerchief to his pocket. "Got a bad cold—monstrous bad cold," said he, shutting back the window. "Susan, my dear, what time have you ordered the carriage?" The Duke thought to give Mrs. Flather a hint, but she was not the person to take one.

"Mrs. Flather wishes to have a little conversation with you, my love," observed the Duchess.

"Pray sit down," said the Duke, wheeling Mrs. Flather in a chair as he buttoned up his waistcoat. "Wants a commission for a son, I suppose," thought he to himself, forgetting she had just told him it was her daughter she wanted to speak about. Mrs. Flather looked at the Duchess, and was silent. Her Grace then withdrew. Mrs. Flather seated herself.

"It is a very delicate subject I've come to speak to your Grace about," observed Mrs. Flather, arranging the fringe of her shawl on her knee, and dressing it out as she spoke; "but I'm sure your Grace will excuse the freedom I have taken."

"Make no apology," observed his Grace. "Make no apology," repeated he encouragingly.

"You are doubtless aware," continued Mrs. Flather, still arranging her fringe as she spoke, "that there has been a certain something going on for some time between my daughter and your son."

"What, Jeems?" exclaimed the Duke, starting, and staring with astonishment.

"The Marquis of Bray," faltered Mrs. Flather, staggered at the Duke's amazement.

"*Indeed!*" exclaimed the Duke, in a subdued tone; adding, with a solemn shake of the head, "sorry to hear it—monstrous sorry to hear it."

Mrs. Flather was nonplussed. The parching dryness again closed her lips, and she sat pulling at the shawl fringe till she drew out a bunch.

"Well," said the Duke, wheeling his chair nearer to hers as she achieved this feat, " tell me all about it. When did it happen?"

"Oh, it's been going on for some time," sobbed Mrs. Flather, drawing her cambric from her bag.

The Duke paused to let her have her cry.

"Well," said the Duke, when she seemed about done, " I'm sorry for it, monstrous sorry for it. Jeems is a naughty boy—monstrous naughty boy; am angry with Jeems—monstrous angry with Jeems; had no business to do anything of the sort—gave him my Lord Chesterfield's 'Letters to his Son,' with the passage recommending young men to attach themselves to married women, underlined in red ink, and marked in the margin. Great pity—monstrous great pity," added the Duke, with a succession of nods of the head—"fine girl—monstrous fine girl. However, I'll tell you what," continued he, in an undertone to Mrs. Flather, laying his hand confidentially on her arm, "*it's no use making a row about it—the less said the better.*"

"Indeed!" sobbed Mrs. Flather, pulling out another bunch of fringe.

"No," said the Duke, with another batch of shakes and shrugs, "*none whatever.*"

Mrs. Flather sobbed in silence.

"I'll tell you what," said the Duke, "the best thing you can do is to take her abroad—go a little tour—up the Rhine—into Switzerland—

down to Milan—on to Florence, if you like. I'll pay the expenses—draw upon me for five hundred, a thousand if you like. May marry her perhaps—Swiss colonel—Italian count— French general—no saying; fine girl—monstrous fine girl; but if you don't, why, you'll come back at the end of a certain time, and no one will know anything about it—be any the wiser. These sort of things are unpleasant, no doubt—monstrous unpleasant; but accidents will happen—youthful indiscretion—more cautious in future; sorry for it, I assure you—monstrous sorry for it; but rely upon it, it's no use making a row about it—*hush it up*—*hush it up*—as the Duke of Wellington said."

"But your Grace misunderstands me," said Mrs. Flather, as soon as the Duke's fringed face began to settle on his shoulders; "your Grace misunderstands me, I think," repeated she, "it's my daughter's affections the Marquis has engaged; and——"

"I understand," interrupted the Duke—"perfectly understand; but what can we do, you know? What can we do?"

"I supposed it was with your Grace's knowledge," sobbed Mrs. Flather.

"Not at all, I assure you, not at all," rejoined his Grace; "on the contrary, always recommended Chesterfield to Jeems. Good book— monstrous good book: Chesterfield knew the world. But, however, what's done can't be helped."

"But he came over to Hillingdon with your Grace's knowledge, I suppose?" asked Mrs. Flather.

"Undoubtedly he did," replied the Duke; "un-doubtedly he did: but that was to see old Mr. Jorrocks—talk about farming—improve the breed of husbandry horses—study agricultural chemistry, and so on. I suppose then had been the time he had come over your daughter."

"Oh, it was only talking," observed Mrs. Flather, anxious to remove the impression under which the Duke laboured.

"Only talking!" said the Duke, with surprise; "talking's nothing— talking's nothing."

"It's a great deal to an innocent young country girl, your Grace," observed Mrs. Flather.

"Don't see why it should," said the Duke, "don't see why it should. Of course it depends a good deal upon what is said," added he.

"Of course," replied Mrs. Flather. "He certainly gave Emma to understand that he was very much attached to her."

"Foolish boy, foolish boy," observed the Duke, with a series of nods, of the head; "however, there is no putting old heads on young shoulders. I remember my poor father—the eighth Duke—heaven rest him!—saying the very same thing to me—no putting old heads on young shoulders; and so it will be to the end of the chapter—so it will be to the end of the chapter."

Mrs. Flather measured the fringe with her knuckle. It was three-quarters of a yard.

A long silence ensued.

"Well, I suppose we can make nothing better of it," at length said the Duke, with a yawn, wishing Mrs. Flather would take her departure.

"Then I fear we cannot make anything better of it," at length said Mrs. Flather, remeasuring the fringe and looking intently at the Duke.

"Upon my word there seems to be nothing to make better of," observed the Duke. "There's no harm done that I can see."

"None if your Grace encourages the match," observed Mrs. Flather boldly.

"*Encourage the match!*" exclaimed the Duke, starting up. "What! Jeems marry a commoner!—a—a—a— IMPOSSIBLE!" and the Duke stamped as though he would rouse his dormant ancestry to avenge the insult.

Mrs. Flather shook with fear. What might have followed must remain matter of surmise; for, fortunately, the Duchess's pride could no longer restrain her curiosity, and she returned to the library just at the critical moment. She had advanced far up the spacious apartment before either party was aware of her presence. The Duke saw her first.

"Susan, my dear!" exclaimed he, in a towering passion, "Mrs. Flather has done us the honour of coming here to claim our son in marriage for her daughter."

"Indeed!" replied the Duchess mildly, well knowing there was no occasion for them both to set on her at once.

"Compliment! great compliment! monstrous great compliment! isn't it?" asked the Duke, white as his whiskers.

The Duke's horror at the marquise marrying a commoner

"Perhaps if you are satisfied *now*," observed the Duchess with an emphasis, to Mrs. Flather, "you had better retire; his Grace is not very well to-day," added she, in an undertone, "and does not like to be disturbed."

Mrs. Flather took the hint and trotted away with the Duchess, nothing loth to leave the obstreperous Duke.

"I think I would like to go home," said Mrs. Flather, half sick with mortification, "if you will allow me to ring for my carriage," continued she, making for the bell as she spoke.

"Pray sit down a little and compose yourself," observed the Duchess, drawing a chair towards her—"you are agitated."

"I shall be better as soon as I get into the open air, thank you," observed Mrs. Flather, in a tone of the deepest despondency.

The Duchess tried to get her to talk on various subjects, from the weather down to the portfolio; but Mrs. Flather was dead beat; "yes" and "no" were all she could say; and sometimes she said one when she ought to have said the other.

The footman's "Your carriage is at the door, if you please, marm," sounded a welcome release; and the Duchess, by no means sorry to get rid of her pertinacious visitor, offered her arm to accompany her to the door.

From the loop-hole window of his dressing-room above, Jeems saw his "ma-in-law" ascend the lofty steps of the antiquated landaulet and drive away amid the adieus of the Duchess.

XXXVI

He wot prigs what isn't hisn,
If he's kotched, 'ill go to prison.

NEWGATE LYRICS

AWAY FROM THE SCENES WHERE our mistakes arise, away from the friends who prompt their course, how soon the mind sees its errors, and points to the path we should not have deserted!

Ere Mrs. Flather's rattle-trap jingled under the castellated gateway of Donkeyton Castle Park, she saw how Emma and she had mutually assisted in deceiving each other, how their wishes had been father to their thoughts.

Before she got two miles on her road, she wondered that she could have been so silly as to go. It wasn't likely the Marquis should have seriously thought of Emma; still more improbable that the Duke and Duchess would sanction, much less wish for such a match. Most likely there were places in London where great people met, and though Emma's and her knowledge of high life was confined to the Donkeytons, she began to suspect that great people were more numerous than they imagined. They might not be so great as the Donkeytons, perhaps, but still great enough to prevent the Marquis from being so desperately put to as to have to seek the country for a wife.

Mrs. Flather was greatly distressed—distressed that she should have made such a fool of herself, and vexed that she had not checked instead of encouraging Emma. Then there was Mr. Jorrocks, and his odious matter-of-fact questions, and Mrs. Trotter's still more odious curiosity. Altogether, Mrs. Flather was in a bad way. The Duchess was sure to tell; she would tell the Marquis, the Marquis would tell Mr. Jorrocks, Mr. Jorrocks would tell Mrs. Jorrocks, and Mrs. Jorrocks would tell all the world. Horrible idea!

Then Mrs. Flather thought how she should meet Emma; what little consolation she might expect from her. And again she deplored having encouraged instead of checking her folly.

It so happened on this eventful day, that there had been a very small attendance of the Justices of our Sovereign Lady the Queen at Sellborough Petty Sessions, Mr. Green and Mr. Jorrocks being the only ones present; Captain Bluster had got the lumbago, Mr. Smith had gone to look at a horse, and Mr. Somebody else to look at a cow, and a third gentleman's wife was ill.

Mr. Green having popped into court a few minutes before our worthy friend, had got possession of the chair, and was sitting in state when Mr. Jorrocks arrived. The Clerk too was away, and his place was supplied by a subordinate. A case had just been called on under the Vagrant Act., disposable of by one magistrate. It was a charge by Farmer Goosecap against some of the independent, itinerant tribe—Hannah Hardy, Jane Hardy, William Hardy, and Alfred Hardy, very swarthy ringletty people—of trying to make free with his poultry; and Goosecap, having had that compliment paid him before, wanted the full measure of vengeance—*nunc pro tunc*, as Captain Bluster would say.

It seems the ladies had held Goosecap in fortunetelling talk, while the men inspected the poultry-yard; but in trying to catch old chanticleer, he made such a noise as disturbed the servants, who gave the alarm; and, wonderful to relate, they took the whole troop.

Goosecap had got to about the middle of his story when Mr. Jorrocks entered, but seeing the people, and hearing the latter part of it, Mr. Jorrocks had no difficulty in comprehending the case, and entering fully into it.

"They'd have a jackass, I reckon?" observed our Squire interrogatively, as the complainant finished.

"Yes, sir, they had," replied Goosecap, "tethered in the lane, about a quarter of a mile off."

"I thought so!" exclaimed Mr. Jorrocks, grinding his teeth, and looking as if he would eat the whole troop. "I thought so," repeated he. "Every man," continued he, most sententiously, "wot keeps a jackass is a waggabone; every man wot keeps a jackass keeps a pair of big panniers also, and there's no sayin' wot on *airth* goes into them. I'd conwict them all as rogues and waggabones," added he, turning to Mr. Green, "and give them full measure—three months to the 'ouse of C., 'ard labour, and all that sort o' thing."

Mr. Green was an indiscriminate humanity-monger, a man who made as much to do about committing a hardened vagabond as others would with a reclaimable first offender, and always tried how little justice he could do and how great a show of feeling he could make. Many men do the same. It is a cheap way of gaining credit for kind-heartedness.

Finding Mr. Jorrocks was in the trouncing mood—not always the case with the old gentleman either, particularly when the offenders happened to be females—Mr. Green waxed uncommonly merciful, and in reply to Mr. Jorrocks's hint, observed that he couldn't do it under the Act. Thereupon a long wrangle ensued between our worthy friend and his colleague, as to the difference between idle and disorderly persons and rogues and vagabonds, but which we will let Mr. Jorrocks explain when he tells his story to Mrs. Flather, which we will now accompany him to do.

The business of the day being over, Mr. Jorrocks bethought him, as he repaired to the inn for his machine, to ask where the job-carriage was gone to, and finding that it was bound to Donkeyton Castle, as Benjamin said, Mr. Jorrocks drove very quietly in that direction, and soon ascertained at the first turnpike gate that the well-known vehicle had gone through, and not having returned, our friend kept moving leisurely on, commenting on the husbandry of the district, and the stupidity of Mr. Green in not knowing the difference between an idle and disorderly person and a rogue and vagabond.

At length he espied the old posters, bobbing their heads up and down at a sort of walking trot, while the driver's right arm went out at regular intervals, laying the pig-jobber whip-thong straight along the carcass of the off-side one.

" 'Ere she comes," said Mr. Jorrocks to himself, as the old vehicle neared him. "I'll give her an agreeable surprise." So saying, our friend drew up under a now leaf-shedding sycamore, and quietly waited her coming. Could he but have seen into Mrs. Flather's mind, he would have spared her the infliction; but Mr. Jorrocks having no cares himself—at least none superior to the interests of his bull—it never entered his head that other people could have any, certainly not ladies, who, he thought, were only meant for amusement.

"YOUR MONEY OR YOUR LIFE!" roared our worthy friend, rising in his vehicle, as Mrs. Flather, in a state of utter dejection, came jingling past where he sat.

"Scream! help! scream!" went Mrs. Flather, to the convulsions of the coachman and Benjamin, and the great amusement of Mr. Jorrocks.

"Oh, Mr. Jorrocks! how could you?" exclaimed Mrs. Flather angrily. "You don't know how you've frightened me."

"Nonsense, my leetle dack, nonsense!" said Mr. Jorrocks soothingly. "*It's only me!*"

"But you don't know how you frightened me, Mr. Jorrocks," sobbed Mrs. Flather, diving into her reticule for her pocket-handkerchief.

"Nonsense, my darlin'!" continued Mr. Jorrocks, "nonsense, it's only fan."

Mrs. Flather sobbed violently, glad to get a vent for her tears. Mr. Jorrocks looked foolish at the result of his practical joke.

"*You* take the reins," said Mr. Jorrocks to Benjamin, "and drive quietly on arter the chay, and I'll ride 'ome with Mrs. Flather," continued he, getting out of his own vehicle, and opening the door of Mrs. Flather's.

"Shall I help you, sir?" asked the coachman, looking down from his box at Mr. Jorrocks's movements.

"You don't take me for a cripple, do you?" replied our friend snappishly, "that I can't get in by myself?"

Thereupon Mr. Jorrocks let down the long flight of steps, resembling Robinson Crusoe's ladder, and prepared to ascend.

Up he got.

The thing then was to get the steps back again, and this rather puzzled Mr. Jorrocks; his short fat arms could not reach low enough to get a sufficient purchase to pull them up in a heap so as to fold them like a map, or a joiner's foot-rule, and it was no use attempting them at the top. Head downwards, he tried in vain, each effort drawing ill-suppressed bursts of laughter from the coachman and Benjamin, as the Jorrockian jacket's fan-tail flew up, and the Squire seemed likely to land head-foremost on the ground.

It was no go.

"Vy don't you come and shet Mrs. Flather's chay door for her, Binjimin?" at last exclaimed Mr. Jorrocks, starting up, and throwing the fan-tail back, as Benjamin snickered right out. "The devil's in these servants," muttered Mr. Jorrocks, seating himself by Mrs. Flather; "they seem to think they're kept to do nothin' at all. I'll skin you alive," muttered Mr. Jorrocks, with a shake of the head, as Benjamin refolded the rattling, ill-jointed, iron steps. "Now," said Mr. Jorrocks to the coachman, as the door banged to, "drive quietly 'ome; don't 'urry, for my quad. is a followin', and is rayther tired."

There was little need for this humane injunction, for coachee had no idea of hurrying—indeed his cattle were incapable of it, and having jerked and flopped them into motion, on they went at the

> We're a' nodding,
> Nid, nid, nodding

sort of pace that they had hove in sight at.

"Well, my leetle dack," said Mr. Jorrocks, in an undertone, scrudging up to Mrs. Flather and squeezing her hand; "well, my leetle dack," said he, "you've recovered your fright, I 'opes."

"Indeed I *haven't*," replied Mrs. Flather snappishly; "you've almost thrown me into hysterics—made me shockingly nervous."

"That's a great pity," observed Mr. Jorrocks, "werry great pity; I only meant it for *fan*."

"I don't like such horse fun," said Mr Flather, anything but pleased at our friend's intrusion into her carriage.

"*Only me*," said Mr. Jorrocks soothingly.

Mrs. Flather pouted her lip and was silent.

"And when's Emma to be a marchioness?" at length asked Mr. Jorrocks, thinking to say something to please Mrs. Flather.

"Don't talk nonsense," replied Mrs. Flather.

"Nonsense!" exclaimed Mr. Jorrocks; "I 'opes there's no nonsense in the matter; real, good, substantial, downright matter-o'-fact-ism I should 'ope. You've been to the Castle, 'aven't you?" asked Mr. Jorrocks.

"Never you mind, Mr. Curiosity," replied Mrs. Flather, colouring at the question. "And pray where have you been?" asked she, anxious to turn the conversation.

"Oh, why, you know, I told you i' the mornin' I was goin' a beakin'. It's our beak day, you know," added the Justice.

"And had you much business?" inquired Mrs. Flather, anxious for any subject rather than the Castle one.

"Not much," replied Mr. Jorrocks, "not much; this alteration in the New Poor Law, I expect, will make more. We had a case too that puzzled Mr. Green, and do all I could I couldn't set him right."

"What was that?" inquired Mrs. Flather, glad to lead our friend on to what, at any other time, would have been a dreaded subject.

"Why, it was this," replied Mr. Jorrocks, taking off his hat and placing it between his legs, "it was a case under the fifth o' George the Fourth, chapter eighty-two, commonly called the Wagrant Hact, being a Hact for the punishment of idle and disorderly persons, and rogues and waggabones. Now, this fifth o' George the Fourth, chapter eighty-two, in my opinion, is the finest piece o' legislation extant; beats old Magna Charta, new charter, and all other charters into fits. In fact, there's nothin' like the fifth o' George the Fourth for keeping things straight."

"Indeed!" observed Mrs. Flather, who had never heard of its efficacy before.

"Well then, you see," said Mr. Jorrocks, "this fifth o' George the Fourth diwides offenders into three classes, jest as railway directors diwide their passengers. First," said Mr. Jorrocks, pressing the forefinger of his right hand against the thumb on his left, "is the great cock offender, called 'INCORRIGIBLE ROGUE,' a chap wot's too bad for anything he has passed through the other two coaches and got to a first-class carriage. Next to him," continued Mr. Jorrocks, putting his forefingers together, "is the 'rogue and waggabone;' and lastly, comes the idle and disorderly person. You twig?" asked he, looking at Mrs. Flather.

"Perfectly," replied she, thinking what a wigging she would get from Emma.

"Well then, you see," said Mr. Jorrocks, "this fifth o' George the Fourth—a Hact wot may be jestly called the true palladium of our rights—describes what shall constitute the three classes of offenders. Idle and disorderly persons are not those wot leave their keys, work-bags, and pocket-hand*ker*ches about, but beggars and people wot won't work—people wanderin', abroad, or placin' themselves in any public place, street, 'ighway, court, or passage, to beg or gather haims; and these it is lawful for a jestice to commit on his own view, as it is called, to the 'ouse of C., which means Correction, there to be kept to 'ard labour for any time not exceeedin' one calendar month. You understand all that?" asked Mr. Jorrocks, looking in Mrs. Flather's face, who had fallen into a reverie.

"Perfectly," replied the lady.

"Then," continued Mr. Jorrocks, "comes rogues and waggabones; this is where Green got wrong to-day. The clause describin' rogues and waggabones sets out by referrin' to the precedin' one about the idle and disorderly persons, it being the intention o' the statut'-makers that no person should be idle and disorderly twice."

"Indeed!" exclaimed Mrs. Flather, thinking that would be a grand secret to possess.

"No," said Mr. Jorrocks very gravely, "the rogue and waggabone clause commences by enactin' that every person committin' any of the idle and disorderly offences a second time, after having been conwicted in course afore, instead of being any longer considered idle and disorderly, shall thenceforth become rogues and waggabones. Then it goes on to enact that certain offences committed the first time shall make the offenders rogues and waggabones. Every person, for instance, pretendin' or professin' to tell fortins, or usin' any subtle craft, means or dewice, by palmistry, which means examinin' the marks i' the palm o' your 'and, jest as the dark-eyed ladies do at Hepsom or Hascot Races— whiles, indeed, with the Surrey 'unt—well, usin' any subtle craft, means, or dewice, by palmistry or otherwise, to deceive or impose on any of Her Majesty's subjects; every person wanderin' abroad and lodgin' in any barn or out'ouse, or in any deserted or unoccupied buildin', or in the open hair, or under a tent, or in any cart or waggon, not havin' any wisible means o' subsistence, and not givin' a good account of himself or herself, and every person bein' found—and this," continued Mr. Jorrocks, pressing Mrs. Flather's arm, "is the point on which Green and I differed—and every person bein' found in or upon any dwellin'-'ouse, ware'ouse, coach-'ouse, stable, or out'-ouse, or in any enclosed yard, garden, or harea, for any unlawful purpose, and many other sitivations," continued Mr. Jorrocks, with a wave of his hand, "shall be deemed rogues and waggabones within the true intent and meanin' of the Hact: and it shall be lawful for any jestice o' the peace to commit such 'fender (bein' thereof conwicted before him by the confession of such 'fender or by the evidence on oath of one or more credible witness or witnesses) to the 'ouse of C., there to be kept to 'ard labour for any time not exceedin' three calendar months."

"Indeed!" observed Mrs. Flather, as Mr. Jorrocks paused for breath.

"Quite true, I assure you," continued the Squire. "Us beaks have great powers. But you will perceive that we have less power over rogues and waggabones than we have over idle and disorderly persons. Idle and disorderlies we can 'quod' on our own view, but rogues and waggabones we must have witnesses against. Well, but howsomever that isn't the pint. Green and I differed about the offence. Four sturdy wagrants, two men and two women, were brought up at Petty Sessions—the women, charged with palmistry—bamming Farmer Goosecap about a gold-mine under the hill at the back of his 'ouse, while the men tried to rob his 'en-roost. Well, the case was as clear as crystal, and I said to Green in a visper, for he was chief jestice to-day, owin' to my bein' a few minutes late, I said in a visper, the jestice o' the case I think will be satisfied by giving the ladies a month, and the gentlemen two months in the 'ouse of C.; for palmistry, you see," continued Mr. Jorrocks, crossing one leg over the other, "albeit improper, p'raps, is more absurd than mischievous—nothin' at least compared to robbin' the 'en-roost; besides, the palmists were ladies—one rayther good-lookin'—and the men were stiff, sturdy, bull-dog-lookin 'ounds, that would be better for *three* months, if not for total imprisonment. But wot do you think

Green said?" asked Mr. Jorrocks, leaning forward and looking full in Mrs. Flather's face.

"Can't tell, I'm sure," replied Mrs. Flather, wearied with Mr. Jorrocks's prattle.

"Why, Green got the fifth o' George the Fourth in his 'and, and readin' the rogue and waggabone clause, insisted that no person could be conwicted as a rogue and waggabone wot had not been previously conwicted as idle and disorderly!"

"Indeed!" said Mrs. Flather.

"Quite true, I assure you," continued Mr. Jorrocks, warming at the recollection of it, "and not all I could say could conwince him that the opening part of section four—'And be it further enacted, that every person committin' any of the 'fences hereinbefore mentioned, after havin' been conwicted as an idle and disorderly person,' referred to the previous section, prohibitin' people being considered idle and disorderly a second time, and makin' them rogues and waggabones instead Green insisted that no person could be conwicted as a rogue, and waggabone wot had not been previously conwicted as idle and disorderly; so to give these parties a step towards the second-class carriage he conwicted them as idle and disorderly, givin' the ladies a week and the gentlemen a fortnight apiece on the mill."

Our Cockney Squire having exhausted his talk, bethought him what he wanted to say to Mrs. Flather. He couldn't hit upon it at first.

"The Markis, to be sure," at last exclaimed he aloud to himself, causing Mrs. Flather to shudder. She would rather have heard him recite the statutes at large, and comment upon them as he went, than return to the sub of her misfortune.

"You thought yourself werry sly, I dare say," observed Mr. Jorrocks, putting on his hat and laying hold of her elbow, "stealin' a march to the Castle. Couldn't gammon me though, I guess—am bad to 'umbug. Howsomever, never mind—tell us about the Duke—was he glad to see you? Monstrous glad to see you? Queer chap that Duke—*monstrous* queer chap, as he would say—*mad* I should say—mad. 'Ow's his farm? Did you see his roan ball, Tiberius? Noble quadruped I understand."

"But 'ere's the Marchioness!" exclaimed Mr. Jorrocks, as the chaise suddenly stopped, on encountering *la dame blanche* on the top of a piece of rising ground, up which the horses had thought necessary to walk.

There was Emma sure enough, in white, with blue ribbons in her straw bonnet, and a blue silk scarf drooping from her shoulders, her clear complexion partaking of a slightly roseate hue, and her eyes brightened up with the animation of anxiety. Seeing Mr. Jorrocks with her mamma, the first brush looked upon his presence as an omen of success, particularly as there was a broad grin on his good-natured countenance, as he took off his hat and addressed her as her ladyship. " 'Ow does your ladyship do?" asked Mr. Jorrocks, as Emma stood transfixed by the carriage.

She did not know what to make of it. Her mamma looked smilingly serious—it might be the affectation of humility after conquest, but Mr. Jorrocks was grinningly smiling. He seemed to partake of the triumph.

A landaulet, a post-chariot, with three, is a very inconvenient carriage for diplomacy. People must turn their heads to communicate even by looks, and a third person hears and sees all that passes. Moreover, Mr. Jorrocks insisted upon riding bodkin—a very awkward-sized bodkin he was—especially as he would have all three to sit back, so that the conversation might be general.

"Well, you'll be gettin' your coronet ready, I s'pose," observed Mr. Jorrocks, turning to Emma, and shutting out the view of her mamma, whose vacant countenance she was trying to study by a sidelong sort of glance. Emma smiled.

"Don't talk nonsense, Mr. Jorrocks!" exclaimed Mrs. Flather snappishly.

"Well, but don't get your 'ead turned," observed Mr. Jorrocks, squeezing Emma's ungloved hand. "Don't cut your old frinds," continued he; "and wotever you do, send me a good slice o' cake."

Emma smiled. Women always smile at the mention of bride-cake.

"The custom o' sending cards and compliments may be werry conwenient when there isn't much tin," observed he; "but you'll 'ave no 'casion for sich lose shavin', so tell them to hice it well, and let the halmond paste be a hinch thick at least. Never mind about Cupids or cherrybins, or none o' them gentry; for me, at least," added he.

With this pleasant sort of *badinage*, pleasant to Emma, but excruciatingly painful to Mrs. Flather, Mr. Jorrocks rattled and talked on till the driver looked down from his perch as he arrived at the turn of the road leading up to Mrs. Flather's, and asked if Mr. Jorrocks would go to the Manse or get out there, very handsomely offering to drive him down to the Hall if he preferred doing so.

Looking at his watch and finding it wanted but ten minutes to dinner-time, Mr. Jorrocks decided upon vacating his bodkinship and driving home in his own vehicle.

Taking an affectionate leave of the Marchioness and her mamma, and charging them above all things "not to let their heads be turned," Mr. Jorrocks opened the door, and unfolding the long string of steps (like a tailor's pattern-book), descended from the altitude of the old landaulet. Having boxed mother and daughter up again, he sought the culinary comforts of his own house in the humble lowness of his own machine.

XXXVII

Still harping on my daughter.

"AND HOW IS IT TO be?" asked Emma eagerly, as Mr. Jorrocks's low-crowned hat disappeared past the landaulet.

"Oh, don't be silly, Emma," replied Mrs. Flather snappishly, thinking she had better take the high hand, and see if that would prevent Emma attempting it.

"Nay, my own dear mamma," said Emma coaxingly, "you surely won't be angry with your own Emma on such an important day."

"Important day, forsooth!" muttered Mrs. Flather; "*I've* no desire for such importance."

"Nay, mamma, wouldn't you like to see your daughter a duchess?"

"Duchess, indeed," retorted Mrs. Flather; "you are counting your chickens before they are hatched, I think."

"Well, *marchioness*, if you would like that any better," replied Emma; "for my part, I really think marchioness sounds not only as well as duchess, but is longer and more imposing."

"I wish you would get such nonsense out of your head, child," snapped Mrs. Flather, looking very down cast.

"Nay!" exclaimed Emma, alarmed at her countenance, "you don't mean to say it's not to be? Speak— tell me," cried she, looking deadly pale. The carriage then stopped at the door. Emma descended the jingling steps with the feelings of a malefactor going to execution. She hurried into the house, hardly knowing what she was about.

Her mother tardily followed.

"You don't mean to say," exclaimed she, as her revered parent entered, "that you've made a mess of the thing?—offended the Duke or the Duchess—put them against it any way?"

"Do *not* worry me, Emma," replied Mrs. Flather, calmly but sternly.

"Nay, then!" rejoined Emma, "I see what you've done! I was sure you would!" exclaimed she, clasping her hands, and, with upturned eyes, bursting into tears.

"*You would go,*" sobbed Emma.

"I couldn't help it, my dear," replied Mrs. Flather.

"*Don't tell me!*" screamed Emma, at the top of her voice, her choler rising as her mamma softened. "I told you you would make a mess of it—your common place matter-of-fact way of going to work, just as if you were bargaining for butter. *You would go!*" screamed she again, at the top of her voice, throwing herself into an easy-chair.

A copious flood of tears deprived her for a time of further utterance.

"And I dare say you've irretrievably ruined it," sobbed Emma, looking out of her pocket-handkerchief.

Mrs. Flather was silent.

"I was sure you had!" screamed Emma, jumping up, and stamping violently on the floor with both feet. "Oh, what a thing it is to be led by a person without feeling or discretion!"

Another shower of tears followed this filial observation.

"Oh dear! oh dear! that I should ever have let you go by yourself—I might have been sure what would happen."

Mrs. Flather looked foolish, not knowing whether to vindicate her conduct, or let her daughter have her "fling." At length she spoke.

"My dear child," said she, "you do me great injustice."

"Don't injustice me!" screamed Emma; "it's you that's done *me* injustice. Why can't you let me manage my own affairs my own way?"

"I did it all for the best," observed Mrs. Flather calmly.

"I know nothing about best—you couldn't have done it worse if you tried. I'll be bound to say, you've disgusted the Duke, and the Duchess, and the——" Here Emma again burst into an overpowering flood of tears. This continued for some time, during which she tried to command her temper, and summon resolution to bear the sad *dénouement*.

"Come, tell me all about it," said she at length, folding her wet handkerchief in a heap, and fixing her red eyes on her disconcerted mamma.

"Well, my dear, I've nothing more to tell," said Mrs. Flather vacantly.

"Nothing more to tell!" exclaimed Emma; "why, you've told me nothing—you left me to conjecture all."

"And very well you've guessed it," thought Mrs. Flather; but this she kept to herself, fearing a missile at her head might be the reward of her temerity.

"Well, my dear," commenced Mrs. Flather again, "I just went as we arranged, you know."

"Well, and who did you see first?" interrupted Emma.

"Oh, the Duchess," replied Mrs. Flather; "you know I couldn't ask for the Duke."

"Well, and what said the Duchess? How did you begin?—tell me *all* quickly, or I shall die of suspense."

"The Duchess was very polite—extremely polite."

"Oh, that's all understood—all matter of course—great people are always polite," sobbed Emma. "And how did you begin?" asked she; "did you blurt out at once what you'd come for, or felt your way?"

"*Of course not*," replied Mrs. Flather; "I talked about indifferent things, and got gradually on till we talked about James, and then I broached the subject as delicately as possible."

"And what said the Duchess?" asked Emma. "How did she take it?"

"Why, she was very civil—extremely civil; but she evidently didn't wish for it, at least she wasn't anxious about it."

"Odious woman! I always thought she would be the difficulty," observed Emma. "The Duke's worth fifty of her."

"Thought James was too young to settle," continued Mrs. Flather; "didn't know his own mind perhaps. Still if the Duke wished it, she had no objection."

"And did you see the Duke?" asked Emma eagerly, still hoping there was a chance.

"I did," replied Mrs. Flather firmly.

"Well, go on!" said Emma eagerly.

"*And he wouldn't hear of it.*"

"*The old beast!*" exclaimed Emma. "What reason did he give?"

"None, I think," replied Mrs. Flather; "he got into such a passion that I was glad to escape to the Duchess again."

"*Odious old infidel!*" ejaculated Emma, bursting into a fresh flood of tears. "And is there no hope?" sobbed she, again looking out of her wet handkerchief, like the sun from the watery clouds. "Did you see James?"

"No," replied Mrs. Flather, "he never appeared."

"He wouldn't use me so," sobbed Emma, thinking of the kiss and squeezing he gave her.

"The Duke will never hear of it, I'm sure," observed Mrs. Flather. "You don't know what a passion he was in."

"Horrid old man!" replied Emma; "looks like an old savage."

Mother and daughter sat silent for some time.

"It's one consolation to think the people down street won't get him, at all events," at length observed Mrs. Flather, still pondering on her misfortunes.

"I don't believe he ever thought of *her*," pouted Emma.

"The Duke will never hear of a commoner, I'm sure," said Mrs. Flather.

"It's hard upon James that he mayn't marry who he pleases," observed Emma.

"It is," assented Mrs. Flather.

"Hasn't the privilege of the poorest peasant on his estate," observed Emma.

"However, the offer's always something," rejoined Mrs. Flather.

Emma was silent.

"I suppose there's no doubt he did offer?" observed Mrs. Flather inquiringly.

"Oh, none," replied Emma.

"Do you remember the exact words he made use of?" asked mamma.

"Why, no, I can't charge my memory with the precise words; indeed, you know, these matters are managed as much by looks as words."

"Well, but you have no doubt in your own mind that what he did say related to marriage, and amounted to an offer, have you?" asked Mrs. Flather.

"None whatever," replied Emma confidently.

"You couldn't well be mistaken in that matter, I think," rejoined her mother, "seeing you have had so many and such eligible offers before."

"Certainly not," pouted Emma, determined to stick up for her offer.

"The best thing you can do, I think," observed Mrs. Flather, after a pause, "is to write to the Marquis himself."

"Why so?" asked Emma, thinking the Marquis might deny the soft impeachment.

"Because," replied Mrs. Flather, "in the first place, the affair is his, and not his father's or mother's."

"Very true," said Emma.

"And in the second place, we have had no communication with him on the subject. It will only be right to give him the option of fulfilling his promise in spite of his father and mother."

"I should doubt his doing that," observed Emma, not feeling inclined to press the tender point too closely. "His father might disinherit him, and that would be awkward for us both. We couldn't live upon air."

"Oh no; these great people can't disinherit," replied Mrs. Flather. "Their affairs are tied up tightly before they are born."

But still I shouldn't like to appear too eager," observed Emma coyly.

"Well, that's very noble of you, my dear," said Mrs. Flather, looking approvingly at her daughter; "but still it would only be fair towards the Marquis."

Emma was silent, thinking how it might act.

"He might think himself badly used," observed Mrs. Flather, after a pause, "if he was not allowed the opportunity."

Emma was still silent.

"Besides," continued Mrs. Flather, "you must remember you have nothing to show for your offer. People—and there are plenty of ill-natured people ready to do so—will dispute it; whereas, if you have your letter and his answer to show, there is proof positive."

"Don't you think the best plan will be," asked Emma, "as the Duke and Duchess are both so disagreeable, for me to write to James and release him; and then I could show the letter doing it."

"A very good idea indeed, I think, my dear," replied Mrs. Flather smilingly.

"I could write it so as not to require any answer," observed Emma.

"What, putting an end to the thing altogether?" asked Mrs. Flather.

"Yes," replied Emma.

"I don't know that that would be the best course" observed Mrs. Flather, after a pause; "it would rather, I think, partake of the objection I urged against not applying to him at all. He should be allowed the option, I think, of declaring his adhesion to his promise. You should not blame him for the acts of his father and mother."

"True," replied Emma; "but did he appear to have talked to them about it?"

"Why, no, I should say not," confessed Mrs. Flather unwillingly.

"That's the awkward part of it," thought Emma. "Then they would be surprised when you broached the subject, I suppose?" asked she.

"They were," replied Mrs. Flather, "the Duke particularly; he was the worst of the two by far."

"Nasty old man," ejaculated Emma.

"Not but that the Duchess was quite as determined," observed Mrs. Flather; "but she wasn't so rude," added she.

"Then you think there is no hope from them; no chance of their softening?" inquired Emma.

"None whatever," replied Mrs. Flather; "the Duke seemed perfectly frantic at the idea."

Emma then again thought of the letter. "You know I could write such a letter," observed she, "as he could answer or not as he liked."

"Well, my dear," replied Mrs. Flather, "you are a better scribe than me. The sooner it is done, you know, the greater will be the appearance of independence on your part."

Emma sighed as she thought of the loss of all her greatness. She then got up to look for her portfolio. Of course it was in one place—her paper in another her pens in a third—and the ink in the *other* room.

Having got them all scraped together, and having selected a pen that would write from the many that would not, she squared her paper before her, and prepared for a start.

"What shall I call him, mamma?" asked Emma, as she looked at the nib of her pen.

"What you generally call him, my dear, I should think," replied Mrs. Flather.

"Oh! why, you know when I'm speaking to him I call him my Lord; when *of* him, I call him Jeems, as the Duke does."

"Of course, then, you'll call him my Lord."

"But must it be my Lord, or my dear Lord?" asked Emma.

"My dear Lord, of course," replied Mrs. Flather; "you've had no quarrel with *him*, you know."

"Or dear Lord Bray, which do you think would sound best?"

"My dear Lord Bray, perhaps," said Mrs. Flather.

"I think it *would*," replied Emma, writing it at the beginning place of her sheet—half-way down of course—"My dear Lord Bray."

"But you are not writing to send, surely!" exclaimed Mrs. Flather.

"No, only the copy," replied Emma; "but I like to see how it looks, as well as how it reads."

"My dear Lord Bray," she read again, and then looked about for a thought. "What shall I say next? it must be something high-flown. 'My dear Lord.' I don't know but I like 'my dear Lord' best," observed Emma: "it looks better to begin rather stiffly—you know I can finish off differently—or postscript a little. I think I'll begin, 'My dear Lord,'" added she, striking her pen through 'Bray.'

"My dear Lord," she read again.

"So long as I conceived your attentions were sanctioned by——" wrote Emma.

"Shall I say 'attentions,' or 'visits'?" asked she. "So long as I conceived your visits were sanctioned by your parents."

"I think I'll put 'visits,'" continued Emma, answering herself, striking out 'attentions,' and substituting 'visits.' She then wrote on—" 'I freely confess I was proud to receive your attentions.' Does that sound bold, do you think, mamma?" asked she, reading it over—

"So long as I conceived your visits were sanctioned by your parents, I freely confess I was proud to receive your attentions."

"No, I think not, my dear," replied Mrs. Flather; "perhaps you might put—'sanctioned by the Duke and Duchess of Donkeyton,' instead of 'parents,'" suggested Mrs. Flather.

"No, I think 'parents' better," observed Emma, after a moment's consideration.

"Well, my dear, you know best. It depends altogether upon the terms you have been on together."

"But," wrote Emma. "Now I want to say," said she, looking at her mother, "that I can't have anything to say to him without their approbation: of course it must be put in better language than that."

She then read over again—"My dear Lord—so long as I conceived your visits were sanctioned by your parents, I freely confess I was proud to receive your attentions. But," she wrote on, "no power on earth—no rank—no title—could induce me to receive them clandestinely."

"What do you think of that?" asked she, looking up at her mamma.

"Very good indeed, I think, my dear," replied her approving parent. "Perhaps, instead of 'clandestinely,' you might put, 'without their consent.'"

"Do you think so?" asked Emma, twirling her pen, thinking her own a better-sounding word.

"It would look more regular," observed Mrs. Flather—"more as if they had *all* known about it, at all events."

"Perhaps it would," assented Emma, striking out the word "clandestinely" and substituting "without their consent" for it.

"Now I think we had better not let out that you had gone to-day for the purpose of putting the question point blank," observed Emma, after a pause—"make it appear rather as if their objection had come out accidentally; or as if it was more a hint than a downright refusal."

"That would hardly do, I'm afraid," observed Mrs. Flather, "for they neither of them minced the matter."

"Well, but the letter is more to *show* to others than to enlighten them," sighed Emma.

"It is so," sighed Mrs. Flather in return. "You might speak about the difference in rank," she added, after a pause; "lay their objection upon that."

"Just so," said Emma, thinking how she could embody the sentiment. She then read the sentence over again, and thus proceeded—"I could not be insensible to the objections difference of station might create, though perhaps I had reason to believe that they would be overlooked in my case; finding, however, from my dearest mamma's interview with the Duke and Duchess this morning that such is not likely to be so, I lose not a moment in declaring that I will never enter any family without the full approbation, nay, encouragement of its members."

"What do you think of that?" asked Emma, looking up, as she got to the end of the long sentence.

"Very good indeed, my dear, I think," replied Mrs. Flather. "You might say it was as much my determination as your own," observed Mrs. Flather.

Emma thought she wouldn't—she would take all the credit to herself. "This being the case," she continued, "you will not be surprised at receiving this hurried communication, relinquishing, as I now do, all—what shall I call it?" asked Emma, looking up with tears in her eyes.

"All claim, perhaps," said Mrs. Flather.

"Or pretension," suggested Emma, feeling that was more like the thing. "Relinquishing, as I now do, all claim and pretension to your hand," wrote she.

Emma then took a cry.

"I cannot conclude without wishing your Lordship, in all sincerity," she continued—"I want to wish him what Mr. Jorrocks calls better luck next time," sobbed Emma, folding and refolding her pocket-handkerchief—"I cannot conclude without wishing your Lordship, in all sincerity, a more exalted and more fortunate choice. Your merits, your wealth, and your connections forbid any doubt on this subject, though I am certain you will never meet with any one more sincerely, devotedly attached than your

EMMA"

She then went off in another cry.

Tea then came in, and the love-sick damsel ate half a loaf of bread, with a pot of strawberry jam, and butter to match. The letter was then copied with the best pen, on the best wire-wove paper, sealed and directed most becomingly, and given to the boy to take to the post the first thing in the morning.

We need hardly add that Emma had a nervous headache next day, and did not show.

XXXVIII

I tell it you in strict confidence.

MRS. JORROCKS COULD NOT MAKE out from Mr. Jorrocks's story whether Emma had accomplished the Marquis or not. Mr. Jorrocks himself was inclined to think she had; but Mrs. Trotter, who had dropped in to hear all she could, and Mrs. Jorrocks, thought otherwise in consultation. They agreed that Mrs. Flather would not have been able to contain herself if she had—certainly not over that morning. At the same time, the undoubted journey to Donkeyton, and the seeing by the Duchess herself of Mrs. Flather back to her carriage (duly reported by the driver), puzzled the consulters not a little. Such a thing had never been heard of before as any one going to Donkeyton Castle without a regular invitation.

Mrs. Trotter was in a desperate state of agitation. If Emma had captured the Marquis, it only showed what Eliza might have done if she had had a fair chance. "Certainly," she observed, with upturned nose, "if *all* people were as regardless of decency as Mrs. Flather, they might all get marquises for their daughters," thinking of the night his lordship had spent at the Manse after the harvest home ball.

Mrs. Claudius Sacker, the doctor's wife, dropped in too, the flying rumours having rendered her uneasy at home. She had not been able to "settle" since she heard of the letter to the Marquis. This was news to the others, and the discussion was resumed with great vigour. Doctors and their wives generally try to keep in with all parties, indeed they would be great fools if they did not, and Mrs. Sacker had called to consult Mrs. Jorrocks whether she ought to go up to the Manse to tender her earliest congratulations to the marchioness elect and her mamma.

Mrs. Jorrocks "didn't know;" Mr. Jorrocks and Mrs. Trotter thought she better had, and our gallant Squire offered to accompany her. Just, however, as his worship was starting, the constable brought a troop of vagrants for him to administer some of his "Daffy's Elixir" to, in the shape of the fifth of George the Fourth.

Mrs. Sacker was just the person Mrs. Flather would have selected for the propagation of her story, for, independently of the delicate situation she filled, Mrs. Sacker had a wonderful capacity for believing all she heard. There was no story too wild, no tale too improbable for her to repeat—not only repeat, but almost to vouch for.

Mrs. Flather received her with more than usual pleasure, and in reply to her inquiries after Emma, pleaded, the ladies' usual pocket complaint—a sick headache. The two then sat commonplacing it for some time, each wishing the other would lead to the point. At last Mrs. Flather hemmed and spoke.

"I suppose you've heard about Emma and the Marquis of Bray?" observed she, eyeing Mrs. Sacker.

"Why, yes—no—certainly, I've heard *something*," replied Mrs. Sacker.

"And what have you heard?" inquired Mrs. Flather. "Why, that I have to congratulate you on his becoming your son-in-law," replied Mrs. Sacker, "which I have very great pleasure in doing," added she, tendering both hands to Mrs. Flather for a hug.

"Thank you, my dear Mrs. Sacker," replied she, shaking them. "I'm sure we have your best wishes at all times—Mr. Sacker's too. At present, however, you are—are—are——"

"A little premature, perhaps," suggested Mrs. Sacker.

"Not altogether *that*," replied Mrs. Flather, but a little—a little—misinformed rather."

"How so?" inquired Mrs. Sacker.

"Why, the truth is, that the Marquis is an extremely fine young man, a very well-principled, genteel young man, and one that I'm sure any mother might safely intrust a daughter with, but he's young and—and— and—you understand."

"Perfectly," replied Mrs. Sacker, who did nothing of the sort.

"The Duke wishes him to travel—go to Switzerland—see Venice—Florence—thinks he might pick up a princess, perhaps."

"But I'm sure an English wife would be much better for him," observed Mrs. Sacker, who was a capital judge of what was good for other people.

"Well, I think so too," replied Mrs. Flather; "but of course that is for the Duke's consideration; he must settle that. All we had to do was to ascertain whether the Duke and Duchess liked the match or not, because I could never suffer my daughter to enter a family where she was not likely to be well received."

"Certainly not," observed Mrs. Sacker, with a shake of the head.

"Indeed, she herself would never hear of such a thing," added Mrs. Flather, recollecting the terms of the letter.

"I'm sure not," observed the complaisant Mrs. Sacker.

"The Marquis, of course, is very much attached to Emma," continued Mrs. Flather, "and I'm sure I pity him most sincerely; but that golden rule of doing by others as we would be done by, precludes the idea of my encouraging the thing in opposition to his parents. For my part, indeed, I should much prefer her marrying a man more in her own rank of life; but these attachments will spring up, despite of all the care we can take; nor would parents, perhaps, be altogether right in discouraging them where no obstacle persented itself. When there does, as in this case, there is but one course for us to pursue."

"Very honourable of you, I'm sure," observed Mrs. Sacker.

"Hard as the task is, I'll not shrink from it," rejoined Mrs. Flather, unbagging her pocket handkerchief—out came the copy of Emma's letter.

"There's a copy of her letter releasing the Marquis," observed Mrs. Flather, picking it off the floor; "you may take it home if you like," added she, handing it to Mrs. Sacker; "perhaps your husband might like to see it."

"Thank you," said Mrs. Sacker, rising and meeting Mrs. Flather with the proffered document.

"I may again say, I was never very anxious for it," observed Mrs. Flather, with a composing sigh.

Mrs. Sacker stared as if she could hardly swallow that.

"Unequal matches," continued Mrs. Flather, "are not desirable things."

"Perhaps not," observed the cautious Mrs. Sacker.

"Seldom productive of happiness," sighed Mrs. Flather again.

"Hem!" coughed Mrs. Sacker.

"Not that I wish to say a word in disparagement of the Marquis of Bray," added Mrs. Flather; "and if the Duke and Duchess had been anxious or agreeable, of course I should have thought it my duty to stifle my feelings, and meet them half way; but the slightest symptom of an objection determined me, and I assured the Duke and Duchess at once that they had nothing to fear and everything to expect from me; for, hard as the task was of putting an end to the rational attachment of two interesting and amiable young people, I would not shrink from it."

"Very noble of you, I'm sure," observed Mrs. Sacker.

"Not at all," replied Mrs. Flather; "on the contrary, I assure you, were it not for the unhappiness the step must occasion the young people, I would *infinitely* prefer, as I said before, seeing Emma marry some nice steady young man in the neighbourhood in her own rank of life," Mrs. Flather thinking she would have to fall back on James Blake as soon as possible.

"No fear but there will be plenty delighted to have her," observed the obsequious Mrs. Sacker.

"Oh, she has had many excellent offers," replied Mrs. Flather; "Emma might have been married over and over again if she'd liked."

"I am sure of it," replied Mrs. Sacker.

"James Blake, for instance," said Mrs. Flather, "is dying for her."

"So I hear," assented Mrs. Sacker; "and a very fine young man he is," added she.

"Very," replied Mrs. Flather; "good-principled young man. It may seem strange, perhaps," simpered Mrs. Flather, as if doubting whether Mrs. Sacker could swallow it or not—"it may seem strange, but I have always told Emma I would rather see her marry Mr. Blake than the Marquis of Bray."

"I hope she will still do so, then," replied Mrs. Sacker; "I'm sure I wish she may, for they are both great favourites of mine."

"Emma's hard to please," observed Mrs. Flather.

"She's young, and has plenty of time to look about her," replied Mrs. Sacker.

With these and such like honest observations, the two ladies beguiled the twenty minutes' sit of which the visit was composed, and Mrs. Sacker finally took her departure with the warmest expressions of attachment to mother and daughter, and the strongest assurances that the copy of the letter would be considered "strictly confidential," a term too well understood among ladies to require any explanation from us. Mrs. Sacker then took her departure.

A party of pleasure, consisting of our worthy Squire and Mrs. Jorrocks, Mrs. and five Miss Trotters, and James Blake, met Mrs. Sacker at the turn of the road leading up to the Manse, and nearly worried her with questions as to the result.

"*And 'ow's it to be?*" bellowed Mr. Jorrocks at the top of his voice, advancing towards her; adding, "*ar'nt I right?*"

"*Yes or no?*" asked Mrs. Trotter, rising up and down on her toes, with anxiety depicted on her fine, bright, olive complexion. Eliza's black eyes sparkled brighter than usual.

"Tell us all about it," said Mrs. Jorrocks, seating her self on the milestone.

"For goodness' sake, don't make such a noise!" exclaimed the cautious Mrs. Sacker; "consider, if Mrs. Flather should hear of this meeting she'll blame me altogether—think we are all in league."

"Never mind," said Mr. Jorrocks, "I'll underwrite you."

"Do tell us!" "Don't kill us with suspense!"

"What's the use of making a mystery about nothing?" and similar inquiries, now flew at Mrs. Sacker, who, panting with the haste she had hurried away to communicate the news, could hardly articulate.

"*Pray* don't make such a noise," gasped she; "consider, if Mrs. Flather should hear—what *would* she think of me?"

"That you're a werry pretty little 'ooman," replied Mr. Jorrocks; adding, in a whisper to himself, "at least I do."

"You don't know *who* may be watching," ejaculated Mrs. Sacker. "It isn't right—it *really* isn't—you shouldn't have come. She'll think we are all in league; that it's a preconcerted plan. Pray walk quietly down," urged she. "Divide into two parties. Come, Mr. Jorrocks, do," urged she, addressing herself to the Cockney Squire. "You go first, like a good man," added she, giving him a gentle push of the arm.

"Tell us about it," replied Mr. Jorrocks, "and we'll go 'ome like lambs."

"Tell you what?" said Mrs. Sacker, in full flutter. "Whether Emma's caught the Markis or not," responded Mr. Jorrocks.

"Caught the Marquis!" repeated Mrs. Sacker. "Yes, *no doubt she has*."

"Hurrah!" exclaimed Mr. Jorrocks, throwing his hat in the air. "Hurrah!" repeated he, catching and throwing it up again; adding, "*I told you so*. Won two 'ats!"

"I don't believe it!" exclaimed Mrs. Jorrocks.

"Nor I," responded Mrs. Trotter.

"Nor I!" added James Blake.

"*Nor you!*" roared Mr. Jorrocks, looking irately at the last speaker. "Vy shouldn't you believe the lady, sir?" adding, "is that your Christian doctrine, sir?"

"Do you mean they're a goin' to be married?" asked Mrs. Jorrocks, sidling up to Mrs. Sacker.

"I didn't say they were going to be married," snapped Mrs. Sacker, dreading the consequences of this unexpected and unwelcome *rencontre*.

"Then vot did you say?" snapped Mrs. Jorrocks in return.

"Oh, do walk quietly on," entreated Mrs. Sacker; adding, "and I'll tell you all about it. Only don't make such a noise and hubbub."

"Vell, tell me quietly," said Mr. Jorrocks, poking up to Mrs. Sacker, and putting his arm through hers; adding, as they walked on together, "is she goin' to be married to the Markis or not?"

"*No, she's not*," replied Mrs. Sacker, in an undertone.

"*No, she's not!*" screamed Mr. Jorrocks; "vy, didn't you say this werry minute that she was?"

"No, I said she'd *caught* the Marquis," replied Mrs. Sacker.

"Caught him!" ejaculated Mr. Jorrocks; adding, "vy, vot do you call catchin' on him if they don't tie him hup? Safe bind, safe find, I say."

"Oh then, she's not!" screamed Mrs. Trotter and Mrs. Jorrocks, clapping their hands and exulting. Joy beamed on the faces of the rest.

"The 'ooman's mad—mad as a March hare," muttered Mr. Jorrocks, taking his arm out of Mrs. Sacker's.

"Tell us 'ow it is?" asked Mrs. Jorrocks, supplying her husband's place, and trying the soothing system.

Well, you see, the Duke and Duchess are *rather* against it," said Mrs. Sacker; "and Mrs. Flather won't hear of it unless they are agreeable."

"'Ookey Valker!" grunted Mr. Jorrocks; adding, "whoever thought they'd be for it?"

"And vot was she doin' at Donkeyton?" asked Mrs. Jorrocks.

"I don't know that," replied Mrs. Sacker; "possibly went to talk to the Duke and Duchess about it."

"What a fool the woman must be," observed Mrs. Trotter, glad that Mrs. Flather had had the errand instead of herself.

"Why, there's no doubt that the Marquis was desperately attached to Emma," observed Mrs. Sacker.

"Just as much as he was to half-a-dozen other girls," observed Mrs. Trotter, looking at Eliza, who was busy looking at James Blake.

"*Then it's no go*," muttered Mr. Jorrocks, putting his hands behind his back, preparing to saunter home alone.

"*Quite finished*," observed Mrs. Sacker. "Miss Emma, indeed, is quite of her mamma's opinion, and has written a most proper letter to the Marquis on the subject."

"Vot about?" asked Mr. Jorrocks, turning short round.

"Releasing him from his engagement," replied Mrs. Sacker.

"That's all nonsense," observed Mrs. Jorrocks.

"They were never engaged," added Mrs. Trotter.

"Only wanted to be," rejoined Mrs. Jorrocks; "that's to say, *she* wanted."

"I assure you it's the fact," replied Mrs. Sacker.

"Who told you so?" inquired Mrs. Jorrocks.

"Mrs. Flather herself. Indeed, I've a copy of the letter in my bag," added she, recollecting herself, and diving into her reticule for it.

"Let's see it," said Mr. Jorrocks, taking it out of her hand as she tumbled it up above the miscellaneous collection of the bag. "I'll read it to you," said he, stopping short. "I'll get on to this 'ere gate," added he. So saying, he climbed up, and seating himself on the top-rail, unfolded the wire-wove paper, and read the well-written document to the anxious circle below.

"My dear Lord——"

"Faith, but they've been pretty frindly," observed Mr. Jorrocks, looking down at the group.

"My dear Lord," repeated he, "so long as I conceived your wisits were sanctioned by your parents, I freely confess I was proud to receive your attentions."

"Wisits!" exclaimed Mrs. Jorrocks—"he never made no wisits to them! It was to Jun and me."

"Except after the farmer's ball, when he slept there *by mistake*," sneered Mrs. Trotter.

"Does she say she was proud to receive his attentions?" asked Eliza of James Blake.

"Silence in the court," cried Mr. Jorrocks; adding, "or I'll commit some on you."

"I freely confess, I was proud to receive your attentions. But," read he, "no power on airth—no rank—no title—(no nothin')," added Mr. Jorrocks, "could induce me to receive them without their consent."

"That's comin' it strong," observed Mr. Jorrocks, looking down on the anxious faces of the auditors. "There must have been summut in it."

"I don't believe it for all that!" exclaimed Mrs. Trotter.

"Nor I neither," rejoined Mrs. Jorrocks.

"The girl's always fancying the men are in love with her," added Mrs. Trotter.

"She's none so captiwatin'," sneered Mrs. Jorrocks. Mr. Jorrocks read on—"I could not be insensible to the objections difference of station might create, though, perhaps, I had reason to believe they would be overlooked in my case——"

"I wonders what that means?" observed Mr. Jorrocks, looking knowingly up at the sky. He could not hit upon the reason, so he resumed his reading—"Finding, however, from my dearest mamma's interview with the Duke and Duchess of Donkeyton this morning, that such is not likely to be the case, I lose not a moment in declaring that I will never enter any family without the full approbation—nay, encouragement of its members."

"There's for you!" exclaimed Mr. Jorrocks. "She'll 'ave it all on the square. 'Love me, love my dog,' and so on."

"Sour grapes, I think!" observed Mrs. Trotter.

"I say ditto to that," added Mrs. Jorrocks.

"I say silence! " retorted our Squire; adding, "or I'll horder some on you hout o' court."

He then read on—

"This being the case, you will not be surprised at receiving this hurried communication, relinquishing, as I now do, all claim and pretension to your hand."

"Ay! ay! but that's comin' to the pint," nodded Mr. Jorrocks.

"Story of the well-bred dog, I think!" observed James Blake.

"I cannot conclude without wishing your lordship, in all sincerity, a more exalted and more fortunate choice."

"'Umbug!" grunted Mrs. Jorrocks.

"Your merits, your wealth, and your connections forbid any doubt on that point, though I am equally sure you will never meet with any one more sincerely, devotedly attached, than your Emma."

"God save the Queen, Prince Halbert, et kids," added Mr. Jorrocks, folding up the letter, and descending from his gate to return it to Mrs. Sacker. "A werry pretty letter, and werry well written," said he, handing it back to her with a bow.

XXXIX

Take a friendly cup of tea with us.

M RS. FLATHER HAD A LITTLE tea-party a few evenings after, as soon as the model of propriety's sick headache enabled her to see company.

Mr. and Mrs. Jorrocks, Mr. and Mrs. Trotter, Mr. and Mrs. Sacker, and Miss Emily Badger, a cousin of Mrs. Sacker's, were the guests.

The model of propriety was decked out for the occasion in plain white muslin, with a little lace cap with blue flowers and ribbons.

Mr. Jorrocks, though not much of a "tea and turn-out man," was glad to go to anything to vary the monotony of evenings at home with Mrs. Jorrocks. As the days shortened, and farming pursuits relaxed, he felt more keenly the difference between town and country.

In London a man of business's day does not commence till the evening, when everything is over in the country, save the easy-chair and the newspaper. The Londoner has his theatres, his billiard-rooms, his libraries, his reading-rooms, his houses of call, his convivial meetings—something fresh for every night in the week; but night draws its sombre veil over everything in the country, and the winter dulness is only helped along by anticipation of parties for the next full moon.

"Mind, you are engaged to us the next full moon."

Mrs. Flather's *soiree* being extra, there was no full moon—no moon at all, indeed.

The copy of the letter to the Marquis having been intrusted in confidence to Mrs. Sacker, and shown by her in a similar spirit, of course the rest of the party felt bound to be ignorant of it, and Mrs. Flather being equally constrained to believe that they were so, matters threatened to be rather awkward at starting.

"Now mind, Jun, you don't let out that you knows anything about the match being off," observed Mrs. Jorrocks out of her calash, as they call the cab-head things tea-drinking ladies in the country put over their smart turbans and flowered caps. "Now mind, Jun, you don't let out that you knows anything about the match bein' off," observed Mrs. Jorrocks to her spouse, as, in company with the Trotters and Miss Emily Badger, they trooped up to the Manse.

"Do you think I can't keep a secret as well as you?" grunted Mr. Jorrocks, buttoning his zephyr about him. "The evenin's are a gettin' cool," observed he to Mrs. Trotter—"the dew'll be strong as we return, and there's never no broughams, nor patent safetys, nor nothin' to get."

"We never care about those sort of things in the country," replied Mrs. Trotter out of her cab-head. "Cloaks and thick shoes," added she, "are all we want."

The ladies having to put the finishing stroke to their toilettes, were met by a maid, who showed them up stairs, where, with the aid of a looking-glass, they repaired any little derangement of costume the cab-heads and cloaks had occasioned. Mr. Jorrocks and little Trotter were shown into the parlour.

Mr. Jorrocks, who still had a *penchant* for Mrs. Flather, and moreover saw that the women wanted to run her down, met her with more than usual *empressement*, and squeezed Emma's and her hands with sundry winks and contortions of countenance, meant to indicate "never mind, better luck next time."

The ladies presently came in, and their inquiries were exchanged about each other's healths, and hopes that Emma's headache had left her, with many "so sorries to hear she had been indisposed—so glad to see she was looking so well."

They then formed themselves into a circle round the pocketful of fuel they called a fire, and an agreeable circle it was, the ladies longing to pull caps, and the gentlemen staring vacantly at the yellow gassey smoke as it curled up the chimney. The ladies tried hard to drive a conversation—talked of worsted-work, patch-work, and all sorts of work.

At length the tea-tray made its appearance, and things began to brighten up—more candles too came in. The hissing urn followed, and then came bread and cakes of various forms and composition. The party adjourned from the fire to the round table on which the things were placed, Mrs. Jorrocks squeezing in next Mrs. Flather, Mr. Jorrocks got between Mrs. Trotter and Mrs. Sacker, while Emma and the other two filled up the remaining places. The women talked, the men talked, they all talked together. Cup succeeded cup, and toast succeeded cake, and cake succeeded toast. Conversation became general. Claudius Sacker was a great talker, and did his best to earn his hyson. Mr. Jorrocks talked, Mrs. Sacker talked, and they all talked.

Mrs. Jorrocks got Mrs. Flather into a quiet mumble—in what is called a conversational chair—after the din of cups and saucers had subsided, and very soon led the way to the Marquis and Donkeyton Castle.

"Well," said she, "and is it to be a match between"—(nodding to Emma, who was patronising Miss Badger) "and the Markis?"

"No," faltered Mrs. Flather; "haven't you heard?" asked she involuntarily.

"No," replied Mrs. Jorrocks, with the greatest composure.

"It's a long story," observed Mrs. Flather.

"Is it?" replied Mrs. Jorrocks; "I should like to hear it."

"Well, but you'll have the kindness not to repeat it," said Mrs. Flather.

"Certainly not," replied Mrs. Jorrocks.

"Promise me that!" said Mrs. Flather, clearing her throat with a hem.

"Not for the world," responded Mrs. Jorrocks.

"Why, you see, I was never particularly anxious for it," observed Mrs. Flather.

Mrs. Jorrocks coughed.

"Not that I think there is much against the young man," added she; "but I don't think these unequal matches are desirable; besides, the Marquis is very young."

"He'll mend o' that," observed Mrs. Jorrocks.

"Still, youth is volatile," continued Mrs. Flather, "and exposed to the many temptations of London, there is no saying but he might have repented, and then what a shocking thing it would have been for Emma."

"But she would have been a Marchioness for all that," observed Mrs. Jorrocks.

"Wealth and titles won't compensate for the want of domestic happiness," sighed Mrs. Flather.

"She'd have had diamonds," observed Mrs. Jorrocks, "powdered footmen, and a coachman with three rolls of curls to his vig."

"Indeed," said Mrs. Flather, imagining it was part of the equipage of a Marchioness.

"Been a Lady Patroness of Almack's," added Mrs. Jorrocks, considering whether they were all duchesses or marchionesses, or how.

"Well, for all that," sighed Mrs. Flather, anxious to put an end to Mrs. Jorrocks's tantalising catalogue, "I cannot but think I did right in putting an end to the thing."

"Then was it a reg'lar engagement?" asked Mrs. Jorrocks incredulously.

"*Decidedly so*," replied Mrs. Flather. "What made you ever doubt it?"

"Because our friend over there," said she, nodding towards where Mrs. Trotter sat hard at work trying to coax Mr. Jorrocks out of a subscription, "thought she had got him for Eliza."

"*Eliza!*" sneered Mrs. Flather—"Eliza had just as much chance with him as you have."

"Emma had booked him before then, had she?" asked Mrs. Jorrocks.

"The Marquis had booked Emma rather," whispered Mrs. Flather. "Emma's not a girl that everybody can gain," added she.

"Not unless they are well gilt," thought Mrs. Jorrocks.

"It don't do for women to be too easily caught," observed she. "Men think nothin' on them. Jun sutored me amost three years afore I would 'ave him."

"That was a long time," replied Mrs. Flather, who had heard Jun say it was only three weeks.

"I had a many grand offers," observed Mrs. Jorrocks, with a shake of the head, as if she ought to have done better.

"So has Emma," rejoined Mrs. Flather, anxious to keep to the subject of her daughter and the Marquis.

"Emma will do well yet," observed Mrs. Jorrocks, looking at the model of propriety, who was now pretending to talk to little Trotter, but in reality was cocking her ears to catch what she could of the dialogue between Mrs. Jorrocks and her mamma.

"No fear of that," responded Mrs. Flather. "She's in no hurry, and has plenty of time to look about her."

"There are as good fish in the sea as ever came out on't," observed Mrs. Jorrocks. "She'll get a markis yet, or at all events a baronet."

"Oh, I don't wish for any such thing," sighed Mrs. Flather. "Let her keep single, or marry some quiet respectable man in her own rank of life, who'll appreciate her for her worth; for she's an angel of a girl," added she.

"So everybody says," replied Mrs. Jorrocks, thinking whether it was the last Sunday or the Sunday before she heard Emma had given the cook a good beating for not letting her eat the apple tart she had made for dinner at luncheon.

"There will be plenty glad enough to get her," observed Mrs. Flather, with a toss of her head.

"Plenty!" replied Mrs. Jorrocks.

"James Blake, for instance, is dying for her at this moment."

"James Blake is a goin' to marry Eliza Trotter," observed Mrs. Jorrocks, with a most malicious grin, unable any longer to contain herself.

Mrs. Flather almost fainted. James was the only real card they had in view. What might have followed remains matter of speculation, for just as Mrs. Jorrocks announced this destructive intelligence, our Cockney Squire, who had been in close confab with Claudius Sacker for some minutes, caused a diversion throughout the room by calling out at the top of his voice to little Trotter, "I say, Trot! 'ow old do you say the Markis o' Bray is?"

"How old!" repeated Trotter, who had been pottering to Emma about double primroses, much to her annoyance, for just as she got hold of the beginning of a sentence, so as to guess what her mamma and Mrs. Jorrocks were talking about, he was sure to put her out by returning to the subject. "'Why, he's just of age," replied Mr. Trotter.

"No, not the man Markis; the ball Markis; my Markis, in fact," retorted Mr. Jorrocks.

"Oh, your Marquis," repeated little Trotter; "why, he's two year old—rising three."

"You're sure of that?" asked Mr. Jorrocks.

"Why, I can't *swear* to it," replied little Trotter, fearing the justice wanted to entrap him as a witness; "I've always heard so. Why do you ask?" added he.

"Vy, because Sack, here," punching the doctor in the ribs with his thumb, "has picked up a cock and bull story, I may well call it, about his bein' three year old, and says Tommy Clotworthy, who had the second-best two-year-old at the show, is a goin' to claim the premium from me."

"Indeed!" ejaculated several.

"That will be very awkward," observed Mrs. Trotter.

"*Werry*," replied Mr. Jorrocks, diving into his breeches pocket, and stirring up his silver.

"Not that they'd get a wast," added he, "if they only took wot I brought 'ome; for wot with his lordship's expenses—wot with Pigg's—wot with my own; and wot with drinkin' of his lordship's 'ealth, I was amost two punds out o' pocket; at least there was one pund eighteen and ninepence unaccounted for. There might part on it ha' rolled out o' my breeches pocket, to be sure," observed Mr. Jorrocks, "for while I was hup speaking, some idle and disorderly person took my seat out from an under me, and I couped my creels out o' the back o' the tent. *Haw, haw, haw*," added he, "thinks I never got sich a capsize i' my life. *Haw, haw, haw*," continued he, laughing at the thoughts of it.

"Well, but what will you do about the premium?" inquired Trotter, still fearing Mr. Jorrocks might call upon him, from what he had said.

"Vy, I don't know about that," replied Mr. Jorrocks. "I doesn't care nothin' about the prize," added he, "but in course I shalln't see the reputation of my ball compromised without a tussle. If the Duke o' Donkeyton's farm gentleman says he's only a two-year-old, vy, I'll let Clot do his worst. I'll bring the ball into the Court of Exchequer, and let Baron Halderson have a look in his turnip-trap. Haw, haw, haw," chuckled he; "I'll get Murphy to defend him!" continued he. "Crickey, but I fancy I see his lordship rollin' about clearin' the big-wigs Sand all the spectators out o' court, like so many cobwebs."

"It's 'alf-past eight," at length observed Mr. Jorrocks, looking at his great noisy watch; "time we were a toddlin'—night hair's bad for the chest."

"Wouldn't you take a little wine and water?" inquired Mrs. Flather, at length finding her tongue, after the shock Mrs. Jorrocks had given her.

"A leetle brandy and water, if you've no objection," replied Mr. Jorrocks.

"I'm afraid we're out of brandy," rejoined Mrs. Flather.

"Never mind," said Mr. Jorrocks, "rum'll do as well."

"I'm sorry we haven't any rum either," replied Mrs. Flather; "the cat broke the last bottle yesterday."

"I thought I smelt it as I came in," observed Mr. Jorrocks, sniffing about. "Howsomever," added he, "never mind, we shall be all the better without it in the mornin';" with which philosophical reflection Mr. Jorrocks gave the signal, and the party were presently on their legs; the ladies scuttling away for their cab-heads and shawls—the gentlemen pocketing their pumps, pulling on their thick shoes, identifying their hats and zephyrs.

Having transformed themselves into as many "guys," there was such saluting and squeezing of hands—such good-nightings among the present, and best lovings to the absent—the more they disliked each other, the greater being the *empressement*.

At length the guests got into the open air, and after waiting a second or two staring up at the dark starless clouds, they declared it was only the first coming out that made it look so black, and they had no doubt they would manage well enough after they had been out a little.

The proffered lanthorn being declined, and the receding footsteps sounding in the dark, amid reiterated "good-nights," and hopes of "safe arrivals at home," Mrs. Flather and Emma closed the door upon their dear departing friends.

XL

Night, sable goddess! from her *ebon* throne
In rayless majesty, now stretches forth
Her leaden sceptre o'er a slumbering world.

"THE MARCHIONESS DON'T LOOK SO far amiss considerin' her misfortin," grunted Mr. Jorrocks to the first cloaked figure he ran against, who happened to be Mrs. Trotter.

"She's not one that will die of love," retorted the rival parent.

"But she might die of the loss of a coronet," observed Mr. Jorrocks; "they are far wuss to meet with nor men in 'ats."

"She never tad any chance of him," snapped Mrs. Trotter.

"Humph," grunted Mr. Jorrocks, recollecting the consultation Mrs. Trotter and he had had together respecting the Marquis and Eliza. "Then you think Emma's not one o' the dyin' sort," observed Mr. Jorrocks, running foul of a tree.

"Not she!" exclaimed Mrs. Trotter.

"P'raps you'll take my harm," observed Mr. Jorrocks, thinking Mrs. Trotter's bright eyes might guide him safer than his own.

They then joined arms.

"I vish old Hursa Major would 'ave the kindness to show us his mug," observed Mr. Jorrocks, looking up at the dark firmament. "Us farmers call him the *plough*," added he, "and I think he should return the compliment by lightin' us 'ome."

"I think so too," replied Mrs. Trotter; adding, "you don't think Emma pretty, do you?"

"Pretty!" repeated Mr. Jorrocks, "pretty well—nothin' to set the Thames on fire;" adding, "are you much of a star-gazer?"

"*Not at all*," replied Mrs. Trotter, vexed at Mr. Jorrocks's shirking.

"I am," said he; "crazeyologist, bampologist, starologist, wenusologist, all that sort o' thing sort o' man," added he.

Mrs. Trotter was silent.

"The Shepherds in the beautiful plains o' Egypt and Babylon were the first persons wot paid much attention to the stars," observed Mr. Jorrocks, "partly for want of amusement, not having no theatres, nor masquerades, nor circuses to go to, and partly to enable them to scrimmage about the country at nights."

Mrs. Trotter was still silent.

"I confess I should ha' liked to ha' been a shepherd i' one of them shires," continued Mr. Jorrocks; "'specially if I'd 'ad a fine 'ooman to darn my stockings, and so on," added he in an undertone, and a squeeze of Mrs. Trotter's arm.

"Mrs. Flather, perhaps," observed Mrs. Trotter.

"No, not Mrs. Flather," replied Mr. Jorrocks, with an emphasis; "some 'un nearer 'and."

"You old goose," thought Mrs. Trotter.

"It's confounded dark," observed Mr. Jorrocks, grazing a gate-post with his shoulder. "If Saturn has his five moons as they say, I'd wish he'd show a light to-night."

"You should have accepted Mrs. Flather's offer of her lanthorn," observed Mrs. Trotter.

"I think we did wrong not," observed Mr Jorrocks; adding, "I'd no notion it was so dark."

"It's lucky the road's pretty good to find," observed Mrs. Trotter.

"Ay, but roads look werry different at nights to what they do by day," observed Mr. Jorrocks; "summut like women in that respect," added he; "nothing personal, in course," continued the gallant Squire.

"Of course not," replied Mrs. Trotter. "Perhaps you think Mrs. Flather does," added she.

"Can't say I've ever examined Mrs. Flather particklar by candle-light," observed Mr. Jorrocks.

"Nay, you saw her to-night," replied Mrs. Trotter.

"True; but there was sich a bevy of beauties that I never had time to look her over—*narrowly*, at least," added Mr. Jorrocks.

Mrs. Trotter was silent. She saw our friend would not be trotted out.

"That Miss Hemily Badger ar'nt a bad lookin'-girl," observed Mr. Jorrocks, after a pause. "Well-set-up gal, I should say; good figure-'ead too."

"As fine as Emma, do you think?" asked Mrs. Trotter.

"Finer nor Emma, I should say," replied Mr. Jorrocks. "More expression, more animation," rejoined Mrs. Trotter.

"Hemma's more sedate-lookin'," observed Mr. Jorrocks.

"Emma's a cold-blooded one," observed Mrs. Trotter. "I doesn't like a cold-blooded 'ooman," replied Mr. Jorrocks, squeezing his companion's arm again.

"I wonder whom she'll take up with next?" observed Mrs. Trotter.

"Isn't this her first?" inquired Mr. Jorrocks. "*First!*" exclaimed Mrs. Trotter, "not by a good many—not, I dare say, that she ever had an offer, but she's tried for them hard enough."

"Humph!" grunted Mr. Jorrocks, thinking the mothers' stories didn't tally.

"Perhaps she'll be trying Mr. Blake again," observed Mrs. Trotter.

"Perhaps," replied Mr. Jorrocks.

"She may save herself the trouble of that, though," chuckled Mrs. Trotter.

"He's not to be catched, isn't he?" asked Mr. Jorrocks.

"*He is caught,*" said Mrs. Trotter, with emphasis.

"Who by?" inquired Mr. Jorrocks.

"Who do you think?" returned Mrs. Trotter.

"Miss Badger, p'raps," observed Mr. Jorrocks, thinking Eliza would not have him after her Marquis *coup.*

"Guess again," said Mrs. Trotter.

"Eliza, p'raps," said Mr. Jorrocks.

"You have it!" exclaimed Mrs. Trotter.

"And doesn't Mrs. Flather know?" asked he.

"Not yet," said Mrs. Trotter. "He only offered this afternoon."

"Yes, she does," interposed Mrs. Jorrocks, who, aided by the darkness of the night, had fallen into line with our hero and his fair friend.

"What, you haven't blabbed, have you?" exclaimed Mrs. Trotter.

Mrs. Jorrocks was silent, feeling she had committed herself.

"Well, now, I must say that is very wrong of you!" exclaimed Mrs. Trotter, "*very wrong indeed!* I told it you in the strictest confidence, and she was just the last person under the sun that I should like to have had it told to," added Mrs. Trotter, from the depths of her calash.

"But she was sure to 'ear of it," snuffled Mrs. Jorrocks from hers.

"*Sure to hear of it!*" repeated Mrs. Trotter, boiling up; "no doubt she was; but there was no reason why you should deprive me of the pleasure of telling her."

"That woman, Mrs. Flather," said she to Mr. Jorrocks, "has spited me more than words can tell; and just as I was going to have my revenge, I'm done out of it in this way. *It's too bad!*" exclaimed she, in a loud tone of voice.

The parties behind hearing something going on before, now pressed to the front, and at this critical moment, a rope that had been tied across the road just as it led into the turnpike, took the front rank by the heels, who were immediately followed by those behind. Down they all went, two layers of them. Great was the scramble!

Mr. and Mrs. Jorrocks, with Mrs. Trotter between them, made the first layer; then came Claudius Sacker and his wife, with Miss Emily Badger. Little Trotter had a tumble to himself at the side. Mr. Jorrocks lost his wig, Mrs. Jorrocks's front came down over her nose, and Claudius Sacker's gold-headed cane went into Miss Emily Badger's mouth.

A reward of two pounds was offered, next day, for the discovery of the wig and the offender or offenders who tied the rope across the road, but without success. Popular opinion pointed to Benjamin; but his worship never suspected him.

The wig was taken from a Scotch terrier, who, having fought with two other dogs for the retention of his prize, it may be supposed not to have been worth much when Mr. Jorrocks got it back.

XLI

On us each circling year doth make a prey.

"FROM ROME TO TERRACINA, FROM Capua to Naples," observed the Duke of Donkeyton, travelling with his eye-glass down Orgiazzi's map of Italy, along with young hopeful, the Marquis of Bray, with whom he was arranging a route for a tour.

The Duke and Duchess had had long and anxious confabs relative to their hopeful scion, caused, not a little, perhaps, by Mrs. Flather's invasion. They thought he would be getting into mischief, and, painful as the separation would be, they had determined to send him abroad for a year, under the superintendence of a steady old file, Professor Yarnington, one of the old straight-cut coat, upright-collared, pig-tailed, silk-stocking, short black-gaitered breed of tutors; a most orthodox-looking bear-leader.

The Duke and the Marquis had set off on their travels after luncheon, and had advanced as far into the bowels of Italy as indicated in the opening sentence of this chapter, when, just as his Grace, with a twirl of his eye-glass, was throwing himself back in the luxurious depths of his arm-chair to twaddle about the wonders of Naples, and his own exploits there as a youngster, the library door opened, and the groom of the chambers approached at a somewhat hurried pace for a well-trained menial, bearing a rich salver with a black-sealed letter upon it.

His Grace broke the seal, and proceeded to read it. Thus it ran:—

REFORM CLUB

DEAR DUKE,—Poor Guzzlegoose[1] has succeeded in killing himself at last. He had been living at the Castle, at

Richmond, for a fortnight, and died this morning of a most inordinate dinner. I happen to be passing through town, and despatch a special messenger with this by the evening train, as, of course, no time should be lost.—

Truly yours,

LOOKALIVE

"God bless us!" said the Duke, throwing up his white-whiskered head; "sad thing! Very sad thing!" handing the Marquis the letter; "sorry for him, monstrous sorry for him."

"Pay the messenger. No answer," added he to the servant.

"Poor man!" said the Marquis, with a laugh, handing back the letter; "he has long been trying to do it."

"Great eater! monstrous great eater!" said the Duke.

"He was that!" rejoined the Marquis.

"Great drinker! monstrous great drinker!" added the Duke. "However, my dear Jeems," continued he, folding up the map of Italy, we must improve the opportunity—be moving; important event! monstrous important event! Kind of Lookalive to send us the intelligence; monstrous kind of Lookalive to send us the intelligence!" added he, ramming the map back into its case without regard to the folds.

The first thing a great man does is to send for his lawyer. The lawyer is to the mind what the doctor is to the body. The king sends for his chancellor, the duke for his solicitor; accordingly, a messenger was despatched to Sellborough for Mr. Smoothington; and the Marquis was recommended to wipe away all trivial fond records of Rome and Terracina, Capua and Naples, from his mind, and prepare for the great struggle of political life.

Mr. Smoothington, though what is called a man of information—that is to say, a great gossip—a man who knew everybody's affairs in the county—was rather behindhand in getting the news on the present occasion; and several people had arrived in breathless haste at the Castle to announce the death of Mr. Guzzlegoose ere it reached Mr. Smoothington's ears at his office.

Having examined and cross-examined the parties who brought the intelligence, and satisfied himself of the truth of it, he had just sent his clerk footman to order the lofty landaulet, when the Duke's messenger arrived, requiring his immediate presence.

It needing no conjurer to proclaim what would be wanted, Mr. Smoothington made a hasty selection of popular addresses, and in his best black suit, with a fresh sprinkling of powder, was soon on his way to Donkeyton Castle.

Mr. Smoothington affected the Duke—indeed he was generally called "The Duke." He powdered his iron-grey locks, and kept the hair at the back of his head as full as possible; had a large crop of whiskers under his chin—now brushed up in full view. He also wore eye-glasses, though not at all short-sighted.

Thus arrayed, he stepped into the lofty landaulet, and sitting well forward, as if fussing in the particular pocket that happened to be next a neighbour's house, he jolted away to the Castle. As he went, he thought of Guzzlegoose—recalled his start in life, when, at the Marquis's age, in the bloom of youth, and the plenitude of looks, he was returned for the county. Thought of his maiden speech—his early promise—his maturer standstill—his later failure. Remembered his Grecian nose, when there wasn't a speck upon it—his waist when it resembled an hour-glass—thought how succeeding sessions had blotched the one and swelled the other— could hardly have believed the pale taper lad of one-and-twenty could have filed into the gross, overgrown, rubicund monster of five-and-forty.

"No constitution, however strong," said Mr. Stnoothington aloud to himself, "can long withstand the united effects of eating and drinking."

He then looked at his watch—calculated what time he would arrive at Donkeyton—wondered whether the Duke would ask him to dine. If so, whether he would produce any burgundy; and, if not, why not, or how otherwise.

The man of law was so long in getting to Donkeyton that the Duke began to fidget and think he could almost do without him. "Tiresome man—monstrous tiresome man," said he to the Marquis, as he paced hurriedly up and down the spacious library. "Could do it ourselves—could do it ourselves—do believe we could do it ourselves," observed he to young hopeful.

Just as they were preparing pens, ink, and paper, and the Duke and Duchess were busy fussing among a drawerful of papers containing the genealogical tree, and the bills and squibs connected with his Grace's first election for the county, the oracle arrived, and, hat in hand, waved his salaams up the room.

Smoothington was a great courtier—bowed extremely low—tried to back out of rooms, an attempt which generally ended in his tumbling over a footstool, or almost cutting himself in two against an open door. When his hands were disengaged, he employed them in rubbing them one over another as if he were washing them. He had a long, pale, but not unpleasant face, and taking him altogether, he would have commanded five-and-forty or fifty pounds as a butler.

If he had not kept the Duke waiting, his Grace would certainly have shaken hands with him, strongly symptomatic of electioneering, and a compliment he had not paid him since Mr. Smoothington attended with the eight-and-thirty skins of parchment containing his Grace's marriage settlement. As it was, the Duke exclaimed, "Ah, Mr. Smoothington, come at last!—come at last!—glad you are!—monstrous glad you are—pray be seated!—pray be seated!"—bowing him into a vacant chair in the neighbourhood of the throne.

"Well," said he, squashing himself into the throne, and wheeling it close up to Mr. Smoothington, "you've heard poor Guzzlegoose is dead—sorry for it—monstrous sorry for it—young man—quite young man—sure he would kill himself—ate so much Perigord pie—Perigord pie—continual Perigord pie."

"Yes, he was extremely fond of Perigord pie, your Grace," observed Mr. Smoothington, with a broad grin on his face, as he deposited his hat under his chair, and began working his hands.

"Well, now," continued his Grace, putting a sheet of paper before Smoothington, "the first thing I suppose will be for the Marquis of Bray to issue an address, offering himself to the county."

"The first thing for the Marquis of Bray to do will be to issue an address offering himself to the county, as your Grace observes," replied Mr. Smoothington, working away at his hands.

"And, perhaps, the less we put in it the better," added the Duke.

"The less we put in it the better," bowed Mr. Smoothington.

"Then just draw up the form of what you think will do," rejoined the Duke, handing Mr. Smoothington a pen.

Mr. Smoothington took it—looked at the nib—held it up to the light—took out his knife—pruned the feather thus having collected his faculties, drew the roll of precedents from his pocket.

"Whether shall we call them, Freeholders of the county, or Free and Independent Electors; or address them as the Gentry, Clergy, Freeholders, &c., of the county, does your Grace think?" inquired Mr. Smoothington, dipping his pen in ink to obey the Duke's dictation.

"Freeholders of the county," replied his Grace. "Freeholders of the county, I think," wrote Mr. Smoothington; adding, "we must allude, I suppose, to the death of Mr. Guzzlegoose?"

"Of course," said the Duke.

Mr. Smoothington then wrote—

TO THE FREEHOLDERS OF THE COUNTY OF ——

GENTLEMEN,—A vacancy having occurred in the representation of our county by the lamented death of Mr. Guzzlegoose, I hasten to offer my humble services in endeavouring to supply the loss that melancholy event has occasioned.

"Will that do, does your Grace think?" asked Mr. Smoothington, looking up.

"I think it will," replied the Duke; adding "read it over again."

Mr. Smoothington read it over again.

"Perhaps we may put in *my friend*, Mr. Guzzlegoose—lamented death of my friend, Mr. Guzzlegoose," observed the Duke.

"I think it would be better, your Grace," observed Mr. Smoothington, inserting the words.

"Looks as if we identified ourselves with his opinions," added the Duke.

"It does, your Grace," replied Mr. Smoothington. "May gain the extreme party," observed the Duke; adding, "Guzzlegoose went farther than we do."

"He did, your Grace," acquiesced Mr. Smoothington; "rather of the whole hog order."

"We had better deal in generalities now, I think," observed the Duke.

"I think we had," agreed Mr. Smoothington. "Suppose we say, 'It is, I trust, unnecessary for me to enter into any detailed explanation of the principles by which my public conduct will be governed,' " observed the Duke; " 'suffice it to say they are those which have been maintained by my family throughout many succeeding generations,' " added he.

"*Very good*," observed Mr. Smoothington, reducing the sentence to writing as quick as possible.

"Then," said the Duke, "we might say, 'In those principles I have been educated, and it is upon my sincere attachment to them that I ground my claim to your support.' "

"Admirable!" exclaimed Mr. Smoothington; "nothing can be better," writing it down.

The Duke then threw himself back in his chair as if overcome with fatigue, his whiskered face turned up to the rich fretwork ceiling.

"Shall we say anything about a personal canvass, do you think?" suggested the man of law.

"Personal canvass!" repeated the Duke; "personal canvass—I. don't know what to say about a personal canvass."

"We, of the Liberal party, generally make a show of canvassing," observed Mr. Smoothington.

"Very true," replied the Duke, "very true; might promise them one—no occasion to make it, you know—no occasion to make it."

"Not unless there were symptoms of an opposition," replied Mr. Smoothington.

"No fear of that," rejoined the Duke, "no fear of that. We are popular—monstrous popular. Not like as if we were attempting the

Tory seat. The seat is ours, you know—the seat is ours. We returned Guzzlegoose."

"Mr. Guzzlegoose always acknowledged the great obligations he was under to your Grace," observed Mr. Smoothington.

"Might say that he would take the earliest opportunity, consistently with the decorum to be observed on so melancholy an occasion, of paying his personal respects to every elector, and affording them an opportunity of ascertaining the details of his political creed, or something of that sort," observed the Duke. "It would look as if Jeems intended doing it, and yet not bind him."

"It would," replied Mr. Smoothington.

"Canvasses are nasty things," observed the Duke. "Remember a drunken fish-fag taking me in her arms, and hugging and kissing me before the crowd," added he, with a shudder.

"It is a season of great freedom," observed Mr. Smoothington.

"Might do the same by Jeems," continued the Duke; "give him the Scotch-fiddle perhaps, or some such nasty complaint. Nasty business canvassing altogether," added he; "should have abolished it with the Reform Bill. However, there's no fear of a contest. No one would be fool enough to risk a crusade against our popularity. We are popular—monstrous popular, I suppose?" asked he of the keeper of his popularity.

"Oh, *very popular indeed*," replied Mr. Smoothington, with due emphasis.

"Should think so," said the Duke—"should think so—have subscribed to two organs, two churches, three races, and I don't know what else of late."

"The Corn-Law League might trouble your Grace perhaps," suggested Mr. Smoothington.

"I think not," replied the Duke—"I think not," repeated he. "They don't know but Jeems, the Marquis, may be for immediate and total repeal. That address pledges him to nothing—that address pledges him to nothing."

"It does *not*, your Grace," agreed Mr. Smoothington. "I don't think we can do better," added his Grace, after a pause. "Time enough to speak out when we're pressed—time enough to speak out when we're pressed."

"It is so, your Grace," assented Mr. Smoothington. "Just run over a fair copy of the address, then," said the Duke, "and let us hear how it reads. While you are doing it I'll order you some wine and water, and a biscuit—a cutlet, or anything you would like to have."

"Not anything, I am much obliged to your Grace," replied Mr. Smoothington; "I never eat luncheon," added he, making an effort for a dinner.

He then made the following fair copy:—

To the Freeholders of the County of ——

Gentlemen,—A vacancy having occurred in the representation of our county by the lamented death of my friend Mr. Guzzlegoose, I hasten to offer my humble services in endeavouring to supply the loss that melancholy event has occasioned.

It is, I trust, unnecessary for me to enter into any detailed explanation of the principles by which my public conduct will be governed. Suffice it to say they are those which have been maintained by my family throughout succeeding generations. In those principles I have been educated, and it is upon my sincere attachment to them that I ground my claim to your support.

I will take the earliest opportunity, consistently with the decorum to be observed on so melancholy an occasion, of paying my personal respects to every elector; and, in the meantime, I have the honour to subscribe myself, gentlemen, with every sentiment of respect and esteem, your very faithful, humble servant,

Bray

Donkeyton Castle

His Grace then took and read it.

"That will do very well," said he, returning it. "And now have the kindness to put it in the printer's hands immediately, and let it be advertised and placarded about the county. Much ob*leged* to you for your attendance—sorry you can't stay dinner—hope we shall be more fortunate another time!" With which tantalising politeness his Grace rose to witness Mr. Smoothington's backward retreat up the room, which he accomplished with a bump against a globe, and upsetting a banner-screen.

That modest body, the "Anti-Corn-Law League," no sooner saw the Marquis's address, than they inquired, through their chairman, his lordship's opinions relative to their pet subject—the Corn Laws; an interference that the Duke could not brook from parties unconnected with the county, and therefore desired the Marquis to take no notice of their application.

No answer was returned. A second and third letter followed with similar success. This nettled the great lawgivers, who pulled the strings in London, and set all their men of weight a going in the county—men in whom the greatness of the leaders was well reflected.

Reports of these meetings were duly brought to the Castle, but the Duke's cue being known, the parties underrated them as much as possible. "Contemptible! monstrous contemptible!" the Duke said they were.

The next thing was his Grace reading in the Whig paper, *The Dozey Independent, or True Blue Patriot*, a paragraph announcing that the League had determined upon starting a candidate in the person of "William Bowker, Esq. of Whetstone Park, in the County of Middlesex, a merchant of great weight and respectability in the City of London"— respectability in City parlance meaning money. The reader will be astonished how Bill, the "snuff-shop man," could have jumped so suddenly from the humble region of Eagle Street into the magnificence of Whetstone Park, in the County of Middlesex. Some may suppose it was with the League money, while others will put it down as an improbability. Let any one, however, take his hat, and a cab (if one can get up), and explore the alley running parallel between High Holborn and Lincoln's Inn Fields, consisting, as it does, of a heterogeneous collection of stables, with garrets above, joiners' shops, cobblers' stalls, and tenement houses; a street or bye street, or back street, a few shades worse then Eagle Street. This wretched alley is dignified by the name of "Whetstone Park," and thither Mrs. Bowker and her sister had taken refuge when their too frequent visitor, the appraiser, came again to seize for rent and taxes.

It was a lucky turn, however, for Bill, who now called himself a retired merchant living on his property. His League excursions so far had not benefited him much; he was too far gone to rally in a short time, and the more money Mrs. Bowker thought he got, the more brandy she drank, and the more mosaic jewellery she bought.

But to the Duke.

His Grace was dumfoundered when he read this announcement, nor did he recover much when, on turning to the front, or advertisement page, he read Mr Bowker's address, announcing that, in compliance with a numerous and highly respectable requisition, he was induced to come forward to endeavour to supply the vacancy caused by the lamented death of Mr. Guzzlegoose. It then proceeded to denounce all restrictions upon trade, more especially upon that connected with the food of man, and concluded by announcing Mr. Bowker's intention of being speedily in the county to make a personal canvass of the electors, and pledging himself to give every man an opportunity of registering his vote in favour of enlightened and rational policy. It concluded, "Believe me to be, gentlemen, with unfeigned esteem, your faithful and sincere friend,

WM. BOWKER

WHETSTONE PARK

"God bless us! who ever heard such a thing!" exclaimed the Duke, dropping the paper lifelessly from his hand. "Who ever heard of such a thing!" repeated he, with a sigh; "bearded in one's own county by the Lord knows who! These are the blessings of the Reform Bill. To think that I should have lived to see such a thing! Told Grey and Russell, and all of them, that they were going too far. Never thought to get such a return for giving up my boroughs. Oh dear! oh dear! what will the world come to? To think of Jeems being defrauded of his birthright!"

"*Shalln't be the case*, though," added the Duke, boiling with indignation. "Will spend my last shilling before I'll give up my seat."

Thereupon his Grace took another look at the hateful address.

"William Bowker!" said he, with a sneer; "wonder who the fellow is. Some millionaire—some opium smuggler—some impudent upstart millowner! Oh, that Jeems should be brought in contact with such a man. Had it been a member of some old county family, with their bigoted pride and Tory prejudices, one could have tolerated it; but to be bearded by William Bowker, of Whetstone Park, in the County of Middlesex—a man of yesterday—a mushroom—a nobody, in fact—it's disgusting!" Thereupon his Grace threw the paper on the floor.

After a few minutes spent in a reverie, during which the Duke passed rapidly through his mind the political events of his early life, contrasting the comfortable arrangements of those days with the angry struggles of the present, he again roused himself, and determined to do something, though he didn't know what. A man in that situation generally rings the bell, and his Grace did so.

"Send Binks here," said his Grace, as a footman answered the summons.

"Binks is out shooting, your Grace," replied the man. "Out shooting!" repeated the Duke; "that's awkward—want to see him particularly," his Grace's wishes increasing as the means of gratifying them diminished.

"Send a groom up to the valet's covert to desire Binks to come here directly," said his Grace impatiently.

"Tell Binks to get on to the groom's horse and ride," exclaimed the Duke, as the astonished footman vanished like lightning.

"The valet's covert" was a wood kept exclusively for the amusement of those useful gentry "upper servants," and there not being many strangers in it in the course of the season, it fell more immediately to the share of Binks and the Castle "gentlemen," who were now giving the pheasants a rattling. Binks was the Duke's oracle; he knew, or professed to know, everything.

Great was Binks's astonishment when the hurrying groom interrupted the "*Heigh! cock! cock! cock!*" of the beaters, by exclaiming, "Mr. Binks! Mr. Binks! come home directly! come home directly! the Duke wants you! the Duke wants you!"

Out came Binks, all bustle and briars, with a face like a turkey-cock, wondering what had happened.

"Get on to my horse and ride!" exclaimed the groom, jumping off and lengthening the stirrups.

"What's happened?" inquired Binks, turning deadly pale; "the Duke's not ill, is he?"

"I don't know," replied the groom.

Off went Binks at a gallop.

Arrived at the Castle, he hurried up into the presence, attired as he was, with his whistle dangling at his velveteen jacket button-hole.

"Binks," said the Duke, "do you know where Whetstone Park is?"

"Whetstone Park!" repeated Binks, standing transfixed.

"Whetstone Park, in the County of Middlesex," said the Duke.

"Yes, your Grace," replied Binks; "I should say it's near Isleworth."

"Isleworth!" repeated the Duke. "Isleworth, Isleworth, that's near Sion House."

"The Duke of Northumberland's," replied Binks. "Do you know anything of a Mr. William Bowker living there?" asked the Duke.

"Mr. William Bowker," considered Binks—"Mr. William Bowker; can't say I do. Perhaps he's a City man," suggested Binks, as a reason why he should not know him.

"*He is*," replied the Duke; "the paper here," holding up old *Dozey*, "says he's going to stand for the county."

"Indeed!" exclaimed Binks, in astonishment. "What! oppose the Marquis?" asked he.

"*So the paper says*," replied the Duke, with a shrug of the shoulders.

"Must be mad," said Binks, with a toss of the head.

"I should think so," rejoined the Duke, with another shrug of the shoulders. "Send for Mr. Smoothington," added he.

Binks hurried away to execute the order.

The messenger met Mr. Smoothington at the Gothic lodge. That eminent solicitor had been shocked, on awakening in the morning, at finding his whole front covered with enormous placards, containing Mr. Bowker's address, and great bills, printed in blue ink, with "BOWKER FOR EVER!" pasted over his nice green door.

The town of Sellborough was in a perfect ferment—far surpassing anything it had ever seen even in the palmiest days of borough ascendancy. The League didn't spare paper. Every house-end—every dead wall was covered with their blue bills. A cart-load had been put up during the night. As day advanced, a band paraded the streets, and public-houses were freely opened.

Mr. Smoothington was hustled by a party of drunken men, shouting "*Bowker for ever!*" as he stepped into the rickety landaulet that was again to convey him to Donkeyton Castle. Worse than all, some wicked wag posted a great "BOWKER FOR EVER" placard against the back of the carriage.

Mr. Smoothington was terror-struck—Whetstone Park had told upon him. A man in his frame of mind was ill calculated to advise the Duke, who was just in a state to be turned either way. If Smoothington had shown a bold front, the Duke, who had seen none of the preparations, would have determined to show fight; as it was, his own inclination being for temporising, Mr. Smoothington's advice would determine him that way.

His Grace rose from his easy-chair as Mr. Smoothington entered the library, and welcomed him with a shake of the hand.

"Tell us all about it," exclaimed the Duke, hurrying the man of law into a chair. "Tell us all about it," repeated he, resuming his own seat and drawing his chair close to Mr. Smoothington's. "*Who is this Mr. Bowker?*" asked the Duke, before his factotum could get out a word.

"Really, your Grace, I don't know," replied Mr. Smoothington; "the whole thing has come upon me like a clap of thunder. I certainly did hear that the League people had held meetings in Sellborough; but knowing the parties, I really looked upon them as too contemptible for notice."

"So did I," exclaimed the Duke, "so did I—impudent people—monstrous impudent people—wrote to Jeems to know his opinions—took no notice of them—took no notice of them. Tell me now what have they done? what have they done?"

"Your grace, I presume, has seen Mr. Bowker's address," replied Mr. Smoothington, pulling one of the enormous placards out of his pocket, unfolding, and handing it to his Grace. His Grace read—

"To the gentry, clergy, freeholders, and other electors of the county of——GENTLEMEN,—In compliance with a numerous and highly respectable requisition——"

"Ah, this is the same as we have in *Dozey*," said the Duke, breaking off; "but tell me now," said he, laying it down, "has he arrived? Does anybody know anything about him?"

"He is to make a public entry into Sellborough at three o'clock this afternoon, your Grace," replied Mr. Smoothington, "and the town was in a perfect uproar when I came away."

"You don't say so!" replied the Duke, holding up both hands.

"The country the same," continued Mr. Smoothington; "all along the road the people kept shouting 'Bowker for ever!' even the children in the villages!"

"*Great heavens!*" exclaimed the Duke.

"Quite true, I assure your Grace. Two or three fellows that overtook me bawled into the chaise 'Bowker for ever!' as they passed."

"You don't say so?" exclaimed the Duke.

"He is a rich man, I suppose," observed the Duke, after a long pause.

"I should think so," replied Mr. Smoothington. "At all events he seems inclined to spare no expense. He's taken the whole of the 'Duke's Head.'"

"Why, that's our house!" exclaimed his Grace. "How could Tucker ever let him in?"

"There's dinner ordered for six. Champagne in ice—wax candles and rose-water—saw the order myself," observed Mr. Smoothington.

"Indeed!" said the Duke, with a chuck of the head.

"Feather bed atop of the mattress—seems a most particular gentleman," added Mr. Smoothington.

"Well, what do you think is best to be done?" asked the Duke, after conning the great placard. "We must do something."

"Upon my word it's a critical position," replied Mr. Smoothington. "A contest's a disagreeable thing."

"*Monstrous* disagreeable!" exclaimed the Duke, with an emphasis.

"This has the appearance of being an expensive one," observed Mr. Smoothington. "Money seems no object. Public-houses opened, and ale flowing like water."

"The expense is not the worst of it," replied the Duke. "I dread the canvass! I dread the canvass!"

"They are nasty things," replied Mr. Smoothington.

"Jeems is not strong," said the Duke. "Jeems is not strong; might knock him up—might knock him up."

"Very true, your Grace," replied Mr. Smoothington. "Might get insulted," observed the Duke, thinking of the kissing he got from the fish-fag.

"He might so, your Grace," assented Mr. Smoothington.

"Do you think we could enlarge upon our address so as to meet the views of the League, and get rid of the opposition?" asked the Duke, after a pause.

"Let me see, your Grace," said Mr. Smoothington, producing a printed copy of the address.

"You see there's very little in it," observed the Duke. "Very general, your Grace," replied Mr. Smoothington, conning it over.

"I said we'd put as little in it as possible, you know," observed the Duke.

"You did so, your Grace," assented Mr. Smoothington; "and a very prudent and fortunate resolution it was."

"The least said soonest mended, always," said his Grace.

"The least said soonest mended," repeated Mr. Smoothington, working his hands.

"Well, now, what do you think?" asked the Duke, anxious to have something for his three guineas and chaise-hire.

"There will be two points to consider," observed the man of law, after a pause; "first, whether Mr. Bowker wants a seat in Parliament independently of the Corn Laws; and secondly, whether, by the Marquis of Bray declaring himself against the Corn Laws, he might not stir up an opposition from the landed interest."

"Ha!" said the Duke, "I see. The first will be the difficulty—getting rid of Bowker; I'm not afraid of an opposition among ourselves. Who's to do it? Who's to do it? We are popular—monstrous popular! I suppose, ar'nt we?"

"Very popular indeed," replied Mr. Smoothington.

"I think if we could enlarge our liberality so as to satisfy the League, we might get rid of the opposition," observed the Duke. "*I really do*," added he.

Smoothington now saw which way the wind blew, and prepared to trim his sail accordingly.

"If it hadn't been the League, we shouldn't have had an opposition," observed he.

"Very true," replied the Duke, "very true."

"Get rid of the League—get rid of the opposition," observed Mr. Smoothington.

"Perfectly correct," said the Duke; adding, "accurate view—monstrous accurate view!"

"No time should be lost," observed Mr. Smoothington.

"No time should be lost," repeated the Duke.

"The thing is how to set about it," observed Mr. Smoothington,

"There's the difficulty," said the Duke.

"If one knew anybody who knew this Bowker that one could set to sound him," observed Mr. Smoothington.

"That would be the way," said the Duke, "but I'm afraid that's not possible. London man—not likely to have any acquaintance down here."

"You might go to him," said the Duke, "with another address—similar to the one now in circulation, with the addition of a reference to Free Trade, and pretend that the omission was accidental, and say that you hope, as the Marquis of Bray and himself are quite of the same way of thinking, he will bow to his Lordship's superior claims, and let him in without a contest."

"Very good," replied Mr. Smoothington, looking at the Marquis's address, saying, "where shall we add it?"

"Here in the second paragraph," said the Duke, reading—

" 'It is, I trust, unnecessary for me to enter into any detailed explanation of the principles by which my public conduct will be governed. Suffice it to say they are those which have been maintained by my family throughout succeeding generations—the liberal improvements of our institutions, the enlargement and removal of every obstacle to the extension of our commercial prosperity,' " said the Duke. "Don't name the Corn Laws," said he; "put it generally, and then the farmers won't be frightened. Then go on again as before. In those principles I have been educated, and it is upon my sincere attachment to them that I ground my claim to your support,' " concluded the Duke.

"I understand your Grace," said Mr. Smoothington. "Then I must wait upon Mr. Bowker with a copy of it?"

"Just so," said the Duke. "Tell him either that the omission was accidental, or that we left it out for brevity's sake."

"I'll do as your Grace desires," observed Mr. Smoothington.

"Be civil to the man, you know," added the Duke.

"Certainly, your Grace."

"The sooner it is done the better," observed the Duke, applying his hand to the bell, saying at the same time—"Would you like a little refreshment?"

"Not any, I am much obliged to your Grace," replied Mr. Smoothington, tying up his papers.

"Then order Mr. Smoothington's carriage," said the Duke, as the servant answered the summons.

"Despatch a messenger the moment you have anything to tell," said his Grace, shaking hands with Mr Smoothington, as that gentleman took his leave.

Two shakes in one day.

1.   The county member.

XLII

When creeping murmur, and the poring dark,
Fill the wide vessel of the universe.

IT WAS TURNING DUSK AS Mr. Smoothington reached the hill above Sellborough on his way back from Donkeyton Castle, but the wind setting towards him, sounds of music and drunken revelry were borne on its wings.

Mr. Bowker had made a grand entry into the town at three o'clock, amid the most enthusiastic demonstrations from the populace. They met his carriage at the turnpike gate, on what had been the London, but was now called the Smoke Station road, and, having taken the four panting posters from it, had drawn him through all the principal streets, preceded by numerous splendid banners, and two bands of music.

The honourable gentleman had made a most favourable impression. He was dressed in the height of the fashion—a mulberry-coloured frock-coat with a rolling velvet collar, and a velvet waistcoat of a few shades brighter colour than the coat; an extensive flowered satin cravat, with massive electrotype chained pins, fawn-coloured leathers, and Hessian boots. His touring excursions having supplied him with an abundant stock of health, he presented a very different appearance to what the generality of country people imagine a London merchant to be like.

Altogether, he created an indescribable sensation; and as he passed along, standing up in his barouche, bowing gracefully to the ladies, they waved their handkerchiefs, and declared he was "a most charming man." Then, when he got to the "Duke's Head," he appeared in the balcony of the drawing-room, and addressed them on the importance of the privilege they would soon be called upon to exercise. After alluding touchingly to the lamented death of Mr. Guzzlegoose, he called upon them to exercise the elective franchise in such a way as would be beneficial to themselves, their posterity, and their country at large, when the elegance of his manner, and the graceful flourishes of his lavender-colour kidded hand, carried all before it, and men, women, and children hurrahed, and shouted "Bowker for ever!"

But when he came to expatiate on their wrongs, pointed out the injury they sustained by the operation of the Corn Laws, exposed their exclusive workings for the benefit of the landlords, and called upon them to support a candidate favourable to their immediate and total repeal, the enthusiasm of the mob knew no bounds, and every hand was held up in favour of Mr. Bowker—"Big-loaf Bowker," as he christened himself.

After partaking of some light refreshment, he then commenced his canvass, amid the ringing of bells, the rolling of drums, the twanging of horns, and the shouts of the populace; and if unregistered promises could have brought him in, Mr. Bowker would certainly have been member for the county.

Thus he spent the day—shaking hands—praising and admiring the children, chucking damsels under the chin—promising all things to all men. At length, tired of the din and flurry of the proceedings, Mr. Bowker was glad when five o'clock came; and with his old friend Mr. St. Julien Sinclair, and his committee, Mr. Lishman, a bankrupt baker, Mr. Grace, an insolvent painter, Mr. Moss, a radical schoolmaster, and Mr. Noble, a sold-off farmer, he left the streets to enjoy the evening repast at the "Duke's Head." The landlord, Mr. Tucker, in a white waistcoat, followed by his waiter and both in their best apparel, met the distinguished guests at the door, and conducted them to the drawing-room.

Mr. Bowker, after begging to be excused a few minutes while he went and washed his hands (a thing his committee never thought of doing), retired to his bedroom, and made a perfect revision of his costume. When he returned he was in an evening dress, smart blue coat with club buttons and velvet collar and cuffs, white neck-cloth, superbly embroidered waistcoat, with black silk tights, and buckled

Mr. Bowker's personal canvass

shoes. He dangled a pair of prim rose-coloured kid gloves in his hand.

"We may as well ring for dinner," observed the florid swell, entering the drawing-room, and surveying the seedy crew sitting round. He gave a pull that sounded through the house.

The dinner was quickly served, and as quickly despatched by the hungry guests, several of whom had not tasted meat for a week. Champagne, hock, claret, sparkled on the board, and was swallowed by some whose stomachs were much more accustomed to beer.

As evening shades made the sherry indistinguishable from the port or claret, and Mr. Tucker, in obedience to the Squire of Whetstone Park's summons, was bearing a branching candelabra through the passage on his way upstairs, Mr. Smoothington arrived at the door of the hotel, and begged Mr. Tucker to carry his card up to Mr. Bowker.

Accordingly that functionary did so.

"Smoothington!" said Bill, glancing at the gilt-edged pasteboard with the easy indifference of a man accustomed to callers. "Smoothington! who is he?"

"Smoothington!" exclaimed the bankrupt baker and sold-off farmer, each of whom was undergoing Mr. Smoothington's polite attentions.

"Is he an elector?" inquired Bill, considering whether he should see him.

"He's the Duke of Donkeyton's solicitor," replied mine host.

"Indeed!" observed Mr. Bowker; adding, "show him into a room, and I'll ring and let you know when it's convenient for me to see him."

"Yes, sir," said Mr. Tucker.

"Help yourselves, gentlemen," said Mr. Bowker, filling his glass, and passing the bottle.

"We'd better cut our sticks, I think," observed the baker, significantly, to the Corn-Law ruined farmer.

"I think so too," replied the latter.

"And I'll go with you," added Mr. Grace, the insolvent painter, who lived in a house belonging to the Duke.

"Oh no, gentlemen," said Bill, "don't disturb yourselves—don't disturb yourselves—I'll receive Mr. Smoothington in the other room."

"We'll go there!" exclaimed all three—"we'll go there!" thinking to avoid meeting Mr. Smoothington on the stairs.

"Take a bottle of wine with you!" said Bill; pushing the port towards them.

"Thank ye—we'd prefer glasses and pipes," observed Mr. Lishman.

"Ah, you are the right sort, I see," replied Bill; "nothing like baccy."

They all then bundled out.

"Just put the table right, and take these dirty plates away," said Mr. Bowker, as the landlord answered the expected summons.

"Now, give a couple of clean glasses, and tell Mr. Smoothington I shall be happy to see him," said Bill, twirling the card about.

Mr. Smoothington's creaking boots presently sounded on the stairs as he ascended two steps at a time. Another moment, and he was bowing and scraping in the room.

"Mr. Smoothington, I believe," said Mr. Bowker, rising and bowing to the stranger.

"The same," replied the man of law, making one of his best Donkeyton Castle bows, and laying his hand on his heart.

"Pray, be seated," said Mr. Bowker; "pray, be seated," said he, laying his hand on the back of the chair, by the clean glasses and plate.

Mr. Smoothington put his hat under the chair, and obeyed the injunction.

"Take a glass of wine," said Mr. Bowker, passing the bottle across. "That's claret without the label; you'll find it better than the port."

"Thank you, sir," said Mr. Smoothington, helping himself to the claret.

"Confound these country inns," observed Mr. Bowker, "they've no notion of doing things properly. Only fancy! they sent up champagne without being iced!"

"Indeed!" exclaimed Mr. Smoothington.

"*Did, 'pon honour,*" said Bill, with a shake of the head. "The claret's not what it should be, but the landlord says it's the best he can give. I'm sorry I can offer you no better dessert than these filberts and biscuits," added he; "but to tell you the truth, I've had the misfortune to lose my footman and part of my luggage."

"Indeed!" exclaimed Mr. Smoothington, with a look of concern.

"He's either left behind at a station, or carried past the right one; at all events, when I wanted him he was not to be found. The worst of it is," added Bill, "he had a couple of pine-apples and some fine grapes, that my gardener—poor fellow—thought would be a treat for me in the country."

"Indeed!" rejoined Mr. Smoothington; "that *is* a loss;" as much as to say, the footman was nothing.

"Why, it is a loss, as things stand," said Bill, "for I should have liked to have offered you a slice. As for myself, I care nothing about them; but we are supposed to grow the finest in England."

"You are very kind, I'm sure," replied Mr. Smoothington; adding, "have you much glass?"

"Three houses, I think," said Bill; "three pineries—that's to say, three vineries; peach-house or two. But I care very little about a garden."

"Pay more attention to your park, perhaps," observed Mr. Smoothington.

"*Ay, there you have it!*" said Bill, brightening up; "there you have it," repeated he. "My friend, Lord Scampington, pays me the compliment of saying I've the finest venison in England."

"Have you indeed?" exclaimed Mr. Smoothington, who dearly loved the cut of a haunch, particularly when he could get a glass of Burgundy after it.

"Help yourself," said Mr. Bowker, pushing the bottles towards him, thinking his friend would want something to wash the lies he was telling him down with. Mr. Smoothington did as desired. Pending the gulp which followed, he bethought him of business.

"I hope you are not tired with the exertion of your canvass," observed Mr. Smoothington, rubbing hand over hand.

"Why, not tired," said Bill, with an air of indifference; "not tired—*rather* bored."

"You are on the Repeal interest, I perceive," said Mr. Smoothington.

"Repeal decidedly," replied Bill. "By the way, did you see my little English and big American loaf dangling from the balcony as you came in?"

"It was dusk," replied Mr. Smoothington; "and there was a great crowd about."

"Looking at it, I dare say," said Bill. "The best dodge yet."

"The Corn Laws must be repealed," observed Mr. Smoothington; "every thinking man must be satisfied of that. I think, however, it is rather a pity for two champions to start in the same cause when only one can come in."

"How so!" exclaimed Mr. Bowker; adding, "what! is there another Richard in the field?"

"The Marquis of Bray and yourself," observed Mr. Smoothington.

"The Marquis of Bray's the other way," replied Mr. Bowker.

"Pardon me," rejoined Mr. Smoothington.

"He wouldn't declare himself, at all events," observed Bill, "and we politicians generally consider those that are not for us are against us."

"It was partly out of delicacy to the memory of Mr. Guzzlegoose, and partly a mistake of mine!" observed Mr. Smoothington.

"How so?" asked Bill, filling himself a bumper, and passing the bottle.

"Why, I prepared his Lordship's address, the draft of which I now produce," said Mr. Smoothington, diving into the back pocket of his coat, and producing some ominous red-taped papers. "In this draft, as you will perceive," continued he, opening it out, "distinct allusion is made to *all restrictions* on trade, including, of course, the Corn Laws; but, by an unfortunate clerical error, that important sentence was omitted, and the bill printed and posted without——"

"That's very odd," observed Mr. Bowker; adding, "shows great inattention on——"

"I was called away at the moment to attend a relation who was dying," interrupted Mr. Smoothington.

"Well, but why didn't the Marquis answer the League letters?" asked Bill; adding, "great body of that sort is entitled to respect, even from a Marquis."

"That *was* a pity, certainly," replied Mr. Smoothington. "If I had been at home it would have been otherwise. These young men, you see, are unused to business—inattentive. I can answer for it, however, that not the slightest disrespect was meant to the League."

"*Hum!*" considered Bill.

"It certainly seems a pity," continued Mr. Smoothington, "that two candidates of the same opinions should offer themselves for the same seat; to say nothing of the probability, nay, certainty, of the Tories putting up a man, and getting it from them."

"I'm not afraid of the Tories," replied Bill; "as a party they are contemptible against the League."

"Single-handed, they are, I dare say," agreed Mr. Smoothington; "but if the League interest is split, a very small party will defeat it."

"True!" observed Mr. Bowker, seeing how the thing would cut. "Well, then, the best thing will be for the Marquis of Bray to retire," added he; "can be no difficulty about that, you know."

"Except that the Marquis's interest has always been paramount in the county."

"Time there was a change then," observed Bill. "The Reform Bill ought to have put all that right."

"I'm afraid I could hardly advise the Marquis to retire," observed Mr. Smoothington, after a long pause.

"You can hardly expect me to do it, I think, after all the expense I've incurred," replied Mr. Bowker.

"Perhaps we could accommodate matters," suggested Mr. Smoothington, helping himself to the proffered bottles. "The Duke has great interest in the neighbouring borough of Swillington, and a dissolution can't be far off; his interest there might return you comfortably for a long session, without trouble or expense."

Mr. Bowker sat silent, apparently considering the matter.

"County representations are very troublesome," observed Mr. Smoothington; "people never done asking—schools, churches, hospitals, infirmaries, races, plays, farces, devilments of all sorts—no gratitude either. At Swillington there's nothing but a dinner, and a guinea a-head to the voters; five hundred pounds would do it."

"I should still lose all the expenses I have been at here" observed Mr. Bowker.

"That could be accommodated too," replied Mr. Smoothington.

"Consider the trouble, though," bristled Mr. Bowker. "What can compensate me for my trouble, mental anxiety, and so on?"

"True!" assented Mr. Smoothington, unable to price it.

"Separation from family," urged Mr. Bowker.

"Very true," replied Mr. Smoothington.

"Leaving one's own comfortable home for a filthy frowsy inn, where they haven't even the common decency, I may almost say, necessary of life, ice for champagne."

"This, I fear, is beyond the reach of our control," observed Mr. Smoothington, rolling his hands over and over.

"Money can't put that right," said Mr. Bowker. Mr. Smoothington shook his head. "It's an unfortunate thing that the Marquis and you should have come in collision," said he.

"It is," said Mr. Bowker, "*most* unfortunate."

"The Duke is a most amiable person," observed Mr. Smoothington; "so is the Duchess; you'd like them if you knew them."

"Faith, I'm not a great man for the nobility," observed Mr. Bowker. "Am very much of an old friend of mine's way of thinking; who says that they first try to make towels, and then dish-clouts of one."

"The Duke of Donkeyton doesn't," replied Mr. Smoothington; "he's always the same."

"Good fellow, is he?" asked Mr. Bowker.

"*Very*," replied Mr. Smoothington.

"And the Marquis, what's he like?" asked Mr. Bowker.

"Very fine young man," said Mr. Smoothington.

"Indeed!" mused Mr. Bowker.

"Perhaps you'd go over with me and talk to the Marquis?" observed Mr. Smoothington, after a pause.

"Why, I don't know," replied Mr. Bowker; "I dare say we can do all he could."

"No doubt," rejoined Mr. Smoothington; "no doubt. The Duke will ratify whatever I do."

"You are his factotum, I suppose," observed Mr. Bowker.

"The Duke does nothing without consulting me," replied Mr. Smoothington, with a self-complacent smile.

"It's an awkward business," mused Mr. Bowker; "commenced my canvass—extremely popular—great disappointment—enormous expense."

"The expense should be *no* object," replied Mr. Smoothington, "if you could only get over the rest."

Mr. Bowker meditated.

"Nay, I don't want to drive a hard bargain," at length said he, with an air of indifference.

"It's only *right* you should not be out of pocket," replied Mr. Smoothington; "indeed, I should consider it my duty to see that you were not, the mistake having originated partly with myself."

"Well," said Mr. Bowker, again helping himself, and passing the bottle, "your proposition appears reasonable—fair, I may say."

"I am glad you think so," replied Mr. Smoothington; "there is only one way of dealing with gentlemen like you."

"Let me see," said Mr. Bowker, rubbing his hands; "it is that the Duke returns me for Swillington at the general election, and pays my present expenses—that's to say, up to to-night?"

"I'll agree to that on behalf of his Grace," replied Mr. Smoothington, bowing and helping himself.

"It may save trouble," said Bill, "if I take a sum down. There are expenses in town as well as here," added he.

"As you please," replied Mr. Smoothington. "What shall we say?"

"Put it in at your own figure," said Bill, with a shrug of the shoulders, and an air of indifference. "A thousand! *say* a thousand!" added he.

This was a good deal more than Mr. Smoothington expected; but coming from a man with three pineries, and the best venison going, he thought it better to close than to haggle; especially as he was dealing for a Duke.

"Agreed," said Mr. Smoothington.

"Help yourself," said Mr. Bowker, again passing the bottle, "and drink success to the Marquis of Bray." Mr. Bowker drank it in a bumper.

"His lordship will be much flattered when I tell him the compliment you've paid him," said Mr. Smoothington, filling his glass and doing the same.

"You may as well give me a cheque for the money to-night," said Bill, "and let me get out of this noisy place before they resume their racket in the morning."

"With all my heart," replied Mr. Smoothington, thinking he had better clench the bargain and get an agreement of resignation at the same time. Pens, ink, and paper being then produced, Mr. Smoothington filled up a cheque for the required sum, and took a memorandum of the agreement from Mr. Bowker, who got a duplicate signed by Mr. S., on behalf of the Duke of Donkeyton.

Exulting in his diplomacy, Mr. Smoothington shortly after backed out of the room, not, however, without receiving a pressing invitation from Bill to visit him at Whetstone Park.

With a somewhat swimming head, Mr. Smoothington descended the inn stairs; and, after ordering an express to come to his house, as soon as he could get ready, he sat down at his desk at home to write his letter to Donkeyton Castle just as the market-place clock chimed midnight.

XLIII

Thus far our fortune keeps an onward course,
And we are graced with wreaths of victory.

SHAKSPEARE

MR. SMOOTHINGTON FELT AS IF he had performed the greatest feat in his life. Single-handed, he had saved the county from a contest. Thus he announced the victory to the Duke:—

MY LORD DUKE,—I have the honour to acquaint you that, after a long interview with Mr. Bowker, I have at length succeeded in inducing that gentleman to retire from the contest.

I found him most genteel, affable, and urbane; but his ambition of obtaining a seat in Parliament, and the great expense he had already incurred, together with the popularity he had acquired, made him reluctant to lose his hold upon the electors. After, however, pressing upon his consideration the similarity of the Marquis of Bray's (amended) political opinions and his own, together with your lordship's old family claims upon the county, Mr. Bowker, in the most gentlemanly manner, consented to retire, on the understanding that your lordship affords him your interest at Swillington, at the general election, and pays the costs of the day. These, to save trouble, and for the sake of round numbers, he has put down at one thousand pounds, be the same more or less, for which sum I have given him a cheque on my banker, and I now most sincerely trust that the Marquis of Bray may succeed to the seat of his ancestors without further let, suit, trouble, molestation, hindrance, or delay.

I have the honour to subscribe myself, my Lord Duke, with the greatest respect, your much obliged and very humble servant,

PETER SMOOTHINGTON,

Sellborough

To the most noble the Duke of Donkeyton,
Donkeyton Castle
IMMEDIATE. BY EXPRESS. ONE O'CLOCK IN THE
MORNING

His lordship had retired to rest at his usual hour, hoping to drown in sleep the painful subject that had occupied the Duchess's and his attention since Mr. Smoothington's departure, having first given orders to Binks to send up any letter that might arrive the moment it came. Sleep, however, was banished from his eyelids. The horrible phantom of a monstrous bloated citizen passed continually before his vision, and "BOWKER FOR EVER" sounded in his ears.

Sometimes, when just dropping off asleep, he fancied himself in the clutches of the fish-fag, and his efforts to disengage himself awoke him. Twelve, one, two, three, and four o'clock, he successively heard strike, and he began to long for daylight. Towards five, just as he really was likely to succeed, a little, gentle tapping, that could hardly awake a mouse, sounded through the thick oak door, and, in obedience to the Duke's "*Come in!*" Jeanette, the Duchess's pretty little French maid, tripped noiselessly into the room, and, by the aid of the rush-light, deposited Mr. Smoothington's letter on the table at the bedside. The Duke was presently at it.

"Bravo!" exclaimed the Duke, as he read the first sentence, announcing that Mr. Smoothington had succeeded in inducing Mr. Bowker to retire.

"That's a good job," said he, "however."

He then proceeded with the rest of the letter.

"Very good!" said he, "very good! well done indeed—monstrously well done," said he, reading the borough arrangement and the thousand pounds. "Smoothington's managed that well." So saying, the Duke lit the wax-candles in the dressing-room, and forthwith proceeded to exercise his gratitude by the following letter to his conjurer:—

DEAR SIR,—I beg to return you the Duchess of Donkeyton's and my very best thanks for the admirable arrangement you have effected with Mr. Bowker. We ratify it in every respect. I enclose an order on Money-boys & Co. for fifteen hundred pounds, begging your acceptance of the five hundred. With respect, sir, I have the pleasure to be, your obedient servant,

DONKEYTON

Having directed and sealed this, the Duke rang his bell, and, after desiring that the messenger might have it, he turned into bed, and slept like a top until twelve.

This being the second time within the four-and-twenty hours that the bow-legged postboy and rat-tailed roan had been at the Castle, the former thought it necessary to refresh his inward man very considerably; and he drank so much strong ale that he was greatly indebted to his horse's discernment for getting him home. He was stupidly drunk. Daylight, fresh air, and the ride made him staring drunk. He looked like an owl. Great placards met his eyes at intervals as he went, but all he could settle respecting them was that they were not "signs." Gradually his vision improved, and his mind began toying with the letters. The placards were all alike, and the frequency of their appearance so far familiarised him with them, that he blurted out on tumbling from his horse in the inn-yard, "Great fat Duke o' Donkeyton total repealer."

After comers saw more clearly. It was market-day at Sellborough, and consternation was depicted on the farmers' faces as they entered the town, and the ominous placard—

A GREAT FACT!
THE DUKE OF DONKEYTON
A
TOTAL REPEALER!

met their gaze at every turn. The League again were prodigal of paper.

The farmers stared, and asked each other what it could mean. It must be a hoax—it could not be true. The Duke, the bulk of whose income was derived from land, would never cut his own throat. One thought one thing, another another.

Mr. Smoothington, like the Duke, indulged in a good snooze after his over-night exertions; and the morning was far spent ere in the progress of his shave his eye met one of the enormous placards on the opposite wall—

GREAT FACT!

THE DUKE OF DONKEYTON

A

TOTAL REPEALER!

Smoothington was horror-struck. He saw the error he had committed. He stared and stared and could not finish his shave; knocks sounded at his door, and rings pealed at his bell; and when he got downstairs, he found the passage and clerk's office crammed full of farmers. Just then the bill-sticker went by with his paste-can and pole, putting up the Marquis's amended address. Boys were distributing it in hand-bills about the streets, and shouts of "Bowker for ever! Big-loaf Bowker!" still sounded in the streets, as "open houses" closed their accounts by turning the topers out of doors. Mr. Bowker had taken his departure soon after the bank opened, leaving the English and American loaves dangling from the inn balcony. The drunken, frantic violence of the debauched town populace contrasted with the sober staidness of the farmers.

Some people may fancy farmers simple fools; but where self-interest is concerned, they are quite as sharp as their neighbours. To be sure, they do sometimes make absurd propositions to their landlords, but that is more a sign of their thinking their landlords fools than of their being so themselves. Did any landlord ever know a tenant make a proposition that would tell against himself?

Mr. Smoothington could not humbug the farmers. He could not make them believe that the Marquis's fresh address had nothing to do with the League placard, or with Mr. Bowker's departure. Moreover, being plain spoken men, they frankly told him so.

The market commenced, and the effect these proceedings had upon the prices will be best understood by the following extract from that excellent agricultural paper, *The Mark Lane Express.*

> SELLBOROUGH.—Our market was well supplied with wheat, for which the farmers expected high prices; but owing to the unexpected announcement of the Duke of Donkeyton's accession to the Corn-Law League (proclaimed by large placards throughout the town before the market commenced) a panic ensued, and it could hardly be got off at any price. Barley, oats, beans, and peas shared a similar depression.

It so happened that this was the monthly meeting day of the farmers' club, when they dined together, smoked, drank, and discussed farming topics. There was a large muster of the body towards two o'clock, at the sign of the "Bull's Head." The subject fixed for discussion—"How much more potent lime was when supplied by the landlord than when found by the tenant?"—was forgotten altogether in the excitement caused by the announcement of the morning. Mr. Heavytail was chairman of the day, and entered the room in a high state of perturbation, caused by the untoward depression of prices. His voice was heard upstairs before he had well got into the passage below.

"AR NIVER KNEW SUCH A THING IN ALL MY LIFE! FOLKS ARE ALL GONE MAD TOGETHER! HAVEN'T TAKEN AS MUCH MONEY AS WILL PAY MY GATES!"

Johnny Wopstraw came in, greatcoated and overalled as usual, with his canvas sample bag in his hand, declaring—"Upon the who-o-le, he was ruined!"

Haycock of Haziedean, Farbridge of Cow Gate, Snewkes of Heckley Heath, Brick of Dobble Heath, Brick of Rushley, Clotworthy of Wooley Grange, Dick Grumbleton of Hawkstone, and some twenty others, all declared the same thing. Murmur rose above murmur, till the joints got upon the table, and the meat stopped their mouths. Heavytail was hid behind a baron of beef. The clatter of knives, forks, and plates, the callings for ale and beer, and the thanking each other for further supplies, stopped the grumbling for a time.

The cloth being drawn, and the favourite beverage of each man placed before him—wine to the wine drinker, spirit and water to the humbler—Mr. Heavytail rose and gave the "Health of the Queen" in a tone that plainly told how depressed he was. Her Majesty's health having been drunk, Heavytail presently rose again, and in his usual stentorian voice, exclaimed—

"UPON MY WORD, GENTLEMEN, I'M SO TROUBLED IN MY MIND, THAT I CANNOT GO ON AS I SHOULD. I THINK I NEVER HEARD SUCH A THING IN MY LIFE, AS FOR A NOBLEMAN LIKE THE DUKE OF DONKEYTON—A MAN THAT HALF THE COUNTY BELONGS TO—TO GO AND JOIN A DIRTY RUBBISHIN' RADICAL SET OF DIVILS, WITH SCARCE A COAT TO THEIR BACKS" (applause). "OH DEAR, I'M BAD," continued Heavytail, panting for breath, and pressing his stomach with his left hand. "I THINK," continued he, in his roar—"GENTLEMEN, I'D BETTER GET THROUGH MY TOASTS, AND THEN WE CAN TALK THE MATTER QUIETLY OVER; SO I'LL PROPOSE THE HEALTHS OF 'PRINCE ALBERT,' 'ALBERT, PRINCE OF WALES,' 'ALL THE YOUNG 'UNS,' 'THE QUEEN DOWAGER,' AND 'ALL THE REST OF THE ROYAL FAMILY;' " with which comprehensive toast Mark sat down.

Farmers then began laying their heads together in knots of threes and fours. Some thought one thing, some another. All agreed they could not compete with foreigners.

"I'VE PUT TWENTY THOUSAND DRAININ' TILES UNDER GROUND THIS YEAR," observed the chairman; "AND WILL ANY MAN TELL ME THAT I'M NOT CONSARNED IN THE QUESTION?"

"Upon the who-o-o-le," observed Johnny Wopstraw, "I think the farmers are the most so."

"And the labourers!" rejoined Mr. Clotworthy of Wooley Grange. "I employ upon an average eight men upon every hundred acres of arable land, winter and summer; and I should like to know how many I should want if it was all in grass."

"WE MUST HAVE A MAN THAT'LL PROTECT US!" observed Mr. Heavytail from the presidential chair.

"*So we will, so we will!*" exclaimed several; and thereupon glasses began to dance, and spoons to clatter on the table, with the applause the observation called forth.

More wine, more spirit, and pipes, were then called for.

"WE MUST SHOW FIGHT, OR THEY'LL FLOOR US!" observed the oracle again.

"We will, we will!" exclaimed several, amid renewed applause.

"Such a man as Squire Wheatfield, or Mr. Hay of the Mount," observed Mr. Brick of Rushley.

"Squire Wheatfield don't farm," replied Mr. Farbridge.

"Squire Hay don't either," said Mr. Brick of Dobble Heath.

Several other Squires were then talked of: Haycock named his landlord; but the proposition did not meet with much success. Snewkes named another, Brick a third, and Dick Grumbleton objected to them all.

"I think, upon the who-o-o-le, we must have Mr. Jorrocks," observed Johnny Wopstraw.

Great applause followed the observation.

Mr. Jorrocks next day having got up very early to write an ode to his Bull, was interrupted by the constable coming to say that two men had quarrelled and fought, and each wanted to lay a charge of assault against the other.

"Quarrelled and fought! what about?" exclaimed our Squire, darting an angry glance at the intruder.

"About—about—*nothing*, I think," said the constable.

"*Humph!*" grunted Mr. Jorrocks. "They'll both be in the wrong, I s'pose?" added he.

"Indeed, I don't know, sir," replied the constable; "they both think themselves in the right at the present time."

"That's jest wot *convinces* me they are both in the wrong," rejoined the Justice, thinking how he could get rid of the case without bothering himself.

"Tell 'em," said he, after a pause, "to go to the public-'ouse, the Jorrocks's Harms, and drink a pint o' hale together, and try to make it hup; and if they can't, to come back here, and I'll commit 'em both."

"Yes, sir," said the constable.

"Send 'em to the Sessions," added Mr. Jorrocks.

"Yes, sir," replied the constable.

"And bind you over to *per*secute," continued Mr. Jorrocks.

"Yes, sir," replied the constable, with a duck of the head.

"Troublesome dogs," said Mr. Jorrocks to himself; "they're *always fightin'*."

"Please, sir, here's Mr. Good'eart wants to speak to you," said Benjamin, entering the sanctum with his usual hang-gallows look, just as Mr. Jorrocks was resuming his poem.

"Mr. Goodheart, Binjimin!" exclaimed the Squire, starting up. "I've not seen Mr. Good'eart these six weeks. Show him in."

Presently the venerable old man made his appearance, drooping with the weight of years.

"Vell, Mr. Good'eart, and 'ow are you?" asked Mr. Jorrocks, in a cheerful tone.

"Thank ye, sir, I'm middlin'—canna complain—not so strong as I was, p'raps—am rather gettin' on in years you see—I'm turned of seventy-two."

"Well, but that's nothin'," observed Mr. Jorrocks.

"Why, no, sir it's not, sir," replied Goodheart; "but we are nabbut a short-lived family, you see. My father was cut off in the prime of life at eighty-two."

"Poor young man!" exclaimed Mr. Jorrocks; adding, "come, sit down, and tell us all about it. You'll be wanting some fifth o' George the Fourth, I presume."

"No, sir," replied Willey, not knowing what the Squire meant.

"Your rent raised, then, p'raps," suggested Mr. Jorrocks acting on Pigg's recommendation of anticipating complaints.

"No, 'deed do I not, sir," replied Goodheart, with emphasis; "us farmers, I think, will all be ruined."

"Vot's 'appened now?" asked Mr. Jorrocks. "They harn't been a firm' of your stack-yard, 'ave they?"

"Far worse than that! far worse than that!" exclaimed Goodheart. "I've been readin' in the *Grampound Gun* of a thing they call a League, for takin' the duty off French corn."

"Ah!" said Mr. Jorrocks, smiling, "you've read up to *that*, 'ave you?" recollecting Willey was always a year or two in arrear with news.

"To think," continued Willey, "of my ever livin' to see such a thing as the French and English on such terms. I, that hate the French, so that I would never eat a French roll or grow French beans in my garden. Why, sir, I was a volunteer in the times of Bonaparte."

"So was I!" exclaimed Mr. Jorrocks. "So was I!" repeated he, "in the City Light 'Oss."

"But you mustn't *allow* it," observed Willey, thinking a magistrate could do anything.   "You must *speak* about it," added he. "What's the use of your being a magistrate if you can't stop such work as that?"

"I fear it von't come within the fifth of George the Fourth," observed Mr. Jorrocks aloud to himself.

"Please, sir," said Benjamin, coming in again, "here's Mr. 'Eavytail and some more gentlemen want to see you."

"*More* gentlemen!" exclaimed Mr. Jorrocks. "It must be the ball they want to see! Confound, that hanimal's werry expensive. Cost me a hocean o' sherry. Shall have to get some Marsala."

"Tell Mr. 'Tail and the gen'lmen," said Mr. Jorrocks to Benjamin, "that I'm partickier engaged—inwestigatin' a dreadful bugglary—but the Markis'll be 'appy to see them, and you go and show him—or get Pigg, if you're afeard he'll toss you again."

"Yes, sir," said Benjamin, taking his departure.

"Please, sir, Mr. Wopstraw says, upon the who-o-ole, it's *you* they want to see," said Benjamin, entering the room and imitating Wopstraw.

"Cuss the chaps," muttered Mr. Jorrocks; adding, "I never 'ave a moment to myself. Vell, send them in," said he in disgust.

"Your sarvant, sir," roared Heavytail, entering the room, followed by Wopstraw, the Bricks, Snewkes, Grumbleton, Haycock, Clotworthy, and a whole host more.

"Good mornin', gentlemen," said Mr. Jorrocks, astonished at the number; "I'm afeard you'll hardly get chairs," added he, looking round the room.

"Never mind, sir, we can stand," roared Heavytail. "We've come to see you about this Parliament business."

"Humph," grunted Mr. Jorrocks; "and who are you for?" asked he.

"You!" roared Heavytail.

"Me!" exclaimed Mr. Jorrocks. "Ah, I twig," added he. "You mean you're willin' to wote as I wote. All right and proper—much obleged to you."

"No, sir," observed Wopstraw. "We think, upon the who-o-ole, we'll have you for Parliament man!"

"Me for Parliament man!" exclaimed Mr. Jorrocks " 'ow can that be? The Markis is to be Parliament man."

"He won't do for us farmers!" roared Heavytail, producing the Marquis's amended address.

"I twig," said Mr. Jorrocks. "Goes against the Corn Laws."

"Upon the who-o-ole, we must have a man that's for them," observed Wopstraw.

"There's been meetings of the farmers all over the county," roared Heavytail, "and they're all for you."

"Indeed!" exclaimed Mr. Jorrocks, "that's werry purlite on 'em; and who'll pay the shot? Parlument's an expensive shop."

"We'll all poll at our own expense," roared Heavytail.

"Ay, but the pollin' ar'nt the great damage. Livin' in London; givin' of dinners; bespeakin' of plays in the country, and I don't know what else."

"Upon the who-o-ole, we think, as you have a house up in London, you can do it cheaper nor anybody else."

"Vell," said Mr. Jorrocks, "but it's an enormous sacrifice you are a callin' on me to make. Consider 'ow 'appy I am in the country, tendin' my flocks and 'erds, guanoin' and nitrate o' soberin' my land, and all that sort of thing."

"But there's a deal of honour in it," roared Heavytail.

"No doubt," replied Mr. Jorrocks; "no doubt," repeated he; "and so there should—and so there should be; but honour, you know, may be bought too dear."

"Well, but it's no use argufyin' the matter," observed one of the Bricks; "for you we've fixed upon, and you we'll have."

"Vell, but," observed Mr. Jorrocks, after a pause, "you've taken me all aback—you've taken me all aback—thought you'd come for to see my noble ball— there's a deal to consider—there's a deal to consider— Mrs. Jorrocks to consult—Mrs. Jorrocks to consult— consult Mrs. Jorrocks."

"There's no time to lose," roared Heavytail. "Let the Marquis get a start, and it's all over with us. you may give your land away, if you can get anybody to take it, that's to say."

"Oh dear," exclaimed Mr. Jorrocks, "that would be a bad go—that would be a bad go. Get little enough as it is. Howsomever, you must give me a leetle time to consider; meanwhile, take a valk, and see the ball, and Mrs. J.'s bantams, and all that sort of thing. Then come back, and have a leetle sherry and seed cake, or something of that sort, and we will talk the matter quietly over, for I declare you've taken me so by surprise, I don't know vether I'm standin' on my 'ead or my 'eels."

XLIV

Bring me no more reports.

PEOPLE IN CASTLES HEAR DIFFERENTLY to the world at large. The real truth seldom penetrates castles.

When the whole country was in a state of ferment at the appearance of the League's "great fact" bill, and the Marquis of Bray's address, the Duke, ensconced within his park walls, fancied all was over and quiet, and that the Marquis had nothing to do but walk quietly in.

On the day following the issuing of the bill, his Grace took a saunter up to the model farm to give directions for some new experiments on nature, and hear the result of some recently made. Mr. Jobson had notice of his coming, and the whole establishment were full fig to receive him. Mrs. Jobson had her lavender-coloured silk curtains unbagged, and the drawing-room arranged in apple-pie order, in case his Grace should condescend to take a little refreshment.

The important experiments being discussed, the Duke, still full of his admirable diplomacy in putting so little into the Marquis's address as to enable him to get rid of Mr. Bowker by a little enlargement of it, could not resist the temptation of saying a few words relative to the late threatened contest.

"All quiet again now, I suppose," observed he to Mr. Jobson, "since *that* Mr. Bowker took himself off?"

"I hope so, your Grace," hesitated Mr. Jobson.

"What, is there any doubt about it?" exclaimed the Duke. "Is there any doubt about it?" repeated he, alarmed at Jobson's manner.

"Oh no, your Grace," replied Mr. Jobson; "at least, I dare say not;

what we hear are most likely lies—in fact, it does not do to believe everything one hears."

"But are there any reports current?" asked the Duke.

"Why, there are reports, certainly," stammered Mr. Jobson, finding the Duke was ignorant of the feeling of the county; "but I can't trace them to any good authority."

"What are they?" asked the Duke impatiently. "What are they?" repeated he.

"Why, I've heard that the farmers threaten an opposition," faltered Mr. Jobson.

"Farmers threaten an opposition!" exclaimed the Duke. "That's something new. That'll not do, I think," added he; "not against the Marquis of Bray, at least."

"That's what I think," observed Mr. Jobson.

"Ridiculous!" observed the Duke; "monstrous ridiculous. We are popular, I suppose? monstrous popular?"

"*Extremely* popular," replied Mr. Jobson; adding, "it would be very extraordinary if your Grace was not so."

"Well, I think so too," replied the Duke. "I think so too. But tell me, who do they talk of? Who do they talk of?"

"I have heard two or three named," replied Mr. Jobson. "Captain Bluster, I think, seems the most likely man."

"Bluster! Captain Bluster!" exclaimed the Duke. "Why, that's the man with the whiskers on his chin—the man I made a magistrate of."

"You did, your Grace," replied Mr. Jobson.

"Impudent dog!" said the Duke to himself.

"I gave him a bull too!" added the Duke, after a pause.

"No, your Grace—Mr. Jorrocks was the gentleman your Grace gave the bull to," observed Mr. Jobson.

"True," replied the Duke, "true—Jorrocks is the man I gave the bull to—Jorrocks is a good fellow— Jorrocks is a gentleman—Bluster's a blackguard—Bluster's a blackguard. Impudent fellow—monstrous impudent fellow."

"Do you really think there's any truth in it?" asked the Duke after a pause.

"Upon my word I don't know, your Grace," replied Mr. Jobson, anxious to soothe, but hardly daring to deceive. "Upon my word I don't know," repeated Jobson. "We live in queer times, your Grace."

"We do indeed," replied the Duke—"we do indeed; that cursed Reform Bill turned the world upside down—always told Russell and Durham, and all of them, that they were going far too far. Well, it can't be helped," added he resignedly, after a pause—"it can't be helped. If they prefer Bluster to Jeems, they must have Bluster." So saying the Duke turned from the model farm in disgust, and, letting himself into the park through the little green door in the wall, wandered musingly homeward, without doing Mrs. Jobson the honour of calling on her.

He had not been long gone ere the news arrived at the model farm that Mr. Jorrocks had acceded to the wishes of the farmers, and was about to declare himself for the county.

Anxious that the Duke should have the earliest information he could give him on so vital a point, Mr. Jobson ordered his hack to be saddled, and followed the line his Grace had taken across the park.

He soon overtook him.

"Your Grace!" exclaimed Mr. Jobson, reining up his thoroughbred, and taking off his hat. "Your Grace," repeated he, "I've just heard that Mr. Jorrocks is the gentleman who's coming forward for the county!"

"Mr. Jorrocks!" exclaimed the Duke; "Mr. Jorrocks! That's the man with the whiskers on his chin."

"No, your Grace," replied Jobson; "the man with the bull; Bluster's the man with the whiskers on his chin."

"Ah, true!" exclaimed the Duke, "the man I gave the bull to. The man I made a magistrate of, eh?"

"Your Grace made magistrates of them both," observed Jobson.

"So I did," replied the Duke, "so I did. And do you say that that Jorrocks, the man I gave the bull to—the man who can't speak English—is going to have the effrontery to oppose the Marquis of Bray?"

"So they say, your Grace. He's the man they call the sleeping partner in Mother H's," added Jobson, with a grin—Jobson having a cross of the cockney himself.

"Audacious dog!" exclaimed the Duke. "Then it's Jorrocks, not Bluster?" added his Grace, conning the matter over.

"Jorrocks, not Bluster," replied Jobson, with an emphasis on Jorrocks.

"Ah, I thought it wouldn't be Bluster," observed the Duke. "Bluster's a good fellow. Bluster's a gentleman. Jorrocks is a blackguard! Jorrocks is a blackguard!"

Jobson stood silent by the side of his hack.

"It's a nuisance," said the Duke, after a long pause "monstrous nuisance; may involve Jeems in a nasty beery canvass."

"It may so, your Grace," replied Mr. Jobson.

"Couldn't we get rid of this man Jorrocks somehow?" suggested the Duke; "he'll most likely have his price," added he, thinking of Bowker and the thousand.

"We might try him," replied Mr. Jobson.

"You might ride over and sound him," said the Duke. "Put it to his good feeling not to annoy parties who have been so civil and condescending to him. Talk about the bull I gave him, the dinners he's had here, the honours I've conferred upon him. Tell him I hope he'll not give me cause to suppose I have fostered a viper in my bosom."

"I will so, your Grace," replied Mr. Jobson. "I'll do all I can."

"The sooner the better," observed the Duke.

"I'll go directly," said Mr. Jobson, preparing to mount.

"Tell him he's not fit for anything of the sort," said the Duke, as Jobson mounted.

"I will, your Grace," replied the obsequious Jobson.

"You might try him with a deputy lieutenantcy, if you can't get rid of him without," added the Duke, as Mr. Jobson bowed and rode away.

XLV

Oh, monstrous beast! how like a swine he lies!

Tired with the exertions of a long day's canvass, Mr. Jorrocks had seated himself in an easy chair, to enjoy a bottle of strong military port, of recent emancipation from the wood, when Mr. Jobson's noisy peal at the bell threw him into alarm.

"Cuss them, 'ere's some more on 'em a comin'," exclaimed he, bolting upright, half resolved not to be at home.

"Please, sir, here's Mr. Jobson, sir," said Benjamin, opening the door.

"Mr. Jobson," repeated Mr. Jorrocks. "Mr. Jobson! That's the Duke of Donkeyton's farm gentleman; show him in, and bring candles—wax un's, you know, Binjimin;" adding, with a shake of the head, "expensive work this electioneerin'."

Mr. Jobson came bowing and groping his way into the dining-room.

"'Ow are you, my frind?" exclaimed Mr. Jorrocks, rising and greeting him with a shake of the hand. "Allow me to solicit the honour of your wote and interest?" added he, coming out with the usual form.

"I am afraid I can hardly give that," replied Mr. Jobson, taking a proffered chair; "I'm afraid I can hardly do that—not but that I'm quite independent, do exactly as I like; only from what I read of your address, I fear your opinions and mine don't exactly tally."

"*Humph*," grunted Mr. Jorrocks. "Independence is a werry fine thing to talk about; but there's precious little on't in the world. The only real independence I knows on, is the independence of furnished lodgin's, thick shoes, and a shootin' jacket."

Benjamin then entered with the candles.

"Take a glass o' wine," said Mr. Jorrocks, helping himself, and pushing the bottle to Jobson. "There's *sher* i' the sideboard, if you prefer it, to blackstrap."

Mr. Jobson preferred claret, if there was any out.

"Claret I never keeps," replied Mr. Jorrocks. "Can soon make you some, though," added he, "with water and winegar, and a little drop o' port."

Mr. Jobson then took port.

Mr. Jorrocks drank Jobson's health, and Jobson drank Mr. Jorrocks's.

"Fine stuff that," said Mr. Jorrocks, smacking his lips, after the glass of hot, sweet, fruity wine. "And 'ow goes on the farm?" asked he. "'Ope Mrs. Job and all the little Job's are well?"

"Quite well, I'm much obliged to you," replied Jobson.

"We'll drink Mrs. Jobson's 'ealth," observed Mr. Jorrocks, helping himself, and passing the bottle.

Mr. Jobson presently returned the compliment, and proposed the health of Mrs. Jorrocks.

"We'll now drink the 'ealth of all the *leetle* Jobsons," observed Mr. Jorrocks, in due time.

Mr. Jorrocks afterwards proposed the health of "The Queen and her stag'ounds," and then of "Prince Albert and his beagles." The glasses being large, another or two apiece finished the bottle.

"*Port!*" said Mr. Jorrocks, as Benjamin answered the bell.

"I've now got a toast to propose," observed Mr. Jorrocks, as the wine came, and he held the decanter up to the candle, to see that Benjamin had not done him out of any. "I've now got a toast to propose," said he, "that I'm sure will find its way to your 'eart, without any soft sawder from me"—("Hear, hear," exclaimed Mr. Jobson). "It is," continued Mr. Jorrocks, "the 'ealth of one both near and dear to me—one wot occupies, wakin' and sleepin', an unkimmon portion o' my thoughts. Oh!" continued he, aloud to himself, "the greatest pang wot I shall suffer in goin' hup to Parliament will be the separation from that henergetic, that hamiable quad—I'll give you," said he, turning to Jobson, "the 'ealth of my ball in a bumper!"

"Nay, fill hup!" said Mr. Jorrocks, as Jobson stopped half way up his glass. "A bamper to the ball, whatever you do!"

Mr. Jobson then filled, and drank as desired.

"He's a fine animal," observed Jobson, as, with a wry face, he set down his glass.

"He is that!" replied Mr. Jorrocks, "a *real* fine animal."

"The Duke wouldn't have given him to anybody but yourself," observed Jobson.

"Vot, he was particular fond on him, was he?" asked Mr. Jorrocks.

"No, but he had such a high opinion of you," observed Mr. Jobson.

"Don't see why he should," muttered Mr. Jorrocks aloud to himself, adding—"We'll drink his Greece's 'ealth in a bamper," filling his glass and passing the bottle.

"Nay! no skylights!" exclaimed he, as Jobson again shirked filling. Jobson then did as desired.

"The mention o' that hinterestin', that hamiable hanimal," observed Mr. Jorrocks, as Jobson again accomplished his measure with a shrug, "reminds me of a most hamiable young gen'lman after whom he is called; one that I'm sure will emulate his ball lordship in his honourable career, and make their common name transcendently wictorious. I'll give you the ''ealth of the Marquis o' Bray,' " added Mr. Jorrocks, again filling a bumper.

"I suppose you mean transcendently victorious in the coming contest," observed Mr. Jobson, who did not altogether approve of the Marquis's career among the ladies; particularly about home.

"I means, celebrated—distinguished," observed Mr. Jorrocks, tapping the decanter to draw Jobson's attention to his duties; adding, "come, drink your young master in a bamper."

Jobson did not like this description of their relative positions; but fearing Mr. Jorrocks might say something more offensive, coolly submitted.

"Nay; no 'eel-taps!" exclaimed our friend, seeing Mr. Jobson preparing to fill upon a half-emptied glass, adding—

> This is liberty 'all, do as you will,
> Fill wot you please, but drink wot you fill.

"But you won't let me do as I will," observed Jobson tartly; "you will make me fill bumpers."

"Bumpers in course to toasts," observed Mr. Jorrocks; "arter we've done drinkin' toasts we shall come to the sentiments, and then you can do as you like, you know."

"I wish we were at them," thought the refined claret-drinking Jobson.

"In considerin' the toasts we've already drank," observed Mr. Jorrocks after a pause, during which Jobson had been arranging a plan of attack in his own mind, "I'm somewhat—that's to say, a good deal flabbergasted to find that we've altogether omitted the name of a lady wot ranks werry 'igh in the peerage of the kingdom, and the estimation of the county (hiccup). I'm cock sure I need say nothin' to recommend that illustrious (hiccup) lady to your consideration, because livin' under the family you'll know a deal more about her nor me; but I should be werry (hiccup) sorry to have it (hiccup) said, that one of her servants and I should 'ave passed a conwivial evening together, without so much as drinkin' of her 'ealth; I therefore beg to propose the "ealth of the (hiccup) Duchess of Donkeyton in a bumper.'"

"Oh dear," groaned Jobson, with throbbing temples, as he shirked the filling.

"Now, we'll jest 'ave another bottle," observed Mr. Jorrocks, turning the bottom of that one into Jobson's glass, so as to make him up a bumper, "and then we can drink good evenin' in a glass of (hiccup) brandy and water or two," added he, ringing the bell again.

"I'm afraid that will be trespassing too largely on your time," observed Mr. Jobson.

"Time's of no importance with me," hiccuped Mr. Jorrocks, with an air of indifference.

"Indeed!" exclaimed Mr. Jobson; "then you've given up the idea of standing for the county?"

"I did not say that," replied Mr. Jorrocks. "I means night-time's of no walue: can't canvass day and night too."

"I was in hopes, from the handsome manner in which you have spoken of our people," observed Jobson, "that you had given up the idea of opposing our friend the Marquis."

"No doubt," hiccuped Mr. Jorrocks; "speak well o' them wot uses one well."

"Undoubtedly," said Mr. Jobson; "and *use* them well too, I hope."

"To be sure," hiccuped Mr. Jorrocks.

"Then you don't mean to oppose the Marquis?" asked Mr. Jobson.

"Not if the Markis'll stand up for us poor farmers," replied Mr. Jorrocks, helping himself out of the fresh bottle, and passing it to Jobson saying, "Let us think prosperity to hagricultur," adding, "it's like the hair we breathe—if we have it not we die."

Mr. Jobson took a little.

"Nay, a bamper to that at all ewents," hiccuped Mr. Jorrocks.

"I thought you said I might fill as I liked to sentiments," observed Jobson.

"No doubt," hiccuped Mr. Jorrocks; "but that ar'nt no sintiment! it's a *toast*—nothin' but a toast; so take a bamper. Sintiments," hiccuped he, "have reference to the ladies, sich as sweethearts and wives, honest men and bonnie lasses, the fair o' Middlesex (hiccup), or summut o' that sort."

"The Duke will take it seriously amiss, I'm afraid," observed Mr. Jobson, "if you put the Marquis to the trouble of a contest."

"Can't 'elp that," hiccuped Mr. Jorrocks. "If the Duke has a mind to cut his own (hiccup) throat, can't afford to let him (hiccup) cut mine too. 'Elp yourself, and we'll drink his Greece's (hiccup) good 'ealth again," added Mr. Jorrocks, setting the example by filling and passing the bottle. "Bamper toast," hiccuped he.

Mr. Jobson eyed his glass as if it were poison.

"The Duke will think it very ungrateful, I'm afraid," observed Jobson, raising the glass to his lips and setting it down again.

"I don't see that," hiccuped Mr. Jorrocks, adding, "howsomever drink your wine, and show your (hiccup) attachment to him."

"He made you a magistrate," observed Mr. Jobson.

"He did so," replied Mr. Jorrocks, adding—"Showed his sense there; for real, substantial (hiccup) jestice—fifth o' George the Fourth sort o' jestice—no man can compete with (hiccup) J. (hiccup) J. With your permission, I'll give you a (hiccup) toast—a bamper—the last bamper

I'll (hiccup) call for. I'll give you 'The fifth o' (hiccup) George the (hiccup) Fourth,' real (hiccup) palladium of our (hiccup) rights. That (hiccup) Graham will play the (hiccup) deuce with the (hiccup) fifth o' George the Fourth, if he won't let us jestices do any more (hiccup) jestice at 'ome. Here's 'The (hiccup) fifth o' (hiccup) George the Fourth,' " concluded Mr. Jorrocks, filling a bumper and drinking it off.

"That's a sentiment, I presume," observed Jobson, filling a very small quantity.

"(Hiccup) toast or (hiccup) sentiment, as you please," observed Mr. Jorrocks, seeing his friend's eyes looking very glassy.

"I suppose we shall be having the bull back," observed Jobson, after a pause.

"What'n ball?" inquired Mr. Jorrocks.

"The bull the Duke gave you," replied Mr. Jobson. "Of course you won't keep it if you oppose the Marquis."

"I don't see that at all," observed Mr. Jorrocks, cured of his hiccup at the bare idea of losing his treasure. "I don't see that at all," added he, looking at the decanter as if he saw two. "If the ball," said he, looking very wise, "was presented to me to buy me off-standin', it would be another (hiccup) pair o' shoes altogether; but it was presented to me as a (hiccup) undeniable (hiccup) token of undeniable esteem. With your (hiccup) permission," continued Mr. Jorrocks, "we'll drink (hiccup) his 'ealth, if you please."

"We have drunk it already," observed Jobson, sick at the thoughts of another drop.

"Never mind that," hiccuped Mr. Jorrocks; "we (hiccup) drank the Duke's health twice, and we'll drink the (hiccup) Duke's (hiccup) ball's health twice too; twice two's four, and one's sivin," added he. "No man can say I'm (hiccup) drank, I think."

"Then you don't mean to return the bull?" observed Mr. Jobson, speaking very thick, and pouring the wine over the side of his glass.

"No!" roared Mr. Jorrocks, in a tone that startled Jobson, adding— "'Ow can you ax sich a question? I loves that Markis-ball too well to part with him. It may be wanity on my part, but I flatters my-(hiccup)-self his (hiccup) lordship re-re-re-reciprocates the (hiccup) sentiment."

Mr. Jobson stared, and shortly after, in attempting to reach a piece of biscuit, lost his balance and fell on the floor.

Mr. Jorrocks rang the bell.

"Tell that (hiccup) Pigg to carry this (hiccup) shockin' drucken chap to (hiccup) bed," hiccuped Mr. Jorrocks; "and let him 'ave a (hiccup) glass o' (hiccup) sober-water, and a (hiccup) red 'erring in the mornin'."

"Yes, sir," said Benjamin, eyeing Jobson's contortions on the carpet.

"And 'ave (hiccup) Cobden ready for (hiccup) me at half-past (hiccup) six," added Mr. Jorrocks, lurching off to bed.

XLVI

The farmers are with us to a man.—LEAGUE LIE, No. 91

THE BITTER, ANGRY PERSONALITIES OF the canvass were at length stopped by the arrival of the writ.

The Duke of Donkeyton, after resorting to every expedient to get rid of our pertinacious friend, had at length been compelled to let Jeems undergo the degradation of a canvass, and the latter had endeavoured to counteract the success of Mr. Jorrocks's early start by the splendour of his retinue, the bounty of his expenditure, and the lavishness of his promises.

Money flew in all directions. He would buy a parrot of an old woman for twenty pounds whose husband was difficult to come over, or outbid Mr. Jorrocks's promised subscription to races or hounds by offering to give a gold cup, or to hunt the country himself. He would do anything!

The country was in a complete ferment. The farmers and landowners pulled well together, but the Duke's large interest, backed by the Radicals and part of the manufacturing interest, made it fearful odds against our commercial Squire.

Mr. Smoothington fortunately made light of the matter, and in his daily reports to the Castle, of the success of the canvass, he repeatedly assured the Duke there was not the shadow of a doubt of the Marquis's success. As the canvass advanced he grew more confident; said that he considered the election as good as over—that old Jorrocks would never show at the hustings; and when that assertion was contradicted by one of our friend's facetious addresses, thanking the freeholders for their promises of support, and pledging himself to go to a poll, Mr. Smoothington accompanied the document by a return from the Marquis's canvass book, showing a clear majority of three hundred.

Our friend, on the other hand, had bet as many as seventy hats that he would win. The accuracy of their respective opinions was now about to be put to the test.

On the nomination day the whole country was in commotion. It rose to a man. It was a time of year when farmers have a little leisure after harvesting, and the fineness of the later autumn tempted the denizens of the manufacturing towns to indulge in a holiday on so exciting an occasion. A sharpish frost in the night loosened the fading leaves, leaving them ready to fall at the least breath of wind. Down they dropped, one after another, twirling round and round as they fell leisurely to the ground.

At an early hour in the morning of the nomination day, the tide of population began to flow into Sellborough. Not a chaise, not a gig, not a car, not a van, not a horse in the country but what was put in requisition. Farmers' nags stood three in a stall. The nomination was fixed for twelve o'clock, and before that hour the respective candidates had entered the town from different sides, escorted by their friends, and preceded by bands and banners. The Marquis's set-out was most splendid. All the flags from the district committees at the different towns and villages were gathered together, forming a perfect forest of silk and gold, which were stationed before and after the barouche and six in which his lordship rode. His colours were pea-green and yellow, the rosettes and favours being composed of gold tinsel instead of yellow silk.

He was accompanied by Mr. Smoothington and his proposer and seconder, Captain Bluster and Mr. Prosey Slooman. The latter had made an unsuccessful attempt to grow whiskers under his chin. Captain Bluster's bristled most importantly red. He had been a protectionist, but the judicious representation by Mr. Jobson of what the Duke had said about his being "a good fellow and a gentleman," had driven him the other way. Bluster was now a red-hot Leaguer—far hotter than his Grace; who, indeed, was anything but a Leaguer at heart. Mr. Jobson headed the tenantry on horseback; who, with slouched hats and downcast looks, followed the carriage, looking uncommonly sulky. Mrs. Jobson, in a flaming clarence drawn by a pair of the Duke's blood bays, dressed in a beautifully made pea-green pelisse, with a yellow velvet bonnet and a green feather, and a twenty guineas point-lace veil, chaperoned a bevy of country belles; while the Duchess's pretty little French maid escorted a troop of the household dolly-mops in the break.

Altogether it was a splendid procession. The Marquis's colours waved from the balconies, windows, and shops, and appeared on the breasts or the bonnets of the fair occupants; while beards or whiskers on the chin denoted that the few men who appeared without cockades were for the young duke, as they called the Marquis.

Twenty-three young ladies were regularly annihilated by the captivating smiles and bows of the Marquis as he passed slowly through the streets, each fair recipient thinking the smile she got was the sweetest. That *old* Jorrocks had no chance, was the firm conviction of every one who saw the splendid cavalcade pass along.

Mr. Smoothington smirked, and chuckled, and rubbed his hands over and over, at the thoughts of the drubbing they would give him.

"The county will be ours for ever and a day," exclaimed he to the Marquis, as they passed under the old archway leading into the market-place.

As they entered the spacious arena, tremendous applause rent the air from the front of the spacious hustings on the far side, before which a whole army of drab-coated horsemen were assembled, with some half-dozen bunting and glazed calico flags in the centre.

It was Mr. Jorrocks, alighting from his fire-engine, in which he had driven from the house of his proposer, Mr. Hamilton Dobbin, who had been wicked enough to break away from the Duke's ranks, in spite of the dinner he had eaten.

"Now, another shout for t'ard Squire!" exclaimed Pigg, waving the only silk flag they sported, and who acted as fugleman to the party. "Now another!" repeated he, as Mr. Jorrocks advanced to the candidate's place in front of the hustings.

"*Hurrah! Hurrah! Hurrah!*" shouted the drab coats.

Mr. Smoothington's countenance fell as he surveyed the dense mass.

"Now three for Squire Dobbin!" exclaimed Pigg, as Mr. Jorrocks's head left off acknowledging the compliment they had paid him.

Three cheers were then given for Mr. Jorrocks's proposer.

"Now three for ard 'Tail!" roared Pigg, flourishing his flag with "JORROCKS, THE FARMER'S FRIEND!" upon it. Three hearty cheers followed for Mr. Heavytail, who had been chosen by the farmers to second the nomination.

The farmers then bustled away to put up their horses, and get back to secure places in front of the hustings. Mr. Jorrocks availed himself of the opportunity to pull his wig straight, and adjust a large bunch of wheat-ears he had stuck in the Jorrockian jacket button-hole (as emblematical of his creed), and which had got rather deranged in his passage through the crowd from the fire-engine on to the hustings.

He then conned over his speech.

The Marquis having arrived at the "Duke's Head," where his central committee sat (at least sat towards dinner-time, when they liberally dispensed champagne and everything expensive); the Marquis, we say, having arrived at the "Duke's Head," alighted, to add the committee as a tail to the head he had brought with him, and having called for a glass of hock and soda-water, his example was followed by those who durst trust their stomachs with such flatulent compounds. Bluster had a glass of brandy.

The party being formed, the Marquis set off for the hustings, walking between his proposer and seconder amid deafening shouts of applause from the dense crowd through which they passed.

Mr. Jorrocks rose to receive his quondam farmer friend, as the Marquis made his appearance at the back of the hustings; his lordship's dandified garb contrasting strangely with our friend's uncouth attire.

"Well, old boy!" said the Marquis gaily, extending his hand to Mr. Jorrocks, "so you won't be satisfied without a beating!"

"I'm not sich a glutton as all that," replied our friend. "Suppose I give you one instead."

"Will you, indeed!" exclaimed the Marquis.

"I'll bet you a 'at I do," replied Mr. Jorrocks, looking very confident.

The High Sheriff's appearance at the back of the hustings put an end to the dialogue, and that functionary, advancing to the front, divided the belligerents.

Silence was then called for, and at length obtained from the sea of heads in front and the crowd upon the hustings. It was broken occasionally by an observation from Pigg, who, having availed himself of the opportunity afforded by the farmers putting up their horses, to get a few glasses of rum, had now returned with his flag, loquaciously drunk. Johnny Wopstraw, Willey Goodheart, and a few more of Mr. Jorrocks's tenants, clustered round the gaunt fugleman, whose tobacco-streaming mouth was conspicuous above the crowd.

The High Sheriff came forward, and, after observing that he had called them together in obedience to Her Majesty's writ, in order that they might choose a fit and proper representative to supply the vacancy caused by the lamented death of Mr. Guzzlegoose, begged that they would give to every gentleman, however they might differ from him in political opinion, a fair, impartial, and uninterrupted hearing; and concluded by calling upon any gentleman who had a candidate to propose to come forward and do so.

Captain Bluster then presented himself to the notice of the meeting. After looking angrily towards James Pigg, who saluted him with a cry of *"Now, Ginger toppin!"* as he took off his hat, the Captain commenced by saying, that unless he had seen it with his own eyes, he could not have believed that an almost total stranger to the county could have had the vanity to conceive himself the fittest champion of its battles, and he certainly did not think Mr. Jorrocks was likely to add much to his character by his appearance in opposition to the popular son of the most popular parents under the sun—(loud cheers from the whiskerites, and roars of laughter from the drab coats).

For his part, he thought Mr. Jorrocks was the last man who ought to have thought of filling such a position—*he* who had received the lavished honours and favour of the parent ought never to appear in opposition to the son (renewed cheers, mingled with hisses). He who had feasted at Donkeyton Castle—eating the Duke's venison and drinking his wine, might surely make some better return than attempting to defraud the Duke's son of his birthright.—(Renewed applause, with increasing disapprobation.)

The Captain then referred to a card which he carried in the palm of his hand for "the word," and again went on.

He had the honour of proposing a candidate to fill the vacancy in the representation occasioned by the lamented death of Mr. Guzzlegoose, and he would not pay the valued friend he was about to put in nomination so poor a compliment as to say, that he challenged comparison with the competitor opposed to him—(Captain Bluster looking at Mr. Jorrocks as if that gentleman would make him sick); but he would fearlessly assert that, look where they would, north, south, east, or west,—they could not lay their hands on a gentleman more pre-eminently qualified than his much-beloved and highly-exalted friend (cheers and great uproar, mingled with cries of "Where's Big-loaf Bowker?" from the drab coats). That friend was the nobleman now standing on his right—one whose every interest was identified with theirs—whose vast possessions must suffer if their interests were injured, and who had, therefore, every reason for advocating such measures as would best promote their common prosperity.

"Weal done, ard Ginger toppin!" exclaimed Pigg, flourishing his flag amid roars of laughter.

"I see," said Captain Bluster, eyeing the inscription on it, "Jorrocks, the farmer's friend, painted on that flag," pointing towards where Pigg stood, with his tobacco-stained mouth gaping wide open to catch every word the Captain said. "I see," repeated he, "Jorrocks, the farmer's friend, painted on that flag."

"It's not painted—it's *geelt!*" exclaimed Pigg, giving it another flourish, amid great shouting.

"I see," said Captain Bluster, for the third time, "Jorrocks, the farmer's friend, in gilt letters on that flag."

"Ay, *that's* it!" roared Pigg, jealous of the honour of his banner.

"But will any man tell me," continued Captain Bluster, "that my noble friend is not as much the farmer's friend as this self-elected champion, John Jorrocks? Who, let me ask, is Mr. Jorrocks, that he should all at once set up as the champion of the farmers' interests? What has he done to forward agriculture? Has he, like my noble friend, the Duke of Donkeyton, a model farm, on which every new machine is exhibited, every new experiment tried? where every species of manure— Hunt's bone dust—Hunt's half inch—soap ashes—rape cake—rags—new Bristol manure—Chie fou—guano— nitrate of soda——"

"*Hoot ye and your nitrate o' sober!*" roared Pigg; "MUCK'S YOUR MAN!" an exclamation that caused such an outburst of laughter as completely to put the Captain out. The Under Sheriff pointing Pigg out, desired the man with the dirty mouth, and "Jorrocks for ever" round his hat, to hold his tongue, or he would order him into custody.

Captain Bluster, after a long pause, again resumed—

Not only was his dear and noble friend, the Duke of Donkeyton, an active promoter of agricultural improvement, but the noble lord beside him—a worthy son of a worthy sire—trod in the footsteps of his Grace. The Marquis of Bray was well known to scientific farmers as the inventor of a valuable—an unequalled draining-tile.

"Never sich a thing!" exclaimed Mr. Jorrocks; "I inwented it!"

The Sheriff called Mr. Jorrocks to order.

Captain Bluster repeated what he said: he had it on the authority of a gentleman behind him (Joshua Sneakington), that the Marquis of Bray had invented a most valuable—a most durable draining-tile; and yet, not content with attempting to defraud the noble Marquis of what he (Captain Bluster) designated his birthright—the representation of the county, this farmer's champion, because the noble lord had proclaimed the discovery at his (Mr. Jorrocks's) house, now wanted to filch the Marquis of his draining-tile too. (Great uproar, mingled with hisses, and cries of "Oh, you horrid old cheat! Oh, you shocking bad man!" and other symptoms of disapprobation from the whiskerites.)

"THAT'S A LEE!" roared Pigg, who immediately ducked under.

He (Captain Bluster) felt satisfied the county would visit such conduct with the punishment it deserved, and with that firm conviction he felt equal pride and pleasure in proposing to the electors, as a fit and proper knight to represent their interests in Parliament, James Frederick Charles Fox Plantagenet Russell Bolinbroke Bray, commonly called the

Marquis of Bray, of Donkeyton Castle.

Mr. Prosey Slooman came forward to second the nomination, with an uncommonly lengthy, well-rounded speech in his pocket; but unfortunately, when it came to the point, he had studied it so much that he could not let it off; so, after gaping a few seconds at the crowd, he simply seconded the nomination, leaving much good abuse of Mr. Jorrocks unsaid.

It was now the turn of the gentlemen at the other end of the hustings, and, accordingly, Mr. Hamilton Dobbin presented himself to the meeting, and was received with cheers from the drab coats, and hisses from the whisker-on-chin-ites.

He commenced by saying that he should occupy a very brief portion of their time in proposing the gentleman who had been unanimously adopted by the party he belonged to, to fight the battle of their interests because, while he felt his own incompetence to go fully into the question that now agitated their attention, he had every belief that the candidate he had to propose was quite able to do so; he therefore felt great satisfaction in leaving the arguments in the hands of his esteemed friend Mr. Jorrocks, whom he begged to recommend as a fit and proper knight to represent their interests in Parliament.

The nomination was received with great applause from the farmers, and hisses from the whiskerites.

Mr. Heavytail then raised his voice to its utmost pitch, and spoke in such a tone as to be clearly audible to several ladies and gentlemen on the church tower across the market-place.

"GENTLEMEN," said he, "IF YOU WANT TO CUT YOUR OWN THROATS, YOU'LL VOTE FOR BRAY; IF YOU WANT TO LIVE AND LET LIVE, YOU'LL VOTE FOR OUR SQUIRE (great applause from the drab coats). I SECOND OUR SQUIRE!"

The High Sheriff then inquired if any other gentleman had a candidate to propose, and being answered by a volley of negatives, he called on the Marquis of Bray to address the meeting.

In compliance with the High-Sheriff's requisition, his Lordship then uncovered his well-waxed ringlets, and throwing back his silk-lined blue dress-coat, bowed, and placed his primrose-coloured kid-gloved right hand upon his heart, in return for the deafening huzzas and waving of handkerchiefs, ribbons, and hats, that greeted his appearance.

"Ladies and gentlemen," said he, when the applause had somewhat subsided; "ladies and gentlemen," repeated he, looking sweet at Mrs. Jobson and party, who were drawn up a little on the left, "permit me, in the first place, to return my most heartfelt and cordial thanks for the kind, the flattering reception you honoured me with on my arrival this day; a reception so cheering, so enthusiastic and exhilarating, that we cannot but admire the indomitable courage of my farmer friend on the left—the god of corn, as his followers call him"— the Marquis looking at our rosy-gilled friend, with his bunch of wheat-ears under his nose; "we cannot, I say, but admire his indomitable courage in coming here to receive the hearty drubbing his temerity is certain to ensure him."

"Are you goin' to bet me that 'at we talked about?" inquired Mr. Jorrocks.

"For," continued the Marquis, without noticing the interruption, "when I look at the splendid array of beauty—an array that I firmly believe no town of this size ever before contained; when I reflect that those bright eyes and sweet looks respond to sympathising hearts arrayed in the cause of the poor man's home, whose interest I stand here to advocate, I say it is morally impossible to doubt, for one moment, what will be the issue of this great and virtuous contest; a contest in which the legitimate laws of nature are ranged against unnatural monopoly and close-fisted selfishness!" (Great applause, and renewed fluttering of handkerchiefs, flags, and ribbons.) "But, ladies and gentlemen," continued his lordship, "let me not be led away by those enchanting smiles, and those applauding cheers, from the important duty that has brought us together this day; and first, let me return my most cordial thanks to my proposer and seconder, for the kind and flattering terms in which they introduced me to your notice; terms that I cannot but feel are infinitely superior to any humble merits of mine, but which will stimulate me to such acts as will render me worthy of your approbation." (Renewed applause, and waving of handkerchiefs.)

"Gentlemen," continued the Marquis, addressing himself to the male sex alone, "you are met here this day, as our worthy High Sheriff has told you, to exercise one of the most important privileges of life—that of choosing a representative of your opinions in the House of Commons; and in proportion to the magnitude of the occasion ought to be the vigilance and circumspection of your conduct in the exercise of so sacred a trust. (Great applause.) It may appear almost superfluous in one, born and bred among you, whose ancestors have ever been conspicuous in the cause of legitimate improvement and good government, to enter into any lengthened explanation of his political opinions."

"*Quite* superfluous! *quite* superfluous!" exclaimed Mr. Smoothington.

"Quite superfluous! quite superfluous!" repeated Joshua Sneakington, and several others behind.

"My political opinions," continued the Marquis, "are the political opinions that in bygone days were wont to secure the confidence of the freeholders in those who have gone before me—opinions from which no member of my family has ever swerved, and which I trust—confidently trust—will secure me the honour of your support." (Great cheering.)

"True it is," continued his lordship, "that the god of corn," turning towards Mr. Jorrocks, "impelled by the fear of alarmists, and perhaps the mischief of the frolicsome, has decked himself out in wheat-ears and poppies."

"There ar'nt no poppies in the case!" exclaimed Mr. Jorrocks, adjusting his bouquet, adding aloud to himself—"who ever see'd poppies at this time of year?"

"Has decked himself out in wheat-ears," bowed the Marquis, "and stands forward as the farmers' friend; but who, gentlemen, I ask you, is more likely to be truly and sincerely the farmers' friend than the humble individual now addressing you, and whose every interest is identified with agriculture—whose best hopes are centred in the soil? (tremendous applause). Agriculture, gentlemen, is a pursuit that has been fostered and encouraged by the greatest men, by all whom the page of history records as famous in the annals of countries (great applause). The greatest statesmen, the greatest scholars, the greatest generals have each found, in turning from their schemes of government, their studies, or the toil of warfare, solace and enjoyment in the harmless simplicity and the interesting relaxation it affords (renewed applause). Every man whose opinion is valuable—every man whose breast glows with a genuine feeling of patriotism, joins in testifying the importance of agriculture." Immense applause, followed by Mr. Wopstraw drawling out—

"Upon the who-o-le, I think I've heard that before."

This rather put the Marquis out, and in the hubbub that ensued he got time to collect himself and turn on another tack.

"Gentlemen," said he, "the only point of difference, as you are perhaps aware, between my honourable competitor and myself is that of corn. On all other questions I believe our opinions coincide, and, but for this solitary question, the god of corn would have followed our banner, with most likely the majority of his supporters. Far be it from me, gentlemen, to treat with levity the honest, conscientious fears and opinions of any class of men, unfounded and groundless though I believe them to be. Recall to your recollection, gentlemen, the panic that prevailed on the importation of foreign cattle! see how visionary were your views and conjectures then! The same, I venture to predict, will be the case with the importation of foreign corn. It will come in; your fears will pass away, or will only be remembered as matter of surprise—surprise that you could so blindly have stood in the way of your own interest." (Loud applause, from the whisker-chinites, and cries of "No, no," from the drab coats.)

"Upon the who-o-le, the climate's against us," drawled Wopstraw.

"The farmers are not the only parties called upon to make a sacrifice," continued the Marquis, "if any sacrifice there is to be. Every article of consumption, every article of wear—the hat on your head—the shoe on your foot—will come down in price, and all things accommodate themselves to the new era (loud applause). If farmers yield the trifling duty on corn, a duty that many of the most intelligent of their body consider is no protection whatever, they, in their turn, will have the duty taken off seeds, and they will get their canary-seed, their aniseed, their grass-seed, their mustard-seed, their parsley-seed, and my friend the god of corn will even get his poppy-seed duty free (great laughter and applause). So the housekeeper will get her spices—her cloves, her ginger, her mace, her nutmegs, her cinnamon, and her pepper. And *you*, my fair friends," continued the Marquis, addressing himself to the ladies, "you will get your ermine, your chinchilla, your swan-skins without a tax. Silks, velvets, and sarcenets will come in at continental prices; and gauzes, tulles, crapes, and lawns no longer continue matters of luxury" (great applause and waving of handkerchiefs). "All things," continued the Marquis, "will be placed upon a new footing, and the dawn of that young and stirring mind which so engages the attention of the public will burst upon the astonished world in all the splendour of meridian day (immense applause). But beyond—far beyond—all these considerations will be the feeling of patriotism the act will engender. You will be the poor man's friend—you will invest the poor man's home with plenty—you will bring joy and gladness to his humble hearth—you will convert the squalid victims of penurious fare into stalwart sons of Albion's isle, and cause the

> Happy tenant of a humble shed,
> To smile at the storm that whistles o'er his head.

His lordship concluded amidst the most uproarious demonstrations of applause.

When they had subsided, a loud cry was raised for Mr. Jorrocks, who, on hearing the Marquis break off about the greatest statesmen, the greatest generals, and so on, had availed himself of the opportunity for retiring to the back of the hustings to drink a glass of brandy-and-water, and he had now got blocked out. Mr. Heavytail having made way for him, our friend at length showed at the front, and was greeted with loud cheers from his own supporters, and the most discordant yells and hisses from the Marquis's party. Silence being at length restored, he essayed to proceed.

"Gen'lmen," said he, looking very indignantly at a knot of hissers who still kept interrupting; "gen'lmen," said he, "afore I opens my private account with you, I wish to make a few observations on a few of the observations that have been made upon me. I doosn't like Captain Bluster's speech; he had no business to speak o' me in the way he aid. He looked at me, too, jest as if I was a bag o' guano. It wasn't the ticket at all. I'm sure when we've had anything to transact together, any fifth o' George the Fourth, or anything of that sort, he's always found me quite agreeable—quite the lady, and I don't think he had any business to ax in sich a himperent tone who I was. I pays every man twenty shillins in the pund, and I never heard no one's respectability doubted wot did that (applause). I've been brought here at a great personal sacrifice, both of cash and comfort, to fight the battle of the farmers—and fight it I will."

"That's reet, ard 'un!" exclaimed Pigg; adding, "Three cheers for t'ard Squire!"

Three tremendous huzzas followed. When they were done, the Marquis's party gave three cheers for the Marquis.

"I've been brought here," continued Mr. Jorrocks, by a great lot o' farmers; they came and 'unted me out at my 'ouse at 'ome, and would have me. That shows the hopinion they 'ave of me. I never axed to be made Parliament man of. The farmers came and said that they were like to be beggared, and axed if I would stand quietly by and see 'em? (Loud applause.) I said, the farmers and I rowed in the same boat—that wot was bad for them would be bad for me, and wice wersa (cheers). The Captain talked as if the guano and nitrate o' sober dodge was all the Duke's; but I appeals to those around me, if guano, nitrate o' sober, or any of them hartificial compounds 'ave a more hardent—a more enthusiastic supporter nor myself!"

"Upon the who-o-o-le, I should say not," drawled Johnny Wopstraw.

"MUCK's YOUR MAN!" roared Pigg.

"Nay, more," continued Mr. Jorrocks, "I did wot the Duke never did—I inwented a machine of a most wonderful capacity. A machine that I really dirsn't set a goin' for fear it should swamp field labour altogether. I mentions that to show that I'm a practical farmer and a friend to the poor. My friend the Markis," continued Mr. Jorrocks, "has made you a werry beautiful hoily oration—one wot called forth the applause both of pit and boxes," Mr. Jorrocks looking towards the carriages and balcony in which the ladies were ranged. "It's the privilege of young gen'lmen in

Mr. Jorrocks addressing the crowd

ringlets and primrose-coloured gloves to obtain the plaudits o' the fair
sex—fine flowery language is sure to find customers with them. Now,
I may fearlessly say that the ladies haven't a more hardent admirer nor I
am; but gen'lmen like myself, of maturer years, must rest our claims to
public favour upon the broader and better basis of sound sense rather
than of heloquence." (Laughter, hisses, and applause, above which Pigg's
"Gan it, ard 'hun! Jorrocks for ever!" rose conspicuous.)

"My noble friend—for friend I must still call him, for he gave me
the most unim bull wotever adorned ring and chain—my noble friend,
I say, in the plenitude of his humour, has christened me the god o'
corn; but I will tell my noble friend that hargument is as far above
heloquence as corn is afore flowers (cheers). We can do werry well
without flowers, but corn we must 'ave. It sounds werry well talking
about bein' the poor man's friend, but I say he is the best poor man's
friend wot gives him a good day's pay for a good day's work (applause).
Vot signifies it to the poor man gettin' a heightpenny loaf for fourpence

if he has not fourpence to buy it with?" (Renewed applause.)

"Gan it, ard 'un!" exclaimed Pigg; adding, with a grin and shake of his head, "'a sink, but he's *a good 'un* to jaw!"

"Then I would like to ax my noble friend," continued Mr. Jorrocks, "'ow he thinks to improve the breed o' the 'uman race, if he makes us poor farmers lay our land down to grass or pine-apples, throwin' the corn-trade into the hands of mouncheer, and drivin' the chaws into mills and print-works. Wot 'un a man, for instance, would Mr. 'Eavytail 'ave been," asked Mr. Jorrocks, patting Mr. Heavytail's broad back as the latter stood beside him, "wot 'un a man would Mr. 'Eavytail ha' been if he'd been brought up a shuttle-weaver?" (Loud applause.)

"I am old enough, gen'lmen, to remember the time," continued Mr. Jorrocks, "when that great man, Napoleon Bonaparte—a man whose werry name worked one wuss nor a whole box o' Morrison's pills—I'm old enough, I say, gen'lmen, to remember the time when that great man, in the plenitude of his imperence, climbed up the column on Boulogne 'eights, and shakin' his mawley at England, swore he'd pitch into her like twenty thousand bricks." (Roars of laughter and applause, Mr. Jorrocks suiting the action to the word, and menacing the crowd with his fist.)

"Then, gen'lmen," continued he, "my frind Good'eart and my frind Wopstraw—John Jorrocks himself— all the true and undeniable tramps—rose to a man, and swore we'd *be blank'd* if he should!"

Roars of laughter and applause followed this delicate announcement, which were again roused by Johnny Wopstraw drawling out, "Upon the wh-o-o-le, I wasn't a soldier!"

"Who knows," continued Mr. Jorrocks, without noticing the observation, "who knows but the Prince de Johnville or Prince de Tomville, or whatever they call the chap, may brew up another storm, and in the row and racket that ensues, who knows but another Napoleon le grand may turn to the top, who'll swear that we shalln't 'ave another grain o' corn from the Continent? Then, gen'lmen, if you've laid your land down to grass, and turned your stout yeomanry into stockin' makers, who's to supply us with bread? and where are you to find Good'earts to wop Johnny Crapaud?" (Thunders of applause, lasting for some seconds.)

"Wot consolation will it be to the starvin' population for frind John Bright to point to his many-windowed ware'ouse, and say, 'Oh, never mind, my 'earties! that's chock-full o' calico at a penny a yard'?" (Renewed applause.)

"Gen'lmen, I can't eat calico," observed Mr. Jorrocks, with uplifted hands, amidst the most outrageous laughter.

"*Nor I nouther!*" roared Pigg, stuffing a fresh quid into his mouth.

"Gen'lmen," continued Mr. Jorrocks, "cheap bread's a capital cry, but wot's the use o' cheap bread to the poor man, if he harn't got no money to buy it with?" (Great applause, with cries of "That's the rub!" "Go it, Jorrocks!" "Now another!")

"Bambazeens and sarc'nets, wot the Markis promises so cheap, will not compensate for the want o' wittles! 'You take my life when you take the means whereby I lives,' observes Hudibras, or some other gen'lman; and you'll destroy the 'usbandman if you annihilate hagriculture.

"My noble frind talked about the legitimate laws o' natur' and close-fisted somethin'," observed Mr. Jorrocks. "I'm more a fifth o' George the Fourth than a law o' natur' man, but it strikes me if the manufacturers want to try a new system, they should pay the National Debt off, and let's all start fair, as the parson said to the Cornish wreckers as he stole down from the pulpit.

"I think, gen'lmen," continued Mr. Jorrocks, after a pause, "that's about all I've got to say to you. It's for you to say whether you prefer the luxtery o' cheap bambazeen and carraway-seeds for nothin', or the old English beef and barley loaves of our forefathers. It's true the Markis has some werry pretty gals on his side howsomever, it's fortinate they haven't got no wotes, otherwise they'd a been sure to have been given in the 'aberdashery line. As it is, we'll have a fair stand-hup fight for it; and as the great Tom Spring would say,

May the best man vin!"

Mr. Jorrocks concluded an animated address by throwing up his hat amid very general applause.

An artisan, in his working dress, with a leather apron tucked round his waist, and a faded green neckcloth about his neck (an active member of the Sellborough Anti-Corn-Law League), here climbed on to the hustings, and intimated that he wanted to ask Mr. Jorrocks a few questions.

"Questins!" exclaimed our Squire, eyeing him with surprise. "Questins! I don't think," added he, pulling out his watch and looking at it; "I don't think I'm a-goin' to answer no questins."

"Not answer any!" repeated the man with surprise.

"No," replied Mr. Jorrocks; adding, "I've got a Muscovey duck for dinner, and I'm afeard it'll be overdone."

"Well," observed the man in astonishment, "I certainly shalln't vote for you."

"P'raps you wouldn't ha' done that anyhow," replied our Squire.

"Upon the wh-o-o-le, he hasn't got a vote," observed Wopstraw.

"Ye come down there!" cried Pigg, giving the fellow a thump on the head with his flagstaff; adding, "de ye think a Parliament man has nought to de but talk to such rubbish as ye? Grou whiskers on your chin like Ginger toppin' yonder, if ye maun make yersel conspikious."

The High Sheriff then called for a show of hands. A forest of them was immediately held up for the Marquis, amid thunders of applause, waving of handkerchiefs, and rolling of drums. The Sheriff then called upon those who were for Mr. Jorrocks to hold up theirs.

A very small number appeared in comparison to what were held up for the Marquis; and after the roars of applause the triumph produced had subsided, the Sheriff declared the show to have fallen in favour of his lordship.

"AR DEMAND A POLL!" roared Heavytail, with such a thump of the fist on the hustings as would have felled an ox.

XLVII

For whom do you poll?

IN LESS THAN AN HOUR the late densely-crowded town was occupied only by its own inhabitants, and the few drunken topers who filled the public-houses—men who, at election times, drank from week's end to week's end. The Marquis set off in great glee to Donkeyton Castle, accompanied by the party who attended him in the morning, to tell the victory of the day: and the farmers quietly got their horses, and wended their way home by twos or by threes, as occasion suited.

"Upon the who-o-ole I think the Marquis'll be hard to beat," observed Wopstraw, as he mounted his mealy-muzzled bay.

"We mun never despair!" replied Willey Goodheart. "I always said in Boney's time, it's never no use being afraid. I really believe, if the French had thought we were frightened, they'd have come over and ate us all up; terrible people for eatin', they say."

"We must stir ourselves to a man," said John Brick, clattering away, much to the astonishment of his great black horse.

Many a heavy-heeled carter went home at an unusual pace that day.

The printing-presses of the respective parties were now hard at full work. It was the eve of publication-day of both papers, and the great "WE's" of the *Dozey Independent* and the *Church and State Gazette* sat in their back rooms, combing and riddling the speeches of the respective candidates into English. Independently of the newspaper reports, each party printed handbills for general distribution, containing their own version of the story. The Marquis's procession was detailed in glowing colours. The bands, the banners, the ribbons, the ladies, the enthusiasm that prevailed, and the surpassing talent that characterised his address.

The *Dozey Independent* "WE" treated poor Mr. Jorrocks very small.

"This curious old codger," said the editor in his leading article, "an amalgamation of a cockney and a countryman, half buck half hawbuck, addressed the assembled multitude with a vehemence and an energy truly surprising for a man of his years, but in a dialect perfectly unintelligible to our reporters. It is lamentable to see a respectable-looking old gentleman, with, we understand, many amiable qualities, making a merry-andrew of himself at the bidding of a desperate and expiring faction. 'Has the old gentleman no friends?' was the question we repeatedly heard asked; and, in sober earnestness, we ask it ourselves—*has he no friends?*"

On the other hand, *The Church and State Gazette* eulogised Mr. Jorrocks, his sayings and his doings, and made a perfect hero of him.

"We heartily congratulate the county on the creditable exhibition Mr. Jorrocks made on the hustings this day. His reasoning, his language, his manner, his dress, his address, was all that could be wished by the most zealous patriot. We never listened with greater pleasure to any speech. It was a perfect masterpiece of impassioned eloquence. Bold, vigorous, and concise, it had all the fervour of a Stanley, with the subdued pathos of a Canning.

"We will not detain our readers from the gratification its perusal is sure to afford by any further observations of our own, but conclude by again congratulating the county on the fortunate selection it has made."

The paper then went on to give the following version of the proceedings, and of Mr. Jorrocks's speech, which we recommend to the notice of all other editors of Church and State Gazettes throughout the kingdom, some of whom send their champions out much worse mounted than they find them:—

SELLBOROUGH

At eleven o'clock to-day, John Jorrocks, Esq., of Hillingdon Hall, one of Her Majesty's Justices of the Peace for the county—the chosen champion of the agricultural interest—made his public entry into our town, attended by an immense cavalcade of yeomanry, and farmers on horseback. The procession was preceded by numerous rich and beautiful flags, and a full brass band in uniform (three trumpeters in dirty ducks and high-lows). The honourable gentleman rode in an elegant triumphal car (the old fire-engine), and was attended by his proposer, Hamilton Dobbin, Esq. His seconder, Mr. Mark Heavytail, of the Pet Farm, one of the oldest and most extensive farmers in the county, headed the horsemen. In number they far exceeded a thousand; some thought two thousand: but, perhaps, fifteen hundred would be about the mark—all free-holders!

Precisely at twelve o'clock the High Sheriff appeared on the hustings; and the usual formalities having been observed, the respective candidates were proposed and seconded.

The Marquis of Bray addressed the vast assemblage first; but we regret that the total want of accommodation for the gentlemen of the press prevented our reporter catching a single word of what he said.

Mr. Jorrocks then came forward, and was received with the most deafening applause, accompanied by the waving of handkerchiefs, and general signs of approbation. When silence was at length restored, the honourable gentleman spoke nearly as follows:—

'Mr. High Sheriff and Gentlemen,—Before I advert to the important business that has brought us together this day, allow me to notice an inquiry made by the proposer of my noble friend, the Marquis of Bray, as to who I am (cheers). I was in hopes, gentlemen, that the time I have now spent among you—the intercourse I have had with you, coupled with the interest I have taken in the promotion of agricultural science, and, I trust, the faithful discharge of my magisterial duties, would have exempted me from such an inquiry; but, gentlemen, lest the unanswered question of the gallant Captain should lead any to suppose that I am an ambitious adventurer standing forward for the mere gratification of my own vanity, or the still baser motives of personal aggrandisement, permit me to say that I am closely connected with the landed interest of this county; and that I was sought in the retirement of private life by the spontaneous requisition of a large body of my brother landowners and farmers to fight the battle of our common cause.' (Immense applause, with cries of 'So you were! So you were!')

'The gallant Captain,' continued Mr. Jorrocks, 'spoke in glowing terms of the Duke of Donkeyton's devotion to agriculture and the expense he incurred in trying experiments, but he (Mr. Jorrocks) fearlessly appealed to the assembled county to say if the farming interest had a truer or more liberal patron than himself!' (Cheers, and cries of 'No, no!—it hasn't! it hasn't!')

'Without wishing to detract from the merits of the Duke of Donkeyton, he might refer to his own labours in the cause of good farming and scientific improvement. He had invented a machine so curious in its structure, so comprehensive in its operations, that, trembling at the monster he had called into existence, he had not dared to use it, lest it should supersede manual labour, and so throw thousands of industrious poor out of employment!' (Great applause.)

'The noble Lord had addressed them with great talent and eloquence. Though opposed to the opinions his Lordship had urged, he (Mr. Jorrocks) could not be insensible to the ability with which he had advanced them. If he (Mr. Jorrocks) felt himself unable to compete with the noble Lord in the display of flowery metaphor, he trusted to supply the deficiency by the use of sounder arguments (cheers). He stood there the defender of British agriculture, and, in his opinion, argument was as superior to metaphor as the yellow waving corn was to the gay *parterre*. Flowers we could do without, but corn was a matter of vital necessity. The noble Lord talked of his sympathy for the poor, but he (Mr. Jorrocks) yielded to no man in attachment to the lower orders (applause). He wished to see the labouring man fully employed and well paid. What matter did it make to the poor man that he could buy an eightpenny loaf for fourpence, if he had not fourpence to buy it with? Would it increase the demand for labour to throw all the arable land out of tillage? He thought not; neither would it be prudent to depend upon foreigners for food.

'I am old enough, gentlemen,' continued Mr. Jorrocks, 'to remember the time when that great man, Napoleon Bonaparte—a man at whose name princes trembled and empires shook—I am old enough, I say, to remember the time when that great man, in the plenitude of his power, menaced England from Boulogne heights, threatening to close the ports of Europe against us. Wars, gentlemen, have been, and wars may be again; and if a second Napoleon should arise, how should we manage if he were to do what his predecessor threatened? Would it appease the hunger of the starving millions for Mr. Bright to offer the contents of his ware house to clothe them? Again, if the stalwart yeomanry, who in former days joined the flower and chivalry of England, were annihilated, who should we get to fight the battles of our common cause? Shall we be unmindful of the poet's truism—'

That a bold peasantry, their country's pride,
When once destroyed can never be supplied?

'Never, gentlemen!' continued he; 'never! (loud cheers). Let us not be deluded out of the substance of our national independence by the shadow of foreign advantages; let us adhere to the flag that for a thousand years has "braved the battle and the breeze," and, in the coming contest for this county, let every man remember the emphatic language of Nelson—

England expects that every man will do his duty.

The honourable gentleman concluded amidst the most enthusiastic demonstrations of applause.

A show of hands was then called for and taken, but our reporter has omitted to supply us with the result. From what we saw, however, we have little doubt it would be greatly in favour of Mr. Jorrocks.

Now for the election.

The polling commenced with great vigour on both sides, but the result of the first day fully justified the confidence with which Mr. Smoothington had assured the Duke, as they quaffed their Burgundy and Bordeaux after the nomination, at Donkeyton Castle, that the Marquis's success was quite certain. There not having been a contested election in the county since the passing of the Reform Bill, the machinery was not in very good order, and the returns from the different polling-places were badly made; but all accounts agreed that the Marquis was considerably ahead, and Mr. Smoothington, taking the highest number that he heard, told the Duke his son was more than a hundred ahead. His Grace was rejoiced—was sure "they were popular—monstrous popular!"

On the other hand, the agricultural interest, nothing daunted by their candidate's position on the poll, moved heaven and earth to reverse his situation on the second. Agents and canvassers scoured the county during the night, and every voter was looked after that could be got to the poll.

The League distributed tons of tracts.

A very unusual activity, for a second's day's polling, prevailed throughout the county, and drab coats and whisker-on-chin-ites, who had never been looked for, cast up most unexpectedly at the different polling-booths; many absentees arrived, some out of gaol— debtors, of course.

Still Mr. Smoothington was confident they couldn't beat the Duke.

A splendid chair was fitted up for the chairing—green velvet with gold lace; and a grand procession arranged from the Castle, for the declaration of the poll day.

"We'll annihilate this old Tom Jorrocks," said the Duke, as the lengthening procession drove from the door; "impudent man, monstrous impudent man!" added he, hurrying away to his library.

Many rumours were afloat as to the ultimate result of the poll. Mr. Jorock's committee had published a statement of the first day's one, which left our Cockney Squire in a minority of twenty only; still it was the general opinion that the Marquis was far more ahead. In this opinion our friend participated, and had it not been for the convenience of arranging the payment of his hats, he would hardly have taken the trouble of returning to Sellborough. As it was, the Marquis's dazzling procession had entered, and his Lordship and friends had taken their place on the hustings before the Squire made his appearance. A vast concourse of persons filled the spacious market-place, and compliments passed current while the Sheriff was superintending the casting-up of the poll-books. At length he appeared on the hustings, and pencils begin to appear to take down the numbers as they issued from his lips. A breathless silence ensued as he declared the numbers to be—

> For John Jorrocks, Esq.   2617
> For the Marquis of Bray   2615

Each party was struck dumb with astonishment.

"Impossible!" "Wrong!" "Mistake!" "Can never be!" issued from the whiskerites; and "Thame! thame!" was lisped by the ladies. A rotten cabbage was thrown at the Sheriff. This roused him from the stupor into which he also seemed to have fallen, and after calling for order, a semblance of which was at length obtained, he declared John Jorrocks, Esq., to be duly elected.

Our Cockney Squire stood in a state of apparent bewilderment receiving the congratulations of his friends, amidst the greatest uproar from the populace. He did not know what he was about. Many of the public-house mob were perfectly furious, and would have torn the Jorrockian jacket off his back if they could have reached him.

After some time spent in dumb show by our friend, each party exerting their lungs to the utmost, the Sheriff sent him word, if he wished to address the meeting, he should now do so; otherwise he would adjourn the court in order to make his return to the writ.

Our friend then stood forward, and uncovered, amidst the most discordant yells and a volley of missiles. That being a game at which two can play, a rotten egg speedily closed one of Captain Bluster's eyes, when all hands on the hustings began to be particularly anxious for order. Mr. Jorrocks's friends rallied round him.

After some seconds spent in dumb show, he at length articulated as follows—

"Mr. 'Igh Sheriff and gen'lmen, I'm perfectly flummoxed at the announcement jest made. I can't think it's true. There must be some mistake, the bookkeeper must 'ave cast hup his accounts wrong! It can never be true that I've beat a Markis."

Cries of "No, no!" "Yes, yes!" "All right! all right!"

"Howsomever, beat or not beat, I'm quite beat for words. Sich a thing never entered my calkilation. John Jorrocks an M.P.!"

"Whe'd ha' thou't it?" exclaimed Pigg.

"Ay, indeed, who would?" replied Mr. Jorrocks.

"Friend!" exclaimed a Quaker (Mr. Obadiah Brown), "friend!" repeated he, "thy footman there," pointing to Pigg, "told me an untruth respecting thy habits of life."

" 'Ow so?" inquired Mr. Jorrocks.

"He assured me thou wert a teetotaller."

"Ne doot!" said Pigg, "ne doot!"

"How canst thou say so, when thy master was drunk the night before last?"

"Why! why!" replied Pigg, "that's nou't again' his bein' a tea-to-taller."

"But, friend," continued Mr. Obadiah Brown, appealing to Mr. Jorrocks, "my brother and myself voted for thee on the understanding that thou wert a teetotaller."

"Sorry you should 'ave 'ad so bad an opinion on me," replied Mr. Jorrocks.

"But thou surely wilt not retain the votes?" rejoined Mr. Brown. "They were obtained under false pretences."

"*That's a lee!*" roared Pigg.

"*I say they were*," retorted Mr. Brown, with vehemence.

"Ar say they *warn't!*" roared Pigg. "Thou axed me when ar canvassed thee, gin wor ard Squire was a tea-totaller, and ar said Yis!"

"Then he's not, I say!" retorted Mr. Brown. "He sells tea ony how," replied Pigg.

The High Sheriff called the parties to order, observing that it was Mr. Jorrocks should address the meeting, if he were inclined; otherwise the Marquis of Bray had the privilege.

Mr. Jorrocks begged pardon. "He really was so struck in a heap that he didn't know wot he was about. He would be werry much obliged to any one who would tell him what to say. He was never in such a pucker afore. Yes, once! No, it wasn't! It was summut like though. He had arranged a beautiful speech to return thanks for his ball winnin' a prize, instead of which they axed him to return thanks for his losin' it, and he couldn't. It was too much for his feelins. So now he'd come to tell his friends where to apply to for their 'ats, instead of which he had to trouble them for them, and to thank the electors who had so gallantly won them for him. (Loud cheers.) He believed there were seventy of them. As many as would last him his life, he thought. It was, indeed, a great wictory! The League, too, had gained a great wictory—a great *moral* wictory! Nothin' could be better. Two great wictories! Both parties pleased! They had elected him to Parliament, and he was ready to sacrifice the plisures of retirement and the luxury of pure country hair, in the enjoyment of which men grumbled if they died afore they were a 'undred. He was ready, he said, to sacrifice these at their biddin'. He didn't exactly know who he'd support when he got hup. Young England, at one time, had favour in his eyes; but they lost it by steeple-chasin'—above all, by Conin'sby ridin' a steeple-chase in Hautumn.

" 'Upon the who-o-ole,' as his friend Johnny Wopstraw would say, he didn't know but he'd support Sir Robert. It was no use doin' things by 'alves. He would go the 'ole 'og—over shoes over boots. He'd been a Vig all his life, and thought to have died a Vig; but inwestin' money in land, and findin' he was likely to be done out of his land, had changed his opinions on that pint. He really thought Sir Robert was a downright clever man. He had found the country reg'larly hup the spout, and had now restored it to hunexampled prosperity. If Sir Robert 'ill stick by us poor farmers, I really think I'll stick by him," continued Mr. Jorrocks. "Be wot they call Conservative. 'Tory men with Vig measures,' as Conin'sby says. Sir Robert had played him rayther a dirty trick about his ball, but he could forgive him. He could forgive him, and he believed the generous hanimal could forgive him. Partin' with his ball would give him unmitigated pain, but he couldn't take him hup to Parliament. He must, however, be partin' himself. It was past two o'clock, and he should like to be chaired, for he'd promised to dine with his neighbour, little Trotter, whose beautiful darter had been married that mornin'. It would be a great surprise to Trot to find him returned to Parliament as well as to dine with him. He should, however, never forget the kindness of the farmers. He would keep a watchful eye on their interest. He would make his trusty Scotch bailiff, James Pigg, manager of his property. He should establish a model farm, like the Duke of Donkeyton's. Guano, nitrate o' sober, Willey's dust, Clarke's compost, petre salt, all scientific mextures should have a fair field and every favour; and he would come down annually twice a year to lector and report on them!"

"MUCK'S YOUR MAN!" roared Pigg, as his master bowed his adieus to the meeting.

[Advertisement]
To Parents and Guardians

Professor Pigg, of the Royal Caledonian Uniwersity, having been appointed by John Jorrocks, Esq., M.P., to manage his extensive agricultural concerns, begs to announce his intention of receiving a limited number of MUD STUDENTS, who will be instructed in the newest and most approved farming mysteries, particklar the use of guano, nitrate of sober, and other hartificial mextures.

The young gentlemen's linen and morals will be under the immediate superintendence of Mrs. Pigg, and they will in every respect be treated the same as the little Piggs.

For terms and further particklars, apply to the Professor at Hillingdon Hall.

THE END